Twisting his shoulder into the man's throat, the man from Havensdale managed to slip his sword free and throwing his weight onto his opponent, he broke free of his grip.

With his fury in his face, Kallum gripped his sword in both hands and raised it high above his head.

The Carwellian soldier's eyes were wide with white terror and he raised a pleading hand to protect his face.

"Don't," the man sobbed imploringly.

Baring his teeth madly, spittle flying from his lips, Kallum Campbell hesitated, then buried his sword with a scream.

Also By Anthony Lavisher

The Storm Trilogy
Whispers of a Storm
Shadows of a Storm

With Jamie Wallis
Vengeance

Anthony Lavisher

Vengeance of a Storm

Book Three of the Storm Trilogy

First print edition published by CreateSpace 2016.

Published in the United States by CreateSpace.
www.createspace.com
ISBN-13 978-1539024385
ISBN-10 1539024385

To Jamie

For showing me the true meaning of courage.

Acknowledgements

There are so many people that have helped contribute to the Storm trilogy, have encouraged, supported and journeyed with me on this wonderful adventure. To all of you reading this, I thank you.

Special thanks should also go to Emma Hatton, my wife Amy, Nathan Shaw, Belana Sa and Margaret and Ted Sherborne for all their hard work, their attention and feedback on what, in the end, proved to be a weighty manuscript.

I would especially like to thank Richie Earl, for his help with Shadows and to all the readers who have taken the time to tell the world about my tales.

When I started the Storm Trilogy back in 2009, I could have never imagined the level of kindness and enjoyment my writing would come to receive. I never dreamt that my tales would capture the imagination of so many people.

Kerry Singleton was one such reader who sadly passed away in 2015, before I could finish the finale. Not generally a reader of fiction he absolutely loved Whispers and Shadows.
I hope he, and you all, will approve.

PROLOGUE

"I don't like this," Arrun Hawksblade hissed through grinding teeth, as he dropped to the ground and placed his back against the wooden palisade for reassurance.

Rellin, but a shadow at best, leant in close, gripping his friend's shoulder tightly.

"Nor do I," he said, his breath barely forming words in his terrified friend's ear. "But what choice do we have? If we stay, we will be arrested and hung."

And if we flee, we will be hunted down like dogs, Arrun thought grimly.

They stared at each other through the darkness of the deepest night, the low clouds forming a heavy blanket of the blackest sky over them. Arrun shook his hooded head, cursing his stupidity and held his friend's eyes meaningfully.

"You can go back, I won't blame you," Rellin whispered, looking briefly up the wall at the rope that dangled there enticingly.

Any response was yanked from his friend, as the third member of their party of would-be fugitives stalked over to them.

"Will you both hurry up," Jessica snarled, her fury cutting through their nerves and forcing them to look about guardedly. "We have been through this already – to stay is to die, bringing death to the innocents of the town."

"I'm an innocent of the town," Arrun whined indignantly.

Despite their situation Rellin grinned and attempted to shake the madness of their actions from his head.

"Come on," he sighed. "Let's get into the forest and head to Bowen's hut. He is away hunting to the north at the moment, but we should find more supplies there for our journey."

They had debated for hours since the Carwellian commander had issued his threats and whilst those in town argued over everyone else's futures for them, the young recruits had decided to take matters into their own hands.

"But by fleeing, you will only look more guilty," Sara Campbell had hissed, perplexed at the decision they had made. "You are my dearest friends, but I will not abandon my family, I cannot. I am so sorry!"

In the end only Rellin, Arrun and Jessica had decided to flee the besieged town as Tess Varun would not leave her home either, preferring to stay behind as well. After a tearful farewell the new recruits had parted ways, both Sara and Tess covering for their friends duties on the south gate to enable them to slip unnoticed over the north-eastern edge of the town's defences.

From her vantage point at the top the palisade, Tess heard her friends' collective sigh as they drew in their breaths for one final draught of courage and slipped through the darkness towards the shadowy, misty protection of the Moonglade Forest.

Her hands shook as she pulled up the rope and she did not see the Carwellian scout, as he slipped from his hiding place in the fields to the south and hurried away to make his report.

CHAPTER ONE

Blood of a Crescent Moon

Cassana woke with a start as the scream split the silence of the night and cut through her dreamless sleep. As she sat up in bed, her heart pounding rapidly, she attempted to blink through her sleep and chase away her confusion. Somewhere off through the darkness of the room, Shadow growled in warning and she heard the hound stalk about in agitation.

In the deathly silence that followed, Cassana felt the familiar taste of fear well up inside her and casting silken sheets aside, she swung herself from the bed, touching her feet to the cold marble floor below. Allowing the chill to wake her properly, she let her eyes adjust to the darkness and slid the knife from under her pillow. Shadow padded quickly to her side and nudged her urgently, his yellow eyes bright and wide with worry.

"What is it boy?" she asked reluctantly. Steeling herself, Cassana rose and followed the dog to the door of her bed chambers. Opening the door nervously, she could see the sanctuary of the lounge beyond, thin shards of a pitying moon splitting the dark. Hurrying over to the door away to her right, she unlocked it slowly, the catch sounding thunderous in the eerie silence of the keep.

Where are the guards? Cassana thought nervously, why was there no investigation of the scream? Her worry drew her on through her rising concern and clad only in her flimsy nightdress, she slipped out into the cold corridor beyond.

With her guardian padding along at her bare heels, Cassana stole through the night, her sickness and fear rising through her body with each faltering footstep. It felt as if the keep was deserted and that only she and the hound now remained.

As she slipped down the corridor, lit by a single torch burning erratically in a brazier, she reached out with her right hand, to touch the cold stone wall for comfort. Cassana's body was now numb, her skin rippled by fear and taut with a whispering warning that chilled her further... she was needlessly putting herself in harm's way.

Each footstep she took only drew her deeper into her anxiety. Something was seriously wrong. Where *were* the guards? Surely they would have been alerted to the scream by now?

Shaking her head, her tangled locks falling about her shoulders, Cassana's tongue clicked against the back of her teeth chidingly.

"You were probably dreaming," she said, snorting foolishly. "You really should..."

She peered round the corner, towards the open doorway and choked on her words.

Bright moonlight spilled through the pointed window at the end of the long corridor, casting a mournful, silvery light on the still form beyond.

Reaching for a breath that was not there, Cassana ordered her hound to stay and stepped warily into the moonlight. As she did, a strangled gasp escaped her lips and the knife slipped from her hand, clattering onto the stone floor.

"NO!" she screamed, her voice bounding down the corridor ahead of her. Cassana raced towards the crumpled form and as she did, she slipped in a pool of spreading blood and crashed heavily to the floor.

Shrieking, Cassana crawled through the blood and pulled Karlina into her arms.

"Oh no! Oh no!" she sobbed, caressing the girl's sodden hair, wiping it from her eyes with shaking fingers.

Cassana looked about helplessly. There was blood everywhere, so much blood she could see her own reflection, glistening in the moonlit crimson pool.

"HELP!" Cassana screamed, looking about her surroundings frantically again. "Help us!"

"Cass?" Karlina murmured faintly, her eyes flickering open briefly, before closing slowly again.

Sobbing from relief, Cassana caressed the girl's pale face and let out a startled breath. "Oh Karli, what happened to you, lovely?"

Moaning, the young girl stirred and she opened her eyes again, staring up through Cassana's protective veil of hair.

"I'm sorry," Karlina whispered, fighting for each word. "I had to come... home, b-but she was here."

"Who was here?"

Karlina shuddered, her dull, emerald eyes flashing with brief, bright anger. "She took Arillion's knife, s-she recognised it, she..."

Cassana frowned. "Who did?" she pleaded, her eyes drifting to the girl's stomach and the deep wound there. Gasping, Cassana clamped one hand over the wound and felt Karlina's warm life slipping through her fingers.

"A woman, b-blonde hair – scar on her face..."

Cassana's head roared from the echo of hasty panic in her chest and her skin crawled as she detected distant shouts of alarm and the sound of hurried approach.

Shadow, ignoring his mistress's orders, padded to their side and began howling.

"Help is coming Karli," Cassana said, weeping heavily. She held the girl close as she began to fight and writhe in agony. "Save your strength, you are going to be alright. Just hold on a little longer."

"It's ok, Cass," Karlina said suddenly, her voice as clear as a clarion call. She grinned impishly. "I'm going to see grandpa and Flotsam, again. They'll look after me now..."

Karlina's body went taught momentarily and as the smile slipped from the girl's freckled face, her final breath chased reluctantly after it.

William Bay gripped his sword tightly as he raced up the spiral staircase, the screams of panic above echoing down to him. Behind, Erith Taye hurried after him, the torch he carried casting writhing, menacing shadows onto the curving wall ahead of them.

Chasing after his own flickering shadow, William hurried on, nimbly so for a man of his years. Above him, somewhere in the distance he could hear the echoing wails and screams for help continuing, rising desperately and falling away ominously between each reaching, imploring breath. The sounds cut through his nerves, chilling him to his bones and as they turned to reach the landing above, his heart hammered with frightful expectancy at what they were about to discover.

The corridor that swept across before him was dark, lit only by a faint, reluctant moon that reached into the keep through an arched window. As the dancing light from Erith's torch spilled gleefully into the darkness, scattering the shadows away, William's eyes were dragged to his left.

On the ground, a large pool of blood drew his

concern away to the left and, shuddering, he led his companion on, following the trail of blood that suggested someone had dragged themselves, or a body, across the cold stone.

Following on past a darkened doorway, the trail led them to an archway. As they neared warily, the distant, pleading screams cried out again and sharing a determined look, the two men rushed on, the bobbing flames of Erith's torch lighting the way for them.

With his sword forgotten in his left hand, Lord Byron's closest friend stared in horror at the scene that greeted him as he stepped into the corridor beyond.

Cassana, her face a mask of utter panic, was on her knees, the lifeless body of Karlina cradled tightly in her arms. There was blood everywhere and Cassana rocked back and forth in shock, her mouth wide open, her raw throat searching for the screams that would no longer come. Tears streaked down her cheeks as she looked imploringly, futilely, at the newcomers for help that was no longer needed.

Behind them, the old hound turned about in confusion, leaving a trail of bloodied prints on the stone as it howled away mournfully.

Erith gasped as he stepped beside William Bay and looked aghast at the lifeless girl in Cassana's arms. Her eyes were closed, her face serene almost, not in keeping with one who had just been torn cruelly from this world. Gripped by his shock Erith just stood there, his burning torch trembling in his hand.

"My lady," William's voice slipped free, as he moved hurriedly forward. "Are you hurt? What has happened here?"

Cassana looked up blankly at him, still searching for the scream that heaved violently in her stomach. She shook her head free of the madness in her eyes.

"Assassin," was all she could manage, her words barely a whisper.

William felt the stab of urgency from her words and stiffened. He turned to Erith, his face a grim mask, taut with apprehension.

"Fetch my wife here," he snapped. "Raise the alarm and seal off the keep immediately."

Forgetting to salute, Erith Taye spun on his heels and hurried away, his booted feet echoing as the torchlight chased after him.

"Wait here, my lady," William said softly. Grimly, he turned and hurried away along the corridor to the right, his sword keen and gleaming in the moonlight as it led the way.

Cassana trembled, holding Karlina close for a warmth that was no longer there, as the first distant cries of the alarm rang out across the keep. Dumb from shock, she shook her head in despair and looked down at the girl in her bloodied arms. Karlina looked asleep and for the briefest, cruellest of moments Cassana thought it all a bad dream.

She knew it wasn't; that the realisation of this night's events would scar her deeply for many years to come with wounds that would probably never heal. But her hollow, exhausted body and mind could not allow her to come to terms with what had happened. She tried to focus on the rational, to step away from herself and sift through her thoughts long enough to grasp on to something that would give her the focus she needed – but her strength was spent and exhausted, she had nothing left to give. Cassana slipped back into her despair and simply held on to the dead girl in her arms.

As he raced alone through the darkness, William Bay was aware of the fear that was creeping up his spine. It sat on his shoulder for a time, whispering warnings as he stepped into another hallway. The torches on the walls were dead in their brackets, when they should have been bright with life.

William's fears roared their concerns in his head, his legs feeling suddenly heavy, slowed by his years and leaden from the sense that he would not like what he was about to discover.

The events in the city had stretched the keep to their limits that night. The voracious fires that had broken out in a warehouse in the east district had demanded that many of the keep's guards were needed to bolster a watch that were trying their best to keep order in the streets below. Those who were left behind, himself included, had been called to muster, to see to Lord Byron's protection.

As William passed the turning for his friend's study, he saw the first signs of blood on the now-carpeted stone floor. A thick trail of it led away to a closed door to his left and resisting the desire to investigate further, he felt renewed urgency chastise his faltering steps.

By the time he came close to Alion Byron's private chambers, William knew that something was seriously wrong. There were no guards on duty outside and the hallway was cloaked in shadows. At the end of the hallway, next to an upturned stool, a dark, lead-lined window rattled open in a stiffening breeze.

Creeping cautiously towards the chambers, William could see that the door was slightly ajar. Each step that took him closer fell into tandem with the hammering of his heart and the door loomed large before him. Caught in his throat, his breath slipped onto his trembling lips as he pushed his way into Lord Byron's quarters beyond and then stole into the night on his strangled, anguished gasp.

By the time Elisabeth Bay found her, Cassana was as pale as the girl in her arms. Stifling her horror with her free hand, Mistress Bay hurried forward, her wide eyes flicking despairingly at the scene before her. Dressed only in a blue night-robe, she placed her candle holder carefully outside the wide pool of blood that had now ceased spreading and watched briefly as the thick candle protested and sputtered, before settling down to shed its warm light calmly again.

Outside, the night was alive with the sounds of distant cries, as the guards that remained searched the grounds and keep for the perpetrator. The tramp of hurried feet in the centre courtyard below distracted her for a moment and, as the desperate cries took the searching guards away again, Elisabeth ran a shaking hand through her unpinned, dark hair and knelt before her charges.

"Oh, Cassana," she murmured sadly, leaning close to brush the hair from the sobbing woman's eyes. She gently tilted Lady Byron's face upwards. "Who would do such a thing?"

Cassana's eyes were raw and wild, the sharpest blue that pierced the shadows. Her lips trembled as she tried to force some strength into her breath, but she could not find the words and simply broke down once more, firmly wrenching her chin away as she hid in the arms of her despair again.

Dropping her unwanted hand to Cassana's shuddering shoulder, Elisabeth Bay silently offered her support as she focused her attentions on the dead girl. Reviled, her breath caught in her throat. She could see that a deep wound had been slashed across the girl's stomach; a wound so terrible, that even the most skilled surgeon could not have stemmed it.

Karlina's fate that night had been sealed from the moment she stepped into the corridor and whatever had occurred here, would resonate through their lives for many months to come.

"I am so sorry," Elisabeth whispered solemnly and then started, as Cassana reached up with bloodied fingers and squeezed her hand gently in thanks.

"No." Cassana hissed vehemently as Elisabeth Bay tried, once again, to coax Karlina's body from her arms. They had spent a long time in silence, lost within their shared grief and awaiting William Bay's return.

"Please, Lady Byron," the older woman persisted. "You must let me take her. You will catch your death if you don't try and get some rest."

"I will not leave her," Cassana murmured, her eyes bright with fresh tears. "I just cannot..."

Elisabeth nodded, allowing her own tears to crease her face for the first time. Nodding, she leant in close to kiss Cassana on her forehead. "I understand, my lady. We shall both see to her, together."

Cassana smiled faintly and drew in a deep, calming breath. She nodded and slowly, reluctantly, relinquished her grip on Karlina. Elisabeth Bay gently took the body and watched as Cassana closed her eyes and licked her lips, breathing some determination back into her trembling body as she started to slowly rise.

"Oh my," Cassana said, as she swooned and fell back against the wall for support.

With gentle encouragement, Elisabeth coaxed her mistress to steady herself, to calm her emotions long enough to find her balance. Breathing deeply for some time, Lady Byron closed her bloodied eyes again, gathering her wits patiently and obediently.

When Cassana opened her eyes once more, her focus was drawn immediately to the scene before her and, despite her steely growl of defiance, she gave in to her emotions and broke down again.

Elisabeth was about to speak when she caught movement out of the corner of her right eye. Turning her head, she saw her husband step through the open doorway and stumble through the moonlight towards them. As the silvery rays illuminated his face for a moment, she could see that it was clenched tight with emotions that she could not discern.

"Husband?" she called out worriedly, dragging Cassana's attention to his arrival.

William Bay walked towards them, ignoring Shadow's need for attention. His eyes were hooded as he slipped his sword back into the scabbard at his right hip with a shaking hand.

He came to stand before them, the candlelight reflecting in his glistening eyes as he turned them slowly, reluctantly to the Lady of the house.

"I-I," William began, his usually clear voice shackled by the words he had to say and his desire not to say them. He dropped to his knees before Cassana and grasped her bloodied hands in his own.

Perplexed, Cassana stared down her bare arms at him, feeling his calloused hands shake uncontrollably.

"I regret so very, very deeply my lady, that your father is dead... has been murdered this night."

Blinking in disbelief, Cassana's eyes glazed over, rolling sedately in her head. She passed out before her scream could even touch her lips.

CHAPTER TWO

Betrayal

Fawn Ardent watched the slow dawn that crept ominously in from the east. A subtle shift in the darkness at first, it slowly spread its searching fingers across Havensdale, offering little hope to those gathered on the ramparts of the town.

Watching her breath cloud before her, Fawn did her best to calm her nerves and studied the clouds that were scattered across the sky by a playful breeze. She licked her dry lips nervously and shuddered at the omens. The rising sun, but still a blushing thought on the horizon, was slowly, ominously edging the clouds with the deepest red.

Scowling, Fawn tied her unruly hair back at the nape of her neck, her trembling fingers fighting to hold onto the tresses that fretted in the wind. Eventually satisfied, she rubbed the rawness of a sleepless night from her eyes and turned her attention reluctantly back to the west.

Shrouded in a creeping dawn mist that drifted from the still waters of the River Haven and clung to the land, Campbell's farmstead was silent, offering no clues as to what had happened inside the previous night.

Following their ultimatum, the Carwellian forces had taken up residence in the farmhouse, their hostages acting as reluctant hosts for the night. Forcing those gathered on the ramparts of the town to watch on helplessly, Commander Gardan had stridden about the western bank confidently, organising the men and women under his command with stabbing fingers and cold, snapping barks.

Half the forces took up position before the south of the town, pitching tents on the side of the road and waiting silently for what would surely follow the next day. Several ladders had been taken from the large barn at the rear of the Campbell's home, offering a stark warning to the defenders.

Fawn gripped the palisade and growled, ignoring the look Sergeant Manse dealt her. Wrapping her dark cloak tighter about her frame, she watched the solitary guard outside the farmhouse and shook her head forlornly.

Leaving several guards on the walls, Fawn and her father had held a meeting in the Arms of the Lady, a meeting that had quickly spiralled out of control. Many of the town's residents had attended, all crying out their demands, most of them fearful of what the mayor's defiance to Carwell would mean for them.

In the end, Dekan Ardent had brought order to the proceedings with a furious fist upon wood. As the disputes faltered and faded away, he strode about the crowded taproom, silencing any dissent with angry, withering eyes.

"I understand all of your concerns," he had begun, his eyes flashing in the inn's lamplight. "I share all of them... how could anyone not? But make no mistake, if we open our gates and hand over what the Carwellian Commander demands, we shall live with the bloody stain of our actions on our hands and consciences for the rest of our lives."

Nobody had offered a response and from her position at the bar, standing beside the barkeeper, Joseph Moore,

Fawn had hung her head. She could sense the eyes falling upon her, could see the doubt already sown into them.

'*Was she a traitor*?' many of them wondered. 'Was she working with the Reven?'

On her honour, Fawn knew that she was not, had only sought to help Cassana Byron, when the young woman's need was greatest. Nothing more than that! Had she known what she was getting herself and the people of Havensdale into, she may well have chosen a different path.

No she wouldn't...

Durnast Brogan, the proprietor of The Well and Joseph Moore's erstwhile rival had risen then, drawing everyone's attention to him. Short and stocky, his fierce countenance and fiery temper commanded wary respect in the town. He had taken a long draw on his pipe and held it there for many moments, his stern gaze sweeping about the inn.

"You all know me," he had growled, his words almost forming in the smoke before him. "I have lived in this town for many years, bled for it and helped to keep it safe. I speak to you today, however, not as a member of the council, nor even as the most prosperous businessman in the town..."

At her side, Fawn had felt Joseph Moore bristle at the barb that his rival had sent his way. Scowling, Joseph had continued to furiously polish the bar with a cloth to divert his anger.

"...but as one who has seen war, experienced the madness that can descend when people are scared, fearful of what will happen if they stand up to those who would stamp their authority all over them," Durnast had continued, tugging at his thick beard. He had jabbed his pipe at the faces that surrounded him. "Mark my words, if we try to keep the peace by betraying our own, we *will* suffer for it in the end, this is the beginning of something

– I can smell it!"

The retired warrior had returned to his seat and his pipe, leaving the rest of the room to attend to their thoughts.

Dekan Ardent had nodded, taking the floor again whilst the momentum was there to be had. "I agree with our friend. We are governed by the law and must continue to be so, lest we give rise to the rule of fear from an iron fist. We *must* stand together. We must not bow down to these threats and give in to these Carwellian demands. We have nothing, or no one to hide and Highwater will defend our stance."

A lone, solitary crow dipped and raised its head, as it cried out a mournful salute, bringing Fawn back to the present. Glaring at the bird, perched on the palisade away to her right, she tried to find some sense somewhere amongst all the madness.

The meeting at the inn had broken up with a fragile, collective pledge of defiance, one that would see Havensdale stand firm and resolute, no matter the cost. The thought that others would now suffer with her did little to ease Fawn's anguish, however, and she had spent a long night awake, searching for answers in the dark.

The revelation from Sergeant Manse that Rellin, Arrun and Jessica had fled the safety of the town in the night had dragged her from her turmoil in the deathly hours. It had done little to ease her fears, only given rise to them, especially when the recruits had been seen fleeing into the Moonglade Forest and Gardan had sent five of his men into the shadows after them.

Hanging her head, Fawn sighed. Lost in her despair, she barely felt the sergeant's hand upon her leather-clad shoulder.

"They will be alright," Larne whispered, reading her thoughts. "Rellin knows the woods better than most; he will lead them to safety."

Fawn looked up, sensing the belief in his words, but detecting the worry in his eyes. She forced a smile and straightened crisply.

"You are an awful liar, Larne," she said. "But I thank you for it."

They fell silent and looked to the west again. Around them, several of the militia soldiers paced the wall, trying to stretch the nerves from their legs and flex the cramp from hands that gripped weapons far too tightly.

After a time, Larne let his hand slip from her shoulder and looked back towards the south gate. Six militia soldiers guarded the walls, one below at the gate. A cart had been overturned and placed just inside the south gate, to halt any mounted assault, should their defences be breached.

Shaking his head, he swept a bitter gaze about the town and, though everyone still kept to the safety of their homes, he expected that none had slept well in their beds that night.

Along the wall, the crow tired of waiting for something to happen and took to the sky, winging its way northwards in silence.

Not everyone in Havensdale felt the burden of the morning's gloom, however. Commander Renald Gardan strode from the broken doorway of Campbell's farm and stepped into the waking morning with a smile on his face. Breathing in the crisp freshness of the day, he nodded towards the sentry and, holding his leather gloves in one hand, slapped them purposefully into the palm of the other.

On the roof of the farmhouse behind him, an old black and white cat stirred from its curled slumber, cocking a curious ear towards the sound. It opened one eye slightly and viewed the stranger sceptically.

Scanning the town before him, Gardan could see the defenders stir worriedly at his appearance and he smiled happily. *The delay had been a masterful one*! Had he simply slit the throat of the farmer, they would have reacted with the clarity of force and any chance of claiming his prize would have been surely lost. Giving them a sleepless night to mull over their fate, however, increased his chances that the Ardent girl would still be his. The town's inhabitants would be plagued by fear, arguing amongst themselves at what should be done to resolve the matter. They would, Gardan thought, a smile creasing his harsh features, most certainly hand her over, once the blood started to flow and the walls were breached.

Ignoring the warning that berated him for his over-confidence, Commander Gardan pulled on his gloves slowly, theatrically.

He had the hand of the Brotherhood on his shoulder and, whilst in the eyes of his brothers and sisters some might think he acted hastily, they would all applaud his efforts once the day was done.

His gleeful anticipation was tempered momentarily with the thought that their brother inside the town had not acted to let them in, had not even sent a signal. *Perhaps he was not even there?* The five men he had sent after the *traitors* had not returned yet, either.

No matter! Gardan thought, smiling. It was of no consequence, as their numbers and experience still gave them the advantage.

"By my hand, the Brotherhood's will be done," Gardan whispered, bolstering his confidence again.

By the day's end, one way or another, Fawn Ardent would be dead and trouble them no more.

Aren Bray stepped out into the rising dawn alongside his commander and, after slowly taking in the view across the bridge before him, turned his gaze to the sword-thin man he would follow to the end.

"Ah, Aren," Gardan said merrily, turning his steely gaze towards him. "Shall we begin?"

Aren felt the slow rhythm of his heart begin to quicken and swallowing down the last of any doubts he may have had, he turned on his heel and went in search of their prisoners.

Fawn Ardent's skin stiffened with fear as Commander Gardan strode to the edge of the bridge. He stood there silently for a time, sweeping his gaze along the line of defenders. His blue eyes flashed balefully, in contrast to the affable smile that spread slowly across his drawn features.

"Have you come to your senses, lady?" he called out, his voice clear, as it rang out over the silence of the morning.

Gardan stood there for a time, waiting for an answer he was sure he would not get. Cocking his head to one side, he listened patiently and idly leant upon the bridge.

"Well, there you have it," he said, eventually. Straightening, the commander stood there, glaring across the bridge at them, his hands on his hips. With no answer apparently forthcoming, he shook his head and returned to his men, who were now gathering outside in the misty morning.

Fawn looked to her sergeant, then along the wall, as her father and Durnast Brogan joined them. The mayor was dressed in the studded leather garb of the Havensdale militia. He carried his trusty Valian Longsword in his right hand and wore an old, battered wooden shield off his left arm.

Behind him, Durnast Brogan was clad in a tight-fitting shirt of chain mail, one that would have once offered him more room to breathe. His leather trousers were clad in steel greaves and his forearms protected by dented, iron vambraces. Coming to stand before them, the old, retired warrior leant upon the haft of his large, upturned axe and studied the farm beyond.

"Perrin has joined the south gate," Fawn's father reported, puffing out his pale cheeks. "He will lead the defence there."

Fawn nodded her thanks, unable to find a smile. Perrin Hawksblade, the town's sword master, was of venerable age, but well respected in Havensdale. Despite the worry he must have about his missing son, she was glad to count him amongst their number.

"What's the bastard up to now?" Durnast asked, eyeing the Carwellian forces.

"We are about to find out," Fawn replied in a whisper.

The mayor of Havensdale eyed his daughter. "We will stand together, Fawn, no matter the cost," he said, bending in close to kiss her on one cheek. "Carwell will soon discover that his men cannot threaten people whenever and however he chooses."

Snorting, Durnast Brogan hefted his axe up and rested it on one shoulder. "Gardan's a notorious whoreson," he said, his bald head wrinkling.

Hawking, he spat his disdain over the wall. "We'll be doing the Vales a service if I plant my axe in his skull."

"Let's hope it doesn't have to come to that," Larne Manse offered forlornly.

Moments later he was painfully certain that the cantankerous, retired warrior might well get the chance.

Despite her fear, Sara Campbell was aware something was happening on the west gate. She looked past her brother, following his turning head as they listened to the distant cries and pleas that carried to them on the south gate.

Sara made to move, adjusting the weight of the shield on her arm as she stepped past her brother. Realising what she was about to do, he grabbed her shoulder roughly.

"We have orders to stay here," Kallum said grimly. His eyes were wide with worry and betrayed his desire to go with his sister.

Sara twisted under his hand and her lower lip trembled with fury. "How can we just stand here and let them do these things to mother and father? How can we not act?"

Kallum looked about, his eyes falling on the Carwellian forces before them. They were readying themselves now, spreading out across the road in a disciplined and watchful line.

Around them, Kallum and Sara's comrades offered them looks of sympathy, but remained silent, helpless and unsure what they could do or say to ease their torment.

"We should attack them," Sara hissed, her mind racing. "We have the protection of our walls, we could chase them away now with our spears and arrows."

Kallum had to admit his sister had a point. But their captain's orders, as she sent them away from the west gate, was that Havensdale would react to any attack with '*vigour*' and '*determination*' – but its inhabitants would not instigate the battle, as Lord Carwell would have the excuse he needed to return to the north and burn them all to the ground.

Sara had almost swallowed her tongue in rage, very nearly spitting out words she did not mean. Beyond the safety of her family, what did she care for the politics of the situation? Innocent lives, her loved ones' lives were at stake and be damned all else.

Fortunately for all concerned, her elder brother, despite his own misgivings, could see that the political ramifications of openly attacking the Carwellian forces was something that nobody needed right now. Highwater, and most certainly the high duke in Karick, would be furious when they heard of Commander Gardan's actions here. Better to let him hang himself through his actions, than plunging the north into war with the East Vales.

But at what cost..?

Perrin Hawksblade came to them and took the girl in his arms as she began to cry.

"There, there, my girl," he soothed, his thick white eyebrows arching tightly over his concern.

Kallum watched the old man fondly. Perrin was in his seventieth winter, but had the athleticism and vigour of one forty years younger. His thinning, white hair ranged across his liver-spotted scalp and you could forage for more of it in his large, wrinkled ears.

Perrin's kind face, lined by his full years, was one that all quickly warmed to and his dry wit could ignite laughter whenever he was in the mood. His long, drooping moustache still held some subtle hints of what colour his hair had once been and presently, his green eyes were filled with a deep sadness at what his beloved town was about to endure.

Skilled with many weapons, Perrin Hawksblade was a sword master and he was dressed in fine, elegantly stitched, dark leather armour. His favoured rapier hung off his left hip and a long, thin knife was belted to the other, a twin for the one sheathed inside his right, high leather boot.

Despite his skills, the old man was losing his sight and a joke amongst the younger militia soldiers was that Perrin had the '*ears of a hawk*' but sadly the '*eyes of bat.*'

Hiding his smile, Kallum nodded his thanks to his old tutor, as their eyes met. The old man tilted his head in response, his moustache twitching as he wetted his lips to dilute his own fear.

"It will be alright, girl," Perrin said, kissing the young recruit on her forehead.

Sara looked up at him, sniffing. They shared a look that suggested neither of them believed that for a moment.

Commander Gardan smiled in satisfaction as the farmer and his wife were dragged out into the mud before him. Both were exhausted, their eyes ringed by desperation and rigid with fear.

The tall farmer looked up defiantly, his green eyes blazing away. Gardan met his glare smoothly and smiled sardonically. The man was still dressed in his soiled clothes from the previous day and had been locked in a store cupboard all night with his wife and youngest daughter. Up on the roof, the old cat, sensing something was amiss, scurried up the thatching to be away from the commotion.

At the commander's feet, the farmer's wife sobbed, avoiding his scrutiny by looking, panic-stricken, towards the town for help. Her face was white from the starkness of her terror, but Gardan guessed that with her deep black hair, she was always that pale.

"They won't help you, my lady," Gardan said casually, following her gaze. He smiled, as his keen, hawkish eyes picked out his prey on the ramparts.

Looking to Aren and the gruff, long-haired man... *what was his name?* Gardan shrugged. No matter. Looking to the two men, he jerked his head towards the bridge and he stalked away. Behind, his men followed, dragging their prisoners through the mud.

"Good morning," Gardan called out, brightly. He swept his gaze about his surroundings and drank in the splendour of what promised to be a very fine day.

The land was silent and a breeze, chasing away the clouds like retreating crimson footprints in the sky, rustled the crops in the fields about Havensdale. The mist on the river Haven had lifted slightly and its waters were beginning to sparkle with life as it meandered southwards through the tension.

Outside Havensdale, to the south, he could see that

his man, Faran Cawl had already mustered the men. Upon their commander's signal, they would attack the town, as planned the night before. The four archers they had selected would cover their comrades' advance and keep the defenders busy, as they used their ladders to scale the walls.

"Have you decided to hand yourself over?" Gardan shouted. Turning slightly, he let a gloved hand rest gently on the farmwife's head and patted her tenderly. She shuddered under his touch, her breath heaving and plunging down rapidly through her shaking body.

"Or, Fawn Ardent, will you condemn the *innocents* of Havensdale to suffer for your crimes?"

Gardan looked up at the walls, scanning the faces disinterestedly.

With no answer forthcoming, the commander slowly, very slowly drew his sword and stepped behind his prisoners.

"No," the farmer pleaded, offering his hands up to the sky. "Please! My wife, she has children to look after! If you must do this, let it be me."

Gardan was actually touched by the man's offer of sacrifice to save his wife. The woman sobbed, begging her husband to be silent.

The commander straightened, looking up at Fawn Ardent.

"Well, my lady?" he roared, his face flushing with impatience. "Shall we end this civilly?"

He could see the captain clearly now, her eyes wide with worry, her face twisted with the situation he had placed her in.

She reached out to grip the palisade and closed her eyes, pulling in a deep breath. When she opened her eyes again, Gardan could already read her response.

"If you want me," Fawn Ardent called down. "Come and get me."

Sighing, Gardan looked to his men. "Then it begins," he smiled and raised his sword.

Aware of the commotion above him, Colbin Wicksford fought hard to stay at his post, underneath the south gate. With some people trapped in Havensdale from other towns and villages, Fawn Ardent had been very expressive in her wants when she said that she didn't need anyone trapped inside the town suddenly deciding they wanted to return home before any fighting began.

Colbin huffed in frustration, rubbing his bearded chin, as he fought with his own desires. His home and his family were trapped on the west banks of the river, currently free of the Carwellian gaze. He wondered, however, how long that would remain so if the day did not go as planned and the resilient defenders repelled their attacks.

He heard the ruthless commander call out and muttered to himself, as the man's demands went unheeded. Shaking his head, Colbin peered through a narrow gap in the wood, studying the Carwellian patrol amassing at their door.

Colbin cursed, touching his forehead to the cool oak and closed his eyes. Ever since that Seer had come to the town, things had started to go wrong... the weather, the morale of the town, little Milly Ford getting trapped under the wheel of Lestarn's wagon; and now this. The words spoken to him by the Seer flashed in his mind and growling, Colbin scattered them, pushing aside his rising fears. It was all bluster, none of it true – just the ramblings of an old man who could conjure up fanciful riddles to play on one's hopes, their fears and dreams.

No! Colbin decided, after many days of torment. It was better to focus on what was real; keep his wits and head in one place, for what was now, surely, ahead. He needed to focus.

He found himself thinking of the woman they had escorted to the capital and decided that the troubles growing large on their doorstep had probably been sown all those weeks before... long before that old relic had come looking for coin and minds to play with.

The sounds of approach touched his ears and he turned, looking in confusion as a man stumbled drunkenly past the narrow gap afforded by the upturned wagon.

Colbin felt a pang of sympathy as he recognised the man. Roland Ford had been at the meeting last night, venting his spleen and frustrations to those present on his apparent '*incarceration*' in the town. He had been in Havensdale for the past week now, working on the leaking roof of his uncle, Trent Ford, and had been keen to return home to Colden, before anything untoward started to happen. When things had not gone in his favour, Rol Ford, as he was more commonly known in the region, had sought the answers to his dilemma in a barrel of *Campbell's Own*.

"Rol," Colbin called out affably, offering his hands up to the man, stumbling towards him. "Come on, we've been through this, man. We can't let you home! It's too dangerous, for all of us."

The man was deep into his fifties and clothed in the loose fitting garb of a labourer. He tripped as he stumbled forward into Colbin's arms.

"I juhst want to get home to me wife and lad," he slurred, his eyes lolling as Colbin steadied him.

"I know, I know – I'm sorry," Colbin said, patting the drunk on the back of the neck. "We'll have you safely home to them soon, I promise."

The man's head came up, the stupor clearing from his eyes suddenly as one of his arms jerked violently.

Colbin stiffened, staring in shock at the sudden transformation. It wasn't until Roland Ford twisted the knife he had driven deep into his neck and clamped a rough hand over his mouth, that the militia soldier realised he had been stabbed.

The gatehouse above him began to spin and a furious heat spread through his body, fleeing from the biting chill that chased after it. Speckles of piercing light clouded his vision and as Colbin was lowered gently to the ground, he turned his head, his lips trembling as he fought for a final breath to raise the alarm.

As the last of his strength slipped away, Colbin's final memory was of Roland Ford, looming large before him, as he lifted the crossbeam off the gates and quietly pulled them open.

CHAPTER THREE

The Darkest Day

Kallum Campbell threw a fearful look at his sister as fresh screams rose from the west. On the south gate the guards tensed, gripping their weapons for reassurance as the Carwellian forces before them started moving slowly forward. Scanning the approaching line, he could see ladders hoisted onto shoulders and felt his skin harden as he spied the skulking bowmen among their ranks.

"Archers," he hissed, drawing Perrin's attention to them. The old man squinted and shielded his failing eyes with a wrinkled, thin hand.

The advancing line suddenly stopped, as if waiting for a signal or the order to attack and the defenders, to the last, waited nervously with wild, punching hearts that threw their rising fear into their mouths.

"Steady now," Perrin said, his voice calming as he spoke. "Breathe, clear your minds and your body and sword arm will do the rest for you."

Something suddenly stirred below them and the movement caught Sara's eyes.

"What in the..?" she said, blinking in disbelief.

A man hurried into view below them from the shadows of the gatehouse, a large wooden beam balanced on one shoulder as he made towards the enemy lines.

At her side, Sara's brother swore, dragging forth another breath as the cold realisation of what was happening swept through him.

"What are you doing, Roland?" he roared, hefting his spear up.

The man spun, almost losing his balance. With a wicked grin on his face and the betrayal flashing in his eyes, he threw the crossbeam from his shoulder and bowed mockingly. Turning, he limped for the Carwellian line, Kallum's spear catching safely in the muddied ground behind him.

Perrin drew in a rattling, horrified breath as the traitor, a man who had relatives living in Havensdale, was swallowed up by the enemy as they dropped their ladders and charged eagerly towards the town.

"To the gates!" the sword master shrieked. He turned and moved in timely fashion, as the dark, feathered shaft of an arrow struck the wall behind him.

Sara ducked as a second shaft buried deep in her shield and as she closed her eyes, her fear completely consuming her, two short, piercing blasts from a hunting horn sounded, before being drowned by the roars of the advancing soldiers.

Commander Gardan's arm faltered as he was about to slice his sword through the back of the woman's neck. His heart and body pulsed with joy as the sound of the horn echoed across the stillness of the day. All eyes turned towards the south gate, be they prisoner, attacker or defender and the air was thick with both tension and exultation.

As Faran Cawl and his men raced towards the town, Gardan's keen eyes picked out the retreating figure of a man, as he fled along the road towards the south.

With eyes wide, the commander looked for Aren Bray and grinned maniacally. "We are in," he cried, the woman he was about to execute momentarily forgotten.

Aren looked down at the farmer he was holding by the scruff of his collar and grinned as he shoved him disdainfully down into the mud.

Flicking a look to his men, amassing eagerly behind them now, Gardan smiled smugly, the kind of smile that filled a face when the person knew they finally had what they had always wanted.

"Come, my brothers and sisters," Renald Gardan cried, his raised sword gleaming with anticipation. "Let us claim our prize. ATTACK!"

Gardan turned through his triumph to lead his forces across the bridge and then stopped abruptly...

Tess Varun, her spear gripped tightly in both hands, had watched on helplessly as the Carwellian commander was about to kill Sara's mother. Unable to drag her eyes away, she stood watching, transfixed, barely hearing the blasts from the horn, almost not registering the command to stay at her post as Fawn Ardent and half the defenders raced away to protect the south gate.

The reluctant witness watched on as the scene before her unfolded and she dealt a horrified look at Sergeant Manse, as he prepared the defenders with words of encouragement that she did not hear.

She drew some strength from his blazing, angry eyes and then noted the surprise and confusion there, as he looked to the ground before the bridge.

Tess followed his eyes and drew in her shock with a gasp of disbelief.

"Oh my," she whispered.

A hooded man walked with casual confidence towards the

eastern banks of the river, his muddied leather boots splashing through a rutted puddle, as he came to stand before the bridge. Cloaked in garb of woodland brown and green, his features were hidden in the shadows of his cowl and the tall man waited silently, his hands pulling the dark embroidered cloak tighter about his frame.

Commander Gardan, his confidence tempered by his surprise, wrinkled his face in annoyance at this newcomer's petulance. He licked his lips, dining once again on the glorious anticipation of his impending success, despite the momentary interruption.

"You are either a fool," Gardan called out pointedly, as the man tested the wooden bridge with a booted foot, "or an idiot! I can't quite decide. This is no concern of yours. Move on stranger, or my men will cut you down where you stand."

The early morning fell eerily silent, the sounds of the Carwellian charge to the south forgotten as all who witnessed the bizarre exchange became drawn to the drama unfolding at the bridge.

The stranger turned his hood to the south, as if jostling his thoughts to order, before looking back across the bridge towards the farm.

"They will try," the man's calm, clear voice responded. Up on the walls of Havensdale, the defenders shared incredulous looks.

Gardan stepped back, as if physically struck. He looked at the men beside him and then snapped his attention back across the bridge.

"Do I know you, stranger?" Gardan demanded, his eyes narrowing quizzically.

The hooded man's shoulders rose and fell inconsequentially. "Why don't you come closer and find out."

To the north, a skylark suddenly rose up into the grey skies above some fields. It sang beautifully for a moment, as it rose slowly through the air. As if realising its joy was out of place, it fell silent and dropped down into the crops to hide away again.

Glowering impatiently, Gardan flicked a bored, exasperated look about and then waved his sword forward in a determined, sweeping arc.

"Kill that imbecile," he screeched.

As his men streamed around him, Commander Gardan's eyes glittered balefully. He smiled faintly then, vile images of the stranger's impending death flickering in his mind. His prisoners were now forgotten, much like the sword raised high in his hand.

Kallum Campbell leapt the remaining steps to the ground and made for the gatehouse as the first attackers spilled round the upturned cart. Behind him Perrin Hawksblade's breath scratched in his chest, as the old man sought to keep up with him and the hasty tramp of boots signalled others followed impatiently behind.

A Carwellian soldier, dressed in riding leathers and a vest of silver mail, made towards them, his face a grim mask as he gripped his cavalry sabre in gloved hands.

He came at Kallum who, despite his bravery, had never fought another man for his life before and as their blades met, singing in greeting, the attacker swept their locked steel to one side, hammering an elbow into the side of the militia man's head.

Kallum staggered back, his vision spinning as the man, his long dark hair flailing wildly about his shoulders, quickly recovered his balance. With his fear numbing his arm, Kallum's blade came up slowly, far too slowly and as the Carwellian soldier's sword flashed for his throat, he tried to throw himself back.

Perrin Hawksblade appeared at his shoulder, elegantly turning the man's blade aside, before countering swiftly to pierce him through the heart. Kallum watched in disbelief, time seemingly catching up with him again as the clamouring roar of chaos surged anew in his ears.

With wide, startled eyes, the attacker dropped to his knees, staring at the two men before him. Grim-faced, Perrin pulled his thin blade free and looked quickly about the market area, as the dying man pitched forward into a spreading pool of his own blood.

Before Kallum could thank his saviour, they were overrun by more attackers...

Fawn Ardent reached the bottom of the steps by the west gate, to be met by Joseph Moore, the proprietor of the Arms of the Lady Inn. The reluctant barkeeper had been guarding the gate, but had left his post to come to her aid.

Fawn glanced at him, as four Carwellian attackers split away from their comrades who were fighting at the south gate and made across the market place to capture the west as well.

"No matter what, they must not open these gates," Fawn panted, trying to calm herself down.

Gripping his short blade, Joseph nodded his reply, his face ashen and his hands shaking.

Fawn's father joined them and the three friends spread out in a resolute, defensive line before the upturned cart. In the distance, she could see the overwhelmed defenders fighting bravely and the stocky form of Durnast Brogan, as he roared an old battle cry and raced across the cobbles to help them.

Overhead, the breaking clouds slipped unnoticed away to the east, as the first light of the rising sun cast its attentions on the day.

As the men surged across the bridge towards the hooded figure, the man stepped forward to meet them, his arms slipping free from their concealment. As he threw a knife at the first Carwellian attacker with his left, the hooded man drew a long bladed sword with his right. The knife took the charging man high in the chest and his momentum took him several more steps closer, before he went down, tripping the man behind.

Grabbing a loaded crossbow from its resting place against the wall, Sergeant Manse raised it, ignoring Tess's gasps, as the stranger raised his sword in salute to his enemies, kissed the steel hilt and strode boldly forward across the bridge to meet his opponents.

He barely registered what was happening on the bridge, as the Carwellian tide surged towards the mysterious rock that stood in their way. Before they came together in the centre of the bridge, the sergeant found his mark, who stood watching the unfolding battle with a mixture of annoyance and astonishment on his haughty face.

"I've got you now, you bastard," Larne hissed and letting out a steadying breath, he pulled the trigger.

Turning aside a sweeping attack, the hooded man punched his opponent in the jaw. As the old warrior buckled, he was pitched from the bridge into the river with an accompanying boot.

Barely recovering, the hooded man ducked low under a blade that nearly took his head off and buried his sword deep in the offered armpit. Blood splashed his concealed face as he reclaimed his steel and his opponent fell, his screams drowning out the furious cries of the soldiers coming towards him. Backing away, the man threw back his cloak and pulled free the shorter blade that hung from a leather sheath off his right hip.

The next attacker to step over the dying man was a woman and she came at him with grim menace in her blue eyes. Behind her, four more attackers came forward warily, their ranks reluctantly thinned to two abreast on the bridge.

With the early sun catching in her short, rusted hair, the woman's blade flicked out, almost catching the hooded man off guard. Silently, he offered her a testing blade that probed her defences, and she turned that aside easily. Grunting, she came at him again, and her flashy lunge offered him far too much, as he twisted by it and hammered the steel from her hands. As the blade clattered to the wooden bridge, she looked up in horror at him.

The man shook his head sadly as he cut his blades across her lovely face.

With his aim true, the bolt from Sergeant Manse's crossbow punched into the Carwellian commander, spinning him away and sending him to the ground. Angry shrieks rose from the crumpled form and his second in command, who had been watching the battle on the bridge with folded arms, turned in shock to aid him. Amidst the confusion, Robert Campbell rose up, throwing his head back into the face of his captor.

Sensing the desperation of their plight, Larne Manse began hurriedly reloading his crossbow, his shaking fingers fumbling as he fitted the bolt to the weapon.

Tess hefted her spear, but a despairing shout from the other man at her side, Jerrin Wicksford, stayed her hand.

The eldest brother of three Wicksford lads, Jerrin, unlike his boisterous brother, Colbin, was a quiet, unassuming giant of a man, whose calm, gentle face and curly, sandy hair made him a popular man with the local girls.

"Too far," Jerrin said, shaking his head. "Wait for the fighting to open up, or you'll hit the swordsman."

Tess baulked, dragging her eyes to the focus of their attention. As they watched him, his blades cutting deftly into the ranks of attackers that were slowly forcing him back across the bridge, they heard the sounds of fresh battle joined behind them.

Without thinking, father and daughter stepped apart and rushed forward to protect Joseph Moore, who shrank away as the Carwellian soldiers charged them.

Stepping in to meet her opponent, Fawn Ardent put him off balance with an attack that was meant to claim his life. As he tried to recover, she slashed her sword across his right shoulder and the man growled in pain as he recoiled.

Another man forced Fawn back, his short blade hissing as it rasped by her face, kissing her cheek. With her heart pounding and her adrenalin coursing, Fawn did not feel the sting of pain, nor notice the blood that began spilling down her face.

At her side, Dekan Ardent moved with a grace and fluidity of one who had rediscovered his youth. With his sword guiding stiffened muscles, he cut his first attacker's charge down with a vicious blow to the gullet and then caught the next man's axe on his shield.

Two more men from Carwell broke from the throng at the south gate and began hurrying away from the mad axe-wielder coming towards them, to help their comrades at the west gate.

Fawn blocked an attack from the large man she faced and felt the force of his blow ride up her arm. With his comrade on one knee behind him, clutching at his shoulder wound, the bald-headed man grinned, noting the fear in his opponent's eyes.

"You should have come quietly, girl," Faran Cawl growled. As Fawn went to reply, he sprang forward, his swirling, twisting attack forcing the sword from Fawn's hand.

"No!" Joseph Moore cried out desperately, as the man from Carwell raised his sword and stepped forward to finish their mission.

CHAPTER FOUR

The Tangled Webs We Weave

Savinn Kassaar tapped his fingers together, distracting his impatience as he waited for his guest to arrive. It was dark in the elegant room, the candles burning low on their wicks to suggest it had been another long night that had slipped away to dawn, adding further to the merchant's mood and anxiety.

Closing his eyes, he slowed his breathing, seeking to settle his heart, and winced when his worry rose up and quickly smashed aside any fleeting respite.

The news brought to him the day before by the girl was, quite frankly, still hard to believe. At first he thought the letter a ruse, a cunning subterfuge to draw him out into the open by the chancellor, and, ultimately, the Brotherhood. He settled his thoughts for a moment and sighed. Perhaps it still was...

Savinn shook his head to clear away the fog of uncertainty. If Khadazin was still alive, which in itself was astonishing, if he were, then the information he held could prove to be invaluable – should he live long enough to unmask the traitors in the high duke's halls.

Savinn scowled. Khadazin was, perhaps, the key, but the door of betrayal he sought to unlock was well beyond their reach at this time. Already, Savinn's contacts had reported that prominent Reven had been *taken* to the high duke's keep for questioning. As of yet, none of them had been returned safely to their homes.

Only two days before, Savinn's own home had been raided, the soldiers who had come the previous morning with polite demands, returning with strength of purpose to batter down the doors to his mansion.

Thanks to Dia's intelligence, of course, they had returned to their master empty-handed.

Savinn forced a bitter smile. Dia's tenacity and bravery had saved him. Had he been in residence when the crows had come for him, he would now be in chains, no doubt, used as a pawn for this game being played, ready to be sacrificed when the Brotherhood needed him to be.

Make no mistake, Savinn warned himself. *The danger has only just begun.*

In hiding now, it would be difficult for him to have any calming influence as matters started to spiral out of control in the city above. He was caught between his desire to publicly fight what was slowly happening under the Valian people's noses and the temperance of, he hated to admit, his own fear.

Even now his estate was being watched, as the chancellor's men waited for his return. As soon as he showed himself, Savinn would be taken in chains. Trapped under the city in his hideout now, he felt that there was little difference in his predicament. Consequently, if his absence and whereabouts remained a mystery, Savinn knew that he could well be used as a scapegoat for this new Reven '*rising*' that was purportedly happening.

The merchant tugged nervously at the golden earring dangling from his left ear and sighed. What really troubled him was that Khadazin, even though he had telling evidence to unmask the traitor to the high duke, did not have the voice to say it loud enough to be heard.

With the chancellor's hands about his own throat, Savinn was painfully aware that he no longer had that voice, either.

Savinn now knew, of course, that the chancellor was behind the plot, rapidly manifesting itself in the high duke's marble halls. Relan was the puppeteer, pulling the strings for the Brotherhood, orchestrating their designs for his master, whoever he was, so that they could turn the people against those of Reven blood or heritage, who lived in the Four Vales.

The storm clouds that were gathering overhead and about to batter the capital were dark omens, indeed.

Savinn shook his head slowly, feeling the sorrow well up in his throat. Stifling the scream of frustration that threatened to ruffle his composure, the merchant growled.

He needed to remain calm. The cards he held may well appear ineffective at this moment of the game, but, should he wish to better his hand, he would need to be patient and wait for Dia to get a look at these '*Reven Lists*' and for Khadazin's safe return to the capital.

Thinking of the Redani made him smile. His caustic, dour friend was the last person that needed this trouble to befall to him. The stonemason had never felt at home in the capital, always finding barriers in his way, ones far too high for him to climb over alone. After the Redani had saved his life, that fateful day all those years ago, Savinn had done all he could to help his saviour – putting contracts his way when none would willingly offer them, using his influence to make those with enough coin buy from the talented stonemason, even though they winced at the thought of having one of such '*heritage*' let freely upon their property.

Savinn had helped him, not just out of some sense of

duty, but also because he had suffered the same fights, the same persecution when he first came to Karick...

Casting aside dark thoughts from a bitter past, the self-exiled merchant puffed out his frustrations.

Savinn was in no doubt that the wax seal on the letter, the stamp of a jagged lightning bolt, was certainly the stonemason's mark. *But was it from him?* Or was it indeed a cunning ruse to draw him out into the open? The timely arrival of the girl suggested that it could be.

The hurried approach of desperate footsteps scattered aside his deliberations. Before he could decide the next move in this game, he would have to take further steps to ensure the legitimacy of the letter that, even now, would not reveal the full extent of what the Redani had overheard.

If he listened to his heart, it suggested that Khadazin was indeed still alive and seeking to remain that way.

Shame-faced, Cullen knocked his way into the study before the echoes had faded. His face was flushed with exertion and his eyes darted away furtively as Savinn stared menacingly at him.

"Sorry, boss," Cullen began lamely.

Savinn leant back in his chair and cut the man's excuses off with a glare as the girl stepped nervously into the room.

Immediately Savinn's demeanour changed from that of snarling wolf to affable, charming host.

With a flourishing wave of one hand, he motioned for his guest to be seated. The young huntress stepped gladly away from the fat man labouring hard at her side and sat silently in the offered chair.

Sensing he wasn't needed before being told, Cullen bowed low and backed away, closing the door slowly and taking his rasping wheezes with him.

"You are rested well?" Savinn asked his guest over a smile.

"Yes, thank you," the girl responded, her dark eyes lowered to the hands clasped nervously in her lap.

Savinn rested his elbows on the desk before him and clasped his own hands together. "You need not fear me, child," he said softly, as she looked up at him through long lashes. "Khadazin is my friend and you can trust me, as much I dare say as he does you to bear such an invaluable letter."

The girl's eyes opened wide and then flicked away in embarrassment as she scuffed a toe of one boot across the carpeted floor.

"He has suffered greatly," Tania managed to say, her throat dry and her mind spinning.

Savinn's sympathetic eyes became hooded, as he sought to keep the fear from them. The letter mentioned little about his condition, only that he was alive and hiding from his enemies at the sanctuary where all who were ostracised by society normally sought to escape to.

"Is he well, lady?" the merchant dared to ask.

Gathering up her strength, Tania recounted how she came to meet Khadazin and his charges, how she had arrived in timely fashion to save the stonemason's life, but, she added with downcast eyes, not his hand.

Clearing his throat, Savinn eased the girl's guilt. "You saved his life, Tania Drew," Savinn smiled. "Had you not gone after them, it would have not just been the Redani who would have suffered..."

The girl looked up at him again momentarily, before becoming nervous under his unfathomable scrutiny. "I don't understand."

Savinn nodded. "I would not expect you to, but I would urge you to discuss it with Khadazin when you return to him. I believe he, at the very least, now owes you the truth of all things."

Tania blinked rapidly. "I am to leave?"

"Of course," Savinn said, adding a chuckle to ease his

guest's nerves further. "You came to me, my lady. I am not holding you prisoner here, you are my guest."

Tania's relief was evident on her dusky, lovely face and before she went to speak, Savinn stopped the words on her lips.

"I would see you safely back to the Redani," he began, as he pulled open a drawer and produced a rolled parchment. He stared at it for a moment, before passing it across the desk to the girl. "But in return, I would ask you speak not of our meeting and that you see this safely into Khadazin's hands for me, if you would be so kind?"

Tania picked up the scroll and turned it in her hands slowly, marvelling at the elegance of the black waxed seal and the mark of a wolf that if bore.

"I will, I promise," she nodded, smiling through her relief.

Savinn studied her intently, drawing her eyes to him. "I must, however, insist that you are accompanied on this journey by two of my most trusted men."

The girl frowned and her face was stained by irritated confusion.

Savinn smiled sweetly. "Whilst the news you bear is of great comfort to me, my lady, I need two of my own to verify that the letter is indeed from the Redani. When they have their certainty, they will return to the city with him."

Tania glared. "Of course it's Khadazin! Big and black – a face like thunder most of the time."

Savinn laughed heartily, a rich, smooth peal that quickly settled the tension in the dark room.

"That's the man," Savinn said, his smile flashing in the dancing candlelight. He held up a placatory hand.

"Khadazin is very important to me, to a great many people. I need to ensure he is safe and well, that he remains to be so. My men will journey with you, they will see you safely to Khadazin and him back safely to me."

"I can look after myself," the feisty girl bristled, her

tumbling dark hair framing the anger on her face.

The merchant-thief chortled. "I am sure that you can my lady." he said, shaking his head with rueful certainty.

Chancellor Relan Valus stopped on the twisting staircase and reached out to touch the cool stone for support. With his breath rasping in his throat and his chest burning from the effort of his climb, he took several moments to regain his composure and strength.

Leaning against the curving wall, he touched his sweating forehead to the smooth stone and sighed as the coolness of the granite spread across his face. The day outside was blisteringly hot, a stifling, close heat that drained every ounce of water from your body and pressed down on you, leaving you weak and fatigued, your head throbbing with dull agony. Deep into his fiftieth summer, Relan cursed his aching limbs and lost youth, chastising himself for not finding the time to drain a jug of water before attempting the climb to the top of the Moon Tower.

Dragging his remaining strength together, he forced himself on, his sandals scraping the stone as he slowly, wearily continued his ascent. As he neared the top, some time later, he could already feel the heat of the morning, waiting there to embrace him once again.

Gathering close his thoughts and composure, he stepped into the marble chamber.

"There will be a terrible storm this night," the high duke said without turning, as his chancellor appeared behind him.

Relan nodded his agreement and stared about the chamber, marvelling at the black polished marble floor, its engraved constellations bright only with the sun, not the moon for a change.

"Yes, my lord," Relan responded. To his mind, it was

the first time he had ever been up in the Moon Tower during the day.

He glanced up at the open roof, staring for a time at the dark clouds, broken by the defiant sun as they darkened in annoyance and the morning slowly progressed. There was no wind to offer respite to the people of Karick this day and the sky gathered close, warning of things to come.

"You wanted me?" the high duke asked, jostling the chancellor from his musings.

"Oh," Relan said, startled, as he flicked his attention back to the high duke, who stood staring down into the city below, his hands clasped behind his back. "Yes, my lord. I have been searching for you and was starting to worry."

The high duke raised a hand up to silence his chancellor further. "Save your simpering, Relan," he said softly, dropping his hand again. "I am fine. I just needed to be alone with my thoughts for a time, to get away from my guilt at what we are doing."

Relan Valus felt suddenly cold and he stepped towards the high duke, appearing at his side quickly, to try and settle his fears. As he approached, the chancellor banished the image of the tall man before him falling to his death on the cobblestones, hundreds of feet below. It would certainly hasten things in the capital, but would not serve the Brotherhood well in the long term.

"I know that the decision is a terrible one," Relan began and then trailed off as the high duke turned and silenced him with a weary glare.

Relan hung his head and hid his relief. The high duke was exhausted, his once strong face weak from countless wakeful nights, plagued by the turmoil of the burden and responsibility he carried for all. These were decisions that, had he been thinking clearly, the high duke would have never chosen to make. But he was now sinking deep into the arms of his paranoia and the desperate cravings that his drugged tea was reducing him to.

Deep lines creased his haggard features and his unkempt beard was streaked with grey guilt. As he looked away from his chancellor, he stared out across his city and idly toyed with an embroidered cuff of his elegant surcoat.

"What is it you want?" the high duke sighed, his irritation broiling away underneath his words.

"The Merchants Guild have offered their thanks and support for your wise decision to postpone the games," Relan said, adding cautiously, "and of your firm resolution to find those behind the threats and attacks."

Relan studied Karian's face, seeing the scowl grow there and watched joyfully as any resentment was quickly replaced by relief.

"Well, that is one less thing to worry about," the high duke said, shaking his head. "I have only just managed to shake off my cousin, Ceren Mal, so to have a second thorn removed gladdens me. Pen them a response for me when you find a moment, Relan. Tell them that I will report any findings I have into the '*alleged*' fixing of the games and that I appreciate their support at this most difficult time."

"Yes, my lord," Relan replied obediently, drawing in a deep breath to steel his nerves. "There is one other matter I need draw to your attention..."

The high duke turned, his bright eyes darkening with annoyance. "Now what?"

Relan twisted his nerves through his hands and wetted his lips before speaking.

"Investigations are continuing, with some success. We have questioned several prominent Reven citizens, receiving encouraging help and support from their community."

The high duke nodded subtly. "But?"

"Well, ah," Relan began, swallowing his uncertainty

before continuing. "Well, my lord, I regret to inform you that when we called to invite Savinn Kassaar to the keep for interview, our messenger was told that he is currently not in residence."

The high duke looked away thoughtfully and ran a trembling hand through his beard. "He is away on business?"

"His wife said so, my lord," Relan replied. "He is away to Ilithia, checking on his business interests there."

Relief spread across the high duke's face. "Then we shall await his return, before talking to him, Relan."

The chancellor waited, just a few heartbeats, before chasing the relief from the high duke's face. "His wife said he left three days ago, my lord. I thought it prudent to check with the captain of the watch and the men who were on gate duty that day... and it appears that none can recollect seeing him leave the city."

For a time they stood in silence, the high duke staring down into the city, its vibrancy muted by the oppressive heat, the sounds muffled and distant. Relan Valus searched the high duke's grim face for tell of his thoughts, but could read nothing there.

When he did finally respond, the high duke's question caught him by surprise.

"Is there nobody I can trust?"

"My lord, of course there is," the chancellor was quick to reassure. "The council have backed your plan to interview those of Reven heritage, the people, even now, applaud your difficult decision."

The high duke rounded angrily, his face twisting and fraying from his rapidly short temper, these days. "And yet I discover that all is not well," he snapped, forcing his chancellor to step back. "You bring me this news, that perhaps I have indeed been mistaken in my trust of one man and whilst you do, I hear troubling reports that my own captain has openly voiced his disgust at the decision.

News, I hasten to add, I heard tell from other sources."

The high duke let his words hang dangerously in the air. He studied his chancellor's pale features for a time, watching the bead of sweat that trickled from his furrowed brow, ran down his nose and dripped to the marble floor.

"Forgive me," Relan blurted, wiping his brow with the sleeve of his robe. "I only sought to save you any further worry, before I had time to talk to Captain Varl personally, to try to settle our differences on the matter and bring him to reason."

"Lucien Varl is a man of honour," the high duke sighed. "I wonder, no, I fear that we have started to lose ours... It is no wonder he is reviled by our path."

"My lord," the chancellor baulked. "Whilst the taste of our actions may seem a bitter one, they are only laced, I assure you, with the noblest of intentions."

"I am well aware of that, but we shall see, Relan," the high duke replied evenly. "The die is already cast and we shall have to wait to see if it falls favourably for us."

"And what of Captain Varl?" the chancellor dared pursue.

"Your dislike for one another is well known, Relan," the high duke said impatiently. "I had hoped this whole affair would bring you together as one, both working towards the same common cause. I wonder if my faith has been seriously misplaced?"

"I can assure you, my lord, that for my part, I want nothing more," Relan countered defensively. "There is much to concern ourselves with, that which is far more important than any prior, petty rivalry. I will talk to him this very day. You have my word on it."

The high duke shook his head. "No Relan. I shall send for him this afternoon. I need to bring this problem to a close. I cannot have my own men openly defying me in public, no matter how they privately view my decree."

Relan Valus was barely able to keep his exultation in check and lowered his head to hide his emotions. Such a meeting would serve only to drive a wedge between them. Rather ironically, having recently lost his patience and ordering the mayor of Eastbury Ceren Mal back home to take *responsibility* for his people, Karian Stromn's list of allies was becoming a self-imposed short one.

"I am sorry, my lord," the chancellor said softly. "I should have come to you when I heard whispers of the dissention. I sought only to ease your burdens."

Relan started as he felt a hand on his thin shoulder and looked up at the high duke in surprise.

"What would I do without you, Relan? You bring me to my senses," Karian said, his sombre face forcing a rare smile. "Your services to me and the Valian people have been invaluable. I, and they will not forget it, I can assure you once again."

Relan hung his head. "You humble me, my lord, with flattery that is not deserved."

The hand slipped away, as did the high duke's mind, as he returned his gaze to the city and the people below him.

"If that is all, Relan," Karian asked, not looking back. "I would be alone with my thoughts for a little while longer."

Bowing, Relan Valus backed away, offering his assurances that he would report all information that came his way to him in future.

Without waiting for the reply that did not come, the chancellor retreated to the stairwell, casting one last look at the high duke, before slipping away.

As he bounded down the stone steps, with renewed vigour in his legs, Relan Valus struggled to keep up with the joyous seeds of the idea that had just been planted in his head by the unsuspecting high duke.

CHAPTER FIVE

The Cold Reality of Steel

Perrin Hawksblade stumbled back, desperately turning aside a lunge from his left. He stepped to his right, somehow catching another blow on the defensive dagger in his left hand.

There were several dead around him now, both friends from Havensdale and enemies from Carwell, and his aging body was wracked with pain and sorrow. Blood ran down his neck from the blade that had almost ended his life and he puffed out his lungs, as he faced the four attackers circling him.

Away to his left, Kallum Campbell killed one of his own attackers with a cut to the face. He wiped the matted hair from his eyes as his adversary twitched and gurgled on the ground, his lifeblood flowing freely from the ragged hole in the side of his cheek.

With eyes widening in horror over his own disgust, Kallum blocked the next opponent's high cut and fell back as the young man he faced stumbled over his own attack and crashed into him.

Both men tumbled to the muddy ground in a

desperate heap and they began screaming and fighting wildly as each sought for the telling blow amidst the tangled madness.

Perrin, aware that his attackers were trying to overwhelm him, spun in a full circle, meeting the eyes of his opponents. He could see their fear, edged with respect there and he used that hesitancy to find some more energy for his failing strength.

The first man to break free of this caution suddenly came at him, his broad blade light and surprisingly agile as he sent a dangerous back-handed cut to the old man's face. Perrin easily blocked the attack, but sensed the ruse, as another man came at him from behind. Turning, Perrin threw his dagger at the man and as the others surged forward he heard a mighty bellowing roar coming towards them.

Head down from his charge, Durnast Brogan threw his fury into his arms and cut both legs from the man he came up behind. The soldier hung in the air for a macabre moment, before crashing to the ground. Spinning with the momentum of his axe, Durnast turned full circle and finished his attack by burying the weapon in the man's back, as he writhed in unspeakable agony.

Perrin's rapier flicked out, opening a man's cheek, but then he staggered forward, as he took a sword in the back.

"Too slow, old man," a voice rasped in his ear.

Grunting, the old sword master dropped to his knees as the blade was pulled slowly free. He looked up across the battle, catching the fearful look in Durnast's eyes, as the retired warrior tried to reach him in time.

Perrin sighed and then smiled in acceptance, waiting for the telling blow that, to his surprise, never came.

As Durnast killed another Carwellian soldier that was in his way, Perrin looked to his left. The man who had stabbed him in the back fell to the ground, his triumph stolen away by a deep wound in the small of his own back.

Finding a breath, Perrin turned his head, ignoring the fiery pain in his body. Before he pitched forward into the arms of his agony, he saw Sara Campbell standing there, her sword red with blood and her face white from her own shock and revulsion.

On Havensdale Bridge, the mysterious swordsman was losing ground badly and, despite the carnage before him, he would soon be overwhelmed. A few more steps back and he would be forced onto the muddy soil, the Carwellian soldiers then able to surround him.

His crossbow now loaded again, Larne Manse raised the weapon, training it on the stocky man who was fighting with Robert Campbell, as the farmer's wife crawled away to safety. As the tall farmer tried to wrestle the sword from his opponents arm, they twisted about.

The sergeant cursed, his desperation to help them stayed by the caution of the shot he wanted to make, but was one too dangerous to take. His hesitancy cost him dearly, as the man tending to the Carwellian commander came up behind the combatants and yanked the farmer back by his hair.

Sergeant Manse turned his head away, but not quickly enough to avoid witnessing what followed.

Faran Cawl chuckled as Fawn Ardent jumped back again from his lunge. Undeterred, he easily knocked aside Joseph Moore's attack as the proprietor of the nearby inn came rushing at him. Punching him in the face, Faran turned his attentions back to his prize as the portly man crumpled to a heap on the ground.

Grinning, Faran stepped forward and then stopped, confusion creasing his features as he looked down at the thick shaft of the spear that had appeared in his chest.

Snorting his disbelief, he took two more steps forward, his sword raised weakly as Fawn Ardent backed away some more.

As Faran went to speak, a smaller shaft took him in the right eye and dropped him silently to the ground.

Fawn barely had time to glance up at her saviours on the west gate, before she was forced to pick up her sword and fight for her life once again.

The heels of the hooded man's boots slipped onto the muddy ground beneath his feet as he caught a sword in crossed blades above his head and twisted the weapon from his opponent's hands. Sensing he was about to die, the unarmed warrior from Carwell backed away, jostling nervously into the men behind him.

With a moment's time to think and draw breath, the hooded man could see that the old man he had pitched into the river was crawling slowly onto the east bank, clawing at the reeds that offered him the safety of dry land. Realising he would soon be outnumbered, the hooded man turned, his dark cloak sweeping after him as he ran towards the sanctuary of the town. As he approached the western wall, two spears arched over his head to cover his retreat.

"Open the gates," he yelled, looking up into the brightening day.

A man waved his arms madly, pointing along the wall towards the south.

"Gate's already breached," the nameless man called down to him. "Hurry, we'll meet you there."

Cursing, the hooded man sprinted away to the south, a chorus of angry roars and shouts chasing after him.

Kallum Campbell felt the man's breath steal from his body, as he managed to find purchase for his elbow in the man's ribs. Flailing madly, both their eyes wide with fear, they rolled on the muddied ground, Kallum's desperation screaming from his lips as he felt a madness sweep through him. His opponent, sensing he was in trouble, began to yell desperately, as Kallum found movement in his sword arm. Twisting his shoulder into the man's throat, the man from Havensdale managed to slip his sword free and throwing his weight onto his opponent, he broke free of his grip.

With his fury in his face, Kallum gripped his sword in both hands and raised it high above his head.

The Carwellian soldier's eyes were wide with white terror and he raised a pleading hand to protect his face.

"Don't," the man sobbed imploringly.

Baring his teeth madly, spittle flying from his lips, Kallum Campbell hesitated, then buried his sword with a scream.

The sounds of battle were raging on as Rellin Steelblade slipped from the fields to the east of Havensdale and padded nervously towards the town. Behind him, Arrun and Jessica followed, casting wary looks about, their young faces, once full of youthful lustre, now pale and stained by the events of the previous night.

Three bowmen headed for the open south gate as they approached, leaving their forgotten comrade dying in the mud behind them.

"What do we do?" Arrun hissed, his blades hanging forgotten at his sides.

Rellin drew back the string of his bow and nestled the white, feathered shaft under his chin. A shallow breath slipped from his nose, pinched by the bowstring, as he tried to calm himself down. With shaking hands he raised the bow higher, staring into the grey sky above, as he reluctantly loosed the shaft.

He closed his eyes in regret, as the arrow sang in farewell.

"You missed," Jessica scowled, her broken Valian failing to hide her disgust as the attackers charged under the protection of the gatehouse.

Rellin sighed. He had hunted many animals in the forest during his tutelage, had seen many gruesome sights as he became accustomed to the path he had chosen and the animals he would be forced to gut and skin. But, until last night, he had never taken the life of another, had never even contemplated the terrible thought that one day he may have to, and of the effect it would have upon him...

His dark thoughts were scattered, as Jessica stepped by him and turned to the two young men before her. With narrow Reven eyes that regarded them both with disdain, she turned and waved her sword towards the town.

"Come on," she snapped, racing away, her dark hair trailing in a stiffening breeze.

Arrun, his heart in his mouth and his eyes bright with fear, looked to his friend. He went to speak, then shook his head sadly.

"I don't know if I can," he began.

Rellin moved to his friend and gripped his shoulder tightly.

He nodded his head. "I know, I know!"

They turned to the clamour of rising, angry shouts. As they reluctantly followed after the Reven girl, they saw their mysterious saviour race into the town, several Carwellian soldiers close behind him, their weapons gleaming dully in the grey, early morning light.

Sara Campbell stared in horror as Perrin pitched forward and groaned weakly. His sword arm was stretched out before him, his rapier gripped defiantly, as if he still sought to fight on.

Durnast growled angrily. "Come on girl, we need to close the gates before we can see to him."

He turned purposefully, grunted, and looked down at the dark shaft sticking from his chest.

"That's not supposed to be there," he snarled in disbelief. Tearing it free, he threw the arrow away and looked towards the gatehouse. His face widened with fear as he saw the three archers spread out into the town, their bows bending meaningfully in his direction.

With heavy legs and a mind pleading with her to flee and hide, Sara moved bravely to stand beside the retired warrior and raised her shield defiantly.

As they waited for the inevitable, a hooded figure suddenly appeared from behind the upturned cart and leapt upon one of the archers.

"Drop it," he hissed, pressing a blade to the startled man's throat as he spun them about to face the other attackers.

As the man obeyed, the hooded man backed away towards the defenders, his steps slow and purposeful as he took his prisoner with him.

"Stand down," the hooded man ordered, pressing the steel closer to the soft flesh of his captive's neck.

The two Carwellian archers looked to one another and they shared an uncertain look. They were about to make a sensible decision when several reinforcements swarmed around the cart to join them and changed their minds.

There was a silent, brief moment when a cloud of uncertainty hung between the two parties before one of the Carwellian soldiers, an old, aging warrior, raised his sword and scattered aside any doubt.

"Kill them," he yelled, the river Haven still dripping from his beard.

Kallum Campbell collapsed beside the man he had been grappling with and fought hard to find his breath. His sword was buried deep, nearly to the hilt, in the ground beside his opponent's head. As they both fought for breath, aware of the battle being joined about them, the young man coughed and turned his head.

"Why didn't you kill me?" he asked the man from Havensdale, his dark eyes flashing brightly with confusion.

Kallum lifted his head and turned towards the Carwellian attacker, the man who probably would have killed him if circumstances had been reversed. They were of similar age, the young man's face clearly defined by a strong jaw line and high cheekbones. His eyes, the colour of the darkest brown, narrowed and widened as he flicked through the thoughts tumbling through his head. His small nose flared rapidly as he panted away, desperate to keep his wild heart in check and his dark, shortly cropped hair was thick with mud.

Kallum shrugged. "I do not know," he admitted, unable to decipher his conflicting emotions. Sighing, he pushed himself up onto his elbows, then onto his knees, reaching for his sword. "But if you want to live through this day, I suggest you stay down, until the fighting's done."

Without another word, the man from Havensdale rose up, pulling his blade from the ground and raced to help save his hometown.

Shaking his head, the young man from Carwell drew in a deep breath and marvelled at the clean air that filled his lungs. Sometimes life had the sweetest of tastes to it.

Fawn felt the first stab of pain, as she dragged her sword from the man she had just killed and tried to wipe the blood from her face. Shuddering, she felt her throat fill with revulsion as she surveyed the scene before her. The men that had come to claim the west gate were now dead, slain to the last by the reluctant defenders who had been forced to such deplorable acts.

Away to her right, her father was on his knees, his

chin resting on the pommel of his upturned blade as he sought to find his feet. Blood ran from a cut to his side and his battered shield lay beside him, forgotten and broken beyond repair.

Her concerns dragged Fawn away from her own despair and clearing her mind, she went to his side. Larne Manse and Jerrin Wicksford, both cut from blades themselves, had come to aid them, but were now running towards the south gate as furious fighting rose anew.

"Father?" Fawn whispered, placing a trembling hand on one of his sagging shoulders. "Are you alright?"

The mayor looked up and smiled, though the warmth of it did not reach his eyes. "Nothing your mother can't sort out, girl," he said, then scowled bitterly. "I never thought I would see such times again, Fawn – when Valian fought against Valian."

Fawn knew her history well and she nodded despairingly, feeling her shame and guilt stir again. "This will not be the end of it, father, I am certain of it."

Dekan Ardent rose, grimacing as fresh pain cut through his side like a new wound. "Well, let's at least put an end to this one, shall we?"

Nodding her head forlornly, Fawn Ardent followed her father across the market place as Joseph Moore groaned and stirred from his unconsciousness.

The hooded man cut the hand from the attacker who came at him from the left and then spun, twisting past the arrow that flashed past him as he charged down the archer, reaching vainly for another shaft.

At his approach, the bowman dropped his weapon and backed away, his hands fumbling for the blade at his side.

Scowling, the hooded man motioned for the archer to draw his weapon and the Carwellian soldier stumbled over his surprise as he quickly drew the short sword.

Satisfied his honour was intact, the hooded man stepped in to meet his opponents attack, easily turning aside the blade with his left sword. Before the man could recover, the hooded man's long blade flashed in the rising sun and deftly stole his life away.

With one shaft in his quiver, the remaining archer fled, racing for the shadows of the gatehouse. Too tired to give chase the woodsman let him go, turning his attention to the battle around him as Kallum Campbell chased after the fleeing bowman. Only several attackers remained standing now, as many of their number were dead, or incapacitated. As the melee danced before him, swaying to and fro to the brutal rhythm of clashing steel and piercing cries, he spied the old warrior he had pitched into the river. Their eyes met across the fighting, fighting that seemed to part for them as they made for each other.

"Enjoy your swim?" the woodsman enquired casually, grinning as the old man's face quivered with anger.

"Not as much as I will enjoy watching you swim in your own entrails," the old warrior spat in response.

The woodsman chuckled as they exchanged blows, lunging and parrying back and forth across the market place. Not finding a mark with his steel, it was the hooded man's mocking laughter that cut the deepest.

With his opponent's rage building, the woodsman let the old man swing the strength from his arm, easily blocking his attacks and spinning by him, to leave behind a cut on the thigh, or a gash in his chest. Slowly, deliberately, he allowed the old warrior to fall into a pattern; a lunging thrust, followed by a step back, countered with a high, back-handed cut, that rose up to try and take his head from his shoulders.

He had seen it many times before, and from warriors with far more skill than the man he faced. He had been taught, all those years ago, that your sword was a servant of your will, one that, should you lose your patience and your focus to anger, was no more use than a roll of parchment in your hands.

The woodsman waited for the high attack one more time, before he stepped beneath the wicked cut and came up under the old man's defences to plunge his short blade deep into his stomach.

"You should have stayed in the river," the woodsman said sadly. Stepping away, he watched as the old warrior stepped backwards, clutching at his wound, his sword falling to the cobbles. He looked up at the mysterious swordsman and his eyes widened as the man raised his sword in salute.

The woodsman turned and did not wait to see his opponent drop to his knees and topple sideward.

Tess Varun watched the mayor and his daughter hurry away towards the fighting at the south gate, fighting with her own desire to go and tend to her foster-father, who was slowly stirring from his unconsciousness. Puffing out her relief, she remained reluctantly at her post and trained the crossbow, given to her by Sergeant Manse, across the bridge.

A solitary Carwellian archer picked his way hurriedly across the bridge, stepping carefully past the bodies of his fallen comrades. He reached the other side and bent low to make his reluctant report.

As she watched, the three men gathered close around the fallen commander and helped him to his feet. Even from atop the wall, Tess could hear the fury in his rising voice and saw them step back, as the tall man waved his free hand condescendingly at them and clutched tightly at the bolt, sticking from his right shoulder.

There was a brief debate, before the commander cast a withering gaze across the river towards her. He stood watching the town for a time, his face a stiff mask of unchecked fury, as the man who had killed Robert

Campbell fetched horses for them. Waving aside offers of help, the Carwellian commander hauled himself up onto his saddle and turned his mount full circle, as he brought it under swift control. As the other men leapt hurriedly onto their own mounts, Tess raised the heavy weapon in her hands and trained it on the commander.

The bolt went wide, very wide of its mark and the commander looked dismissively at where it had struck, before turning his head again to glare at her. Drawing a finger promisingly across his throat, the commander kicked his heels to his mount's flank and led his men across the fields on the western banks of the river.

Tess shuddered, watching helplessly as they rode away into the lifting gloom and was certain that it would not be the last time she saw the horrible man.

Across the bridge, Sara's mother's screams pierced the silence as she crawled through the mud towards her husband.

By the time Fawn Ardent reached the gatehouse, the battle was won. Havensdale had survived, somehow, and as she slowed, her father labouring hard at her side, she could see that the town had paid a very heavy price for its loyalty to her. With several injured Carwellian attackers groaning and writhing in agony on the ground, she counted reluctantly, searching for those that still stood.

Sara Campbell, her face spattered in blood, stood leaning on her brother's arm – both of them exhausted, but still alive and ready, should any further attacks come.

Durnast Brogan was sat on the ground, surrounded by the dead and the broken shafts of the two arrows jutting from his chest and left shoulder. As he fought for a breath he could not find, he held on to the outstretched hand of Perrin Hawksblade. Away to her right, Sergeant Manse was talking to a man dressed in woodland garb who stood by quietly, his arms folded, listening attentively and nodding his hooded head occasionally. Beyond them, Jerrin Wicksford was hurrying towards the open gates to close them up and stopped when Jessica, Rellin and Arrun appeared, their pale faces masks of sorrow and tears spilling down their cheeks as they stared in horror at the devastation before them. Arrun screamed as his wide eyes fell upon the still form of his father and he rushed to the fallen man's side.

As Fawn approached, her relief at the youngsters safe return quickly stolen from her face, she saw the hooded man sheath his blades to shake the hand that Sergeant Manse offered him.

"I don't know who you are stranger," Larne Manse said, gripping the hooded man's hand tightly, "but I thank the Lady for your help."

The newcomer nodded his head faintly and they both turned as Fawn and her father approached. Fawn sent a look at her father, whose eyes were narrowed with scrutiny. She detected something there, as Sergeant Manse drew her attention away again.

"This man," Larne began, his face full of his evident admiration, "faced down the Carwellian forces on the bridge, alone!"

Fawn's eyes widened and the hooded man raised a hand, to stop any further words from the excited sergeant.

"Please," the man said, his voice calm, but tinged with irritation. "I did what I had to do, that was all."

"Who are you, stranger?" Fawn asked, feeling uncomfortable as the hooded head turned towards her question. "You would have our thanks, sir, for your timely aid this day."

Rough hands slipped from the man's dark cloak and reached up to slowly lower the hood. As Fawn regarded the strong, handsome face before her, her father drew in a startled breath and gasped in astonishment.

CHAPTER SIX

Trust

Elion Leigh led the remnants of his patrol in silence along the quagmire that was now the North Road, his thoughts distant as they made swift, yet reluctant progress towards their destination of Havensdale. Overhead, clearing skies offered pastel blue hope to the weary group of riders, warming their anxiety and chasing away their tension for a time.

Elion drew in a ragged breath and cast a reluctant look at his sergeant, who rode along at his side, his face still drawn tightly together in thunderous silence.

With a sigh, Elion looked away to the plains to the east, feeling his sergeant's eyes fall upon him again as he tracked the low flight of some geese as they flew in disciplined wedge formation towards the south west. They had barely spoken for two days, since their departure from Eastbury and, even now, the echo of Ashe's fury still rang in his aching head.

A gentle breeze picked up his senses for the briefest of moments, freeing him from his fatigue, allowing him to forget, momentarily, how jaded and filthy he felt. Elion's hair was matted, clinging to his scalp, much like his clothes, and he could smell the sweat, the muck, the mud and the blood of the last week upon him. If he smelled this bad to himself, only the Lady knew how he would smell to the others.

They, of course, were feeling the same. Since their encounter with the outlaws in Greywood Forest, the patrol had been continuing on with sheer determination alone. Each and every one of them were physically exhausted and mentally drained beyond any measure. The worrying events that unfolded in Eastbury before they left, had wrung any last drop of strength from them.

Elion caught the low whispers of Bran and Bren's hushed discussion, as they leant close in their saddles at the rear of the straggled patrol.

Turning stiffly in his saddle and allowing his mount to lead the way, Elion's eyes were drawn instantly to the thin ghost that rode along silently beside Liehella on a tall, brown Palfrey.

Even now, Elion could not fully believe the words the girl had spoken – even though, somehow, he had been able to see beyond her rising madness, her panicked desperation that her saviours would ride away to their deaths, taking her with them.

Clearing his throat, Elion closed his dry eyes and shook his head. Despite the ridiculousness of Elissen's accusations, when he was able to actually listen to what she was saying, it made uncomfortable, perfect sense.

A hollow pit opened up in his knotted, empty stomach and churned his thoughts over for him. That Commander Gardan despised him was no secret to him. Elion was already painfully certain that his superior was using this whole affair to ridicule him and finally finish his career, returning the young upstart to the gutters where he belonged.

But to despise him enough to want him dead?

Despite the man's nature and reputation, Elion could still not believe it and even the slightest hint of truth to Elissen's warning left a very uncomfortable taste in his mouth.

Elion swallowed his disgust, but it rose back up immediately. Whatever the truth of it, they would find out the answer when they got to Havensdale.

And that was the problem. They did not know what they would find once they reached the town. If what the girl was saying was true, then knowing Gardan, he would have what he wanted, no matter the cost. That in itself left another problem. What in the Vales would they do when they arrived there?

When Elion had recounted Elissen's tale to his comrades, they had, once they recovered from their disgust and shock, to the last, wanted to go after Gardan and confront him with the evidence. Ashe wanted to do more than that...

When their emotions had settled down to listen to reason, however, they were silenced by the reality of what pursuing such a course would mean for them all.

Elion's career was already finished and, if they were to discount the girl's testimony and return to Carwell safely, they would be separated and disbanded. Of course, Elion would insist that the brave men and women under his command be spared any punishment, but he doubted his wishes would carry any weight in the city anymore.

Riding west to go after Gardan and stop whatever was happening in Havensdale would immediately put them all on a charge of sedition. Not only were they abandoning their posts, they were also directly disobeying orders.

The young captain growled angrily. Faced with the evidence of Elissen's words, Elion could not let Gardan get away with it. He was going to falsely accuse innocent people in Havensdale, just to cover up the fact that, so it appeared, he was working with the raiders and knew all about the attack on Eastbury.

To any rational person it would sound absurd, Elion knew and, even now, he was plagued with doubts that he was being duped. But if that was indeed the case and the desperate girl was making it all up just to stay alive, then why did what she was saying feel so compellingly, uncomfortably, true?

Fearing he was going to drown in a sea of confusion, Elion scattered his thoughts and focused on the one thing he was sure of... and that was that Ashe was furious at him for bringing Elissen with them.

He looked back at his sergeant and Ashe held his apologetic gaze for a moment, before dismissing it with a disdainful turn of his head.

In truth, he had wanted to leave the girl behind, but, little short of locking her back up again, how was he to stop her? Elissen's delight that Elion had believed her story was tempered somewhat by the fact that he could tell she would seek revenge for what had happened to her loved ones, for what Gardan and his allies, whoever they were, had orchestrated and inflicted upon the unknowing inhabitants of Eastbury.

Elion had warned her that they rode only to Havensdale to seek the truth and honourable justice, nothing else. Elissen had meekly nodded her understanding, but her wide eyes had flashed with the truth of her harboured desires.

So, despite a furious debate and row, with only Jarion Kail and the brothers Bran and Bren Fal agreeing with their captain, they had left Eastbury with Elissen in tow, leaving their posts, their careers and their prisoners behind to be guarded by Reyn Cross and his two companions. Reyn, having heard what the girl had to tell, had wanted to ride with Elion, but the captain had refused him.

"You have a little one on the way," Elion had reminded him pointedly. "I would have you see the child enter this world."

In the early mist of the following morning, Elion and his patrol had slipped from Eastbury before the villagers knew they were gone. Riding westwards, they had made slow progress through the storm ravaged East Vales and had reached the Northern Crossways half a day later than they normally would have. Shadowing Greywood Forest, they spent the next day heading north, stopping for the night at the village of Colden to resupply and regain some lost strength and conviction for what was to come.

"Elion?" Ashe said, his voice strained by their current estrangement, but full of rising concern.

The captain followed his friend's jabbing arm to the road and the hazy horizon ahead. As the patrol began to stir, he picked up the distant form of a rider coming towards them from the north.

Nodding his thanks, Elion regained control of his mount, and gripping the reins, he led the patrol on cautiously.

As the approaching rider came close enough to recognise, Elion shared a questioning look with his sergeant and, calling the patrol to a halt, they waited silently for Lucas Rhee to reach them.

Raising his hand above his head in greeting, the portly rider reined in his mount and walked her forward through the mud to join them.

Elion could see the confusion in the man's deep set dark green eyes, hiding there behind his forced smile. Lucas's mount laboured heavily, suggesting that he had ridden her hard that morning.

"Lucas?" Elion welcomed him warmly, adding just enough surprise to the greeting. He didn't know the man well, but word about the barracks was that he was a studious, dependable man, loyal to Carwell and the commander he served under.

Lucas smiled, casting a swift look at the weary group before him. His eyes widened as they fell upon Elissen and then flicked hastily away. The girl hid her eyes from him and picked at the stitching of her saddle.

"Captain," Lucas smiled, returning his attention to the sallow rider who studied him intently. "I thought you were headed for Carwell? Forgive my surprise."

Elion smiled sweetly. "Those *were* my orders, granted. But events have dictated we seek out Commander Gardan... where is he? Why are you not with him, Lucas?"

Lucas swallowed nervously and ran a shaking hand through his unkempt, curly brown locks. He wetted his lips.

"Well," the rider began, smiling in apology for his hesitancy. "We were refused entry to the town and Commander Gardan decided that we would have to use any means necessary."

"What do you mean by that?" Ashe barked, cutting across Elion's response.

Elion cast a fretful glance at his sergeant then returned his attention to the round face of Lucas Rhee, who was starting to sweat nervously under their scrutiny.

"We were ordered across to a farmstead, over the river," Lucas began, faltering. "He gave us a speech, saying that to uphold the law we would have to step outside its boundaries... or something like that."

Behind him, Elion heard the sharp intake of collective breath and he shook his head as he felt his skin crawl up his arms.

"He gave everyone the option to leave, if they didn't want part of it, without stain upon their reputation," Lucas continued, stumbling hastily over his explanation. "I didn't like the feel of what was about to follow, so I took his offer and left."

Elion guided his steed forward and placed his hand on the rider's wide shoulder, as he tried to find his shame somewhere in his lap.

"You don't have anything to be ashamed of, Lucas," Elion said softly, restoring some pride to the man's eyes. As they held each other's gaze, their mounts began nuzzling each other and snorted softly in greeting.

"If what we have discovered turns out to be true," Elion continued reluctantly, "you will not regret your decision."

Lucas frowned, his rounded face wrinkling. "I don't like the sound of that, captain."

Withdrawing his hand, Elion looked back at his companions and sighed. Elissen hid behind a veil of her hair, but he could see that she twisted the reins she held tightly in her hands, her knuckles white with fury.

"I think it best you not know," Elion admitted, returning his gaze back to the rider. "Suffice to say that things are about to get a lot worse and I would spare any who need not be involved, what is to come."

Lucas Rhee's broad chest rose and fell from his indignant huff. "Well, I thank you for that, captain, but I believe I have the right to know why you are escorting the prisoner to Havensdale, when you had orders to see her to Carwell?"

Before Elion or even the bristling Sergeant Garin could respond, Elissen cried out, her near-hysterical shriek of anguish cutting through the tension and panicking the mount she rode. Liehella reached across and brought the Palfrey quickly under control and did her best to calm its rider, as well.

Elion felt his hands trembling as he hastily dragged Lucas's attention back. "Because we have evidence that had we returned to Carwell, we would not have reached there safely."

Reluctantly, Elion told the rider of what Elissen had overheard, of her claims that Gardan was party to the raid and that he was travelling to Havensdale to cover up his involvement in the failed attack on Eastbury. As Elion recounted all Elissen had told him, Lucas's wrinkles quickly vanished, chased away by his rising astonishment. When Elion had finished, Lucas sat back in his saddle and blinked, shaking his head incredulously

"I can't believe it, Elion," he said, again forgetting he was talking to one of rank. "This cannot be! I mean... it just..."

Ashe Garin rumbled his agreement. "I know, it sounds bloody madness to me as well... but we all know Gardan, we know he's a ruthless bastard – the man is capable of anything."

Jarion Kail nudged his mount past Janth and Tristan to join the debate. "I can believe it! I don't want to – but what are the alternatives? If we ride to Carwell, we could be killed along the way. Are we to take that chance and hope that all of this is a misunderstanding? I think not."

Elion raised a hand, as Bran tried to offer his thoughts. "We have debated this matter at length and I do not want to discuss it again." He looked to Lucas Rhee and held the man's gaze.

"You see now why we seek our answers in Havensdale. From what you say, it sounds like we are travelling a road that will not lead back to Carwell."

Lucas Rhee raised his hands, waving them about to signify his helplessness. "I-I don't know what to say, captain. This is all too much. I can't believe what I am hearing, nor can I reason why."

"Neither can we," Ashe growled, muttering. "All we did was save Eastbury from a worse fate than had visited it and captured the leader behind the said atrocities."

Elion nodded his head subtly. "Well, we shall ride on to Havensdale and seek our answers there, Lucas. I would ask only that you assist Reyn Cross with the prisoners and see them safely to Carwell for justice."

Lucas Rhee nodded his head hurriedly, his small green

eyes flashing with relief. "What should I say if I am asked about you?"

Elion chewed his bottom lip thoughtfully for a moment before responding. "Say only that we remain in Eastbury, to protect her borders and tend to our injured who are too wounded to ride."

Lucas Rhee nodded and letting out a deep breath, he glanced about the weary patrol. "I give my luck to you, Elion Leigh." He reached out and shook Elion's hand briefly.

"My luck to you all," he said, his face pained.

With a nod, he steered his mount away and jabbing his heels into the mare's flanks, he rode southward, nine pairs of eyes following forlornly after him.

"Have a drink for me when you get there," Ashe said, licking his lips in remembrance. "It could be a while before I can properly enjoy a tankard again."

"Just the one?" Tristan said, grinning.

Elion laughed.

Commander Gardan's guttural scream echoed through the stillness of the late morning as he writhed in furious agony.

"Just pull it out," he snarled, spittle flying from his thin lips.

Looking up apologetically, Aren Bray gripped the bloodied shaft in his slick hand again and drew in a breath. Behind him, Esten and the fourth member of their party, the archer Garin guarded the hollow they had stopped at, watching the plains to the north for signs of pursuit.

With his free hand, Aren pushed down on Gardan's left shoulder and wrenched the bolt free.

"About time," Gardan hissed, spitting angrily as his second threw the shaft away. Tears filled his eyes and he wiped them away hurriedly as Aren cleansed the wound with some water from a skin, before tearing some clean cloth from his cotton shirt to plug the gaping hole in his commander's shoulder.

Uncharacteristically, Gardan waited patiently whilst Aren worked on his wound, all the while his mind tumbling through the events that had unfolded before him and quickly turned the tide against them.

Never one to shy away from adversity, Gardan chewed his tongue thoughtfully and quickly calmed his disappointment that he had failed the Brotherhood and, ultimately, lost the chance to be rid of the captain once and for all.

The past was lost to him now and although at some point Havensdale would surely burn, he needed to turn his mind and focus on what he should do with the future.

The game had started in earnest now and by returning to Carwell, he would not serve the Brotherhood best. With the political tide turning towards the hardliners and more targeted raids to come, he needed to become more involved.

If he was honest with himself, Gardan hated the thought that someone else would steal all the glory for themselves. When the dust had settled from what was to come, he wanted to be the one standing on top of the pile of bodies, the one covered in the most blood. There were going to be legacies on offer in the coming seasons and he was going to ensure his name was the one carved deepest in the Reven lands.

Aren's enquiry of the two guards on whether they were being followed was met with relieved, thankful shakes of their heads. Gardan, despite the fire in his chest, relaxed a little. The rest of his patrol, dying inside the walls of the town had given him the chance to escape, to fight that other day and by the storms he was going to make the most of it.

Closing his eyes, the commander listened to his heart for a time, losing himself to its erratic drumming. When he was in control, once again, he opened his eyes, staring up at the clearing sky above him and watched the geese that flew silently overhead, sedately winging their way to the west.

Waving a hand cantankerously at Aren for assistance, the man helped him to his feet and stepped back hurriedly. Stalking from the hollow, Gardan swept a steely gaze about his surroundings, picking out the distant, snaking line of shimmering blue that was the River Haven, far away to the east as it meandered across the flatlands towards a broad forest.

Turning his thoughts westward he caught sight of the geese again, their shapes dark now against the horizon, as they quickly flew over the distant line of trees. Spinning slowly, he cast his attentions on their weary mounts, ridden hard to make good distance from Havensdale.

"Your orders, commander?" Aren enquired, seeing Gardan's piercing blue eyes narrow, as he picked out the low hills to the south.

Placing his hands on his hips, Gardan listened silently to his own thoughts for a time, before smiling.

"We head south," he said, turning to his men. "We will cross the River Haven beyond those hills and make good our time to the south."

Aren shared a look with the other men and nodded.

"Our destination, sir?"

"We head for Karick to make our report." Gardan said, a slow, wicked smile cutting across his face.

CHAPTER SEVEN

A Question of Honour

The woodsman raised the silver tankard to his lips for a moment as he thought about taking another sip of the lovely, piquant ale, before putting it down on the table again. Pushing the ale away, he leaned back in his chair and winced, the feeling beneath him strange and uncomfortable. It had been many years since he had sat on a chair, having become accustomed to sitting and sleeping in the cradle of nature's embrace.

The inn, brightly lit by lanterns, was busy tonight, many of the tables filled with sombre faces that kept quietly to their thoughts and were aware only of the drinks clasped tightly in their hands. To the common ear, the silence was oppressive, but for the woodsman, it was the perfect tonic for his dark thoughts.

The longest day the town of Havensdale had ever witnessed was drawing to a close now, the skies overhead dark with wistful reflection. The woodsman shook his head sadly and sighed, running a thoughtful hand through his stubble, soon to be beard.

Havensdale would eventually recover from this day. It

would move on, its people would endure and one day the grandchildren of those who had witnessed such times would reflect on the stories told to them with a disbelief that such horrors had ever happened in their town. But for now, for a long time to come, the memories would remain open and raw like the deepest of wounds.

The woodsman felt his throat thicken with his sorrow and he blinked his eyes dry rapidly. The town of Havensdale was in shock, not mourning. That would come when realisation settled in and those who had died were given back to the land. The events that followed the defence of the town were blurred, even now, and after the carnage had been dealt with, the dead removed to the chapel and the wounded tended to, the people of Havensdale had come together in the market square for a silent, sombre show of strength and unity.

There were no words that could ease the horror or dilute the disgust they were feeling. There were no words that could stem the flood of tears for those that mourned for their loved ones.

The woodsman had helped remove the bodies, both friend and foe, to the chapel, but there was little else he could do to help them. Thankfully, the mayor of Havensdale had quickly recovered from his shock, diverting any suspicion of his apparent familiarity with him, by offering his swift apologies.

"Forgive me," Dekan had said, though his eyes conveyed a different message. "I thought for a moment I knew you, but I fear I am mistaken."

Masking his relief, the woodsman had offered raised hands and a smile as his acceptance, reluctantly looking to those gathered close. The sergeant seemed to accept the ruse, but his daughter, however, harboured the traces of suspicion in her eyes.

Any further enquiries of his identity were quickly dispelled by a young man's cries for help as he knelt by his dying father. As the captain and her sergeant had rushed to his aid, the woodsman caught the mayor's attention with a thankful nod of his head.

Stepping in close, the mayor had whispered "We will talk later," and then he was gone, swept along by the rising tide of horror that was quickly gathering Havensdale up in its arms.

Blinking free of his thoughts, the woodsman turned his attentions to his surroundings. A sea of nameless faces crowded the bar and filled the tables, but none dared to sit with the hooded stranger who sat in a shadowy corner of the inn and had faced down the Carwellian forces on his own. The two old men who sat in the chairs before the fireplace, turned their thoughts towards the cold hearth, clutching at their tankards as they stared into imaginary flames. Flicking his eyes away, the woodsman admired the fabulous painting of the Great Divide hanging above the fireplace for a time and wished he was there at this moment, striding the slopes and exploring the ridges and twisting mountain trails.

The woodsman scowled bitterly. *So much for hiding away...*

He had dismissed the appearance of the doll at his camp as a parlour trick, played by the Seer who had probably been whispering while he slept, planting the seeds of his dream in his mind. It sounded ridiculous, but what other explanation could there be?

A day of brooding and little else of note had found the woodsman sinking deeper into a dark pit of consternation. The Seer's words were already settling deep in his soul, eating away at his strength and resolve. As the following day slipped away into the next, he began to worry about how in the storms the Seer knew about the girl. It had been weeks since he had saved Lady Byron's life and he had almost forgotten about her. *Almost...*

Uncertain of what all this meant and to ease his

frustrations, he had decided to head for Havensdale to find out what had happened to the Byron girl. It was putting himself at risk, the unnecessary danger of being recognised, but if it helped to ease his anxiety and give him some peace, it was worth it.

He had reached the vicinity of Havensdale too late to gain entrance the night before, and had set up camp in the forest, a few miles from the town.

With a dark sky and forest playing on their fears and thinking his fire belonged to someone else, the youngsters from Havensdale had stumbled wildly into his camp, fearful of pursuit. Tripping over their haste to tell him what was happening to their town, the youths were clearly desperate for aid, from anyone. They were imparting their desire to head to Highwater to report what was happening when the woodsman spied the dancing flames of five bobbing torches, splitting the shadows behind them.

For the briefest of moments, he had toyed with turning his back on the terrified youths, safeguarding his peaceful existence and leaving them to their fates. But his code, his honour, shrouded these past years by his own mantle of fear, was still ingrained deep in his veins. With a sigh and the Seer's words echoing in his mind, he had told the three youngsters from Havensdale to hold fast to courage and ready themselves.

Picking up his tankard to divert the memories of the bloodshed that had followed, the woodsman drained the ale and smacked his lips in delight. For a time, he searched the taproom for the comely waitress and when he finally caught her eye, she dealt him a weary smile that, for a fleeting moment, lit up the oppressive gloom of the inn.

As she began filling a fresh tankard for him, her father busily serving others at the crowded bar, the woodsman felt his skin prick with apprehension as Dekan Ardent entered the inn. Scanning the faces that turned at his entrance and finding what he was looking for, the mayor started wending his way towards the shadowy corner, his steps stiffened by agony, his hand clamped over his bandaged side to smother the pain that hid beneath.

One of the old men at the hearth voiced his desire for another town meeting and the mayor stopped momentarily to reassure the white-haired old man with a gentle pat to one shoulder that there would be.

The woodsman looked helplessly for the serving girl and scowled as the mayor intercepted her, taking the tankard from her hands. He smiled and said something softly to her, before turning his attentions back on his destination. The dark-haired beauty spun deftly on her heels and limped heavily back to the bar.

"May I?" the mayor asked, as he came to stand before the table. He offered a disarming smile and placed the tankard of ale on the knotted wood, sliding it across as an offering.

The woodsman remained impassive, but gently inclined his head in thanks and invitation.

Dekan Ardent sat down, waiting patiently for the interest from the other patrons to wane. Once the majority had returned their attention back to their sorrow and their drinks, the mayor leant across the table. Resting his elbows on the wood, he clasped his hands together to form an arch.

"It was a brave thing you did today," he began over a smile.

The woodsman shrugged and tested his ale. "I didn't have time to think, I just acted," he offered with a nonchalant shrug.

The mayor of Havensdale ignored the off-handed comment and fell silent as the serving girl brought him a fresh tankard.

"Your cider, Mayor Ardent," she said with an accompanying smile. Her hazel eyes were bright like amber as they caught the lantern light and flicked briefly to the mayor's scowling guest.

"Thank you, Scarlet," Dekan Ardent said, smiling warmly. "And thank you for all your help today."

The smile slipped from her lovely face as she swept her steadying cloth onto her left shoulder and murmured her thanks. Curtseying, rather elegantly, Scarlet retrieved the stranger's empty tankard and slipped away.

The woodsman watched her leave, feeling the stirrings of an old ache in his chest.

"She *does* look like her," the mayor whispered, snatching the woodman's thoughts up and uttering them for him.

The woodsman's eyes widened and then blazed with fury. Leaning close, he held the mayor's eyes.

"Do not speak of her," he hissed, though in the quiet of the inn, it sounded almost a shout. At the bar, Scarlet registered she had heard the exchange by inadvertently glancing in their direction.

"Forgive me," the mayor whispered, holding his hands apart in apology. "I had never noticed before, until I saw you again, Evan. It has been a long time, my friend."

Lost to the past, it appeared that the woodsman did not hear him, though, after a while, he slowly returned to the present with a bitter wince.

"It has been many a long year since I have heard that name," he whispered, flicking a guarded look about the inn. "I have wondered, sometimes, if it actually belongs to me, or is part of someone else's life."

Dekan Ardent studied the hooded man before him, noting the deep lines under his eyes and the grey now in his beard. The dark hair, once perfectly kempt with scented oils, was now tangled and rugged, his nose crooked by a past that had violently hewn out his future.

A shadow of his former self, there was still tell of the man that once was, burning away in the woodsman's dark green eyes, chiselled there in his demeanour and bearing.

"I thought you had died," the mayor admitted, recoiling as his companion fixed him with a venomous look. "That is what they said."

Calming himself, the woodsman took a long pull of his ale before replying.

"After today, it would probably be better for all of us if I had."

The mayor's eyes narrowed. "We shall deal with Carwell in due course, make no mistake," he said. "If he thinks his men can ride through the Vales, carrying out his whims without compunction, then he is seriously misguided."

"What will you do?" the woodsman asked, watching as the mayor unclasped his hands, balling them into angry fists.

Regaining his composure, Dekan sighed. "Unlike Gardan, I will not act outside the law and I will not demean that law further by sinking to his dishonourable depths. Innocent lives have been lost this day and I shall head to Highwater in the coming days, to report what has happened here. Alion Byron will be furious when he hears and will surely sponsor our case for justice in the capital."

"If I know Gardan, he will seek a similar course," the woodsman warned quietly, pointing a finger meaningfully at his host. "You would be better making haste to Karick, as, in the end, it will ultimately be Carwell's word against Havensdale."

The mayor fell silent, his head shaking his thoughts through his mind as a pained look creased his weary features. In truth, there were plenty more dead on Carwell's side of the battle and Gardan would certainly play on that. At the end of it, would it even matter that Havensdale was only defending herself against an unwarranted show of force? And what were they to do about the traitor? The man who had let the enemy into Havensdale by murdering poor Colbin Wicksford? Justice was needed there, also. There was much that needed his attention and in the coming weeks, he would have to be strong, both for his daughter and for the people of the town.

Dragging his words out on a sigh, Dekan Ardent shook his head.

"Sadly, I must look to the north for aid," he said, holding the woodman's eyes. "The capital is in turmoil and the high duke buckles under the strain."

Immediately the woodman's face twisted and he sat back in his chair, retreating into the shadows of the corner, his eyes glittering from within the depths of his hood.

"I care not for word of the games played in the capital," he hissed, waving a hand dismissively. "They have always been played there and much better, I dare say, than those who sit at the table today. I came seeking only word of the Lady Byron, whom I helped some many days ago now."

Dekan nodded. "My daughter heard tell of your noble actions from Lady Byron herself, *woodsman*. You most certainly and inadvertently, I dare say, thwarted the first move in a dark game that was about to be played. Sadly, however, I fear your heroic actions only delayed matters."

"What do you mean by that?" The woodsman's eyes flashed with reluctant concern.

Leaning close across the table, the mayor replied. "Lady Byron reached Karick safely, thanks to you, my daughter and her men. But, following threats to the council members, she was kidnapped in the night by those who still to this day remain unknown."

The woodsman frowned, his face pale. He kept to his thoughts for a time, before he spoke.

"And what of Lady Byron?"

"That mystery deepens further," Dekan whispered. "She has recently returned home safely and her father, who was attending the council meetings in the capital, has hurried home for a reunion, seeking, I expect, answers to this mysterious riddle."

Looking away, the woodsman stroked his stubble thoughtfully. When he looked back again, there was tell of his dormant fire again, blazing away there in his eyes.

"I am certain to regret this, but you had best tell me what you know," the woodsman said wryly, a ghost of a smile playing across his lips.

Tess Varun burst into the inn sometime later, as the mayor was finishing his recount of all, to his knowledge, that had been happening in the Four Vales these last few months. The distraught girl blenched, as the entire inn looked towards her and as she regained herself, Dekan Ardent rose up stiffly, the pain in his side forgotten, or at least dulled for a time by the cider he has consumed.

"Tess?" the mayor asked, feeling a knot of worry tighten in his belly.

"Riders approaching from the south again," she stammered in response as she searched for Scarlet in the crowd.

For a moment, the stunned silence was palpable and then, as one, the inn surged to its feet, forgotten stools scraping angrily on the wooden floorboards and the clamour of muttering defiance dragging the townsfolk out into the night.

Tess hurried away from the inn, lest she be trampled underfoot and, on leaden legs, she led the reinforcements to the wall.

As Dekan Ardent joined his daughter on the ramparts, he was actually touched by the solidarity being shown. The night before, when they had held council in the Arms of the Lady, it had been decided that only the militia would guard the walls against Carwell, so as not to endanger more innocent lives.

After the terrible events of the day, he would have a hard job tasking Havensdale's defences to the militia alone.

Fawn was barely awake on her feet, her face ashen and haunted, the cut on her cheek angry and thick with fresh, congealing blood. She met her father's enquiring look.

"We make out at least six riders approaching," she whispered, straining to number the distant riders in the darkness.

The woodsman appeared alongside them, shouldering his way impatiently through the throng, gathered too close on the ramparts.

"See these people armed and spread along the walls," he hissed, surveying the lands to the south. His keen eyes could pick little out with the lanterns burning on the walls.

If the mayor was annoyed at being ordered about, he didn't show it and he began seeing to the woodsman's suggestion. As he moved away, Sergeant Manse joined him to help organise the defenders and Fawn moved closer to the woodsman.

"Thank you," she said softly, searching for his face in the confines of his hood.

The woodsman nodded. "You should also douse this light, my lady," he said, staring up at the cloudless night sky. "You are only making targets for yourself. Use the stars for your light."

He looked about, pushing past Tess to pick up one of the torches, stacked in a barrel against the wooden palisade, away to his left. Moving to the lantern hanging from the watch-post, he opened the glass door and lit the torch.

A hush settled on the wall and many eyes turned to watch, as the flames licked hungrily at the torch. When it was blazing brightly, a gentle wind shaping the fire, the woodsman hurled the torch out into the night.

Fawn watched as the torch arched in a slow trail of fire into the darkness and landed on the muddy road. It sputtered indignantly for a time, before rallying and casting its glow out strongly once again.

The woodsman turned to Fawn. She read the intent in his eyes and nodded, turning to those gathered nearby.

"Spread out along the walls," she ordered quietly. "Light several more torches and toss them out onto the ground before us. When that is done, douse the lanterns. I would see better who approaches this night."

As several defenders hurried to follow her orders, Fawn turned her head and nodded her thanks to the stranger again.

"We have not had time to talk, woodsman," she said softly, stepping close to his side. "I should like to, if the Lady allows it."

The woodsman turned away, his eyes adjusting to the darkness as the lanterns were put out. Overhead, he could start to discern the tapestry of stars, beautifully weaving its way into slow focus.

"I should like that also, my lady," he replied, though he certainly didn't sound like he relished the prospect.

Smarting, Fawn turned away from him and listened to the rumble of distant hooves, her heart gently starting to drum out a beat to accompany her rising apprehension as they drew near.

"That's close enough," Dekan Ardent called out, as the riders slowed their mounts and guided them warily forward. The silence was unbearable and the dark skies and stars overhead gathered close to survey what would follow.

On the cusp of the light offered by the carpet of flickering torches, a man dismounted and guided his steed forward.

Fawn stifled the fear on her lips, as she made out the crest of Carwell on the breast of the man's leather armour.

The man stopped abruptly as the mayor's words echoed down and he glanced up into the darkness, his blue eyes bright from the torchlight as he scanned the town's defences.

"We mean you no harm, we come seeking only answers," the man called out, his clear voice echoing through the night.

A dog barked in response, somewhere inside the town and Fawn looked to her father. Dekan gripped the palisade, his breath heavy in his chest.

"You would not be the first from Carwell to seek answers here recently," the mayor said frostily. "Speak now of your business, or return the way you came."

The young man hesitated, glancing back towards the line of riders who waited patiently behind him. When he turned again, he held up his empty hands and moved slowly forward.

"That's far enough," Sergeant Manse said, pointedly raising his crossbow.

Abruptly the man stopped, drawing in a steeling breath as he stepped back a few paces.

"I do not know what has happened here today," the rider began, "but I can only vouch for my own intentions. I come seeking answers from my... former commander and wish no ill upon Havensdale or her inhabitants."

Fawn shared a glance with those gathered close by. Larne met her questioning look and scowled.

"Do not be fooled," he warned, hissing through gritted teeth. "A rider went for reinforcements and this could be a ploy... a different approach, Fawn."

Fawn saw her father nod thoughtfully and looked to the woodsman. She frowned when she realised that he was not there. Scanning the line of grim faces, she could see that he was gone.

"You say *former* commander?" Dekan Ardent called down.

The man's haggard face hardened and he nodded. He looked about his surroundings for a time and then edged forward again, his hands held high in placid submission.

"Judging by your welcome, I fear, however," he dared, "that we have arrived too late to stop the injustice he would mete out upon your town?"

Fawn felt her temples tighten painfully with confusion. She drew in a calming breath, touching her father gently on one shoulder. He dragged his tired eyes to her as she signalled her intent to speak. He nodded once, returning his focus to the man below them.

"If you come in peace, sir," Fawn said, drawing the rider's attention to her, "then you and your patrol must lay down your arms. Do this now, and you may enter the town with one other and we shall discuss the matter civilly."

The man lowered his hands and a smile of relief stole across his weary, yet handsome face.

Fawn quickly chased the smile away. "Betray this trust, however, and on my honour, you will not leave the north alive."

Swallowing, Elion Leigh reluctantly nodded his acceptance. As he unbuckled his sword belt, he turned to his companions to give out his orders.

In Havensdale, alone now in the Arms of the Lady Inn, the woodsman sat back down in his chair and drained his ale quietly, his thoughts dark, his hands shaking.

Above all that had happened this day, the mayor's words kept haunting him, raking up the ashes of a fire he had long since tried to bury. Hiding his face in his hands he closed his eyes, trying desperately to banish the images that flashed in his mind.

With a growl, he dropped his hands to the table, his

breath suddenly calm, his eyes narrowed by controlled fury.

"And thus it begins, my love," he whispered sadly.

CHAPTER EIGHT

Solace

Arillion winced and ran a finger over the fresh stitches in his shoulder, tracing the ragged line of the tight wound with a gentle, curving finger.

"Not bad," he admitted, looking up at the old woman and grinning. "I think I'll be able to use this again, someday soon."

The woman's thick, white eyebrows knitted together and she fixed her patient with a look of consternation.

"Only if you rest and regain your strength," she chided him. "If any more of those stitches come out again, you will have to do them yourself."

Arillion wrapped his good arm behind his head and lay back on his pillows, arranged against the headboard. He flashed a broad smile up at the woman, watching absently as she busied herself about the cluttered wagon, tidying up the bloodied bandages and broken threads she had left on the stool beside his bed.

"What? And miss out on the chance of getting your hands on me again," he chuckled finally, his grey eyes glinting mischievously. "Many a maiden would jump *on* the chance." He winked at her.

Despite the hour, there was still some life left in the evening and the last breath of a dying day spilled through the drawn curtains of the wagon.

Mother Shale, as Arillion called her, ran her failing eyes over the man's naked body. His legs and decency were hidden away under the bedsheets, but his torso was bared and gleamed, somewhat, in the last light.

He was a handsome man, she had to admit and in her day, she would have been trembling at the thought of his offer. But now..?

"It will take more than your pretty smile and words to light my fire again, swordsman," she snapped, with just a touch of regret lacing her words.

Arillion shrugged. "Well, I guess you will never find out. Shame really, I like a bit of experience."

He smirked and his infectious smile danced across his features, before being chased away by his rising pain.

"I jest, lady," Arillion grimaced. "Just trying to liven the day."

Mother Shale straightened loose hairpins and smiled as she took a tinder and flint to the candle in a brass holder on the table to the right of the bed. It must, she reflected, be torture for a man such as he was to be trapped in his ruined body, confined to his bed when all about him the sounds of merriment and life danced on.

"Rest, swordsman," she soothed him. "If you do, in a few weeks you will be free of your bed."

Arillion opened his curving mouth and went to say something pithy, but she threw clean bandages at his face and hurried from the wagon.

Chuckling, Arillion swept the bandages from his face and dropped them in his lap. Fighting against the pain, he glanced about the wagon, feeling the dark walls close in about him again. Not one to be usually troubled by his own company, of late, the assassin had found that he longed for the old woman's visits, yearned for Kaspen Shale to come to him, bearing scraps of information about what was happening in the city.

"Getting soft," Arillion muttered, scowling. He needed a few throats to slit, that would help set him on the right path again.

He rubbed his tired eyes with a curled forefinger and stifled a yawn. All this inactivity was killing him. He had work to do and a great deal of money to claim. The fact Cassana was home, despite the nature of her arrival, meant that she owed him a lot of coin and the lingering promise of more. Even better than that was that he had fulfilled, in a fashion, his contract with Savinn Kassaar and that meant he could collect the remainder of his fee, should he ever see Karick again.

Arillion cursed his luck. Confined to his bed, rising only for the briefest call to nature, he had little to do to influence matters now, other than dwell on his boredom and the past. Something he despised doing, as despite everything else on his mind, all he could think about was her...

Arillion growled, focussing his attention on the sounds outside his wagon. The distant strings of fiddle and harp, the ribald chatter and song, helped sooth his impatience for a time, as he too listened to, and wistfully imagined, the merriment taking place in the temporary city beyond. Deep into the festivities now, Arillion knew that once the Solstice celebrations had finished, Kaspen Shale would have trouble finding an excuse to remain in Highwater. If it proved impossible for him to remain, then Arillion had best be on his feet again.

He glared at the hidden shape of his splinted, ruined leg and raised one eyebrow sceptically.

Not a chance!

Arillion's thoughts, rapidly returning to the shadowy image of her beautiful face, stirring emotions he could do without, scattered as he detected the nearby whispers of a guarded conversation. Picking up only fragments because of the rising frivolity, he focused on the muttering tone of the unfolding debate and felt a warning chill steal down his neck.

After a time, he heard the reluctant approach of one who did not really want to be there, and then a tentative foot on the wooden steps outside.

Kaspen Shale paused, and then finally stepped into the wagon, closing the door gently behind him. Sweeping off his wide-brimmed hat he bent low to avoid the cold lantern hanging from the curved roof.

"My friend," he greeted, coming to his guest's bedside.

Arillion looked up at him, studying his troubled countenance. "Well, wayfarer? Why the face?"

Kaspen recoiled slightly and then smiled ruefully. "You are a perceptive man, Arillion. A talent that, I daresay, has served you well in the past."

Arillion ignored the wayfarer's flattery. "What's happened, Kaspen? I can see it in your eyes, if nowhere else."

Smoothing down his forked beard and rising irritation, the wayfarer sat down on the stool and drew in a deep breath.

"As you know, Tomlin has been watching the keep and following Lady Byron's movements of late," Kaspen reiterated, not for the first time recently.

Arillion nodded, not trying to hide his impatience and Kaspen smiled disarmingly, quick to continue.

"The city was in chaos last eve, the fires that swept through the merchant's district not helped by the riots that broke out across Highwater."

Arillion nodded. "Is she alive?" he dared to ask.

Kaspen's dark eyes widened, before settling down. He shook the appreciation from his face and nodded slowly.

"She is, my friend. But I fear for her now... her father has been murdered."

For once, Arillion was lost for words and he looked away. Chewing his top lip thoughtfully, he calmed his trembling, good hand, but could not stop his numbed left from twitching.

He was silent for a long while, as he sifted through the connotations and calmed his raging heart. Shaking his head and cursing his fateful slip in the mountains, he looked back at his host, who was watching him like a hawk, his eyes glittering in the candle light.

"So, the die has been cast," Arillion said, holding Kaspen's eyes, "the Brotherhood have finally begun in earnest. I feared, or rather I had hoped, that last night's chaos was nothing more than just timely coincidence."

Kaspen watched as Arillion punched back at the board behind his head, waiting for him to regain his composure. When the swordsman was finally calm again, he leant forward.

"What does all this mean, my friend?" Kaspen asked, though in truth, he was reluctant for the answer.

Arillion fixed him with a glare, his grey eyes piercing the gloom and burning with barely contained anger. "It means that we need to find the spy, and we need to find him... or her, quickly."

"How do we do that?" Kaspen asked, feeling his own frustration rise. "We have tried to locate your contact, this Morgan Belle, but there is no sign of her. She has not been seen since last winter."

Arillion frowned. Morgan ran a brothel in the west of the city, '*The Nest*', and he had laid a few eggs there in his time. She had quickly taken to his charms and over the years they had shared a relationship of mutual respect, trading information that led to coin and often, contract. The feisty woman, with the waist-length sable hair and long, blood-red painted nails, had her claws in a rich vein of information that was readily whispered in the ears of her girls and boys, by their needful, lustful clients.

She had interests in Carwell also. But such a long absence for her was troubling. Arillion's brow furrowed deeply and he fought against the emotions broiling away in his stomach. Had the Brotherhood silenced her, aware that she might well have been party to knowledge that could lead those who were looking, to the spy in Byron's Keep?

Arillion sighed and dismissed her face from his mind. She was probably dead and of no use to him now. He held Kaspen's questioning gaze for a time, before smiling faintly.

"We should focus our attentions elsewhere," Arillion said quietly. "I need you to find out what is happening in the keep, see if you can find out more about what happened. Who killed Alion Byron would be a bloody good place to start."

Kaspen rose and swept his hat back up onto his head. He straightened the brim between thumb and finger.

"I shall see what we can find out," Kaspen replied, inclining his head subtly. His face was impassive as always and Arillion could not tell if he was losing his enthusiasm for the hunt.

When the wayfarer was gone, Arillion let out a deep breath and fought against his frustration. He wasn't going anywhere for a while, so he had best get used to it. For now, he was at the mercy of Kaspen Shale and he would have to trust the wayfarer to find out all that he could.

Alone, and losing himself to the past again, Arillion could not shake the clawing, unsettling worry that stirred in his throat. Since his escape from Smuggler's Gap, he was beginning to suspect that Tobin's involvement in all of this ran deeper than he had hoped. And if it did, then that could only mean that...

"Well?"

Kaspen was heading back to the merriment at the campfire, slipping unnoticed through the shadows when a larger, dark shape stepped into his path and nearly sent him to an early grave.

"By the storms," Kaspen cursed, clutching at his clothes to try and hold on to his heart.

Agris Varen flashed him a broad grin and clapped his friend on the shoulder with a huge hand.

"If we are going to continue treading this path, my friend," Agris said, withdrawing his hand, "you had best watch the shadows in future."

Kaspen eyed his large friend and said nothing, as he planted his hands on his hips.

"Is it true what Tomlin says about Alion Byron?" Agris dared to ask, his ruined face twisting worriedly.

Kaspen nodded. "I am afraid so, my friend. I am beginning to wonder what we have got ourselves involved in."

Agris grunted. "Too late for that and I, for one, do not."

The wayfarer leader smiled ruefully. Agris was spoiling for a fight and he would not back down now. For years, since his brother had been caught by Carwell's men for stealing horses and hung without fair trial, his giant friend had been waiting impatiently for a chance to get back at those who upheld the law. If, what Arillion had said was true, then this *Brotherhood* must have their hands on reins in very high places.

Wincing at the thought of what was to come Kaspen began to worry that his friend may well soon get the chance.

"We need him back," Agris stated, dragging Kaspen's dark thoughts away.

"My mother is doing all she can," he protested.

"She is," Agris agreed. "But, and with the greatest of

respect to your mother, he will not heal quickly enough. Arillion needs fire in his blood to fuel his recovery."

Kaspen felt a wisp of apprehension stir on the back of his neck. "Why do I feel like I am not going to like what you say next?"

Agris Varen's grin was bright in the shadows. "Because you won't," he said. "Send him your daughter. She will tend to his needs and he'll be on his feet within a week."

Kaspen Shale recoiled and fixed his friend with a warning, baleful look. "I would not send her anywhere near his bedside." he hissed.

As Agris turned and wandered away, chuckling, Kaspen frowned. He turned his head, looking back over one shoulder towards the dark wagon and then trailed thoughtfully, reluctantly after his giant friend.

CHAPTER NINE

Storm Clouds

The first light of a cold dawn slowly clawed its way to life on the horizon, along the dark coastline to the east. From what was fast becoming his favourite vantage point on the Hermitage Retreat's curtain wall, Khadazin watched the thin shards of opaque light spread out slowly along the coast, probing the shoreline and rock pools for shadows, chasing them away along the jagged shore towards the west.

Wrapped in a heavy fur cloak, to ward away the chill in the coastal air, the Redani watched the breath-taking scene for over an hour, marvelling as the sedate waters of the Low Sea began to capture the grey dawn in its mirrored canvas. Khadazin had watched the dawn come every morning since they had arrived at the monastery, each one seemingly more beautiful to him than the last.

The wondrous sight before him was, he reminded himself sadly, the one thing he longed for each sleepless night, and yet, today, was the one the thing he had hoped he would not have to see.

Khadazin's slow, calm breath formed his thoughts

before him and he closed his eyes, listening to the sounds of the waves rolling up the shore, the seabirds shrieking noisily as they searched for their breakfasts. On the island that would one day be a colony for those shunned by society, its current inhabitants, the Low Sea's Dusky Seals, sang their mournful tune and sent tears spilling down Khadazin's cheeks.

'Sam Geddles would not see the dawn,' Brother Markus had warned him the previous evening, as they sat their silent, candle-lit vigil by the leper's bedside. James was bereft of any emotion, his young face drawn so tight from his sorrow that Khadazin feared the boy would pass out.

In silence, they had spent many hours by Sam's bedside. A fearful son, a brooding guardian and a sombre patron; all lost to their own thoughts, all reluctantly listening and watching for the last breath and final fall of his shallow, barely stirring chest.

It was testament to Sam's strength and tenacity, that Khadazin had eventually been forced to take James to his bed in the wagon, when the boy had fallen asleep at his father's bedside, his head drooping to rest on the dying man's chest. Nodding his head to the monk, the Redani had borne the boy away to the wagon, tucking him up in his blankets and ruffling his sandy mop of hair with his remaining hand.

Screwing his eyes tighter still, Khadazin banished his self-pitying thoughts and focused on the day ahead. Since Tania's departure with his letter for Savinn Kassaar, he had busied himself with James's welfare and his own, slow recovery. Despite the fact that his wounds, inflicted upon him by his captors so many days ago now, were but numb, fading reminders, Khadazin was beset by frequent headaches and a fiery tightness in the back of his neck that hampered his movements. Fighting with his guilt, the stonemason had distracted his worry for the girl with his concern for Sam's rapid decline. For the better part, until he tried to dress himself, or found that simple tasks were no longer that simple, Khadazin had not even dwelt too heavily upon the loss of his hand...

Feeling dark, fresh wounds tear open in his thoughts, he calmed himself, dragging in a deep breath of the fresh salty air and opening his eyes as he held it there for a while.

Blowing out his cheeks, Khadazin stomped some life into his sandalled feet and the toes that were so cold they felt like they weren't even there. He glanced down to reassure himself and wondered how he would have fared at Borin's, the torturer's hands, if he had not escaped when he did?

The hurried approach of booted feet upon stone chased him from the past and dragged his attention back to the monastery, still shrouded in shadows and silence.

Owyn, the thin, pale guard who had greeted them when they had first arrived, waved up to him as he hurried up the steps to the ramparts. Khadazin felt his heart begin to hammer and he hurried to greet the copper-haired guard.

"Forgive me, Redani," Owyn panted, his eyes still full of sleep and his chest tight from exertion. "Brother Markus is asking for you, he is with your friend."

Khadazin, his face a grim mask, gripped the guard's shoulder in thanks and hurried past him, as the man stepped respectfully aside.

Brother Markus looked up, his kind, yet fierce face stained by the long hours of a sleepless night as Khadazin entered the tiny cell, James trailing reluctantly behind him. Respectful candles burned low on the table at Sam's bed side and they flickered gently in the wake of their arrival.

"It will not be long," Markus whispered sadly, searching for the boy in the shadows, as he hid behind the giant Redani.

Khadazin swallowed, feeling the cold bite of realisation sweep through his body. He turned to look down at James and saw the tears glistening in his wide, fearful eyes.

"You do not have to be here," Khadazin said forlornly.

James nodded, sniffing. He wiped his eyes and rubbed his nose on the sleeve of his left arm.

"I know," he said softly.

James moved past the Redani and hurried to his father's side. Picking up a limp, bandaged hand, he sat down and began to cry.

Tania rose from her bedroll and glanced about the camp. Dawn was still but a hopeful promise and the only real light was coming from the embers of the previous night's campfire and the fading memory of the stars, once scattered in the sky overhead. Kneeling on her bedroll, she stretched the stiffness of a poor night from her body for a time and tied her tangled locks back behind her neck. The woods were dark and quiet; the only thing disturbing the solitude was her disgusting companion's deep, thunderous snoring and one of the horses tearing amiably at the dewy long grasses of the small clearing.

Reluctantly, Tania looked to where Cullen was sleeping, his broad back towards the fire, his eyes, for once, not turning in her direction or lingering on her body.

The huntress shuddered. Since slipping from the sewers and heading away from Karick, the trio of riders had made good time of their journey, leaving well behind the towering presence of the city and the dark storm clouds that menaced it.

It soon became apparent to the girl, however, that her

journey back to the monastery would not be an easy one, as the disgusting creature, his beady eyes leering and his quivering lips always quick to offer some suggestive remark, left her stomach nauseated and her nerves sharper than the knife she had hidden in her left boot.

The only foil to her anxiety came in the form of the third member of their party, the quiet, vigilant young man, who had not said a word since their departure and only answered to Cullen's barking orders with obedient nods and calming gestures.

Turning her distaste and thoughts away from the snoring figure, she found Riyan, sat on his haunches, near to the tethered horses, his attention on their woodland surroundings.

Tania smiled. The young man seemed on edge, out here in the expansive wilds of the South Vales, preferring, it appeared, the cluttered confines of the city and sewers. She shook her head in confusion. How anyone could live in such a choking, bustling city was beyond her. During her search for Savinn Kassaar's whereabouts, she had not been able to catch her own thoughts for any length of time, constantly pestered and plagued by peddlers, hawkers and worse.

Free of that madness now, she was thankful for the time to be able to hear her own thoughts again, even if she didn't currently want to listen to them.

Not wanting to risk waking Cullen and keen for some respite for a time, she rose on steadying feet and stretched languorously. Hearing the whispers of movement from her clothes, Riyan turned, a faint smile lighting the gloom for a moment.

Tania returned the smile, studying the man. He had a plain face and a broad forehead, crowned by fair hair that was far too thin for one of his age. His high cheekbones swept down a cheerful jaw line to a square chin, dusted by a reluctant beard. A fulsome mouth spread widely under a sloping nose that was quickly forgotten when drawn to the bright sapphire eyes that were usually alive with curiosity.

Dressed in travelling clothes that consisted of cloth breeches, a dark shirt of leather and matching wrist-guards and boots too soft for riding, he clearly had not been outside the city much. Tania had seen him shivering as they ate the broth she had prepared for them the night before, as he huddled too close to the flames for a warmth that would only make him feel worse in the cold heart of the night.

Riyan raised an arm in silent greeting and Tania padded carefully over to him.

"All quiet?" she asked, as she knelt beside him and looked out into the shadows, searching for signs of life.

Riyan nodded.

"I am going to go hunting," she told the man, with a look that dared him to stop her. "I am, ahem, keen to avoid Silver Falls and, if given a couple of hours, will be able to put *fresh* meat in our stew tonight."

Riyan nodded his encouragement and smiled.

"You don't say much, do you!" she stated softly.

Riyan smiled and shook his head. He fell silent for a time, looking away, before turning his eyes back.

He raised a hand, tapping his fingers to his open mouth and shook his head again.

Tania's eyes widened with comprehension and she just about managed to stop her mouth hanging open.

"Ah, you cannot speak," she surmised and the man nodded.

He shrugged, putting a fore-finger beneath one eye and dragged it down his cheek a couple of times, before shaking his head emphatically.

Tania's eyes widened again and she offered him a smile that suggested comprehension, but revealed the opposite.

Riyan smiled in understanding, waving her away to the forest encouragingly. He raised three fingers to his mouth quickly several times and then raised his thumb.

Tania rose stiffly, keen to be out in the woods and stretching her legs once again. She turned reluctantly, looking back at Cullen's sleeping form, and her breath caught in her throat as he coughed and rolled over.

She looked at Riyan, then nodded towards Cullen as he began snoring again. Cocking one eyebrow, she dealt the mute a questioning look.

Screwing his face up with distaste, Riyan glared at their companion and waved a dismissive hand in his direction.

Tania chuckled silently and carefully, quietly, went to retrieve her quiver and bow.

Balan Ford cursed, steadying himself as he struggled with his balance and the large bundle of thatching on his aching shoulders. Straddling the roof, he loosened the bindings on the yelm he had hauled up on his own and spread the wheat out across the hole in the roof, torn free by the angry storm that had rampaged through Colden but two nights before.

Catching his breath, Balan wiped the sweat of his exertions from his face and looked about the village. The tiny community was alive now, as people hurried about their lives, many trudging eastwards through crop-laden fields towards the ghostly looming presence that was Greywood Forest, to fetch fresh water from the natural spring there. Balan watched his mother as she chatted incessantly to their neighbour, Mary Wren, as they wandered away, bearing empty buckets in swinging hands.

Ignoring the frustration that broiled away suddenly, Balan turned his head to the ringing sound of the smithy and the giggles of the children, as they chased the chickens across the village square again.

Balan picked up a twisted willow spar and stared at it for a time, allowing himself to calm down. With his father mysteriously gone, leaving behind his vain efforts to repair the roof, damaged a year previously in the Great Storms, it had fallen upon the young son of the house to fix things that were promised time and time again. Mary's initial pleasure that her son had returned safely from the mountains, was soon replaced by her desire to make the most of her husband's absence. Stripping the hours away with her furious tongue, she had her son fixing this and fetching that – '*Just recompense*' she had said, for the fact that he had not returned home with any *worthwhile* coin for his efforts. Handing over what little coin he had found, Balan soon began to feel like he had never been away.

The only difference in his mother's daily routine was that she did not have a drunken, abusive husband to contend with for a time. When Balan questioned her about where his father had gone, she simply looked away and shook her head.

"Knowing your pa," she had answered, her weary voice devoid of life, "it could be anywhere."

Balan cursed, shaking his head as images of the fight in the mountains stirred in his thoughts. He had feared going away, had been terrified when the swordsman had pressed a sword to his throat, his life hanging on the whim of his blade. Up there, in the twisting confines of Smuggler's Gap, Balan had feared, was certain he would die. But now, back home and dragged down by the apathy and shackles of his mundane life, he realised that, for the briefest of time, he had never felt more alive.

The young man's face fell and he closed his eyes, allowing the rising wind to soothe his frustrations, as it ruffled his hair for a time. There was little to keep him here, Balan knew. It was only a son's sense of loyalty to a mother who ambled her way through life, awaiting a release from the bonds of her despair, that did. If it wasn't for her, he would have left by now.

Angry at the taste of his own excuses, Balan turned his disgust to good use and spent the rest of the morning finishing off the repairs under a blue sky that brightened with hope as the hours slipped slowly away.

Finally, called down for lunch by his mother, Balan gingerly stepped across the thatched roof and slipped deftly down the rickety ladder to the ground below. Tossing his tools into a wooden box, relief chasing his arm, he dunked his head in the barrel at the side of their home and shuddered in delight, as the cold water chased his weariness and dark mood away for a time.

Balan was returning with another bucket of water from the spring, under the shade of the forest, when he first saw his father. Feeling his nerves spike and his throat thicken with worry, he slowed his approach to the village and loitered in the fields with only the swarming flies for company.

Finally, however, with shaking hands and a sky overhead that appeared to darken, Balan trudged back into Colden, catching his father's brash voice, as he barked out his demands to a wife who slipped obediently away into their home to fetch him some food.

Balan winced as his father wandered around the side of the old hut to relieve himself and he tarried in his approach, his sandals and feet thick with the mud of the square. Steeling himself, Balan remembered his vow, when he had defended his life, and hauling up his frame, he strode purposefully towards his home.

His father appeared in timely fashion as Balan approached, his eyes darkening as he spied his son and wiped a wet hand on his shirt that was already covered in a dark stain.

"There you are!" he said, his words devoid of any joy.

"Well? What happened? Did they get her? How much money did I make?"

Balan slowed, putting the heavy bucket down with a shaking hand. He straightened, not able to meet his father's accusing eyes, filling, even now, with his customary rising anger.

"I, I mean, they," Balan mumbled. Not the best start to his supposed newly discovered confidence and strength.

Stalking close, limping heavily on his left leg, his father's face loomed large in his eyes. "Spit it out! It's a simple question that even your fancy tongue could cope with."

Balan bristled and felt his hands tremble. "They did not," Balan whispered, his eyes narrowing. "And *you* did not make anything."

His father stepped back slightly, seeing the look in his son's eyes, noting the gleam of defiance there. He rallied quickly, however, as he grabbed his son by the shirt and dragged him about roughly.

"What in the storms does that mean?" he roared, as Balan struggled back, his own face dark with rising anger.

Pulled about, Balan clutched at his father's clothes and searched for his breath and balance. When he found it, his words were brittle, cracking upon his fear at what would surely follow.

"The girl escaped," Balan faltered, tripping over his words. "Everyone died, there was a swordsman..."

His father blinked. "Dead? But there were nigh-on thirty swords in that hunting party? How?"

He released his son, shaking his head in confusion. When he gathered his wits, he looked back at his son, his eyes clouding with dark fury.

"Then how is it that you still live, son?"

Balan backed away, sensing his father's rage, hearing the accusations in his words.

"If they all died, where is the money? Where are their horses?" his father snarled, spittle flying from his lips.

"Three men went after the girl, once Tobin and the swordsman were dead," Balan said hastily. "They did not return, father, so I came home. I thought you would be pleased."

"Empty handed?" his father roared. "I am out, bloodying my hands and risking my life and you... YOU flee like a coward, without wit enough to make good our fortunes?"

Balan went to speak, but his face was filled by his father's fist.

With his surroundings spinning and his eyes lolling, Balan was aware that he was falling. As the soft ground reached up to catch him, he heard his mother's futile protests as a shadow loomed over him. Before he could regain his senses, he was hauled up and dragged inside, his father's fury ringing in his ears. Groaning, Balan fought with the flashing speckles of silver light in his eyes and as the dark wooden walls of the cluttered kitchen spun about him, he was thrown roughly against one of them.

"Stop it, Rol," his mother pleaded, though, with his face dragging down the splintered wood, Balan could not see what was unfolding. "You will kill him."

"It's more than he deserves," Roland spat and Balan could hear his heavy approach. "We need that money! It will be some weeks before they cough up the crowns I have just earned us!"

"What do you mean?" his mother asked, dragging his attention away. "What have you done this time?"

From his heap on the wooden floor, Balan could hear his father stalking about. Moaning, Balan touched at his face and he grimaced in agony as he felt the blood spilling from his ruined mouth. Shaking, his face on fire, Balan spat thick blood and some teeth from his mouth.

"It doesn't matter what I have done," his father was snarling, though, through the fog, to Balan it sounded like he was worried. "We just need to get away for a time. We have powerful friends now, but it is best if we head to Carwell for a season."

A chill stole up Balan's spine and he could hear the fear in his mother's voice as she shied from away from his father, across the wooden fasting table, riddled with more holes than it had oak these days.

"Husband, what *have* you done?" she demanded. Balan heard three quick steps across the wooden floor and winced, as he heard the ringing slap of hand against flesh.

His mother shrieked and Balan could hear her sob as she curled up under her husband's rage.

"Stop it!" Balan snarled, pushing himself to his knees. The room spiralled, as he looked to see his father dragging his mother to her feet.

"Leave her alone, father!" he shrieked, rising unsteadily.

Roland's head turned, his eyes balefully fixing on his son, as he hurled his wife away. Rising up to his full height, he hauled the table aside and came at his son, grabbing him by the throat.

"You are no son of mine, coward," he hissed.

Balan fought for breath under the firm grip of the hand about his throat. "I would rather die, than lay claim as your son."

Roland baulked, his face filling with rage, his eyes blazing with hatred.

"Stop this, Roland," Balan's mother was at her husband's arm, clawing at him with nails that raked along his bared skin. "You will kill him."

Roland's eyes swung to his wife and he flung her away. He turned his eyes back on his son, his disgust flashing there. Finding a breath, he hurled his son towards the sideboard that stretched under an open window and watched disdainfully as he crashed amongst the pottery and dough his mother had been kneading to bake fresh bread.

"Get your things," Roland bellowed, rounding on his wife who was crawling away across the earthen, straw-strewn floor, sobbing. "I would finally be rid of this whelp."

Balan's mind was racing, his face ruined by broken clay. As his father dragged up his mother by her lank, greying hair and threw her towards the back rooms, he rose up, his hands curling about a rusting cleaver. Before he realised what he was doing, Balan was stumbling across the spinning room, his rising fury a distant rumble, like thunder on the horizon.

Roland Ford heard him coming and turned, far too slowly however, to stop the blade that his son planted in the top of his head.

CHAPTER TEN

The Enemy Within

Edren Bay strode purposefully through the keep's gardens under the scrutiny of a bright summer's day. With the furious rain now gone, dragged southwards by impatient clouds, the city could breathe again, alive with the clear freshness that only such a storm's passing could bring.

Following a marble path, edged on both sides by beds of beautifully bright flowers and bushes of oleander, he listened to the thrumming sounds of the foraging bees and tracked the flight, momentarily, of a dancing, yellow butterfly. He smiled faintly. When Highwater was his, he would make certain that the gardens continued to flourish.

Passing under an archway of white roses in full bloom, Edren made his way towards the summer house and the backdrop of the dovecote beyond. A blackbird sang merrily overhead from the highest branch of the old apple tree, which was heavily laden with offerings this year, and, as he hurried by the statues in the former duke's private garden, a horde of sparrows bickered noisily in the hedgerow that surrounded it.

Edren blanked out the feelings that surged up within

him and gritted his teeth. The last few days, gone it seemed in a heartbeat, felt nothing more than a dream to him now. He half expected to wake up each morning to discover that Alion Byron was still alive and that the Brotherhood's plans were just whispers and shadows... a promise of the glorious days to come.

Calming himself, Edren came to a stop by the Byron summer house and frowned when Cassana was not there. The alarm had been raised quickly, when his mother had taken breakfast to the lady of Highwater's chambers and the keep was now being searched frantically for her.

Edren sighed and ran a hand through his hair, before smoothing down the sleeves of his finely cut, scarlet tunic. Absently adjusting the black lace trims, he went and sat on the marble bench in the summer house.

Cassana was not in any immediate danger, as far as he knew. The assassin was long gone by now, Edren's diversions working masterfully, and, as the city tried to contend with the shock of those bloody events two nights ago now, he could not help but think it would be better for all in the long run if she had gone to find a tree to hang herself from.

Guilt rose up in his throat and Edren spat it away, lest he choke on it. Alion Byron was dead. It was always going to happen and once Cassana had escaped, it was inevitable. The Brotherhood were moving their pieces carefully about the board now, and there would be many more pieces sacrificed in the coming weeks, if the game was to be finally won.

Edren had intercepted Lord Astien's note when it arrived in the city, had very nearly burnt it, as he had with so many others of late. But, for some reason, he had not. It wasn't out of some waning loyalty to a doomed Alion Byron. It wasn't even that he hoped to delay the inevitable with some subconscious sense of duty to the man who had treated him almost like his own son. No! If he was honest with himself, he knew it wasn't anything to do with that at all... it was because of Cassana.

Her face came unbidden to his mind and he shut his eyes, seeking to banish her. Despite his allegiance to the Brotherhood, his betrayal to his family and lord, he had preserved the message only because he wanted to ensure that Alion Byron had time to protect his daughter.

Edren was sure that if he had destroyed the letter and Highwater had remained unaware of the events unfolding in the capital, the Byron bloodline would now be wiped out. It would have been the easiest soloution, probably, for all concerned... but, despite his willing subterfuge and betrayal, Edren could not bring himself to allow Cassana to die also.

Slipping away to easier days, Edren lost himself for a time, his conscience taunted by his past. They had grown up together, Cassana and he, almost like the brother and sister that both had lost, sharing adventures and also, many times, the venom and punishments that came with such mischief. Was he strong enough to turn his back on all of that? Could he dismiss everything they had done together and so easily cast aside the personal secrets and trauma they had shared and consoled each other through?

Although he knew he must, Edren was certain that he could not. Had he shared his feelings with the chancellor or the Brotherhood, he too would also now be laying in state, awaiting burial in the family vaults. It was bad enough that he and his cohort had persuaded his friend Elan to take Cassana to Karick on a lesser-travelled road, cajoling him to seek passage through the Moonglade Forest where the Reven were waiting. It had all sounded so easy when they and the chancellor had planned the strategy, all those seasons ago. Cassana would be spared, used only as a bargaining tool when the Valian armies amassed outside the gates of Highwater. Once the Reven lands were conquered, Relan Valus had promised she would be returned, unharmed and unspoilt to him.

Edren buried his face in his hands and growled. *Was he truly that naive?* Did he really think that Cassana would be allowed to return to a normal life after all of this? Did he honestly believe that once he, Edren Bay, became the lord of Highwater, that she would sit willingly by his side, sharing the stewardship as friends and, perhaps one day, as husband and wife?

"You stupid fool, Bay," he snarled, punching himself furiously in the side of his head.

Of course she would not! She would despise him, perhaps even more than his own parents would come to do and he would sit at the head of his table alone, surrounded by his thoughts and the dishonour of his actions.

Feeling himself drowning in his self-pity, he rallied himself and glared about his surroundings. He was still alone. None had chanced upon him and witnessed his weakness. Calming himself and ignoring the pain in his face, he straightened himself and rose brusquely.

Highwater would be his and there would come a time soon when all who stood in his way would either be dead or locked up in the city's dungeons. If Cassana was not to accept the future he had planned for her, then she would join her mother and father in the family vaults.

Edren found Cassana, moments later, as he explored the dovecote. Beyond the court being held by the pigeons and doves inside the beautifully carved, domed marble structure, he detected the playful bark of a hound.

With his heart rousing to a wild beat, Edren entered the small, lawned area on the far side of the dovecote and let out a breath as he found the source of his consternation.

With Shadow, the faithful old Byron hound watching on, and annoyed by the inattention, Cassana stood with her back to him, her bow gripped confidently in her right hand, as she fitted another arrow to the string. Her long tresses, longer than he remembered, were loose, tumbling down her back like a dark waterfall. She was not adhering to her status, dressed again in the common clothes she had been wearing when she stumbled into the keep in *secret*, all those days ago now. The leather breeches had been expertly mended, waxed and treated, the blouse boiled clean and its torn seams stitched. Soft dark boots swept up her legs, helping to frame the allure of her slender figure and Edren stood where he was, under the shade of a cherry tree, his arms folded across his chest as he watched her fluidly draw back the string to her left cheek and let fly.

He tracked the shaft's flight as it flashed across the lawn and joined several other arrows there in the centre of a round, straw target. Edren felt a momentary surge of pride and then fought it back down again as Cassana reached for another white-feathered shaft from her quiver.

Drawing in a faltering breath, Edren began walking towards her, his hand hesitantly straying to the pommel of the Valian Longsword, belted at his waist.

It would be so easy now, he thought, to plunge his blade into her back and end all of his uncertainty and turmoil. His hand curled around the dark leather hilt...

"So you found me, then." Cassana stated, without turning and Edren flinched. Shadow wagged his tail eagerly in greeting.

Edren forced a smile, even though she could not see it. "I have, my lady," he said, his relief disguising his words. "We have been sick with worry, we..."

Cassana turned and Edren fell silent, his heart stopping momentarily. He had expected to see a ghost before him, a woman broken by grief and ruined by her fear for the future. But as Cassana's stony face regarded him curiously and her eyes flicked quizzically about his face, Edren began to wonder if he had underestimated her. Back someone into a corner long enough, tear their life apart enough times and they will either break, or they will temper, hardened by their adversity and forged by their desire for retribution.

"I have been lax of late," Cassana said, a trace of a smile on her dry lips. She turned away again and reached for another arrow. "I have been a prisoner in my own home for far too long."

Bent bow, swift motion, left centre of the target.

Cassana turned back, her eyes bright with anger. "I will return shortly, Edren. I must practice some more, ready myself for the days ahead."

"Cassy?" Edren croaked and then politely cleared his dry throat.

"I have funerals to arrange," Cassana said evenly, though her voice was strained and distant. "I have the city to address... and most importantly, I have a future to protect."

Edren's mind was raging, pulled apart by confusion and worry. When he spoke, he winced, as his words tumbled out too hastily. "I know you are suffering and I know that I cannot possibly understand what you are feeling at this time... but I know you, I know the fire that clouds your mind when you are angry. You need to take time to digest things. You have to make time to think clearly about what you will do next."

Cassana looked over her shoulder at him, her features stony pale and hard as marble. "I know, Edren. I will. Your father has already spoken to me at great length, advising me on our best course from here."

Edren hid any worry from his face and distracted his thoughts for a time by ruffling the hound's ears, as it sat patiently at his feet.

"I am so, so sorry, Cassy," Edren said eventually,

unable to look up at her. "After all you have been through recently, to have this happen... I just want you to know that I, like my father, am here for you. I always have been, I always will be. You know that, don't you?"

He dared look up and was relieved that his shame, masked by his embarrassment, was eased by the soft smile warming her face.

"I know," she responded, swallowing her tears before they could rise.

Edren moved to her, opening his arms wide. She slipped into his embrace and drew strength from him.

Holding her close, the spy sensed her relax, felt her ragged breath as it tickled his neck.

"I worry about you, Cassana," Edren admitted, stroking her hair. "You will have a great burden to carry now that you are alone. My father has told me what will be expected of you in the wake of your father being killed and–"

Cassana stiffened their embrace and recoiled, pulling away from him.

Her eyes blazed dangerously. "Come now, sir, my father was murdered, plain and simple. Let us not dress our words..."

Edren held up a hand in apology. "Forgive me, I did not mean anything by it."

Cassana, her hands on her hips, regarded him for a time, before she finally calmed down.

"I know, Edren, I know," she whispered, before anger caught her thoughts again. "I have much to think about and would be alone for a while longer. I have letters to write and people to find. I would ask only that you look to my safety and that of my family in the coming days."

"Your *family*?" Edren's question was past his lips before he could stop it.

Cassana drew forth an arrow and fitted it to the string of her bow. She held her friend's eyes meaningfully.

"Highwater is my family now, and I will not let them down. There is a dark menace tainting the halls of the capital and I will not allow it to spread here also."

Edren's heart was racing. He knew that she would not be able to resist the storm that would batter at Highwater's gates, she was not strong enough. She did not have the heart or the allies to withstand the inevitable. But, if she tried to, she would be swept away by it. She would be *killed* by it.

"My Lady Byron," Edren said pleadingly. "It would be unwise to resist the will of the council, it would..."

"My father's letter will probably already be on the high duke's table," Cassana responded calmly. "It states his desire to defy any attempt to go to war against the Reven. I firmly believe he was right in his misgivings. After what has just happened, I am certain of it."

"But..."

Cassana cut him off. "I will not lend Highwater's support to such madness, when it inevitably happens, as I believe it shall. I will no longer be a pawn in this game. I will honour my father's wishes. I will lend my strength to his belief and I shall stand against the storm when it comes."

"Go to Karick, Cassy," Edren pleaded. "Speak to the high duke, tell him your concerns. He will listen to them. You are your father's daughter. I see that. He will see it, too!"

Cassana shook her head sadly. "He will not, I fear and I would not put myself in harm's reach again. If they can strike at us here, I would not survive a second journey to the capital. If the high duke wishes to engage in peaceful debate, then he will have to come to me."

Edren's stoic composure, the narrow-minded ambition that had seen him safely this far, was in tatters. He knew what this meant. The Brotherhood would come for her and he would not be able to save her a second time.

"But my lady, it is too dangerous for him. The threat to the council members still stands. With the raids and attacks happening, he will not come and such defiance will surely mark you. Whoever ordered your father murdered, they will also come for you."

Cassana spun and her shaft sang as it buried in the centre of the target.

"Let them come," she hissed and her words, carrying all her grief and anger in them, chased Edren back to the keep without another word.

CHAPTER ELEVEN

Catalyst

Dia hurried through the grounds of the high duke's keep, her shawl wrapped tightly about her. In the oppressive sky above, the glowering clouds continued rumbling their discontent and another jagged flash of lightning lit up the dark skies as it stretched out over the west of the city.

She felt the cobbles under her feet tremble as a huge peal of thunder roared and echoed across Karick. If she didn't hurry, she would be caught out in the storm that was about to wash the capital away. It was only late afternoon and already it felt like the depths of the night. Dia wished it were, as her task would have proven a lot easier, or at least, would have felt as if it was.

Allowing her feet to guide her whilst her mind wandered, Dia headed to the Records Office. As she neared, her heart began to pound, drumming in her head enough to drown out the thunder for a time. Glancing up, she studied the myriad of clouds knotting together angrily above her and she marvelled at the raw power that waited there, hidden away in the almost beautiful tapestry of dark blacks, greys and subtler blues.

She had been waiting several days now for her chance to slip into the Records Office, to finally discover what was really going on inside what was once, the Royal library. At last her moment had come, and she needed one last draught of courage, one more moment of deceit before she finally had her answers.

Chancellor Valus was attending an urgent meeting with the high duke, Lord Astien, and the other council members who had stayed in the capital to attend to the rising problem of the Reven threat. In the last few days, troubling news had reached the city, telling of more attacks on prominent members of the city of Ilithia. The worst, it was being reported, was that the mayor of the city had been kidnapped by '*Savage*' looking individuals, as he visited outlying towns and villages to reassure them that all was being done to safeguard the region from further Reven attacks. As of yet, no demands had been made...

Following the more worrying news that another murder had taken place in the capital, the tension in Karick had become more intense than the storm about to erupt. Only a day's past, a Reven family's house was stoned by youths, who shouted obscenities before fleeing the watch that chased angrily after them.

Savinn Kassaar had contacted her with news soon after, saying only that the stonemason was still alive.

By the Lady that news gladdened her heart. She had thought, as so many others with him, that the Redani was surely dead. Remembering a summer day, long since forgotten, Dia recalled that she had only met the stonemason once, bumping into him as he searched vainly for the chancellor's office to report to work. Had she known what ill fortune would befall Savinn's giant friend and saviour, she would have sent him home, not directed him on towards his fateful meeting with his destiny in the high duke's gardens.

It took her a while, but after recovering from her surprise and shock that there was still the possibility of stopping the rising madness, Dia had drawn on her newfound hope to give her the courage she would need to find.

She was almost at the office before she realised it and only just managed to smile at her lover, as he grinned at her hurried approach. Dealing him her most winning smile, she felt her heart quicken as he shared a look with his fellow sentry, Wen. The older man smiled in recognition, but his warmth did not reach his eyes.

"Gentleman," Dia greeted them, smiling. "I fear you have drawn short lots this day."

The three of them looked up at the rampaging clouds overhead and shared their concerns in the form of a bitter nod.

"Very short," Eran winced, his handsome features creasing, "especially when the chancellor is not even here."

The two guards shared a disgruntled look, before the older man fixed her with a curious one. "What can we do for you, miss?"

His tone was enquiring and yet laced with irritation. Dia smiled sweetly. He was probably fed up with hearing Eran prattle on about her constantly during the long, tedious hours they were forced to spend together. Dia felt her heart race and looked briefly at Eran, seeing the affection and more, gleaming there in his bright, blue eyes.

"The chancellor has asked me to tidy up matters for him whilst he is detained elsewhere," Dia replied, slipping the keys from the folds of her long skirt and jingling them in front of Wen's eyes as evidence.

The older guard studied the keys, then searched her impassive face for tell of what she was about. After a time, he shrugged nonchalantly.

"As you will, my lady," he said, stepping aside

dismissively.

Dia offered her thanks and met Eran's grin as he watched her knowingly.

'Grumpy bastard' he mouthed silently. As Dia moved to the old, wooden door, Eran stepped aside, reaching out to touch her shaking hand tenderly.

She smiled at him, brushing by slowly. As she reached for the keyhole, her heart began to hammer. *Two keys, which one?*

She chose the larger, more worn key and slipped it falteringly into the lock. With her breath in her throat, she turned the key, letting out a silent gasp as it gave and the lock slowly released.

Closing her eyes momentarily, Dia gathered herself, before turning to the two guards. Wen was witnessing the fresh lightning to the west, whereas Eran was watching her, the hunger left from their lovemaking that morning still burning in his eyes.

"Gentlemen," she grinned, winking. Shoving on the heavy door, she slipped into the shadows of the stone entrance hall beyond. Closing the door, she stood with her back to the wood for a time, gathering her wits. The passion of the morning's tryst trembled through her body again and she felt a stab of pain in her breast. If she was finally about to find what Savinn wanted, she would not need Eran any more...

As she lit the candle in the cold lantern, forgotten on the windowless ledge to her left, Dia wondered, when the time came, if she would actually be able to give him up.

Chancellor Relan Valus fell into the comfort of his chair, his head pounding furiously. With his office spinning wildly about him, he buried his face in his trembling hands and fought to focus his mind.

The meeting with the high duke had gone well, very

well. But as Karian Stromn slipped further into his paranoia, so did his spontaneous outbursts and flashes of uncontrolled temper. The tension in the room, attended by the Lords' Astien and Farrington, the Lady Rothley and, much to the chancellor's annoyance, Captain Varl, had broken down after a messenger delivered a letter from Highwater in timely, orchestrated fashion.

With his eyes widening incredulously over the short message on the note, borne hastily by wing and kept back for two days by the chancellor, the high duke drew in a breath before tearing the parchment asunder.

"This is unacceptable," the high duke had roared, rising angrily and hurling away his chair. "Even my old allies turn against me, at a time when we need unity and strength."

When he was calm enough, the high duke recounted Alion Byron's words bitterly for those gathered about the meeting table.

'Highwater will not give its blessing to this madness, Karian, and we will not support the victimisation of innocent Reven citizens. I will not come back to the table unless reason returns to the capital.'

With the high duke ranting at the apparent '*disloyalty*' and '*betrayal*' of his old friend, the chancellor had worriedly studied the horrified looks shared between Astien, Farrington and Varl. As his eyes, however, met Lady Rothley's, he accepted her nod of congratulations with a calmer, faint smile.

There had followed a heated debate about what to do and to where the council should divert their efforts next. By the end of it, Captain Varl had been dismissed with warnings that he and his men had better find some evidence of who was behind these threats soon, or they would be replaced by those who could.

As Varl left, casting a withering look in his old enemy's direction, Lord Astien and Farrington rose together, both offering their need for a more calm and measured approach to resolving matters. The high duke had dismissed them without so much as a look in their direction.

When they were gone, Lady Rothley had turned to the high duke, her pale face haughty and cold.

"My lord," she had said, stirring the chancellor's heart with her words, "now that those spineless imbeciles have left, shall we talk about what really *needs* to be done?"

Relan smiled, feeling the tightness in his temple ease somewhat. The high duke was slowly falling into madness, losing all grasp of reason and reality. The pressure building from the people was starting to take its toll. Attacks were already starting on the Reven citizens and soon, very soon, the people of Karick would start rounding the scum up for them. If he didn't despise them so much, he might actually feel sorry for them.

He just needed to make a couple of more careful moves and the madness could begin...

Relan poured himself a wine from the carafe on his desk and sipped idly at the strong, rich red. Smacking his lips in appreciation, he stared at his shaking hand for a time and then put the glass down carefully.

He had not heard any word from Highwater and would not, he supposed, until the Kestrel returned, or news winged its way to the capital. Feeling his pulse race, the chancellor tried to calm himself, but failed miserably. When news reached the capital of Alion Byron's murder, the high duke would break and it would be time, then, for the chancellor to play his hand.

Any thoughts of the days to follow were quickly scattered by the angry, crisp bark of annoyance and the sound of someone forcing their will upon the guard outside the chancellor's chambers. Opening a drawer, Relan slipped a slim-bladed knife out of its velvet sheath and placed it from view in his robed lap. The door burst open and as a pile of limbs and bodies tumbled hastily into the room, the startled guard offered his apologies hurriedly.

"Forgive me, sir, this man..." he began, but was dragged roughly from view by a large man in the corridor beyond.

Straightening himself, a tall, lean, hawk-faced man slammed the door on them and focussed his annoyance on the thin, pathetic man sat before him.

"If you won't do it," the man hissed angrily. "I will have that idiot flogged before sunset. How dare he deny me entrance?"

Relan Valus smiled faintly and leant across his desk, placing the knife on some forgotten parchments.

"He was obeying my orders," Relan began. "Like all good soldiers should."

The man stood watching him, his temper tighter than the arms folded across his leather-clad chest. When it appeared that he was about to erupt, the chancellor offered him a seat, which, after a moment's consideration, he thankfully accepted.

"I have to say, Renald, that I did not expect you here," Relan Valus began, watching as the man pulled off his gloves and tossed them on the desk between them. The newcomer helped himself to the bottle of wine and drank hastily from it. "Why are you not heading back to Carwell?"

Commander Gardan's eyes narrowed painfully and he slammed the bottle down on the wood.

"I have news, obviously!" he growled, wiping the wine from his twitching moustache.

"Obviously," the chancellor observed, threading his hands together.

Relan Valus watched the silent man for a time, as his face filled with annoyance. Knowing the man well, he waited for the customary disdain to paint itself on his weary features, looked for the spark of anger that was never far from his eyes.

He hadn't seen Gardan for several seasons and was taken aback by how the lines that creased the corners of his eyes looked deeper now and the thin hands, that wielded so much power in the east, were calloused and shaking, their nails dirty and unkempt.

Gardan scowled, forgetting his pain, irritated by the chancellor's scrutiny.

"We are both all the more older now, Relan," he snapped. "If you have finished, I shall begin."

"What happened to you?" Relan enquired, noting the hole in his leather armour and the dried blood there.

Gardan glanced at his wound, licked his lips and sighed. "A lucky shot, that is all." He waved away any concern. "I have survived worse."

Relan nodded, sipping his wine. "Tell me then, brother, what news of Havensdale?"

Drawing in a breath, the commander calmed his rising frustration and leant across the table. When he spoke, his eyes blazed with guilty tell of his failure.

"Things took a turn in Eastbury," he began slowly. "That fool Raven allowed himself to be captured and was dragged back to the town in chains."

The chancellor's concern rose up over his arching eyebrows, throbbing nervously in his head.

"But that should not have altered the plan," Relan probed, tapping the long stem of his wine glass thoughtfully with a twitching finger.

Gardan scowled, waving away his concerns. "Of course not, the plan remained the same. I took over from the patrol that had captured him and the other raiders, making sure that he *understood* what we were about and what was expected of him."

Relan Valus failed to see what the problem was and he glared at the commander impatiently.

"I have a lot to do, Renald," he said wearily. "Just get to the point, will you?"

Gardan's face coloured and he recoiled in his chair. He held the chancellor's eyes for a time, before reining in his temper.

"As you will," he said coolly, spreading his hands on the desk. "Fawn Ardent lives, Havensdale repelled our attack. Is that short enough?"

Relan Valus blinked, then rose up into the arms of his anger. "You fool!" he spat angrily. "It was a simple task and you had more than enough men to achieve it. All you had to do was frame the captain and bring her to the noose."

Gardan rose swiftly and they glared at each other across the parchments. "Choose your next insult carefully, brother. You should not be so quick to deal out such condemnation. It is only by our lord's will and your confounded luck that you still breathe. I am doing what I do best, making the most of the situation and turning it to our advantage."

Relan uncurled his fists and searched for the calm in his lungs. "Then, pray tell, share your wondrous plan with me. How are we to make the most of this?"

Gardan smiled. "Fawn Ardent is finished, mark my words and Havensdale will burn, once our armies march north. When I report to the high duke all that has happened, of the men they have murdered to cover up their treachery, they will be marked as traitors and rebels. With Alion Byron dead, they will have nobody to turn to. They will have no evidence to deny the claims I take before the high duke."

Relan Valus relaxed, his mind already working away, seeking further ways to turn this to their advantage.

Seeing that the chancellor's infamous mind was at work, Commander Gardan proceeded to recount the attack on Havensdale, how they had breached the walls, thanks to their man inside, but of how the tide was turned by the arrival of the mysterious swordsman.

Relan waved away Gardan's concern. "One man will not stop what is to come, my friend."

Gardan frowned. "And yet it is one man's testimony that could still bring our plans to ruin. There was something about this man... I do not know, I cannot put a finger on it."

Tilting his head thoughtfully, Relan offered a smile. "Make no matter of it, brother. Captain Ardent will no longer be a problem for us, despite the setback. Alion Byron is most likely dead as we speak, his daughter with him. With no leader in the north, Havensdale will have no voice strong enough to dispute your claims and, rather fittingly, because of your *failure*, our story will ring all the more loudly with the truth of her supposed betrayal."

Gardan smiled thinly, trying to ignore the insult, but his bitterness chased after his words. "Agreed! She will not be able to get Lady Byron's account on the matter - she will, if she has the courage to try, hang herself for us."

"Indeed!" the chancellor smiled. "I am about to play my highest card, one which will see that the Reven taint is stamped out in these lands, forever."

Gardan saw the flicker of desire dancing in the chancellor's eyes, framed by his certainty and perhaps the glint of madness. "Which card is this?"

Relan Valus put a thin finger to his lips, smiling from behind it. "The one that will kill two birds with one very cunning stone."

Gardan felt his wound throb and watched the chancellor for a time. When it appeared that he would find out no more, he shrugged.

"Play your card, brother," he said, rolling the tension from his neck. "I should report to the high duke, tell him my side, lest others beat me to it."

Relan nodded his agreement. "I shall come with you,

Renald. There is much we need to discuss on the way."

"I will go alone," Gardan said, his tone suggesting no response was expected. "It would not look good if the high duke thinks I came to you first with this news."

The chancellor bit his tongue and reluctantly nodded. "So be it, brother. One matter, before you go. Captain Varl is yet to be fully discredited. Your arrival has proven most timely. I think it best you stay here for a time, as Karick will soon need a strong arm."

Gardan grinned and they shook hands firmly. "Work on that for me, Relan. Dispose of Varl and stake my claim for me. Once I am in charge of the investigations here, we can start dragging the Reven to the blocks."

Relan held up a hand. "Let us take one step at a time, brother. Captain Varl knows the location of the high duke's family and I have been unable to find out where they are myself."

Gardan scowled. "By the Storms, then deal with him, man! Burn the information from him if you must, so that we can begin in earnest. I yearn for this, Valus, so let us not rest on our laurels. Together we will carve a glorious name for ourselves and the Brotherhood."

The chancellor's heart was pounding and he had to resist getting swept along with him. "We shall, my friend, we shall. But first, a word of caution, though. Before you see the high duke, you should know that he is unstable and you need be on your guard with him. He is prone to outbursts and irrational behaviour, beware of his rising madness."

Gardan snorted, swept up his gloves and turned, two long strides taking him to the door. When his hand was on the ringed handle, he turned.

"Do not concern yourself with me, Relan," he said, nodding his farewell.

"I work for a madman, remember?"

Dia carefully replaced the parchment back where she had found it, hesitated, then shifted it to the left a fraction. Satisfied, she sat back in the old, high-backed chair and shook her head. Things were spiralling away from her, events happening far too fast in the capital for her to keep up with. Savinn Kassaar, despite his need for information was, she hated to admit, no longer in a position to influence matters. His self-imposed exile would only hamper his efforts to thwart the chancellor and the Brotherhood and raise unwanted attention and suspicion. Only yesterday, the merchant's family were smuggled from the city, taken far away to someplace safe. For him to have acted in such a way spoke silent volumes to her.

He hadn't said it in his last message, but Dia could tell that Savinn was worried, more worried than he had been when the hardliners had acted swiftly to block his nomination to join the council.

Feeling her exhaustion and the burden she carried for him pressing heavily upon her, Dia sighed and tried to stop her hands from trembling. It was cold in the records office, despite her shawl, the heaving shelves of scrolls, parchments and tomes, lost to the shadows, were mere grim sentinels that gathered about her solemnly and waited to see what she would find.

A rasping breath from the storm outside rattled through the room and the lantern light failed momentarily, plunging the musty stone chambers into nothingness, before spluttering defiantly back to life.

Urgency chased her hands back to the rough lists of names, scrawled upon the sheaves of parchment, next to the huge quill and ink pot. Stacked to her left, forgotten now, were piles of heavy tomes and several empty bottles of ink.

Dia returned her thoughts back to the parchment she had kept aside, the first parchment she had discovered. The rough Reven Lists the chancellor had been working on were not needed now as she knew neater copies were safely in the high duke's possession. But she dared not take anything, lest Relan Valus notice something was amiss.

Reluctant to tarry any longer, she looked at the parchment one last time, scanning the names again, lingering over several of them.

Shaking her head, Dia returned the parchment back on top of the pile of books, then placed the quill back on top of it. Rising stiffly, she dragged the chair back to the position she thought she had found it and picked up the lantern.

As Dia hurried away through the lacklustre swirling light, she was certain she would never return to the room and could not shake the fear and worry from her mind. Three names in particular, jumped out from the list, all of them underlined by an angry hand. Two of them were not even of Reven heritage.

As she stepped back into the entrance hall and fumbled with the lock, Dia felt the sickness in her stomach. Many of the names included on the lists were wealthy families in Karick, those who had some connection to one of Reven heritage, be it by blood, marriage or association. Savinn Kassaar's own name was top of the first parchment, underlined several times to punctuate further the danger her employer was in. She worried for him, she feared for him. But, as she hurried to blow out the lantern and made for the door to escape outside, she found herself worrying for the other names that had garnered her attention.

Lucien Varl's name was there, underlined also, as was Fawn Ardent's. Lady Byron's name was second on the list, scribbled out and then hastily re-written. Other prominent members of the council were also on the list, but, more telling, were the names that were not.

Fighting against her despair, Dia stepped into the

arms of the storm raging outside. As she weakly sent a smile to the sodden sentries, she could not get one name from her mind.

It was Alion Byron's... the lord of Highwater, the high duke's oldest and closest ally. And there was a definite, meaningful line drawn through it.

CHAPTER TWELVE

Awakenings

Cassana stared at the woman, searching her face as she glared accusingly at her. The woman was plain, many would say, though some might find more than just beauty in the eyes that flashed with something deeper than anger. Dark hair framed a pale face, marred by untold horrors and stained by more than just tears. The line of a scar cut across one cheek, still angry, but fading with time and her cheeks, once full of laughter and smiles, looked hollow, drawn tightly together by a mouth that curled in disdain, framed by dry lips that were cracked and wetted by blood.

"I am so sorry," Cassana said, holding her words together. She raised her hands up feebly in apology and the woman countered with her own, her pale face filled with fury.

"Save your pity," she hissed. "I want nothing from you."

Cassana sighed and turned away from the mirror, leaving her guilt behind. Crossing over to her sofa, she collapsed into its embrace and groaned. For a brief moment her mind was clear, free from her thoughts, spared by her turmoil. But then, inevitably, she heard distant whispers, as her thoughts began to return and the shades of the departed began to cry out for justice.

Cassana did not cry. She had not shed a tear for several days now and with the state funeral of her father approaching, she knew she would have to lock away her emotions for a little while longer and hold fast to the strength that her anger gave her.

William Bay had come to see her but an hour before, updating her on how Highwater had reacted to news of her father's murder. As always, his own face was troubled, haunted by the loss of a dear friend, a sword brother, but led primarily by his concern for the well-being of his charge.

Whilst the citizens of Highwater were naturally in shock, mourning for a leader who treated them justly, fairly and honourably, there were angry calls rising from them now, demands for answers, answers to questions that would need to be addressed swiftly.

Cassana's thoughts slipped away from their brief meeting and from the final image of William's worried face as he reluctantly left her chamber. Her father's old friend was lost, devastated by the loss, so why wasn't she?

Reaching inside herself, Cassana knew she was still in shock, her mind unable to deal with the terrible events five nights before. She could still not actually believe it had happened, that those dearest to her had been ripped from the world, stolen away by the cruel edge of an assassin's blade. It still felt like it was all just a terrible dream, played out sickeningly in a mind tormented by the fear of what was to become of her now.

The numbness of her sorrow was hard to come to terms with. It would come, in time, when her heart could cope with the reality of what had happened and the shadows no longer held the threat of dangers that were still so very, very real.

Before she realised it, Cassana had dug the broken, untended nails on her left hand, deep into her palm. She stared blankly at the marks for a time, before the pain caught up with her. Sighing, she shook her hand and looked about her chambers. The morning sun peered through the drapes, trying to entice her out into what promised to be a fine day. It was a tempting invitation, but Cassana had much to think about.

Her mind drifted away, before it could be dragged back to the dilemma of how Highwater could stand against Karick. How she could gather enough allies to support and protect her, whilst she sought the evidence she needed to bring the rising madness to an end.

Unfortunately, her thoughts formed a hazy image of a young girl with bright red hair and freckles that wrinkled impishly around a mischievous smile.

The cold kiss of reality lingered on her bare arms and Cassana hugged herself. She had spent her emotions at the cruel murder of Karlina, even though she somehow wanted to honour her passing with more. Every time her throat and eyes welled with sorrow, however, her anger and shame rose up to steal the moment away.

One thing was not lost on either Cassana or William Bay, the terrible realisation that had Karlina not come home unexpectedly that fateful night, the assassin would have claimed her life, also. There was no doubt that the woman had been heading to Cassana's chambers and had been disturbed by Karlina's return, her opportunity inadvertently thwarted.

The assassin, whoever she worked for, was long gone by now, William had reluctantly admitted to Cassana. Whilst they had deliberated over how she had managed to get into the keep, both of them had begun to wonder at the timing of the chaos in the city below.

"I would warrant, my lady," William had said, his wearied face glowering, "that there is no coincidence in these events."

Cassana had simply played with a tangled lock of her hair, her thoughts and eyes far away. She had managed a faint nod, but added little else to the discussion and the unsaid mention of Highwater's spy.

Sighing, Cassana rose stiffly and headed for her wardrobe. There was much to be done and she still needed to decide upon the words she would say at the funerals.

She slipped from her dress, allowing the fine silk to tumble about her ankles. Before stepping free, Cassana thought of her encounter in the gardens with Edren. She knew her reaction had shocked him and she felt her shame rise at the thought that she had taken her anger out upon him. He had not spoken to her for days now and on the one occasion she had seen him, Edren had turned from her path and made haste in his retreat.

Chewing her top lip, Cassana reached for her leathers. She had need of her bow and the calm distraction it offered her. She did not, however, regret what she had said to her childhood friend. There would be no reconciliation with Karick until they separated reason from madness. And until that day came or her enemies called at her door, each arrow she loosed, each shaft she buried in the target, was a barb of revenge in the conjured, imagined heart of a blonde-haired woman with a scar on her face.

Fawn Ardent stirred sleepily from her thoughts, ruffled to the present by the soothing easterly wind that rampaged briefly over the ramparts and stole across the farmsteads to the west.

With a deep sigh, she tucked a wild strand of her hair behind an ear and gripped the palisade tightly, staring south along the empty road. With the storms gone now, dragged away by impatient clouds, the land was finally recovering and the road, once a quagmire, was now dry and kind to the merchant Lestarn Corbus' wagons, as he made reluctantly for the capital.

Not wishing to think about what she had also asked of him, Fawn turned her attentions away to the fields, still heaving with crops that yearned for sickle and scythe.

Fawn shook her head.

Was it any wonder?

The events of the attack on Havensdale had left the townsfolk devastated, a lasting damage worse than any storm could have inflicted upon them. With all of the funerals recently, the people's strength was gone, lost to the blades of their Carwellian attackers, drained by their sorrow and the bleak prospects for the future.

Fawn bit her lip angrily, enjoying the brief pain before she calmed herself. Leaning heavily against the lantern post, she grasped vainly at one of the thoughts jostling for attention in her weary mind and tried to hold on to her waning strength.

The meeting following the attack, held in the crowded Arms of the Lady Inn, had been a heated one. Dekan Ardent had struggled for a time to bring order to the proceedings and it wasn't until the stonemason and local trouble maker Culwin Oakwood had been dismissed from the meeting that calm and reason were allowed to return.

Understandably, many of the townsfolk wanted justice for the attack on Havensdale, for Carwell and, more importantly, for Renald Gardan to be brought before the courts in Karick and punished for his unwarranted actions.

As the debate unfolded, many people voiced their unhappiness at the continuing presence of the Carwellian forces that had been allowed into the town and, to stop a lynch mob forming, Dekan Ardent had revealed that the young captain and his patrol would be leaving the following morning.

Surprised at this turn of events and not privy to this information, Fawn had dealt her father a questioning look.

"Now that I am fit enough to ride, I will head to Highwater in the morning, to report what has happened to us to Lord Byron," Dekan Ardent had announced, forcing a wry smile as he continued. "Captain Leigh has invaluable information that will only strengthen our case and he and his patrol will escort me safely north."

The rumble of discontent and scepticism that swept through the inn was mirrored on Fawn's face. With a grimace, her father had leant close.

"It is the only way to keep them calm, I fear," he had whispered quietly. "I trust the captain, as I sense you do also, daughter. He will not betray us, I am certain of it."

Fawn blinked and forced a bitter smile. After the meeting, as everyone drifted silently away, she had argued at length with her father, demanding that she journey north with him.

If she was honest with herself, she was keen to leave Havensdale and take away the excuse that Carwell needed to return and burn the town to the ground. If she wasn't there then they could have no *justifiable* quarrel with the town. *Could they*?

The woodsman, silent throughout the town meeting, had spoken then and she had glared at him, as his words ended the debate.

"If Carwell wishes it so, my lady, Havensdale will burn now, with or without you here," he had said, his dark eyes flashing with regret.

Dekan Ardent had winced, adding also, "and I think it unwise, for now, that you and Lady Byron reunite, Fawn. There is more than just coincidence in this attack and I fear, as I have already said, that you have marked yourself a target because of the help you gave to Cassana."

"It would be better if you stayed away from her for

the time being," the woodsman had suggested meaningfully.

Focusing her bitter thoughts elsewhere, Fawn watched as Rellin Steelblade trudged along the wall underneath her, a brace of conies slung over one shoulder. His face was troubled and it looked as if he carried a heavier burden. As he reached the gates to the town, he banged heavily upon them.

Fawn peered over the wall and watched as the young hunter waited for Jerrin Wicksford to open the gates for him. She heard the weary, muffled greeting from within as the gate was hauled open and noted the brief hesitation, as the youth reluctantly tarried.

Looking away, Fawn couldn't blame him. He and his two friends had found Colbin's body as they returned to help defend the town. The shock of what had occurred the night before and their reluctant return, ignoring the woodsman's wishes, had plunged them deeper into their despair.

Fawn blinked her tears away as she thought of Colbin and those who had died. She still couldn't believe what had happened, could still not forgive herself for not handing herself over. Even now Perrin Hawksblade lingered on death's door and Durnast Brogan, badly pierced by arrows, threatened to accompany him on his journey.

And as for Robert Campbell...

Fawn began to taste the tears that ran down her face and grimaced as the cut on her cheek smarted. Closing her eyes, she fought against her guilt and the chasm that was opening up before her.

If she wasn't careful, she knew she would fall into that gaping pit of despair and if she allowed that to happen, she would be of no use to anyone. The people, despite their lingering doubts about her, needed her to be there for them now. The people of Havensdale, in her father's absence, needed a strong leader to guide them, not a weak one, plagued by doubts and shackled by her own selfish guilt.

She suddenly thought of the Seer and of how, since his arrival, things had started to turn sour for Havensdale.

'There is a storm coming,' he had warned her. Fawn gritted her teeth angrily.

He had meant Gardan and his men, she knew that now. But what would follow in their wake?

"Everything alright with you, lad?" the woodsman asked the young hunter, as he made his way past the militia headquarters.

Rellin jumped back, clutching at his chest with his free hand. As he fought to calm his fright, the woodsman nudged himself away from the side of the building, walking from the shade to intercept the young man.

Rellin managed to nod as the woodsman gripped his shoulder and searched his eyes for tell of his thoughts.

"How are you coping?" the woodsman enquired, letting his hand fall away.

The youth looked to his dusty boots and shrugged. "I-I am not sure how I should be feeling right now," he admitted, mumbling somewhat.

The woodsman sighed and looked up to the ramparts, noting Fawn Ardent's interest in their exchange.

"Well, that is to be expected," the woodsman said softly, looking away. "You have witnessed the worst side of man these last few days and it is never an easy thing."

Rellin glanced up from his boots and his eyes flicked about the woodsman's features.

"I still cannot believe what has happened," he began falteringly. "How Colbin was murdered, why we were attacked and..."

"And?" the woodsman prompted. He knew full well what would follow if he allowed it to and was keen to stop the youth falling back into the arms of his fear.

He bent low as Rellin looked down again, searching for his face and chasing his head back up to meet his gaze.

"I cannot stop thinking about that man in the forest," the youth blurted out hastily, "he was going to kill Arrun – I had to do something."

The image of the Carwellian tracker, bearing down upon his friend, flashed in his mind. Arrun was stood ready to meet him, the night gathered in close like their enemies, his swords raised, but his fear draining his arms of the strength he would need to fight. Rellin saw himself, as clearly as if he was there again. Reaching for a shaft, he draw back on his bow...

Trembling, Rellin turned away from the memory and of what had followed. He drew in a breath, knowing full well he would recount the fight in the forest again, later that night in his dreams.

The woodsman was watching him quietly, his arms folded across his chest now and his stern face softened by understanding.

"How do you come to terms with killing another person?" Rellin asked, his throat thick with shame.

The woodsman shook his head sadly. "You cannot, Rellin," he said quietly, his eyes staring far away. "There can be no reconciliation for taking the life of another, only the slow easing of guilt over time."

Rellin felt a chill sweep through his body and he shuddered. "But how could those men attack us? How could someone kill Colbin like that?"

The woodsman moved close again and placed a hand on Rellin's shoulder to comfort him.

"The fact you have to ask that question means that you are not like them, Rellin," the woodsman offered. "Be thankful for that. To those who have to live with such a thing, killing to stay alive is a necessary burden to carry. It will stay with you always and it will remind you of who you *truly* are. If you ever find yourself forgetting the face of the man you killed, then you must walk away from your path, Rellin. Hang up your sword and shoulder your bow."

The young recruit sniffed back his sorrow and blinked his glistening eyes free from their turmoil. Drawing in a deep, steadying breath, he nodded his thanks and made to leave.

"Never be ashamed that you saved your friend's life," the woodsman stated, as the youth hurried away. It was better that he lived with the guilt of killing a man, than with the shame of letting his friend die.

Evan blew out his cheeks and looked up at Fawn Ardent. She was still watching him, the same curious look on her face that Cassana Byron had worn, all those days before. She would want that talk with him soon, he knew that. He had managed to avoid her, thus far, but with her father away now, he knew he would not be able to avoid her for much longer.

Nodding slightly to her, the woodsman turned away and headed for the Arms of the Lady. He knew he shouldn't, that it was better to head out into the forest for a time and be alone with his thoughts once again. But, to his disgust, he had to admit that he was thankful for the company and was reluctantly getting used to being around people again.

As he strode across the market, he heard the sound of a child's laughter. By the well, a mother fetched water from the depths below, her daughter playing with a white kitten on the cobbles, by her feet.

The sound of the child's laughter was eerie, yet welcoming, as it merrily filtered across the respectful silence of the day. Smiling in greeting, the woodsman raised a hand to the mother, as she turned and sent a lovely smile in his direction.

At the exchange, the child, her russet pigtails bobbing

about her head, looked round and regarded him with quizzical eyes of the brightest blue.

The woodsman stopped, his chest tightening with fear and the colour draining from his face. With a monumental effort, he wrapped his cloak tightly about his frame to ward away a chill in the air that wasn't even there. Without a word, he hurried on his way, his heart pounding fearfully as it chased him across the square.

The woodsman had seen that girl before and would never forget those eyes. How could he?

He still had her doll in his knapsack.

CHAPTER THIRTEEN

Unlucky For Some

Relan Valus forced a smile as William welcomed him home. Shutting the wild storm outside and taking his sodden cloak from him, the butler fussed about his master, helping him dry off with the warm cloth he had waiting for him.

Relan accepted the amiable conversation, his mind drifting away as another roar of thunder shook the city. The man, faithful and loyal for many seasons now, enquired on his day and his master's needs for the evening.

"Would you like me to bring your supper to your study, sir, or shall I have your guest join you in the dining hall?" William enquired, turning politely away to shake the rain water from his cloak.

The chancellor frowned. "My guest?"

William turned back, the cloak forgotten in his hands. "Yes, chancellor, the lady arrived earlier this evening. She said that you were expecting her and would wait in your study for you. She was very adamant and seemed to know the way..."

Relan felt his pulse quicken, heard his temple throb. He forced a smile and it chased William's concern away.

"Fetch my supper in an hour, William," he said, passing back the cloth as he hurried away. "Until then, I am not to be disturbed."

"Yes, sir," William acknowledged. He suppressed a shudder. It wasn't his place to say, but the woman unsettled him and he would be perfectly happy if she was long gone by the time he brought his master his supper.

"Ah, Chancellor Valus," the Kestrel purred, as her thin, pale host hurried into the study and locked the door behind him.

She could see the anger flashing in his eyes, long before it reached his lips and with a sigh, she vacated his seat and meekly crossed round the table to sit in the chair opposite.

The chancellor hurried to his comfortable leather-backed chair, but did not sit in it. With shaking hands supporting him on the desk, he leant forward, his face twisting with rage in the candlelight.

"You grow too bold, Kestrel," he hissed, spittle flying from his lips. "You cannot walk so freely about the city. You should not risk showing your face so openly."

"And what's wrong with my face?" the Kestrel asked with a shrug. Smiling, she leant back on the chair and placed her booted feet on his desk.

She was wearing her short skirt again, showing far more leg than she wanted to, but she knew it would distract him long enough to calm him down.

The chancellor's eyes flicked reluctantly to the promise higher up in the shadows of her thighs and he lost his next words in a swallow.

"You look tired, Relan," she observed and, for once, there was no malice lacing her words, no rough edge to her tongue. The last time they had met, in the chancellor's offices, the man had looked almost dead on his feet. *But now?* Well, she wasn't quite sure if he was actually alive. His face was skeletal. His eyes, still bright with ambition, flashed from sunken sockets and his cheeks were barely skin, hollowed like dark caves in his face.

With a sigh and subdued by her beauty and concern, Relan Valus slumped into his warm chair. He reached for the decanter to his left, glowing with the amber promise of the *Burning Leaf* inside.

With a shaking hand that clattered decanter and glass, he poured himself a drink, reaching across to refill his guest's, too.

"I hope you bring us news to gladden a weary heart," the chancellor said softly, flicking his eyes to her.

The Kestrel reached for the glass and took a long, deep mouthful of the brandy. Running a tongue over her lips, she shaped them into a faint smile.

"Alion Byron is dead," she whispered, but the relish in her words did not fill her face.

Relan Valus bowed his head, shook it from side to side slightly and then drained the brandy from his glass in one go. Allowing the fire to burn his throat a while, he eventually poured himself another full glass and sat back with a moan.

The chancellor held the Kestrel's glittering eyes for a time, then nodded.

"The Brotherhood thanks you, Kestrel," he said quietly. "You have struck a deep blow for our cause and it shall not be forgotten."

"As will my payment not be!" the Kestrel pointed out bluntly.

Relan Valus remembered his anger. "You shall have your just reward, Kestrel. Have no fear of that, assassin. I forget that it is the coin that ties you to us, not your loyalty to the cause."

"Do not mistake my thirst for coin as being stronger

than my desire for power, Valus," the Kestrel hissed dangerously. "The Brotherhood finally rises from the shadows, where it has hidden for many years. I will lead them into the light, but I shall have my share of the spoils when the Reven Lands are divided amongst us."

Relan Valus raised his glass. "Indeed you shall, Kestrel. Indeed you shall." He licked his lips in anticipation. "What news of the Byron girl? Please tell me that she no longer draws blood from our side."

The Kestrel's eyes fell and she sipped at her brandy for a time. When she looked up again, there was something in her eyes that the chancellor could not read.

"She lives," the Kestrel said, her features twisting with regret. "I was disturbed on my way to her chambers and had to change my plans."

Relan Valus frowned, noting the faint edge to her voice and seeing the bloodied bandage on her hand for the first time. He leant forward again, his glass clasped tightly in both hands before him.

"What happened to your hand, Kestrel?" he asked, trying not to show his delight in her injury.

She was fallible, after all.

The Kestrel looked at her bandaged hand for a time, her eyes distant and guarded.

"As I said already," she snapped, after a time. "I was disturbed... nothing to concern yourself with."

"What is it?" the chancellor demanded, sensing there was something she wasn't telling him. He was starting to worry, as she was normally a lot more composed than this.

The Kestrel sighed and she reached beneath the desk with her injured hand. She retrieved it moments later and tossed a knife on to the table between them.

Relan Valus looked at the glistening, crescent-shaped blade and then looked up at the assassin, fear evident in his eyes, worry staining his face.

"Where did you get that?" he hissed, his eyes flicking from her to the blade and back again.

The Kestrel swallowed hard. "It was in Highwater, in the hands of a girl."

Relan Valus frowned. "A girl?" he shook his head free from its confusion. "What was it...?"

"It does not matter who had it," the Kestrel growled hastily. "What we should be concerned with is how she came by it and why it has suddenly appeared after all these years."

They shared a knowing look, trading their worry and rising fear over their drinks for a long time. After a while, Relan put his empty glass down and did not attempt to steady his hand.

"I thought you said he was dead?"

The Kestrel licked the fear from her lips. "He probably is... I should know. But we should not overlook the coincidence of this, Relan. Lady Byron somehow manages to get home, our hunting party slain to the last, we..."

The Kestrel trailed off, staring into the flames of the candle, dancing on the corner of the desk. As her mind reeled, she saw the bodies in the mountains again, remembered the first one she had found hidden in the thicket, a single, definite cut to the throat. The skin rippled on her bare arms as she angrily rubbed her concern from them. *It couldn't be*! It just wasn't possible.

Without realising it, she traced the cut on her face with a thoughtful finger and glanced at the blade again.

"If it is him," she said finally, "then we need to watch our backs from now on and get on with things. Humour me, chancellor, where are we with it all?"

Scowling at her, the chancellor tried to dismiss his worry and focussed on the events of the day. He was drained by his meeting with the high duke, as each discussion they held was becoming more difficult as the high duke's need to quell his cravings increased. Banishing the thought of the furious storm he had weathered in the high duke's chambers, he held on to the threads of hope that had arisen from it.

Relan smiled. "The merchants' guild is now ours," he began, trying to rein in his joy. "With the promise of the spoils to come, I have managed to bring them onside and, more importantly, I have managed to coerce that fool Loren Kalis into hanging Savinn Kassaar for us."

The Kestrel blinked and could not help but admire the chancellor's cunning. Kalis was head of the Guild of Independent Merchants and an old fool. A fool who had lost the majority of his fortunes on a single, reckless bet, some summers ago. He had wagered all his coin on his belief and love for his son, believing that the boy would win the sword tourney. A competent, but not fine swordsman, he had inevitably lost, taking his father's fortune with him. Ever since that day, Loren Kalis had convinced himself that the games had been fixed somehow, rallying his guild members about him to try and force a postponement to the games.

"How in the storms will he do that?" the Kestrel asked eagerly. Savinn Kassaar had been allowed to attain far too much power and wealth and the numerous attempts by his enemies to kill him had all failed over the years.

Relan Valus' face spread wide from glee and he grinned, almost maniacally.

"Thanks to me, Kalis has found evidence that Savinn Kassaar was behind irregular betting in the games. He has uncovered written proof and gathered testimonies from money-lenders, who will support his claims, to the high duke."

The Kestrel smiled, trying to calm herself. "Kassaar will not take this lying down." She pointed out. "It would be better for us all if you just let me slit the bastard's throat."

The chancellor held up his hand and stayed her anger. "Leave Kassaar be, Kestrel. He is going to prove very useful to us, the perfect torch to set fire to the streets of the capital."

Sensing the chancellor was beginning to enjoy his web-spinning, the Kestrel glared at him meaningfully.

"Spare me your subterfuge, Valus," she hissed. "Get to the point."

Smiling sweetly, Relan Valus spread his hands wide on his desk. "Very well, I am sure your limited mind will be able to cope with this... so humour me a while longer, would you?"

His guest dealt him a murderous look that suggested he had better get on with it.

Relan licked his lips hastily, before continuing. "Only today, an anonymous source revealed that the Reven were behind the attempt to abduct, or kill Lady Byron on her journey to the capital. The high duke is naturally distraught, as any faint, misguided hope he had left that peace with the Reven was still an option, is now in ruins."

He paused long enough to cleanse the disgust from his throat. "It is bad enough that Reven are attacking all across the Vales, it is even worse now that all on the council know that he and Alion Byron kept that information from them. It will be worse still for the high duke in the coming days when news of Alion Byron's death reaches the capital and evidence of Savinn Kassaar's criminal involvement in the fixing of the games, of the vast amounts of money he made at the expense of others, is made known."

"Kassaar will contest this evidence," the Kestrel pointed out, keen to rein in his excitement. "He will use all of his influence and power to refute these accusations."

Even as she spoke, the Kestrel knew the chancellor had another card to play.

"He would," Relan Valus smiled, "if he hadn't gone into hiding to avoid being dragged to the city's dungeons for *questioning*."

The Kestrel drained her brandy and coughed to cover her rising arousal at the prospect. "And when he surfaces to fight these claims, we shall have him."

Relan Valus nodded. "In time, yes. But before we can coax him out of his hole, we shall spread the word of his treachery through the streets, stoke up the fires of hatred beginning to burn for those of Reven heritage. We shall sow the seeds of his involvement in the attacks, whisper the warnings that a Reven, albeit a bastard, should never have been allowed free rein to claim such power. The mob will rise, I am certain of it – especially since only yesterday a *witness* came forth having seen a Reven running away from yet another murder in the Lower Quarters of the city. In the end, I firmly believe that Savinn Kassaar will be forced to come to us."

The Kestrel dropped her feet to the carpeted floor and drank in the glory of the silence that followed. The promise of such an outcome was too much for her. Her hand had long been stayed by the Brotherhood, prevented many times from killing him. In fact, at the start of his rise, the Brotherhood had actively encouraged the high duke to support the Reven merchant, slowly building his stakes in companies that would not have normally traded with him. How far reaching were their ambitions? How long had these plans actually been in place?

The Kestrel, for once, did not even try to disguise her admiration for the man and his scheming.

"Amazing," she whispered incredulously. "What you have achieved for our lord is truly incredible, Relan! I am glad that prior attempts on the merchant's life have been unsuccessful, giving the Brotherhood time to realise his worth in all of this."

Chancellor Valus nodded his head sagely. "I agree,

Kestrel. It is a good job we did not react in haste, as without him, I fear we would still be far from realising our ambitions."

The Kestrel did not really hear him, as she was lost to the promise of the glorious future ahead. Aroused by the thought of those who would need to die before the end, she allowed herself to relax, her mind to wander.

She snorted suddenly with a thought. "It's ironic, really, isn't it? The one man who could still bring us down is the one that saved Savinn, all those years ago?"

Relan Valus blinked. "What did you just say?"

"I said," the Kestrel growled, her eyes flashing impatiently, "that it's ironic the stonemason saved Kassaar. If he hadn't, then where would we be?"

Relan Valus' eyes widened and he clicked his fingers thoughtfully at the woman sat across from him.

"Where would we be, indeed, Kestrel," he said, a wicked grin spreading across his face.

CHAPTER FOURTEEN

With Friends Like This...

He was watching her again.

Tania could feel Cullen's eyes on her, as she swung from her saddle and dropped to the dusty ground, which would soon be washed from the hillside by the angry storm clouds that chased after her.

The last few days travel had been hard for her and she shivered, as she fed her mount some grain and allowed her mind to escape its concerns for a time. As the stallion gently accepted the food from her shaking hand, Tania heard Cullen's heavy approach, heard his rasping breath as his long shadow stretched on the ground before her.

"Going to get supplies, girl," he leered in her ear, his breath stinking. He brushed by her and made for the small hamlet she had not expected to see again so soon.

She did not look at Cullen as he began talking to one of the villagers, near to the tree stump with the wishing-coins hammered into the ancient wood.

Before they left the hamlet, Tania promised herself, she would offer another coin to the wishing wood and make one of her own.

A gentle hand on her shoulder startled both her and the horse. Jumping, Tania clutched at her breast and glared at Riyan as he stepped away, raising one hand in apology. She had quickly learnt that the mute was as silent in his comings and goings as he was with his words.

Riyan must have detected the look of disgust on her unusually pale features, as he looked briefly towards Cullen then returned his attention, offering her a sympathetic look. Tania followed his gaze, shuddering as she was once again reluctantly forced to look at the focus of her discomfort.

Cullen had made his intentions clear from the outset, once he was away from his master and the choking confines of the city. At every opportunity, he watched her, said as much with his good eye, as he did the tongue that often wetted the appetite on his sun-blistered lips. During their journey he would offer suggestive comments whenever he could, and he was near to her, far too near to her, as often as physically possible.

On their second night out under the stars, when the fiercely hot day had cooled to a bitterly contrasting night, Cullen had suggested that she cuddle up under his blanker, as he could *clearly* see that she was cold. The fire had gleamed in his eye as it ranged hungrily over her breasts and with her anger, her fear and revulsion all flashing in her eyes, Tania had wrapped her blanker tightly about her body to cover herself up from his disgusting attentions.

Riyan cleared his throat and Tania switched her attention back, stroking her mount's strong neck and brushing wild strands of her hair from her eyes.

Riyan pointed southwards across the moors, the horizon lost to the haze of a bright sun. He looked back at her questioningly.

"If we are lucky, we should reach the monastery by sundown," she offered, the relief evident on her lovely face.

Riyan nodded, smiling his encouragement. He accepted her words with a slight nod and wandered quietly away to join Cullen, as the fat creature haggled aggressively over the price of the mead he would need for the remainder of their journey.

Tania sighed, shaking her head. She couldn't wait to reach the Hermitage Retreat, was desperate to see her friends again and be finally rid of the man who had been preying on her for several days now. The thought of spending another night in his company made her feel sick and she was only thankful that after this evening, the Lady willing, she would be back in Khadazin's company and could be rid of the disgusting man, once and for all. Cullen was becoming bolder with his advances, the closer they came to their destination and should things get out of hand, she doubted either she, or Riyan, would be able to control him.

Tania shuddered, clenched her fists and scowled. If things did get out of hand, which she feared they might, she would put an arrow in his good eye and leave him for the crows.

The forest was alive with excitement as the young man stumbled along the trail. With his breath ragged in his throat and his surroundings spinning wildly about him, the fugitive hurried on his way, his battered face pale, his clothes torn and his nerves shredded.

A gathering of birds screeched their protests from the high branches overhead as he picked his way through the tangled thicket and found the trunk of a suitable tree to rest against. He had spent the night out in the forest, fleeing from imagined pursuers and he knew with certainty that he would run out of breath long before he ran out of trees to hide in. Groaning, the young man collapsed against the ancient wood and slid down the rough bark into the arms of his exhaustion.

After a time, he was asleep and the crows overhead became bored, returning to their debate with low squawks as they bickered about the day's news. Foraging insects appeared as the sunlight rallied and pierced the shadows again, searching the wildflower and garlic with renewed vigour. A solitary butterfly, its wings as bright as the sun, danced near to the dishevelled form and then fluttered lazily away to inspect the last of the summer's foxglove.

As the forest slowly returned to a natural calm, a shadow detached itself from the protection of a large, grizzled oak and padded silently over to the sleeping form. As it neared, the shadow bent the bow it carried meaningfully in the intruder's direction, the drawn arrow glinting dangerously.

Reaching the sleeping youth, the shadow kicked him roughly awake and stepped back two paces.

Gasping in fright, the youth started and scrambled back into the trunk's arms, his face and eyes wild with fear and panic.

"Don't kill me," the young man screamed, irritating the crows overhead. He raised his filthy hands pleadingly.

"Don't kill you?" the shadow chuckled. "Judging by your look, I'd say I would be doing you a favour!"

Balan stared up at the giant shadow, the sun at his back blinding his vision. Shielding his eyes with a trembling hand, the young man waited until he could pick out the face between his fingers.

The man was tall, his face strong and fierce to match his frame. A dark beard covered his jaw and his long hair was held back by a leather headband. Serious dark eyes regarded the young man with a mixture of irritation and pity.

"Who are you?" the giant demanded, his rising impatience chasing after his gruff words. He returned the notched arrow to the quiver at his side and slung the large bow over one shoulder. "What are you doing in *our* forest?"

Balan's mind raced and he began stammering, his words incoherent as he spluttered through a pathetic explanation that made no sense even to his own ears.

"I have no idea what you are talking about, boy," the giant growled. He looked the youth over, noting the dried blood that stained his clothing, hearing the tremor of fear and madness in his voice.

Sighing, the giant looked about and muttered something under his breath. After a time, he returned his scrutiny back to the youth.

"I've lost my bet now, anyhow," he snarled. "Won't be able to hunt anything out here with the noise you made crashing through the trees."

Balan sniffed, relaxing slightly. He looked up at the man, stared at the huge hand he offered him.

"Come with me lad," the man said, waiting for him to grasp his offer. When he did, Balan was yanked roughly to his feet and just about managed to keep his arm in its socket.

"W-where are you taking me?" Balan stammered, looking back the way he had just come from.

"To the boss," Trell said, dragging him off. "He'll have to decide what to do with you now."

Kerrin Thorn rose stiffly from the stump of wood near to the campfire as Trell sauntered into camp, a young man trailing forlornly behind him.

Flexing the dull ache from his injured shoulder, the tracker moved over to the scrawny donkey on the fringes of the clearing and absently scratched at his pricking ears.

"Looks like another stray to look after," Kerrin chuckled softly. The donkey regarded him for a moment, before returning his attention to the long grass and flowers that were to be his lunch.

Kerrin slapped the donkey fondly on his broad back and smiled. Since Elion Leigh and his comrades had reluctantly left him behind, the old tracker had made a slow recovery from his injuries. During this time, he had formed a strange bond with the donkey that Devlin Hawke was fattening up for winter. Both he and the scrawny animal were outsiders, one viewed as an enemy, the other a supper, or three.

It was a strange companionship, but the two must have sensed their place in the outlaw camp and both drew strength from the other's affections and company.

Kerrin watched as Trell ordered the lad to warm his bones by the fire and headed off to chat quietly with Col, the only other outlaw present today. The big man nodded to his '*guest*' as he strode by and Kerrin returned the greeting with a smile.

After he was able enough, Kerrin had set about proving his worth. If, for some reason, Elion Leigh was so busy he forgot about him, the old tracker wanted to make sure that Devlin Hawke had good reason to turn him loose, or find use for him.

He had not seen the outlaw leader much, several times at best, but each time, Kerrin found himself drawn to the wit and charm of the most wanted man in the Four Vales. Devlin was a man who viewed the world around him as he found it and, judging by the way the outlaws had been treating their guest thus far, Kerrin was not about to do anything to change that. As soon as he was able, Kerrin began to show his worth to his hosts and after a week, the men of the forest viewed him with open respect and warmth. His skills as a tracker were '*Uncanny*' as Devlin Hawke put it ruefully, and, with his unnamed friend, the donkey in mind, Kerrin had set about helping the men of Greywood put more food on their plates and in their stores for the coming autumn and winter.

During this time, as their smiles towards him broadened and his nerves began to ease, Kerrin found himself torn between the feelings he was having for his newfound friends and the stain upon his lifelong service and undying loyalty to his lord, Henry Carwell. The ruthless lord of the East Vales wanted nothing more than to see Devlin Hawke swing from a gibbet. If Kerrin was ever allowed to return home and his betrayal, his failure to bring the notorious outlaw to chains, made known, the old tracker expected he would join Devlin Hawke on the end of a tight noose.

As he struggled with the shame of his conflicting emotions, a thought struck the man from Carwell, as he made his way over to the newcomer.

If Devlin Hawke did not allow him to leave, the old bachelor would not be sorry to stay...

"So, what brings you to the forest?" Kerrin asked the youth, as he grunted and sat on the ground beside him.

The young man stared into the flames of the fire, his hands holding his head, his knees drawn up under his chin. He did not respond to the question, simply shaking his head and muttering to himself.

"Are you alright lad?" Kerrin asked softly again, drawing the youth from his reverie with a start and rapid blink.

The young man looked round at him and Kerrin could see the haunted look in his wide eyes, the look of one who had witnessed something terrible, been party to something unmentionable.

The youth shook his head, but could muster little else and hid his bruised and battered face back in the shelter of his hands.

Kerrin reached out and patted the newcomer's shoulder reassuringly. He flicked his eyes to Trell and Col, who were regarding them surreptitiously. With a final hiss, Col snatched up his bow and loped reluctantly away through the trees to the south. Trell looked back over towards them, his eyes relaying his irritation.

"Just rest a while and get yourself warm, lad," Kerrin whispered. "I'll fix you some porridge in a while – but first, what's your name?"

"M-my name's Balan," the young man said quietly from within his hands, his shoulders heaving as a sob strangled his response.

"Kerrin," the tracker replied, offering his hand in greeting. "Well met."

Slowly, the reclusive youth returned to the world. With a shaking hand, Balan grasped him weakly and the tracker could not help but notice the dried blood under his filthy nails.

"What will happen to me?" Balan dared to ask, tears beginning to streak down his swollen cheeks. He looked down at his empty hands, still shaking and heavy from guilt. Moaning, he hid his face in them to hide away from his own shame.

"That depends on you, lad," Kerrin muttered, as Trell began making his way over to them. He leaned close. "But no matter what happens next, you must tell them the truth..."

By the time Devlin Hawke stalked in to the small camp, the young fugitive was warm from Kerrin's porridge and huddled over the fire, blazing away under a failing summer sky.

Sweeping his gaze about the camp, Devlin pulled the hood from his head, but left his scarf in place as he strode forward purposefully.

Col slipped into camp behind the outlaw leader and headed for a seat, across the fire from the youth. From the thickening shadows in the entrance to his tent, Kerrin looked on nervously, seeing Balan tense as Devlin Hawke stood over him. He flicked a questioning look towards

Trell, who was keeping watch on the cusp of the clearing and the big man shrugged in response.

"So," Devlin Hawke said, drawing everyone's attention to him. He let his word hang in the air for a time, his eyes bright like sapphires as they regarded the dishevelled youth, struggling to rise before him. "Who have we here now, I wonder?"

The outlaw leader stroked the beard hidden away under his scarf thoughtfully. The youth did not hear it, terrified as he was, but Kerrin could detect the trace of amusement in his voice.

"Well, boy?" Devlin's mood began to turn as the newcomer stared blankly at him. "I am a busy man and a rapidly growing impatient one with all the comings and goings in my forest of late. Speak now, lad, or I'll drag you to the trees and leave you for the foxes."

Balan cowered away and raised his hands pleadingly. "P-please, sir, I beg of you, don't hurt me. I seek only the sanctuary of the forest and your protection."

"Do you now?" Devlin Hawke's eyes widened and he placed his gloved hands on his hips. "And, pray tell, why should I, the lord of this forest, grant you such a boon?"

The young man began to cry and he raised his shaking hands towards the outlaw leader. "B-because I have k-killed and will hang for my crimes..."

Devlin Hawke frowned, looking for Trell. The big man looked on in amazement and from his seat at the fire, Col drew a long knife and planted it in the ground between his own feet.

After a long period of contemplation, Devlin sighed and pulled his scarf down. His face, usually jovial and engaging, was now cold and serious. He motioned for the youth to sit and joined him by the fire with a weary grunt.

"Tell me your name and tale, lad," Devlin ordered him softly. "Then we shall see what is to be done with you."

Balan Ford struggled through his tale and a tankard of cider, when he became lost in his fear and beset by his grief. He set about, as best as his scattered mind could, recounting all he could recall. Lost to the flames, he did not see the look that crossed Devlin Hawke's face as he told of the hunting party he had joined at his father's behest, did not see the outlaw leader baulk and drain a tankard himself, as he stumbled through his account of the bloody events in the mountains and of the, still to this day, astonishing duel he had witnessed.

Despite his questions, of which there were many, Devlin Hawke let the lad have his time at the fire. He knew that if he interrupted him, the boy would falter and valuable information might be lost in his ravaged mind. Despite his own fear, thrumming away in his stomach, pounding hard at his temples, Devlin reined in his impatience as best he could.

With his voice barely beyond a whisper, Balan Ford recounted how he had killed his own father, how, when he needed her support the most, his own mother had screamed at him – tearing at his face with her nails, as she cried murder and called furiously for aid to arrest him. Sobbing openly now, the young man told of how he had fled his home of Colden, with angry shouts and his own shame chasing after him into the forest.

At this, the young man retched, his guilt too much as he fell onto his knees and brought up his disgust. In the heavy silence that followed, the outlaws watched on sympathetically, but did nothing to help.

It was late by the time the youth had finally gathered his wits to finish his tale and from underneath eyebrows stiffened by shock, Devlin Hawke whistled lowly, shaking his head.

After a time, when all at the fire had gathered their composure, the outlaw leader placed a calming hand on the heaving shoulders of the grief-stricken young man.

"I am sorry, Balan," Devlin said. "Such horrors have drawn many of us to the forest, binding us to one another under Greywood's protection. You have suffered greatly, I can tell that and I am truly sorry for the burden you carry. I would give you that protection you seek, but first, I would have answers that only you can offer. Speak plainly and truthfully to me now and I will offer you my hand."

Balan blinked away his tears and sniffed. He drew in a faltering breath and nodded. "What would you have of me, sir?"

Devlin sent a guarded look about the campfire which fell, eventually, on Kerrin, who had long since joined them. He stared at the man from Carwell for a time, before looking back at the lad.

"You mentioned a man in your tale, Balan, a man called Tobin," Devlin began, licking his top lip nervously. "You said he fought to the death with a swordsman, the one who had spared you your life?"

Balan nodded. "I did!"

"You also said he seemed to recognise this swordsman. Did he mention a name, anything of note that could shed light on this mystery?"

The fugitive's eyes became distant as he stared into the snapping flames of the fire. After a time, he blinked free of the past and searched the flickering shadows for the outlaw leader's attentive eyes.

"Tobin mentioned his name," Balan said finally. "He called him Arillion and they spoke about an unnamed woman they both knew."

Devlin's eyes widened and he traded shocked looks with his men. Kerrin looked from one horrified expression to the next, finally allowing his curiosity to fall back on Devlin Hawke. The tracker could see something in his flashing eyes, but could not discern what it meant.

Shaking his head, Devlin scowled and drummed the fingers of his left hand across his knee.

"So his luck finally ran out," the outlaw muttered, almost sadly. He fell quiet for a very long time and when he spoke again his face was pinched by the worry spreading across his features.

"Arillion was known to me... I had dealings with him many times and would have had more, had he not betrayed me and then, later still, turned his back on me."

Scowling, he ignored the look everyone gave him and continued. "I had already surmised that he had decided to take the girl to Highwater, not to me for ransom, as we had arranged. At first, I thought he sought to claim the reward for her safe return for himself – but now I wonder whether he knew he was being pursued and sought to spare us the trouble it would bring."

Trell spat his disagreement on the fire. "That bastard cared not for us, Devlin. He was after the money, plain and simple."

Devlin shrugged, but his face twisted in regret as he ran a hand through his unkempt hair. "Well, no matter now. The news you have brought me, Balan, offers up more important questions. Why, for example, would someone go through so much trouble to capture the girl? You said yourself there was a larger reward for her being taken alive, so who ordered this and why?"

Balan's weary face looked confused. He went to speak but the outlaw leader whipped up a silencing finger.

"I also know of this Tobin, I knew of him many years ago. But, again, his involvement in all of this asks more questions than it answers..."

Devlin Hawke rose from the fire and wandered away, shaking his head. On the fringes of the camp, he stood in the shadows quietly, his arms folded across his chest in deliberation.

Kerrin looked at Balan, watching the exhausted young

man as his eyes lingered on the outlaw leader. The lad was traumatised by everything that had happened to him and who could blame him? Recalling all he had, though, told the old tracker that there was great strength lurking there, too. As he waited for the outlaw leader to return, Kerrin felt a chill steal up his arms to settle on his shoulders and neck. His mind drifting, he began to think about the attack on Eastbury again. Of what had become of Elion's prisoner, the man they knew only as Raven and, more importantly, what had become of his captain and friends.

Were they safe? What had happened to them upon their return to Carwell?

Before Kerrin realised it, Devlin Hawke was back at the campfire. He stood regarding everyone present with a look of cold apprehension.

"I did not say before, Balan," Devlin began, "but I knew of your father. I am led to believe that he was a man with a dark reputation, had more than the stain of blood on his hands. Whilst I am sorry for the scars of guilt you will always bear for him, I am not sorry, I have to say, that he is dead."

Lost for words, Balan simply nodded as the outlaw continued. "Is there nothing else of note you can recall, Balan Ford?"

"*Note?*" Balan gasped suddenly, his eyes widening. Sitting back on his haunches he fished about in one pocket and pulled forth a worn, folded letter.

"I found this letter in Tobin's saddlebags," the youth said, passing it to his host. "It meant little to me, but I kept it anyway."

The outlaw leader opened the letter and turning towards the light of the fire, he read it silently. After a moment, he shook his head in rueful disbelief.

"By the Storms," Devlin Hawke whispered.

CHAPTER FIFTEEN

The Departed

Elion Leigh felt his heart race as he surveyed the ragged, cloudless range of the Great Divide for the first time since he made his stand against the Reven raiders in Storm Pass, all those years before. Framed by a beautiful blue sky, summer had rallied in the north once again, the storms swept away to the South Vales by bitter clouds and harsh, spiteful winds.

"Been a while, I guess," Ashe Garrin said, nudging his mare forward to follow his captain along the heavily rutted road that cut through the rising plains and snaked away over the hills to the north. Despite the rising heat of the day, the summer air was fresh with a gentle breeze that stirred up the heady scents of the wildflower and chased away the patrols' own stench for a time.

Following the revelations in Havensdale, they had quickly put aside their differences and settled the tension between them over an ale (or two) in the Arms of the Lady Inn. Hearing of Gardan's further treachery, Ashe had quickly concluded that, whilst he had been angry at his friend for bringing the girl with them, she was, it quickly transpired, an important witness. It would be better to keep her close and safe, lest anything happen to her before she could testify against Carwell's brutal commander.

Ashe barely heard Elion's soft confirmation and they fell silent again, as the party of riders made for the hills. The sergeant was worried, though not for himself any more. They had all made their choices, back in Eastbury, when it appeared that there was no other alternative to be found.

No! He was worried now for the wider implications, for what it all meant for the future. If Alion Byron sought justice for the attack on Havensdale outside the halls of the capital, it could mean civil war between the north and east. That in turn would force the high duke's hand. Would he be able to bring both parties back to the table, should fighting ensue? How could he, when there were justified questions on the credibility of the attacks on Eastbury, of the murders committed and the testimony of a girl who sought only revenge for what had happened to her family.

Ashe groaned, his head pounding from the tension and not helped by the high sun, rising unchecked in the cloudless sky above them.

Elion Leigh watched his friend, as they rode northwards across the plains, the thunder of their group rumbling along behind them. The burly sergeant was exhausted, his beard flecked with grey and his pale face marked by his worry.

Elion sighed, running a hand through his thickening beard. They were all worried – they needed to be.

Casting aside his own misgivings, the former Carwellian captain focused his thoughts on the mayor of Havensdale, riding in close, orderly formation behind them. Dekan Ardent had been silent for the last two days of travel, offering only polite answers to any questions that came his way. Grim-faced and fighting with the pain from his injury, the mayor was lost to his thoughts, his eyes haunted and flashing from the worry he held for his daughter and for the people he had been elected to govern. He was taking a great risk, Elion knew, seeking aid from Alion Byron, when Commander Gardan was most surely in the capital making his own case against them. If for some political reason the lord of Highwater did not listen to Dekan Ardent's concerns, where then could he take his claim? Who else would be willing to risk Carwell's wrath, in search of a justice that might not ever be found?

From what Elion had seen, and from what little he knew of the mayor, he took him to be a man of his word, a loyal supporter of the high duke and a direct, honest man. He had not met many men in Carwell he could mark as such and for Elion that was more than enough for him. Despite what had happened and the concern, naturally, from the people of his ravaged town, Dekan Ardent had ignored the protests and welcomed them into Havensdale.

It was a rare thing, to find a man willing to listen first to reason, rather than react hastily from fear. After what had happened to them, if Havensdale had attacked them, Elion would not have blamed them.

"Look at that beauty," Ashe whistled softly, dragging Elion's thoughts back to his surroundings.

Shielding his eyes from the sun, Elion followed his sergeant's arm and picked out the distant, hanging shape of a Valian kestrel, as it hunted the lower plains to the west. Sharing a wry smile, they watched the bird, as it quartered the land for prey, and they let their mounts find the road for them for a while.

"It has been a long time since we have had a safe road." Elion's words slipped away on a weary breath and Ashe nodded his agreement.

After a while, the hunter dropped from sight and with

a sigh, Elion sent his friend a knowing smile. As if reading his thoughts, Ashe said.

"Aye, it's lovely! I have never been to the north... but I could easily come to like it here."

Neither voiced the dark thoughts that rose from his statement, but they shared a grimace at the prospect that they may well be forced to seek a new life here in the coming days should the storm clouds return to haunt them.

At the rear of the group of riders, Elissen watched the captain and his sergeant, seeing the look on their faces as they watched the elegant raptor. Despite her numbness to everything happening around her, she somehow found a smile. She had never been away from her home, no more than a few miles at best and her memories, the scars of what had occurred there, felt almost as if it had happened to another person. *Almost.*

Feeling her anger rise and the haunted images of what she had witnessed flash before her eyes again, the broken young woman forced a calming breath from her dry lips. With her heart racing, she struggled to banish her demons, whispering at her from the recesses of her scattered mind, and they were well over the hills before she could regain her composure. Every time she felt herself relax, was able to clear her mind enough to forget for a while, she heard Commander Gardan's voice, dripping with disdain for the lives he held in his hands. She recalled fleeting, ghostlike images of the murder he had committed and she had unintentionally witnessed in Eastbury. With yet more white fury in her knuckles, the young woman twisted her failing sanity through the reins, forgotten in her hands.

Sensing the tension in its mistress, Elissen's mount became agitated and began testily taking his frustrations and nerves out on Jarion Kail's stallion.

Bringing the large black under control, Jarion dropped

back to ride along beside the pale woman and reached out to touch her hand. With two rapid blinks, Elissen returned to him and she attempted a smile that failed miserably. Jarion warmed her with a broad smile of his own and took in her dishevelled, haunted features.

Her once lustrous locks hung in filthy, snaking tendrils about her shoulders. Marred by recent events and the horrors she had witnessed and endured, her face was cold and harsh, all beauty drawn from it by her need for a night of sleep that did not end with her rising from her blankets and sobbing hysterically.

Jarion realised he was staring and found his breath, looking about their surroundings as their two mounts eyed each other warily.

"I am sorry," Jarion said quietly, dragging his eyes back to her. "I did not mean to stare."

Elissen calmed her mount and reached out with thin trembling fingers. She took Jarion's gloved hand and squeezed it gently.

"Please, Sir Jarion," she said, her mirth burning in her eyes, eyes that could have belonged to another person, "there is nothing to apologise for. I should be the one..."

Seeing the flash of the girl that once was and not wanting to draw her fragile mind back to the flames of the madness that was destroying her, Jarion simply nodded.

He held on to her hand as long as was deemed acceptable, then reluctantly let her go.

Drawing in a steadying breath, he focussed on the land spreading out beautifully before them and suddenly found himself thinking of his friend, Eban Dahl. A well of sorrow formed in his empty stomach as the realisation that he would never see him again finally settled there. With everything that had happened, these last terrible weeks, Jarion did not even attempt to wipe away his tears.

The remainder of the journey to Highwater for the weary

group of riders offered them all some needed respite. Rather curiously, they did not meet another soul on the Northern Road, did not encounter any signs of life until they were in far sight of the great city and its outlying hamlets and farmsteads.

Cradled in the lower foothills of the Great Divide, Highwater was a beautiful, sprawling city. Tall towers reached to the skies like stretching, ivory fingers and black pennants fluttered gently from them in a gathering breeze. As they came within a few miles of the city, Elion found his gaze drawn to the mountains, once again, and his breath caught in his dry throat.

Clouds had settled on the ragged peaks now, drifting lazily along the range that stretched as far as his eyes could see. Passing through a tiny hamlet, Elion flicked a look at Dekan Ardent, as the mayor guided his mount alongside him. With the road narrowing somewhat, Ashe tilted his head and respectfully dropped back to ride alongside Liehella.

"Sir?" Elion enquired, seeing the deep furrow in the mayor's brow.

Dekan Ardent swallowed. "Something is not right," he said quietly, eyeing an old man who sat on his porch outside a hut, drawing thoughtfully on an antique pipe. The mayor raised a hand in greeting, but the sullen smoker just regarded him with dour, milky-white eyes.

Elion glanced about the hamlet as they rode through. "What is it? I have never been to Highwater before, so I..."

As they cleared the hamlet, a dog snapping in their wake, Elion fell silent. The small group of riders slowed.

"This is not good, captain," Dekan Ardent said. He grunted in pain as he twisted in his saddle to regard those behind.

Ahead, on the low horizon, they could see a sprawling, makeshift city of tents and wagons, spread out before the walls of the city in a chaotic show of civilization. For one terrible moment Elion thought Highwater was under siege, then relaxed as Dekan Ardent continued.

"The Solstice Games finished days ago and the roads should be full of people returning to their homes. I wonder why they have all stayed."

The patrol shared looks that ranged from open worry to guarded concern and they remained silent as the mayor of Havensdale shielded his eyes and scanned the breathtaking view before them.

"We have made good time because of the empty roads," he said eventually, drawing his attention back to the young captain at his side. "Come, my friend, let us continue with haste and find the answers to our questions."

Raising his hand, Elion signalled for the small company of riders to continue. As they rode off, Elion felt his uncanny itch begin to flare again and he shook his head worriedly. Behind them, the barking dog, satisfied with its defence of his homestead, turned and padded back to its master for a well-deserved rest.

As they neared the city of tents and hazy speculation sharpened to fine detail, Elion could tell that Dekan Ardent was right to be worried. The huge sea of tents and wagons were smothered in silence and those few people who were present huddled solemnly about wistful campfires, or gathered together, talking in hushed, guarded tones.

Elion's itch of worry was on fire as they made towards the city gates, the air laced with the acrid smell of wood-smoke, pipe-weed and someone's late attempt at breakfast. People looked up as they rode quietly by, all of them, to the last, dressed in dark clothes and wearing grim expressions on their absently curious faces.

"I don't like this," Janth hissed.

Elion's attention was drawn to a cluster of brightly painted wagons, far away to the east. There was a large gathering of people there, all sat listening intently to a tall man, dressed in black, who held court before them.

The man's words were lost to the oppressive silence of the sombre day, but the weaving, articulate twists of his hands suggested that a great debate was unfolding there.

"Wayfarers," Ashe offered, his voice painfully loud. The sergeant winced, casting a wary look to the east.

Elion nodded, turning his head as Dekan Ardent muttered something. They held each other's gaze for a time and the young captain could read his fear there.

"Highwater usually flies the colours of Alion Byron, a rearing black horse on a red field," the mayor said, his voice failing. He rallied himself and shook his head. "They are flying black pennants, which can only mean one thing..."

The tension was palpable and they rode in hasty despondency towards the towering gatehouse of Highwater, the furthermost warden city of the Four Vales.

Seeing the large party of riders making towards them, four guards, dressed in mail and wearing black tabards strode from under the shade of the gatehouse to meet them. Bobbing glimpses of the city beyond revealed a bustling plaza, heaving with life, but all subdued by events unfolding within.

"Off you get," one of the guards ordered, raising a free hand to halt their approach. He tapped the haft of the spear he carried meaningfully on the dusty ground. The man, deep into his winters, kept his hand raised until the party of riders had obeyed.

"Well met," Dekan Ardent greeted, striding forward to grip the man's hand. He glanced about curiously. "What news, friend?"

The grim looking man, his youth long-since gone,

licked his lips nervously as he cast a furtive look over the newcomers.

"No news that is good, I fear," the man said, his pock-marked face stained by sadness. He caught the emblem on Elion's leather and raised an eyebrow.

"Carwell?" he observed. "You are a long way from home."

Dekan Ardent reined in the man's attention, still gripping his hand needfully.

"They are," he admitted. "They have escorted me safely from Havensdale and we carry urgent news to the lord of Highwater."

If they held any doubts that something was awry in the city, they were dispelled as the guard look behind at his fellows. The three men swapped dark expressions and looked to their boots.

"I fear you have come too late, sir," the old guard said, swallowing back his emotions as he returned his gaze to them. His grip, much like his resolve, failed as he let go the mayor's hand. "Alion Byron was murdered, seven days past."

Dekan Ardent stepped back into his shock, covering his mouth to stifle his gasp. Elion's heart raced, as a wave of despair washed over him and his skin stiffened with worry.

Behind him, he heard Elissen's strangled, choking sob and he cast a despairing look at Ashe.

This cannot be happening, he said to him silently. The sergeant's eyes were wide, his mouth hanging open.

Alion Byron, *dead?*

Seeing the effect his words had had upon them, the guard stepped forward and placed a hand on Dekan Ardent's shoulder.

"The funeral is happening today," the man reported, his throat thick with sorrow. "I fear your news will have to wait, for today at least. Lady Byron now rules the city and it is to her you should deliver your news."

Dekan Ardent's resolve slipped from him in an anguished sob and he staggered. Elion leapt quickly to his side, as both he and the guard steadied the distraught mayor.

"I'm alright," Dekan growled, waving away their concerns. "It's just the shock, that's all. Alion and I are old friends..."

The guard stepped back respectfully and bowed his head. "You are all welcome to join the city in its farewells today, but I must ask that you leave your weapons and horses outside the city."

He directed their attentions to the makeshift stables that had been set up under the high limestone walls of the city. Stablehands and grooms busied themselves with the care of their charges and Elion could see hundreds of horses tethered to posts and fencing, as far to the east and west as he could see.

Elion shook his head in disbelief. They thanked the guard for his help and stepped respectfully away to confer about what they should do next.

"Well, now what?" Ashe hissed, as they all gathered close. He found the mayor's sombre face in the sea of grim expressions before him.

Dekan Ardent was silent for a time. When he finally spoke, his voice was stretched thin across his weariness and laced with the bitterness of his deep sense of loss.

"I need to speak to Lady Byron, today if possible," he said, though his words bore little hope.

"That will be difficult," Elion said, then regretted his words as the mayor glared at him. "But we shall try."

Chewing his bottom lip, Elion rolled the cramp from the bunched muscles of his neck and winced as the bones cracked. He let his gaze wander about those gathered close, before finally settling them on the mayor again.

"I will accompany you," he told the mayor, quickly

finding his sergeant as he heard his sharp intake of breath. "Ashe, I want you and the others to stay outside with the horses and weapons... please, let me finish! We may need to move on quickly and it would be best if you all stay here whilst Mayor Ardent and I seek an audience with Lady Byron."

"But that's not going to happen today, Elion," Ashe growled, holding his hands up to register his frustration. "Be realistic, man. Let the girl bury her father before you bring our shadows to her door."

Elion and the mayor shook their heads in unison.

"We have to try," the captain said, stealing the words from the other's lips. "If we cannot gain an audience today, we shall return immediately, you have my word. In the meanwhile, send someone into the city for supplies. We do not want to get caught out again..."

He fixed his friend with a look that told him the matter was concluded and finally, with great reluctance, the sergeant nodded his accord.

Smiling at the others gathered close by and seeing the worry in their faces, Elion unbuckled his sword belt and passed the weapon to Bran. The young, dark-haired rider took the weapon. Holding it close to his chest, he met Elion's fearful look with one of his own.

"We should hurry," Dekan Ardent said, passing his long blade into Ashe's reaching hands.

With a nod of silent farewell, the mayor clapped Elion on one shoulder and steered him off to report to the guards, who had made their way back to the shadows under the gatehouse.

Ashe watched the pair leave, joining in with the steady trail of arriving mourners and then turned back to the faces looking in his direction.

"Let's find some shade," he said, grumbling. "We look to our horses then see to ourselves."

As one, the remnants of the party that had set out

from Havensdale returned their attention to their mounts and made for the spreading shade under the towering walls of the sombre city of Highwater.

Under the ever-watchful, towering presence of the distant peaks of the Great Divide, Elion Leigh waited patiently in the heaving, writhing mass of mourners. The main square was full of hundreds of grim-faced, solemn citizens; all crowded together, all sharing their grief with silent looks or respectful, guarded whispers. Away through the sea of strangers, Elion could just make out the familiar face of Dekan Ardent, as the mayor talked in quiet, hushed tones with a street vendor. The tall, thin-faced man sensibly wore a straw hat with a wide, drooping brim and his eyes scanned the crowd for potential customers as he bent in low to the mayor of Havensdale's ear and shared some gossip from the corner of his mouth.

Elion felt the sharpness from an old woman's elbow as she used the excuse of her advancing years to force her way through the throng. Calming his temper in the rising, stifling heat, Elion stepped onto his aching toes to survey his surroundings.

A line of silent, black-garbed guards kept the crowds away from the marble fountain in the centre of the large cobblestoned square. On either side of the square, the guards marshalled the streets, as far as he could see. Shielding his eyes from the sun, Elion's gaze followed the crowds northwards, as their writhing mass swept away from him along a wide street that snaked away into the city beyond.

Falling back onto his heels, Elion shook his head, feeling the sickness broil in the pit of his stomach. With Alion Byron murdered... with him gone, their hopes of finding any support in Karick were in tatters.

Lady, what will become of us now? Elion asked silently, his vain question echoing hollowly in his ears.

Wincing, the former captain looked about the crowd, fearing his thoughts louder than the oppressive silence of the day. Normally, Elion observed, his ears would be ringing with the raucous assault to his senses, the bark of dispute, the merry laughter of greeting, the general song of civilization. Today there was nothing, only the low whisper of anticipation – the quiet, speculative rasp of rumour and conjecture, broken only occasionally by the cry of a newborn.

To Elion Leigh, the absence of mundane life and the silence of a respectful, disconsolate city was the most terrifying thing he had ever heard.

The only one of his senses that was working today, it seemed to Elion, was, unfortunately, his smell. Despite the drifting, enticing fare of those hawkers who hoped the crowd's stomach would be greater than their sorrow, any fleeting reprieves were smothered by the stale aroma of sweat from the unbearable heat. The lingering, unpleasant reminder of the recent flooding that had dragged the sewers up into the streets, did little to improve matters.

By the time Dekan Ardent prised himself away, Elion was ready to fight his way out of the city and rejoin his comrades. With a grim smile, the mayor leaned close, his breath also noticeably stale.

"Alion Byron lies in state," he began, casting a fretful look about at those gathered close enough to overhear. "He is in the Chapel of the Lady, where the people of Highwater have been able to pay their respects."

Elion followed the mayor's eyes as he flicked them meaningfully across the square towards a wide lane to the west, closed to the public now by a stoic line of guards.

Licking his dry lips, Dekan continued. "We should make for the keep. My friend tells me that the funeral cortège will bear his body there soon, for burial in the family vaults. Before this happens, Lady Byron will break from tradition and address the crowd. We should make sure we are there, before the streets become choked and impossible to traverse."

Elion felt his hopes fade. "How in the Lady's name will we gain an audience?"

"I know this city," the mayor said, ignoring the despondent look on Elion's face, "and it knows me. I just need to get near to the gatehouse and find a friendly face."

Without another word, Dekan Ardent began heading off through the crowd of mourners. Casting a wistful look at the large gatehouse, Elion drew in his resolve and threaded his way northwards through the masses.

Ripples of whispers stirred the silence, sweeping along the rising, twisting street known as Merchants Walk. On a futile, waning breeze, the sounds of wailing began to rise, carrying the loss of a city up to those waiting quietly on either side of the wide street.

Stirred by the sound, several pigeons roused from their roosts on top of one of the tall, huddled buildings. Snapping their wings in a salute of their own, they swept away from the rising tide of sorrow and winged away to the east.

Elion stopped as Dekan Ardent slowed and turned to look over his head, back the way they had just came. The slow climb through the crowds had taken its toll on him and the mayor's face was pale, covered in a thin sheen of dripping sweat.

"Are you well?" Elion asked, his face flashing with worry. The mayor nodded subtly, his eyes filling with tears.

Elion followed his head, his body, once dripping from the heat, suddenly cooling. He began to hear the sobs and wails rise, as the sounds of the slow approach of horses and the distant rattle of a carriage drew near.

Following the mayor's eyes, Elion could just make out the approach of a rider, above the tide of turning heads.

As the funeral cortège drew near, Elion could see a cavalcade of riders following behind, guarding the black carriage that was drawn along by two horses. Elion felt his emotions churn as the crowd of black dropped to one knee in respect as the riders and carriage swept past.

Closer now, Elion could make out the solitary rider, who he suspected was Lady Cassana Byron. She rode at the front of the procession on a tall, magnificent black stallion. With his breath lost in his throat and Dekan Ardent's sobs rising behind him, Elion was pulled down on to one knee by his sorrow for a man he had never met, but had heard only the best about.

Lady Byron was, Elion noted curiously, dressed, not in finery, but in travelling leathers and a blouse of the starkest white. No jewellery adorned her neck and ears, no rings sparkled in the sun from her fingers. High riding boots swept up her calves and a short blade was sheathed off her right hip. Her face was pale from her loss, but her eyes were bright with determination, as she guided her mount slowly along. Her long black hair was tied back in a plaited tail, her loose tresses pinned behind her ears. She tilted her head gently to either side of the street in acknowledgement as she rode by and Elion felt the hairs on the back of his clammy hands rise. Lady Byron was dressed, it seemed, not as her status would warrant and society would expect – no! She was dressed for a fight, Elion noted, feeling his hopes rise.

The riders escorting the carriage, driven by a ghost of a man, clattered by and Elion caught the one and only glimpse he would ever have of Alion Byron, the lord of Highwater. With his ears drowning in the wails and cries of protest surging up from the crowd kneeling about him, Elion saw the body, lain out on the carriage, dressed in antique, polished battle armour, his cold lifeless hands grasping the sword resting on his still chest. Even in death, Alion Byron's face radiated strength and as the cortege swept by, Elion could see that a black scarf had been draped across the Lord of Highwater's throat.

"Lady Byron led the procession and my old friend William Bay drove the carriage," Dekan Ardent whispered, his throat thick with emotion as the cobbles rang from their passing. "We need to hurry, Elion. Follow me."

The mayor rose up quickly and began picking his way through the mourners, many of them still down on one knee, their heads bent respectfully. Feeling his guilt rise with him, Elion followed his comrade up the winding street of Merchants Walk and to the keep, rising up into view on the hill before him.

As he approached, the heat of the sun draining from his body, Elion hesitated. His head pounded from the worry raging in his heart. He had already become involved in something well beyond his perception, something greater than his own concern. But there was still time! Time to escape what was to surely come, time to find a life that offered him the peace and sanctuary he knew that would always elude him, should he carry on.

"Lady," Elion muttered, wringing his hands together nervously as he looked up at the bright sky above him. "You have shown me this path and in your will I shall always place my trust."

With his honour chastised and his code and belief flowing anew through his veins, Elion Leigh, former captain of Carwell, the hero of the assault on Raven's Point, picked up his faltering composure and followed the mayor of Havensdale up the winding street to find his own destiny.

CHAPTER SIXTEEN

Precipice

Arillion felt himself stir as the woman entered his wagon. Sitting up in his bed, he forgot the agony in his body for a time, as she stole his pain away with a dazzling, flashing smile.

With her hair tumbling about her in a thick, ebony veil, Lia came to him, bearing a bowl of steaming pottage. As she approached, Arillion allowed his eyes to range over the slender curves of her body, hidden away like a promise beneath a long plain, dark dress.

"How are you feeling today, swordsman?" she enquired, her bright eyes dancing with mischief as she sat beside him.

"Suddenly very stiff," Arillion admitted, a lopsided grin creasing his handsome features.

With colouring cheeks and averted eyes, the beautiful woman leaned close and he could smell the jasmine on her. "Would you like me to feed you, swordsman?" she asked, her voice husky and teasing. "Or can you manage on your own today?"

Arillion grinned, enjoying the game. Flicking his

hungry eyes about her face, he lost his answer there for a time, before he scowled.

Not again! He scolded himself. Smiling sweetly, he took the hot bowl from her with his good hand, feeling himself stir again as she brushed a finger over his hand.

"I'll manage," Arillion said, wincing, as fresh pain stabbed reproachfully at his injured shoulder.

Lia Shale sat back on her stool and watched as Arillion tucked into the stew. With the bowl in his lap, he hungrily spooned his steaming lunch down, dealing her questions between mouthfuls.

For three days, the beautiful wayfarer had come to his bedside, tending to his needs and the needs of her father. Despite his obvious reluctance to allow his only daughter anywhere near the handsome swordsman, Kaspen Shale had relented to the wisdom of his friend's suggestion. Glad to be relinquished from her duties, her grandmother had imparted only one piece of advice for her granddaughter's new role.

"Keep your wits around him girl."

Lia smiled at the thought and of the fear and reluctance in her father's eyes when he had imparted his own wishes, and the details of the man she was to nurse back to swift health.

It was clear to her, seeing the look in her father's eyes, that it wasn't her wits he was worried she might lose...

When the bowl was empty and his belly full, Arillion passed it back without thanks. Fighting down her annoyance, Lia settled the bowl in her lap and watched her patient, as his eyes, those startling eyes, held her with a gaze that said much, yet revealed very little.

"The funeral is taking place as we speak and father has declared a grand party this night," Lia imparted, keen to dilute the fire smouldering in his eyes. "Should you wish it, Arillion, you are welcome to join us and say your own farewells to the lord of Highwater."

The swordsman's face was impassive as he looked away for a time, lost to his memories. When he finally flicked his attention back, his features had softened into a smile.

"I should like to join you, my lady," he said, his eyes wandering again. "Perhaps I'll even manage a dance..."

Lia chuckled, the sound light and musical. "I doubt that, swordsman! You know our ways and I daresay you have a few more weeks before you can keep up with me."

She rose swiftly, her eyes burning in the lamplight, as she glided effortlessly towards the door. Spinning, she offered her patient a graceful curtsey and a mischievous grin.

Arillion watched her, marvelling how the shadows framed her dark hair and beautiful features, how the lamp reflected in her bright, lively eyes.

"Guess I'll have to find another way to keep you with me then," he grinned, licking his lips hungrily as she slipped away to the bright day outside.

By the time Elion Leigh and Dekan Ardent fought their way through the crowds to reach Byron Keep, they were both ready to throttle the next person who shoved them aside. Finding some calm amongst the clamouring chaos, the two held on to each other's waning strength as they slowly, but surely threaded their way nearer to the gatehouse.

"Nearly there," the mayor of Havensdale panted. Their eyes met briefly and Elion feared for him. If they didn't find some shade and water soon, the injured man would most likely faint from the heat.

A half-moon wall of more than thirty guards held the crowds at bay with shield and spear and the mourners, hushed by their expectation, nervously, yet patiently waited for the moment when Lady Byron would break from centuries of tradition and address the people before laying her father to rest.

It took quite some time, but they eventually came within three heads of the front of the crowd, halfway down the east side of the cobblestones, towards the gatehouse. Elion could see the guards on top of the curtain wall, watching the crowds gathered below intently, their crossbows readied, lest more assassins lurk there.

Were there assassins here? Elion wondered, scanning those nearest to him. Would they risk such a public attack, with so many people to bear witness? Feeling his skin prick worriedly, he looked back over one shoulder, studying the dark windows of the buildings nearby that were in range for a good archer.

Elion prayed to the Lady there would be no attack. If there was, they would be trampled to death in the ensuing panic.

Dekan Ardent was more intent on the guards, his weary features pinched by concentration as he searched vainly for a familiar face. He met Elion's questioning look and shook his head apologetically.

"Nobody," he sighed, ruefully adding, "I should have spent a bit more time in the barracks."

Elion forced a smile, bitter images of a lonely corner in the officer's mess in Carwell flashing before his eyes. He had spent many a solitary evening in that corner, hoping to be accepted by his betters and yet shunned by them for his apparent lack of '*breeding*'.

Swallowing back his pride, Elion's attention was dragged away, as was the writhing crowd, towards the gatehouse. The large, double doors creaked slowly, ominously open, revealing glimpses of the courtyard and keep beyond. From atop the keep, Elion could see that the Byron Pennant fluttered proudly in a breeze. Its statement was not lost on him.

Alone, a solitary figure waited in the shade, gathering her composure about her before drawing in a steadying breath and striding out from under the shadows of the gatehouse to address the crowds waiting anxiously to hear what she had to say.

Elion felt his pulse quicken as Lady Byron strode with ever-increasing, purposeful steps to stand in the sun before the wall of guards. From his vantage point, Elion was sure he could see her shaking and his heart reached out to her. He noted her chest rise as she drew in a deep breath and then fall as, quietly at first, she spoke.

"I thank you all for the honour you have shown my father this day," she began, pausing to lick some courage onto her lips. "He was a proud, honourable man, loved by all who knew him, respected by those who were protected by him."

Cassana let her words echo about the deathly silence and began pacing, bringing her words to those on the west side of the crowd.

"I believe none of you here would argue that my father, Alion Byron, was a fair and just man. He guarded this city and cared deeply for the welfare and prosperity of you, its citizens, as if you were his own. He never stopped caring, he never stopped championing all that has made Highwater what it is, all that you, and he, have made it together."

A ripple of respectful approval skipped across the crowd, as Lady Byron's words gained volume and purpose. "As a daughter, I shall grieve a father's passing, and I shall never recover from the loss. But as Alion Byron's daughter, I have promises to keep, promises to my murdered father, promises to care for you all as he did before me."

The crowd stirred uneasily at this, the word *murdered* echoing loudest of all.

"Before my father was killed, he was in dispute with

the direction those who sit on the council in Karick would take the Four Vales. As far north as we are, many of you will not have heard news from the rest of the Vales. There is much unrest and there are dark stirrings from a supposed spectre of the past. In the coming weeks, you will hear tell of a Reven uprising, how there have been brutal attacks, kidnappings and murders of prominent figureheads of Valian society. You will hear of how an assassin nearly claimed the life of Lord Carwell himself. These reports would be compelling evidence, taken as they are. But I stand here before you today, with a promise that they are not to be trusted."

Allowing the implications of her words to settle, Lady Byron strode to the east of the crowd. Elion's heart was in his throat and he looked to the mayor of Havensdale. His shock was mirrored there and they looked back expectantly, drawn by the spell this young, inexperienced woman was weaving before them.

With her hands clasped before her, her eyes blazing away with controlled anger, Cassana Byron continued.

"My father was murdered for his belief, only seven days ago, by those who would send the Valian people to war. But he was not killed by a Reven as some might have you believe! He was slain in his bed by a Valian woman, a woman with a scar on her face. Had the Lady not intervened, I would be dead now, also..." she paused to calm her rising haste and rein in her fraying composure. "Some weeks ago, whilst journeying to the capital, I, myself, was attacked by Reven in the Moonglade Forest. I was saved, thank the Lady, and escorted safely to the city, where my life was put in even greater danger. Eventually, with help, I made my way back home, but I truly believe, as did my father, that I was meant to be used as leverage against him, when he stood firm to his code and honour. It seems that there are those in the Four Vales who would want war with the Reven, who want those living this side of the Great Divide with any Reven heritage tossed back over our walls to await our blades when we come for them. They will offer you more compelling evidence to support their claims, there will be further attacks, I can assure you, more killings and new kidnappings to bolster their cause. Having witnessed, first-hand, one of these attacks, I could let myself become swept away by tell of this Reven threat. But I shall not. I *will* not and with your support and strength, we shall not let this happen."

Shocked, startled faces turned in the crowd, sharing silent thoughts with friends, neighbours and strangers alike. Elion swallowed his doubts down, his worry that when the armies came calling at their gates, the people of Highwater would not have the same resolve as the lady governing them.

"My father, a man of his word, a man for his people, believed and has tellingly died for his belief, that there is a plot to steer the Valian people to war, a war with a ghostly menace at best. It lurks in the marble halls of the capital, it whispers in the ears of those who hold the reins of our fragile destiny in their hands... but we are not alone. There are those who will also stand by us, those who believe that the Reven insurgency is but a ruse, orchestrated by those who would have you believe otherwise. I have come before you today to ask only that you trust in the daughter of the man you loved, as she searches for the evidence that will stem this madness. My father told me, on the day he died, that he truly believed the claims to be a lie, and I will not stop until I have proven them to be so."

She strode back to the centre of the cobbles and faced the crowd, her fear and her emotions flushing her face.

"Will you honour my father's wishes and stand firm with me whilst I search for the proof he sought? Will you stand alongside me as I seek to stem the tide of madness and dilute the flood of propaganda that would wash over our beloved city and sweep us all to war? Will you? What say you my friends?"

In the deathly, uncomfortable silence that followed, Elion Leigh could see that Lady Byron thought she had made a terrible mistake. That was until the first rallying cry went up from the crowd, an old man with one eye, the other socket hollowed and sunken. His face was wrinkled by his years, his head liver-spotted and haunted by the wisps of his youth that had probably seen him to the last war.

"Aye, lady," he cried, raising a thin, bony fist and shaking it defiantly.

A chorus of cries began roaring out, freed from the shackles of uncertainty and as their calls of support and unity rang out, the crowd began shouting their determination and pledges of support for the man they had loved and the woman who would now lead them.

Elion found himself swept up in the euphoria and shouted his own declaration of determination. At his side, Dekan Ardent grinned, his eyes alight with hope once again, his wound and pain momentarily forgotten.

"There's still hope," he said, nodding to himself.

Lady Byron clasped her shaking hands to her lips and kissed them, offering her thanks in a wave to the swelling, writhing sea of faces before her. With an elegant bow, she turned, as the man Dekan had identified as William Bay, strode from under the gatehouse to escort her back inside. Cassana, tears creasing her cheeks, raised a hand in farewell to the crowd and took William's offered arm. Though grim-faced, his eyes betrayed his pride, or perhaps relief, and as they turned, Dekan Ardent rose up onto his toes and roared out a greeting.

"WILLIAM BAY!"

The man's head turned at his name, searching for a familiar face in the sea of strangers. If he spied the mayor's waving arms, he did not show recognition and turning away, he swept his charge back into the safety of the keep.

"Bugger!" Dekan Ardent cussed, as Elion bent close.

Above the din of the crowd, the young captain could not hear what followed. Cupping a hand to one ear, he nodded for the mayor to repeat his words.

"I said, he didn't see me, we shall have to wait for the crowd to disperse before announcing our presence at the gates."

Elion nodded forlornly and looked sceptically at the gathered throng. With a sigh, he began searching for a vendor so that he might purchase some water, or perhaps find something a little stronger to help them while away the time.

Elion managed to find some water for the waning mayor and they slipped away to find some shade, whilst they waited for the crowd of mourners to disperse. In hopeful silence, they studied the hundreds of people closely, watching the way humanity went about its business and conducted its affairs. Many stood in hushed groups, discussing the events of this dark day and the momentous events to which they had borne witness to. Most, it seemed, were unable to tear themselves away, all clinging to one another as they debated what the seeds sown by their new steward would mean for them in the coming days and weeks.

The old man, who had stoked up the support for Lady Byron, soon succumbed to the heat, and with an old soldier's salute towards the keep, he allowed himself to be swept down the hill to the city beyond. Dekan Ardent watched the man disappear from view and then bowed his head, lost to a memory of a day when he and Alion Byron had shared the battlefield together.

Elion Leigh watched the mayor for a time, then averted his attention, his own guilt rising as Dekan began to weep. Calming his emotions, Elion studied the waning crowds and soon spied the man who was searching the faces for someone of note. As the man, dressed in a heavy ring mail shirt and piecemeal greaves came near to them, Elion gently touched the mayor of Havensdale on his left shoulder and startled him from his reverie.

Nodding towards the man, they rose from the cobbles and stretched the aches from their taught muscles.

Letting out a thankful sigh, Dekan Ardent dealt him a smile.

"I know this man," he grinned, as he turned and caught the man's attention with a relieved wave. "Here, Erith!"

The man's face creased into a smile and he came over to them. "Captain Ardent," he said, gripping the hand offered to him.

Dekan smiled, as he shook the warrior's hand gratefully. "Mayor Ardent these days, but it's good to see you, my friend. I am only sorry the circumstances were not better."

Elion saw the man's weary face fall and his eyes flick momentarily towards him. Dekan noticed, slapping his thigh in annoyance.

"Where are my manners," he scolded himself. "Erith Taye, this is Elion Leigh, a captain from Carwell, who has kindly escorted me here. Elion Leigh, Erith Taye, a loyal friend and damned good at chess, so don't play him for money."

They shook hands and traded smiles through the mayor's introduction. Erith momentarily studied the young man before him and was taken aback by his dishevelled, haunted appearance. Before he could hide it, his dark eyes filled with questions.

"All in good time, my friend," Dekan said quietly, dragging the man's attention away with a clap to his shoulder.

Erith nodded and remembered himself. "William

asked me to fetch you to him. As you can appreciate, there is much to attend to this day, but he can spare you a few moments."

The relief on their faces told him much, and without further word, Erith escorted them through the crowds and the line of guards, who parted obediently as they approached.

As they followed behind their guide, Elion dealt the mayor a look. Dekan Ardent's face, once grey with agony and stained by sorrow, was now full with hope. He nodded his silent agreement.

A few moments would be enough.

Elion Leigh did not have enough time to appreciate the grounds of Byron Keep, as Erith Taye quickly escorted them through the gathered throng of dignitaries and busy servants, who were enjoying the sun and drinks being served to them. Passing through the gardens, they hurried by an elegantly carved stone bench, from where a harpist played a gentle, sombre piece. The haunting strings spread across the grounds and blanketed the low conversation of the guests with its beautiful and emotional chords.

Entering through the western side of the keep, their escort took them up the full length of a twisting staircase and along a lushly carpeted hallway. Reaching a heavy oak door, he knocked once and when a muffled voice responded from within, he opened the door and motioned for them to follow him inside.

William Bay rose from behind his neat desk and hurried to greet his old friend. As Erith Taye said his farewells and left, closing the door gently behind him, Elion flicked his eyes about the brightly lit study. A large window, its glass lead-lined and crossed by diamond shapes, filled the shadows with the bright day outside, revealing the heaving burnished shelves of old books and parchments that filled every available wall and seemingly held up the ceiling. A table, just inside the room, away to Elion's right, was home to a silver, brightly glowing candelabra and a crystal decanter full of a golden, amber spirit. Six matching crystal glasses were neatly arranged around the decanter and four comfortable looking chairs were tucked under the antique looking table.

His rising thirst was drawn away as Dekan Ardent held his old friend close. After a time, they clapped each other on the back and drew away from each other at arm's length, regarding the lines and the grey that had settled on them both since their last meeting.

"I would say that I am glad to see you, Dekan," William began, then lost his words to a sad shake of his head.

"And I you, my friend," the mayor of Havensdale responded bitterly. "For what it is worth, you have my deepest sympathy, William. I know how much you and Alion loved one another."

Williams eyes clouded momentarily from his loss then were cleared quickly by his rising anger.

"You heard the speech, I take it?" he asked guardedly.

Dekan nodded and stepped back. "We did, and I must say I was as impressed as I was horrified by what she said."

William nodded and sighed. He suddenly seemed to notice the other guest in the room and he flicked a curious look at his friend.

"My manners, again," Dekan Ardent cursed. Introductions were hastily given, polite handshakes exchanged, but seats were not offered, hinting further at the short time they had to impart their news.

Sensing the urgency in their host, Dekan Ardent drew in a deep breath. Elion's heart began to hammer in his chest.

"I know this is terrible timing, William," Dekan began reluctantly, tugging at an earlobe, "so I must apologise for bringing this to you today. We had heard no news of Alion's murder, nothing, until we reached the city gates. I know today is not the day for it, but I must speak to Lady Byron – it is of the upmost importance that I do before we leave."

William searched his old friend's eyes, his face twisting worriedly. He looked at Elion, also, and then took a pace back and sat on the corner of his desk.

"You must understand, and expect, that this will not happen today, Dekan," William said grimly. "But you can, at least, tell me. I cannot guarantee it, but should I deem your news to warrant it, I will speak to her on your behalf when I can."

Elion felt his hopes rise as his heart calmed. He had not expected to get this far today and was sure the news they bore would quickly change the man's mind.

Softly, calmly and, to Elion's surprise, without any emotion, Dekan Ardent told of the attack on Havensdale by Commander Gardan and his men, of the claims he brought to their door and of the carnage and murder that had ensued.

As the mayor spoke, William Bay's face stiffened with shock, then paled as the implications of such a conflict began to settle in his stomach. After Dekan Ardent had finished talking, William blinked free of his shock, then, with his brow furrowing, he looked at Elion Leigh.

"But this man is from Carwell?" he stated, confused.

Elion smiled. "I am, sir. But, my tale brings even more shadows to these events and I would save them for the Lady Byron, if it is at all possible?"

William rose from the desk and looked between his guests. His sigh was deep and long and, as he massaged his aching temples, he resigned himself to act with a slow nod.

"I will see Lady Byron as soon as she returns from her vigil at her family's tomb and arrange a meeting. Help yourself to some brandy. I will send a servant with some food and then we can see about getting someone to look at your wound, Dekan."

William shook their hands and hurried from the room, his voice calling out commands as he retreated down the hallway.

Elion's relief escaped his lips, carried away on a smile. Grinning broadly, Dekan Ardent added his own relief and moved towards the decanter.

"I need a drink," he gasped, picking up an empty glass. "For medicinal purposes, obviously," he added with a painful smile.

Pouring a couple of glasses, the candlelight burning in the glowing liquid, he passed Elion a glass.

"To Alion Byron," the mayor of Havensdale said softly, raising his own glass in a toast.

Elion clashed their glasses together, the contact echoing about the room like a shrill, high-pitched cry. He countered Dekan Ardent's grim face with a wry smile.

"To the fallen," Elion said and drained his glass in one pull.

CHAPTER SEVENTEEN

Piece by Piece

Lord Astien was not sure how he reached the long hallway leading to the high duke's offices. His head was throbbing, his throat dry and his eyes raw. Like a dream, he chased his leaden footsteps towards the guard on duty outside, not sure if he was actually awake, not wanting to believe that he was.

The terrible news from Highwater had finally reached the capital, borne on the wing and delayed by the terrible storms that drowned the city. With its streets running like rivers, choked by rubbish, effluent and two more bodies resulting from attacks on Reven citizens, Karick was as taut as a bowstring, waiting for that telling shaft that would sever the fragile strands of peace and plunge the streets into chaos.

The guard, somehow familiar to Bryn Astien, looked haunted, his cheeks drawn, not full of their usual smile.

"He awaits you," was all he said, as he reached tentatively for the ringed handle.

With barely a nod, Lord Astien was admitted to the study beyond and the sight that greeted him stopped him in the doorway.

Weakly lit by a single candle dying on its wick, the perpetual dark from the storm outside strangled the room and suffocated its usual elegance and finery. Papers were strewn haphazardly across the carpeted floor and it appeared as if the lashing rain outside had somehow stolen in through the large window and rushed about the study causing eager mischief.

The guard forced him into the room as he began to close the door and Bryn Astien searched the shadows, noting the upturned chairs, the broken glass on the carpet and the books, torn from the shelves that lined the east wall.

"My lord?" he dared to ask.

The silence, disturbed only by the heavy rain lashing at the window, was broken by a weak call, away to his right. Searching the dark, he picked out movement and a looming figure rose up from the arms of a deep, low-backed leather chair.

"I am here, Bryn," the high duke greeted weakly. He shuffled from the dark, stepping into the grey gloom.

Astien recoiled, unable to hide his shock at the ghost that stumbled into view. Karian Stromn, the guardian of the Four Vales, the heart of the Valian people, was a broken man. His long hair was matted, his beard untrimmed and his eyes as wild as the storms outside. Dressed only in a scarlet silken robe, it appeared as if the high duke had not left his chambers for several days, his gauntness suggesting he had not eaten much in that time either.

"Have you heard?" he said weakly, his voice distant, lost almost in the storm.

Bryn Astien nodded and followed the high duke slowly over to the desk. With one hand on the huge desk for support, the high duke stumbled around to the chair beyond and collapsed into it.

"Be seated," Karian said, motioning faintly to one of the upturned chairs.

Pulling one upright, Bryn sat down slowly, the concern in his wide eyes gleaming in the faint, flickering light.

The high duke watched him for a time, one hand clutching at his temple. When he finally spoke, the high duke stumbled over his words and shook his head angrily.

"My lord, you are not well," Bryn Astien observed. "Should I send for your physician?"

Karian glared at him. "The man is a fool. I have already sent him away twice today. All he wants to do is bleed me! I can do that myself – the only thing that seems to work these days is my herbal tea. It helps me to calm down for a time, to rise above this sea of uncertainty I am drowning in."

Losing his response in his throat, Bryn Astien simply bowed his head helplessly. As his mind raced, he heard the high duke groan.

"Damn this," the high duke snarled, pounding a fist on the old wood and startling his visitor. "Damn it all, Bryn." He held Bryn Astien's worried look with an imploring, desperate gaze.

"What will we do without him?" the high duke asked, his emotions thick in his throat. "I needed his strength for this, I needed his counsel... and he left me, he deserted me, he betrayed me when I needed him the most. How could he do this to *me*?"

Lord Astien felt his own grief fall away as he was overcome by fear and worry for the man who held the last chance of peace in his trembling, weak hands. As he studied him, Bryn Astien could tell that the man he had sworn loyalty to, the only other person he would have followed to his death, if his honour bade it, was falling foul to a madness from which he would never return.

"My lord, you must rest," Bryn began hesitantly. "You

are in shock, we all are. Alion's death is a blow to us, to everyone. But he never betrayed you, he only ever sought to protect and counsel you."

The high duke shook his head. "No! No! You are wrong. I had the letter, you heard it. He would not come back to the table – he would rather let the Reven run rampant through our lands, cutting away at our stability whilst hiding behind his walls, pointing accusatory fingers at those seeking to restore order."

The high duke was ranting, his once-calm, reasoned tone shrill and laced with delirium. Unable to intercede, Bryn let the high duke talk himself hoarse, listening to his mad ramblings as he bemoaned those who had turned their backs on him, of the treachery of Savinn Kassaar, who it was now clear was behind this Reven uprising.

Rubbing the chill from his hands, Bryn Astien shook his head bitterly. The news that evidence had been *found* to support these claims sounded all but false in the ears of those who were willing to listen. But, with the increased news of further attacks, the *Reven* murderer still at large in the capital and now, the death of Alion Byron, there were fewer people who wanted to listen.

Bryn waited patiently for a while further, before cutting off the high duke, as he was spitting in anger about the failure of Captain Varl, of how finally, with the arrival of Commander Gardan, the things that were needed were finally starting to be done.

"I am leaving, my lord," Bryn Astien said firmly, before the high duke could begin seething at the reported uprising in Havensdale, of the traitors the mayor was purportedly harbouring there.

"Leaving?" the high duke whined, blinking in confusion.

Lord Astien rose up swiftly. "Yes, my lord. There is little I can accomplish here, now that Carwell's influence has returned to the capital." Ignoring the dangerous gleam in Karian Stromn's dark eyes, he pressed on. "With your leave, I shall return to Highwater, to speak with Lady Byron. I will try to make her see reason and bring the north back to the table. If I can do that, which I believe I can, it will ease your troubles and unite the council once again."

For a brief moment, the fog of madness lifted from the high duke's face and he settled back in his chair wearily. "You are right, Bryn. That would be a boon to us all." He waved his hand dismissively. "Hurry back to your home, speak to Cassana Byron on my behalf, bring her to reason and settle this tension between us."

Hiding his relief, Lord Astien bowed gently. "My thanks," he turned away, making slowly for the door, his head keen to be away, yet his heart reluctant to be going. He paused in the shadows, then turned.

"Shall I bear your sorrow to Lady Byron, my lord?" he asked quietly.

From his chair the high duke nodded. "Words cannot truly carry my grief to her, but I give you my consent to at least try, my friend."

Smiling sadly, Bryn Astien inclined his head politely and hurried from the room. As he swept wordlessly away from the guard, down the long hallway, he was suddenly aware of the lingering thought that he may not set foot in the capital again after this night was done.

The three men sat thoughtfully in their chairs, nursing their drinks as they discussed recent events. Unlike the high duke's study, Bryn Astien's chambers were brightly lit and once his visitors had arrived, they adjourned to the well furnished lounge for their secret meeting.

"I understand your haste, I really do," Lucien Varl said in answer to Bryn Astien's announcement. "But I fear for the future of the council and the Vales if you go."

The three sipped at their wine and listened to the

storm for a time, before Lord Astien responded.

"You did not see the high duke this night," he said softly, drumming nervous fingers across his left knee. "He is not well and he is not listening to reason. The chancellor has his claws deep in him now and with Gardan stirring up trouble and chaos in the city, it is only a matter of time before the high duke sees other traitors where there are none to be found."

Lord Farrington nodded his head in agreement as he ran a hand through his russet hair. "The hardliners have played their hands well, moving their pieces to a place they have not been for many years. Alion's death has only aided that."

A sombre hush settled on the room and glasses were raised, drained and re-filled. Eventually, as the rain relented outside, Lucien Varl rose up and paced about the room worriedly.

"If what you say is true, then I fear we are at a bleak crossroads, my lords," the estranged captain said, eyeing them both meaningfully. "If the balance of power in the capital is shifting towards the hardliners, then we shall also be moving towards war."

"It is what Alion Byron believed at the end," Bryn Astien said, bowing his head. "If we are to stem this madness, we must look to our safety first, before we try to find the evidence we need to unmask the traitors."

Henry Farrington cleared his throat. "I have already made plans to leave tonight, to slip away before the other council members realise that I have gone. I need to return home, to fortify my position, before the political divide weakens and undermines me. Having played my hand early at the council meetings, my list of allies grow thin. I need to speak to Baron Kern, to warn him of the trouble we may have ahead of us."

Bryn Astien looked towards the curtained windows. "Is it wise to risk the storm? Dusk approaches. Leave at first light, it will be safer then."

Farrington bobbed his head from side to side, as if juggling his thoughts. Draining his glass in one pull, he rose stiffly and smiled.

"I have tarried here far too long my friends," he said apologetically. "My enemies grow strong around me and I would have the safety of my keep before we plan our next move."

Lucien Varl nodded. "I am home, so I shall stay and do all I can to influence matters where I can, though I fear that I no longer have any kind ears that will listen. I will send regular word of what is happening, on the wing and in secret."

Bryn Astien grunted his agreement as he rose and strode forward. He took Farrington's arm by the wrist and shook it firmly.

"May the Lady watch over you, Henry," he said, smiling thinly. "Safe journey to you. I will update you on matters when I get to Highwater."

"Watch your back, my friend," Farrington said, pulling him close. They embraced briefly, clapping the other heartily on the back before pulling away brusquely.

"Lucien," Farrington said. They shook hands and then, with a graceful bow, the lord of the South Vales was gone.

When they heard the door close, Lucien turned.

"When will you leave?" he asked, trying to hide the worry from his words, failing to mask the fear etched on his face.

"In the morning," Bryn replied. "I have the high duke's blessing and I hope that it will carry me home safely," he paused, swallowing his nerves. "If it does not, you must get out of the city and make for Highwater."

Lucien Varl shook his head. "I have the care of the high duke's family to attend to... it may be the only card I have left to play. Should things fall apart here, I will look to them first, then follow you to Highwater."

They shook hands firmly and Bryn Astien eyed the man closely. "Be careful, Lucien and watch for the chancellor. He hates you and as the power in the capital shifts, he may make his move."

Lucien Varl's eyes shifted nervously under the scrutiny and he waved one hand flippantly. "He had better watch for me..."

Sharing a grin, they walked from the lounge and Lord Astien showed his guest to the chamber door.

As their farewells faded away, Lady Rothley used the temporary quiet to rise up stiffly from the hidden listening hole she had been attending for some hours and slip silently away along the narrow secret passageway to make her hasty report.

Dia woke from her slumber. Raising her weak head from the pillows, she allowed her eyes to find their strength in the dark room for a time, feeling the warmth of her lover beside her. Smiling demurely at the thought of their fierce love-making, she moaned softly, snuggling in to Eran with a smile.

He was sat up and with a considerable effort, Dia propped herself up on her left elbow, eyeing his naked outline in the dark.

"What's wrong?" she enquired softly, stifling a yawn.

She felt him tense as he drew in a deep breath, felt his body finally relax as he let it out again.

He shifted, turning his thoughts to her and she could feel his arms slide about her and pull her gently into a warm embrace. With their bodies entwined, Eran kissed the top of her head.

"I don't like what's happening in the city," he began, hesitating, fearing to continue.

Dia made a sound to comfort him and she hid her

own anxiety as she detected his on his body.

"It's this Gardan," Eran whispered. "He's forced Captain Varl out and is running amok in the streets with his men. It's not right, Dia. It's not honourable."

Dia held him tighter and nodded. She was well aware what had been happening of late, as was Savinn Kassaar, and none of it was good. With all the political turmoil, the news of Alion Byron's death and the apparent cracks of division splitting the council, there was nothing to comfort them, no news to settle their fears for the days ahead.

If Eran sensed her body and mind at work, he chose to ignore it and lost himself to his own deliberations.

"The news from Highwater has done little to ease things, my love," he sighed deeply. "Only yesterday, Gardan's men, men of Karick I hasten to add, dragged a Reven family from their homes in broad daylight. A crowd had gathered to watch and the family were pelted with horse dung and rotten vegetables as they were led away."

Dia ran a calming hand over his broad chest, attempting to distract him. When he tensed at her touch, she dropped her hand and let him have his say.

She felt him shudder. "I have been relieved of my duty by the chancellor," Eran said heavily. "Wen remains, but tomorrow I must report to Eagle Watch Barracks again, as I am *needed there*."

Dia freed their tangled limbs and sat up hastily. She could pick out his features in the shadows now, twisted with worry.

"What does that mean, Eran?" she dared to ask. She reached out to caress the turmoil from his face.

Closing his eyes, Eran forced a smile. "Tomorrow, I fear I will be amongst the men who hound the Reven, or those who have any links to them, from their homes. How will I live with myself?"

Dia felt the breath of her fear as it whispered on her naked body. She felt her heart race, felt her own emotions for the man she no longer needed, rising to the surface. Eran was an honourable man, much like the estranged Captain Varl. He was a kind man, tied only to his duty and the care of the city. To think that he may be forced to do unspeakable things...

It was true to say that the Carwellian commander's arrival in Karick had brought the storms with him. News of the '*nest of vipers*' in Havensdale, as he had put it, had done much to fan the flames from the fire of vigilantism that was spreading through the city. Couple his timely arrival with news of Savinn's apparent fixing of the games and the murderer at large in the city conveniently being marked as a Reven, and things were turning very sour, very quickly.

Eran thought her rising fear was for him and he drew her into his arms again.

"I am sorry, Dia," he said softly. "I should not have said anything. We have the night, for once, to ourselves and we should make the most of it."

Dia felt their passions rising and as she lost herself to his gentle, needful touch, a distant peal of thunder boomed out prophetically.

Lord Farrington turned in his saddle. Pulling the hood from his head, he looked back over the heads of his escorts, towards the dark, towering walls of the city. As the distant rumble of thunder died away, he returned his thoughts to the darkness ahead and the quagmire that was the South Road.

It was dark now, thank the Lady and the heavy rain that had battered the region beforehand had eased to a fine drizzle that left horse and rider soaked to the bones. Raising his face to the dark sky, he allowed the fine, damp air to cool his fears for a time, losing himself in the darkness above, blushing softly from the radiance of a hidden half-moon.

"A grim night, my lord," the hooded man at his side observed, eyeing the swirling cauldron of clouds overhead.

Pulling the hood of his long cloak back onto his head, Farrington nodded in agreement as the small column of riders rode towards the subtly darker tree line of the distant Whispering Woods.

"Aye, Thomas," Henry muttered, his voice nearly lost below the swirling wind and the splashing gait of their mounts. "A poor one, but a necessary one I am afraid!"

Thomas Gyles was a stoic, dour companion – the perfect companion on such a similarly natured night. His pock-marked face was lost to the depths of his hood, but Henry could picture his consternation of having to leave at such an hour, and in such terrible weather.

With the raised torch in his right hand swaying and dancing in the rain, Thomas nodded grimly.

"I daresay we shall be thankful once we are home in our own beds, my lord," he muttered, the closest thing Henry would get to an agreement this night.

Smiling, Farrington urged the column on, the torches several of the party carried casting writhing shadows in the swirling mist and darkness.

It was quiet in the Whispering Woods that night. The trees dark and menacing, the skies overhead brooding and watchful as the small group of riders made their way through the rain and mud.

Lord Henry Farrington felt his fear rise as they made haste along the twisting South Road and held on to the thought that he would feel much safer once they were out in the open plains beyond the woods.

To the west, an owl screeched suddenly and the patrol tensed, keen to be off, but reticent to ride foolishly into any unknown danger.

Lord Farrington cursed his thoughts and forced a rueful smile. The circumstance of their hasty departure and the rising tension he was leaving behind in Karick was playing on his mind.

He allowed a nervous chuckle to escape his lips and watched amiably as his breath clouded before him.

Thomas turned his hooded head and Farrington could see his eyes shining nervously from within.

"A fell sound, my lord," Thomas said. "All we need now is a fox..."

Before Henry could respond, a feathered shaft appeared in his companion's chest. It quivered there for a time as Thomas stared down at it.

His senses numbed by shock, Farrington reached out to the injured man as dark shapes moved in the shadows and more shafts sang from the trees.

With a roar, black cloaked figures rushed from the woods and as Thomas spilled from his saddle, another shaft protruding from his right shoulder, Farrington brought his mount under control and kicked his booted heels deep into its flanks.

"Ride," he screamed and as his mount bore him away, he left Thomas and two of his men behind in the mud to fend off the attackers that quickly cut them down.

With his sword in one hand and the misting rain swirling about him, Lord Farrington broke through the line of attackers blocking the road ahead. His blade came down, ripping the life from a hooded head and he and his five surviving men broke through the lines.

With hearts galloping madly, the riders splashed through the mud, dark shafts filling the night. A pitched scream rose and sounds of a heavy fall behind signalled they were paying a heavy price for their flight.

Keeping low to avoid being plucked from his saddle by an arrow, Farrington urged his mount on. The stallion,

Tempest was nine summers and he had reared him from a foal. They trusted one another like siblings and as one they raced from the danger, leaving the shouts of pursuit behind.

"Keep close," Farrington roared to those following behind. As they rounded a broad turn, only one torch now to light their path, he began to hope they were safe.

With his sword still gripped in his hand, Henry let Tempest find the road as he scanned the woods about them for further sign of danger. Fairly certain that any pursuers on foot were now far behind them, he reached for a breath and found a smile instead.

Farrington sent a rallying grin over his shoulder and did not see the rope that snapped up across the road before him...

CHAPTER EIGHTEEN

Resolve

The crisp night was alive with merriment, laughter and song, an unfitting tribute, one might say, on a day when a city had said farewell to their beloved lord.

After the mead he had drunk, Arillion would disagree.

The Wayfarers, true to Lia's promise, had gathered together as one around a huge camp fire, built earlier that day whilst Alion Byron was being laid to rest in the family's vaults. Erected almost like a great pyre, it was a fitting way to send off the lord of Highwater as only they could.

The assassin was finally lured from his wagon by the celebrations, long after the sun had drawn its curtain on the sombre day. Leaning heavily on a staff, given to him that afternoon by Mother Shale, Arillion had gingerly stepped out into the night, glad to be finally free of his confines, finally able to find the strength to escape them.

Receiving only welcoming smiles and nods at his appearance, Arillion had moved over to join in the celebrations. Sitting in the shadows, it had taken a long while for his host to realise that Arillion was even there and rising from his seat, beside a raucous Agris Varen, Kaspen Shale had wandered over to him. With a grunt that hinted at his indulgence, the wayfarer had sat down beside him.

Without a word, Kaspen had passed him a flagon of mead. Nodding his thanks, Arillion had sipped at the honeyed liquid, marvelling at its taste and aware of his sudden eagerness for more.

For a time, they had sat in contemplative silence, both watching the dancers weaving and whirling before them to the swift, rousing string of Tomlin's fiddle and song.

"Well?" Arillion had finally asked, cocking a curious eye at his host.

Sipping at his horn of mead, the tall wayfarer had turned from the merriment, the fire aglow on his face, the writhing flames bright in his shadowy eyes.

Kaspen had sighed, shaking his head. "Lady Byron gave a rousing speech today, her words igniting the flames of defiance we shall need, greater than any we could have hoped for."

Arillion had sipped at his mead, curling his lips into a subtle smile.

Head before heart...

"The coin we are spreading about the taverns and streets have offered up some news this day, also," the wayfarer continued. Playing reluctantly with the gold earring dangling from his left lobe, his face had fallen somewhat, leaving Arillion's pulse to stir uneasily.

When Arillion had glared at him, Kaspen Shale had dropped his hand to his lap, shaking his head sadly.

"I'm sorry to say this, swordsman," he began, "but the young girl you saved in Greywood is also dead."

Arillion blinked himself back to the present, looking at the empty space beside him, full, even now, with the words of the vague account of what had happened to her. Even now, his chest knotted with sadness, his throat thick with regret. He shook his head angrily and, much to his surprise, managed to clench both of his fists.

If only I hadn't slipped in the mountains...

Aware his emotions and his clarity were being clouded by the mead coursing through his veins, the assassin allowed himself a moment of weakness.

He *had* slipped and nothing was ever going to change that. There was no point wondering had he not, how things in Highwater would have turned out. How quickly he would have uncovered the spy.

The spy?

Kaspen's men had finally managed to find him some hope. The name *Teal* meant nothing to Arillion and, had this mysterious man been anyone of note on the streets, he would have already known of him. Granted it had been a couple of winters since he had been in the city, but still, he found it hard to imagine that someone could have risen to such prominence without him, or his contacts, having known. But at least they had a name now and plans were under way to draw this man to a meeting in the lower reaches of the city. If this Teal's thirst for coin was as great as suggested, then they should not have too much trouble.

Before Arillion found himself drowning in pointless musings about Morgan Belle's fate again, he found himself thinking about Karlina.

Bitterly, Arillion lost himself to the image of the freckled redhead, her impish, infectious smile and her refreshing strength of character, despite the cards life had seemingly dealt her. Closing his eyes, the assassin let out a heavy sigh.

It would have been better to leave her to the outlaws, Arillion thought, shaking his head free of his rising sorrow.

Around him, the dancing became more frenetic, more lively as the passions increased and the mead flowed, but Arillion sank deeper into his thoughts, hearing nothing, focussing only on the tragedy of her murder, of the implications, once more, of what Alion's Byron's death meant for Cassana.

For the first time in some days, Arillion lost himself to his worry. She was, it appeared, in even more danger now than she had ever been. Her father was dead, she too would have been, had it not, it was rumoured, been for Karlina's fateful intervention. Left alone, without her father's guidance, how could Cassana become the woman Arillion believed she could one day be?

His honeyed throat filled with bile as he thought of the assassin, of the description Cassana had given to the crowds that day outside the keep.

"...a Valian woman with a scar on her face."

Despite the huge fire, Arillion felt the chill of the past sweep through his body and heard all of those bleak, buried memories clamour for his attention again.

Growling, Arillion reached again for his tankard and distracted himself by watching the dancers. Banishing the images of her beautifully cold face, the assassin lost himself to the frivolity writhing before him.

As he watched, the pounding music coursed through him, the fiddle screaming, rising faster through the chords, sweeping up all that still sat and listened into its embrace.

A sea of bodies swirled and writhed to the tune, drawing all under its spell, stirring Arillion's excitement and passions, forcing him through his pain to rise.

And then she was there.

Arillion saw Lia, as the dancers seemingly parted for her. Dressed in a flowing skirt and silken blouse that showed more than it covered, the beautiful wayfarer stood in place, her face hidden by the masses of ringlets tumbling about her bare shoulders. As Arillion watched, she danced where she stood, her body twisting with mesmeric moves, as she weaved and twisted her hands above her head. Swirling silks flashed from her wrists as she writhed and spun alluringly, her eyes bright from the fire, her body filling with her desire as she was seduced by the rhythm of the music and sucked in all who were watching her.

Arillion stood watching, his heart thundering in his chest, his own desires rising up through the music as Lia's beauty bewitched him.

As Tomlin's fiddle died for dramatic effect and the dancers stopped, Lia dropped her arms slowly to her side, caressing her body as they fell.

With her breath lost in her heaving breast, she licked her full lips slowly, lingeringly, and a hungry, passionate smile flashed across her face.

The fiddle flared up again and the sea of bodies became swept up once more.

As Lia started to spin slowly towards him, Arillion saw a different face each time she turned. First Cassana, then Lia, then Cassana again and then A...

Arillion grimaced, running his good hand over his stubbled chin as he fought with himself and his rising needs.

"Getting old," he sighed finally, shaking his head.

With a rueful, apologetic grin, Arillion turned away from the beautiful wayfarer and limped back to his wagon, taking his resolve and his desires with him.

It was near midnight by the time Lucien Varl made his way back through the east wing of the high duke's keep to his quarters. Following the secret meeting, the captain had made his way down into the city, to find out first-hand what was going on, but returning home some hours later with only the storms for company and the thunder to answer his questions.

All was quiet on the streets in Karick. The city was

slumbering, sheltering from the storms and awaiting the chaos that would return the next day. Only the hardy or foolish were abroad and, having stopped in one of his favourite taverns along the way, his frustrations only increased. He had met with several of his men, loyal to him, well-liked by him. Despite their warm, hearty greetings and offers of ale, they had nothing to tell, or had little they were willing to part with.

Lucien was no fool! He saw the guarded looks they shared as he probed them for news, noting their fear as much as their worry, as he nodded in regretful understanding.

Leaving coins to help dull their shame, he left them alone and made his way home. *Home*?

When it seemed that High Duke Stromn could not do without his services, some seven winters ago, he had left his family home, just off the Valian Mile, to take up residence in the keep. Leaving his mother alone with her embroidery and her memories, the ambitious, dutiful young captain had made a new life for himself in the keep.

Banishing the childhood memories away before they could come flooding back, he reached out and slipped his key in the lock. Glancing about the empty, stone hallway, he turned the key, entranced by a nearby torch that rallied in a chill breeze and danced hypnotically in its iron bracket. Glad that the servants had remembered, for once, to light his way home for him, he pushed his way into the chambers beyond.

It was dark inside. His late return had meant that he had not lit a large candle, earlier that evening, to welcome him home. Closing his eyes, Lucien allowed his senses to gather for a time, before taking four steps to his left, towards the table he knew was there. As he fumbled for the tinder and flint, he felt the air in the room shift subtly and stopped worriedly.

The silence in the room was strange, somehow, and as

he listened to it, he became uneasy. After a time of uncertainty, he began to relax, and his searching fingers closed about the cold tinderbox. Turning, he faced the room, allowing the first few strikes to light the dark briefly, revealing phantom images of his lounge and the dining table, where a cold candle waited for him to bring it back to life. He approached slowly, not wanting to stumble in the dark, and he struck the flint on steel again.

As the room lit up, several shapes appeared from the shadows, rushing at him as he stood trapped by his shock. They came silently for him and as he dropped the tinderbox, reaching for the Valian Longsword at his side, something slammed into him, bearing him to the ground. With the wind ripped from his lungs, he crunched an elbow into the weight on top of him and was rewarded with contact and a dull grunt of pain.

Growling angrily, Lucien struggled free, his eyes sensing, rather than seeing, the other assailants coming for him.

With a cry, he was free and as he rose up, dragging his sword into his hand, something struck him in the side of the head. The shadows exploded with sparkling silver light and as he recoiled, he heard movement behind him.

"Too slow," a voice hissed in his ear.

Darkness returned...

One moment Henry Farrington was flying to safety, the next he was crashing heavily onto the road, his fall crushing the breath from his body. Bruised and winded, he rolled onto his side and tried to find the strength to move. As his senses returned, he could hear the sounds of battle joined about him, could see the rearing horses and the dark cloaked shapes that ran amongst them.

Cursing, Farrington spied his sword, where it lay in the mud and crawled slowly towards it. As his fingers slipped about the hilt, he saw his mount free itself from the rope that had plucked him from his saddle. As Tempest reared up, scattering several attackers with warning hooves, Farrington rose up sluggishly.

A cloaked assailant came at him, long blade raised and flickering in the dying torchlight. Turning the attack aside easily, Farrington ran one shoulder into the assassin's throat and as the man recoiled back, he cut him down with a deft slash to the belly.

With his blood raging now, but his anger tempered by his years of training, Lord Farrington spun, as another attacker came up behind him. As the lord of the South Vales cut the hand from his adversary, then dealt a wicked deathblow to the man's face, he caught glimpses of his men, surrounded and outnumbered by many assailants. Growling, blood running down his face, Farrington strode forward and then stopped, as a blow took him in the back, an arrow piercing his reinforced riding leathers. Grunting in pain, Farrington turned to find the archer as he reached vainly for the shaft that was deep between his shoulder blades. As he made for the retreating archer, he was struck from behind again. A second arrow dropped him to his knees and the sword slipped reluctantly from his hand.

The sounds of battle surged about him as the archers turned their attentions to those who still fought. In the ensuing chaos, Farrington crawled away towards the tree line, each pull through the mud wracked by fiery agony, but filled with the desperation of one who did not want to die this night.

With the screams of the fighting and dying echoing behind him and his nostrils filled by the rank smell of rotting leaves, Lord Farrington crawled away through the mud towards the safety of the trees. Grimacing, he tore at the land with desperate, clawing fingers, hauling himself over the rough muddied ground towards the distant sanctuary of the woodland. He was almost there when he heard the slow, careful splash of a pursuer following him through the mud.

"And where do you think you are going?" a rich, feminine voice enquired.

Grabbing Henry Farrington roughly by the hair, the Kestrel yanked his head back and drew her crescent blade deep across his throat.

CHAPTER NINETEEN

...no matter the cost

Elion Leigh dealt Dekan Ardent a nervous look as Erith Taye led them along a wide, carpeted corridor, bright with still lamplight. Ahead, they could see two guards, flanking a high pair of double doors, framed by ornate carvings that depicted some sort of hunting scene, the story of which Elion could not quite make out. As they reached the guards, Elion's chest was hammering wildly from his rising fear. Once they crossed that threshold, there would be no turning back from this path.

They had waited for the better part of the evening, long into the night, if truth be told, their hours slipping tediously away in the quiet of some quarters that had been offered to them. Left for many hours before their summons, Elion and the mayor had discussed at length the options that Lady Byron could realistically offer them? Eventually, however, when they began to chew over the same worries and misgivings of their venture, they slipped away into their own reflective silence and focused on what had passed, not what was to follow.

In that time, as promised, Mayor Ardent's wound had

been cleansed and dressed in fresh poultices and bandages by a young, shy woman with sunshine tresses, who had kept quiet for the better part of her visit, offering only shy replies when spoken to.

After she had gone, two servants had arrived, offering hot baths for them both, hinting further that they may have to wait some hours for an audience with Lady Byron. Elion Leigh had gladly accepted the kind offer, but the mayor had declined, preferring some solitude for his troubled thoughts.

An hour later, Elion was relaxing in a brass tub of steaming hot, rose-scented water, trying to ease his guilty thoughts about his comrades, trying to find warmth and shelter in the cold night outside the city.

After his bath, his aches soothed and his cramping muscles content for a time, Elion had stood at a mirror, staring at the stranger that looked back at him. He was startled by the apparition before him, the flashing blue eyes haunted and ringed by dark circles, each new line on the face tell of a horror witnessed or a reminder of yet another sleepless night haunted by anxiety.

Turning away, Elion had reached for the nearby razor, keen to restore some youth to his face, then hesitated. Bitter images of his dealings in Eastbury with Gardan, memories of what Elissen had overheard in the woodshed there flooded his mind and, with a wince, Elion had run a hand over his thickening beard.

He was a marked man now and, had he allowed Elissen to swing from a noose, would probably also be a dead one. Elion had sighed, painfully aware that if Gardan already knew that he still lived, he would also be branded a traitor, a conspirator who dealt with outlaws and supported Reven sympathisers.

Better to keep the beard, he had thought nervously, trying to steady his trembling hand.

Erith Taye nodded to the two guards, who stiffened

with respect as they approached them. Turning, he brought Elion back to the present, with a soft request for them to remain outside. Without waiting for a reply from his charges, the soldier turned and knocked firmly on the door. Moments later, he slipped into the room beyond and closed the door behind him.

Dekan Ardent leaned in close. "I'll lead for us, my young friend," the mayor whispered. "Once I have hopefully had my say, I shall hand the reins over to you for your tale. Stay strong, stay to the truth and all will be well."

Elion nodded dumbly, his head swimming with a maelstrom of possibilities of what the truth may actually bring for them.

Before he could grasp hold of a sensible thought, Erith was back.

"Lady Byron will see you now," he said without offering them a smile.

Cassana was weary. Weary beyond words, exhausted far beyond any emotion she could feel. She looked up from her lap, where she clutched at an empty wine goblet and had been seeking her thoughts there for a time, as her guests entered. She studied them intently.

"My Lady Byron, may I introduce Mayor Ardent of Havensdale and Captain Elion Leigh of Carwell."

Erith Taye motioned them forward into the Byron family lounge with a sweeping arm and then stepped back towards the door to await his orders.

Cassana put her empty goblet down on the reading table beside her chair and rose up sluggishly. Trying to find some last reserve of strength for what was to follow, she offered her guests a smile, seeing the look of worry that flashed in the eyes of the two men before her as they noted others present in the room.

Drawing in a breath, Cassana turned to the woman

who sat regally on a divan, away to her left and was studying the newcomers intently with her bright, amber eyes.

"Lysette?" she said falteringly, drawing her friend's attention to her.

Lysette Astien, her dearest of friends had *finally* arrived in Highwater two days before the funerals. Trapped by her own duties in her father's absence and much to her consternation, she had been unable to come to her friend's side until then.

Upon her arrival, Lysette had quickly set about trying to alleviate the worry and stress her dearest friend was under, sharing deeply in her sorrow, but bringing smiles to her face with her ready wit when no other could.

For Cassana, Lysette had been the strength she needed for her speech, had been her guiding, strong hand for the funeral and the lonely hours leading up to it.

"My lady?" Lysette enquired, her pale brow knitting together with only the subtlest hint of imperfection.

Cassana offered her an apologetic smile and crossed to her friend, who rose gracefully and took her hands.

"I cannot thank you enough for your love and support this day," Cassana said softly, so only her friend could hear. "But I would ask that you retire for the evening, so that I might talk to these gentlemen alone."

If her friend was upset, she hid it well and offered only a dazzling smile and kisses to both of Cassana's cheeks.

As they parted, Lysette gathered up her dignity and swept a dark silken shawl about her shoulders.

"Until tomorrow, my love," Lysette said, offering Cassana and her guests a slow curtsey.

Cassana turned and looked to the grand fireplace, where Shadow stretched out on the giant bearskin before the roaring hearth. Edren sat near to the hound, his attention distracted by the dancing flames and the old dog's rumbling snores.

"Edren," Cassana called out gently. "Would you please see Lady Astien to her quarters for me?"

Edren Bay rose swiftly, nodding his accord, but his eyes narrowed with annoyance at being dismissed. He crossed hurriedly to his charge's side and offered her his arm gallantly.

"My lady," he smiled, though his words carried less warmth.

Lysette took his arm and together they bade goodnight to those present in the room as they departed reluctantly.

Elion Leigh watched the exchange, noting the look on the man's flushed face. He had a sullen look about him this night and was clearly upset, but managed, despite the day that had been and the hour that it was, to rein in his frustrations.

Elion's attention was drawn to the woman as she departed and he felt his throat tighten as she regarded him with her bright, alluring eyes.

She was like a statue, stony pale and yet beautifully captured, her face free of lines and graced only with the blessing of the Lady. Taller than Lady Byron, she was dressed in a simple, long, flowing black dress, that rose up under her slim throat and was edged by pearls. Her bare arms were slim, also, her left wrist bearing jewels to match those at her throat.

Her hair was golden, cascading about her shoulders in wild, bright ringlets that caught the hues from the fire. To Elion, such a lady should not have worn such unkempt hair and he guessed it freed now, perhaps, from the style she would have worn earlier that day for the funeral.

As she swept by them, Elion saw her smile, but her face was stained with the perceived pinch of haughtiness that many of her wealth and status often radiated. Elion had met many ladies of such note in Carwell, when he hid in his corner in the mess. He had spent many an hour observing their behaviour, as they courted would-be suitors, revelling in the attentions from those of rank and status who fawned drunkenly over them.

Elion could tell that Lady Astien enjoyed the affect her beauty had on those about her and he politely, yet pointedly turned his head away from her. Her escort met his gaze briefly, but Elion could not tell anything of the man from his guarded, yet somewhat curious expression.

Lady Byron also dismissed Erith Taye and as the doors closed quietly behind him, Elion could see the relief on her weary face. She came forward then and tilted her head to her right, where William Bay nursed a goblet of wine.

"Gentlemen," she greeted, her voice clear and full of strength again. "I apologise for the lateness of the hour..."

Dekan Ardent strode forward and took Cassana's hands gently in his own.

"From the depths of my heart, Lady Byron, I offer you my deepest sympathy," he said, struggling with his own grief. "Your father was a dear friend of mine and I am only sorry that news of his death did not reach me sooner."

Elion saw Lady Byron's face harden as her defences came up again. She accepted the mayor's kind words with a grateful nod of her head.

"I wish circumstances were better for our reunion," Cassana said sadly. "I am only sorry that we did not have the fortune to meet when I was in Havensdale. William tells me the last time I was in your company I was a young girl with too much anger in my veins to pay any attention to those I met."

Dekan cast his mind back to the day in Alion Byron's study, all those years ago now, when the young firebrand that was the lord of Highwater's daughter had received a furious scolding for setting fire to a cat's tail to see how fast it could run.

Releasing the mayor's hands with a bitter smile, Cassana stepped back, offering her guests a seat and wine. Positioning himself on the divan, still warm from its previous occupant, Elion accepted a goblet of wine from William Bay, who offered him a courteous nod before returning to his chair.

Dekan Ardent did not accept the offer and when Lady Byron was seated again, he took up the waning momentum of the day.

"I would presume that William has already told you of our reason for coming to you this day, my lady and I beg your forgiveness for the timing."

Cassana held up a slender hand to placate his apologies and as she sat forward, he could see her eyes narrow angrily.

"William has told me, Dekan," she whispered, shaking her head sadly. "I cannot believe what has happened to you, to the people of Havensdale and to my dear friend Fawn. Be assured that Highwater will not take this belligerence lightly."

She glanced away to the fire, losing herself for a time, before William Bay cleared his throat. Rising stiffly, his goblet still in one hand, her advisor wandered to the fire, drawing his dark robes about his frame with his free hand to ward away an unseen chill.

"Sadly, my lady, I can." William muttered. "Gardan is a ruthless, if you permit, bastard. He and his lord are well known for their methods, for their hard-lined approach to the law and the politics that govern this land."

Dekan Ardent nodded. "I must agree with William, my lady. When Gardan came to Havensdale with his claims, he would not waste time with Highwater, would not come to William, our Justicar here in the north, and seek his justice there."

William turned, scowling. "The man will do anything he can to get his way, even if it means war with the north."

Cassana stayed any further words with a raised hand. "Gentlemen, please," she said, her face weary. "I understand your anger, your urgency, but before we decide on what has happened, what we must do, I would hear what Captain Leigh has to say."

All heads turned to Elion and he shifted uncomfortably under their gaze. As Lady Byron nodded for him to proceed, Elion drained his glass for courage and then, as best he could, recounted his tale. At first, he lost himself to the raid on Eastbury, of the horrors visited upon its' inhabitants and of his patrol's pursuit northwards. He did not see the looks on those gathered close as he spoke, seeing only the past and feeling, once again, the emotions of all he and his comrades had been through since then.

Cassana watched the captain as he spoke, her face becoming more horrified as he journeyed deeper into his recount. She felt the familiar chill of helplessness steal up her arms and neck, began to feel the tightness in her chest, as her worry took hold at his words. When Elion came to the part of his tale about Gardan's treachery, of his seeming collusion with the raiders, she let out a strangled gasp, looking urgently for William's face and counsel.

"I cannot believe what I am hearing?" she gasped, shaking her head. *How can this be true*? "You are telling us that Commander Gardan, the confidant and general of Lord Carwell's armies was in league with the raiders, knew of their attacks... and would kill brave Valian citizens to keep it so?"

Elion blinked twice. Even to him it sounded utterly preposterous. He attempted to clear his doubts from his throat, but when he replied his words were stretched thickly over his nerves.

"Yes, Lady Byron. As ridiculous as it sounds, I believe the girl to be telling the truth, despite her need for revenge."

Cassana sent a pleading look to William as she rose up and took her glass and thoughts to stand by the fireplace. Shadow raised a sleepy head as she approached and snorted in greeting.

William wrung his worry through his hands and shook his head. "For many years Carwell and his supporters have probed and tested the high duke's desire for lasting peace, hoping for a time when they could find an excuse to change his mind," William paused and licked his lips, "I believe their chance has finally arrived."

Elion looked to Dekan Ardent, who met his fearful gaze and nodded his agreement. All heads then turned to the young woman, who stood staring into the flames of the roaring fire and sipped thoughtfully at her wine.

"The truth often travels more slowly than a lie," she began, turning to them, "so before we discuss what must be done, what path we are forced to take, I should tell you what may not have yet reached your ears." She continued, ignoring the looks that Dekan and Elion traded. "My father and the high duke were in the process of discussing plans to trade peacefully with the Reven, an agreement which, if supported by the council, would have potentially ensured many years of peace and prosperity for the nations on *both* sides of the Great Divide.

On my way to the council, in my father's stead, I survived a kidnap attempt, as you already know Dekan. Having listened to my speech today, although now I hear it was *somehow* already common knowledge in Karick, you will also know that it was Reven who attacked me."

Elion dealt the mayor another look and could see that this last news was just as shocking to him.

Cassana used their shock to press on. "As it is very

late, I shall spare you the finer details of what followed by saying that after Fawn Ardent and her men guided me safely to the capital, my life was put in even greater danger. Drugged in my room by a woman, Madam Grey, I was kept from seeing the high duke by a threat that had been made against the council. My life was again put in danger, but, and I feel this could serve us well in the days to come, I was rescued from the high duke's keep and spirited to safety before those behind this rising threat in the Vales could use me as leverage against my... father.

My allies, whom I have sworn to keep anonymous, ensured my safe return northwards... though the danger had not yet passed. Again, my companions and I were attacked whilst travelling through the Great Divide, by a substantial band of Valian, not Reven, mercenaries. I survived... but my protector did not."

Whilst their guests digested the information, their faces taut with horror, William rose and took up the momentum.

"It appears that whoever was behind these initial threats against the council are now also behind the attacks that are happening across the Four Vales. There can be no coincidence that hatred is being stirred up against any of Reven heritage living this side of the mountains. The attempted murder of Lord Carwell, the attacks on Eastbury and Havensdale, with many others following, all point towards, I am afraid to say, one thing..."

Dekan Ardent recovered from his shock. "And what is that?"

Cassana turned from the fire, her cheeks burning from the heat, or perhaps her anger.

"That my father was right," she glowered. "He believed that all of this has been orchestrated to send the Valian people to war. Think on it a moment! My attempted kidnap, twice, to use me, no doubt as a pawn against my father. Highwater is the gateway to the Reven

Lands, a valuable staging post for any potential invasion... but my father was a man of peace and would have never agreed to such a course."

But now he is dead... Elion concluded sadly.

As if reading his thoughts, Cassana fixed her steely gaze on the captain, but her face softened into a smile.

"With your testimony today, Captain Leigh and news of what has happened in Havensdale," she began, "we know that my father was right. What is even clearer to me now is that we have a clue as to who may well be behind it all."

Elion swallowed hard and the answer rang true in his ears as William Bay uttered it.

"Carwell?"

Cassana nodded, chewing her bottom lip nervously as she sifted through her tumbling thoughts for the pieces of the puzzle that still eluded her, dare she look for them.

"I cannot believe that Commander Gardan would be acting out of his own interests. He lacks the subtlety, so I am led to believe, to orchestrate such a deep-rooted, carefully thought out plan. Loyal to Lord Carwell, Gardan must be taking his orders from others. Who better than the ruthless steward of the East Vales, whose man, Lord Astien writes, has already started rounding up Reven citizens and *questioning* them."

Lady Byron, sent an apologetic look towards Elion, who twisted his empty goblet in his shaking hands nervously.

"Forgive me, Captain Leigh," Cassana said, crossing to him and placing a gentle hand on his shoulder. "I did not mean to besmirch your honour by casting such aspersions, but the evidence is starting to become quite compelling."

Elion shook his head sadly. "I am a loyal citizen of Carwell, my lady, but I fear that I am no longer her captain."

Cassana met his glistening eyes as he looked up at her and she smiled again. "From what you have told me, I fear that may be so. But, Elion, should you ever wish it, Highwater would always welcome an honourable captain to protect her."

Elion rose and took Cassana's hand, kissing it lightly. He looked up his arm at her, trembling subtly under her scrutiny and smiled. "You honour me, Lady Byron and I shall certainly consider such a generous offer."

William Bay flicked a conspiratorial look at the mayor of Havensdale and they shared a wink as Elion released Lady Byron's hand and rose.

Cassana swept her gaze about the three men and swallowed hard.

"So gentlemen," she began falteringly. "We must now decide on what must be done. If Carwell and his allies in the capital are trying to undermine the high duke with this apparent *Reven* uprising, we must find the evidence we need to prove otherwise.

It is far too dangerous for me to risk retuning to Karick in person, so in the morning, I shall send a letter to the high duke, detailing all of your claims – of the girl from Eastbury's testimony, of the attack on Havensdale and Gardan's false claims. My letter will seek just reparation for Gardan's actions and demand that he be brought to trial for his actions and part in the attacks."

Both Elion Leigh and Dekan Ardent tilted their heads in thanks as William Bay drained his wine in one pull and rose up swiftly.

"Evidence will be hard to come by," William warned. "It will be dangerous, as we may be forced to obtain confessions from those involved..."

Cassana turned her head, regarding her friend darkly. "Then so be it! A Valian woman murdered my father, the high duke's most trusted ally – a most timely attack, do you not think? But who ordered his death? I fear we may never find out, but there is a spy in Highwater and we must root him or her out first, before we can even begin to unravel any of this."

William nodded his agreement. "My thoughts entirely, my lady. Once we have the spy, we may well find out who is behind much of this, or at least obtain the information we need to find them."

Dekan Ardent nodded. "In the meantime, I shall return to Havensdale in the morning, Lady Byron. If war is coming, it may well come to Havensdale first. I need to be with my daughter, a daughter I hasten to add, who wanted to bring this terrible news to you herself."

Genuine warmth flooded Cassana's face with a beautiful smile. "I would dearly love to see Fawn again, Dekan and rest assured I will do all that I can to refute these ridiculous accusations. I can see in your eyes you think our reunion a bad idea?"

The mayor of Havensdale nodded. "Sadly, I do, my lady. You are both important pieces in this game and I would not want to place you both together on the board at this time."

Cassana looked away, twisting a lock of hair about her left forefinger. "I fear you are right, sir," she sighed wistfully. "I will send a company of men to Havensdale in the coming days, to help you bolster your defences and strengthen your numbers."

"Your lady is most kind," Dekan accepted, bowing deeply. He straightened, fishing through his leather tunic to pull out the sealed letter he had been asked to deliver. "In return, I have a gift for you."

Taking the letter, Cassana turned it in her hands, staring at the neat, elegant handwriting that bore only her first name and offered no clues as to the writer. She looked up questioningly.

"From an old friend," the mayor said, his eyes hooded.

Cassana thanked him and turned to the young man from Carwell, casting more than a passing, appreciative eye over his tired, yet handsome face.

"And what of you now, Elion Leigh?" she asked. "Will you seek your answers elsewhere, now that Highwater knows your tale and, I hope, is counted your friend?"

Elion bobbed his head. "Yes, Lady Byron. I will keep Elissen safe, until we can all be sure of a fair trial in Karick. Until that time comes, I will seek further information on the attacks, of Gardan's involvement and the wider implications. I shall gather the allies we will need to aid us in the coming struggle, should it turn into a fight."

"Where will you go?" Cassana asked him worriedly.

"I will travel to Greywood Forest for my allies, lady," Elion said, his eyes bright with determination. "They may be wanted men, but their word is true and I believe they may be of great use to us."

William Bay looked sceptical, but dared to ask. "And your information?"

Elion turned to him.

"I will go to Carwell for my answers."

"Thank you, sir," Lady Astien said, smiling as Edren escorted her to the door of her chambers. She slid from his arm and moved away slowly. Placing her hand on the wood, she turned to look over her shoulder, a sultry look dancing in her eyes.

"Are you coming in tonight?"

Edren nodded, though his eagerness was absent this time. He watched her as she unlocked the door, his dark eyes ranging over her slender curves, hidden away beneath her mourning dress, but waiting there for him again, nonetheless, should he wish to take her.

With the door open, she led him into her elegant

quarters, its paintings and tapestries lost to the shadows, the four-poster bed awaiting them in the centre of the room. Servants had lit candles and the light of the room swirled gently from a rushing of air.

Lysette wandered towards the bed, her hips swinging extravagantly as she walked. Swallowing hard, Edren stood in the doorway watching, his heart fighting against his rising desire.

"Close the door," Lysette commanded and before he could help himself, Edren obeyed. With the draught repelled, Lysette pulled her shawl from her shoulders and dropped it on the bed.

"Some wine, I think," she said, moving over to a cabinet to fetch some glasses.

Edren shook his head. "Not for me, we should talk about what just happened."

"Uh huh," Lysette agreed, ignoring his request and filling a glass for him. Putting the bottle down, she crossed over to him and placed the glass in his hands.

"I need to find out what they wanted," Edren said hurriedly, his features pinched from worry. "This could mean trouble for us, it–,"

Lysette silenced his ramblings with a slender finger and laughed, her voice sympathetically mocking. "Don't worry about it, Edren, I'll find out all we need to know tomorrow. Cassana's so happy to see me, she can't help but tell me everything. How else did I know that you were not talking to her?"

Edren recoiled, his face clouding angrily. "Do not mock me, woman. You need me more than I need you. It has been hard for me, these last few days. I knew the day would come, when Alion would be killed, but it does not mean that it has not affected me."

Lysette laughed and purred as she slid an arm about his neck and drew him close. "Oh, my lover, of course I understand. You have grown up here. Alion Byron was like an uncle to you. It's only natural that you would have these feelings... and yet, you still opened the door for the Brotherhood, still allowed our assassin into the keep to kill him."

She felt him tense and held on tightly to him, her breath hot on his neck.

"I did," Edren hissed, pulling back to hold her gaze. "And I would do it again."

"Good," Lysette replied, sipping at her wine. "If she does not stand aside when the time comes, you may need to."

Edren looked away, his heart faltering, his head roaring. Lysette watched him for a time, then pulled away.

"Worry not about such things, Edren," she said softly. "The pendulum is in motion and there is nothing we can do to stop it now. Soon, you will be the lord of Highwater and I, should you wish it, will be your confidant, your mistress and who knows, perhaps one day, even more."

Edren looked at her, seeing the ambition burning in her eyes, rising and falling rapidly in her chest. He desired and yet hated her, all at the same time.

Edren knew what she was, had allowed her to seduce him all those years ago with the promise of riches beyond his wildest dreams and more power than he could ever hope to wield. He knew all of this and yet he had still succumbed to her charms. She had been the driving force behind the plans to use Cassana as a pawn, the one who had seduced Elan and found out when they would be travelling. Edren had then suggested a *safer* route to his friend and with the Reven mercenaries in place they had waited eagerly for the terrible news to arrive.

Edren drained his glass thoughtfully and licked his lips. "We need to let the chancellor know that the mayor of Havensdale has been here... and of this captain of Carwell. Gardan will be very interested to hear about him, I am sure."

Lysette moved away from him and he watched her walk to the bed. As she reached there, the dress slipped from her shoulders and slid down her body to pool at her ankles.

"There will be time for talk later," she said huskily and with a groan, Edren Bay threw his empty glass to the floor and moved towards her.

Tonight he desired her. Tomorrow, he would hate her all over again.

CHAPTER TWENTY

The Return

Khadazin was roused from his sleep by a gentle hand that rescued him from his rising nightmare. Fitful at first, the Redani had slept deeply through the cold night, his weariness chasing him towards dawn and yet another lonely vigil. As his restless mind began to work, he had found himself in a forest, surrounded by tall, silent trees that appeared to close about him. Unnerved, Khadazin had stood there, clenching both of his fists to ward away the fear tearing at him... and then, through the shadows, he had seen a hooded figure, walking slowly away from him, dark robes drawn tightly about a thin frame.

"Wait!" he had called out, his deep voice echoing through the silence. Khadazin had tried to run after the figure, not wishing to be alone in this dark place, but each time he thought he was drawing near to the stranger, he would lose sight of him or her again behind a tree, only to then see the cowled figure reappear, somewhere else in the distance.

With his frustrations building, the stonemason had begun to run recklessly through the forest, always far away from the mysterious stranger, never within easy reach.

"You'll have to try harder than that," the chancellor's voice hissed behind him.

"Khadazin?" Brother Markus enquired softly, his face hidden in the shadows of a grey dawn light that barely lit the Redani's chamber. "You were dreaming..."

Groaning, Khadazin raised himself up on one elbow and ran his huge hand across his broad face, scratching his thick beard.

"Forgive me, brother," Khadazin yawned deeply, sitting up on his cot, keenly aware that he no longer had both hands now he was awake. "Another bad dream, I'm afraid."

The monk stepped away, his features, already scarred, marring further from his concern. He warmed his cold hands within the folds of his robes and nodded his hooded head.

Since Sam's death, five days past now, both James and Khadazin had struggled to cope with the loss. After the leper's burial, high on the bluffs along the coastline to the west, the Redani and his charge had spent their time consoling each other, lost to any real sense of purpose, devoid of any real hope.

James, naturally, was beside himself with grief. He was a young lad, one who had witnessed far too much in his young life already, suffering greatly for his love of his father and because of the man they had chosen to protect them.

Not wishing to go on, James could not come to terms with his father's passing. Having always believed that his father would get better, that the monks at the monastery would be able to save him, James was struggling with the knowledge that the advancement of Sam's condition was beyond even the Lady's help and that his father had only come there to die.

Without Khadazin, Markus wondered how the lad would have coped.

"What is it, brother?" Khadazin asked, rousing himself further with an arching stretch of his broad back.

Snapping from his thoughts, the monk raised a hand in apology. "Forgive me, Redani," he said quietly. "I fear I am still in my bed – you have visitors."

Khadazin's eyes glittered in the dark, chasing the monk's averted gaze for a more detailed explanation. There was warmth in his words, but they were tainted by an underlying worry.

"The young huntress has returned," Brother Markus smiled reassuringly.

He stepped back as the Redani leapt from his bed, his huge, naked frame almost filling the room.

"Khadazin," Tania cried out in relief, rousing herself from where she leant wearily against the side of the wagon that had once been Sam and James' home. The two men standing beside her watched the Redani's arrival silently, sharing a knowing look.

With her features bright with joy and her tousled hair full of a swirling breeze, the huntress ran to the stonemason as he emerged from the infirmary.

"Tania," the Redani cheered, throwing his arms wide and wrapping her in a huge embrace as she gladly jumped into them. Over her head, Khadazin cast a worried look at the girl's two travelling companions and felt his fears flutter restlessly.

Holding each other close, Khadazin and Tania drew strength from one another as they stood in the cold courtyard of the monastery, the sky overhead a morose collage of swirling clouds shaded by the failing night and edged by the rising dawn.

Brother Markus appeared, smiling, as he viewed the scene before him. The girl's return, thank the Lady, was a timely one. Her wilful, feisty nature was the breath of fresh air needed to chase away the clouds hanging over the stonemason's head – clouds that even the winds from the Low Sea could not.

Respectfully, the monk turned away, hurrying to find James and tell him the good news.

"I have missed you," Khadazin said, aware that the girl's presence was already having a calming effect on him. "How was the journey?" He hesitated as he felt her tense. "Is something wrong? Are you alright?"

Tania pulled herself reluctantly from their embrace and she looked up at him, her beautiful face older somehow. Her dark eyes glistened with tears but smouldered away angrily with the young woman that was.

She sniffed and nodded. "I am fine Redani... or at least I will be when you tell me what in the storms is going on?"

Khadazin frowned, his face stiff from the cold morning and an even colder night under furs that barely kept him alive.

He studied Tania's face, noting the hurt, the need there. Khadazin sighed and offered her a smile.

"I owe you that, Tania Drew," he accepted quietly. "At the very least, I owe you that."

A bright smile danced across the girl's face and she nodded her thanks. After a moment's thought, her face twisted. Pulling away, she looked back to her companions.

"Before we talk, Redani, I should introduce you to my friends," she hesitated just long enough to tell the Redani more than he wanted to know. "Your friend sent them with me, to see me safely to you and you safely to him."

Khadazin's heart began to pound, roaring in his ears, clouding his dormant thoughts. He had been waiting for this, from the moment he was set upon by the chancellor's men in the alleyway. Could it be possible that the time for his return to the capital was almost here? His body began to shake at the thought of seeing Savinn Kassaar again. A reunion he had thought many times would never happen.

Whilst Tania was away, Khadazin, with each slow passing day, could feel his desperation rising, the need to return to Karick and exact his vengeance for what they had done to him and Cornelius, despite the obvious dangers such a journey would place him in. It had filled his waking thoughts, plagued his restless dreams and, as his strength returned, the stronger the Redani became, the greater his hunger and desire had become.

Holding his hand, Tania guided him over to the old wayfarer's wagon and introduced the two men to their charge. Khadazin accepted their greetings, the older and somewhat familiar man, the one with an unsettling look about him, offered him a gruff welcome, stating his pleasure to find him almost in one piece, as he offered the stonemason his left hand, swapping quickly to his right. Khadazin was riled by the man's lack of tact as he gripped his clammy hand and found it hard to imagine that a man of Savinn's reputation and standing would entrust his care to such a guardian. As he felt his nerves prick, the Redani accepted the silent nod from the younger, calmer looking man and shook his offered hand readily.

"Cullen and Riyan," the huntress said, a nod indicating each man. "Riyan cannot talk, so don't worry, he's not ignoring you Redani."

The young man nodded and smiled. Khadazin nodded back and then, feeling foolish, he swept his gaze between his designated protectors.

"So what happens now?" Khadazin dared to ask.

Riyan looked to Cullen and the squat man narrowed his eye. "First, you get these limp old virgins to fill our bellies, stonemason. Then, once you and the girl have had your little catch up – we will be off. The boss is keen to have you back as soon as we can… what with things being as they are n'all."

Tania saw Khadazin tense at the oaf's words and swallowed her own distaste. "We'll see you both fed, have no fear."

Before Khadazin could vent his spleen or enquire about what was happening in Karick, she gripped him by one arm and led him hurriedly away. As they retreated, Tania could feel Cullen's eyes on her again and she shuddered.

Khadazin drew the girl close, holding her tightly as her tears fell down her cheeks. The news of Sam's death had been a blow to Tania, as she too had hoped that the brothers of the Hermitage Retreat could have saved him. Saddened by the realisation of what his passing meant for James, Tania's resolve had crumbled before the former stonemason, as they stood on the ramparts of the outer ward, watching the slow arrival of another beautiful day.

"How is James faring?" the huntress dared softly, finally pulling away from Khadazin's embrace.

Khadazin sighed and shook his head. "Not well."

Tania drew in a breath and looked out across the Low Sea, her thoughts drawn away by all that had happened recently. Each time she thought she had found a solution to their dilemma, her memories dragged her back to the fight in the woods and of the men she had killed.

She moaned, shaking in the cold breeze. She desperately needed to get back to her old, mundane life and her woods, but knew it could be quite a while before she was able to. Pulling her cloak tightly about her, Tania studied the small island and listened to the seal colony's haunting wails for a time.

"So Redani," she whispered eventually. "Will you tell me your tale now?"

Khadazin met her needful eyes and nodded. "Yes, Tania – I will."

Sitting on the crenulations, he slowly lost himself to the past, recounting how he and Savinn Kassaar had become friends, of how, when the merchant sought to repay his kindness, he had inadvertently placed him in great danger.

Tania listened to the stonemason's tale, seeing the bitterness that crossed his features as he told her of his costly sleep in the high duke's gardens; of how, when he woke, he overheard the conversation between these mysterious *brothers* and of their plans to kidnap an unsuspecting noblewoman.

Khadazin's tale began to pick up a pace as his anger began to burn fiercely and he recounted his desperate fight in the alley. From there he told Tania of his imprisonment, of his brutal torture at the hands of this mysterious *Brotherhood* and of his friendship with Cornelius Varl.

Tania began to weep, as falteringly, Khadazin told her of their daring escape, of his shame at what they did to the torturer and of Cornelius' death.

"I am so sorry, Khadazin," the young woman said, wiping her eyes. She reached out to touch the stonemason and he smiled sadly.

"Thank you, lady," he replied weakly. Closing his eyes, Khadazin finished off his tale, of how he had buried his friend and then was found, by lucky chance, by James and Kayla in the forest.

Forgetting her sadness, Tania watched Khadazin as his face twisted with remembrance, as he probably started thinking of the other friend he had just lost. It shamed her to think she was being so selfish, wrapped up in her own self-pity at how miserable she felt, how sullied she was from the journey south with Cullen and Riyan. Because of Cullen's attempts at delaying their departure from the village they had stopped off at for supplies, she had seriously underestimated the time it would take to reach the monastery and had been forced to spend another night under the stars with *him*.

"So you have my tale, Tania," Khadazin said, jostling her back to him. "I have spared you only the details of the man I know to be behind the plot to kidnap Lady Byron of Highwater. It is far too dangerous a thing for you to know."

Tania nodded her head in understanding. "Thank you. I cannot begin to comprehend all I have heard, but I can believe what I am hearing. Thank you for placing your trust in me. I realise what it means for you to tell me."

Smiling from obvious relief, Khadazin stood and turned to look out to sea. "I am only sorry I did not tell you before you bore my message for me."

Standing beside him, Tania looked up into his saddened face and dealt him a flashing smile.

"We are in this together, Redani," she stated, her jaw tight with determination. Before Khadazin could respond, tell her that her part in this tale was now done, Tania produced Savinn's letter and placed it in his hand.

"For you, Khadazin Sahr," she said quietly, her words guarded. "I will be down in the courtyard when you have finished."

Turning, Tania hurried away, seeing James appear below her – a bright, thankful smile on his weary features.

Khadazin watched her leave, feeling a cold breeze sweep through him. He waited until he saw the two youngsters embrace, before he turned back to look out across the vast expanse of the Low Sea.

With the sea salt in his nostrils and the breath of a fresh day in his lungs, Khadazin swallowed down his nerves and broke open the black wax seal on the letter with his shaking thumb.

Cullen paced about the courtyard, his impatience showing on his mottled face, his rising anger blazing in his one good eye.

"What's taking him so bloody long?" he riled, casting a look at his silent companion. His anger was not quelled by Riyan's nonchalant shrug of indifference.

With food in their bellies, the morning had slipped slowly away for them both in the rising heat and sunshine of another fine late-summer day. As the monastery came to life and the brothers returned to their fields, their patients and their studies, so did Cullen's desire to be on the road again.

Since the Redani had returned from the ramparts and slipped hastily away into the infirmary, his protectors had not seen or received message from him. They had, just once, seen Tania, as she hurried away from them towards the stables and for a time, Cullen's anger had been replaced by his hunger.

Sighing, Cullen sat on the steps of the wagon and allowed the shade of the eaves to calm his frustration. The boss wanted the stonemason back safely and as soon as possible, but no amount of complaining was going to make him move any faster. And besides, did he really want to upset the Redani before they had even set off? They had several days on the road and he doubted he wanted to stoke the embers of Khadazin's renowned temper.

Cullen scowled and ran a sweaty hand through his filthy beard, still flecked with grease from the fried bacon he had eaten for breakfast. Feeling the soreness in his buttocks from long days in a saddle, he allowed himself to relax for a bit and recover his strength for the journey ahead.

A thought suddenly came to him and he looked over at Riyan, who was watching a blackbird curiously, as it sifted through the straw strewn across the courtyard for any undiscovered tasty morsels.

"I hope the boss has told the Redani in his letter what

is going on in Karick?"

Riyan looked back to him and nodded. He made a few gestures with his hands and Cullen grunted.

"Yes," Cullen said in agreement. He hawked and spat. "I doubt he has, either."

"It seems our time together draws to a close," Brother Markus observed as Khadazin stepped out from under the shaded porch at the rear of the infirmary.

The Redani smiled wryly as the monk turned on his stool, from where he was milking a goat in the small paddock, created naturally by the curtain wall that swept around them.

"I fear so, brother," Khadazin acknowledged, shielding his eyes from the sun and keen to be in the shade that the towering presence of the monastery high above them offered his friend.

"There, girl," Markus whispered soothingly, as he returned to his milking. The goat eyed Khadazin's approach sceptically.

Grabbing a nearby stool from in front of a small pen, the Redani ignored the smell from the pigs wallowing inside and went to sit by the monk. He watched Markus gently work the milk from the goat for a time, before realising that even that task would prove difficult for him now.

Sighing, Khadazin stared at his sandals and wiggled his dusty toes for a while.

"When do you leave?" Markus asked, eyeing him briefly. His pocked face fell somewhat and looking up, Khadazin realised that he too, would be sorry to say goodbye.

"As soon as I can," Khadazin admitted. "My escorts are keen to be away and after the letter I received, I am, also…"

"And yet, my friend," Markus said, turning from his

chores. "I can tell you do not want to go."

The Redani snorted a breath from his flaring nostrils and bobbed his head.

"I have survived, I have endured," Khadazin began falteringly, "and I have regained my strength so that I may have the chance to avenge my friend's death and the wrongs done to me."

Brother Markus studied the Redani's strong, gentle face, noting how well his wounds had healed. Despite all that had happened to him, Khadazin had survived and, as he put it, endured. It was testament to his determination and whilst the monk suspected that the vengeance he sought would not bring him peace, he could not stop him from leaving, no matter how much he wanted to.

"If the Lady wills it, brother, you shall find your destiny and the peace you deserve."

Khadazin put his broad hand on his friend's shoulder, surprised at the muscular frame he felt beneath the habit.

"James is not taking the news well," the Redani admitted. Looking up at the monastery looming above them, he lost his conflicting thoughts to the slow gentle dance of some bickering gulls high above him. "He has only just got Tania back and now he is losing me."

Markus spread his hands across his lap. "James is still in mourning, Khadazin – you all are. He will calm down in time, I am certain of it. It's not as if you won't see him again, is it?"

They shared a knowing look between them, both keenly aware that the path Khadazin had chosen was a dangerous one.

Sighing, Khadazin fished out Savinn's letter. He turned it in his hand thoughtfully for a time, before passing it to the attentive monk.

"I may not return," the Redani whispered sadly. "My friend has written to me with news and none of it is good, I am afraid. Promise me, brother, you will not read it until

I am gone. The news from the north is terrible, there are dark days ahead for all Valian people and, to my utter shame, I realise now I should have taken what I know to the high duke sooner. If I had… if I had not been scared, perhaps none of this would have come to pass."

Brother Markus could see the turmoil on the Redani's face and ignoring the knot of worry in his stomach, he reached out and gripped his friend's hand.

"You have my word, Redani," Markus said, offering a twisted smile.

Khadazin rose slowly. He looked down at the monk, watching him as he slipped the letter into his habit. Offering his hand to him, the Redani hauled the monk to his feet and smiled.

"Look after James and Tania for me," Khadazin asked. "Should I not return, that letter will be of great value to you." He leant in close and whispered a name in the monk's ear.

Markus blinked, his eyes flashing wildly as the Redani stepped away. They shared a nod and without another word, Khadazin turned and strode away.

James was distraught. He followed forlornly behind his giant friend as the Redani shouldered his bedroll and the meagre belongings James had salvaged for him from the old wagon. Following Khadazin reluctantly out into the sunshine, he trailed behind, dragging his feet through the dust and straw.

They had spoken at length about Khadazin's need to return to Karick, despite the danger. Apparently, it was a matter of honour and many people were relying on him now. Not sure what it all meant, James had sulked, withdrawing deeper into his own despair.

"About time, Redani," the short, ugly man with one eye grumbled as they approached the gatehouse. At his side, a younger, friendlier looking man offered them a smile.

"Are these the men who will protect you?" James asked, hurrying to Khadazin's side and looking up at him.

Khadazin nodded, though James suspected it would be his friend who looked after them.

"Let us away," Khadazin said, his voice calm, free of any apprehension or fear.

Riyan came forward and took Khadazin's belongings for him, heading away to the horses tethered outside the settlement, under the shade of the gatehouse.

Nodding his thanks, Khadazin turned and embraced James, feeling the sobs wracking the boy's willowy frame.

"Hurry back," James sniffed and Khadazin nodded, feeling the tears slide down his face.

"I will, James," Khadazin replied, his words choked. "I promise you."

James smiled somewhat. "I am going to miss you, Khadazin. But I will ask father and Kayla to watch over you."

Smiling, the Redani reluctantly released the boy. "I am sure they will," he smiled. As he straightened, he noticed Brother Markus and Tania crossing the courtyard towards them. He frowned when he saw Tania was carrying her bow and knapsack.

Catching the look in his eyes, the beautiful huntress silenced him with a smouldering glare.

"James and I have said our goodbyes, too, Redani," she looked at the boy, who nodded enthusiastically, though he rubbed his red eyes and wiped his nose at the same time.

"She saved us all before, Khad," James stated enthusiastically. "And I will feel much better knowing that she is with you."

"But–," Khadazin began to protest.

Tania headed him off with a dazzling smile. "Not another word, stonemason. I go where I choose and for now, I choose to be at your side."

With his heart pounding nervously, all number of potential scenarios tumbling through his mind, Khadazin looked to Markus for help. Behind him, Cullen sounded his approval, his eye ranging hungrily over the girl's slender curves.

"I can offer guidance only, my friend," the monk smiled, mischief in his eyes. "If the Lady wills it?"

Tania smarted, her hands on her hips. "Yes, she does and she is standing right here!"

Shaking his head, Khadazin nodded reluctantly. He watched, feeling his tears rise again as James and Tania shared a warm embrace. It was as if they were just heading off on a trek, not heading north to become involved in the dangerous game being played out in the capital.

Brother Markus came forward and handed Khadazin his crossbow.

The stonemason shook his head. "No brother, I cannot use it anymore. I shall use the hammer Tania got me from the local mason."

Brother Markus smiled, his marred face filling with something other than serene calm for once.

"I was not always a monk, Khadazin," he stated quietly. "I have fixed a leather pocket under the weapon, so that you can slip your wrist into it. It should allow you to hold the crossbow securely."

Khadazin turned the weapon over, inspecting the pocket. It was true, he could probably hold it, but…

"And I have fitted a crank and handle to the crossbow string. Once it has fired, wind the handle away from you and the string will pull back." The monk pointed out, finishing Khadazin's question for him.

The Redani looked up in astonishment and nodded his thanks dumbly.

"If you have to use it, Redani," Brother Markus said, "and I pray to the Lady you do not. But, it you do, use it well my friend."

Slinging the weapon over his shoulder with the long leather strap that had also been fixed to it, Khadazin nodded and reached out to shake the monk's hand.

"Thank you, my friend," he said, smiling, "for everything."

Folding his hands in his habit, the monk nodded his head graciously and stepped away.

Ruffling James' hair Khadazin turned away from them, looking at Tania. She smiled towards the monk in farewell, before turning her eyes to the Redani.

"Don't say another word," she ordered him, grinning.

Shaking his head, they both turned and followed Cullen out of the courtyard.

As they passed under the gatehouse, Tania reached out to hold the Redani's hand. Gaining his attention with a gentle squeeze she looked up at him, her wide eyes full of determination.

"I'm with you, Khadazin, to the end" she stated simply, then rather sheepishly added, "But I need to stop off in Silver Falls along the way…"

Khadazin turned in his saddle. Tania rode along at his side quietly and followed his gaze as he looked back towards the Hermitage Retreat. The sun was high now in a brilliant blue, cloudless sky. Shielding their eyes, they could just about make out the dark shapes of Brother Markus and James, up on the gatehouse walls. James was waving madly, his voice echoing his farewells.

Tania smiled, feeling her chest tighten. "We will see them again, stonemason."

Khadazin nodded his head and surveyed the beautiful scene before him in wonderment, much as he had done when they had first laid eyes upon it. As before, the walled vineyards swept away to their right, full of robed figures busily working their vines in the heat and the majestic sight of the monastery, perched high on the craggy hilltop, stripped the breath from his lungs. The coastline drew his thoughts away from James for a moment, as Khadazin lost himself in its power, its sheer beauty. *Would he ever witness such a sight again?*

He gritted his teeth, his face stiffening with determination. James had told him before he left that he had gone to see the local mason and stated his desire to learn Khadazin's former trade. Even now, his heart rallied and his chest filled with pride at the boy's declaration. If that was not enough to keep him alive, nothing would be.

"Come on," Cullen growled impatiently.

Sighing, Khadazin waved his hand madly towards the monastery, smiling as he heard James' echoing cheer.

Gripping his reins tightly, Khadazin nudged his mount forward, slipping from the bright sunshine into the shadows of the forest.

CHAPTER TWENTY ONE

Breaking Point

Lucien Varl retched as his lungs reached for a rallying breath and dragged him roughly awake. For a time, as his senses swirled and he choked on the dried blood in his mouth, he had no recollection of who he was and how he came to be there.

Groaning in agony, he searched through the impenetrable darkness, but his head, roaring with pain, drowned out his hearing and he could see or tell nothing of his surroundings.

He suddenly realised he was naked, his body numb and stiff beyond any feeling. Growling, Lucien willed himself to move, then felt the raw, bitter kiss of the manacles that spread his arms wide and hung him, suspended in an abyss of nothingness.

"What in the Storms?" he began then hesitated, as broken, fragmented images of cloaked assailants flashed in his mind.

If they could have, Lucien's shoulders would have slumped, but he was drawn taut between chains that whispered mockingly at him.

Too tired to think about who had attacked him, too badly beaten to attempt a scream for help, Captain Lucien Varl bowed his head in defeat and began to sob.

For what felt like forever, Lucien drifted in and out of sleep, cradled by the cold for a time, then jerked awake on his chains by the distant tell of life. Every once in a while, he was sure he could hear the sound of somebody crying… or was it screaming? He couldn't tell for certain, but the faint, echoing boom of a heavy door suggested that someone was free to come and go as they chose.

As he became accustomed, as best he could, to the terrible sense of helplessness wracking his body, Lucien began to focus on his thoughts. Finally able to hide away from his agony and the terrible cold that bit deep into his flesh, he was able to sift through his confusion and piece together what had happened to him recently.

The last thing he could recall, after his meeting with the Lord's Farrington and Astien, was that he had been set upon in his chambers. That told him a great deal. Their secret meeting must not have been quite as secretive as they had all hoped.

Lucien sent an exasperated breath away into the darkness and shook his head sadly as he wondered on the fate of his cohorts. Were they, too, in such dire straits? Or had the Lady spared them to safety?

A fresh draught somehow stole through the oppressive dark and highlighted briefly the terrible smells that actually resided here. The cold, wet cobbles underfoot were slick with rotting straw and a great deal worse – and the smell of urine and excrement clogged his nose and throat. Lucien gagged on the stale air as the fresh breeze slipped hurriedly away and he hopped from one foot to the other, to try and free himself from the squalor of his unseen surroundings.

It felt as if there were walls close by, his cell no larger

than the reach of his manacled wrists and he was certain, as fresh blood still trickled down his face from the blow to the side of his head, that he had not been moved far from his chambers.

Lucien bowed his head, fighting against the rage that bunched his aching muscles and drew what little strength he had left from his body. He was in the Old Royal Dungeons, deep under the western grounds of the high duke's keep.

Not used for many years, they had remained closed, forgotten and unused when larger dungeons had been built in the west of the ever expanding city, some dozen winters ago now.

Relan Valus' snakelike countenance goaded him in his mind and Lucien banished his enemy with a growl.

"Save your strength for when you need it," Lucien hissed, drawing in a slow, deliberately calming breath.

After a while, he felt himself relax, his raging heart settled by thoughts of his training, the mental exercises taught to him all those years ago to enable him to remain level-headed in battle.

Lucien was wise enough to know that he was still afraid, still furious, but he allowed himself to be fooled for a while, as he focused his thoughts on his survival and the possibility of escape.

Moments later, the foreboding, distant crash of heavy wood on stone rallied his fears again as he heard the purposeful approach of heavily booted feet.

Tongues of flame licked at the edges of Lucien Varl's vision, teasing him with phantom images of his surroundings as the darkness began to steal away into shadows.

As his captors came closer, their feet tramping in unison to the captain's wild heart, Lucien could begin to tell that he was in a small cell, its ceiling low, its walls running with condensation, its floors cluttered by filth, bones and scurrying rats.

Closer still his captors came and their dancing torchlight cast lengthening light into the dark, chasing the shadows away into cobwebbed corners and old, crumbling recesses.

Outside his rusted, barred gaol, Lucien could see only a long wall that stole across his vision towards an archway to his left and a blank wall to his right.

Glancing up, he could see that he was manacled to the ceiling of his cell by chains, bound tightly at his wrists by rough iron that had already cut deeply into them. He tugged frantically at the chains, but the ancient stone was not about to give him his freedom without a fight.

Muffled voices died as his hosts drew near and Lucien returned his gaze to the crumbling archway, drawn by the dancing flames that spread and rolled along the walls and sent menacing shadows into the passageway.

With his heart in his throat, silenced by his rising terror, Lucien Varl was not surprised when Chancellor Relan Valus strode into view, two hooded guards in dutiful formation behind him.

"Bastard!" Lucien spat through gritted teeth, tugging on his chains frenziedly.

Relan Valus smiled wanly, his eyes brimming with glee. He moved forward, gripping the bars with his thin hands as the guards took up position either side of him.

"Now, now, Lucien," Relan chided, shaking his head, "is that a way to greet an old friend?"

"*Friend*?" Lucien snapped, pausing to laugh maniacally. "You are no friend of mine snake, no friend of the Valian people."

The chancellor stepped back, his smile slipping wider across his mocking features. "Ah, but that is where you are wrong, c*aptain*. I have many friends and soon, I, and they, shall have the love of the Valian people."

"The high duke will not stand for this," Lucien hissed and even before Relan replied, he could read the answer on his lips.

"Let us leave the high duke out of this, shall we? I am certain that he is more concerned with your supposed betrayal, of your disappearance to join the Reven traitors you so obviously have been helping. Only yesterday, how did he put it? Ah yes, '*How is it that Gardan can get such quick results, when my captain could not find out anything?*'"

Relan grinned, then added, "What could I say to that? I just had to admit, though it pained me to do so, that your lack of urgency said much more about you than your supposed loyalty did. Why, it was as if you did not w*ant* to find the perpetrators. With Savinn Kassaar and now you, Lucien Varl, in hiding, it would seem we have a very certain direction to point our questioning fingers."

Seething, Lucien watched as the chancellor ran a bony finger thoughtfully down one of the rusted bars of the cell. When he looked up, he studied his prisoner, a mocking smile on his face.

"Ah, the irony," Relan Valus laughed, his thin, snapping voice bounding away into the dark.

Lucien's chains rattled with fury. "What do you mean? Speak plainly man, or be done with it."

Folding his hands within his robes, Relan Valus smiled again. "Like father, like son. You both led different lives and yet, still, you end up in the same place."

"What do you mean?" Lucien hissed, his eyes glittering dangerously. "What do you know of my father?" he shouted angrily.

"I know everything," the chancellor shrugged. "But I digress, we have more pressing matters and I am a very busy man."

The captain's mind reeled, as one of the guards slipped a large key into the lock of the cell and turned it stiffly. He opened the barred door and stepped back as

Relan Valus came into the cell, staring down disdainfully at the squalor he was forced to step through.

"What do you want from me?" Lucien asked in a low whisper, as the chancellor stepped close, his thin, gaunt face aglow with triumph.

"I want you to tell me where the high duke's family is? Where you have hidden them?"

Lucien laughed. "You bastard. So that's your game is it?"

He spat in the chancellor's face and delighted as Relan Valus recoiled in horror. It was a hollow victory, but one nonetheless.

"You *will* tell me, Lucien Varl," the chancellor snarled, wiping the spittle from his face. He regained his control and stepped close again. "If you do not give me their location willingly, I shall send her to you to cut the information from you."

Lucien held the snake's eyes and drew his body up proudly. "I will not yield their lives into your hands, Valus. Whilst the high duke may think me a traitor, I am still his man and will always be."

Staring down his nose at his prisoner, Relan Valus regarded the captain with disdain.

"So be it," he smiled and turning, he swept from the cell and strode angrily away.

"I will have your head, Valus," the captain roared angrily.

Seething, Lucien Varl met the eyes of the guards, as they locked the cell and made to leave.

"Shame on you," he said, shaking his head. "Shame on you all…"

The young boy ran down the twisting street, narrowly dodging the contents of a chamber pot that splashed onto the cobbles before him and sent him skidding to safety.

Ignoring the cry of apology from an upstairs window that chased after him, the boy slipped through the throng, elbowing his way desperately through the gathered crowd.

"The Watch are coming," he hissed, pausing only to wrench the sleeve of his tunic back from insistent, angry hands.

With lowering clouds watching his flight, the lad hurried down a quieter lane towards the large courtyard ahead and the high gates of Lawyer Brook's estate.

"What's chasing your tail, lad?" the solitary guard enquired, cocking a curious eye towards the urchin, as he bowled into him, his breath ragged, laboring hard in his chest.

"You said if I heard or saw anything," the boy gasped, as the guard steadied him with a smile and caring hand. "Well, the Watch are heading this way…"

The guard's eyes widened and fishing a few sceptres into the urchin's grubby hand, he sent him on his way. Casting a look down Wig Lane, lined on either side by tall, ramshackle buildings, the guard could see the bustling crowds clearing, could detect the distant, heavy approach of determined, booted feet.

Growling, the guard headed inside the gated walls to raise the alarm.

Eran Dray looked up at the clouds gathering overhead, as he followed his comrades down Wig Lane towards the Brook Estate. His shield was heavy on his arm as he glanced back over one shoulder and saw that a mob were following in their wake, drawn like flies to the raid that was about to take place – hopeful of joining in the fun, or at least picking up the pieces afterwards.

Since reporting to Eagle Watch Barracks, he had been involved in two 'arrests'. Ordered by his captain, Esten, a man who was not even from Karick, but one of Gardan's puppets, Eran and his patrol had been forced to bring two

Reven citizens in for questioning. Fortunately, both men had come quietly, but Eran could sense that some of his fellows were disappointed they had accepted the warrant's summons so easily.

After they were roughed up and delivered to the dungeons for questioning, Eran had heard little about their fate, only that their homes had been looted the very same day of their summons and that nothing had been done by the militia to stop it.

It was a familiar story all across the city and whilst some of his fellow guards held grave doubts at what was happening, they kept their thoughts to themselves, for fear of being marked as sympathizers or traitors.

Feeling the tension build around him, Eran thought of Dia and felt his chest tighten. Dragged away from his duties at the keep, he had not had leave to see her for some days now and it was eating away at him. Their last evening together had been a solemn one, a quiet, tense night spent in each other's arms, sharing their fears for what was happening.

As Eran slipped from their bed the following morning, Dia had held onto his hand, reluctant to let him go.

"I will be fine," he had assured her, but her beautiful face twisted sadly, her eyes revealing his own lie.

"Do not drown in the madness," she had pleaded him and as he left and closed the door, he could already hear her sobs.

Eran was dragged away from his thoughts by his captain's bark.

"Our warrant requests that Lawyer Brook and *all* his family and staff be brought in for questioning today," Captain Esten Oswald cried out and Eran could already see the gleam of anticipation in his eyes. "It's not for us to question why, but I would remind you all that there is a stain on this land and to cleanse it, we must remain strong and loyal to our cause. There are Reven allies everywhere and we must draw them out swiftly, or their poison will run too deeply in our veins."

Eran looked to the man beside him and felt his heart sink. Fuller was a large brute of a man, who had already roughed up a couple of their warrants on the way back for questioning. As the bald-headed man rolled the tension from his neck, he crunched the relish through his knuckles.

Eran shook his head. A Valian man, Lawyer Brook was marked a friend of Savinn Kassaar, the merchant reportedly behind the uprising and troubles. He had hoped that because he was not of Reven blood, today would go quietly. But, as he looked at his comrades gathered about him, tasted the anticipation and excitement in the air, Eran feared that it would not.

The guard held on to his nerves as long as he could, refusing to open the gates and ignoring the warrant waved menacingly under his nose.

"My master is not home today," the man mumbled, too quickly to mask his lie and Eran could feel the anger build around him.

"Open these gates," Captain Oswald hissed. "The longer you delay, the worse it will be for you, I promise you that."

Swallowing, the man looked for support, but the two guards that had been standing beside him moments before, had melted back into the estate. With eyes wide, the guard nodded dumbly, cold sweat dripping from his hooked nose as he fumbled for the lock.

As the tumblers clicked, the gate was hauled open and with a growl, Esten Oswald stepped forward and punched the guard in the face.

"Have at them," the captain grinned and with a roar of delight, the rest of his patrol surged through the gates.

Blinking in disbelief, Eran watched as the guard crumpled to the cobbles and, before his captain could see the horror on his face, he drew his own sword and rushed forlornly after his comrades.

Screams stole through the silence as Eran stepped into a wide entry hall, a majestic oak staircase sweeping up to a balcony and chambers above him. Feeling soft carpet underfoot, Eran fought against his desire to berate the two men who were dragging a maid-servant by her dark hair towards the courtyard outside and hurried reluctantly after Fuller, who was roaring what sounded like a battle-cry, not a call for people to show themselves.

Not wishing to see how he went about his business, Eran was drawn to him by the vain hope that he would have the strength to stop any over-zealous arrests the brutish soldier may seek to carry out.

With his hearing drowning in the rampant panic in his ears, Eran Dray struggled to keep up with Fuller as the militia man kicked open an oak door that led into a large kitchen. As his frame filled the doorway, Eran could hear the fear from those hiding within.

"Come here, you," Fuller growled, charging down stone steps into the room. Eran leapt after him, putting his sword away as he saw Fuller haul aside the large long table in the centre of the kitchen, scattering pots and pans and a pile of recently peeled potatoes across the stone floor.

Above the screams, Eran watched helplessly as Fuller punched a tall, reed-thin man, dressed in a loose-fitting apron and tunic. The hawkish man tumbled from view and the impact of Fuller's fist echoed about the chamber.

A rotund woman with a corn-coloured bob for hair knelt hurriedly beside the stricken man and shrieked up at Fuller as he towered over them.

"FULLER," Eran cried, moving to his side. Grabbing the huge man by the shoulder, he hauled him away.

Fuller spun on him, his eyes wide with shock. "Take your hand off me boy," he spat.

Despite the fear in his throat, Eran stood firm. "We are here to take them in for questioning – *not* to beat them senseless."

At that, Fuller's flushed face split into a toothy grin. "Is that what you believe boy?" he chuckled, looking down at the husband, cradled in his wife's fat arms. Their daughter had scrambled to her parents now, having been hiding behind a barrel near the pantry.

Fuller wrenched his arm free and, finding a calming breath, he sent a disdainful look towards the family.

"I've bigger prizes to claim," he growled, his dark eyes sweeping back to Eran. He stepped in close, jabbing a thick forefinger into his comrade's chest. "Have a care, Eran. Wouldn't want to be marked as a sympathizer now, would you?"

Fuller shoved him aside and stalked from the kitchens. With a deep sigh, Eran turned to the family, who were watching him closely.

He smiled vainly, offering his hand to them. "You had better come with me," he said. "If you don't, I am not sure how long I can guarantee your safety."

After delivering the family outside to his captain and the several militia men who watched over the guards who had already surrendered, Eran hurried back into the estate house, just in time to hear the raucous commotion from upstairs. As he reached the bottom of the sweeping staircase, Fuller and several other guards appeared, dragging an elderly gentleman to the top of the stairs, his protestations lost amongst his gasps for breath and the boots that several men planted into his body.

"This is an outrage," the man spluttered angrily,

choking as Fuller shoved his companions aside and grabbed the man by the scruff of his robes.

"It's an outrage Valian people have dealings with Reven scum, that's what it is," Fuller snarled.

"You cannot do this," the man boldly protested. "I have surrendered to your care willingly. You may not lay a finger on me."

"Tell that to the judge," Fuller laughed, pleased at his own apparent joke. He caught sight of Eran, as he put a tentative foot on the lowest step on the staircase.

"Catch," Fuller called down and before Eran or his startled comrades could react, he threw the old man down the stairs.

Eran raced up the stairs, halting the old man's tumbles far sooner than Fuller would have liked, but not before he heard the lawyer's wrists buckle under his body and snap like twigs.

Cradling the screaming old man in his arms, Eran looked up at Fuller.

"What are you doing man?" he raged. "Have you lost your mind? He was coming quietly – this is not honourable."

Fuller turned, ignoring the looks on the faces of many gathered near. "Next?" he roared, as he stalked hungrily from view.

Waving some of the startled men down to him, Eran ordered them to get the screaming old man to safety and find him some care. With ashen faces, two of them gently scooped up the lawyer and bore him hurriedly away.

Rising, Eran gathered up his fallen shield and watched helplessly as three men dealt him a look of disgust and hurried after Fuller. Drawing his sword, Eran Dray rushed up the staircase to try and find the rest of Lawyer Brook's family, before anyone else did.

Three chambers were empty, filled only with the opulence

of a lawyer's income. Lost to the shadows and the grey day outside, Eran found no sign of Lawyer Brook's family.

On the other side of the estate, all was quiet and Eran assumed that Fuller and his pack were having little success, which calmed his nerves somewhat. He was just turning away from the last room in the east wing, when he heard something behind him.

Turning slowly, he listened to the silence, disturbed only by his heavy heart's drumming. As he cleared his senses, he heard a pleading whisper, coming from a large, tall closet on the far side of the chamber. Moving quickly to the door, Eran sent a look along the landing and could see that Fuller and his men were heading back towards the last room on the west wing.

Turning, Eran hurried back to the closet. Large enough to walk in to, he scanned the gowns and garments hanging up and began pulling them aside. Halfway down the left side, he was startled by a muffled scream, just as much as the people hiding there were.

A woman with greying, long, plaited hair, elegantly dressed and deep into the autumn of her life, cradled a young boy in her arms. At her side, a dark-haired pale beauty clung to them both, a gentle hand stifling the fear of her child.

"P-please sir," the older woman pleaded, her piercing blue eyes bright with tears. "We are innocent and have done nothing wrong to warrant such treatment."

Her fear receded somewhat when Eran cast a fretful look over his shoulder, as Fuller's barking orders grew loud behind him.

Eran turned back, his words catching nervously in his throat as he knelt beside them.

"You must stay quiet," he whispered. "I will try to distract them. When we are gone, you must flee this place quickly. Take only what you need… is there another way out for you, lady?"

The old woman nodded and she clutched at Eran's hand as he rose. "Thank you, sir," she said, kissing his fingers gratefully.

Eran quickly pulled the garments back into place, the younger woman's lovely eyes flashing with bright thanks as they were lost from sight.

"Found anything?" a voice called out, as Eran stepped out into the room. One of his comrades, Garn, was silhouetted in the doorway.

"Thought they might be hiding in the closet," Eran responded, hoping that he had masked his fear enough. As Garn stepped into the room and went to say something, Eran scooped up a handful of jewellery from an ornate box on the dresser beside him and tossed them to the militia man.

Catching a necklace deftly, Garn grinned and stooped to gather up some fallen jewels. When he straightened, Eran was by his side to distract him.

"Come on," Eran said hurriedly, we had better report back in – before things get out of hand."

Pocketing his prizes, Garn followed Eran out of the chamber and went with him to lend credence to their report.

A large mob had gathered outside the estate, warned back by the words and swords of Captain Oswald and his men. Fuller and the remnants of his band had been persuaded by Garn that the final room was empty and Eran had reported to his captain that the lawyer's family had probably been moved somewhere safe before they arrived.

With his disappointment etched on his face, Oswald looked down at the lawyer and his staff, all cowering on the cobbles before them. Brook was still crying in agony and Fuller, feeling his captain's eyes turn to him, shrugged.

"He tripped on his robes as we brought him down the

stairs," he offered lamely, then mirrored his captain's subtle grin.

Looking about the estate, Captain Oswald nodded his head. "Good work, men," he called out, waving a gloved hand towards the gates. "Let's get our prisoners out of here, whilst we still can."

Prisoners? Eran thought, failing to hide his disgust. As the militia men hauled up the lawyer and his staff, the crowd parted reluctantly. With tension in the air and the eyes of the mob on them, the captain led them through the throng, ignoring the hisses and curses that were hurled their way.

As they reached the safety of Wig Lane, the captain waved his men through. As Eran passed, Captain Oswald turned back to the crowd.

"It's all yours now," he called out and spun away as the mob rushed into the estate.

Savinn Kassaar picked up his goblet and sipped at the strong red wine. A particularly good vintage from the South Vales, the bottle had not lasted long, despite the merchant-thief's desire to make this one last. Setting the goblet down again with his trembling hand, Savinn massaged his throbbing temples and groaned.

"What are you doing?"

He let his question go unanswered and stared about his study, deep in shadows now, lit only by the flickering flames of a candle, drowning slowly on its wick. Savinn shook his pounding head ruefully, bitterly aware of the irony of his observation.

He felt a lot like the candle – still burning with desire, still clinging on to hope, but destined, ultimately, to be swallowed up by the darkness.

The news from the city above was not good and the merchant-thief consoled himself with another sip of wine and the fact that he had managed to get his family to safety before the madness had truly begun. There were dark reports from his allies about the raids taking place across the capital, of the hundreds of Reven and Valian citizens who had been dragged away for questioning and had not, as of yet, been seen or returned to their homes.

Savinn scoffed, clenching the nerves from one hand angrily. From what he had heard, they would have no homes to return to, should they ever be released. Looting was rife, mobs stripping homes as soon as its inhabitants had been led away – the militia doing little, if anything, to stop them. With Renald Gardan's arrival in the city, things had started to happen quickly, his iron fist and boot stamping a brutal, Carwellian authority on proceedings.

Savinn's concerns had shifted quickly to the news from Dia of the names that were on the Reven lists, of the names that were not, and he had started to form some idea of who he could count his allies and who, undoubtedly, were now his enemies.

Scowling, Savinn fought against his rising anger, tempered only by the sense of his own futility. He had been naïve, perhaps vain to think that his wealth and influence would count for anything once the Valian people began to turn against him. Marked as the lead agitator in the phantom Reven uprising, his mantle of position had slipped quickly away into nothingness, leaving him with few moves, if any, left that he could make.

Drawing his thoughts away from the poster on the table before him, he found himself thinking of Lady Byron and of Arillion. With Cassana back in the capital, but ostracised from the high duke by a father, murdered cruelly, no doubt, by the Brotherhood, he wondered if anything he could tell her would actually help? He doubted it. The Reven lists the chancellor had drawn up would prove nothing, other than prudence and foresight on his part and with still no clue as to who was really behind the plot, no strong evidence to support their claims, Savinn and his allies would be retaliating from a weak position – one that would appear more fantastical than the claims of those who whispered in the ear of the high duke.

And as for Arillion? There was still no news on the fate of his right hand, no word from the assassin. *Was he dead?* Savinn smiled sadly. He still owed the rogue a great deal of money and, so driven by coin as he was, Savinn could not understand why, if Arillion was still alive, why he hadn't returned to the capital to claim the second half of his reward. It led the merchant-thief to surmise that maybe the assassin's luck had indeed finally ran out.

Savinn's head swam with his dilemmas and the wine as he tapped a finger thoughtfully on the desk. High Duke Stromn's absence from public life of late was also worrying. Had the chancellor and his allies removed him from power without the Valian people realising it? Thinking of the chancellor left a bitter taste in his throat and he wished that he had hired Arillion, or ordered Dia to slit the bastard's throat before he had sunken his claws too deeply into events.

Dia could offer little information to ease his fears, either and, with Gardan running amok in the city now, he wondered how in the storms anyone was going to stop them. How was he to avert the looming threat of the Valian armies marching north to war? There were already worrying rumours of conscripts being called for, the rallying cry for loyal '*Valian*' heroes.

Savinn's sigh was long and hard, full of a deep regret laced with anxiety. After many days of incessant rain, the storms had flooded the sewers, cutting off what little access he and his followers had to the world above them. Tomorrow, he would have to find a way out and up into Karick. Since the raids had started, the Reven inhabitants in the city had called for calm, demanded that the high duke stop these unwarranted arrests, cloaked in the public guise of polite *invitations*. As the anger on the streets rose and seemingly daily news of new Reven attacks reached their ears, the people of Karick were short of patience and reason.

To counter this madness, for several days Savinn had been sending messages to those in the city he could trust, asking them to arrange a protest, a rally that would gather at noon on the sixty-eighth day of summer and march peacefully on the high duke's keep to demonstrate their worry about the unjust treatment of loyal Valian citizens. Surely a large group of citizens, both Valian and Reven, would draw the high duke out of hiding, make him see reason and find shame at his actions and the way his people were being treated?

It was a risk. One Savinn had deliberated over for many days. If he was recognised amongst the crowds, he would be dragged away and tortured. But what choice did he have now? He had to try something, something that would offer hope to those who were not caught up in the rising madness.

Any faint flicker of hope Savinn had was quickly snuffed out as his eyes fell upon the poster, delivered to him by one of his men, who had braved the sewer's rivers of filth and excrement. The poster, reportedly distributed readily about the city, had sent Savinn fleeing deep into the depths of his wine cellar and he had not come up for two days now.

Shaking his head, Savinn held it up and winced. He snorted derisively as he held the notice over the waning candle and watched as the flames licked hungrily at the effigy of a dark-skinned Redani, wanted to the sum of ten thousand gold crowns by the authorities for his part in aiding the '*Reven fugitive*' Savinn Kassaar and for his involvement in the attempted kidnapping of Lady Byron.

"Well played, chancellor," Savinn hissed, allowing the flames to burn his fingers.

"Well played, indeed!"

CHAPTER TWENTY TWO

Alliances

Elissen stared in wonderment at her surroundings, not really believing where she was and still not certain she had willingly allowed herself to come along. Up ahead of her, through the twisting maze of trees, her protectors rode single-file in wary silence, their hooded heads sweeping about the silent forest, searching for a danger that was not there, or was perhaps not yet ready to show itself to them.

Gripping her reins tightly, Elissen breathed a slow, steadying breath and attempted to hide her fears from her mount. The palfrey, called Rook on account of his colour, had finally become her friend and after many days on the road together, the two of them had agreed to share a respectful truce, of sorts.

It had been a tense journey back from Highwater for them all. News of Alion Byron's murder and the ramifications of Elion's and Dekan's meeting with Lady Byron had broken the final strands of the weary groups' resolve. Slipping away from the arguments that ensued, Elissen had lost herself to the hollowness of the angry debate ringing in her ears. All she could think about was her revenge, her need to somehow send her father and sister to their rest with the knowledge that justice was meted out to those truly responsible for their deaths. Elion Leigh's news that it appeared Gardan was not the one fully in charge of the attacks and that it may well be Lord Henry Carwell, steward of the East Vales, left any hope she had of a satisfying resolution in tatters.

Her thin hands began to tremble and she allowed the calming chatter of her surroundings to soothe her demons. Events in the Four Vales, it appeared, were darker, far more dangerous now than her petty problems and selfish quest for closure. She needed to find her strength again, be there for those who had saved her, put their trust in her when others would have let her dance a final jig on the end of a short rope.

Elissen shuddered, guiding her mount into some dappled sunlight and warming herself there for a moment. If the Lady willed it, if there was any justice left in this life for her, Gardan and his master would be brought to account for the blood staining their hands. It may not be her testimony now that would sing loud enough to bring them down, but she would add her voice to the rising chorus of shouts and aid those seeking to stop the slow march to war.

Blinking free from the quagmire of thoughts that threatened to drown her clarity of thinking, Elissen became aware of Jarion Kail, as he dropped back to ride his mount alongside her.

She met his captivating eyes with a timid smile, unnerved at his increasingly bold attempts at conveying his appreciation to her, and yet at the same time not entirely unhappy with them, either.

"So how are you finding Greywood, my lady?" Jarion enquired, a smirk on his face and no doubt mischief on his mind.

Elissen studied the tall, sun-dappled trees for a time,

breathing in the heady scents of the wildflower, transfixed as a shard of sunlight caught on the broken strands of a spider's web. Marvelling at the calm serenity that seeped through her veil of worry she listened to the soothing drone of a roaming bee.

"Despite its reputation," Elissen began, meeting his smile as she turned to him again, "I feel… relaxed? Though I daresay once we are prisoners of Devlin Hawke, I may change my mood again."

They smiled at each other and shared a chuckle which was loud enough to draw a thunderous look from Sergeant Manse in their direction.

"That's the dishes for me tonight, then," Jarion muttered, winking.

Elissen realised there was a bright smile on her face and her guilt quickly drew it away again. Stiffening in her saddle, she tilted her head towards her companion.

"If you would excuse me a moment, Sir Jarion, I need to ask your captain a question?"

Jarion went to reply, but Elissen had already dug the heels of her boots into her mount's flanks and was heading away from him.

Shaking his head at his stupidity, Jarion cursed his haste and chewed angrily on his tongue.

"It won't be long now," Ashe Garrin said quietly, sweeping his eyes about their surroundings, wondering if every shadow he saw was an outlaw about to put a shaft through his heart or welcome him with a tankard of mead.

Diverting his fragile nerves, Ashe sent a look back at his captain who was riding thoughtfully along behind him, an all-too-familiar distant expression on his bearded face.

My how you have aged, the burly sergeant thought as he studied Elion's face. Despite his captain's luck at having a bath and that his body was now free of the deep grime and stale stench from their road, his face still held his worry there – deepening the lines of his boyish features into the weary countenance of one who had the weight of the world on his shoulders.

His wife's own features flashed in his mind and Ashe felt an ache of longing rise, his need to see his Cath and their children again. Before he could stop himself, Ashe counted where he was in the season and how, with each day that passed now, the arrival of his next child drew close.

"Sergeant?" Elion's voice cut through the image and as his wife faded from his view, Ashe blinked.

"Sorry, miles away," he apologised, raising a gloved hand.

"I need you here with me, Ashe," Elion said quietly, holding his friend's gaze long enough to gently chastise him.

Since their departure from Highwater, they had spent two days escorting Mayor Ardent back to Havensdale. The relief was evident upon all who welcomed their return, no clearer shown than on Fawn Ardent's pale features as she rushed into her father's arms.

Leaving them to have their reunion, Elion had gathered his companions about him in the dust outside the town and told them of the decision he had deliberated over on their return journey.

Despite their protests, Elion had announced that Jarion, the brothers Bran and Bren, Liehella, Tristan and Janth would stay in Havensdale to help protect the town. Only Elissen and Ashe would journey with him, as he went in search of allies and answers.

Elion sighed, thinking back to the hurt he had seen in their eyes, the sense that he was abandoning them, leaving them after all they had gone through together, all they had sacrificed to get them this far.

Jarion's anger had rung the loudest and he had, in no uncertain terms, told his captain that he would follow them, whether he liked it or not. Seeing the worried look Jarion dealt Elissen, Elion felt his chest tighten with something other than frustration. Finally, casting aside his own emotions, he had relented, allowing Ashe to step in and head off the protests from any others who had then sought to disobey their captain.

From Havensdale, they had cut eastwards across the plains, coming into Greywood Forest from the north to ensure they did not risk meeting the other outlaw group operating in the region.

"I am here, Elion," Ashe growled, hurt etched on his grizzled face. "Despite everything, I am with you to the end, you know that."

Nudging his mount forward, Elion reached across and gripped his friend's broad shoulder. "I know, Ashe, I'm sorry, it's just I cannot believe what we are doing? I know we must and whilst we are doing it I realise that we have to ensure Elissen's safety, but–,"

"–you are not sure if this is the right way to go about it?" Ashe finished for him.

Elion nodded, looking back towards Elissen, as she slowly guided her mount through the trees to join them.

"We could not risk leaving her in Havensdale, should it be attacked again. Whilst we may never get the chance to bring her to Karick for her testimony, we must protect her in case we ever do."

Ashe frowned, his voice dropping to a conspiratorial whisper as he eyed the girl's reluctant approach. "She'll be safe here, although she may not like it."

Elion grimaced. "That's what I am worried about."

The four riders spent the next hour traversing a rising ridgeline up through Greywood Forest. All about them the land was alive, uncaring of its guests' concerns as the wildlife went about its daily business. At one point, riding alongside Elion Leigh, Elissen had spied a deer through the trees up the slope from them and they had stopped for a while to return the doe's curious stare with breathless awe.

After a while, as the deer trail they followed became choked by thicket and the low branches of the silver birch forced them from the saddle, Elion picked a path for them back down the hill to lower ground. On the sodden and leafy, lower forest floor once more, it wasn't long before the captain announced that he was lost.

Attending to their mounts, the four of them soothed their frustrations with a hearty lunch of rough bread and cheese, washed down with some *Campbell's Own.* With bellies content and their troubles forgotten for a time, the small party continued on their way with renewed vigour and fresh determination.

"That's far enough," a voice warned, the statement echoing about the forest as Elion drew back on his reins in fright.

Snapping his head about, Elion searched for the speaker, but could not see anyone in their dense surroundings.

Ashe flicked a glance at his captain and with a nod of understanding they both raised their empty hands above their heads.

"We are here to see your master," Elion called out after wetting his dry throat. "We come in peace."

To the east a shadow stirred and a figure dressed from head to boot in woodland leathers of brown and green stepped onto the muddied, twisting path before the riders.

"Is that so?" the man called out, his face hidden beneath his hood and behind a dark scarf. He bent his bow in their direction, aiming the nocked shaft at Elion's chest.

Elion cocked one ear towards the speaker in recognition and lowered his hands slowly. "Col?" he asked.

Relaxing his bowstring and putting his arrow back in his quiver, the outlaw raised a hand and pulled the scarf from his face to reveal his grin.

"Sorry, captain," he chuckled. "Just having a bit of fun with you – it's not often I get the draw on Carwell's men… and women."

Elion breathed a sigh of relief, forcing it into a smile.

"I can't say I blame you. How are things? How is Kerrin holding up? I've been thinking of him a lot lately."

Col smiled broadly. "He's doing fine, in fact he's doing great. I've never met a man who could track like him. The boss will be reluctant to lose him."

There was something in the way he said it that sent a chill up Elion's spine, despite the sun that filtered down through the leafy canopy and warmed his face.

"So what brings you back to Greywood, captain?" Col asked, slinging his bow over his left shoulder. "I would have thought not to see you again."

Elion ran a hand through his facial foliage and grinned. "As I, you," he winced regretfully. "But there are matters I would discuss with your boss, if you would kindly take me to him?"

Col folded his arms across his chest, revealing the leather guards on his wrists. He eyed the four riders before him for a moment, before nodding.

"As you wish," the outlaw answered, turning away. "Follow me close, but I'll warn you now – he's not been in the best of moods of late."

Elion Leigh looked across at Ashe Garrin, as Col led them through the trees towards the camp and could tell the burly sergeant was also experiencing the sense they had lived this life before. Once again, wood smoke touched their nostrils, the late-afternoon fire already building in fury, ready for the cold night ahead.

Guiding his mount around a low-hanging branch, Elion caught glimpses of the camp Devlin Hawke had escorted them to as his *guests*, all those days ago now and found himself thinking of the evening they had spent together under the stars. Swallowing his guilt at the memories, most of which were pleasant, Elion scanned the camp and felt his heart begin to gallop as they approached.

Col called out a greeting as he neared and several heads turned towards him, smiles slipping from hardy faces when they realised that their comrade had not returned alone.

Tethering their mounts to the same tree as last time, Elion drew in a calming breath, dealt his comrades an encouraging smile and stepped into the sunlight of the clearing.

"Look who's back," Col grinned, turning as Elion raised a hand in greeting.

Kerrin Thorn rose up from his attendance by the fire, his face wrinkling with merry surprise. Striding forward, he grinned as Elion drew him into a tight embrace.

"Captain," Kerrin chuckled, as Elion withdrew cautiously and looked fearfully at the tracker's shoulder. "Don't worry, she's healing up well, I have to say. Must be all the fresh air I am getting."

Elion shook his head in happy disbelief and held the tracker close again.

"Thank the Lady," Elion said, clapping Kerrin on the back.

Pulling away, Kerrin was dragged into a bear-like hug by Ashe, quickly joined in the embrace by Jarion Kail. Blinking his rising emotions away, Elion's eyes fell upon Elissen, standing timidly on the cusp of the clearing, her hands clasped nervously before her.

She was smiling, such a rare sight these days and as their eyes met, Elion felt his pulse quicken.

"Trell's out with the boss," Col grunted, drawing Elion's attention away as Elissen looked shyly to her toes. "They should be back before sundown, so until then you are free to catch up with your friend and help us prepare the supper."

Elion nodded and moved forward to grip the outlaw's hand. He sent a smile to other outlaws watching on, seeing only their curiosity there.

"Thank you, for everything," Elion replied, flicking his attention to Kerrin.

Col followed his gaze, releasing his hand. "He's a tough one, that one," the outlaw observed, his soft words full only with respect and admiration.

Devlin Hawke's arrival back at the camp was greeted by the sounds of laughter and merriment, which did little to improve his mood. With his anger tight on his lips and his cloak even tighter about his tall frame, he stepped into the clearing, his eyes flashing with the flames of the camp fire.

"What in the–," he began, his words lost as he saw the faces of his guests turn towards him. In his shock, he did not hear Trell's rumbling groan as he stepped into the firelight alongside him.

As one, those gathered about the fire and their tankards, rose up stiffly from the ground and it was Col who found his voice first.

"Found them wandering about the forest again, boss," he grinned. "They were heading west and towards trouble, *again*."

Dragging the hood from his head, Devlin Hawke planted his hands on his hips, sweeping his cloak back. His dark eyes ranged about the camp, noting those present, falling eventually on the thin woman, hiding at the rear of the camp behind the burly sergeant, her eyes wide with fright.

Sighing, the notorious outlaw strode forward and

gripped Elion Leigh's offered hand. As he tightened his grip, he searched the captain's face, his expression softening from annoyance to one of curiosity.

"I would say it is good to see you, my young friend," Devlin said, as Trell stalked by them and reluctantly shook Ashe's hand, "but judging by your look, I fear I may come to regret it."

Elion smiled wanly. "We shall see, my old friend. Perhaps we should supper first, before I spoil our reunion?"

Allowing Elion to have his hand back, Devlin Hawke sent a look about the outlaws gathered close, noting the evident calm in the camp, absent the last time the Carwellian men were here.

"Supper it is, then," Devlin said finally, scratching his beard thoughtfully. "Come, my friends, let us share some food and a few tankards before I have my appetite ruined."

Elion met the outlaw's eyes and they shared a knowing look.

After their gracious host had filled his guests' bellies with supper and mead, he allowed them a while to dance about the rising anticipation with polite conversation. Swatting aside Elion's words of thanks for looking after Kerrin Thorn, Devlin Hawke fell silent for a time, studying the captain intently and trying to ignore the chill that settled on his arms. Elion Leigh was a changed man. His eyes betrayed him, far more than his dishevelled appearance and the pathetic beard he was trying to grow. Something terrible had happened to him since their last meeting, he could see it there in the way Elion's smiles did not reach his eyes, in the slump of his shoulders, once stiff with duty and honour.

Cutting across Kerrin's tale about how he was trying to stop the outlaws from eating his new friend, the donkey, Devlin Hawke rose up, drawing everyone's attention with him.

"So," Devlin began, warming his hands over the flames of the fire, "let us spoil the moment, Captain Leigh. What brings you back to my forest? Loyalty to your man would have done so one day, I am certain, but so soon? I think not?"

All heads turned to Elion Leigh, apart from the donkey loitering on the cusp of the firelight. He bowed his head and continued munching on his supper.

Setting down his tankard of mead, Elion licked his lips slowly.

"Perhaps we have come to join your band of men?" he said, grinning.

Devlin chuckled, pacing around the camp fire, coming closer to the captain.

"If that were the case, my boy, I would gladly welcome you… but I can see that it is not."

Elion swallowed hard, as Devlin came near. Though the outlaw's face was fixed with a roguish smile, he could detect the anger in his usually calm demeanour.

Elion looked up as the outlaw stopped beside him. Reaching down, Devlin Hawke picked up a jug of mead and filled Elion's empty tankard for him. The outlaw took a long pull of the honeyed brew, before passing it back to the Carwellian captain.

"There," Devlin Hawke said quietly. "I have shared my supper and now my drink with you, Elion Leigh. It is time for you to share something with me."

Sipping at the mead, Elion nodded, forcing a smile.

"Very well," he sighed, looking to Ashe for support. "But you may want to sit down for this."

Devlin Hawke listened to Elion Leigh's account of all that had happened to him since the outlaws had handed over the murderer, Raven, to them. Despite the mutters of shock from his men when the captain told them of Commander Gardan's treachery and, it appeared, thanks to Elissen's testimony, his involvement in more than just the raid on Eastbury, Devlin Hawke remained silent. Tugging thoughtfully at the earring in his left ear, he listened calmly to Elion's tale, raising only his eyebrows when the Carwellian attack on Havensdale was told.

It wasn't until Elion recounted their arrival in Highwater and of Alion Byron's murder that he broke his silence, whistling softly, as he sat back on his haunches.

"That has stirred up the nest," Devlin observed, finishing his statement with a profanity. He looked over at Elissen and raised a hand in apology.

Elion nodded, still unable to believe what he had told them, still not ready to accept that what was happening was even true. "There is dark talk of the threat of war again, of the shadows drowning the marble halls of the capital."

"I bet there is," Trell broke in, draining his tankard and shaking his head. Ashe grunted in agreement.

Devlin eyed them both, raising one brow at them. Smiling, he turned his thoughts back to the former captain.

"Carwell has been waiting for this and he will be the one pulling the strings," Devlin surmised, tossing some twigs onto the fire. He watched the rallying flames for a time, before looking up again. "Before these events, the high duke *was* a man of peace. He would have never countenanced such a direction, without the spectre of a Reven uprising. Even then, he would have had the ear of those with sense, the ones who have always steered his head away from war towards peace. But now, with his strongest supporter dead…"

Elion was already nodding. "The pressure upon him will be far greater. Lady Byron believes that her father was right, that all of the attacks happening–,"

"Lady Byron lives?" Devlin broke in, looking at Trell in shock.

Elion noticed the exchange and frowned. "Yes… she was escorted to safety, despite being attacked in the mountains by Valian mercenaries."

Devlin looked for Balan, who had been listening intently to Elion's tale. His eyes were wide with fear, his face full again of the horrors he had witnessed, of all he had been through since that fateful morning in the mountains.

"Lady Byron is well, despite events," Elion continued cautiously. "Her protectors, however, did not fare as well. But, because of their sacrifice, she was able, albeit briefly, to be reunited with her father once more."

Devlin Hawke rose up again, his hands noticeably shaking as he wandered away to the shadows. He stood by the donkey for a time, ruffling the beast's ears thoughtfully. Finally snapping from his reverie, he slapped the donkey's rump and turned.

"Walk with me again, captain," he ordered. Turning, the outlaw strode into the night, the eyes of the camp following after him.

"Better get after him," Trell muttered, handing Elion a full flagon.

Nodding, Elion accepted the drink and scooping up his own tankard, the former captain of Carwell hurried away into the forest.

Elion finally caught up with the outlaw leader, when Devlin Hawke stopped to sit on the rotting trunk of a fallen oak. As Elion passed him the flagon, Devlin nodded and idly picked some moss from the rough bark of the old tree.

"It's hard to believe, I admit," Elion said eventually, when it appeared the outlaw was not in the mood to talk. Moaning, Elion sat beside him and with a sigh, he raised his tankard.

"To Alion Byron," Elion decreed. Devlin's eyes glittered as he raised his flagon and crashed their drinks together.

Silently, they supped at their mead, looking to the stars, high and bright above them in a cloudless night sky. All about the forest was alive with the sound of crickets, thrumming away merrily as they welcomed the night.

Wiping his mouth, Devlin dragged Elion's attention to him with a curse.

"Damn you boy," he hissed. "Damn you for bringing this to my door."

Elion recoiled, his heart racing as the outlaw turned on him.

"I did not know where else to go," Elion pleaded, holding up his empty hand. "Please, Devlin. There are dark times ahead, not just for me, but for all Valian people. If someone does not do something to stem the tide of this madness, all will be lost."

"And you think I can help you?" Devlin spat angrily. "Grow up, Elion. What can I achieve, that you, Alion Byron and the sane members of the council cannot? What even makes you think that I would want to?"

Elion took a deep mouthful of mead and closed his eyes as the honeyed liquid settled the bile in his throat.

"I thought that maybe there was an honourable man leading these men – the type of man that would stand up against those in power, against those who would wield their authority without care, without compunction and with only greed and malice in their minds?"

Devlin stood and snarled, hurling his flagon into the night. It shattered against a tree and as the crickets fell silent for a moment, an owl screeched somewhere off into the darkness.

For a long while Devlin Hawke stood with his back to him, the air taut with tension. When he finally turned back, there was a grin on his face and a sparkle in his eyes again.

"I do not doubt that what you have brought to me is compelling, Elion Leigh," Devlin began, folding his arms across his chest. "But, when all is said and done, without any hard evidence, it is only supposition, after all."

Elion's heart sank and he averted his eyes, less he reveal his own doubts.

"I know that, Devlin," he sighed, looking up at the outlaw leader. "But what am I to do? I cannot let these injustices go uncontested. If someone does not stand against the tide, we will all be swept aside by the madness. The Four Vales will never be the same again."

"Then I ask again, Elion Leigh," Devlin said evenly. "What can I achieve that you cannot?"

Elion rose up and passed his tankard to the outlaw. "For many years, you and your men have been a thorn in Carwell's side. I would have you apply pressure to that wound in the coming weeks, stirring up trouble that will divert any plans Lord Carwell may have to send the Valian people to war."

There was a gleam in Devlin's eyes and Elion pressed on.

"If we are to stop those who would bring us to war, we need evidence and we need it fast. Tomorrow I shall head to Carwell, to find out what is happening there. With all eyes focused on Karick and Highwater, there has been little news from the east. I have allies there, allies who will be as horrified as I. I will use that friendship and garner their support to find out what is really going on."

Devlin nodded his head thoughtfully. "But Gardan wants you dead, Elion. The girl's evidence, should it be true, confirms that."

"It does," Elion agreed. "But I am willing to risk my life if I can do something to aid Lady Byron in her search for the truth. Will you aid me again, my friend? You did so once before and I would ask for your help again."

Devlin stroked his beard, shaking his head. He chewed on his bottom lip for a time, before sighing. "If you had come to me a week ago I would have said no. I would have sent you from my forest with a kick up your arse."

"But what of this day? What about now?" Elion dared to ask. His heart hammered wildly in his chest and his head pounded furiously from all of the mead he had consumed.

Elion's eyes narrowed. "Today, though I am sure I will live to regret it, I would say yes. You are giving me a chance to bloody Carwell's nose and I would be a fool to turn it down. But know that I do it for my own reasons, not for you, not for Cassana Byron. All I will say is, for now, I am with you and that you can thank the boy Balan for that."

Devlin gripped Elion's shoulder, seeing the relief and further questions rising in his eyes. He chuckled, whipping a finger up before the captain's face.

"Not another word, Elion Leigh. No more of your incessant questions."

Elion grinned, puffing out his cheeks in relief. "Thank you, Devlin. I would ask, however, one thing more of you. Will you and your men protect Elissen, while I am gone? She may still be of use to us and we should do all that we can to keep her safe in the meanwhile."

Devlin's mocking scowl slipped from his features and he nodded. "Agreed. I will have my men guard her with their lives whilst we are gone."

"*We*?" Elion blinked, not certain he had heard correctly.

Devlin Hawke grinned, a dangerous glint in his eyes. "That's right. You and I are going to pay Carwell a visit. We are both wanted men now, you more than I, I daresay. Carwell will be the last place they will look for us."

“But–,” Elion began to protest, but the outlaw cut him off.

“Not another word, Elion Leigh,” he snapped, though now there was only mirth in his words. “If I hear another breath from you, I’ll turn you in for the reward myself.”

They both laughed and Elion silently thanked the Lady as Devlin pulled him into a tight embrace. As they took the remaining tankard back towards the fire of the distant camp, Elion could not help but think it would almost be worth letting the outlaw capture him, just to see the look on Lord Carwell’s face.

CHAPTER TWENTY THREE

The Burning Question

The man sat patiently at a table in the centre of the room, his hands clasped before him on the worm-riddled surface as he faced the door, closed before him. Dressed in shadows, his face was hidden beneath the cowl of a dark cloak that draped about his body, obscuring all but his forearms that were covered in black leather and garnished by silver studs that glinted dully in the poor light.

The clamour of the taproom beneath the man's feet was rising now as the night grew old and its composure slipped slowly away from it. As the ale drained from the tavern's barrels and its patrons soaked up its welcoming taste, the atmosphere, like most evenings at the rundown establishment, became increasingly unstable. Much like the chair he sat carefully forward in, it could break at any moment.

As if in answer to his thoughts, the sounds of breaking pottery and the crashing splinter of a table seeped up through the floorboards, accompanied by the expected cheers of encouragement and the obliging contact of knuckle against skin.

The candle's light flickered erratically in the wake of a draught that breathed softly in the darkness of the silent room. Its spluttering flame burned brighter on its wick, casting a dancing pallor to life on the featureless walls and sent it peering into the recesses of the room's shadowy corners.

Accustomed to the sounds by now, the man allowed the fracas beneath his boots to wash past him without distracting his attentions from the door he fixed his impatient stare upon.

In the hallway outside, the penultimate step of the staircase creaked in protest at the skilful attempt of someone's silent ascent. The man smiled, drumming his fingers on the table, as he heard another in careful attendance.

At last they come, the man thought with relief.

Moments later the torchlight in the hallway outside, already struggling to slip under the doorway and conquer the room, died. Three swift taps at the door, then a pause, followed by a louder rapid knock, jostled the man from his statuesque demeanour.

"Come," the man commanded and the handle turned obediently.

As the door swung open, the waning torchlight from the hallway spilled gleefully past the hooded figures standing there, reaching into the room to drive away the darkness.

At the man's behest, the newcomers stepped into the room, the larger of the two closing the door gently behind him.

"Sorry we are late," the first man said, raising a gloved hand in apology. "We made sure we were not followed, as you requested."

The man nodded his cowled head, motioning for his guests to be seated in the rickety chairs across from him. The first man to speak accepted the offer with a nod, but the larger man stood with arms folded across his broad chest, his gaze flashing from within the shadows of his hood.

"You are a hard man to find, Teal," Kaspen Shale observed, crossing a leg over one knee as he sat back in the chair that creaked with a warning.

Teal offered an obliging nod in response, tapping one finger hastily on the table.

"I like it that way," Teal said quietly. "You never know who is looking for you."

Kaspen nodded. "The night draws long and I would be away before the watch decides to drag their whores upstairs."

"Then get to the point," Teal said evenly. "Your man said you wanted information – I sell information. I find it if I can."

Kaspen searched the shadows of the man's hood, but could only see a pair of dark eyes narrowing there. He looked back over his shoulder and accepted the large pouch that Agris passed him.

"A gesture of our faith in you," Kaspen smiled, tossing the heavy pouch on the table between them.

Reaching across, Teal picked up the bag of coins and tested their worth. With a nod of his head, he slipped the coins from view.

"A fine gesture," he admitted. "Now, wayfarer, what is it you seek from me?"

Kaspen tensed and behind him, he heard Agris shift uncomfortably. They had taken care when sending word out not to reveal who they were. This Teal, it seemed, already had the advantage over them, which was unsettling.

Searching the man's eyes, Kaspen could gauge nothing, only that his accent was educated and from the North Vales.

"Well?" Teal barked. "I am a busy man and my time

costs money."

Dropping his leg back to the floor, Kaspen leant on the table, folding his hands together.

"Very well," Kaspen began, edging his words with warning. "With Alion Byron's death, there are many questions that need answering. Who killed him, for one? How they got in to the keep, for another."

Kaspen paused, searching for a reaction from Teal, but the mysterious information seller remained impassive.

"But what we seek is far more important," Kaspen continued. "There is a spy in the Byron household and we would know their name."

The singing in the taproom beneath their feet was the only sound to be heard, as they eyed each other across the table. After a time, Teal sat back in his chair and threaded his fingers together thoughtfully.

"A curious question, indeed," Teal mused, holding his guest's attention, "and a question that will cost you double what you have already brought to the table. I warn you now that it may take a few days more than you would like. For now, I will answer only with a question of my own. Why would the wanderers of the Vales seek such knowledge? The affairs of court and the politics of this land have never been of interest to your people before? Why now, I wonder?"

Kaspen flashed a devilish smile. "Why now indeed?"

Teal chuckled softly, bobbing his head. "A fine riposte, wayfarer. We have an accord. I will be in touch via your contact, once I have what you seek."

Kaspen rose hurriedly. Looking down at the hooded man, he offered him his hand. Teal stared at it for a moment, before shaking it slowly.

"Bring me the information in two days and you'll have an extra bag of coin for your diligence."

Turning away, Kaspen and Agris strode from the room, leaving Teal to watch thoughtfully after them.

When they were gone, their footfalls' retreat fading away down the back stairs of the inn, Teal propped his elbows on the table, wrung his hands together and let out a long, deep sigh.

The night was alive with the sounds of the city as Arillion waited patiently for Teal to leave the *Guard Room*. The assassin was well aware of the tavern's darker reputation from prior dealings there and it was a popular drinking, whoring house, frequented by the numerous shifts of the city watch whose own guardhouse was not more than two hundred paces away across the courtyard, deep in the poor district of the city.

From where he hid across the lane, at one with the shadows, Arillion watched the run down establishment, his eyes fixed firmly on the rear entrance from which Kaspen Shale and Agris Varen had left, some time ago now. Although they could not see him, Kaspen had sent a subtle nod in his direction, as they hurried west through the streets of Highwater.

By the storms it felt good to be out on the hunt again, Arillion thought, feeling his pulse race. Being confined to the wayfarer's wagon for so long had nearly finished him and when Kaspen told him of the meet, Arillion had insisted he come along, if only to watch from afar. Despite clearly harbouring doubts, Kaspen had wisely relented, Agris Varen lending the assassin his staff to lean on.

Somewhere off through the dark a woman's angry scream pierced the night's blackness that seemingly blanketed Highwater's poor quarters in a veil of suffocation.

Arillion scowled. Yet another poor bastard caught in the web of their own circumstance, dragged into the district's squalor by the cost of living and the hollow opportunity it presented to them.

The poor quarter's vein-like labyrinths of alleys,

narrow claustrophobic lanes and treacherous back streets were harbour to all kinds of activities, all manner of opportunity for those with the strength to take it.

How Arillion loved it. He grinned, his eyes wide with a joy that might have given away his hiding place if anyone was looking.

Morgan Belle had once said to Arillion that there was no difference between night and day on the poor streets of Highwater, only a subtle change in the smell. Arillion was forced to agree. It never seemed to change this side of the street; it was always dark and soulless here in the city. There was never any hope for those trapped within their own lives and little chance for betterment, despite the noble intentions of Alion Byron.

Arillion scoffed at the idea. Of course most of them did little to change this fact anyway. Instead they sat around begging for someone to help them, whining about Alion Byron's lack of help. Complaining that the strong and the rich took all they possessed from them and how they were powerless to stop them as they chiselled their way through their meagre and pitiful existences.

Once upon a time Arillion had been like them and he might have even pitied them at one stage in his life. But now he despised them all. The law of the streets in the Four Vales, no matter what city you lived in, was simple. Take what you can get and kill those who try to take what you have from you.

Money was everything to everyone in Highwater, despite what the monks might preach, or the politicians may tell you. From the painted whores standing on the corner of Charnel Lane, to the beggars and racketeers who descended upon the bustling market streets like diseased vermin, people would do anything they could to get as little or as much as they could get their hands on.

It was no different on the other side of the coin, either. The Brotherhood was clear evidence of that. When it came down to it, it was all about the power, all about the wealth you had and the status you could buy with it.

Arillion licked his lips thoughtfully as Cassana's face flashed in his mind and he shook his head free of his old, bitter view of the world. A few seasons ago, Arillion would have thought nothing of the power-struggle threatening to tear the Vales apart, only of the money to be made from it. But now, after Cassana, with her naive, yet dutiful and infuriating desire to always make things right, Arillion was not quite so sure. Yes, there was still a lot of coin to be made, still plenty of throats to be cut but, for a change, he would be doing it with a purpose, one that was, for once, not solely governed by his desire for wealth.

Arillion smiled. Dress it up as he may, but despite everything, it actually felt quite good.

Lost to his thoughts, Arillion almost missed the hooded figure that had appeared from the tavern and checked carefully from the shadows of the porch that the way was clear for him.

A careful man, Teal, it seemed, was as anxious as Arillion and his companions were to make sure it wasn't a trap or that things were nothing more than a business proposition. Feeling his old senses come alive, Arillion watched his man, not even feeling the dull throb of pain from his broken leg.

Teal checked the lane for many moments, before stepping out hurriedly and moving fluidly past Arillion's hiding place.

Arillion cursed silently, as Teal made swift his retreat and turned left at the end of the lane. He had positioned himself carefully, or so he thought, expecting Teal to head either east or further south into the poor quarter. He had not expected the information seller to head towards the more affluent west of Highwater.

"You bloody old fool," Arillion hissed. With his

padded staff thudding gently, the assassin hopped his way to the end of the lane and swept his steely gaze down the street.

Apart from a dog, snuffling forlornly through the rubbish, the street was empty. Teal was gone.

Arillion puffed out his cheeks, throwing his head to the dark sky and fixing his frustrations on the lone star that managed to pierce the night.

"Next time," Arillion said, calming down quickly. He had only wanted to see where Teal went, and, to a point, he had.

His *questions* would come when they had what they wanted from him.

Chancellor Relan Valus heard the screams, long before he and his escorts reached the lone cell, in the depths of the old Royal Dungeons. Captain Varl's pleading echoes bounded down the rough tunnel towards them, wrapped up in the torchlight that rolled and bobbed around the slick, ancient stone walls.

It had been another day of success for the Brotherhood, each raid, each Reven traitor gathered up by the city, another cut deeper into the fraying resolve of her people. News of the discovery of Baron Crowood's family, butchered to the last, had seen one Reven merchant dragged from his home and nearly beaten to death. Naturally, the chancellor had sent word to the high duke, cowering away in his chambers with only the worst of news to settle his fears and cravings. A few more days and Relan would be ready to make his move.

He had sent a note, congratulating Crowood on his continuing efforts to the Brotherhood's cause and of how gladdened he was to hear reports of the chaos stirring on the streets of Ilithia. Finishing the note, he enquired on how his family were, despite the news of their *apparent* murder at the hands of the savage Reven insurgents.

His attention was diverted as a high-pitched scream set his nerves on edge and his two escorts shared a silent look. Despite his glee at finally having the captain out of the way, he almost pitied him. The Kestrel must be close to the answers they sought by now and it was not a time for honour or duty to stand in their way.

As they neared the cell, Relan stopped, dragging both guards to a halt by the sleeves of their tunics.

"Wait with me," he ordered the man Fuller, softly. Turning his eyes to Esten Oswald, he hissed, "send her to me, I would have a report on her progress."

Captain Oswald nodded, passing Fuller the torch as he headed dutifully away down the tunnel towards the beckoning light of the corridor beyond the crumbling arch.

The Kestrel stepped back from Lucien Varl, aware that for once, perhaps, she had taken him too far. Sighing, she wiped her bloodied hands on a rag and tossed it onto the floor beside the three toes she had just taken.

Wiping her bloodied brow with the back of her sleeve, she stepped back and watched as the former captain hung before her, his sweat soaked, blood-streaked body swaying gently on supportive chains.

For two days he had resisted her attentions, each lick of flame, each delicately placed cut met with guttural screams of defiance that said a great deal about the man.

Unperturbed, the Kestrel worked on his mind, whispering soothing words as he drifted in and out of consciousness, bringing him back with a cold bucket of water here, or a caressing touch there.

Despite Relan Valus' obsessed urgency, she would have the answer. Captain Varl would give her what she wanted, but she would not risk hastening his death before she had the location of the high duke's family.

She turned as one of the chancellor's new thugs came to the bars of the cell, his eyes white with horror as he looked at the dripping carcass that was the former captain of Karick.

"Yes?" the Kestrel snapped, dragging his attention to her.

"Begging your pardon, milady, but he would see you a moment," the man blurted and without waiting for a response, turned away hastily.

Looking back at the captain, the Kestrel ran a thoughtful finger down his bloodied, burnt chest, feeling his heart stirring there.

"We shall talk again soon, my captain," she whispered gently in his torn ear, before turning away.

"Well?" Relan Valus asked, his need burning in his eyes.

The Kestrel walked up to him, dismissing the two guards back down the tunnel with a piercing look.

"And a good evening to you, too," she smiled, standing before the chancellor with her hands on her slender hips.

"Has he spoken?" the chancellor hissed, his anger colouring his gaunt cheeks. "Time is pressing, Kestrel. I have moves to make and I need to know we have them before I begin."

The Kestrel waved away his concern. "I am well aware of the situation, chancellor. But I will not rush my work. It's a pity you did not let me deal with the Redani before you gave him over to Borin and Fenton. Things would have been a lot easier for us now if you had."

Relan ignored the look in her eyes and folded his cold hands within the sleeves of his robes. "We have all made mistakes, Kestrel, but I did not come to listen to you underline my prior shortcomings. As you know, I have taken steps to ensure that the Redani can never speak of what he heard, lest he end up in a cell again. So get me that location and get it soon. We need to send men to kill them before we make our next move. We cannot risk any other delays."

The chancellor made to move past his words and the assassin blocking his way, but she planted a hand firmly on his bony chest.

"You will only strengthen his resolve, leave him to me and hold fast to your patience," the Kestrel hissed. "Once Lady Stromn and her whelp are dead, you can have his head for your gates, I promise you."

Relan Valus looked down at the bloodied hand on his chest and stepped away. The anger building on his lips slipped from his face and he nodded.

"As you wish, Kestrel," he sighed. "Send word, as soon as you have their location."

"Have no fear of that," the Kestrel smiled, imagining her blade deep in the chancellor's back as he turned wordlessly and walked away from her.

Sighing softly, the Kestrel turned and went in search of her answer.

CHAPTER TWENTY FOUR

Shadows Deep

The crowd gathered together talking in hushed tones, their breath filling the courtyard on the cold, crisp morning. Savinn Kassaar, wrapped from head to toe in dark robes and a cowl to conceal his identity, spoke quietly with one of the priests from the nearby chapel of Our Lady's Favour.

"We should begin soon," the priest said softly, his reluctance painted as clearly on his pale features as the blue wash in the cloudless sky above them.

Savinn nodded, but said nothing. Both men knew the risk of their endeavour today and whilst to others it seemed folly, the city of Karick needed a show of calm and humility, one that would hopefully bring it back from the brink.

"The Lady knows we need the high duke to see reason," the priest continued, clasping his hands together. "Our halls are already full with those seeking sanctuary and I fear for what may come."

Savinn placed a calming hand upon the priest's sharp shoulder. The old man, Mathew, had worked tirelessly over the years, helping those who needed it, giving care and guidance to those who were lost. Savinn had donated heavy coin to the chapel for many years, never forgetting where he had come from and always willing to help those who needed it when they arrived.

Dropping his hand, Savinn tilted his head and stepped back into the masses, allowing the priest to address the crowd full of men, women and a handful of children. All of these faces, grim and pale, turned to the priest as he spoke.

"My friends," Mathew began, his hands raised high, "today we rise above our own fears to bring hope to those who cannot. There is a terrible malaise in the streets of our great capital, one which, if not treated, will poison our future and sully the memory of our peaceful past."

Savinn, arms folded tightly across his chest, listened on, his heart drumming heavily at the priest's words.

"Many of our citizens are missing," Mathew continued, "taken from their homes without just cause and, as of yet, not returned. Walk with me my friends, as we take our concerns peacefully to the high duke, to share our fears and hopefully, with the Lady's grace, have them listened to by a man who I know we all love and respect. Come with me all – let us find the man whom many believe we have lost."

Savinn swallowed back his fears as the crowd fell in behind the old priest and the march east towards the Valian Mile began.

As the merchant-thief hid amongst the masses, a child, hanging off his mother's hand, stared up at him, blue eyes wide as they searched his cowl.

Pulling down his scarf, Savinn smiled reassuringly and only hoped that the boy did not read the worry in his eyes.

Commander Renald Gardan sat on his mount, chewing idly at a nail, hidden away beneath his new and rather splendid leather riding gloves. All about him, his men waited silently, their breaths the only tell of the life in their bodies. Reports had been received that the rabble would come to them at the main south market, and then turn northwards up the Valian Mile.

'No need to bother the high duke with this,' he had said to the chancellor earlier that morning, before the first light of dawn had even touched the horizon. Relan Valus had agreed wholeheartedly, wishing the commander and his men well with their entrusted task.

Sighing with impatience, eager for it to begin, Gardan looked to his second, mounted beside him.

"All is in hand, commander," Aren Bray said quietly in answer to the question on his lips. Leaning forward in his saddle, Aren patted the broad neck of his grey mare and ruffled her ears.

Gardan eyed his recently promoted captain and found it hard to fathom that a man who showed no remorse when it came to butchering, could display such affection for a horse he barely knew.

"It had better be, captain," Gardan warned, staring across the silent square to the west. Any hawkers, traders and peddlers had quickly vanished into the early morning gloom at their arrival.

Distracting himself, Gardan studied the magnificent statue of Valan Stromn in the centre of the large market square, the towers of the large south gate filling his view beyond.

An exquisite piece of workmanship, Gardan studied it closely for a time, marvelling at the incredible detail and thinking thoughtfully about the skilled hands that had fashioned it. He nodded his head respectfully and smiled his thanks.

Many of the Brotherhood cursed the former high duke's memory, angry at the years of peace they found themselves entrenched in and never forgiving him for not finishing off the Reven people, all those years ago.

Not I, Gardan thought, clenching his fists tightly about his reins. Without his reticence, Gardan would never have had this opportunity for the riches and glory that awaited him. If the Reven lands were already Valian, its people enslaved or probably annihilated, there would be few, if any scraps left on the table for him to fight over.

But not today – today, the history books would recall this the moment when all it meant to be Valian was remembered, when the hard road, less travelled of late, would be taken, for the betterment of all and for the future of all true Valian citizens.

"Sir," Esten Oswald hissed, drawing his commander's thoughts away from the past as sunlight settled on the statue's stone crown.

Gardan found the man to his left, stood in line on the cold cobbles with the other militia soldiers. The former archer was pointing across the square, towards the crowd that was heading their way through the mist and gloom.

Nodding his thanks, Gardan stood in his stirrups and swept a steely gaze about his men.

"We are here today, only to ensure that these people do not bother the high duke. There is a time and a place for such discussion and it is sat around a table, *not* gathered before the walls of the high duke's keep." Gardan paused, staring at the faces that turned to look at him. There was worry there, he could tell, but, scattered in amongst the uncertainty, there was also the flash of eagerness, the burning glimmer of anticipation.

Sheep and wolves, Gardan observed, satisfied.

Remembering himself, he continued. "If the crowd does not disperse quietly and on its own volition, we are instructed to gather up only those of Reven blood. But, and I stress to you, there will be no repeat of the brutality I have heard reports of recently. There will be no blood spilt by us on these cobbles today. Am I understood?"

As a ripple of obedience swept through his men, Gardan turned his thoughts westwards, sharing a quick, triumphant look with Aren Bray.

The market was silent, the air full of tension as the crowd of Valian and Reven protestors came to a halt, some distance from the line of riders and militia soldiers.

For a time, both groups stared at one another, the only sounds to be heard the hearts raging in each person's head, the jingle of harness and a quickly stilted enquiry of a perplexed child.

Several crows circled in the sky over the square, debating the day ahead, before drifting their way south above the towers of the gatehouse. The dark shapes of the sentries on duty there were silhouetted against the rising day as the tension grew.

Savinn watched as the priest walked forward, the old man's hands slipping from his sleeves as he raised them in greeting to the militia soldiers.

"Lady's blessings upon you all this day," Mathew called out, as his sandals scraped on the cobbles.

"And to you, brother," the tall, hawk-faced man responded, his crisp words echoing across the square as he shifted in his saddle.

"We seek a path to the keep," the priest called out. "May we pass, sir? We travel in peace and hold no malice in our hearts or purpose."

Savinn felt his fears claw at his arms, as the white-haired man who could only be Renald Gardan, looked nonchalantly about the faces in the crowd before him.

"Sadly, father, I must decline your request," the commander responded, his words earnest, but his harsh features haughty and menacing. "By order of Karian Stromn, the high duke of Karick, you must disperse. There will be a time for your concerns to be heard, but it will not be today, it will not be like this."

The priest's features, stained already by sorrow, fell with grief, as he turned back to the crowd. He stepped back towards them, arms falling to his sides.

Whispers of uncertainty slipped through the throng as people began to discuss what to do next. As those with enough purpose gathered together to debate matters further, several hooded people stirred, slipping through the masses hastily.

A cry went up from the throng, as people scattered and as screams began to rise, Savinn Kassaar, much to his own horror, realised what was about to happen.

Eran Dray noticed the commotion and heard the screams of panic from where he stood in the front ranks of the militia line, furthest right from the man who had stamped his mark upon the city. Called to arms that morning, before his planned return to see Dia, he had been ordered to join Fuller and the other members of Eagle Watch at the south market.

Several of the crowd suddenly rushed forward, scattering people in their path as they raised small crossbows and sent a volley into their line. Screams of pain rose from the militia ranks as several men fell and as Eran rose up from behind his shield, he noticed Garn on the cobbles beside him, a dark shaft deep in his neck.

As Eran dropped his shield and fell to his knees to gather his friend in his arms, Gardan's voice screamed out, shattering any hope he may have had for a peaceful resolution.

"Reven assassins – take them all."

All about him, the roar of anger rose from their ranks as the militia and riders charged forward, steel scraping from scabbards, hooves ringing loud on the cobbles.

"Leave it," Garn pleaded, blood bursting on his lips as Eran held him close. His friend clutched at his mail shirt, pulling him down to his ear as he fought with the shaft choking the life from him.

"Don't drown with them," Garn said and then, stiffening momentarily, he sagged low in his friend's arms and slipped quietly away from the madness.

Riders surged into the crowd, scattering people in all directions as their battle cries rose wildly above the pleading screams of terror. Before he could react, Savinn saw a horse bowl Mathew over and heard the crunch as the priest's head was dashed on the cobbles.

Savinn stumbled over the young boy in his haste to be away, hissing for the screaming mother to flee to safety with her child, as he made for a nearby alleyway. One of the dark cloaked crossbowmen was already fleeing the square and scowling, Savinn chased after him, the chaos breaking across the market like thunder behind him.

As he chased the fleeing assassin into the alley, the merchant-thief heard the first of the panicked screams fail abruptly and felt his stomach turn with disgust.

Rising up weakly and leaving his friend's body on the bloodied cobbles, Eran Dray was pulled towards the carnage before him by the acid tongue of his furious commander. With his head spinning and his eyes wide at the madness before him, Eran spied the robed figure fleeing down an alleyway with one of his accomplices. Dragging his horror away from the sights before him, he ran after the robed figures, determined to find the answers that others were not even trying to find.

"Wait for me, brother," Savinn called out, as he pursued the crossbowman down the twisting, cluttered alley.

A beggar looked up as the robed figures rushed by him, cursing them angrily as they slipped from view around a corner.

Savinn's heart was in his mouth as he closed upon his

prey and he saw the Valian man look over his shoulder.

"Get away from here," the man hissed back, waving his crossbow away down a narrow lane away to their left.

Savinn stumbled and with a curse, the man slid to a halt. Muttering, the man hurried back, his deep-set eyes bright with worry as he eyed the alley for pursuers.

"Get up you imbecile, before you cost–,"

The man's curses were cut short as Savinn rose up swiftly and pressed a blade to his exposed throat.

"Who paid you to attack?" Savinn snarled, drawing a thin line of blood from the trembling man's skin as he forced him against some broken fencing.

"Tell me," Savinn demanded, as they heard the beggar shrieking anew and detected the sounds of booted feet coming their way.

The man's eyes narrowed, "Like I would tell you anything, Reven scum."

Their pursuer was drawing close as Savinn leant in close. "So be it," he hissed, pressing his blade deep.

Eran Dray approached the still figure ahead, his arm heavy as he slowly drew his Valian blade from the sheath hanging off his left hip. About him, the tall buildings lining the narrow alley leant in close, observing his faltering approach with scorn, seemingly aware of the fear rife in his body.

Placing a slow boot in front of the other, Eran padded quietly towards the body, noticing the dark pool that was spreading out slowly across the ground and the small crossbow lying forgotten, nearby.

Eyeing the two adjoining alleys and aware of the shadowy doorways that offered him further danger ahead, Eran kicked the assassin over, recoiling as he saw the man's throat, opened to the bone and glistening in the early morning light.

Gagging, Eran recoiled, reaching for breath. The man

was Valian, as he somehow expected him to be and as he felt his stomach lurch, he staggered back.

Savinn Kassaar listened to the man retch from the shadows of the doorway he pressed himself tightly against. His heart was in his mouth as he held his breath and struggled to shut out the distant screams coming from the market square.

Cursing himself, he gripped his blade, allowing his anger to sweep through his cold body. *How could he have been so stupid?* He should have foreseen that Gardan and his allies would have known about the march, would have taken steps to turn it to their advantage and divert the high duke's attention away from the people of Karick who had not yet embraced the madness.

You bloody fool, Savinn, he berated himself, his anger chasing his arm and fuelling his need for revenge.

From his slight field of view, the soldier rose up again, wiping his mouth as his sword rasped against the floor. The only other time Savinn had been in such danger was on that fateful day, all those years ago, when Khadazin had saved his life.

The tall soldier stepped further into his view and looked down the other alleyway, his broad back turned towards him. Feeling his fury rise, Savinn Kassaar raised his blade and stepped from the doorway.

"That's enough, captain," Commander Gardan said softly. Turning his mount away, he dug his heels in deep and headed away from the bloodshed. "Clean this mess up," he growled, as he rode away.

Aren Bray nodded, swallowing hard. Reluctantly, he turned his attention back on the square, watching as the last of the prisoners were rounded up and the wounded dispatched.

On leaden legs, he stepped towards the carnage, his

eyes dragged to the bodies on the cobbles that surrounded Valan Stromn's statue in bloody worship. Many had perished under the swords and hooves of the militia and although everything had gone as planned, Aren couldn't help but think that the price was a heavy one to pay.

No doubt the Brotherhood would spin this their way, reporting of the treachery and *unprovoked* attack on the brave Valian militia. With many Reven dead, no longer needed for questioning, their attentions would have to turn now towards finding Savinn Kassaar. When news of this attack spread, the people would round up the other Reven citizens for them.

Stepping over the broken body of the old priest, Aren felt his hopes rise above his revulsion. If this didn't bring the bastard out into the open, nothing would.

A voice called out, rolling down the narrow alley to send Savinn back into his doorway before he gave himself away.

With his poised blade clutched tight to his trembling chest and his breath trapped in his throat, the merchant-thief listened to his own panic, as a second militia man came hurrying down the lane.

"What you got there, boy?" a gruff voice barked out.

Savinn closed his eyes and did not see the large militia soldier who dragged the other man aside to kick quizzically at the corpse.

"One of the assassins," said the militia solder, the one Savinn had been about to kill. "I–,"

"Good work," the man said. "I knew you had it in you. Come on, there's plenty more work to be done. Better let the commander know we killed another one of them."

"B-but he's not Reven?"

"Yes he is," the larger man growled meaningfully.

Savinn heard a scuffle and then the two men hurried

away, back towards the square. When their arguments faded away, the merchant-thief let out the longest sigh of his life.

Hurrying from his hiding place, he sifted through the corpse's pockets for a letter, a note, anything that could aid him. He cursed when he found nothing more than a few sceptres and a solitary crown. Of course there would be nothing incriminating – no self-respecting assassin would have a letter on him, signed by the chancellor or whoever had hired him.

Shaking his head, Savinn stared down at the dead man. Sighing, he bent low again to close the assassin's eyes, staring vacantly towards his next life.

"What have you done?" Savinn asked sadly. Rising up, he threw a glance down the alleyway towards the market square and tasted the disgust on his lips.

There were no sounds coming from the square now, no screams, no cries of anger, only the telling silence of what had happened. It was the most deafening sound he had ever heard.

With his nostrils flaring from his ragged breath and his hands shaking uncontrollably, Savinn looked back at the corpse, before turning his thoughts to the bloody blade he barely held on to.

"What a wretched species we are," he said, tears spilling down his face.

Turning from the man he had murdered, whose name he would never know, Savinn hurried away from the alley and became one with the city.

CHAPTER TWENTY FIVE

...who needs enemies?

Cassana heard the hurried approach of heavy booted feet long before the discussion outside the library door, giving her enough time to put the letter from the woodsman aside and make herself presentable enough to receive guests. Adjusting the pins in her hair and smoothing down the creases in the skirt of her velvet dress, she rose slowly and crossed to the window. As the ringed handle of the heavy oak door turned, she glanced out across the city of Highwater and thought how calm it seemed today.

Lord Bryn Astien, his face drained, his eyes haunted, strode into the library, the door pulled quietly close by Erith Taye as he passed.

"My lady," Bryn Astien began, his words, prepared at length on the journey northwards, failing him immediately. With his steel helm tucked under one arm, he came forward and offered the lady of Highwater a respectful bow.

"Please, Bryn," Cassana said hastily. Crossing to him, she threw herself into his arms and was relieved when her father's old friend put a strong arm about her.

"I am so sorry, Cassana," Bryn whispered, shaking his head in disbelief.

Cassana looked up into his glistening eyes and nodded her thanks. She could smell the road on his armour, see the dust and sweat on his face and hair, streaked by the sun and laced with his advancing years.

"It has been a difficult time," Cassana admitted, her voice hollow and lost. "I fear that I am still in shock, but I suppose that is a good thing. We cannot allow our emotions to cloud our judgements at this time."

Forgetting his manners, Bryn Astien's eyes widened as he took in the woman who stood before him. No longer the truculent girl who haunted the halls of Highwater Keep, she was the woman her father had always known she could become, more like her mother with each passing day. It broke his heart that she had to discover herself like this.

As if reading his thoughts, Cassana half-smiled and pulled away from his embrace.

"I have had to grow up fast," she accepted, her emerald eyes flashing briefly with the girl that once was.

Bryn smiled, putting his helm down on top of a pile of old, leather-bound books. Straightening slowly, he winced and found her eyes once more.

"I know your father was proud of you, Cassana," Bryn said, swallowing his own grief. "To hear of your safe return lifted the burden of guilt from his shoulders."

Smiling, Cassana wandered to the window again.

"He was, I know," she said, more to herself than her guest. "What brings you home to us, my friend?"

Bryn Astien swallowed hard. "Grave tidings, I fear. The capital is in shadows, danger haunts its streets and poison laces the ear of the high duke."

The fear on Cassana's face was evident as she turned. Searching Lord Astien's eyes, she encouraged him to continue with a furtive nod.

"News of... your father's murder caused uproar in the capital. The high duke sends his deepest sympathies and urges that, in this difficult time, we seek a sensible and peaceful solution to our differences."

Cassana glowered, disdain lacing her words. "It is a little late for that. My father could see what was happening, he tried to prevent what was to come... and look what happened to him? He had to be right about it, he just had to and I cannot return to the table without his proof."

Bryn Astien nodded in agreement, his sigh long and hard. "I fear you are right, my lady. It is clear to me, though I can offer no evidence to support it that, following the vote by the council, there is a move to finish what could have been started, fifty years ago."

Cassana crossed to a magnificent oak sideboard and poured him a goblet of wine. Stepping close to her father's friend, she placed it in his trembling hand.

Nodding his thanks, Bryn Astien drained the goblet and licked his moustache.

"My thanks, lady. It has been an arduous road, one I feared I would not survive."

Seeing the worried look on her lovely face, Bryn recounted all he had heard, all that was happening in the capital. News of the Reven and Valian citizens being dragged for questioning did little to ease her fears and when he spoke of his secret meeting with Lucien Varl and Henry Farrington her face was as pale as the whites of her eyes.

"So at least we are not alone," Cassana murmured, breathing a sigh of relief. "There are those who would stand with us?"

Bryn Astien nodded his head. "Indeed so, my lady. If the hardliners are pushing for war with the Reven, if this is, as I also suspect, a calculated ruse to garner the people's support for such a declaration, then we must stand firm and act swiftly to counter their moves."

Cassana spread her arms wide. "But how can we do this? The high duke will not come to me and I cannot go to him. It is simply too dangerous. If they can reach my father here, they would most certainly be able get to us in Karick."

"Honestly, lady? I do not have the answer – but we must search for it," Lord Astien said, his deep voice full of conviction. "It seems that Chancellor Valus is the man orchestrating things and there is no question that he has managed to sway the high duke. The real concern is who he is working with. I fear, with Captain Varl's recent removal from the high duke's confidence, that it is to Lady Rothley and Lord Carwell we must divert our attentions."

"Captain Varl has been removed?" Cassana blinked in confusion. Her disgust swept aside Bryn Astien's response. "I have been stupid, so *stupid.* I did not see it when I was there, but now, after all I have heard, all that has happened, it is clear to me that Madam Grey was working for Chancellor Valus. It is why I never got to see the high duke, despite the chancellor's assurances. Valus kept me from seeing him, so that his allies might have the chance to capture me again."

Bryn Astien poured himself another wine and drained it hastily again.

"I stopped in Havensdale on my return," he said quietly, his voice guarded. "The news from there is terrible, though I hear tell that you have already been informed of that... and worse?"

"I have," Cassana said evenly. "It seems you are right to direct our thoughts towards Carwell."

Bryn Astien nodded. "Gardan, the man responsible for the raid, these falsehoods, has arrived in the capital. He brings claim of Valian treachery and it is he who has ousted Captain Varl, it is he who now directs the militia's investigations."

Cassana gasped and covered her mouth to stifle the profanity that was about to follow.

She paced nervously, clutching her arms to her breast. "This is grave, grave news, my lord. It seems that we face many foes and whilst we may know some of them now, we must still watch the shadows and hope to find the key that will unlock all of this."

Bryn Astien nodded. "Your father believed there to be a spy here, my lady," he dared ask. "Have you any further news? Any clue as to who it may be? If taken alive, they could shed a great deal of light on this for us."

Cassana shook her head, masking her concern with a casual wave of her hand. "Sadly, as of yet, no, but we seek one who may help us and that is a comforting thought."

Bryn crossed and placed a gentle hand on her trembling shoulder.

"I am with you, my lady," he said, fondness in his eyes and determination etched on his face.

Cassana smiled and stepped on to her toes to kiss both his cheeks.

"Thank you, my friend, it means everything to have you back here with me," she paused, her smile distant. "We both loved my father dearly, and together, we can share this strength for our loss. The road ahead will be a perilous one, but there is still hope. If we can prove to the high duke that he has been duped, the tide will turn in our favour, I am certain of it."

Bryn Astien put aside his goblet and held onto Cassana's hands as he fell onto one knee, offering his strength and support to her.

He chose not to tell her of his fears that, should they not find the Lady's favour soon, the high duke might not have the power or breath left in him to save them.

When Bryn Astien was gone, Cassana sat back down with

a sigh, her eyes wandering to the letter. Distracting her rising thoughts, she picked it up again and read it for what must have been the hundredth time. Simply put, short and honest, it could have only come from her mysterious saviour, his joy at her safe arrival home, tempered by the sadness of her father's death. Hinting at more than a common familiarity with her father, the letter only served to deepen the woodsman's enigmatic past. His final warning in the letter, after he had pledged his support and desire to see her again, was a telling one...

'I have suffered at the hands of those who work from the shadows in Karick. Rest assured, they will not forget you and you must watch for them still, I fear, my lady. Their reach is long and their strength grows daily. I have been a fool, a coward. I shall not hide from them any longer. I will not flee from the past and the pain that rests there. I will do all that I can to aid the justice that is failing this land and I will not fail you, Cassana. My swords, once again, are yours.'

It was signed, simply, '*Woodsman.*'

Cassana's heart raced as she dropped her shaking hands to her lap and slowly folded the letter up. Closing her eyes, she thought back to the woodsman's stand at the brook, of his skill and bravery that day, so long ago now, it seemed.

A hazy image of the woodsman's imagined heroism on the bridge in Havensdale began to form in her mind and as her emotions swept her away, she began to think of another brave swordsman, one who had seen her to safety and the one who had first claimed, then broken her heart.

Edren Bay looked up from his book of poetry as he heard the light approach of heels on marble. Sighing, he closed the book, drinking in the peace and solitude of his surroundings one final time. The summerhouse was the perfect retreat, offering him somewhere he could escape his turmoil and deliberations. It was a quiet corner of the keep where he had only the insects and birds to keep him company.

Had Alion Byron felt the same? He found himself thinking and his mood entirely spoilt, Edren awaited Lysette's arrival.

With the sun shining in her ringlets, Lysette Astien swept into the secret garden, her feigned surprise clearing any blemishes from the corners of her eyes.

"Forgive me, sir," she said, still attempting to play her games. "I thought to find some solitude and all I have done is spoil yours."

Edren scowled, rising as her station dictated. "Spare me the pleasantries, lady. What is it you want?"

The smile stayed on her lips, but her eyes betrayed her anger as she swept up the marble steps to the shade of the summerhouse.

"The heat, I understand," she soothed, sitting on the marble bench, its legs beautifully carved into four oak trees, reaching up to cradle their marble sky.

As Edren sat back down, she unfurled her silk fan and began calming the heat burning her cheeks.

"I thought you should know that my beloved father has returned to us," she said, with only the merest hint of disdain. "He brings Lady Byron the gravest of news, it seems."

Edren dealt her a look of warning, rising up hurriedly. Bounding down the steps, he strode about the hedges and slipped from view for a time. When he returned, Lysette was studying a nearby yellow rose, sniffing its petals deeply.

"Satisfied?" she asked him, as he sat back down beside her.

Edren felt his anger rise again. "Do not mock, Lysette. We should be careful what we say to one other. You know what trouble was caused the last time somebody overheard my conversation."

Lysette fanned her impatience and took his hand in hers. "That is for the chancellor to worry about. The fool thinks he is the master tactician, yet his mistakes have nearly ruined our plans."

"*Our* plans?" Edren cocked an eyebrow.

"You know who I mean," Lysette hissed. "Stop dancing around me, Edren. What is wrong with you?"

Edren looked away and sighed, letting go of her slender fingers. "I fear for the future, our future. We are alone here, with only thugs and mercenaries to watch over us. Can we really achieve what the Brotherhood wants of us?"

Dropping her fan to her lap, Lysette reached up with both hands and gently cupped Edren's face, pulling his attention back towards her.

"Hush now, my darling," she soothed, kissing his lips to stifle his protests. "We can and we must. There is only one way out of this for us and that is to succeed. We are in too deep now and I would have it no other way."

Edren pulled away, his dark eyes blazing. "But at what cost? Alion Byron is dead. *Dead*! Who else must die so that we can open the way for our brothers and sisters?"

Lysette's beautiful eyes burned with her answer. "Whoever it takes, Edren. We will have to bloody our hands some more, before we plunge them deep into the riches that await us."

Edren shook his head, his panic on his bearded face. "Alion Byron had to die, I understand that. B-but what of Cassana? What about your father, my parents? They will not stand idly by and allow us free rein over them."

"I think you value my father's loyalty to the Byron banner too greatly," Lysette chuckled mirthlessly. "He will, I assure you, when the time comes, realise he is beaten and join that which he loathes."

Edren snorted. That did not sound like the man he knew, the man who had been his master, teaching him to become a man of humility, a knight fashioned from all it meant to be honourable.

"I would not be so certain of that," Edren warned, searching her face for tell of what she was capable of.

Lysette turned away, starting nowhere in particular. "Then he will die. I am prepared for that. The moment I pledged myself to the Brotherhood, I knew that it was a possibility."

Edren felt sickened and he swallowed his disgust. "You would watch your own father die, just to have more wealth and power? What of your mother? She would never forgive you?"

Lysette laughed sarcastically. "Oh, my sweet lover, how naive you are. My mother will bathe in the riches I bestow upon her. She hated Alion Byron as much as I, choking on her envy at the power he had, the power he only obtained with my father's help."

The summer fled from Edren's body and he shuddered, horrified at the look staining Lysette's captivating features.

"And what of my parents?" he asked quietly.

She turned her thoughts to him, blinking free from her desires. "They will be spared, as was agreed. Nothing has changed. If they do not comply, they will be exiled."

Edren, his body shaking, rose on unsteady legs. He looked down at the woman who, only the night before had shared his bed again. In the clear light of yet another day, he despised her even more.

"They will not be harmed, lady," he warned her, his hand slipping to the pommel of the Valian Longsword at his hip.

Lysette nodded, fanning her face. "You have my word on that. Have you spoken to the chancellor yet?"

Edren shook his head. "The moon waxes tomorrow. I thought it better to tell him on the stars, rather than with ink."

Lysette smiled. "A wise decision. I imagine he will be very interested to hear about our visitors from Carwell and Havensdale."

Edren nodded subtly. *More blood on my hands*, he thought sadly. Bidding his farewell, Edren turned and hurried from the gardens.

After he was gone, Lysette let out a long, deep sigh. Fanning her annoyance idly, she pulled the petals off the beautiful rose, counting the names of those who still needed to die before her mission was done.

CHAPTER TWENTY SIX

Shining in the Darkness

The Kestrel smiled. Stepping away from the groaning captain, she allowed the echoes of his distraught whimpers to fade away into nothingness. Watching as he hung before her, she marvelled at her handiwork one last time, before turning away from him.

"My thanks, captain," she purred, slipping the crescent blade into her belt as she strode from the cell and pulled the barred gate close behind her. Turning the key in the old lock, she reached for the torch, sputtering away in an iron bracket on the adjacent wall.

Lifting it free, she searched the shadows, finding the bloodied carcass, dangling there. Already the rats were gathering again and she swallowed her sadness down.

"You are a brave man," she whispered. Turning, the Kestrel stalked away down the corridor, hearing the pleading moans chase weakly after her.

Garin Bree watched as the Kestrel came towards him, rising hurriedly from his stool to greet her. She cast a withering look at him, as he ran a hand over his bald head and shifted furtively before her.

"I must see the chancellor," she hissed, her hands still covered in thick blood and her cold face flickering with flame and shadow. "I will return later. Tell the next watch that he must be kept alive at all costs. Do you understand?"

Garin fumbled for his tongue and blurted out he would. The woman searched his face for a time, then nodded once. Pulling her hood over her braids, she made for the stone steps that twisted up from view at the end of the small chamber.

When Garin heard the gate close behind her, he forced his squat frame back down onto his stool and let out his held breath.

The woman gave him the shivers, even more than Gardan did. Thinking of his commander, no doubt enjoying a warm bed and woman somewhere, Garin scowled and picked up the knife and the block of wood he had been carving.

Whilst Aren and Esten were getting promoted and having fun rounding up Reven traitors, he was stuck down here in the dark for hours on end watching over a condemned man.

"S'no justice in it," he grumbled, shaking his head bitterly.

Dia watched from the shadows as the hooded figure closed the rusted gate which led down into the depths of the Old Royal Dungeons. Picking its way through the reaching fingers of the old ruins, left untouched by the former high duke in the western grounds as a warning to all who would follow him not to forget their bloody past, the figure carefully, cautiously surveyed its surroundings, before slipping away into the night.

With a fulsome moon bright overhead, Dia remained where she was for many moments, holding on to her breath lest she reveal her presence. The thorns of the rose bushes tugged at her sleeve as she tried to shift her cramp from one calf to the other and with a grimace, she fell back against the cold stone of the wall behind her, thankful that the storms had finally abated, dragged away by rising winds towards the Western Vales.

Wrapping her cloak tightly about her frame to ward away the chill in the air, Dia looked up at the night sky above her and sighed.

If only everything else was as clear.

News of the bloodshed on the streets of the capital had burned a steady path through the resolve of those still clinging to the hopeful strands of peace. Despite Savinn's account, received only hours before from the barkeep of the Jade Eagle, the word on the streets was that the Reven had attacked the militia without provocation, yet another example of the danger they all *supposedly* faced, the threat all loyal Valian citizens were living under.

Dia felt her disgust rise, holding herself tightly to chase away her fears. She had still not heard from Eran and was desperately worried. *Was he alive*? Had he been one of the soldiers slain the previous day?

Banishing the emptiness inside of her, Dia focussed her thoughts on what she knew. Savinn needed news and he needed it now. The word was that Captain Varl had not been seen for some days now and that the high duke had been confined to his bedchambers with a mystery illness. Her master had finished his letter with a stark warning. Time was running out for them all.

The Lady's providence, it seemed, had already fallen into her lap only two nights prior, as Dia trailed the chancellor and his bodyguards through the keep. Fully expecting Chancellor Valus to retire to his estate for the night, she had stalked them from his office, through the western grounds of the keep. When he and his men unlocked the old gate leading to the disused dungeons, she knew that she was onto something.

Casting aside her duties without care for the ramifications, Dia had watched and monitored the comings and goings every night since. With several hooded figures in regular attendance, changing every night, she knew she had to get inside to find out who was being held there, or what was going on, no matter the cost. Her eagerness was tempered by her fear and the thought ringing in her ears. *Had they taken the high duke?* Was this finally their decisive move to forever change the mantle of power in the Four Vales?

Checking the position of the moon, she judged the watch would be relieved in a few more hours. After they had changed, she would make her move. If the Lady willed it, by dawn she would have news for Savinn, news that would give him back some of the hope he and the people of Karick had recently, violently lost.

Dia's legs felt numb as she followed the spiralling staircase down into the depth of the Old Royal Dungeons. With the flickering light from her candle lantern casting menacing shadows on the wall before her, she followed the broken steps carefully down into the unknown.

The night had slipped painfully away for her, as she waited for the watch to change and as the solitary guard was replaced by two others, she had felt her fears take a choking hold of her determination. Slipping through the night, she had hurried to the kitchens, gathering a tray of cured meat and bread, some cheese and a jug of water to take with her. Grabbing the room key she might need later, she had slipped away before the cook's curiosity got the better of him, making her way back to the western side of the keep's grounds. After many moments of deliberation, fighting with her desire to flee and hide in the comfort of her lover's arms, Dia had drawn in a calming, assured breath and opened the rusted gate.

Each step Dia took down into the depths drained more of her courage, leaving her with only her love and loyalty to Savinn Kassaar to keep her going. Before she realised it, the old steps gave way to a dimly lit chamber, the rough ceiling low and oppressive. Sweeping her hood about the room, she saw the guard hastily lift his head from the table he slumbered at.

"My lady, I beg your–," he began, kicking his stool over as he lurched to his feet. Dressed in a leather tunic and breeches, he was tall, his chest broad and his shoulders wide. The guard's long hair was matted and greasy, clinging to his neck and scalp and as he hesitated, his relief flashed in his dark, button-like eyes.

"Who are you?" he demanded, his voice gravelly. His right hand strayed to the blade on the table.

Dia licked the gamble on her lips. "I bring sustenance to the prisoner," she began, stepping closer.

The guard hesitated, his eyes going to the tray she carried, his thoughts drawn to the promise of the food underneath the cloth. "Chancellor Valus asked me to come."

At the mention of his name, the guard relaxed, offering her an apologetic nod. "They said we needed to keep him alive. What have you got, girl? Shame to waste it all on the condemned."

Dia dealt him a bright smile from within the shadows of her hood. Stepping towards the table, she put the tray and her lantern down. As the guard dragged his prize across the knotted wood towards him, Dia moved back, her right hand slipping to the knife, concealed under the sleeve of her left arm.

"Hmm," the guard said appreciatively, as he lifted off the cloth. "Is that ale?"

Her breath lost, Dia moved close, her heart thundering as she grabbed the man by the throat from behind. Pulling him backwards before his shock gave way to strength, she plunged her blade deep into his right ear.

With a gurgle, the man stiffened in her grasp and she felt him struggle desperately as she twisted the blade. Sickened by the feeling of death she wielded in her hand, Dia fell back as the man thrashed wildly. Stumbling to her knees, Dia lost her grip on him and could only watch as the guard turned – his eyes wide with shock.

Reaching up vainly to the hilt embedded in his ear, he went to speak and then, as Dia rose again, the man dropped to the dusty stone floor and toppled to one side, his body twitching, his eyes wide and staring as blood spilled down his neck.

Her hands trembling, Dia looked about the chamber, her eyes drawn to the two arched passageways that slipped away into the depths of the dank, musty dungeons. Gagging on her disgust and the heavy, stale air, she pulled her blade free, turning away as blood spouted from the deep wound.

With trembling hands, Dia cleaned her blade on the dead man's tunic, his body still clinging to the spasms of life as she slipped the weapon back into her wrist-sheath. Pulling her sleeve down, she replaced the cloth over the tray and picked it up. With nostrils racing, she drew in and let out several long, deep breaths, as she looked towards the tunnel where the distant tongues of flame chased the impenetrable darkness away. Closing her eyes, she attempted to clear her thoughts, struggling with her emotions as she fought against her revulsion.

That man, and one other, had to die this night. There was no turning back now. She had to find out who was being held prisoner here and, more importantly, she had to rescue them, whoever they might be.

The tunnel stretched away for what felt like eternity, slipping by shadowy cells, their barred doors broken and open. As the light from her lantern led her on, Dia felt her anticipation rise. With anxiety in her steps and her concern chasing at her heels, she hurried into the unknown, desperate for the answers she was risking her life for.

Eran's handsome face flashed in her mind and her fears gave way to her determination. She would see him again and they would find happiness in this life, despite the danger that threatened them all.

As Dia spied the distant tongues of a billowing torch, she vowed that to have that happiness, she would do whatever it took to see her Eran again.

Chancellor Relan Valus dismissed the guard, telling him his services were no longer needed that night. Ignoring the puzzled look on the man's tired face, the chancellor sent him away with an irritated wave of his hand, waiting for him to disappear from view, before he drew in a calming breath and let himself into the high duke's study.

It was a cold night outside and his dark robes and cloak did little to warm his fears, rising steadily with each heart beat, following the Kestrel's earlier report.

For so long he had suffered the banality of life in the capital, an apathetic existence that fifty years of peace had afforded the Valian people. With no eyes fixed across the mountains, no ambition, save that of prosperity settled in the heart and mind of the high duke, it had been a long and hard road to get to this point.

Relan felt his eagerness warm his fears, chased on by the hunger the Kestrel's news had barely satiated. Captain Varl had been broken, his strength and honour finally in tatters, his secret no longer his own to guard.

News of where the high duke's family was being protected was the decisive move he needed to finally tip the scales of balance in the Brotherhood's favour.

The Kestrel had done her duty well again, so well that

Relan almost, *almost* felt pity for the former captain who, once the high duke's family were dead, would no longer be a burden to him.

Following his capture, Relan had quickly come to realise that, no matter how much he wanted his old enemy gone, until Karian Stromn's wife and child were dead, they would need to keep Lucien Varl alive. Even now, it was still possible that the captain was fighting against them and that the location he had given them was just a ruse.

The name he had given them was a pointed barb at that, one directed firmly at the chancellor, his most bitter of enemies.

Shutting out the implications and the memories that suddenly came flooding back, Relan Valus swept his angry gaze around the study that was lost to gathering shadows. As he crossed the carpeted floor, his sandals crunched on the broken glass that had not been picked up.

Gagging at the smells emanating in the room, Relan looked for the high duke, finding him slumped over his desk, shivering in the faint candlelight that lit the room.

"My lord?" The chancellor called out, not even bothering to hide the disdain in his voice any more.

Karian Stromn raised his head weakly and stared wildly up at him, through eyes shot with blood.

"Relan?" he murmured, trying to haul himself up.

Chancellor Valus moved slowly to the table, staring down at the man who ruled the Four Vales and who, in a matter of days, would slip from his seat of power and be consigned to the history books.

"Tell me you have some good news," the high duke demanded, shaking uncontrollably. He was gaunt, his features filthy, the unkempt nails on his hands blackened by his self-imposed incarceration.

Relan sighed. The increased dosages in his beloved herbal tea had worked wonders on the high duke, stripping away his strength, instilling a deep-rooted fear and anxiety in him. It was a shame to see it come to this, the man who had given to him the status and position of power he required to carry out the Brotherhood's will.

"A clear message has been sent to those who seek to break the strength of our nation," Relan said evenly, his eyes betraying his malice, however. "Those of Reven blood will soon come to know what it means to betray the Valian people."

The high duke's eyes blazed angrily, rallying with a faint glimmer of the man that was and the chancellor was forced to step back under the weight of his gaze.

"I have heard of what has happened, Relan, don't think that I have not. We should be garnering the Reven community's support, not rounding them up like sheep for slaughter! We should be looking at ourselves before judging others!

The actions we have taken to protect ourselves have betrayed our values and our Valian principles. They are unlawful, unjust and unacceptable. I am ashamed to call myself Valian on this dark day..."

Sensing his moment, Relan stepped close to the high duke, placing a calming hand on his heaving shoulder, glaring down as Karian began to sob in shame.

"What is happening to me, Relan? What have I become?" the high duke demanded, trying to look up at his advisor, too ashamed to meet his pitying gaze.

"You are losing your mind," Relan hissed lowly, not sure if his words even registered. "The streets run with the taint of Reven blood and soon, very soon, the Valian armies will be marshalled for war."

Karian blinked, staring in disbelief. "W-what nonsense is this? I would not give countenance to such an act – neither would the Valian people."

Relan drew his hand away. "Ah, my lord, that is where you are wrong. They await only the strong leader they need, one who will carry the burning torch of their anger for them. The one with the strength to finish off what was started by your father."

The confusion in the high duke's eyes cleared and the bright clarity of realisation burned there for a brief moment.

"What have you done?" the high duke breathed. "What have I allowed to happen?"

"Everything," Relan Valus smiled, stepping back as Karian lurched wildly to his feet, reaching for his chancellor.

The high duke came for him, then stumbled, his strength lost to his drugged body, his mind spinning drearily as he fell to the floor, glancing his head on the corner of his desk.

"Rest, my lord," the chancellor ordered, moving away from the still body. He crossed to the first candle, snuffing out the light between finger and thumb. "You have laboured hard and long for the Valian people, but your betrayal, your weakness will be your legacy, and they will always remember you for it."

Relan crossed slowly over to a book case. Reaching up, he gently blew out the candle that rested there, watching with fascination as a wisp of smoke curled up into the shadows. He turned to the groaning high duke, who raised his head weakly and tried to crawl towards him.

"Help me, Relan," Karian Stromn pleaded, reaching a trembling hand out to him. "W-we can still stop this madness, still make things right."

The chancellor laughed, shaking his head. With glittering eyes, he crossed to the table, to the left of the door, drawn to the final, flickering candle there.

With fingers balanced over the waning flame, he glared back at the pathetic creature that was the high duke of the Four Vales.

"I am making things right," he snarled. Bringing his

thumb and fore-finger together, he plunged the study into utter darkness.

Teren Clay heard the woman's approach, long before she and her lantern arrived. Standing at the bars of the tiny cell, he stared at the man that hung before him, marvelling how anyone could take such torture and yet still draw breath.

For two hours or more now, he had watched the former captain of Karick, chasing off the rats when they came for their supper, lost to his guilt at what was happening to the man most in the city still respected.

There was a time when Teren would have fell upon his own sword to protect the life of his captain, but now, with things the way they were, it was time to think about himself for a change, of his family and the riches he had been promised, despite the stain upon his honour.

The hooded woman came closer and sighing, Teren turned to greet her as her lantern helped chase away further shadows.

"Better stay there, missy," Teren said in warning. Raising his hands, he stepped from the narrow tunnel to meet her. "It's not pretty and I would spare you that, at least."

The woman nodded her hasty thanks, her eyes as bright and wide as the moon outside.

"The chancellor asked that I bring food and water for the prisoner," she stammered, passing him the tray she carried.

"For what it's worth," Teren shrugged, taking it carefully from her trembling hand.

Dia waited until the guard's curiosity got the better of him and he lifted off the cloth. Time froze and all sound disappeared as she reached for the blade at her wrist. Too slow, events seemed to catch up with her and the guard roared, as she pulled the knife free. As the blade lashed out, the guard dropped the tray. Throwing himself at her, Dia's breath was knocked from her body as the guard slammed her heavily up against the wall.

His eyes were wide with hatred as he grabbed her wrist. Pummelling it against the rough stone wall, the guard took Dia by the throat and leant in close as the knife fell to the stone floor with a clatter.

"You bitch," he snarled, spittle flying from his lips.

Dia struggled in his grip, terror racing through her as the man pressed himself against her, his long face furiously thin, his cheeks hollow and pocked.

"Thought you could take me, did you?" the guard rasped in her ear, turning her head to the wall.

Dia sensed his hunger ranging over her body and she shuddered as he ran a tongue down her neck. "Before I hand you over to them, perhaps I'll take you instead? Eh? Would you like that?"

As the man dropped his right hand to cup her breasts, Dia snarled and brought her knee up heavily between his legs. It wasn't a felling blow, but it was enough to shift his attention and as he recoiled in pain, his grip lessening, Dia turned her head, her green eyes wild with madness as she threw herself forward and bit her captor's nose from his face.

Screaming, the guard stumbled away as Dia spat the bloodied flesh from her mouth. The guard was fumbling for his sword and before he could draw it, Dia scooped up her knife and leapt at him, burying her fury deep in his belly.

Teren groaned, slumping back against the wall as he stared down at the wound. Blood pouring from his ruined face, he looked up, disbelief in his eyes.

"Forgive me, Lady," he coughed, looking up at the rough arching ceiling over their heads. Thick blood spilled through the fingers of his hands, clutching futilely at his belly wound and face. With a final, deep sigh, he slid down the wall to the ground.

Falling to her knees Dia gagged on the terrible taste in her mouth. Spitting out her disgust, she heaved and retched, hiding her shame in her hands and behind a thick veil of hair.

After a long time, when the roar of panic in her ears had finally settled and her stomach stopped heaving, Dia drew in a steadying breath, wiped away her tears and did her best to gather her composure. Brushing back her unruly tresses from her eyes, she finally flicked her gaze up.

The guard was no longer moving. Slumped against the wall, his grim face was a terrible, bloody visage that Dia knew would haunt her for the rest of her life. Shuddering, she sniffed and rose unsteadily to her feet. Not wishing to retrieve her knife, she left it clutched deep in the man's belly.

Stumbling forward she turned her attention towards the shadows, hidden away behind the bars of the cell, her heart lurching and her blood raging with apprehension.

Dia's eyes widened, horrified at the image before her. A man, or what was left of him, hung suspended from chains that dug deep into his raw and bruised wrists.

She stood there dumfounded, trying to tell who the prisoner was, but not able to discern where the blood stopped and the man's skin started.

Stifling her shock with a bloody hand, she stood before the cell, chilled to her bones, horrified at what had been done to this poor man. Something scuttled by her heels, startling her, and with a scream failing on her lips she unlocked the door to the cell and quickly hauled it open.

Dia choked as she stepped into the cell, the dancing flames of the torch behind her casting menacing shadows on the prisoner before her.

A rat scurried away on the end of her boot as she

hurried to the prisoner's side and gently lifted up the man's head. The ruined face was covered in blood and cut in many places. One of his eyes was swollen shut, the other blackened either by fist or fire.

Gently wiping some of the congealing blood away from his face, she felt the tears begin to slide down her cheeks.

"Oh, captain," she whispered, shaking her head in despair, "what have they done to you?"

Captain Varl twitched suddenly, startling her as he slipped from his unconsciousness with a groan. Gently steadying his rising thrashes, Dia whispered to him, calming him down as he began to growl madly.

"Save your strength, captain," she pleaded with him, placing her fingers over his blistered lips to silence him.

Lucien Varl moaned and slumped into the embrace of his manacles. After a time, his breath barely catching in his lungs, he raised his head weakly.

"Am I dead?" he asked, his voice faint. He forced open a slit in his left eye, searching the face of the haunted vision of beauty before him.

"You are alive, captain," Dia said, caressing his face. "I am going to get you out of here, to safety."

"Listen to me," Captain Varl sputtered, blood spilling from his lips. "Leave me... you have to get–,"

"Hush," Dia said hastily, aware that if anyone else came now there would be nowhere for her to go. "There will be time to talk later. For now, I have to get you to safety. We are running out of night."

"No," the captain pleaded, his voice rising madly. "There is no time for me."

Dia turned from the captain, ignoring his ramblings as she hurried outside. Steeling herself, she bent low to the dead guard, avoiding his vacant stare as she unhooked the ring of keys from his belt.

Gasping for air, she ran back to Lucien Varl's side,

trying not to look at his wounds, fighting to keep hold of what resolve she had left.

With fingers thick with fear and wet with blood, she finally managed to find the key to the manacle on his left wrist. As it snapped open, Lucien screamed as he swung away from her to hang suspended from his other wrist.

Dia stared in shock as the deep cuts glistening on the captain's back spread wide across his frame like maddened bloodied smiles.

Blinking free of her revulsion, Dia hurried to work on the other manacle and barely managed to hold onto him as he slumped into her arms and bore them to the filthy floor.

Soothing the captain's pleas to listen to him, she tore strips off her cloak, gagging as she wrapped them gently about his feet, several toes missing from each foot.

Choking on her sobs, Dia took her cloak off and wrapped it tightly about his naked frame.

"Come on, let's get you out of here," she whispered, hauling them both to their feet.

As she led Captain Lucien Varl from the cell he thought he would never leave, Dia prayed to the Lady that after all he had been through, the cold night didn't kill him before she could spirit him away to safety.

CHAPTER TWENTY SEVEN

Revelations

Unlike in Karick, the cold night in Highwater was beset by strong winds which cleared the sky and emptied the streets. As the moon-soaked night slipped slowly away and the taverns and brothels of the poor district of the city filled, Arillion soon found himself alone in his vigil.

Word had come to the wayfarers, the morning before, that Teal had the information they sought. Whilst their dismay at his efficiency was well placed, Arillion had cautioned Kaspen Shale that it was not the sort of information you just *happened across.*

Sadly, time was not on their side and following a heated debate which had ended with Agris Varun siding with Arillion, the two men had persuaded the wayfarer leader that it was in their best interests to allow Arillion to question this Teal afterwards.

Arillion grinned, his face stiff from the cold but warming quickly with the thrill of the hunt again. Pulling his scarf up over his nose, the assassin covered his mouth and let out a long breath to warm his numb fingers.

Agris and Kaspen had been in the inn for quite some

time now and he was keen to finally meet this Teal.

"Get on with it," he snarled, wincing as his voice echoed away down the empty lane.

Agris Varen's hulking form stepped out into the lane and sent a firm nod towards Arillion's hiding place. As the giant wayfarer looked up at the clear night sky overhead, he lost himself in the tapestry of stars for a time, before Kaspen Shale stepped out behind him, pulling the door gently close as he moved his large friend out of the way.

Arillion was already heading towards them, his movements and his strength improving, his reliance on the staff he leant on diminishing by the day.

Kaspen frowned. Despite the fact his daughter no longer attended to the assassin, he still feared what Arillion was capable of, what he would lead them to. As that day drew ever nearer, the wayfarer found his faith and determination wanting.

Arillion's eyes were as bright as the stars and they mirrored the moon as Kaspen leant in close and whispered a name to him.

From within his hood, Arillion's eyebrows arched over his uncertainty for a brief moment, replaced quickly by his curiosity.

Clapping both men on a shoulder, Arillion waved them away.

"My turn," he whispered, grinning.

Teal waited for quite some time in the room he had shared with the wayfarers, lost to his thoughts, indifferent to the large bag of gold crowns on the worn table before him. As it usually was in the inn, the rowdy roars of the patrons had now quietened down to faint groans of pleasure, rising in tandem to the knocking timbers of a headboard, or the hasty, rickety creak of a bed.

Scooping a fistful of coins from the leather bag, Teal

tossed them on the table and rose slowly. Slipping the bag from view, he wrapped his cloak tight about his frame and pulled his hood closer about his features. Leaving the room he knew he could never return to, the information seller closed the door behind him, turning to lock it. Putting the key on top of the doorframe, he hurried to the stairs and did not attempt to hide his departure, such was his urgency to be away.

He stepped out into the dark lane beyond the inn, right on to the point of a sword.

"We meet at last," a cold voice said, forcing him back into the stairwell.

"Who are you?" Teal demanded calmly, though the fear in his eyes revealed the opposite.

"That's what I was going to ask you?" Arillion smiled, turning the tip of his blade meaningfully on the exposed throat of the information seller.

"If it's the money you want, just take it. I have more than I can spend..."

"Don't mind if I do," Arillion grinned, offering his empty left hand out.

Teal's eyes narrowed as he handed the bag over, his fury barely unchecked as he watched his assailant spirit his efforts away into the folds of his cloak. If he had watched more closely, he may well have seen him struggle under the weight of the coin, which tugged on the stitches in Arillion's shoulder, reminding him that he was far from fully recovered.

"So what now?" Teal hissed, offering the empty palms of his hands to the mysterious swordsman. "Are you going to run me through, or can we settle this more civilly?"

Arillion cocked his head thoughtfully, then lowered his blade to press the point to Teal's chest.

"I just want to know a few things before I let you go,"

Arillion said softly, chuckling as he heard the final throes of someone's ecstasy echo about the inn.

Teal nodded. "Ask away, then – it's not as if I have a choice."

"No," Arillion agreed, his eyes flashing. "You don't."

With the point of his blade, he forced Teal to sit on the stairs and when he was satisfied that the information seller would not be able to draw the long blade he had hidden beneath his cloak, he continued.

"How is it, after all the years, all the business I have drained from the veins of this city that I have never heard of a man called Teal? How is that, I wonder?"

"Perhaps," Teal retorted slowly, "you are not as good as you think you are?"

Arillion snorted. "Oh, but I am."

Teal shrugged. "Then I can offer you nothing that will put your mind at rest. I am, much like you, good at what I do. I have always been able to hide in the shadows, watching, listening and learning. Having become quite good at it, I have been able to make a lot of money from my skills, also... until now."

"It is always good to be reminded of our mortality," Arillion responded, his voice distant. "So, here's my dilemma. I and my partners sought information that was costly, so very costly in fact, that we did not expect such a swift resolution. You are either, as you boast, very skilled at what you do, or you already knew the name of the Byron spy and held on to it, only to deepen your pockets further for our coin."

Teal glowered, waving a dismissive hand. "Believe what you will, I care not. You have your name and I will, despite your dishonour, refrain from involving myself in this mess any further. You have my word that I will not seek revenge for this, nor will I warn those who may well work against you."

"Generous of you," Arillion said, inclining his head.

"You already have a great deal of my coin and so I will hold you to your word. Break that word, however, and... well, I don't really need to go on, do I?"

Teal shook his head and went to rise. Arillion tutted and forced him back down with a twist of his sword.

"Hold on there, lanky, I haven't finished with you yet. I won't ask you for your source, I won't belittle you with that – but I am curious to know how is it when Alion Byron, his men and his daughter could not locate the spy, that you, a man I have *never* heard of, could find out that the traitor in the Byron household is none other than the daughter of Bryn Astien, Lady Byron's closest friend? How is that possible?"

"How indeed," Teal replied smoothly, clasping his hands together before him.

Arillion sighed. Teal was never going to tell him, no matter what he did to him. He stood there for a time, contemplating the risk of letting the man live. He was about to run his blade through the man's neck when his skin pricked, his old senses coming alive to warn him. If Teal worked for someone, it could mean that they were trying to draw Arillion and his companions out into the open. Killing their messenger would only force their hand sooner. Perhaps it was better to settle matters cordially and deal with the consequences as they arose, should there be any.

Stepping away, Arillion allowed Teal to rise. As he smoothed down the creases to his pride and reputation, the information seller searched the grey eyes, glittering from the shadows of the dark cowl before him.

"Before you go, I would ask you a question, stranger?" Teal said quietly. "Why would you and the wayfarers care for the welfare of the Byron household? What possible gain is there to be had from it? I, as you also probably know, am well aware that there is a change in the air, a change that will forever mark the Four Vales.

Why resist it? Why not embrace it?"

Arillion chuckled again, shaking his head. "What makes you think I won't?"

They eyed each other for a time, listening to the angry spit of a candle, sputtering to sleep on the wall above their heads.

Teal nodded. "I wish you luck, stranger," he said finally.

Arillion smiled. Reaching up with his free hand, he pulled his scarf down and grinned.

"Now we know each other," Arillion said meaningfully.

With a deft flick of his wrist, Arillion opened up Teal's left cheek with his sword.

"And now I know you" he warned with a hiss.

With the fire burning his face, Teal watched in disbelief as the swordsman melted away into the city outside. Slumping back on to the stairs, he reached for a breath that was not there, his skin crawling, his heart racing.

The stinging pain in his face brought him back to his senses and Teal's hand came away dark and wet.

"More blood on my hands," he sighed.

Rising up soberly, Edren Bay hurried away into the night, wondering what he had just done to the Brotherhood's plans.

Ellie raised her head from the riddled surface of the table, her eyes still heavy with sleep, as she looked about her surroundings in confusion. The candle on the table was still burning brightly, casting a proud light about the dusty room she should have been cleaning.

Moaning, the girl dropped her weary head back into the cradle of her arms and tried to reclaim her dream. There was so much to do of late, so many chores and errands to run, now that the sewers were safe again.

Ellie scowled, chasing away her thoughts. She was hoping, with the *beast* away, that her life would get easier, that she would escape some beatings for a time and to be honest, she had the latter...

She was just clearing her mind, falling back into the gentle drift of a dream when she heard the distant, urgent echo of a knock. Snapping up straight in her rickety chair, she listened to the night, wondering if it was just the hammering of her heart that had shaken her awake again.

Tap, tap...tap, tap, tap. Kicking back her chair, Ellie picked up the candle holder and hurried to the top of the stairs, staring down the dark, steep staircase into the shadowy abyss below.

Peering over the naked flame, writhing in protest, she found her courage and started hesitantly down the stone steps, stained from the storms of recent weeks.

As the secret door cracked open, Dia let out a gasp of relief, searching the dank passage behind her worriedly as a pair of bright, fearful eyes peeked out into the sewers.

"Thank the Lady," Dia sighed, offering a weak smile at the waif-like stray that greeted her. Shaking off the memories of a similar stray that had grown up down here, all those years ago, Dia filled her smile with genuine warmth.

"I need to see the boss," she said, with enough urgency in her tone. "But before you do..."

Dia stepped aside and the girl's bright blue eyes almost popped out of her head in fright.

From where he crumpled, Captain Varl was somehow still alive... *barely*, and together the two females wrapped their arms about his waist and helped him up to stagger through the hidden entrance. When the false wall had swung back into place shutting out the terrible stench of the sewers, Dia waved the girl away.

"Fetch help, now," she barked at the waif. With her eyes barely back in their sockets, the young girl darted up the stairs, her sandals drumming out her retreat.

Dia turned her attention back on Lucien. Collapsing under his sagging weight, she sat on the lowest step, cradling the captain in her arms.

She was exhausted and had no clear recollection of the daring flight that had seen them safely through the high duke's keep and up to the Silver Falls Suite – the same quarters that Arillion had spirited Lady Byron away to safety from, all those weeks before.

Dia's luck had somehow held out during the night and the captain's strength had, too, but only by the thinnest of threads. Just the once had they seen a guard, as he strode across their path on his watch. A cursory look had come their way, but at such a distance, it appeared that Dia was only helping her drunken lover back to his quarters.

Her extensive knowledge of the keep had also saved them, allowing them safe passage along halls and corridors that were unguarded, or uninhabited at such an hour... *but which hour?* Having waited for most of the night for her chance to search the Old Royal Dungeons, Dia had lost track of time. Had she been able to see the sky, she would have discovered a faint grey to the edges of the fading curtain of night.

"Stay with me, Lucien," Dia whispered in the only ear the captain had left. She was relieved when the lashes and lids of his eyes stirred at the sound of her voice.

Moments later, Savinn Kassaar appeared at the top of the stairs, his narrow eyes widening in shock as he spied the gift she had brought to him.

The Kestrel raced along the tunnel, the torch carried by Garin Bree chasing the shadows away before her. Returning with enough food to ensure the captain did not die before she had word of the high duke's family's deaths, they had quickly found the absent guard, dragged away from the entrance chamber into the darkness of a disused side-tunnel.

With her cloak snapping in her wake, the Kestrel tried to keep ahead of her panic, unaccustomed to the emotion that was threatening to overtake her. As the torchlight ahead began to beckon to her, she began to slow, her crescent knife gleaming in the flickering light. Behind her she heard Garin's rattling breath and the rasp of his steel as he pulled it from its sheath. She dealt the burly man a venomous look over her shoulder.

"No more prisoners," she hissed. Looking away, the Kestrel padded silently down the tunnel towards the cell.

Putting his torch gently down, Garin Bree did his best to follow quietly in her lengthening shadow, his mind screaming at his stupidity for tempting the Father of Storms scorn with his earlier complaints.

Without a second glance at the dead man, the Kestrel hurried to the bars of the cell, staring in disbelief into the shadows that filled the mocking emptiness before her. As she fought for breath, she grasped on to the cold iron with her free hand, wreathing her fury tightly about it.

Lucien Varl was gone. His knowledge and the power it wielded, stolen away into the night with him by those who still worked against the Brotherhood. It had happened before, with the Byron bitch, but this time it was under her watch.

She felt the fear creep up her arms like a hunting spider and tasted the bitterness of failure on her tongue.

Oh how the chancellor will love this!

The Kestrel turned, her eyes wild with anger, her face twisting with malice. Letting out a guttural, maddened scream, she moved swiftly, slashing her blade across the startled guard's throat.

As Garin clutched at the scarlet line, his shock

staining his face, the Kestrel turned away, chasing her screams and her fury down the dark tunnel.

Coughing up the last of his life, Garin Bree dropped to his knees, staring ahead into the shadows. As his vision darkened and he pitched forward onto his stone deathbed, his last thought was that he should have stayed in Carwell.

At least the madness there was one-sided.

Savinn Kassaar stepped from the room, wiping the blood from his hands on an even bloodier cloth. Searching the hallway to distract his anger and disgust, he found Dia away to his left, sunken on a stool, her head heavy on one shoulder and her face hidden by her tangled tresses.

Giddy from the wine he had consumed earlier that night and now intoxicated by the news Captain Varl had managed to impart to him before he lapsed into unconsciousness, the merchant-thief steadied himself on the cold, rough stone wall with a trembling hand.

Finally catching his breath, Savinn slowly crossed the carpeted hallway and stared fondly down at the girl.

Girl? Savinn found a smile. In his eyes she was still the robust urchin, who had shown such promise when he took her from the streets that would have prematurely claimed her life had he not.

Had he *not* rescued her, Savinn realised, they would not have this chance now. Shaking his head, Savinn listened to her steady breathing, her exhaustion holding her deep in the arms of a fitful sleep.

How in the storms had she managed it? Dia was resourceful, he knew that. He had chosen her for that very reason. But to have found out about the Reven Lists, to have remained free of the Brotherhood's scrutiny and to have now spirited the captain away from under their noses... it was nothing short of a blessed miracle.

Reluctantly, Savinn coaxed her from her slumber with a gentle hand. When she came round, he smiled down at her fondly, his Reven eyes glistening.

"Dia, my child," he whispered, "truly you are a wonder!"

Dia swept her hair from her pale face, still thick with streaks of dried blood and plastered with filth.

"I don't feel it," she groaned, taking Savinn's offered hand to rise.

Massaging her aching back, she fell into Savinn's embrace and held on to him tightly, trying, but failing, to banish the dead men's faces from her mind.

"There, girl," Savinn soothed her, stroking the tangles from her hair. "The captain will live, I hope – but he has survived long enough to give us hope, at the very least."

Hearing the excitement in the merchant's usually even tone, Dia pulled back in his arms and looked up into eyes that were bright with hope, yet framed by concern.

Savinn smiled broadly and his handsome face, drawn and lined, smoothed happily. "Chancellor Valus had him taken, several nights ago and brutally tortured to reveal the whereabouts of the high duke's family."

"Do they know?" Dia pursued, seeing the light fail in his eyes.

Savinn nodded his head, pulling her back close for selfish comfort.

"Yes, I am afraid they do," the merchant sighed, kissing the top of her head.

Stiffening, Dia broke their embrace. "Then we must save them," she said hastily, pacing about.

She wandered away down the hall and then turned, her beautiful face set firm in weary determination. "There are still those who will rally to our cause, we must reach out to them, get them to save the high duke's line..."

"And we will," Savinn said firmly, holding up his hands to silence her. "As soon as Cullen returns, which will be shortly, I hope."

"Cullen?" Dia did not even attempt to hide her

disgust.

Savinn grinned in his customary wolfish manner. "I know you hate him, as do most, but he has his uses. We have all the evidence we need, but not the audience to accomplish it. The chancellor is still strong. He grows stronger by the day. If we are to finish him once and for all, bring the Brotherhood down before they can truly rise, then we must chose our allies and our next move very wisely."

"But they will send men, to kill Karian Stromn's wife and child." Dia pointed out, hurrying back to her master's side.

Savinn nodded. "They will, but with so much going on in the city, we may have a couple of days' grace. They will have to choose their men wisely, not risk the implications of such a move being known to men who still tussle with their loyalty and honour."

Dia sighed, chewing the nail of her left thumb thoughtfully.

"Then let us hope that Cullen proves his use," Dia said, starting to turn away. "If Khadazin is going to name who I am coming to suspect he will, then the stonemason will be invaluable to us, also."

Savinn nodded, fighting back his rising concern, realising that she was leaving him.

"Where are you going?" he called after her. "It is too dangerous there for you now!"

Dia looked back once, her face set in shadows, her eyes glowing with promise.

"I am going to find out what they have done to the high duke. Without him, all of this will count for little."

"And then?"

"I will find the chancellor," Dia said softly. Turning, she hurried away, taking her words with her.

"I will find him, and then I will kill him."

CHAPTER TWENTY EIGHT

Barrowlands

The wind gently picked up Elion Leigh's attention, dragging him from his thoughts as he allowed his mount to guide him over the rough ground, rising steadily before him. Enjoying the fresh air that caressed his face and ruffled his hair, the former captain of Carwell stared in wonderment about his surroundings.

"Beautiful, isn't it?" Devlin Hawke said, as he reined in alongside him. Elion nodded, following the outlaw's gaze back to the scene before them.

As far as they could see, the land before them was a sweeping spectacle of high craggy hills and misty barren moorland, scattered with secretive glens and hollows. Overhead, the sky mirrored the land, a contrasting canvas of clouds, grey and wistful, broken occasionally by slivers of fading blue.

Deep into summer now, the limestone crags of the hills, of which Elion could count thirteen, were covered in bright gorse and swathes of purple heather that swept down steep slopes, stitched together by meandering paths cut into the land by boot and hoof.

On each hill, a mound of ancient stones had been piled wide and high, left there centuries before by those who honoured their dead by giving them back to the land, not sending them to the next life by flame and ash.

It had been many years since Elion had first ridden across the Barrowlands with his father and he had forgotten what a breathtaking spectacle it was. Although only a few days from Carwell, it was a wild, remote place, frequented only by the wildlife that lived there, or the hardy Valians that hunted them. The children's bedtime tales of the Barrowlands and the dead buried there were enough to keep most people away and Elion was happy for it to remain so.

Elion heard Devlin snort at some private thought and he dealt the outlaw a questioning look. Following their tempestuous departure from Greywood Forest, Elion had said little, keeping to his thoughts and rising doubts. Sensing his need for solace, Devlin had been happy enough for the peace and quiet.

The outlaw caught his companion's gaze, but led them on for a time, picking a path up through the heather towards the mound of large rocks that formed the closest barrow.

A lark, startled into the sky to their left, drew their thoughts away for a time, before Devlin reined his mount in and slipped from his saddle with a grunt.

Eager to relieve the cramp in his buttocks, Elion followed the outlaw's lead and together they led their mounts on careful feet towards the barrow.

After they had tied their horses to a gorse bush, they stood before the burial mound, solemnly surveying the eternal, beautiful view that the people had honoured their departed with. Devlin wandered forward and picked up a stone from the dusty ground, adding it to a small pile that had already been placed at the base of the burial mound.

"What are you doing?" Elion asked. They were the

first words he had said for quite some time and his voice sounded like it belonged to somebody else.

Devlin stepped away from the pile of stones and planted his hands thoughtfully on his hips. He bowed his head for a time, then looked back over his shoulder at him.

"He speaks." Devlin's shock was laced with amusement and he ignored Elion's dark look. "Some people, those who still remember the old ways, leave a token of respect at the barrows, to remind others that the dead should not be forgotten and to let the dead know that they are still remembered."

Elion forgot his irritation, the notion and custom appealing to him. With a nod of understanding, he picked up a stone and walked forward to add his respect to the pile.

"It is a beautiful thing," Elion said softly. "I wonder who this is? Who they were? What they were?"

Devlin snorted again. "Little is known, my young friend, save that they were buried in the same way the Reven bury their dead. The historian, Elias Birch, wrote that evidence suggested the Reven may have once lived south of the Great Divide," the outlaw stabbed a scowl at his companion, "you can imagine how that was received! He was vilified by his peers and lambasted by the royalty for his *lunatic* beliefs. The Valian people did not want to entertain such a notion that perhaps some of the Four Vales was not their rightful ancestral homeland after all."

Elion blinked. He had never heard that story and knew little of Elias Birch save that he had been a brilliant man, who was disgraced for some reason at the height of his fame, fading away into the very history books that he had wrote. He reportedly died a pauper, living his last years in the squalor of his shame and ignominy.

"Such a shame," Elion said, looking at the stones. Perhaps Birch had been right all along? The barrows would certainly suggest he was.

"By my reckoning," Devlin said, wandering away to reclaim his horse, "we should reach Carwell in the morning. We had better hope your pathetic attempt at a beard has grown by then, otherwise you'll be snatched away to a noose in no time."

Elion couldn't help but grin, swallowing back down his anger, which was becoming quicker to rise of late. He nodded, running a hand through his attempt.

"A few more days with you and I'll be ready to hand myself over."

Devlin laughed, the sound caught up by the wind and carried several times into the valley below them.

"That's more like it," the outlaw grinned. Swinging up skilfully into his saddle, he turned his mount towards his companion. "I've missed the old Elion Leigh and it's good to have him back."

Elion thought back to the anger of their departure from Greywood, of Trell's distrust and horror that his boss was leaving for Carwell without him. Ashe, equally, had riled at the thought of not travelling with them and the big outlaw and the boisterous sergeant had shared an unlikely alliance.

Since that night, the heat of the fire lost to the fury of the rising argument, Elion had been hiding under his cloud, sullen and aloof. He could still see the hurt on Ashe's face as they left, could see the fear in Elissen's eyes, when she realised she was going to be left behind.

Thinking of Elissen soured the moment, as the only person that seemed happy to be staying behind was Jarion Kail.

Retrieving the reins from the thorns of the gorse, Elion hauled himself up onto the saddle. He turned his mount to the west for a time, scanning the horizon, lost to the haze of the day. Sighing, he swung his thoughts back to the east and followed the outlaw leader towards the clouds stating to gather there.

By the time the clouds had slipped southwards, dragging any threat of being caught in the rain that tarnished the horizon, the heat had been stolen from the day.

Devlin Hawke, despite his earlier indifference to riding towards possible danger, had lapsed into a brooding silence as they neared the end of the Barrowlands and the protection it afforded him. Over a sparse lunch, nestled behind a barrow, in what little shade they could find, Elion and Devlin had shared only a few words, each man realising the risk they had so easily put themselves in.

Elion shifted in his saddle, as they reached the final barrow, the land starting to fall away drastically towards a deep valley known as *The Chalice*. Eyeing the storm clouds to the south of them now, he tucked a strand of his wild hair behind one ear and chewed his bottom lip.

"What's wrong?" Devlin demanded, his words strangely harsh.

Elion sighed. "I am home, though I fear it no longer is."

Devlin looked away, his eyes distant, lost to another time when he had said almost exactly the same words.

"Aye, lad," he said, his irritation slipping away. "Hopefully there will come a time for you, many years from now, when you will look back on what has happened and wonder if it ever did."

Elion sent a look at the outlaw, but Devlin's guard was back up and he was hiding behind his scarf again. Only his eyes were showing from beneath his hood, and they were similarly clad in shadow.

"Now that we are nearly there," Devlin said, checking the sky, "what are your plans?"

Elion twisted his reins nervously. "We view the city from the ridgeline of *The Horseshoe*, then head north several miles to my father's estate. He will, despite his retirement, have a firm finger in things and have news of what is happening in the city."

"And you think your father will be happy to harbour two of the most wanted men in the Vales?"

Elion ignored the outlaw's amusement and scowled. "My father is an honourable man, dutiful to the high duke and loyal to his only son. He will help us when we tell him what has transpired in the west. He will reach out for us and will do all he can to seek what we desire."

Devlin nodded, keeping his doubts to himself. Clapping his hands together, he tilted his head slightly.

"Very well, Master Leigh. Lead on, my friend. Let us seek what I am certain we will not want to find."

Several hours later, Elion would come to wish that they had stayed in Greywood Forest.

CHAPTER TWENTY NINE

Over the Hills...

Khadazin stared ahead at the road, not really seeing it and paying little heed to his surroundings as he allowed his mount to carry him northwards. Since leaving the Hermitage Retreat, the small fellowship had made swift ground, reaching the outskirts of the town of Silver Falls in half the time it had taken Sam and him to flee south to safety.

Reluctantly, at Cullen's behest, Khadazin and his companions had waited in the woods to the east of the town, whilst Tania had slipped hurriedly in for a reckoning with her father. It had taken quite some time and as the Redani was beginning to fear the worst, the young huntress had returned, with eyes haunted by what had occurred and rimmed by a deep sadness.

When Cullen had asked if all was well, Tania had simply nodded her head. Continuing on with their journey, Khadazin had eventually found the girl's eyes and read the truth of her lie there.

"Are you alright?"

Tania's soft voice drew him from his thoughts and

Khadazin returned to his surroundings. She rode alongside him on her tall mare, lost in the saddle somewhat, as she searched his dark face for tell of where he had been.

Khadazin smiled faintly, nodding his head to assure himself more than in any answer to her concern. He wasn't *alright*, but worrying her wasn't going to help them. The closer they came to the capital, the greater his fears, his doubts and worries became.

"I am fine," Khadazin lied. His stomach cramped, his nausea rising in his throat to choke off his desires for revenge and replace them with brittle uncertainty.

How in the storms, even if he made it to Karick, could he ever hope to have his revenge?

From what Cullen had told him, things were even worse than he could have ever feared. Despite the comforting news that, because of his letter to Savinn all those weeks ago, Lady Byron had been rescued from the chancellor's clutches, it seemed that the peace and prosperity of the Four Vales balanced on a failing knife-edge. The people, Cullen had growled, were ready to tear those of Reven blood from their homes and mete out their own justice. The flames of their anger were being fed by propaganda from the hardliners and stoked into a frenzy by reported Reven attacks throughout the Four Vales. Many citizens across the realm were being turned against those of Reven heritage or even any who had dealings with them. The high duke was also strangely absent and the shadowy threat of war was looming large on the horizon.

Left to mull over what Cullen had told him, Khadazin had been struggling with his guilt, though deep down he knew it was misplaced. But, in spite of this, he couldn't help but think that if only he had told Savinn the name of whom he had overheard – perhaps the merchant could have taken it to the high duke, before it was too late?

The former mason tried to shake his doubts from his head but the closer he came to returning home, the further he wanted to be away from that moment.

Tania was still watching him and her beautiful face was full of worry.

"I know that's not true, Khadazin," she said, her eyes bright, "but I won't pry. I can only begin to imagine what you are feeling right now. Just know that I am here for you, whenever you need me."

Khadazin swallowed his self-pity. "You humble me, young lady. You have done more for me than I can ever truly repay, but know that I will at least try."

A thought danced in her lovely eyes and she smiled, shaking her tresses. "You are my friend, Khadazin Sahr – that is enough repayment for me."

Feeling the fading heat of the day rise in his cheeks, the Redani looked away and smiled.

Ahead, Cullen and Riyan rode on in silence, their heads hooded as they looked to the road that wended its way northwards towards a bare hillock that rose up onto the horizon and was framed by clouds, deepening with the promise of rain. Before them, the plains, full of flower, swirled with a gathering breeze and as they followed the rutted road on, several figures stepped from the shade of a copse of trees ahead to the west and wandered slowly out to greet them.

Cullen dragged gently on his reins, slowing their approach just enough to not warrant suspicion. He glanced back over one wide shoulder and fixed Khadazin with his good eye.

"Better leave this to me," he advised gruffly. His face was red from their journey, his breath and jowls thick with apprehension.

Sinking into his saddle, Khadazin pulled his hood tighter about his face and his hand deeper into the sleeve of his robe. He dared a glance at Tania, but her attention was fixed firmly on the five men before them, her left hand straying to the bow, strapped across the saddle in front of her.

With his heart in his mouth, Khadazin watched as they rode close, seeing, for the first time, the weapons that the five men carried in their hands and noting the hard, cold edges to their eyes.

"Hail, friends," one of the men called out, raising his empty hand. He was a short, dark-haired man with a scar deep on his right cheek that creased his features to give him a maniacal look. "What business do you have on the roads, this fine day?"

Cullen reined the small party to a halt, some distance from the band of men. Dragging his hood from his head, he sat silently for a time, eyeing each man in turn.

Finally, he leant forward in his saddle. "S'no business of yours, *friend*."

The unsettling silence that followed was finally filled by several crows, bickering overhead, as they winged their way towards the copse of trees. Khadazin held his breath, feeling the cold chill of fear tingle in his ruined wrist. Images of the fight in the clearing came flooding back and he shifted in his saddle as if he were sat on flames.

The leader of the band of rough looking men turned to his comrades, shrugging nonchalantly. With an even madder looking grin, he turned back and sheathed his blade, opening his hands peacefully.

"Now, there's no need for that, brother," the man said, though his smile was lost in his dark, narrowing eyes.

"It's been many a year since these roads have been filled by such a welcome," Cullen pointed out, twisting the reins he held through his large, stubby hands. "Either tell us what you are about... or get out of the bastard way."

Even the crows fell silent and a heavy tension settled on both parties. Khadazin dared a look at Tania to see that her hand was now curled reassuringly about her bow, the other, sliding slowly down her calf to search for the bag of arrows tied to her saddle bag.

Cullen still sat forward in his saddle, the brow above his good eye cocked, as he dared the men to make their move.

With a nervous gasp, meant to be a chuckle, a red-haired man, long into his winters, stepped forward and dragged the scarred man away from the rash move he had tensed to make.

"Now, come on Beran," the old man soothed, his thin fingers digging into the broad shoulder of his companion. "We were just going to ask a few questions, nothing more. No need for this to get messy. Not as if we really know how to handle these blades, after all."

"Father?" the man scowled, dropping his hand from the hilt of his tarnished blade. He looked down at his boots and then, wrenching his shoulder away, he stepped forward, wetting the apology on his lips.

"Didn't mean much by it," he mumbled, looking up at Cullen, whose bitter scowl did little to ease the apology. "Since the word went out, we have been checking the roads... just in case. I mean, ten thousand crowns? Well, it's a king's ransom I'd say, and given the chance, we'd never have to work the fields again."

Cullen forgot his anger for a time, which was a rare thing, and he shot a look at Riyan, who had been watching the whole affair with a calm, almost disinterested expression on his face.

"That is a lot of crowns," Cullen agreed. "But for what?"

He saw the man, Beran, look past him towards Tania and then, with more interest, the hooded, robed figure of Khadazin.

"I'm doing the talking," Cullen snapped, dragging the man's face and irritation back to him with a click of his fingers. "What's this all about?"

The man scowled and fished about in his pocket. Unfurling some parchment, he held up a poster and passed it into Cullen's grubby, reaching hand. Cullen eyed it for a moment and then chuckled.

"Does it look like we are harbouring a fugitive?"

Beran shrugged and then nodded his head towards Khadazin. "Well, what about that one?"

Cullen followed the scarred man's curiosity. Hawking, he spat onto the road and wiped his mouth with a filthy sleeve.

"There's no black there, man," he said quietly, "only the green and yellow of a dying man."

The scarred man frowned and Cullen put him out of his misery.

"He's a leper," he whispered conspiratorially, "we are taking my cousin to the priests in Karick, so that they can ease him into the next."

The man's face softened and he folded the paper up, slipping it away into his pocket as he stepped back a few paces. "Apologies," he said, bobbing his head to all concerned. Turning in resignation, he waved his group away. "Come on lads, we've pissed enough travellers off for one day."

"Wait," Cullen called out, as the group ambled forlornly from the road and away from their dreams of a better life.

Their leader turned, a question on his lips, as Cullen flicked him a gold crown. Beran caught it deftly and stared at it for a moment, before looking up.

"To help you on your way to your king's ransom," Cullen answered for him and with a wave the two groups parted.

Cullen didn't pull them off the road until they were far from view and in the protective shadow of the hillside.

"What's wrong?" Khadazin dared to ask, his fear thrumming through his veins.

Cullen shook his head and spat his distaste on the ground again. "Seems like someone doesn't want you back in Karick, Redani," he growled, cursing. "Ten thousand reasons in fact."

Khadazin felt sick and covered his mouth to stifle his disgust. So, the chancellor was taking steps to prevent his return, to silence him before he had even had a chance to voice his accusations.

"Clever," the Redani muttered, shaking his head with what was almost begrudging respect.

He looked up at his companions, all of them watching him with differing emotions. Tania's beautiful, if weary face, was full of sympathy and Riyan's with what only could be described as admiration. Cullen's, however, was a mixture of mock-turmoil, one expression tussling with the desire for a great deal of crowns, the other with a rising broil of fury.

"Clever, my arse," Cullen snarled. "If the high duke thinks he is being clever, he is mistaken. By the storms, as if we were actually going to ride in through the south gate with you?"

"Then how are we going to get in the city?" Tania asked and regretted it, when Cullen's eyes ranged hungrily over her, as if he had just found a great treasure.

"Same way you came out, girl," he chuckled, delighting at her horrified expression. He jabbed a thumb at the Redani. "He's already in the shit, so we might as well drown him in it."

Cullen's laughter filled the greying sky, but as they rode away across the plains to the northeast, it travelled alone.

Whether through a subconscious haste to get it over with, or a desire to see his parents again, Elion Leigh guided Devlin Hawke to the hills that bordered the flatlands surrounding Carwell, long before the sun had begun to set.

As their journey and the Barrowlands slipped away behind them, Elion began to struggle with his doubts. He yearned to see his home again, to feel something familiar and be somewhere that he felt safe – not to have to look over his shoulder, or question what was happening to him for a short while. His journey, since that fateful morning on the road to Eastbury, had been a perilous, brutal one and even now he could not grasp the implications, nor believe that it was to him these things were actually happening to.

His doubts about Devlin Hawke's eagerness to become involved were also troubling him. The notorious outlaw, whom he strangely counted his friend, was not a man to meddle in affairs outside the boundaries of his domain so readily... so why was he getting involved?

It never felt the right moment, but he was determined to question the mysterious outlaw about his aid, of his past, and, more pressingly, why Elion had to thank a vagabond boy, wanted for murder, for Devlin's involvement in this mess.

And what a mess!

Sighing, Elion left his horse to feed on the grassy slopes of the hillside, stretching his calves, as he climbed the steep rocky path up to the ridgeline of *The Horseshoe* – so named, as the range of hills curved like its namesake from the northwest of Carwell, sweeping about to flank the flatlands, many miles to the southeast.

Short of breath and his lungs on fire, Elion finally reached the broad ridgeline and joined Devlin Hawke on the rocky plateau, where he stood by the low cairn that marked the highest point of the hills.

His footfalls heavy and his heart racing, Elion approached the outlaw, who stood with his arms folded tight across his chest, his hair and cloak whipping about him furiously as he surveyed the sight before him. Not keen to be near the edge in such high winds, Elion shuffled alongside his friend and swallowed hard.

"Never thought to be back here," Devlin said softly.

Elion had begun to think the same and, almost reluctantly, he looked down into the flatlands that fell away hundreds of feet below them.

The rugged scree slope slipped away onto a broad plain that stretched as far as his eyes could see, failing on a misty horizon to the east as it was cradled by the hills and framed, quite beautifully, by a darkening sky brimming with clouds.

From their buffeted vantage point, they could tell that things were calmer down in the lowlands, its fertile ground heaving with a patchwork quilt of outlying farmsteads and crops. With the harvest well under way, Elion could see the dark shapes of the farmers and the tenants who busily worked their fields whilst the light was still holding. Elion was amazed how, even at this height and with the high winds in his ears that the nearest workers voices still carried up to them. From a nearby paddock, next to one small tenement, he could hear a goat's bell jingling as if it were on the slopes, just beneath him.

Over their heads, the broken clouds had started to gather together again, casting shadowy hands on the lands below like a creeping portent, searching to drag more of the Four Vales into the rising chaos.

Crushed momentarily by a sense of futility, Elion was saved, as thin shafts of the failing sun broke over the hills and stretched away like rays of hope – a reflection, perhaps, of those who were still prepared to stand against the tide of madness.

A sign from the Lady? Elion smiled and shook his head. No! It was just the beauty of the land and the elements that shaped it. A miraculous, simple thing that people had lost sight of – just as many had lost faith in the comfort of peace and the kind hand that had governed them.

Realising that he was tired, so tired that he could no longer think straight and hold on to his thoughts, Elion banished his musings and reluctantly dragged his attention to the Great East Road that slipped by the hills to the south and stretched triumphantly across the flatlands towards the rising colossus that was Carwell.

Carwell...

His stomach knotted as he realised that, had he not listened to Elissen that fateful morning in Eastbury, he would not have survived to see this sight again. Licking his lips, Elion swept his gaze over the scattered villages and outlying hamlets that surrounded the great city and drew in a deep breath.

Unlike the toweringly gentle and elegant beauty of Karick and Highwater, Carwell's presence was ominous and brooding. A sprawling, squat city, lost behind towering walls of dark stone, the capital of the East Vales was a heaving behemoth that threatened to swallow up everything around it.

Elion filled his cheeks nervously. Lost to gathering shadows and crested by angry clouds, it was a fitting vision, in keeping with the darkness stirring within Carwell's walls.

At his side, Devlin Hawke snapped from his reverie and swore brutally. Elion followed his gaze back to the Great East Road and frowned as he saw the dozens of crow cages that now lined the great highway.

"Bastards," Devlin hissed, glaring at Elion.

Chilled to his bones, Elion raised a hand. "This is not good, my friend. I have never agreed with Carwell's methods of display as you know, no matter the perpetrator's crime, but I can tell you when I left the city all those weeks ago, there were no cages on these roads."

The expression on Devlin Hawke's face, free from its

scarf now, did not look like he believed him, but Elion pressed on.

"We should not tarry here," the former captain warned. "It will be dark soon and I would not want to rouse my father's temper from its sleep."

Devlin watched as Elion turned and hurried away, keen to be free of the edge, keener to be free of the city. The outlaw turned back briefly, glaring at the walls of Carwell.

Finally tearing himself away, Devlin Hawke hurried after his friend. If what he suspected was happening proved to be true, he knew that things would never be the same again.

If that were the case, then before Devlin drew his last breath, before his time was done, he would make certain that he buried his sword and his hatred deep into Lord Carwell's heart.

There were no stars in the dark, overcast sky as the guard welcomed Elion Leigh and his guest home. If he were shocked at the lateness of the hour, the old retainer hid it well as he quietly hauled open the twin, iron gates and allowed the riders' entry through the high crenellated gatehouse into the Leigh Estate.

As Elion swapped pleasantries with the guard and the breathless groom, roused from his sleep by the hooves on the cobbles and still not fully awake, Devlin Hawke flicked his nerves about the grand manor house and fought with memories, long-since buried.

Devlin could tell that the inner courtyard, though lost to the depths of night, was protected by a sweeping curtain wall, propped up by several storehouses and outbuildings. A broad pathway led away from the courtyard towards the grand entrance porch of the main house, welcoming him through the shadows with flickering torches.

Fighting with the feeling he was trapped and unaccustomed to his nerves, the outlaw was thankful when Elion took the reins from his shaking hand and passed them to the groom. Nodding his thanks, Devlin, his scarf now firmly in place, followed Elion along the broad path towards the house, his eyes sweeping for signs of a trap, his hand brushing reassuringly over the pommel of his Valian blade.

"Come on, my father doesn't bite," Elion smiled. Clapping the outlaw on one shoulder, he added quietly, "but he might talk you to death."

As it turned out, Marten Leigh, the master of the house and Elion's double, if a great deal older, did not bite, nor did he entertain talking Devlin Hawke to death. After recovering from his shock and well-guarded annoyance of a visit at such an hour, he remembered his manners and held his son tight to him, clapping him heartily, thankfully on the back. Without waiting for an explanation, he ushered Elion and his guest into a large reading room, its shadowy shelves lined with a wealth of knowledge and history to rival even the greatest of collections.

"I will have Oliver fetch us some refreshment," Marten Leigh stated, picking up a silver bell and ringing it briefly. For such a slight, lean, self-made man, he had a deep voice, one that commanded immediate attention. As Elion's father placed the bell back on a side table, Devlin surmised that he must have been well-suited to politics.

A smile filled his face as Marten regarded the man before him. "It is so very good to see you my son. How I have missed you these last few months. Your mother, may the Lady watch over her dreams, is resting. She took another turn today and Father Michael has ordered her to take things easy for the foreseeable future."

Elion's heart sank, replaced by his guilt. He had not thought much of his mother since heading to Eastbury, and his shame tasted bitter in his throat. "I am sorry father. I will go to her, as soon as we have spoken."

Elion noted the worried look in his father's eyes, the familiar tell that he was still not happy, despite his apparent words to the contrary. A bitter memory of the countless arguments over their son's continuing absences from home came unbidden to Elion's mind.

"I sense that you have not returned *just* to see your mother and me, but before we speak, I believe my manners have been lacking," Elion's father's tone underlined his fears as he turned to the stranger in his house. He crossed the carpeted floor and offered his hand in greeting.

"I am Marten Leigh, sir," he beamed, his face full with charm and evident pleasure.

"A pleasure to make your acquaintance," the outlaw said. He shook his host's hand enthusiastically for a moment before offering him a devilish smile.

"And I am Devlin Hawke."

Elion groaned and from the doorway the butler Oliver gasped, dropping the tray of drinks he was carrying with a terrified squeal.

CHAPTER THIRTY

Misplaced Loyalties

Checking the clearing skies for sign of further rain, the woodsman trudged reluctantly along the top of the fresh earthwork defences that ringed Havensdale. Several soldiers, reinforcements sent by Lady Byron as promised, worked the sodden earth with shovels and picks ready for the large stakes they hoped would slow any cavalry charge, should it ever come.

The air was fresh and a great deal clearer than the woodsman's head as he stalked under the south gate and headed through the crowded market square, full of soldiers training and curious children looking on, mimicking the swordplay themselves with wooden sticks.

Permitting a smile, the woodsman wrapped his cloak tight about him and made for the Arms of the Lady and the woman who was waiting for him.

Since the arrival of the troops, Havensdale's charm had slipped quickly away for the woodsman and, accustomed as he was to his own company and thoughts, he spirited himself back into the Moonglade Forest, spending his days at the hut of the absent owner, Bowen.

The young hunter Rellin came to see him daily, giving him the excuse he needed to still involve himself in what was to come. A few days after his escape to the forest, the old woodsman Bowen had returned from his trip north. A wiry, brittle old sod, he was nearly as thin as the great hunting bow he carried and his sun-beaten skin as hard as the leathers he wore.

Though he was clearly not happy to find someone in his home, Bowen soon forgot his anger when news of what had happened in his absence was revealed. Finding a common enemy, they quickly began to strike up an unlikely friendship, one based solely on the fact that in the coming weeks, their skills may well be required, should the town need to be evacuated and the hunting grounds Bowen had been scouting to the north, become their home.

Swatting a fly aside, the woodsman stepped up the wooden steps and pushed his way into the inn. For once, with everyone working the fields or raising the defences, *The Arms* was quiet, save for Joseph Moore, stood idly behind the long bar, his thoughts far away as he wrung a cloth slowly through his hands.

Blinking free, the portly barkeep raised a hand and smiled.

"A *Campbell's?*" he asked cheerily and the woodsman nodded, swallowing his rising thirst. "I'll bring it to you now, sir."

Nodding his thanks, the woodsman turned away, heading to the same corner Cassana Byron had slumbered at, many weeks before, and joined the woman waiting for him there. There was the unmistakable scent of last night's fire in the air and the fresh rushes hanging from the ceiling of the inn.

"My lady," the woodsman greeted, waiting to be shown a seat.

Fawn offered him a strained smile and watched

impassively, as the woodsman sat across the table from her. When their eyes met, she could see that he was already guarded, ready for her questions. She sighed, propping her leather-clad elbows on the table and clasped her hands under her chin.

"I did not think you would come," Fawn stated, aware that Joseph was already coming over to them.

"You think so little of me?" the woodsman whispered, leaning back in his chair as his ale was delivered with a bright smile. Once the pleasantries were out of the way and paid for, he leant forward again to continue.

"Rellin came to find me, I accepted, and now I am here."

"How is Bowen? I hear he did not take the news well?" Fawn asked, her eyes flicking about the woodsman's face.

The grey streaks in his beard and tangled hair were deeper of late, his eyes ringed by a weight that was getting heavier each time she saw him.

"He is angry, lady. Angry and shamed that he was not here to protect his borders when the attack came," the woodsman offered. "We have spoken at length about what may have to be done."

Fawn raised an eyebrow. "Oh? And what might that be, pray tell?"

Ignoring her irritation, the woodsman fixed her with one of his steely looks.

"If our allies do not find the evidence they seek and the weight of protection that we will need, then the Valian armies will be marshalled for war, make no mistake. If that happens, then we must be prepared for what happens next."

"What does that mean?" Fawn pursued reluctantly. She dropped her hands to the table and shuffled her fingers nervously.

Softening the edges to his tone, the woodsman replied, "It means that as Havensdale has been branded a nest of vipers, a den of *traitors*, the Valian armies will march north, not only to invade the Reven lands, but to also stamp out any dissenters that might stand against their conquest."

Fawn reached for her drink and drank heartily from it. The woodsman supped from his tankard also and then raised it before them. Licking her lips, Fawn crashed their tankards together.

"Then we had best make sure that doesn't happen."

The woodsman nodded. "We will certainly try." Shifting his discomfort from one buttock to the other, he asked, "What news from the capital, captain?"

Fawn sighed and shook her head sadly. "Lestarn Corbus, our local merchant, who has dealings with the capital, returned yesterday morning and he returned with nothing good. The high duke has been absent for some weeks now, the city out of control, run by his chancellor and, I am afraid, an old friend of ours..."

"Gardan!" the woodsman breathed the man's name softly and Fawn could see him clench his fists tightly. "That man has more lives than a leprous cat."

"It gets worse," Fawn continued reluctantly. "The former captain, Lucien Varl, a man of quality and who, up until recently had a great deal of support from the ranks, is missing. This has done little to help matters. Anyone of Reven heritage has been taken in for questioning by the militia and many of them have not been seen again. Vicious attacks on Reven citizens have increased greatly, even on people who have ties or dealings with them. Homes have been ransacked, even burnt down in their owner's absence. The capital is in turmoil."

The woodsman vented his fury on the table between them and Joseph Moore nearly dropped the tankard he was polishing.

"Then we are fast running out of time." The woodman's eyes were dark orbs of anger. "First, we had the threat of peril and then there was the supposed source of the trouble. Now it seems, with the naming of Savinn Kassaar, the people have a focus, a point of hatred that will only increase as those that want war stoke up and feed fuel to the flames of chaos that will engulf the Four Vales. Soon, lady, mark my words, the call will go out for conscripts. The politicians and the warmongers will quickly find that they preach their case with growing support, as they knew they would. Without the high duke to calm things down, or Alion Byron as a voice of reason, they will raise taxes on the promise that this Reven threat, this stain upon the land, will finally be washed away. The people will not stop to think what is happening and, like sheep, they will follow their masters' example when they march north – they will even, most likely, thank them for it."

Fawn remembered to breathe and bit her bottom lip. She shook her head, thinking again of the terrible news that her father had returned with, news that had drained the last of her resolve away. With Alion Byron gone, murdered it seemed by a Valian, not Reven assassin, there was little hope that, even with compelling evidence, there would be anyone of sound disposition left to receive it.

"You sure know how to cheer a lady up," Fawn chuckled, her amusement taut and hollow. "Here am I, inviting a friend out for a quiet drink..."

"That is not why you asked me here?" the woodsman cut in brusquely.

Fawn smiled, searching the weary yet strangely handsome face before her. So much had happened that summer, so much pain and sadness that she could barely recall what had transpired. Even now, after the dead of both sides had been burned, there was the threat of worse to come. Even now, despite the early signs, Perrin

Hawksblade still clung to life, his reticence to leave his wife and son clear in his sparkling eyes the last time Fawn had visited his bedside.

Elsewhere, Durnast Brogan was recovering, his fiery tenacity and the promise of having a reckoning with Gardan fuelling his desire to be away from his bed. Across the river, however, the Wicksford and Campbell households were broken, their losses immeasurable, their sorrow unbearable.

Before she could stop herself, Fawn thought of Roland Ford, of the man that the town had counted a friend, bound even by blood. His betrayal sat heaviest on them and even though, when Sergeant Manse returned from Colden with news that Roland had been killed by his own son, any joy she may have allowed herself to have was gone, replaced only by confusion and a broken widow's ramblings at the shocking patricide.

Without even beginning to contemplate her own fate, Fawn shook her head and fought back her tears. *What did it matter if the man before her chose to keep his past his own?* After all that had gone before, all that was to follow, could she really blame him?

"Forgive me, woodsman," Fawn said, reaching across the table to clasp his gentle, yet heavily calloused hands. "I have plagued you incessantly about your past, when I have no right to. You are your own man and it is not for me to judge what you were. I know only of the man you are, and for that I would thank you and also count you my friend."

The woodsman, for once, had no reply and he sat quietly, holding Fawn's hands tightly. Raising her fingers to his lips, he smiled across the table at her, as he kissed them softly.

"My thanks, lady," he said eventually. It was a long time after that when he finally let go of her hands.

Eran Dray cradled Dia in his arms, listening to the calming sound of her breath, as it slipped from her parted lips and she stirred slightly in the grip of a dream. With his back against the cold wall, he ran a hand gently down the curve of her neck and kissed her hair tenderly as his mind wandered over their naked bodies, tangled as one in their exhausted, yet loving embrace.

He fought down his rising desires as he recalled their reunion, long overdue and one that was full of joyous relief as they kissed and fell into each other's arms and then, inevitably, their bed. They had not made love this time, though their desires were raging, both needing the comfort and touch of the other to calm their fears for a time.

With a start, Dia flinched, fleeing from her dream and lay quietly, calming her breathing as Eran stroked his long fingers through her beautifully tangled hair. A solitary candle writhed seductively from its sconce, its wan light casting lulling shadows about the small room.

"How long have I been asleep?" Dia asked, yawning into the back of her hand.

"A while," Eran said, holding her tighter.

Moaning sleepily, she rolled over in his arms, looking up at him with tired eyes filling with promise. "Did you rest?"

Eran shook his head, his soft, handsome features hardening. "I could not," he admitted, closing his eyes. "Every time I do, I see them – I hear their screams and it is something I cannot bear."

"I am so sorry," she said softly. Eran's recount of the bloody massacre at the South Gate Market that was now being called '*The Stamping Ground*' by those who would see every Reven driven back over the Divide, was too much for him to deal with. Through his tears, Dia had done her best to remain strong, to calm his troubled soul, but had been unable to fight back her own despair.

News came daily from the streets of the capital, of fresh beatings, of lynching's and, in one instance, a murder. A Reven trader, who lived in the west of the city, had come out to chase off some youths who had been throwing stones at his shop. When he did, the youths' parents had been waiting for him and they had set upon the man with clubs and staves, beating him to death and leaving his body to drain in the street. Elsewhere, Eran, through his tears of shame and growl of disgust, had told her how one of the watch captains in the east of Karick was too drunk to follow his orders and bring a Reven family in for questioning. Sending a *Street Rat* with a note, the captain had tipped off a local lynch mob of their location and let them do the work for him.

Eran had received no word of the family's fate, though they both doubted it had been a happy one.

It had been said in some corners, also, that at the start of the madness, some Reven families had even sought refuge at the high duke's keep – effectively saving the militia and authorities the bother of coming to find them. They too, had not been seen again and it left a bitter taste in Dia's mouth, a terrible question in her head.

What were they doing with these people?

"What am I going to do?" Eran said suddenly, his words dripping with despair. "Tomorrow, I have to report back to my watch. How can I live with myself, with the things they are forcing me to do, Dia?"

Dia soothed his panic with a tender kiss, pulling away as his passions chased away his concerns. She placed a gentle finger to his lips and smiled.

"You must do what you can, where you can," she whispered, ignoring the chill that stole up her back. "Without men like you, this city will be lost."

Eran was already shaking his head. "But there is nothing I can do, Dia. If I desert, I would be branded a traitor, a *Reven-Lover.* If I stay, I will be eventually forced to do terrible things that I cannot get out of. Without Captain Varl, this Gardan, his methods... it is all too much. The city will not survive his choking grip."

Mention of the captain stirred up Dia's revulsion and images of what had been done to him by these monsters burned in her mind. She pulled away from their embrace. Swinging her legs over the side of the bed, she sat there quietly for a time, brushing her toes over the cold stone.

"I was so worried for you and I desperately wanted to see you," Dia began, her heart racing, her stomach knotting. "There are a few things I need to do and then, if you will have me, we can be together. We could flee the city, head west, perhaps? We could go to help your parents on their farm. Live a life that is free from all of this. Be happy, be one."

Her words were full of desperation, as if she did not truly believe her rising excitement could ever be. Eran knelt behind her on the bed and wrapped his strong arms about her milky-white shoulders, drenched in a cascade of tangled auburn.

"That is a lovely dream, lady," he sighed, though his body tensed with his thoughts.

Dia began to cry and Eran pulled her deeper into his arms.

"Hush there," he whispered, slowly kissing her neck. "Don't cry, Dia. We'll get through this somehow, *together.*"

Blinking back her tears, Dia looked up at Eran, seeing the hunger, the concern and the fear all swirling there in his bright, gleaming eyes.

"I love you," she breathed, giving in to her desires.

The stars were bright, much like the chancellor's anger, as Relan Valus stalked through the grounds of the high duke's gardens, towards his offices. Behind him, at a respectful distance, his bodyguards followed in his wake, sweeping the shadows and the silent night for sign of any who would wish harm to the man whom many said now ruled Karick.

Annoyed at the supposed need for protection, Relan Valus focussed his thoughts away from his distress. News of Captain Varl's escape from certain death left a sour taste in his mouth, one laced by bitter annoyance at the Kestrel's apparent failure. The connotations rising from the captain's rescue asked more questions than it satisfied answers and for two days he had wracked his mind for any tell of who may have spirited him away to safety.

The furious argument he had endured with the Kestrel did little to ease his worries and by the end of their last meeting, they had reluctantly come to an agreement that, whilst his escape could prove troublesome, in his condition, should he survive, there was little that he could do to stop the Brotherhood's momentum now. In a few days time, the high duke's family would be dead and then he could allow the news of Karian Stromn's terminal illness to be made public. The people would need a corpse in time, so that they might pay their respects to the man they had once loved and worshipped, if only to ease their own guilt of how they had turned from him.

Relan scowled. Even now the man refused to die – somehow holding on to the faint strands of life, starving to death in his chambers, with guards watching vigilantly at his door.

"Do your best," the chancellor hissed to his unseen enemies. He looked up at the leering moon overhead and smiled. In two days time the moon would reach its zenith and he could contact his master on the stars, to tell him that all was ready for his arrival.

Fighting back his lust, his need for the moment to finally arrive, Relan turned his attentions to some loose threads that needed tying up. If, by some miracle, those who opposed the Brotherhood somehow managed to find an unlikely voice for their concerns, he needed to be certain that there was no proof left behind of what he had been orchestrating these last ten years. Their enemies would not be that lucky, he knew, as they would die long before any court was called. But, just for a little while longer, it was better to err on the side of caution.

Nearing the records office, lost to the depths of the night but its location lit by a welcoming lantern, the chancellor was surprised that the old guard was still at his post. A brief spark of rare guilt was quickly replaced with admiration at the guard's sense of duty and Relan made a mental note to promote the man when things settled down in the city.

"Lord Chancellor," the thin, sour-faced man greeted, stiffening with respect and saluting sharply. "A cold night, for certain!"

"Indeed it is," Relan Valus replied cheerily, as he came to stand before the heavy oak door. "Forgive the lateness of the hour, but I have been remiss of my duties of late and thought it best to tidy up matters here, before finally relieving you of your post....?"

"Er, Wen, sir," the man responded to the unsaid question in his pause. "Thank you, sir."

Wen stepped back as the chancellor fumbled through his robes under the watch-lantern's light and slipped the iron key into the large lock. He regarded the two escorts that waited on the cusp of the golden light and tried his best to hide his relief at finally being able to get back to his regular duties and be free of his interminable boredom.

The chancellor had the door open and was slipping inside when Wen's hesitant voice dragged him back.

"I doubt you will be late to your bed, sir," Wen said affably. "The girl tidied up in there for you, some days ago now."

Relan Valus slipped back from the darkness and stepped out into the lantern light.

"What girl?" he asked softly, his hooded eyes glittering menacingly.

CHAPTER THIRTY ONE

The Prodigal Son

Cullen looked back at Khadazin knowingly, as they broke from the eastern fringes of the Whispering Woods and the Redani caught sight of Karick for the first time since he had been taken from there in the dead of night, all those weeks ago now. The Redani's concealed face was as grey as the clouds gathering together over the capital and his eyes were white with fear as he tussled with the past and tried to free himself from the uncertainty of his future.

It was still early, the grasslands and outlying farmsteads wreathed in a grim mist, that hung over the land like a watching spectre. Dark birds, crows possibly, stirred from their roosts, but drifted their way silently overhead, as if they, too, did not want the calm of the morning's gloom to be broken.

Pulling his scarf from off his nose, Cullen dropped back to ride alongside the stonemason. Without looking at him, Tania urged her mount away to keep Riyan company.

"Takes my breath away," Cullen offered, throwing a nod towards the towering granite walls of the city. His breath misted before him and Khadazin reluctantly followed his gesture. "I can only imagine what you are feeling right now!"

"No, you cannot," Khadazin whispered, but Cullen chose to ignore him.

They had spent the previous night, deep into the eastern plains, huddled together in the open for warmth as they sought to avoid any who chased the vast amount of coin being offered for Khadazin's capture... or head. As soon as the sky began to lighten, they were off again, already awake and keen to be in the city before too many people were abroad to witness their arrival.

They had not met another soul – though Khadazin was certain they were being watched the entire time.

"Going to make for the eastern side of the city," Cullen explained for the second time that morning. "Once there, we will steal you in through the sewers and get you to a place of safety."

"Thank you," Khadazin said quietly. "You have risked much to come for me and I shall not forget it."

Cullen eyed the Redani for a time, his remaining good eye narrowed. Not used to receiving thanks, he was unsure whether the stonemason was being sincere with him or not. When he was fairly certain that he was, Cullen nodded his head several times.

"You have been through a lot, Redani, on the behalf of many others – I think it's the least we could do."

As they rode on in contemplative silence, Cullen was fairly sure that in the days ahead, Khadazin may well come to regret that they had ever found him.

Khadazin gagged, the terrible stench and fumes of the sight before him filling his flaring nostrils and clogging his throat. Slipping from his saddle, he passed the reins into Riyan's offered hand and went to stand beside Tania. She had the tails of her cloak gathered up, covering her mouth and nose.

“I fear this is the only safe way we can get you to your friend,” Tania guessed, her eyes reluctantly following Cullen. With a great show of balance, the fat, squat man picked his way around the steep grassy slopes of the manmade cesspool and made for the rusted iron grate that would lead them into the dark sewer tunnel and under the towering city beyond. A continuous torrent of filth and excrement spilled over the edge of the narrow cobbled ledge, gathering many feet below in the deep pool of everything the stonemason did not want to think about. Even at this hour, the stench was overpowering and Khadazin was only thankful that they had not arrived during the high heat of the day.

“Why don’t you stay with Riyan and the horses,” Khadazin suggested, but the look Tania gave him quickly silenced any further protestations that may have been coming.

Riyan was going to wait for news from them in a place called *Briar Copse*, somewhere to the east. A common meeting place apparently, though Khadazin was not sure he wanted to know for what.

The first joyous birdsong of the day began to fill the surrounding land and Khadazin, despite his revulsion at the thought of what he was about to endure, felt his spirits lift somewhat. Gripping hold of Tania’s hand and the thought that he was finally going to see Savinn Kassaar again, the stonemason gathered up his courage, dragged in a deep breath and went in search of what he hoped would prove to be his destiny.

The next few hours were spent in the dark, twisting confines of the sewers, lit only by the lantern that Cullen carried, as he strode on purposefully ahead of them to light their way. Several times, the Redani lost his footing on the slick, ankle deep walkways and each time, Tania was there to help him from his knees.

All about them, the shadows dripped with water from the low, stone roof, drumming a warning out on their hooded heads and soaking them through to the skin. As they traversed the warrens that were the city's sewer network, rats scurrying across the path before them, the only thing of hope that Khadazin could cling on to was that the ferocious storms that had battered the Four Vales of recent weeks had now passed on. If they hadn't, they would have been swimming in the river of filth that churned idly by them, not walking beside it.

By now, either Khadazin had become accustomed to the terrible stench of the sewers, or his broken nose was actually proving useful. Either way, despite his deep feeling of despair, the Redani was thankful for it. Tania kept close to him, holding his hand when she could, or stalking ahead of him through the filth, when their pathway became too narrow.

By the time Cullen had stopped to change his waning candle, both Tania and Khadazin were numbed by their exhaustion and from the cold, desperate for somewhere to stop and rest, but reluctant to tarry any longer down here than they had to.

After a time, Tania turned back to Khadazin and her dark eyes flashed with relief.

"We are nearly free, Redani," she said, her muffled voice echoing away behind them.

Khadazin searched their surroundings and failed to hide his scepticism.

"I do not think I shall ever be free of this stench," he muttered, though his complaints were lifted by his grin.

Moments later, Cullen put them out of their misery and turned from the channel of sewerage, leading them away down a narrow side tunnel towards a blank, featureless wall. Striding forward, Cullen hammered on the wall with a hairy fist.

"It's a secret entrance," Tania explained.

Whilst Khadazin knew that the merchant was in hiding from Savinn's letter and the girl's report from her previous visit to the city, he had not realised how desperate things must have become for his friend to be hiding away in such a forsaken place.

As time slipped slowly away and Cullen's patience followed with it, his beating fist became heavier and more frequent. Finally, when it looked as if Cullen would tear the wall down with his bare hands, the wall slid away to reveal the curious face of a tall, thin man with long tendrils of grey hair, pulled back into a ragged tail behind his neck.

"About bloody time," Cullen muttered, adding something else less charitable.

"My thoughts exactly," the man retorted and then, with a grin, stuffed his hand out in greeting.

Tania shuddered in the wake of a gleeful draught of stale air and watched the exchange wordlessly. After many days in the company of Cullen now, she longed to get this over with and be rid of his lecherous attention once, and finally, for all.

"Boss is waiting," the man said. Breaking from their handshake, he eyed Cullen's charges with a look of relief and genuine surprise. He stepped aside to allow the newcomers entrance and offered them a nod of greeting as they stepped warily over the threshold.

"Wait for me in the room at the top of these stairs," Cullen ordered them, without looking back. Before Khadazin could respond, Cullen began to hurry away, his breath stolen by the effort of his rapid ascent of the steep staircase before them.

"Follow me, Redani," Tania said, smiling weakly. As the secret door was swung back into place behind them, Khadazin followed the huntress up into the unknown in pursuit of the retreating, bobbing light of Cullen's lantern.

Sitting at a worm-riddled table in the sparse room at the top of the stairs and with every fibre of his body aching, Khadazin finally heard the distant approach of feet. In the quiet of the room and from across the table, Tania quelled the Redani's rising anxiety with a bright, encouraging smile. As the footsteps hurried closer, each muffled footfall quickened the pace of Khadazin's heart. Closer the footsteps came, lengthening in urgency, drumming out a hasty tune that threatened to lift the beat from Khadazin's chest.

When the robed figure of Savinn Kassaar appeared in the doorway, Khadazin did not truly believe he was there. On heavy legs, he rose from his rickety seat, steadying himself with his good hand, as the merchant's bearded face broke into a broad smile, spread wider by his obvious relief.

"Khadazin!" Savinn roared heartily and the two friends hurried forward into the other's arms, holding each other tightly.

"My friend," Khadazin gasped, not really believing what was happening as his friend clutched thankfully at his broad back and he felt his own tears streak down his cheeks to fall on the merchant's shoulder.

"I did not ever think I would see you again," Savinn admitted, pulling back slightly to check his mind was not playing tricks. He surveyed the stonemason's battered face for a time, noting the memories of what had happened to him, lurking there in his glistening eyes.

"There were times, my friend," Khadazin winced, curling his lips, "when I thought that, also."

Gripping the Redani's shoulder with his left hand, Savinn conveyed his own guilt with a subtle shake of his head, then spied Tania, stood now to one side, near to the open doorway that led steeply back down to the secret entrance.

"My lady," Savinn greeted, his guilt swiftly hidden

away again, saved for a time when privacy would permit further honesty. "I had not expected to see you a second time, but I must admit that it gladdens me so."

Tania shifted nervously on her feet and studied the condition of her boots, before looking up.

"Khadazin is my friend," she began defiantly, daring the merchant-thief to send her away. "And I would be by his side for what is to follow."

Khadazin grinned and Savinn dealt him a knowing look. With a chuckle that echoed about the room and bounded away down the staircase, the merchant-thief stepped away from the Redani and offered the young woman a graceful bow.

"You are most welcome, huntress," he said in earnest, raising his eyes to hold her attention. "You have proven to be a most valuable friend, both to Khadazin and myself and I will not soon forget it."

Embarrassed by all the attention, some colour returned to Tania's cheeks. As she hid away in a veil of her sodden, dark locks, she muttered something that may have been her thanks. Smiling fondly at her, Khadazin forgot about where they were for a time, before the gravity of the situation dragged him back roughly with a bitter reminder of why he had risked coming back to the capital.

Sensing the shift in the air, Savinn met his friend's flashing eyes and straightened again. Raising his hands dramatically, he clapped them together three times and waited for only six heartbeats, before a young waif of a girl hurried into the room. Dressed in loose-fitting pantaloons and a shirt, smeared with grime, the waif stood there with darting, tired blue eyes. Running a thin hand through her short, blonde hair, she flicked a wide look at the huge Redani before her, then shifted her gaze to Tania and found a faint smile.

"Ellie," Savinn said, drawing the girl's attention back.

"Show the young lady to some quarters and fix her a hot bath. I would speak with my friend further, before we break our fast."

Offering Tania a smile, Savinn waited until the two girls were gone, before he turned back to Khadazin. He studied his friend thoughtfully for a time, touching the fingertips on his hands together furtively. Savinn suddenly noticed Khadazin's missing hand and looked up in horror.

"The cost of my life," Khadazin said, glancing reluctantly at his leather-capped wrist. He looked up again, flicking his hazel eyes about the room.

"We have all suffered, it seems."

The merchant nodded licking his top lip nervously. "Come, my friend," Savinn said finally, his bearded, face weary, yet gentle. "We have much to discuss and little time to do so."

Savinn led the stonemason hurriedly through what appeared to be a completely different world – one that Khadazin would not have guessed was deep under Karick, in its ancient sewers. He barely had time to marvel at the magnificent paintings, as the merchant guided him along a luxuriantly carpeted hallway and into his private study, a room filled with great opulence that was but a hint at Savinn's vast wealth.

Falling into the offered chair, the very same Cassana had sat in, all those weeks before, Khadazin looked across the antique desk at his friend and, similarly, his eyes were drawn to the painting of the wolf, hanging on the wall behind his head.

Savinn grinned, as if reading his thoughts and poured them both a glass of deep red wine from a silver carafe. Licking his lips, Khadazin reached for the offered goblet, then hesitated, his heart thrumming rapidly in warning as it chased away the desire rising in his throat.

"No thank you," the stonemason said quietly, sinking back into the embrace of his chair. "I need a clear mind for what is ahead and would not wish to revisit darker days."

Savinn shrugged and drank heavily from his own goblet. Closing his eyes for a time, he savoured the exquisite taste, before putting aside his drink. Clasping his hands together before him, he leant forward and gripped his friend's attention with a withering gaze.

"I shall be as brief as I can, Khadazin," he began quietly, "as much of what you needed to know was already in my letter to you. What was not in the letter, sadly, is that, although your honour and bravery put in motion events that would save Lady Byron's life, it has, I am afraid, set in motion darker times that have ended with the assassination of her father."

Khadazin blinked and somehow stopped his hand reaching for the goblet of wine on the desk before him. He stared at the merchant, his face grim, his emotions reeling.

Seeing his friend's pain and confusion, Savinn continued. "The hardliners have waited many years for the chance to unsettle the stability of the Vales, to find a way to wrestle power from the high duke's line and, ultimately, finish what was started, all those years ago."

Khadazin frowned, snorting bitterly. "I am a simple man, Savinn. You had best spare me any intricacies and lay it out easily before me."

Savinn smiled, sensing some of the old Redani lurking there behind all his uncertainty. The same man who had no friends, save one, in the city and had once spent his time with only his customers and his drink.

"Very well," Savinn said evenly. "To simplify matters, the plot you overheard was the pivotal move that would start a succession of events that, as I detailed already in my letter to you, would shift the mantle of power and its focus away from peace and stability, towards war. Whilst you have been away, the city has stirred with dark unrest, treachery and brutality. Numerous political and well-orchestrated attacks have left the country's nerves on a knife's edge. Recent events have tipped that edge towards the hardliners, who, I am led to believe, call themselves the *Brotherhood.* It has cut through any hope we could have had for a peaceful solution to our problem."

Khadazin frowned, sifting for the right response. "So this *Brotherhood*, these hardliners have duped the people into hating any of Reven heritage. You alluded as much to me in your letter... is this why Reven tried to kidnap Lady Byron? A politically motivated move to undermine..." realisation dawned on the Redani's battered features and his eyebrows arched up in horror, "her father."

Savinn's face softened and reached across to grip his friend's shaking hand. "Do not blame yourself, Khadazin. Had you not sent me that letter, the *Brotherhood* would have taken Lady Byron and matters would now be completely out of our control."

Khadazin snorted and tussled with his emotions. "Are they not already?"

Savinn smiled, his face mirroring the wolf, hanging behind his head. "Not quite... but, before I lay my cards on the table and ask something further of you, I must finally know, my friend, that which you have kept from me."

Khadazin recoiled and his breath caught in his throat. He looked away, dragging his hand from the merchant's grip. After a time, he drew in a long, deep breath.

"Very well," he whispered, letting out his emotions. His face hardened, his eyes narrowed and he clenched his fist tightly. "On the day I fell asleep, I overhead two men talking, plotting to kidnap a woman who I later discovered was the daughter of the *Seventh*, the man I now know to be Alion Byron. I do not know the second man's identity, though they referred to each other as *Brother*, but he was younger, much younger than the man who would have me hunted and tortured, to reveal the identity of anyone I may have told."

Savinn's face was pale and he calmed the fear in his shaking hands by rubbing them together nervously

"Of course, I did not tell them," Khadazin smiled ruefully, "and I presume that, with your aid, Lady Byron was spirited away from them, which added to their desperation to find out who worked against them."

Savinn nodded. "They did not find out, though other events and moves by them have forced me into my present circumstances. I have been marked the firebrand, the leader of this Reven *uprising* and, as you are now painfully aware, I hear you have been marked the man behind the attempt on Lady Byron, when in fact, you are the one who ultimately saved her."

Khadazin growled, his eyes were dark, glittering with malice. "A clever move, though I wonder if more from desperation. Do they still fear my testimony? Do they really think my desire for vengeance worthy of such concern?"

Savinn shrugged impatiently. "Perhaps, my friend, though circumstances may have already silenced your evidence before you can even give it. Who was it, Khadazin? Who has set fire to the Four Vales and, ultimately, put us on the path to war?"

Khadazin barely heard what the merchant was saying. His head pounded furiously, his pulse screaming through his veins.

"It was the high duke's chancellor, Relan Valus."

Those words, guarded for so long, had an amazing effect on both men. For Khadazin, it was a great release, like he had just passed on a heavy burden. For Savinn, it was a key to the puzzle, a valuable piece that he thought he had always had, but did not know where it went until he had found it.

"Know thy enemy," Savinn whispered, shaking his

head. "I have long suspected this, though, without clear proof have had nothing tangible to take before the high duke."

Khadazin swallowed his exuberance. His friend should have been much happier than this at the revelation.

"Then we must find a way to see the high duke! Bring my testimony to him and stop this madness before it is too late." Khadazin's voice was rising, his excitement, his needs, rousing his spirits.

Savinn's words shook the remnants of any last hope he had from his body.

"The high duke is dying, Khadazin! He is a prisoner in his own keep and the chancellor's move to outlaw us both has effectively silenced our evidence before we can give it credence. If we attempt to see him or rescue him, we will be killed, without fair hearing and certainly without fair, if any, trial."

Khadazin silenced his strangled sob and buried his face in his large hand. He sunk into his chair, his broad shoulders heaving with grief.

"Then it has all been for nothing?" Khadazin snarled, pummelling his wide forehead angrily. He looked up at his friend, who, once again, was remaining impassively calm.

"Perhaps not," Savinn smiled, his Reven eyes traced by hope. "It is most likely that the high duke is being drugged, poisoned slowly by the chancellor and his allies. It is a method they have used before..."

Khadazin sat up slightly. "Then we *should* rescue him!"

Savinn nodded. "It would be the right move and perhaps the only way to stop this madness."

"But?" the Redani dared to ask.

Savinn smiled. "We have many allies gathering, in Havensdale and in Highwater. Lady Byron will not open her gates to the Valian armies and I am sure that before the hardliners can send their hatred over the Great Divide, there will first be a great civil war."

"Then what must be done?" Khadazin demanded, his frustrations getting the better of him. He stood up and paced about the room angrily.

"Come with me, my friend, and I will show you," Savinn purred mysteriously.

CHAPTER THIRTY TWO

The Calm before the Storm

Arillion grimaced as he tried to stretch the pain from his injured leg. Sat near to his wagon, he warmed himself by a wistful fire, the early morning chill clinging to him, whilst the bland sky overhead brightened with a teasing promise of the day ahead.

The wayfarers, largely, were still in their wagons, or hidden away under their blankets, nursing their efforts from the night before. Arillion shook his own efforts from his head and traced a tendril of swirling smoke up into the sky. It still amazed him, even after all this time spent with the wayfarers, that their voracious appetites for song, dance and drink did not diminish. Each night, they would come together to listen to Kaspen Shale's tales of the ancient days, to dance to the skilled rhythms of Tomlin's fiddle and his woman's flute. Coupled with their thirst for mead and wine and, well, anything you could get your hands on, there was no time to rest, no time to think clearly.

Arillion eyed his ruined leg and was thankful for a valid excuse, though he played on their hospitality by hiding from them how well the broken bone was healing. He needed Kaspen Shale to stay in Highwater, until the spy, at the very least, was in chains and her allies' identities burned from her.

A shadow stretched across him and the assassin glanced up from the waning fire, startled at the newcomer's silent approach and quickly warmed by the sight that greeted him.

"I thought you weren't talking to me," Arillion observed, as Lia, beautiful even at such an early hour, took her place beside him on his blanket.

"I am not," the wayfarer replied cordially. Dressed in the vibrant skirts and silks of her people, she drew her knees up under her chin and hugged her slender legs as she searched the fire for something.

Dragging his eyes from the obligingly bared skin of her calves, Arillion shifted his focus, turning to trace his attention up the slender curves of her body, to search for her face, hidden away in a tumble of raven tresses.

"So you are not talking to me," Arillion chuckled. "Are you still angry with me then, or can't you resist my company any longer?"

She rounded on him, her eyes, once full of passion and lust, now flashing with hurt and anger.

She said something appropriate, but Arillion had lost himself in her beautiful face and heard not a word from her fulsome, snarling lips.

When she looked as if she was about to strike him, Arillion blinked free of his trance and raised a placating hand.

"Forgive me," he said hurriedly, running a slow hand through his long hair. Rolling the tension from his neck and shoulders, he softened the mirth in his eyes, a little.

"There is nothing to forgive, swordsman," Lia said, though her words were laced with hurt. "I have many suitors, some much younger than you and I will seek one who has the stamina to keep up with me."

Arillion winced, throwing her a look. "You cut deep, lady."

Lia bristled as he smiled mockingly, then bit her lower lip to cut off her choice retort.

"Anyway, enough of our short history, that is now lost to us and I came here only to talk about my father."

Arillion straightened, gathering up his defences. "What about him?"

Lia fixed him with a reproachful look. "I worry about him, about the direction he is taking our family," she began. Looking carefully about at the sleeping forms nearby, she lowered her voice. "People are starting to question why it is we stay in Highwater, what it is that could possibly be keeping us here. They point fingers towards you, swordsman. They are not stupid, they know you are up to something, they know it is your hand that guides us... and they fear for the days to come."

Arillion shook his head, looking up again to hold her accusing eyes in his own hooded gaze. "They should not fear me, they should thank me. A change is coming and they will not be able to avoid it – nobody can."

Lia frowned. "I do not know what you mean and I do not want to know. But know this, if my father does not move us on soon, the people will lose their patience, they will question his leadership and they will stir with thoughts of change. I do not want them to call a vote. You know our ways – you know what that could mean for him... for me."

Arillion, for a brief moment, felt something that might have been guilt rise up, before he dismissed it with the thought of all the money he could make, of the woman he had promised to help and the one he had decided to kill.

"I will warn your father, Lia," the assassin placated her, though he knew Kaspen was already hooked and could not break free.

Lia studied the assassin's ruggedly handsome face for a time, fighting with her annoyance and rising desires. Smoothing the cloth of her bright skirt down over her bared legs, she rose swiftly.

Looking down her small, upturned nose at him, she banished the final coals of her desires away with a curt nod.

"I will hold you to your word, swordsman," she said quietly. Spinning on her anger, the beautiful wayfarer stalked away through the morning gloom.

Arillion watched her for a while, before she slipped away into her wagon on the far side of the camp.

Shaking his head, the swordsman looked to the mountains, running his thoughts over them to the wealth and riches to be had there.

Had he made the right choice? Had he sided with his old enemy fate for a change, spurning his one chance of finding his true destiny?

The image of a red-haired girl and her freckled face flashed in his mind and clenching both his fists tightly, Arillion knew that he had not.

By mid-morn the wayfarer camp was alive, the clearing sky bright with an attentive sun and the air full of the scents of breakfasts cooking. Not hungry himself, Arillion watched the comings and goings thoughtfully, spying a heated discussion between Kaspen and Mother Shale. After the angry encounter, Kaspen threw his hands aloft and stalked angrily across the barren land towards the city. Frowning, Arillion began to flex his injured shoulder, pleased that some feeling was coming back, glad that he would soon be able to grip a sword in his left hand.

Some time later, the assassin saw Lia look in his direction, as she served the few customers, still drawn to her stall from Highwater. Over the last week, trade had dropped off substantially and more and more of the wayfaring family were forced to sell their wares inside the city walls.

Lia fixed him with a fiery look and turned to dazzle the young man she was serving with an alluring smile.

Chuckling, Arillion dragged himself up and wandered away across the fields to find some peace and solitude.

When Arillion returned, the sun was high overhead, pounding the lands below with its fury. Eager to be out of the intense summer heat and keen to rest his throbbing, aching leg, he limped over to his wagon and slipped quietly away from the day.

"There you are," Kaspen observed, from where he sat on the stool beside Arillion's bed. He was flushed from the sun and the assassin judged that he had not long arrived himself.

"Here I am," Arillion agreed. He stumbled over to the bed and sat down with a weary groan.

"Still hurting you?" Kaspen asked and Arillion nodded, gently massaging his swollen shin.

"You needed something?" the swordsman asked, without looking up.

Kaspen cleared his throat for a moment, before forcing his question from his hesitant lips.

"My people are restless, Arillion. When are we to leave?"

Arillion looked up, holding the wayfarer's gaze. He sighed, shaking his head. "Soon, my friend. I understand your concerns. Lia came to see me this morning and she told me that your people are beginning to whisper behind your back."

Arillion could see the worry stretching across Kaspen's weary features, though he doubted it was concern for any mutiny, only the anxiety that his daughter was speaking to him again. Usually guarded with his thoughts, the wayfarer had failed to hide his joy that

Arillion and his daughter were not talking.

"They are always restless, swordsman," Kaspen began, waving a hand dismissively, "but we are wanderers, wayfarers who travel the Four Vales, rarely two nights under the same stars... we have tarried here far too long, though I know why we could not leave."

Arillion nodded, reaching across to grip the wayfarer's hand. "We will leave soon, once we are sure Lady Byron has acted upon our letter. There may be others working with the spy, but we cannot track them all down, it is for others to concern themselves with now. Did the letter get delivered safely?"

Kaspen squeezed Arillion's hand, releasing it. "It is done! Whilst I was in the city, I met with our man, who had some interesting news."

Arillion folded his arms across his chest, signalling for Kaspen to continue.

"It seems that Lady Byron has allies, those who would fight alongside her, should matters slip beyond our control. As we have heard, Havensdale was attacked by Carwellian forces, by Renald Gardan, of all people. It seems they had evidence that a Fawn Ardent, the captain of the Havensdale militia, was conspiring with the Reven uprising and the one who delivered Lady Byron to the capital, into the hands of her enemies."

Arillion frowned, starting with shock. "What horseshit is this? She was very kind to Lady Byron. On our way back to Highwater Cassana even wanted to seek sanctuary there, as she trusted the captain. She may have been young and inexperienced back then, but I judge her worth in measuring people."

"I agree," Kaspen nodded. "Havensdale stood firm, saved, it seems, by the arrival of a mysterious swordsman, a woodsman who fought alongside them."

Arillion's senses pricked. "Woodsman, you say? Hmm! Lady Byron was saved by a woodsman, when the

Reven tried to abduct her... now I am really curious." He caught the look that crossed Kaspen's face. "What else?"

Kaspen sat forward on his stool. "A town in the East Vales, Eastbury, was raided by Reven and Valian mercenaries a few weeks ago. A Carwellian patrol saved the town and pursued the raiders north, seeking to save the hostages they had taken. They did not succeed, sadly, but captured the leader of the raiding party. It seems this is where our friend Gardan comes into the story. He was overheard talking to the prisoner, inadvertently admitting his guilt to his involvement in the raids."

Arillion yawned. "Is this going somewhere, Kaspen? I know Gardan, he is a ruthless bastard and I wouldn't put anything past him. He is Carwell's right hand, after all."

Kaspen stiffened, then smiled. "Yes, he is. It is well known. What is not known, however, is that Gardan killed the prisoner and gave false testimony, implicating Fawn Ardent as a Valian traitor. I may be a roaming imbecile, but that is clearly a move to shift blame onto Lady Byron's allies."

Arillion smirked, ignoring the irritation creasing Kaspen's face and the annoyance in his words. "So we have a thread to tie to Carwell. It makes perfect sense... even if you are an imbecile."

Kaspen drew in a breath, then laughed heartily. "You are a hard man to like Arillion, has anyone ever told you that?"

"Most people I have met," Arillion chuckled, shaking his head. His mind was racing, tumbling through the myriad of connotations. The implication of the length and growing strength of the Brotherhood's reach was not lost on him.

"So Carwell has finally made his move, after all these years. We won't be able to finger him in this plot, not yet. He is too wily a fox for that. But Gardan's involvement in the raids makes for some compelling evidence. How did we come by this?"

Kaspen threaded his hands together. "A young woman overheard Gardan, witnessed him kill the prisoner. She was framed by Gardan as the murderer and was sentenced to hang. When the Carwellian forces moved on to Havensdale to arrest Fawn Ardent, the girl was released by the leader of the patrol that had initially saved Eastbury."

"Dissension in the ranks," Arillion mused. Things were starting to get very interesting. "So, let me guess, the patrol, armed with the knowledge imparted by this girl, go to Havensdale, then word is sent to Highwater for the attention of Alion Byron."

Kaspen's face darkened. "As far as my contact knows, Havensdale and the patrol have joined forces, they have pledged to keep the girl safe, should she be able to testify against Gardan, whilst other evidence is being sought."

Arillion nodded his approval, clearly happy with what he was hearing.

"What about Gardan? Where is that snake hiding?"

Kaspen smiled ruefully. "The word is that he has gone to Karick."

Arillion swore, chewing thoughtfully on a thumb nail. After a long time of contemplation, he spat his efforts away, looked up again and smiled.

"Give me two days, Brother Shale. Let us wait to hear what Lady Byron does with our efforts."

"And after that?" Kaspen dared to ask.

Arillion's flint grey eyes sparked with glee as he spoke.

"We head south to Havensdale, to join this merry band of rebels and traitors"

Cassana studied her reflection in the mirror, as she tied her hair back in a tight braid. With a sigh, she turned away from the woman she no longer recognised and crossed her bedchamber to pick up her bow and quiver. Dressed in her leathers and a clean sable tunic, she moved into her lounge, her eyes sifting through the streaming slivers of sunlight, to fall reluctantly on the mysterious letter.

It had been found under her door, slipped there in the early hours of the morning as she slept, by an unknown messenger. Feeling a chill steal through her and unnerved at the thought that nameless individuals were still able to slip unnoticed through her keep, Cassana turned from the letter and headed for the door.

"By the storms," she shrieked, as she hauled it open to be confronted by William Bay. As they both nursed their shock and found a smile, Cassana stepped back into her chambers, motioning her visitor to close the door behind him.

"You sent for me, lady?" William asked. He no longer dressed in his robes of office, choosing to wear leather trousers and a tunic, its dark sleeves padded and studded for extra protection. His old Valian war blade hung from his left hip and he shifted its position as he took the seat Cassana offered him.

"I did," Cassana replied eventually, putting her bow and quiver aside. She picked up the letter, crossing to William and passing it into his reaching hand.

With her arms folded before her, Cassana watched, her heart galloping as William's eyes widened over the words he hastily devoured. When he looked up his weathered features smoothed across his shock.

"Who gave you this?" William demanded, waving the letter before him.

"It was slipped under my door," Cassana said, shrugging. "But by whom, I know not. All I know is that I do not recognise the hand that penned it."

William was silent for a time and Cassana could tell that he was struggling through the same series of emotions that had kept her distracted, left her sickened for the better part of the day.

"It must be nonsense, lady," William began, though he paused long enough to sow his own doubts. "I mean, Lady Astien? A spy?"

Cassana trembled, feeling the disgust rise in her stomach. Images flashed before her, tumbling away incoherently of her and Lysette lying on her bed as children, playing with kittens – of them dancing together at Lysette's coming of age ball, of the way, even then, that men found her friend desirable and avoided the rebellious, tempestuous spirit that was never far from her side. A multitude of memories rose up, overcoming Cassana again and forcing her to find a seat. William looked on, his face lined with fresh worry, the edges of his old eyes deepened by his rising concern.

"You are both so close," William offered, dropping the letter to his lap. "I fail to see how and why, even if there was the faintest grain of truth to this lie, that Lysette would betray not only her closest friend, but her own father as well."

Licking the fear from her lips, Cassana blinked away her turmoil and nodded her head once.

"Believe me, William, I have agonised over the very same thought, and for many more hours. I love Lysette and I know that she, in turn, shares that love. I have to believe that this letter is false, an attempt by our enemies to undermine my trust in my friends and allies. But... if it is not, then we have allies that work with us, yet hide their identity to safeguard their involvement."

Cassana fell silent, thinking of Savinn Kassaar, of all he had done to help her and of all he had said and done to ensure that his involvement in her escape from Karick was kept a secret. Her mind began to wander.

When she focused on the present again, she could see that William had read something in her face. Recovering her composure, Cassana gripped his attention with a furious look.

"I cannot contemplate that Lysette is a spy, the spy that has done so much to this household, to undermine its strength and position at the council table. After all, Lysette was not in the city when my father, when the–, when he–," Cassana hesitated, choking on her rising grief for a time.

William rose swiftly for a man of his advancing years. Crossing to sit beside her, he took Cassana's hands in his own and gripped them tightly, forcing her to focus on him.

"If she is a spy, then she must have allies," William began, his mind racing. "But we must tread carefully, my lady. Bryn Astien is our greatest ally and he is as loyal to you as he was your father before you. Before we even threaten that allegiance, we must discover more about her movements and of those she has dealings with, both privately and publicly."

Cassana nodded several times, sifting through her thoughts. A chill stole through her body as she realised that Elan had been romantically involved with Lysette, before he had been killed defending his charge against the Reven attackers in the Moonglade Forest. Was it possible that Lysette had found out about which way they would be travelling from her own protector?

Closing her eyes, Cassana let out a deep sigh as yet another heavy burden settled on her young shoulders. When she fixed her eyes on William again, they were bright with determination.

"We must conduct ourselves as normal," Cassana began, clutching William's hands even tighter. "If we have a thorn in our midst we must have a care to remove it slowly. I will treat Lysette as I always have, but throw veiled questions her way, to gauge and seek hint of her true allegiances."

"Agreed, lady," William said quietly. "I will conduct

my own investigations on the matter, but will have a care with whom I speak to."

Cassana smiled grimly. "If we have new friends, we should not dismiss their help so easily. If after our search we discover, however, that they are not, we will have beaten them by not rushing in and throwing fragile accusations about."

"But if they are correct?" William dared to ask. "If they have found out what we could not?"

Cassana's face flushed and William sat back in shock. All her sorrow, all her anger, all the turmoil and horrors she had suffered and witnessed of late hardened there momentarily for him to see, then vanished behind a mask of grim calm.

"Then I will confront this traitor," Cassana whispered. "I will confront her and I will slip the noose about her neck myself."

CHAPTER THIRTY THREE

Hunter's Moon

The guard strode past Dia's hiding place and holding to the caution that had seen her so far that night, she remained where she was for many more moments. Hidden in the shadows of the musty stairwell's antechamber, she gathered together her fraying courage and listened to the fading tramp of the guard's footfalls, as they were lost to the thunderous roar of the nerves in her head.

Gathering her cloak tightly about her, Dia hurried up the twisting stairs on failing legs and settled down on the final step to listen to the night. The air beyond her hiding place was crisp and welcoming, swept about by a clear night breeze. Overhead, the dark sky was scattered with bright stars, glistening in support of the huge full moon, resting proudly at its zenith and casting a silvery light across the city.

Dia shuddered. The city was quiet now, but the day had seen further bloodshed; a dark day that had broken any hope of peace for those that still clung to it. Reports were coming in from the streets that many of the Reven, those still managing to evade arrest, had slipped away over the past few days. Much coin had changed hands and several families had escaped Gardan's clutches, fleeing north towards the promise of sanctuary that was fast becoming Highwater.

Gardan's response had been ruthlessly blunt. The guards who had helped the Reven flee, who had taken their '*tainted coin*', were dragged to the Stamping Ground and summarily hung.

That bitter warning had left its mark on a city which for many weeks had been holding its breath, and it let out its relief in a gasp of violence. As madness swept through the streets, its people, desperate for an end to their misery, went in search of any Reven still in hiding, pulling them from their homes and dragging them, man, woman and child alike, to the keep. Most were beaten badly, but in a few horrific cases they were killed, their corpses dragged through the cobbled lanes of Karick by angry, chanting mobs.

Dia retched quietly at the thought. She had witnessed one such mob as she fled away down the Valian Mile, to pass on her latest note for Savinn Kassaar at the Jade Eagle Tavern. Weaving through the gathered crowd, she was accosted by a drunken brute, who grabbed at her cloak and pulled her roughly about.

"Whatc'ya hiding away in there for?" he had leered, tearing her hood from her head. The man had hesitated a moment when he saw that she was not Reven and Dia had distracted him further with a diligent knee between his legs. Ignoring the curses behind her, she had slipped through the throng and escaped the madness.

The madness. The calming breeze turned to ice as Dia thought about Eran's words that morning, when he had finished his watch for the night and fell in to bed beside her. He was drained, both physically and emotionally and as he wept in her arms, he rambled and blurted out the news that had, ultimately, forced Dia to play her final hand.

Reports from the north gate that night disclosed that during the early hours, covered wagons full of prisoners, most of them Reven, had been shipped out under armed guard to the east. On patrol in the south of the city, Eran had only heard tell from the whisper of his comrades back at their barracks, as he finished his watch.

"Finally getting rid of the stench," one soldier had spat gleefully, his hatred forcing Eran to step away from his own rising anger. Eventually, he had found what he sought from the most unlikely of sources... Fuller.

Through his tears, Eran had recounted that the Reven, gathered up by the city's militia in recent weeks, were being sent to Durrant's Field, to help increase the speed with which the precious minerals and metals were being dug from the mines there.

To Dia this troubling news signified a telling shift in momentum and disgusted at the thought that innocent Reven were being forced into slavery to hasten the invasion on their hereditary lands, she had hurriedly sent her note. Only a few hours before, she had received word from Savinn himself, telling her that '*hope had returned*' – a reference, surely, that Cullen had returned with the renegade stonemason. He had finished his note with the plea that if she could not find a way to save the high duke, she should get away, flee to his side and forget about her other promise, as it was becoming far too dangerous now.

Dia felt her tears rise, thinking of the words she had penned herself in response to her master's letter. She had tried to get to the high duke, but he was heavily guarded and well beyond their reach. But, because of the guards, she had surmised, grasping on to anything that gave her hope, that he must still be alive.

Dia had been going to leave, had decided to let the chancellor hang himself with the rope of his own ambition, when Eran told her of the fate of the Reven citizens of the city.

Her lover was bereft of hope, his calming strength and honour draining away before her. She had to do something, this one last thing to save him from the despair he was drowning in.

Dia sniffed, brushing her tears away with the back of her trembling hand. Leaving Eran asleep in their bed, she had left him that evening, smiling sadly at him from the doorway. When she returned, she would tell him the truth, of what was happening, what she knew and whom she worked for. He would be free then, free to flee with her, free to escape the madness and start a new life someplace else.

But even as she quietly closed the door behind her, she knew he would not flee. Eran was an honourable man, much like his former captain, and he would do all he could to stop the injustices that were happening, even if it meant, ultimately, that it would lead to his own demise.

Before she realised it, Dia was up on her feet and out on the ramparts at the northern end of the high duke's keep. There were no guards abroad, save the one, standing on dutiful watch at the entrance to the Moon Tower. Dia drew in a steadying breath, calming her fears as she sought the courage that would carry her along the curtain wall.

She had been watching the chancellor's office for some time that evening, waiting for him to leave so that she could do this one last thing, this one last act. When the chancellor had finally finished his duties for the night, he had, with a solitary bodyguard in attendance, hurried through the grounds of the keep towards the north-east. Trailing them through the shadows, Dia had observed the chancellor from afar, watching as he slipped into the eastern guard tower.

From below, in the inner ward, Dia had watched Chancellor Valus hurry along the ramparts towards the

Moon Tower, his guard chasing at his heels and the pair framed by the star-filled curtain of night. Unsure of why he was visiting the high duke's tower at such an hour and her curiosity now piqued, Dia decided to investigate what was occurring in the majestic tower. When she had her answer, she would, with one telling stroke, buy Savinn the time he needed to staunch the deep wound that was slowly killing the Four Vales.

The guard stirred at Dia's approach, her shadow cast by the moonlight along the rampart behind her. Lowering her hood, Dia sent him a smile as she neared.

Above them, the Moon Tower reached up into the night sky, its dark, rounded stone walls radiant from the silvery kiss of the glorious moon behind it.

"You have no business here," the guard stated, his breath clouding in the rising chill. He was a plain man, whose face was one you wouldn't usually remember – though, knowing what she had to do, Dia knew she would never forget it. Hefting his shield higher, the guard straightened.

Dia stepped closer and just to calm him a little she dealt him her most apologetic, fulsome smile.

"I am sorry," she said humbly. "I know the chancellor is not to be disturbed, but I have urgent news about the high duke for him."

The guard frowned over his hooked nose. "Well, give it to me and I'll see he gets it, miss."

Smiling her thanks, Dia fished inside her cloak and stepped near. "Thank you, sir. He will want to hear it immediately."

Thinking she reached for a note, the guard nodded hastily, stiffening with shock as Dia drew her knife and buried it under his chin before he could react.

Dia sagged under the blade's weight, as the man moaned and fell against her. Turning him about, she grunted under the strain and lowered him to the floor.

Sending a hasty look along the deserted rampart, she dragged the dead guard inside the entrance to the tower and pulled her blade from the twitching corpse. Turning from her revulsion and the startled, accusing eyes, Dia wiped the glistening flecks of blood from her face with a sleeve and did her best to clean the thick stains from her hands. Reaching for a calming breath, she looked up into the shadows of the twisting spiral staircase.

Gathering in her disgust, Dia gripped the bloodied knife in her hand and with clarity of purpose in her eyes, she began her murderous ascent.

By the time Dia neared the top of the marble staircase, her breath was wrung from her, her chest burning from the effort and her legs heavy with fatigue. With her left hand touching the smooth stone walls to guide her up the Moon Tower and her need for secrecy forcing her to make her ascent in the dark, she was thankful, despite her rising apprehension, when the darkness began to shift subtly, grey shadows forming on the edges of her returning vision.

Her ears detected the distant echo of a man's voice, the chancellor's voice, bounding down the tower to her. It rose and fell periodically, as if in answer to an unheard question. Tussling with her need to flee and her desire to finish what she believed had to be done, Dia wrenched herself away from her uncertainty and stumbled on her way.

The air was cold, her body and clothes soaked with a chilling sweat that bit deep into her cramped, taut muscles. Too tired and weary to contemplate further on what she was about to do, of how her actions would affect the future, Dia crept stiffly up the last few steps to the grey outline of the door above her.

Unable to breathe from the efforts of her climb, not daring to reveal her presence, Dia crept close to the door, silvery grey light spilling through the half-opened doorway.

Above the warning of her racing heart she heard the chancellor speak again, his voice clear, his words attentive and laced with obedience.

"I can assure you, my lord, this set-back has done little to halt our momentum. When they are dead, which will be soon, I promise you we can proceed with our final plans. We will soon start marshalling our army for you and the taxes I have raised today will help fund that further."

The chancellor fell silent and Dia peered through the opening, eyeing the scene before her with puzzlement and then breathless awe.

The roof to the tower was open, the bright moon overhead casting its fullness down into the circular chamber. The dark floor reflected the sky overhead, its marble surface etched with constellations, glimmering like a black, silver-kissed lake. On a moon island, in the centre of the lake stood the chancellor. Dressed in long dark robes, his head was bowed and his arms raised high above his head, as he stretched them out to the night sky above him. A cool wind swept about the chamber through elegant arches and it stirred Dia from her trance.

"Yes, my lord, I understand fully and I will speak to her this very night. I will convey your gratitude for her efforts, but also your displeasure at recent events. I will reiterate the need for further caution, yet ensure that matters are in hand for your arrival."

Dia frowned, her mind racing. *Whose arrival?*

Relan Valus was nodding his head to the unheard speaker.

"The way is open, my lord," the chancellor said finally, lowering his hands to his sides. "We will await your arrival and prepare your throne for you."

Dia's blood froze at his words, her skin crawling as

the chancellor fell to his knees and the cold night air dropped to a gentle caress. Gripping her blade, Dia slipped carefully through the opening, marvelling as the constellations began to slip by under her feet.

The chancellor was breathing heavily, his chest rasping from his obvious excitement as Dia crept across the sky beneath her feet. As she neared him, the knife felt heavy in her hand and rallying herself, she raised the slim blade high.

A whisper of movement slipped through the shadows of one of the arches to her right, dragging Dia's attention away. A cloaked figure, sword in hand, rushed at her, its blade flashing before it. With a roar of anger, the attacker's blade swept down and Dia lurched back as the steel parted the air where she had been standing. As the tranquillity of the chamber broke under the weight of the chancellor's fury, Dia stepped in past the wide blade and slashed her knife through the cloaked figure's raised arm.

A deep scream echoed about the chamber as Dia turned back to the chancellor. His eyes glittered balefully in the moonlight as he stood watching the scene before him far too calmly.

Before she could reach him, another figure stepped out from under an arch away to her left and as Dia leapt back from the opponent she still fought, she could see the thin, hawkish face of the newcomer, the moon bright in his white hair.

"Kill her," Renald Gardan roared, dragging his Valian blade from the scabbard at his side.

Panicking, Dia ducked under a vicious high cut, spinning away under her attacker's armpit and leaving a deep slash in his side as she turned and ran for the doorway. Two more figures raced from the shadows behind her to join Gardan, as he strode confidently and dismissively past the chancellor and the injured man, who dropped to his knees, his sword falling from his hands to clatter on the chamber's polished marble floor.

Dia leapt through the doorway as a wave of hatred swept after her.

They had been waiting for her!

Free momentarily from the trap and her exhaustion forgotten, Dia fled down the twisting stairwell into the depths of the tower, the sounds of pursuit echoing on the stone steps above her. Down she raced, the fingers of her free hand brushing the cold stone wall as she stumbled her way down blindly. Her heart was in her mouth as she choked on the ramifications of what she had heard; and with her enemies quickly gaining Dia knew that though she had failed in one respect, if she could but survive the night, she would also triumph. Savinn would need to know that the Brotherhood were ready, that their master, whoever he was, was now ready to usurp the high duke. It made rescuing Karian Stromn and saving his family all the more important now.

Tripping, Dia dashed her hooded head against the stone as a numbing fire tore down her back and twisted through her ankle. Snarling angrily, she righted herself and plunged on down through her pain, her head giddy from the swiftness of her descent and the steep twisting curves of the stairwell.

Again the darkness began to lighten and Dia knew she was thankfully nearing the base of the Moon Tower. Leaping from the last five steps onto her good ankle and the chamber floor, she tore her eyes away from the man she had murdered and fled from the tower into the night.

With her breath caught in her throat, Dia stopped dead in her flight.

As she raced along the moonlight rampart, a hooded figure stepped out from the eastern guard tower and began walking casually towards her, two guards following close behind.

Dia felt her hopes fail and looked about, her mind racing as the figure came closer. Behind Dia now, the sounds of booted pursuit rang louder. With her dagger raised in warning, Dia watched as the cloaked figure came towards her, a pair of slender arms reaching up to lower its hood.

Dia's eyes narrowed as she regarded the sallow, yet beautiful face before her and her stomach knotted as she spied the scar on the woman's cheek, noted the tight braids of her blonde hair.

"You!" Dia hissed. She choked on her disgust as she recognised the knife that appeared in the woman's left hand and saw the moonlight slip gleefully across its crescent blade.

The woman came to a stop, several paces before her and it was then that Dia spied Wen, lurking in the shadows and his shame, on the rampart behind her.

"Put the knife down," the woman said calmly, dragging Dia's horrified attention back to her. A thin smile cut coldly across her confidence.

Gardan and his men spilled out from the tower behind her and Dia half-turned, brandishing her blade menacingly, as she crouched lower into her desperation.

"Give yourself up to us, girl," Gardan snarled, his hatred edging his words.

The woman raised her empty hand at the commander. "Stay back, Gardan," she warned him. "I'll handle this."

Dia snorted, glaring at the woman as she lowered the crescent blade slightly.

A cool wind swept across the rampart and Dia shuddered, her heart catching on its erratic rhythm. Sighing, Dia looked up at the stars in wonderment and then looked back to the woman as she edged a few more steps towards her.

Eran's beautiful face came suddenly into her mind and her fears were scattered by the joy of their love. Dia smiled and then, with a shake of her head, she gripped the parapets and pitched herself silently from the rampart into the abyss below.

Flinching, the Kestrel walked forward, ignoring the venomous look Gardan dealt her.

"Silly girl," she said with a weary sigh, staring down through the darkness at the body, broken and dashed on the cobbles far below.

CHAPTER THIRTY FOUR

Pieces of Hate

Elion Leigh sat in the shadows of the tiny room, his head bowed, clutching forlornly at the thin, skeletal fingers of his mother's hand. He did not feel the pain in the arch of his stiff back, nor did he notice the agony of his taut, cramping neck. With his head hiding low in his shame, Elion sat by his mother's bedside, furious that he had never been there for her, distraught that, as she slipped away into a deep, tormented sleep, she had not even recognised the stranger holding her hand.

He could vividly recall the first time he had noticed something different about her – the way she would catch herself in mid-sentence, searching for the words that would not come and then, later, forgetting what it was she was doing. Distracted by his training and studies, the young master of the house did not see this frustration building, as his mother, the woman who had borne him to this life, began to lose herself to the world and the people she loved around her.

Following his enlistment into the ranks of the Carwellian army, Elion spent long periods of time away from home and, with his promotion after his heroics during the horrific defence of Raven's Point, he lost himself to the duty of his rank, forgot about his duty as a son.

Elion cursed his honour, raising his head as he studied the face of his mother. Once bright and beautiful, his mother now looked well beyond her years, her dark, lustrous hair, now lank and grey. Her renowned beauty was still there, though, like her mind, lost to the world, surfacing only rarely, when clarity returned and her smile lit up the room.

It had been winter when Elion had last seen her smile.

Losing himself to the sound of her breath, rising and falling sporadically, Elion fought back his tears and cleared his mind. It had been a long night for them all. A night that had tested his father's waning patience to its limits and threatened to ruin all that Elion hoped to achieve, before he had even truly begun.

Discovering that he harboured the most wanted man in the Four Vales, was not something that Marten Leigh was evidently happy about and as his father's anger focused on his son for bringing dishonour to their family name, Elion could see the grin widen on Devlin Hawke's face. When Elion finally managed to calm his father down and the broken glass had been replaced with full glasses of a fine ruby port from the West Vales, Elion found the opportunity to recount everything that had happened during the summer, everything that he and his allies had endured and knew.

Throughout his tale, Elion's father listened with rising incredulity, his glass forgotten in his trembling hand, his wide eyes flicking between his son, stiff in the chair before the fire across from him and his companion, stood in the shadows, next to a tall bookcase, his arms folded across his chest, his head nodding in agreement when clarification was needed.

When their tale was told, Elion's father, a more chiselled, rougher version of his son, had drained his glass and re-filled it hastily with a needy, shaking hand. When he finally looked up from his thoughts, his blue eyes had filled with sorrow.

"I cannot believe what I am hearing, but I can believe what is happening."

Elion's father told them of his sadness, his disgust of hearing about Alion Byron's death. Both Devlin and Elion could see the anger in his face, as Marten told them about the horrors happening in Carwell. Since the supposed, and now, after what he had heard, fabricated attempt on Lord Carwell's life, the unfounded harassment and vilification of the city's Reven populace had become a great deal worse. As the news of the attacks on Eastbury and those further afield across the Vales surfaced, the Reven had been gathered up in earnest, whispers telling of the terrible things that were happening to them in captivity.

When news of Alion Byron's death was received, the shadows lengthened and the crow cages began to fill, bodies of these *Reven Traitors* lining the roads and filling the walls around Carwell.

Seeing the disgust and outrage on his son's face and the calm, unsurprised expression on Devlin's, Marten had shaken his head.

"I can see now why you risk all that you have, my son," he had whispered, draining his glass. "Lady Byron will need her evidence, if this madness is to be stopped. I do not know what influence I still have in the city, but I will send out messages immediately, seeking the assistance we will need."

Elion's relief had slipped deeply from his chest and Devlin had dealt him a roguish wink.

Turning his head, Marten Leigh had risen from his seat and walked forward to the outlaw, stretching his shaking hand out to him.

"Your reputation does little justice to you, sir," Marten said, forcing a smile.

Devlin Hawke had looked down at the offered hand with what could have only been described as contempt. Elion's heart had been nearly in the fire, before Devlin had looked up, smiled broadly and shook Marten Leigh's hand readily.

"It will," Devlin had grinned. "You just wait until I get started."

A gentle tapping roused Elion from his slumber, cutting through his uneasy rest quicker than any blade could have. Raising his head slowly, through his bleary eyes he could see that the first embers of the day spilled through the breaks in the thick curtains, casting faint ribbons of hope onto his sleeping mother.

She was deep into her dreams now and as Elion craned his neck, the door to the room cracked open.

"You have a visitor, sir," Oliver's whispers slipped through cautiously. Waving an accepting hand and smiling his thanks, Elion rose up stiffly.

"I will be down presently, thank you," Elion promised and when the butler was gone, he turned back to his mother, smiling sadly.

Bending low, Elion kissed his mother's forehead gently and slipped from the room with a final, thin smile.

It would prove to be the last time he saw his mother in this life.

Heading quietly away from his mother's chamber, Elion slipped through the shadows and familiarity of his childhood home. Hurrying along the upper balcony of the manor house, he stepped through a dark archway and made haste along the gallery, peering over the low, beautifully carved oak balustrade into the dining hall beneath him.

The early dawn light warmed the grand room, slipping in respectfully through the tall, arched windows to fall on the weary looking figures, sat at the head of the table, sharing hushed words.

Sensing they were being watched, they looked up into the shadows and Elion announced his arrival with a curt wave of his hand at his father and the man who was still wrapped in his travelling cloak.

Feeling his heart race, Elion hurried to the end of the gallery and raced down the narrow staircase to join them.

The portly guest rose up as Elion stepped into the grand hall, smiling grimly as they met with thankful handshakes.

"Lucas," Elion greeted, his relief evident as he clapped the man firmly on his right shoulder. "Thank you for coming so swiftly, I had not thought to see you so soon."

Lucas Rhee's brow furrowed and his handshake tightened. "Circumstances dictated otherwise, captain."

Marten Leigh cleared his throat, drawing their concerns to him momentarily.

"I shall retire for a time," he said, nodding his head slightly. "You have much to discuss and I will ensure you are not disturbed."

Without waiting for a response, Elion's father strode from the room, closing the large, double oak doors behind him as he left. Both men watched the door for a few moments longer, listening as Marten's retreat faded away over the wooden floorboards, before they turned back to each other.

Releasing his hand, Elion motioned for Lucas to retake his seat and then joined him, sinking wearily into the high-backed chair at the head of the table.

"I received your message, captain, and came as soon as I could," Lucas began, shaking his head. "In truth, I was glad to escape the chaos."

Elion nodded. "My father tells me things are out of hand, that the city is on the edge of something terrible."

Lucas puffed out his cheeks and ran a broad hand over his tight temples. "You have seen the crow cages, I take it, and heard the worst from your father?"

"I have," Elion replied sadly. "Had I not seen it for myself, I would have never believed it."

Lucas looked up, his eyes shining with his fear. "The streets, captain. They writhe with hatred, they run with blood. I do not understand how it has come to this."

Elion reached out and gripped his hand. "I am beginning to, my friend, and I need to know anything you can tell me, anything you think might help me?"

Lucas pulled his hand away and sank back in his chair to regard Elion warily. "I will tell you all that has happened since I saw you on the road from Havensdale – but you must tell me your tale, also, captain."

"Agreed," Elion said flatly. He threaded his hands together and rested his elbows on the table.

Drawing a deep breath into his large frame, Lucas ran a hand through his hair and nodded.

"I made swift time back to Eastbury and joined up with Reyn Cross, as you advised. With our prisoners under guard, we made for Carwell and reached the city safely, without any attack."

"Did you see any evidence of a possible ambush?" Elion asked, wringing his hands nervously.

"None," Lucas answered, holding Elion's eyes for a time, before looking away. "The authorities relieved us of our prisoners, giving each of us a sizeable reward and leave for two weeks. No questions were asked, no news of where you were even sought, captain. Before the day was out, the raiders were hung and quartered in Raven Square, as a warning for any who would wreak havoc upon the innocent."

Elion frowned. "They were executed without a trial?

Without hearing the evidence of the townsfolk who survived, or from those who saved them?"

Lucas shook his head. "It seems Lord Carwell has dispensed with lengthy hearings these days, captain. The law, if it is sought at all, is swift and without compunction."

Elion shook his head, running a thoughtful hand through his beard. "This is deeply troubling. Without the rule of law to govern us, we are nothing more than the savages that purportedly threaten us."

Both men fell silent, before Elion tore himself from his dark thoughts. "Have you heard tell of my companion, Clarissa? She was the one who bore news of the attack on Eastbury? I would have expected her to return to me with the reinforcements?"

Lucas ran a nervous tongue over his lips. "I enquired of her, but she has not been seen by her family or comrades for several weeks now, I am afraid."

Elion pounded the table angrily. "Damn this!" he snarled. Rising up into his anger, he paced away for a time to be alone with his grief.

"I have to say, captain, that though I never truly doubted your belief in the course you were pursuing, I am now fully convinced you are right," Lucas said carefully, rising up slowly. "The march for war has begun, taxes have been raised, without the consent of the capital and the call to arms has gone out – a rallying call for '*True Valian Heroes*' to come forth to defend their lands and strike a blow to the heart of the enemy."

Elion turned, his eyes aghast with disbelief. "They are calling for conscripts?"

"Yes. Carwell's forces are already on standby. The orders were received two days ago. The call for recruits has also been raised, sent far and wide across the East Vales... there are hundreds of willing men coming in from the towns and villages daily, many of whom are not even asking how much they will be paid."

Elion's sigh was long and full of despair. "Then it has begun? The long march to war?"

"I am afraid, captain, that it seems it has," Lucas replied sadly.

Elion motioned for his guest to have a seat and began to recount all that had happened since he reached Havensdale. As his words found their mark, Lucas recoiled, shaking his head and questioning the disbelief flashing in his own eyes. When Elion finished, with tell of the events happening in the capital, Lucas began to weep, the revelations of Gardan's actions too much to cope with.

"I am sorry, sir," Lucas said finally, wiping his eyes as he found some composure. "I don't know what to say. I don't know what I can do to help."

Elion leant on the table and looked down at Lucas with sympathy in his eyes. "Neither do I, Lucas, neither do I."

Both men sat for a long while, watching as the rising dawn slowly filled the shadows of the dining hall. By the time Lucas and Elion parted ways, it had been decided that, not to endanger Lucas any further than he already had been, he should only supply information to Elion's father, who would then pass it on to his son and allies.

"I wish you well, captain," Lucas said, gripping Elion's hand tightly. "I fear I shall not be allowed to resign my commission and that I will not be able to avoid the coming war. If that time comes, when all hope seems lost, I shall slip away and seek you in Havensdale."

"And you will be most welcome, Lucas," Elion smiled, embracing the Carwellian rider. "Go now, send word to Reyn for me and tell him all I have told you. He also has his family and honour to protect and I would have you warn him, before the Four Vales descends into civil war."

"Let us hope that it does not come to that, captain," Lucas said softly. "I wish you well with your hunt."

Elion nodded, watching, as Lucas swept from the hall on unsteady legs. Groaning, Elion fell into his father's chair, listening to his heartbeat and Lucas's fading retreat.

"I think it's time to start that hunt," Devlin Hawke said, jolting Elion from his thoughts, as he stepped from the shadows and leant idly over the balcony above him.

Elion glared up at the outlaw. "How long have you been listening?"

"Long enough," Devlin said, curling his lip derisively. "You have your answers Elion Leigh and it is now time for you to stop searching for excuses and actually do something about it."

Elion bristled, rising up from his seat. "And what does that mean?"

Devlin swatted aside the question and slipped from view. When he stalked into the hall moments later, his eyes were bright with malice and Elion swallowed as the outlaw strode up to him.

"It's time to act, Elion Leigh," Devlin said, stabbing an accusing finger at him. "You can achieve nothing in Carwell, other than your death. Things are too far out of control here and it is elsewhere we shall have an impact."

"I disagree, it is not too late," Elion retorted, his words echoing about the room petulantly. "We have allies here, they will stand with us."

Devlin laughed and his words that followed were dripping with scorn. "Wake up boy! This is not some heroic tale of honour and glory. There is just you and I. We came here for information and now we have it. Henry Carwell marches to war and there is nothing here that you and I can do to stop it. With the high duke about as useful as a low piss in a high wind, there will be no political answer to our problem, we will have to seek another solution."

Elion swallowed his anger, eyeing the outlaw suspiciously. "I don't like the sound of this."

"There's no point being squeamish when dealing with rats," Devlin quoted, smiling. "You asked me to help you, you said you wanted me and my men to be a thorn in Carwell's side – well that's what we will have to do. We shall hit his preparations, harassing and harrying his tax collectors, his supply lines and forces wherever possible. We shall buy you some time, whilst your allies prepare their armies to stand against the storm."

Elion's face was pale and he slapped his sides in frustration.

"There must be another way, there has to be! We must abide by the rule of law, or everything that has been achieved, the peace that is the foundation of the Four Vales will be broken."

Devlin folded his arms across his chest. "Then let's break it. You speak of this mythical peace, Elion Leigh, but clearly there are those that will so easily risk it for their own bitter gain. Nothing has changed. It's not in our nature."

Elion scowled. "But the law that I adhere to is a shield, not a sword for dealing out wanton justice."

Devlin chuckled, shaking his head. "That is a noble statement my young, dutiful friend, but sadly a misguided one. How long do you think you can hide behind that shield of yours, when your enemies are all about you and those you love most are being slaughtered before your eyes? There will come a time, very soon, when I fear you will have to strike out from behind your shield, lest all you stand for be lost. Your enemies will break your shield, mark my words. They covet the law when it serves their purpose and cast it aside to suit their needs when it is a burden to them."

Elion looked away, his cheeks burning. When he turned back, his eyes were wet with tears. "Then what must we do?"

Devlin Hawke grinned enigmatically. "We have allies spying for us here, we have strength and determination in Highwater and we have friends in Havensdale. It may not be enough to match the might of Karick and Carwell, but it is a start."

Elion nodded, his mind swamped, his hands shaking.

"But will it be enough?" he dared to ask.

Devlin Hawke smiled and when he spoke, his words were full of ominous relish. "Sometimes the best way to win a fight, my young friend, is to start one and see what happens. I guess we are about to find out."

Scarlet Moore was the first guard to spot the small group of approaching riders, as she limped along the defences of the south gate of Havensdale and held on to the thought that her watch would soon be over and she could fall into her bed for a well-deserved rest.

The mist was clearing now, as the sun appeared on the cold horizon to the east and chased away the memories of a quiet, bitter night, shared around a waning brazier with strangers and friends alike.

Scarlet suppressed a deep yawn and fought against the weight of her heavy eyelids. Since the arrival of the reinforcements from Highwater, Havensdale had turned into an armed camp. People quietly went about their daily business, too scared to stand idle, too worried that the future would catch up with them if they did.

The earthwork defences were now complete and Scarlet had been back in her militia uniform for nearly twenty days. With the losses they had suffered, Havensdale was in need of bodies and Scarlet, during her darker moments, wondered if she had only been asked to rejoin the militia ranks from desperation, rather than any real need for her services.

A stiff breeze picked up her senses and ruffled unruly strands of her pinned locks. Brushing them from her eyes, she sent a look along the wall to her right, to see if anyone else had noticed the riders in the distance, aware only of some of the darting looks that slipped her way when she wasn't looking. Sighing, Scarlet looked away again, feeling her embarrassment chase away the cold. If she had wanted the attention, she had it now, as there were plenty more men in the town to end any perceived rivalry she may have once had with Jessica.

Smiling inwardly, Scarlet looked to her left, seeing the lonely pair of soldiers, stood talking in hushed tones, breaking the monotony of the dawn occasionally with guarded laughter. Scarlet shivered and gripped the palisade. Kallum Campbell's life, since the raid, had been torn to pieces. Caught between his duty to his family and the defence of his home, he was unable to truly mourn the loss of his father and, because of the company he was keeping, had been unable to find the forgiveness of his sister, Sara.

Liyam Tallis was, in the eyes of many in Havensdale, a spy and murderer. Spared by Kallum in the battle, the young rider from Carwell, shamed at the deception of his commander, had stayed in the town to face its inhabitants' wrath, rather than return to suffer the shame of his actions from his family in Carwell. Whilst he had not even drawn blood on his blade that terrible morning, he was still seen by many as the enemy and, despite his newfound friend's attempts, had been ostracised for his part in the attack.

Scarlet sighed. Sara Campbell was inconsolable and her kind, gentle nature had been destroyed. On the very few occasions they had shared a watch, the once affable girl kept to herself, speaking only when the threat of further attacks was mentioned and voicing her desire to '*have her revenge*' as she put it.

Scarlet shook her head sadly. Havensdale would never be the same again. Raising her eyes, she stole a look at Kallum and Liyam, feeling her pulse quicken at the sight of the handsome rider from Carwell.

Snorting softly, Scarlet stared through the lifting mist along the road, stretching solemnly away towards the riders, approaching slowly from the south.

Life was complicated enough these days.

With the alert raised, the sentries concern at the riders slow approach diminished, as they came within a mile of Havensdale. Two riders, Scarlet could see, were flanking a covered cart, driven by one other individual.

"Traders, perhaps?" Kallum offered, leaning on the palisade and flicking a look at the comely girl beside him.

Scarlet shrugged, desperate for her bed, but knowing that she would have to wait another hour, at the very least now. "I hope so," she whispered, hugging herself.

Kallum dealt Liyam a look, only to find him transfixed by their beautiful companion. Shaking his head, he discreetly elbowed his friend in the ribs and suppressed a chuckle when Scarlet dealt them a look and Liyam distracted his embarrassment with a lame excuse about cramp in one leg.

By the time the small fellowship reached the town, Fawn Ardent had joined her sentries on the south gate. Dressed in a long, dark blue cloak and clad in dull ring mail, the captain of Havensdale watched thoughtfully as she regarded the travellers before her.

The lead rider, a short squat man with a flame-red beard and complexion to match, slipped stiffly from his saddle and led his mount forward slowly, until he reached the wooden stakes blocking his path.

"Fair morning," he called up, raising a fat hand in greeting. His voice rolled across the silence of the early morning.

Fawn ignored the looks that came her way and raised her hand. "It may well be, if the clouds lift," she replied affably, looking up at the low clouds gathering above them. "May I ask what brings you to our town?"

The man nodded, shuffling from one foot to the other. He dealt the large, hooded rider behind him a brief look, before turning back again.

"That you may, lady," the man said. Tethering his mount to one of the stakes, he picked his way through the defences and clambered up on top of the earthworks, uncaring of the crossbows now trained upon him.

Gathering his breath, the man shielded his rough, ugly face with a hairy hand, as he searched the faces on the wall.

"We are looking for Captain Ardent," the man announced, drawing his attention back to the woman he had been speaking to.

Fawn dealt Scarlet a look. "Fetch Sergeant Manse," she muttered out of the corner of her mouth. As the girl limped hurriedly away, Fawn gripped the palisade with both hands.

"Then you have found her, sir," Fawn announced, smiling faintly. "What can I do for you? I believe that we have not met?"

Cullen nodded, wiping a hand across his mouth to hide the relish in his smile.

"It's not what you can do for me, though it's a lovely offer. It's what we can do for you."

Fawn frowned, watching as the man motioned back to the young woman who drove the wagon. Standing up, she turned gracefully, pulling the cover from the cart to reveal the wounded man, wrapped in bandages and blankets beneath.

As a mutter rippled along the defenders, the other rider pulled the hood from his head, revealing the dark skin of his Redani heritage.

Even in Havensdale, they had heard tell of the reward being offered for a Redani fugitive. Fawn blinked away her confusion, her mind starting to race.

"Who are you people?" she asked.

The Redani spoke, his deep voice drawing the defenders attention to him. "My name is Khadazin Sahr, lady. I am a fugitive, I am a stonemason and I am the man who can help you have your vengeance."

CHAPTER THIRTY FIVE

Know Thy Enemy

It took the woodsman only an hour to hear tell of the newcomers' arrival to Havensdale. He heard it from Rellin Steelblade, when the young recruit found him in the Moonglade Forest, checking the traps he had set the previous night. Rellin had heard the news from the school mistress, Kitty Sharn, who had in turn heard whisper of their arrival from Tess Varun. Tess had heard it from the baker, Letty Karsis, who had witnessed the strangers heading across the market place, now acting as makeshift barracks for the reinforcements from Highwater. A wounded man was being helped towards the church by Fawn Ardent. A strange trio of newcomers trailed behind them as they spoke, with several militia soldiers in close attendance. Not that she wanted to gossip, of course, the notorious rumour mongerer had told Tess, as she nearly snapped her neck trying to see what was happening from the porch of her shop.

Nodding to the guards on duty, though he did not know their names, the woodsman strode under the south gate and made for the militia headquarters. By now, the town was alive with speculation, those with time to spare huddling together in small clusters, whispering their suppositions and sharing their concerns as the rest of the town slipped by about their business around them.

Knocking on the door of the small, stone building, the woodsman silenced the voices within, before hearing footsteps creak across the dusty floorboards he knew waited within.

Dekan Ardent hauled the door open, a worried look on his haggard face, a cup of the *Burning Leaf* balanced in the palm of his left hand.

"A little early for that, isn't it?" the woodsman chided.

"Come in," Dekan replied, ignoring him. "I'll pour you one as well."

Dekan turned and headed away, leaving the woodsman to slip through the door before it closed on its own accord.

Blinking, the woodsman adjusted his eyes to the familiarity of the small room, its table cluttered with piles of unattended dispatches and letters. Several candles lit the room, one almost falling off the bookcase away to his right. The tiny cell to his left was empty for once, suggesting that people were too busy these days to get into trouble.

Sweeping his gaze through the dimness, his eyes were drawn to Fawn Ardent, sat in her chair, regarding him with a smile that imparted she was more than just happy to see him. Her face was weary, marked by countless nights devoid of any lasting sleep and her usually loose auburn hair was tied back, the ringlets gathered up high on the back of her head.

"Woodsman, I was about to send for you," she greeted warmly as her father shuffled behind her, searching for an empty cup amongst the chaos. She rose up stiffly and gestured to the man sat across from her. "May I introduce you to Khadazin Sahr?"

The Redani rose hurriedly, his large frame casting a broad shadow across the room. Turning, the man stuffed out a huge right hand and as the woodsman gripped it politely, he noted that the Redani's left one was missing.

"A pleasure," the giant said, looking subconsciously down at his empty wrist. He glanced up again and flashed a bright smile across his black, battered features. "Something I lost along the way..."

"Well met," the woodsman replied. Flexing some feeling back into his hand he dealt Fawn a curious look. "I have heard the name, though the poster does you little justice."

The Redani's chuckle was more a rueful snort and he nodded his head as Dekan Ardent wandered back and forced a cup of brandy into the woodsman's shaking hand. Licking his lips, Evan settled his nerves and downed the liquid inside, ignoring the eyebrows raised his way.

"Time, it seems once more, is against us, woodsman, so I shall quickly bring you abreast of matters." She waited for the Redani to take his seat again and watched worriedly as her father leant against the bookcase, heard it protest and moved to lean against the wall, instead. Finding a place on some papers for his empty cup, the woodsman folded his arms across his chest and signalled his readiness.

Looking to the Redani for his acquiescence, Fawn sat back in her chair and rested her hands on the table before her.

"As we have heard recently, our friend here has a sizeable bounty on his head, one that, as Khadazin will no doubt explain, has nothing to do with his involvement in this supposed Reven uprising."

The woodsman threw a look the Redani's way, but his dark eyes were firmly fixed on the captain across from him.

"Normally, Khadazin's tale, the detail of which I

would ask him to save for the moment, would be reason enough to raise our concern, but matters in the capital have taken a sinister turn and we have a pressing road before us now." Fawn paused, wetting her lips. "Khadazin?"

Drawing in his breath, the Redani turned his attention to the woodsman, whose heart was beginning to canter.

"My story is a dark one, one that saw my torture at the hands of those who would send the Valian people to war. The political turmoil in Karick is worse than anyone could have imagined and my... our enemies have a firm grip on the throat of the capital and its people."

The woodsman's impatience began to stir. "This is all very good, but if time is as pressing..."

"Patience, my friend," Dekan Ardent cut in, drawing a slow, apologetic nod from the woodsman. He held up a hand and the Redani continued.

"The high duke has lost his grip on power and he is no longer in charge. His chancellor and Havensdale's sworn enemy now rule the city. Reven people are being rounded up, some have been killed and the streets that were once my home are now full of fear and violence. In the keep, the situation is just as bad and any who still seek peace have been pushed aside, or worse..."

The woodsman's mind was racing, trying to keep up with his heart, which was now galloping away from him. "Gardan made it to Karick, then?" he scowled and the Redani nodded. "Bastard!"

"It is worse than I can say," Khadazin whispered, clenching his fist. "I will be honest with you, woodsman. I have friends in the city, friends who have helped not just me, but an acquaintance of ours, also."

The woodsman cocked an eyebrow in Fawn's direction and he just caught the smile, slipping from her face. He looked back to the Redani, who was also smiling.

"It seems we are connected, the three of us."

Khadazin went on to briefly explain how he had innocently overheard the fateful secret meeting all those days ago, how he had sensed his life was in danger, of his precautions that had allowed others to watch for news of Cassana Byron's fate. Unable to act in time to prevent the attack on her journey to the capital, Khadazin explained (without naming names) how the woodsman's noble actions and Fawn Ardent's kindness, had inadvertently set in motion a series of events that had finally led to Khadazin's friends rescuing Lady Byron and seeing her, almost, safely home.

It was here that the woodsman intervened, marvelling at what he was hearing, gripping the Redani's shoulder.

"Who are our enemies, Khadazin?" he dared to ask.

The stonemason sent a look around the room whilst he regained his composure. When he finally spoke, his words went deeper than any blade their enemies could have buried.

"I knew who the enemy was, or at least one of them. There is, I am told, a *Brotherhood* that has been working secretly for many years, positioning themselves for a moment when they could orchestrate a move towards war. Lady Byron's abduction was the first move in a lengthy game, a game that we have all become involved in. Through our actions, we have all been marked as enemies and, from what I have heard, Captain Ardent, both you and I have suffered for it."

Fawn bowed her head and nodded, drumming her fingers nervously on one of her knees.

"Havensdale has suffered for it..."

Dekan Ardent moved to his daughter's side and comforted her as the Redani turned his grim face towards the woodsman again.

"I was captured and tortured by the Brotherhood, but did not reveal whom I told about the conversation I overheard, or who the speakers were. They kept me alive because of this, I suspect, long enough for me to escape. Fleeing south to the Hermitage Retreat, I found sanctuary there and when I was able enough, I sent word to my friend, the person who had rescued Lady Byron, who knew only of the meeting, not the identity, that I was ready to return, to testify against our enemies. It seems that the Brotherhood are as cautious as they are clever and all of these moves, all that has transpired, has been to stop both I and Lady Byron speaking out against them."

"Who is this enemy you refer to?" the woodsman demanded, though there was only reluctance, not anger, in his question.

"The man I overheard plotting, the man who I suspect is slowly poisoning the high duke, as he had Madam Grey drug Lady Byron, is none other than the very person who penned the Reven Lists and was the ear of the high duke. It is the chancellor, Relan Valus."

As she was looking to her sorrow, hiding her shame away from them, Fawn did not see the reaction on the woodsman's face, the look of abject horror, disgust and anger that stained his rugged features. Khadazin did, as did he see the look that Dekan Ardent dealt him. Sensing it a matter that was none of his concern, the stonemason thought it better not to react.

Reaching for a thought, whilst trying to find a breath, the woodsman ran a hand through his hair and let out a whistling breath. His legs felt weak and his whole body began to tremble. For a long time now, the woodsman had locked his past away, closing it firmly behind a door, happy to hide all of his feelings, his emotions and memories away there. With every day that passed, everything that happened, the door opened wider. As the Redani's words faded away, the door opened wide in his mind with an ominous, slow creak.

"That man has always had ambition, the kind that leaves its mark," the woodsman was not sure if his words carried into the room, but he saw the mayor nod.

Fawn looked up and saw the shadows settling on the woodsman's face. She, too, had been lost to the past, her mind reeling and her skin crawling with disgust, as she thought back to her time with Cassana, of how she had shared a tearful farewell with her in Edward Neve's office, inadvertently handing her over to her enemies.

"Khadazin brings us hope, however," she said, clearing her doubts, as she stood up, "stonemason?"

The Redani smiled. "We have a chance, woodsman, to stop this before it is too late. My friend, who remains in the city and will contact us, should he have news, rescued a man only three days ago, from the Old Royal Dungeons in the capital. This man was Lucien Varl, the former captain of Karick. He was being held by the chancellor and tortured by a woman for the location of where the high duke's family were being kept. Which, I am afraid to say, he unfortunately gave them."

The woodsman's eyes widened. "This man you speak of? He still lives?"

Khadazin nodded. "He does. Lucien's testimony could bring down our enemy, before it can raise its head to strike. With help, I have brought him here, so that we can plan our retaliation, can thwart the chancellor and destroy this Brotherhood before they can react."

The woodsman's mind reeled and he took an involuntary step backwards. When he gathered his wits enough to speak, he shook his head worriedly.

"If the Brotherhood wants the high duke's family, they must seek to kill them. It can be the only reason why the high duke is not dead... we must rescue them before it is too late."

Fawn smiled grimly. "And that is exactly why I was looking for you, woodsman."

With his legs heavy with anticipation, the woodsman

made for the church moments later, leaving the mayor to discuss matters further with his daughter and the Redani. The stonemason's words had torn open old wounds, though honeyed the pain with fresh hope. *If they could get to the high duke's family before...*

Evan shook his head. There was too much to think about, so many things left unsaid, far too much anger and hatred swirling unattended in his head, a head which was already beginning to throb painfully. Clearing his thoughts as best he could, the woodsman approached the church, calmly framed by a clearing blue sky.

Several guards were on duty outside the small, plain stone church and they admitted him without any protest. Once his eyes had adjusted to the dimness of the chapel inside, the woodsman made his way down the vaulted aisle, his boots echoing reverently on the stone. As he neared the altar, dedicated to the Lady of the Vales, he spied the two newcomers, stood outside the door to the infirmary away to his left, talking to Sergeant Manse.

Wrapping his cloak about his body, the woodsman approached, feeling his senses prick as their eyes flicked towards him.

"Well met," Larne Manse said, striding forward to grip his offered hand. Their eyes met briefly and the woodsman saw tell of something unsettling in the sergeant's eyes.

"And who have we here?" the woodsman said, turning his thoughts to the newcomers. A young beauty watched him curiously, her dusky face framed and cloaked by shadows, her eyes flickering brightly in the writhing candlelight.

Larne Manse stepped aside, sweeping an arm to the girl. "Companions of the man within," the sergeant offered lamely, suggesting that he, too, was still unsure of what was transpiring.

The woodsman offered a smile, turning his attention

to the rough looking brute, stood far too close for comfort next to the girl. As their eyes met, the woodsman's chest tightened, as familiarity flashed across the one-eyed man's face.

"Do I know you?" the man asked bluntly, though his tone suggested that he already knew the answer.

Short of breath, the woodsman fought for his words, feeling his throat constrict and his heart begin to flare again.

"I think not, sir," he managed eventually, as he searched his memory for a recollection. The man had a face that you would want to forget, even though you knew that you wouldn't.

Thankfully, Sergeant Manse cut through the rising tension. "This is the woodsman who helped save the town during the attack."

The one-eyed man was clearly not surprised or impressed, though the young woman regarded the mysterious newcomer more appraisingly.

"Woodsman is it?" the brutish man remarked, trying not to hide the mockery in his voice. He offered the woodsman a fat hand on the end of a garishly tattooed arm, which was eventually, briefly taken.

"And you are?" the woodsman asked politely.

"The name's Cullen, the girl's Tania. If you want more answers *woodsman*, you had best seek them inside."

The man's eye sparkled with something and nodding his thanks, the woodsman made his apologies to the sergeant and hurried through the heavy oak door.

Once he was inside, he closed the door behind him, resting his fears against the cold wood, trying to calm his raging heart. Shaking his head, he tried hard to resist, but a distant memory flashed in the woodsman's mind, stirring up the embers of his past again. As his rising anger burnt away his fears, Evan knew that his time in exile would soon be over. With each passing day, each revelation, he was being drawn deeper into the rising storm, unable to escape, powerless to stop it. He felt like he was drowning, being pulled to his death, as the cold weight of his past, the burden of his heavy sorrow finally claimed him – just reward, it seemed, for his shame and cowardice.

Cursing bitterly, the woodsman went in search of the priest, leaving behind the cold realisation that the man, Cullen, had been painfully right.

Though the passing years may have clouded his certainty, the woodsman did indeed know him, after all. He should have remembered him, though time had not been kind to the brute, as Cullen had been one of the men who had saved his life, all those years ago...

"By the Lady's grace, he sleeps now" the priest Lenton Bartram whispered, as the woodsman stepped into the tiny cell. The tall candle on the table beside the bed flickered in a draft, outlining the worry on his drawn face, as he rose from his watchful vigilance and gestured to the man, wrapped up in sheets and asleep on the cot between them.

The woodsman nodded, offering the old priest a smile as the man moved to his side. He was clad in ill-fitting grey robes that hung from sharp shoulder and fell unhindered to his sandalled feet. Greying hair retreated over the crown of his freckled head and his face, drawn tight from the grief of recent days, was pale and sunken.

"I shall leave you for a moment," the old priest said, patting the woodsman on one shoulder as he left.

Evan watched him go, listened to the faint rasp of his sandals, as he slipped away into the shadows. Drawing in a deep breath, the woodsman turned his attention to the sleeping man and sucked in his horror at what he saw.

It was difficult to see where the man was beneath the many horrors he carried, thickly crusted now with dried blood. Sitting on the warm stool beside the bed, the woodsman reached out tentatively to grasp one of Lucien Varl's bandaged hands.

"The years have not been kind, my friend," he said sadly. Bowing his head, the woodsman wept.

Relan Valus sat in the high duke's gardens, surrounded by the shade of a fierce summer's day and wrapped deep in his thoughts. Despite his weariness and the tightness stretching across his temples, he was at peace. Glad to be free of it all for a time, the chancellor closed his eyes and listened to the silence of the afternoon. The only sound was from the gentle breeze rustling through the leaves of the rowan tree above him and, before he realised it, the chancellor was drifting off into a fitful sleep.

Some time later, he was awoken by the kiss of cold steel, pressed gently to his throat. With a screech, he lurched back on the stone bench, his eyes wide with panic.

"Careful now," the Kestrel chided him, her voice mocking, yet light with amusement.

Relan Valus lowered his voice to a dangerous whisper. "Have a care, Kestrel, I do not make light of such mockery."

Slipping her crescent blade away, the Kestrel shrugged and fell onto the bench beside him. He scowled at her for a moment more, before looking away to track a bee across the flowerbeds.

"Have they left?" thc Kestrel asked, finally.

"They have," Relan replied. "They should be there by tomorrow's eve."

The Kestrel's response was a delighted murmur and crossing her bared legs, she folded her hands in her lap.

"You still should have sent me," she said, not trying to hide her disappointment.

Relan turned his thoughts to her, stealing a look at her

slender legs, as she stared up at the tree above them and frowned.

"Gardan wanted his man to lead them," he said, losing himself in the shadows underneath her short, leather skirt. "He... *I* thought it best you keep to the shadows for a time."

Looking back at the scarecrow beside her, the Kestrel nodded, her eyes brilliantly blue.

"And what of the girl?" she asked delicately, seeing the anger and embarrassment flash across his face. "Do we know anything more about her?"

The chancellor looked away, shaking his head free of his disappointment.

"She had no family, no friends of any interest..."

"What of the lover?" the Kestrel purred. "I could have a word with him?"

Relan Valus cocked an eyebrow towards her, smiled faintly and shook his balding head. "I think it best we just watch him. If he is innocent and not involved, as I suspect, then we would do well not to draw any further attention to the matter. Whatever the girl heard, it died with her on the cobbles."

"I dealt with the body," the Kestrel answered, reading the question in his face before he uttered it. She sighed and picked at the stitching of her leather skirt.

Relan Valus looked away, trying his best to unravel the knot of worry in his stomach. It was impossible to ascertain how much Dia was involved and for whom she was spying for. He had spent many hours deliberating over it, trying to find the thread that tied all the things that had transpired to thwart them over recent weeks together. It was clear that there were those who sought to stand against the Brotherhood, but, as of yet, they remained in the shadows, waiting to play their hand, should they have any cards left.

The chancellor scoffed, that irony not lost on him.

"What is it?" the Kestrel asked, seeing the look on his face.

Drumming his hands on one knee, he turned to her, flicking his eyes about her pale face.

"The girl, Dia – she was working for someone, someone we should be wary of. But I cannot see it; I do not know where to start."

Chewing her lip, the Kestrel hesitated, before reaching out a hand to him. She touched his hand and held it briefly for a time.

"I have been thinking about that, it's why I came to find you during the day."

Encouraged by the relief on his face, she withdrew her hand and continued.

"The Byron girl escaped, clearly, and with help she made it home, despite our best efforts. Dia, the spy, she was the one, was she not, attending to Lady Byron, once Madam Grey went missing?"

The chancellor nodded his head, thought for a moment, before shrugging. "She carried out her tasks without raising suspicion, continuing to unwittingly take her the drugged water."

A sarcastic smile danced across the Kestrel's beautiful features as she relished the flavour of her own words. "Like a good spy, she remained invisible, even whilst she had gained your trust."

The chancellor blinked away his rising anger before he could respond. For a long while he sat, staring into the past, wracking his mind for that which he was missing. After a time, he drew in a breath, his eyes widening. He turned back to the Kestrel, hasty excitement chasing his words.

"All this time, we have been unable to find out who helped the Byron girl home, though now, I suspect that it was Dia who actually helped her escape from the keep. She may have been the one to free Lucien Varl, also. She certainly had enough freedom to come and go as she pleased..."

It was the perfect moment to point out his failings to him, but the Kestrel's thoughts were elsewhere. It was true, knowing now that the girl was a spy, that Dia most likely rescued Lucien Varl. The men murdered during his escape were killed by clumsy, reluctant strokes, whereas the guard, killed outside Lady Byron's quarters during her escape, was felled by a clean and efficient cut to the throat...

"I believe she may have freed Varl, but I doubt her skill beyond that."

"That does not help," the chancellor snapped, glaring at her. "I am trying to piece together who the stonemason told. With everything that has happened to thwart our efforts, I am certain now that he must have told someone... but whom?"

Running a hand through her tight braids, the Kestrel nodded. "But, if what you have told me is correct, the Redani was not well liked, he had few friends, if any, besides the man he saved, Savinn Kassaar."

They both looked at each other, sharing widening looks as they grasped onto the answer, dangling before them.

"It couldn't be, could it?" the chancellor rasped. He rose up, pacing away, his hands clasped behind his back. After a time, he spun on his sandals and wagged a finger at the Kestrel.

"Humour me a moment, Kestrel. The Redani saves Savinn Kassaar's life and from that moment on, Kassaar believes he owes the stonemason his life. Could it be that the very man we have marked as our enemy actually *is* our enemy?"

The Kestrel's frown suggested otherwise. "Savinn Kassaar's disappearance might only be a coincidence. He is a wealthy, ambitious man, I accept that. He is a man who, until recently, had a great deal of influence in this city... but do you honestly think he has the desire and power to stand against the Brotherhood?"

Relan Valus was too wrapped up in his excitement to hear what she said. His weary face was full of vigour, his movements, as he paced about again, swift and light.

"Kassaar is half-Reven, wealthy and a man who aligned himself to the high duke. He was friends with the stonemason and even got the man his fateful job in these... very... gardens..."

The Kestrel drew in a breath. "Keep talking, you may have something."

"The stonemason overhears the plot to take Lady Byron, though she is not named. For many days he lost himself in his turmoil, drinking heavily each day. Even after being tortured, he resisted confessing, but, as I have said, he must have told someone. Who better, than the man who had become his guardian, who owed him a life debt and actually had the power and perhaps the political desire to rescue Lady Byron?"

"Kassaar has become rich and fat from the high duke's support, he would not want the high duke to be ousted, nor the daughter of his strongest ally taken and held as a pawn against them."

The Kestrel could not contain her own elation and she rose up. "If Kassaar is the one behind this, the girl was working for him. But with Kassaar in hiding, perhaps not even in the city, we have little else of substance."

When Relan Valus turned, all the stress and strain that had been weighing heavily upon him in recent weeks had been lifted.

"Our brother and sister in Highwater report that Lady Byron has never spoken to them about who helped her home to safety. If Kassaar was the one to instigate such a move against us, he would have been wise to swear her to secrecy. We have a chance, Kestrel, a slim one, but an opportunity we should certainly take."

The Kestrel was nodding. "But how?"

Relan Valus smiled. "I shall send a letter to Highwater this very day and have our brother there deliver it into her hands. It will come from Savinn Kassaar, saying that the situation in Karick is desperate, how he has information for her that could end all the madness and gain revenge for her father's murder. Too dangerous for her and him in Karick, he will want to meet her somewhere safe and in person."

"The Byron girl has proven that she is no fool," the Kestrel scoffed. "She will not fall for that."

"It is a move that does not expose our hand. If she does not fall for our bluff, then so be it, we will be none the better for it." Relan Valus sighed, spreading his hands wide. "But if she takes our bait we will finally, finally have her and our armies can slip into Highwater without having to raise arms."

The Kestrel scowled, looking up pointedly at the rowan tree that shaded them.

"Then send the damned letter, Valus," she snarled. "Our lord will be here in a few days time and the berries are already beginning to turn. Autumn will soon be here."

Relan Valus smiled. "Arrange some hunters for me, my lady. Have them wait in the mountains for her. If Cassana Byron has never met Savinn Kassaar, she will stay inside her keep. But if she has and we are right, then..."

The Kestrel licked her lips. "Then finally that little bitch will be dead and our mistakes will wash away down the mountainside along with her blood."

CHAPTER THIRTY SIX

An Eye for an Eye

"Are you sure you want to do this?"

Khadazin turned his head slightly towards Tania, seeing the worried look on her face. Nodding his head, the Redani offered her a smile that briefly eased the tension gathering about them.

Looking back towards the militia headquarters and the heated debate taking place outside between Fawn Ardent and her father, Khadazin shifted nervously on aching feet and drew in a long, slow breath.

"I know Savinn, were he here," Khadazin began in a low whisper, "would counsel me to remain behind, to stay safe. But what better way is there to prove to the high duke of my innocence, than by rescuing his family?"

Tania threw a look about them, scanning the nearby faces to see if anyone had heard them speaking. Most were focussed on the argument, whilst some stared up at the grey skies overhead and tried to distract their discomfort.

Tania shivered, knowing that, though the sun had been dragged away by the winds rising from the north, it was only her fear for her friend that forced her to pull her cloak tighter about her neck.

Khadazin was right, of course. But it did not make his decision any easier. Cullen was furious when the Redani firmly stated his intentions to go with the woodsman and the other volunteers. Not because he believed the rescue mission was unimportant, just because it meant, as one of the Redani's protectors, that he would be forced to go along.

Thinking of Cullen and wishing Riyan had not stayed behind in Karick, she looked for the bully, finding him saddling his mount, checking through his saddle-bags to make sure he had enough food, mead and weapons. Tania frowned. Ever since Cullen's meeting with the woodsman and their strange conversation, she had begun to wonder about them. It was obvious they knew each other, though, from the woodsman's perspective, it was something that he apparently wanted to forget.

Sighing, Tania brushed a wisp of writhing hair from her eyes and studied the woodsman. He stood alone under the shadows of the south gate, saddling his mount. The young woman watched him for a time, looking hurriedly away when he sensed eyes upon him and turned his head sharply. Khadazin was watching her and, flushing scarlet, she turned away.

Eventually, the debate died down and with a brusque embrace, Fawn Ardent turned away from her father and strode hurriedly over to those who would be riding with her that afternoon. At her approach they all gathered close except for the woodsman, who chose to remain where he was.

"I thank you all for the difficult choices you have made," Fawn began, sweeping her eyes around the ten volunteers gathered before her. "The Four Vales is on the cusp of war, a war which has been orchestrated by those hungry only for the land and riches that wait for them over the mountains. We cannot allow any more innocents to die because of their ambitions and today we strike back at them. If we do not, they will crush us underfoot, sweeping aside all who wish to preserve the peace, the prosperity and the law that protects these lands."

Finding her breath, Fawn looked for the woodsman, seeing his hooded head nod in approval. Unsure why she would seek his approbation, the captain of Havensdale pulled on her riding gloves and accepted the reins of her mount that Kallum Campbell handed to her.

Drawing in a calming breath, Fawn put a heavy foot into one stirrup and, with a reassuring pat to her mare's sleek neck, she propelled herself up onto the saddle, watching as her companions followed her lead. Swinging her mount about, she met her father's gaze, as he came forward and offered her a faint smile. He was still angry, she could tell, as he had wanted to go in her stead, a familiar face to those they sought to warn and rescue and from a father's selfless position of wanting to protect his only child.

"Swift and safe, my girl," he said gruffly. Fawn smiled and reached down to kiss him on the top of his head.

"I'll be back before you can miss me," she smiled, though the fear in her eyes robbed her promise of any real conviction.

Waving a gloved hand, Fawn motioned her companions towards the gates, hauled open roughly by the woodsman. As Fawn was about to nudge her mount's flanks, a ragged voice called out, cutting through the sombre silence of the marketplace.

All heads turned as one, eyes widening in shock at the sight that greeted them. Rellin Steelblade was leading two mounts across the square towards them, his youthful face flushing at the attention that came his way and fell upon the man who was lashed to the saddle of the stallion he led across the cobbles with a raised left hand.

"I am coming with you," Lucien Varl gasped, his ruined face twisting through its pain. The look he sent towards them dragged the last warmth from the day and dared any to protest.

Fawn shook her head, marvelling at the man's spirit, his determination to his duty, his loyalty to his lord, even though that man had, it seemed, turned his back on him.

Lost to their awe, none gathered saw the look that crossed the woodsman's face. None that was, apart from Cullen, who found his gaze and sent him a knowing, spiteful grin.

Fawn Ardent smiled as the Redani, still uncomfortable and looking ungainly in his saddle, dragged back on the reins and slowed his mount, a large bay gelding, so that she might catch up with him.

"It could be a rough night," Khadazin observed amiably, eyeing the dark skies above them worriedly.

Fawn nodded, her breath heavy from the furious winds battering the grey moors that the party from Havensdale rode solemnly across.

"It seems autumn draws her first breath," Fawn gasped, turning her face from the winds, gusting angrily from the west. They were riding into its fury and the good progress they had made since leaving Havensdale that afternoon was quickly being lost.

The stonemason fell silent, wrapping the reins tightly about his right hand, imagining how they would have felt in his left. Even now he could still feel his missing hand, though he loathed looking at his leather-capped wrist and the stark reminder it always gave him.

Fawn watched the Redani, studying his ebony features. It was a strong, if battered face that always looked dour, suggesting he was unhappy or not far away from an outburst. The soft, gentle tone of Khadazin's words when he spoke, however, was always a surprise to her. Fawn, though she knew little of the man, held a great deal of respect for him, for his strength, for the honour he possessed and the hardships he had suffered over his concerns for a young woman he had never even met.

Khadazin sensed the attention and he flicked his dark eyes towards her.

"It is a funny thing," the Redani began, smiling ruefully, "this path we find ourselves on. At the start of summer I was content with my life, though I realise now, not happy with it. I had my business, I had my solace and I had my anonymity. But now? Now I have nothing, only a bounty on my head and the desire to see the chancellor pay for his crimes, for all he has done. Not just to me, but for all of the chaos he has unleashed upon the Four Vales."

Fawn swallowed her nerves, her hair as wild as the look in the Redani's eyes.

"I too seek such justice, though it is Renald Gardan who is foremost in my thoughts. He has inflicted much harm upon Havensdale and its people, has tried to have me killed for my part in Lady Byron's story and though I might want to, I cannot ignore it." Fawn trailed off and her deep sigh was lost to the roaring winds. "I wonder what my part in this story will be, when the final page has been turned?"

Khadazin watched as Fawn struggled with her emotions and forgot his own sorrow for a time. He only had his vengeance, his promise to keep and his love for James, Tania and Savinn to worry about – Captain Ardent had the lives of her town to bear and fret over. She had to struggle with the weight of her guilt at the harm she had brought down upon them.

Licking his lips, Khadazin unthreaded his hand from the reins and reached across to her.

"Our fates are one, it seems, captain. We shall turn the last page together, I promise you."

Fawn smiled faintly and nodded her head. She watched as Khadazin struggled with his balance and politely rode ahead to rejoin the young huntress, who had been watching their exchange with great interest. She saw the dark-haired beauty lean close to say something to him, but looked away so as not to witness them talk about her.

At the rear of the group of riders, Fawn looked ahead to the dark hills, still some miles away to the west. If they were to find shelter for the night, they would have to press on, despite the weather. Though there was no guarantee they would reach their destination in time, there was too much at stake to afford any delay.

Almost immediately, Fawn thought of the danger they might face. If the chancellor had sent a large force to kill the high duke's family, then all would be lost, despite their thirteen in number. The remnants of Elion Leigh's patrol, as the most accomplished riders, had quickly volunteered their services. Having worked tirelessly with the people of Havensdale to build their defences, any suspicion that had initially come their way, had now softened to admiration and respect. All rode in disciplined formation, all silent and focussed on the terrain about them.

It was not so in the town, however, for Liyam Tallis. Kallum Campbell's Carwellian friend, the young man whose life he had spared, was still viewed with open hostility for his part in the attack on Havensdale. Despite his best efforts and determined help, the young rider would not, Fawn thought sadly, ever find forgiveness in the town.

Fawn swallowed back her own mistrust and was thankful that Kallum had come with his friend on the journey.

Looking past the unappealing and squat form of Cullen who seemed very familiar, despite his girth, in the saddle, Fawn's eyes fell upon the woodsman and Lucien Varl, Rellin riding behind them at a respectful distance.

Both rode well ahead of the group, their heads turned to one another in deep, guarded conversation. Again, Fawn felt her pulse stir, burning with suspicion and itching with curiosity.

If she had any doubts as to Cassana's former observations about the woodsman and his lineage, they had been quickly dispelled by his grace and skill on horseback. When Lucien Varl's shock and recognition had flashed in his blood-shot eyes and across his ruined features, Fawn knew that the mysterious woodsman, the man who had saved Havensdale, was no ordinary man. Her father's attempts at hiding his own knowledge of the woodsman's identity had not fooled her either.

As Fawn's curiosity was replaced by rising anger, she remembered her former promise to the woodsman in the Arms of the Lady. Despite that, however, she could not help but want to find out the truth. They were all blindly putting themselves in danger and whilst the high stakes were fully justified, she sensed that there was more to the woodsman's tale than she knew.

Perhaps it would be for the best if she didn't know...

Trying to divert her frustration, she thought of Lucien Varl. His choice for hiding the high duke's family where he had was, it appeared, a masterstroke. Even though it had been at the high duke's behest to spirit them to safety and shield them from the threats made against the Valian Council, Lucien's choice of location, the isolated Ashcroft Estate, even now, hinted that he may have harboured suspicions about his hated enemy, the chancellor, Relan Valus, long before anyone else had.

Fawn frowned, lost to the memory of the dark shadows and tragedy that had fallen upon Baron Ashcroft, a former member of the Valian Council. He had retired from public duty following the scandal that the murder of his daughter had caused in the capital, all those years ago now.

Fawn's mind began to work, twisting through a myriad of threads, listening to the whisper of dared possibilities. There was a loose strand here, a single thread that dangled enticingly in the wind before her. Losing herself to her thoughts, Fawn Ardent tried to reach out and grasp hold of it.

Arrun Hawksblade stifled a yawn as he stumbled up the steps of the Arms of the Lady Inn. Although the skies over the town were choked with heavy clouds, his eyes were narrowed from the apparent brightness of the failing afternoon.

For several days he and his mother had remained at his father's bedside, tending to his needs when the old sword master had been moved to the comfort of the Ardent Estate. Whilst the town struggled to cope with the aftermath of the attack and the demands placed upon them by the threat of further harm, Arrun shut himself away from his friends, tending only to the duty expected of a loving son.

It was hard for Arrun to cope with the thought that his father might slip away without him there and as long as his stamina would allow him, Perrin Hawksblade's son sat at his bedside, holding his still hand, talking incessantly to him, trying to coax him back from the dark path he was on. Each time his father's breath faltered, Arrun's heart failed, rallying as Perrin fought back, stubbornly refusing to let the Father of Storms take him.

Finally, through fear for her son's own waning health, Dehenna Hawksblade ordered him out into the fresh air, promising faithfully that she would send a servant for him, should his father waken. Reluctantly and with some petulance, Arrun relented. Desperate for some ale and the company of his friends, the young Hawksblade headed for the Arms of the Lady.

Scanning the busy tap-room, Arrun found a familiar face amongst the sea of strangers. With reinforcements from Highwater and all that had happened, he knew that his home would never be the same. With the blood and life that had been lost, it would be hard to find, amidst the sorrow, any joy to balance the guilt he carried at taking another man's life.

Tess Varun caught his eye, as she weaved through the throng, supplicating her patron's thirst and rising impatience with a bright promise here, or a foaming tankard there. Ignoring the clamour and barking demands for attention, she made for her friend, dealing him a glad smile that failed to hide her weariness.

"I thought we would never see you again," she began, leaning in close to kiss him on one cheek. "How is your father?"

On any normal day, Arrun would have relished such a greeting, but, too tired for anything other than company, he just bobbed his head. "My father is too proud to ride the last storm. We shan't be rid of him yet."

Tess gave the young warrior a gentle hug, holding him tenderly for a moment, as the inn heaved and writhed around them. When they finally pulled away from one another, Arrun drew in a faltering breath, looking about the crowded inn.

"Where's that rascal hiding?" he asked, an instinctive grin creasing his pale features. "Is he off chasing rabbits again?"

Tess frowned. "Did he not come to see you?"

Arrun planted his hands on his hips and attempted mock consternation. "No! He has been far too busy for his *friend*, following after the woodsman like a lost puppy, sniffing at his..." Arrun trailed off, thinking it better to remember his manners.

"Rellin's gone, Arrun," Tess replied, seeing the hurt, then the shock, register on his face. "He went with Fawn and the others to the Ashcroft Estate, to rescue the high duke's family."

Arrun blinked, drew in a breath and stepped back into the embrace of his rising horror. Looking about furtively, he visibly paled before her eyes, his mouth agape. Dragging his strangled words from his throat, he stumbled back, jostling the two men behind him. Ignoring their angry curses, Arrun Hawksblade fled the Arms of the Lady Inn, his words cutting through the clamour and stealing the warmth from Tess's over-worked body.

"No! He will die! The prophecy, the prophecy..."

Fawn Ardent scanned the hills to the south, watching the distant shadow of a kestrel, as it hunted the grey land. With a crisp, cold night behind them, warmed only by waning fires and sheltered from the winds by the lee of a low hill, the party from Havensdale had made good progress following their early start. Chased from the east by the first light of the day, they rode in silence, their urgency rising with each hour they came closer to their destination.

Exhausted beyond anything tangible, Fawn was thankful that she could no longer feel her aching body. After a sleepless night under a heavy blanket and the attentions of a low sky, she allowed her instincts and her frustrations to guide her on.

Despite her reluctance, she had still tried to coax some truths from the woodsman, met only with an uncomfortable silence, as they sat alone about his waning fire, their thoughts drawn to the erratic flames. With the winds whistling about them, Fawn had watched the woodsman for some time, her heart skipping every time she whetted the need on her lips and failed to find the courage to voice her question. Eventually, too tired to care about angering him, she had cleared her throat, drawn her knees up under her chin and, in a weary, soft voice had asked him.

"How do you know my father?"

For a while she wondered if he had even heard her, so lost to the flames as he was. Eventually, however, he had turned his head to her, his haggard face alive with shadow and flame.

"I served with him," he said haltingly, "back when my life was not my own."

As he looked away again, Fawn drew him back. "And Lucien Varl?"

The woodsman's eyes had narrowed, his head snapping up to hold her gaze with a look laced with irritation.

"He served with me a long time ago, when he was but another sword in the line."

Drawn to his piercingly cold bright eyes, Fawn had tried to calm her heart, skipping away under her armour with more than just her nerves. She had slipped through his defences momentarily and it had been her chance to land a telling question, to prise open the secrets he guarded so tightly.

But, when it came down to it, she knew that she could not. Smiling, she had reached out and took his rough, calloused hands.

"Thank you," she had whispered. Rising up, she had looked down at him, seeing the curiosity flashing across his face. "I am here for you woodsman, should you ever need me."

Swallowing hard, the woodsman had nodded his hooded head slowly, his lips curling ever-so-slightly. Kissing her hand lightly, he let it go. When he had turned away from her, Fawn stumbled back to her bedding and left him to his musings.

Fawn's mount tossed her head, snorting irritably and

bringing her back to the present. Patting the mount's neck in apology she scanned the horizon and found the woodsman, riding alone ahead of them. Over a cold, solemn breakfast of dried meats, rough bread and water, the woodsman had quietly announced that once they reached the borders of the Ashcroft Estate, he would wait for them, watching for any danger that may be shadowing them. Seeing the look on his face and the warning in his eyes, Fawn flicked a glance towards Lucien Varl. The fugitive captain had somehow survived the night and, with each hill and valley they took closer to their destination, had seemed to also gain in strength. The man's broken features twisted with what might have been sympathy and, looking back to the woodsman, she had nodded her accord.

Any questions that may have come from elsewhere in the party were cut off brutally as Cullen, hawking and spitting away to their left, had raised himself off one cheek and broken the discomfort of the silence with a loud and lengthy peal of wind. Fawn had dealt him a despairing look, but the uncouth man had returned her disapproval with a grin and sigh of evident satisfaction.

Recalling her disgust and feeling her aching muscles stir with anger, Fawn urged her mount on, failing to notice the kestrel as it banked sharply in the air and made swift on its wings towards the west.

The Ashcroft Estate nestled in the foothills of the Prospect Range, wreathed in a low mist and framed by ominous storm clouds. As the party from Havensdale neared, they were thankful that the sky was dark only with the promise of rain, not the trailing black smoke from an attack.

Fawn let out a sigh, her relief chasing away her fears for a time. Smiling at Lucien Varl, she gave the signal to continue, watching sadly as the woodsman peeled off from the column of riders and rode silently away to the south towards the low ridgeline, lost to a gathering mist.

Rellin made to ride after him, but Fawn stopped him with a firm shake of her head.

"Do not judge him, lady," Lucien Varl gasped, his face creased with pain.

Fawn shifted in her saddle as the column of riders slipped by them on both sides and made for the outlying buildings of the walled estate.

Fawn studied the former captain of Highwater, marvelling at his spirit and tenacity. In his bright eyes, she could read the sorrow he carried for the woodsman.

"You know him, captain," she began hesitantly. "That much is clear to me."

Lucien looked to the south, and further away into the past. When he spoke, his voice was soft and distant.

"He was my friend," Lucien said, shaking his head slowly. "That is as much as I can say..."

Fawn smiled. "Then that is more than enough for me, Lucien Varl."

With his battered face twisting into what may have once been a handsome smile, they nodded silently at one another and made after their companions.

The guard on the crenelated curtain wall had already raised the alarm by the time the column of riders reached the estate and the heavy double oak doors, wrought with iron bands and large studs, were already firmly shut to them. Several shapes were silhouetted against the misted hills behind and Fawn could see the bows bent in their direction.

"State your business here," one of the men called down, his face obscured by the poor light, his head clad in a leather helm.

Fawn guided her mount forward, Lucien Varl and Khadazin following her lead on either side.

"I am Captain Fawn Ardent of the Havensdale militia and I bring word of ill tidings to Lady Stromn."

In the echoing silence, Fawn could see the man turn his head to the guard stood next to him. As she dealt Lucien a swift look, the man turned back again.

"You are mistaken, captain," he called down, attempting to fill his response with affable confusion. "Lady Stromn is in Highwater, she..."

Snarling impatiently, Lucien Varl nudged his mount forward, grimacing as he fought against the pain wracking his body. "We are running out of time, man! Let me speak to Tristan Malak. I know he is here, as are his charges."

The man bristled. "And how, might I ask, would you know that?"

Lucien Varl smiled, though his countenance was hideous and did little to ease the tension of the men up on the wall. "Because I am his captain and it was I who sent him here."

It took a long time, but eventually the guard sent from the walls returned with another warrior, dressed in a long coat of leather, his broad face twisting with confusion as he stared down at the riders gathered before him. After a moment, he gripped the stone parapet and his face stiffened with disbelief.

"By the storms!" he growled, his revulsion and horror evident upon his face. He turned to the man on his right. "Open the gates! This *is* my captain, Lucien Varl."

Moments after, the gates groaned open in protest and Fawn and her companions rode under the gatehouse to gather in the small cobbled courtyard beyond. A large manor house rose up before them, the sky above mournful with light rainfall now. The morose, unsightly architecture of the manor house did little to improve the tension of the drab day.

Fawn slipped from her mount and, with Kallum

Campbell's aid, helped Lucien from his saddle. Swaying slightly, the injured man waved away their concerns as Tristan Malak came across the courtyard towards them. Fawn watched as the large man hurried to Lucien's side, his high, heavy boots cutting through the stillness.

"Captain," he hissed. His eyes were wide with confusion and his shock sent wrinkles rippling over his bald head. "What has happened to you?"

Lucien gripped Tristan's shoulder with a trembling hand, digging his urgency into him.

"There is madness in the capital," he hissed, falling against his friend. "The chancellor has moved against us and the high duke... he is sending men here to kill Lady Stromn and her son."

There was a sizeable crowd gathered around them now and their gasps and curses filled the silence as they shared horrified looks with one another.

Khadazin looked for Tania. The young huntress was standing by her mount and her face, usually dusky from the sun, was as pale as the moon and etched with worry.

"We must not delay," Fawn Ardent called out, her crisp voice cutting through the rising dismay. "Fetch Lady Stromn and her son for us, we would speak to them and take them to safety before any danger can come to your door."

The guard who had first greeted them tugged nervously at his indecision, before shouldering his way through the throng, his haste chased by his curses.

Fawn turned to Khadazin to find he was already watching her. He nodded in her direction and spread his dark features into an encouraging smile.

Puffing out her cheeks, Fawn listened as Lucien Varl gave orders to Tristan Malak to gather his men and make ready to depart. With the commotion in the courtyard, she did not hear the staccato retreat of Malak's heavy boots. The only sound she could hear was the steady, rising drum of warning in her chest.

The woodsman hunkered down on his saddle. His hood was drawn tight over his head, his long cloak sodden and close against his body as the wind continued to rally and the iron-grey mist swirled about him.

From his vantage point on the southern ridgeline of the Prospect Hills, he could see the riders from Havensdale, as they guarded the covered wagon that made slow progress away from the Ashcroft Estate through the grim evening to the east. Since they had left the estate, he had spent the last hour shadowing them from the ridgeline, as he continued his vigilance and waited for the sighting he sensed would inevitably come.

Cold and cantankerous, his horse laboured hard, snorting heavily and longing for a warm stable, some oats and her brush. The woodsman smiled, patting her long neck.

"There, there, girl!" he soothed, gently. "We'll soon have you home."

Home?

The woodsman scowled, throwing his attention away from the memories, constantly attacking his resolve now. Being here, so near to the Ashcroft Estate, was too much to bear. He scowled again, peering southwards into the lowlands. The horizon was dark now, a thick band of heavy mist blanketing the land. Nothing stirred, not even the cattle from a distant farmstead. They stood like statues, black shapes in the grey, still in their protest at the waning summer.

They would come, he knew. This Brotherhood would not miss their chance and with the cart and their charges to protect, the woodsman knew that even the Lady's favour would not see them safely away from harm.

Cursing, the woodsman guided his mount down the rugged incline, picking an assured path down through the jutting rocks. His heart began to tremor as he thought about the moment he would be forced to rejoin his comrades. When he did, there would be no hiding from his past any longer. Fawn Ardent would have her answers and he would no longer have his solace. There was still time! He could still ride away and never look back...

Men like you should not hide away, the Seer had said to him, that fateful night in the forest.

The woodsman shook his hooded head and growled. As he looked to the east, his breath caught in his throat. Standing on his stirrups, he narrowed his eyes, searching through the bleak lowlands to the east. Dropping onto his saddle, he drew heavily on the reins and swung his mount about, his rising fear chasing him swiftly to the north.

Khadazin stifled a yawn, fighting against his misery as the small wagon was dragged slowly eastwards over the rough ground by two stout Valian ponies. The rain, but a figment of his imagination at first, was now lashing his face, thrown about by a gleeful wind that drowned out all but his thoughts.

It had been a trying afternoon, one that ended with the high duke's family reluctantly, unceremoniously bundled into the wagon with scant few of their possessions. The irritation on Lady Stromn's pale face, as she was dragged from the depths of a book, was quickly dispersed when she saw the condition of Lucien Varl. With her son stood behind them, his hand covering his shock and his eyes wide with horror, Lucien's warnings soon found their mark, striking fast under Lady Stromn's confusion. News of her husband and the peril he faced, should he still live, had her ready to charge to the capital and demand to see him.

Khadazin's intervention and tale of treachery soon put that idea from her and, with Fawn Ardent's assistance, they persuaded the distraught woman that first and foremost they should flee to the sanctuary of Havensdale and the determination and defiance that stirred there. After a moment's deliberation and a fearful, anguished look cast towards her son, Tobias, Lady Stromn rose up on unsteady legs, drew in her determination and accepted the shaking hand that Lucien Varl offered her. As the distraught son and wife hurried to make their preparations to depart, Lucien Varl came to Khadazin and clapped him on one shoulder.

"My thanks, stonemason," he said, smiling in relief.

Khadazin had smiled in return, though he, to his eternal shame, had still not imparted the news he had of Cornelius, the man he knew to be his father. Savinn had confirmed Khadazin's fears, as they looked upon the sleeping captain and, though he knew he should, he had not told Lucien of his father's fate. After all he had been through, all the torture he had endured, Khadazin, from bitter experience, knew that the news would probably have killed him.

Sighing, Khadazin wiped the rain from his face, rubbing his sodden beard ruefully. It was not the right time. They needed Lucien Varl, just as much as he needed them.

Tania's urgent voice scattered his thoughts, as she drew his attention away from his deliberations and pointed to the south. Shielding his eyes from the rain, Khadazin could see the woodsman, head bent low over the neck of his horse, as they charged through the gloom and swirling rain towards them.

Fawn Ardent noticed the girl's keen awareness and gave the order for the column of riders and wagon to stop. Khadazin swept a look about their surroundings, but could see no obvious reason for the woodsman's haste.

"What is wrong, captain?" Lady Stromn's irritation cut through the rising tension, as her face peered through the parted canvas and she hushed her son's incessant calls from within.

She was a beautiful woman, even now, Khadazin mused, and must have truly been a vision in her youth. Long sable hair fell neatly, despite the weather and hurried departure, about her thin shoulders which were draped in a fur shawl. Her captivating features just about held on to the memory of her youth, creased only by the ravages of state and she searched the horizon with narrowed eyes of the deepest jade. Her high cheekbones wrinkled as she elegantly stifled a sneeze and Khadazin, remembering his lowly position, looked away in embarrassment.

Fawn Ardent slipped from her saddle and led her horse back to the wagon.

"Our scout, the woodsman returns, Lady Stromn."

Not fooled by Fawn's attempt to disguise her worry, Lady Stromn nodded. "I see!" she whispered, closing her eyes momentarily.

Their numbers were swelled by Lucien Varl's men now and the twenty one riders waited in silence, listening to the rain as it drummed on canvas. After a time, the sound of sodden hooves rumbled through their apprehension as the woodsman charged across the grasslands towards them, dragged hastily on his reins and leapt fluidly from the saddle to stride towards the wagon.

Khadazin caught the look in the woodsman's eyes as he approached Fawn Ardent, seeing the fear flashing from within the depths of his cowl. A chill stole up his arms as the Redani looked for Tania, discovering that she and Rellin, the young hunter from Havensdale, were both looking towards the south.

Fawn turned to the woodsman as he approached her on failing legs.

"Woodsman?" she enquired, as he stopped before her and lowered his hood. His long hair was plastered to his skull, his once greying stubble, dripping black.

Before he could reply, Lady Stromn let out a strangled

gasp. All heads turned towards her, as she flinched and cupped her mouth to hide her shock. Her eyes widened and then quickly narrowed, burning with hatred.

"You!" she hissed, gripping hold of the canvas with her free hand. She looked about desperately, her eyes wild with anger.

"Guards! Arrest this man, immediately."

The woodsman smiled grimly as all heads turned towards him and Tristan Malak took a dutiful step forward.

The woodsman held up his gloved hands, his eyes fixed upon the high duke's wife, as his heart threatened to burst from his chest. "You may have them arrest me after, lady," he said, offering a curt bow. "But at least allow me to save your life, first."

He turned away from the wagon and pointed towards the south-east where ghostly shapes had begun to appear on the horizon. Forty dark blurs, approaching purposefully through the swirling, driving rain towards them.

CHAPTER THIRTY SEVEN

No Way Back

Arillion sat on the steps at the rear of his wagon, watching and listening as the wayfarers gathered up their camp. The relief in the cool evening air was tangible and the smiles back on many of their faces, as their makeshift home for nearly two weeks now was swiftly, effortlessly packed away.

The night before had seen a heated debate, as the entire wayfaring family gathered together about the large fire, venting their frustrations at Kaspen Shale, who answered their questions with assurances that they would leave the following day. The celebrations that night had been immense and, much to Arillion's amusement, had delayed that which they so longed for, by the better part of the day.

Picking at the stitching of his leather trousers, Arillion looked across the empty plains towards the towering walls of Highwater. Scowling, he shook his head and massaged away the pain that was building in his shin from an afternoon of inactivity.

The word from Kaspen's contacts in the city was that

Lady Astien had not been arrested and, it was reported, had been seen with Cassana in public, laughing and sharing some private joke. Angry beyond words, Kaspen had prevented Arillion entering the city and killing the woman himself, cautioning him on the folly of such a move.

'It may be that she is biding her time,' Kaspen had warned him, forcing him back onto his seat. 'We have done all we can, swordsman. It is time for us to leave the Byron girl to follow whatever path she chooses.'

Despite his annoyance, Arillion had quickly realised that the wayfarer was right. If she had any sense, which he knew she did, Cassana would bide her time, until she had enough reason to act.

Arillion sighed, massaging his temples. He had kept his word to Cassana. He had found the traitor for her and it was time for him to honour his other promise.

Kaspen's relief had been evident when Arillion told him he was ready to depart. After the joy of the celebrations had worn off, however, Arillion was certain that the wayfaring leader's problems were only just about to start.

As if he had somehow known Arillion's thoughts, Kaspen left Agris Varen's side and approached him from across the camp, weaving through the throng of eager wayfarers. Arillion met his broad smile with a subtle nod.

"Feeling better?" Arillion asked, grinning.

Kaspen's face was grey as he swept the broad-brimmed hat from his head. "Not really," he winced, sitting on the steps beside him. "We should be on the road before the hour," he added, finally.

Arillion nodded, folding his hands in his lap and stretching out his aching leg. "Good. I hope your people are happy."

Kaspen frowned. "For the moment," he said, looking about guardedly. "Though, I daresay, once we reach

Havensdale, they may change their minds."

Arillion turned to the wayfarer, as Kaspen added, "What are we going to do, once we reach Havensdale, swordsman?"

Arillion held Kaspen's eyes for a time, searching his features for tell of his resolve. "We will offer them our services and tell them honestly of what we know."

Kaspen scowled. "Let us be honest with each other, shall we? What *do* we actually know?"

Arillion looked away, spying Lia, as she hurried away from them. He ignored the look on Kaspen's face and lost himself to her departing curves for a time.

"We know who the spy in Highwater is, we know, as do they, that Carwell is likely to be behind all of this and, most importantly, I know who killed Alion Byron."

Kaspen watched as Arillion bowed his head, lost to his thoughts. When he did not continue with his explanation, the wayfarer dragged him back by clamping a hand on his taut shoulder.

"And yet I do not," Kaspen growled impatiently. "We are in this together, my brother, and yet, why is it that it feels like I am the one taking all the risks?"

"We are both risking everything, Kaspen. You will just need to trust me." Arillion replied, looking away evasively.

Kaspen leant forward to purse Arillion's averted eyes, ignoring the cold look of warning that flared there as he drew breath to speak again.

"Share with me, swordsman," Kaspen demanded, ignoring the warning. He clenched his free hand to ward away his fear. "You know of this woman, as you say. I saw the look on your face when I told you of Lady Byron's description."

Arillion wrenched his shoulder free and rose up, striding away to stand before the remnants of the great fire. Spreading his hands wide, he warmed them there for a time, his mind raging with a torrent of emotions, emotions he had locked away for the better part of a decade. Kaspen came to stand beside him and he could hear his anger flaring in his nostrils.

Finally, when the wayfarer's patience was wearing dangerously thin, Arillion turned, his face as grey as his glittering eyes.

"I know of her," the assassin admitted, amazed at the release he felt for sharing this news with another. "I will say only that if it is indeed her that killed... that murdered Alion Byron and the girl, then she will have something of mine, something that I will pluck from her cold, lifeless hands."

Kaspen recoiled at the fury, the malice and the venom that filled Arillion's words. The assassin's eyes were full of barely controlled fury, dangerously framed by his anger.

"It will be dangerous, my friend," Kaspen pointed out, hoping to divert the tension between them.

Arillion nodded, clasping his hands before him thoughtfully. "Yes, it will," he said softly, "but we have no choice now. There can be no peaceful resolution to this – surely that much is clear?"

"It is, of course it is! But you must understand that I risk much by aiding you," Kaspen hissed. "When we get to Havensdale, I will have to think long and hard about our agreement. If my people become too involved, it will ruin our way of life."

Arillion grabbed Kaspen's wrist as he turned to walk away and stepped in close, his face full of anger.

"Ruin it?" he spat, holding the wayfarer in his grip. "I am trying to help you save it! After all you have done for me it is the least I can do."

"Spare your lies, swordsman," Kaspen snarled. "Do not try to ease your conscience by pretending what you do is for *our* benefit."

Arillion let him go, gritting his teeth. When Kaspen

did not leave, he let out a calming breath and said, “This Brotherhood, this regime, this new world, will not have room for your kind, Kaspen Shale. There will be no freedom to choose how you live your life, mark my words. If we do not stand as one, we will fall alone and I, for one, would prefer not to kneel and accept what is to come.”

Kaspen swallowed down his anger, sighed and rubbed his tired eyes. “If what you say is true, then I will be forced to fight. I am a rogue, I admit it. But I am no warrior or assassin, Arillion. What are we to do? We cannot just walk into the capital and kill our enemies”

The look that crossed Arillion’s handsome face chilled him to his bones.

“But that is exactly what we will do. If we are to stop this war, we must cut the heads from the snakes,” Arillion hissed. “We must kill them all before they can sink their venom into the Vales.”

“It is likely that we will all die,” Kaspen whispered sadly, his mind full of all he could lose, those he would leave behind.

Arillion’s reply did not ease his fears. “I fully expect to die, Kaspen Shale... but not before my blades have drenched Karick in the blood of our enemies.”

Despite the beautiful evening sunshine that filtered down through the tree canopy and the melodic song of a blackbird, Elion Leigh felt little comfort as he led his horse through Greywood Forest, towards the distant camp that was beginning to feel like home.

Up ahead of him Devlin Hawke strode purposefully on, his determination and long strides putting great distance between them. It had been like that, ever since they had slipped silently away from the Leigh Estate, making for the protection of The Horseshoe range.

Devlin's eagerness to get away from Carwell was evident and he pushed them hard, resting little, travelling as long as the day would allow and then breaking camp before dawn. Little was said on their return journey and Elion was left to struggle with his guilt, of leaving his parents behind again and the fact that in their haste to depart, he had not gone to say goodbye to his mother...

Cries rose from the camp, as the outlaw called out a florid greeting and Elion could see figures stir happily at their leader's safe return. Feeling his pulse quicken, Elion hurried through the trees to catch him up, knowing that once they reported on what was happening in Carwell, there really would be no way back from this.

Trell's gratitude was painted clearly on his broad face as he gripped Devlin's hand and ordered the young fugitive Balan to see to their leader's horse. As Balan led both their mounts away, Elion nodded his weary thanks. Looking about the camp, he couldn't help but smile as he caught sight of Ashe and Kerrin, as they put aside the blades they had been sharpening and rose up from the fireside.

Ashe reached him first, his relief splitting his bearded face and his haste almost tripping him over.

"By the storms, it's good to see you, Elion," Ashe roared, sweeping him deep into an embrace and slapping him warmly on the back. He mercifully pulled back before his captain choked to death. "I was beginning to think I would have to come looking for you."

Elion smiled. "We were delayed a little." Hearing the strained notes in his voice, they shared a look that said much. As Kerrin Thorn joined their reunion, Devlin came over to them and placed a jug of mead into Elion's hands.

"Get that in your belly, lad," Devlin ordered, grinning. "The Lady knows we deserve it!" Raising their drinks, they crashed them together and took eager, deep pulls.

"So what has been happening?" Devlin asked, wiping

his mouth and looking for Trell. The large outlaw came over to them, sharing a smile with Ashe.

"We have been busy, ain't we?" Trell began and Ashe nodded his accord. "We have hit several wagons and a few individual travellers. Got some good loot for our troubles and sent them on their way to Carwell with tales of how vicious we are. When they send some patrols to scout the area, which the Carwellians' reckon they will, we'll hit them hard."

Devlin's jovial expression hardened and he flicked a look around the camp.

"Good!" he nodded, tugging at his beard. He drank thirstily from his clay jug again and tossed it away into the trees when it was empty. "Gather as many men as you can, Trell. Call a meeting, there is much we need to discuss."

Trell hesitated, then nodding, he spun away. Gathering up his bow and a full quiver, he loped off through the trees to the south.

Devlin dragged their attention back by announcing he was going for a sleep – that they should wake him when people started arriving. With an emphasising yawn, he hurried away. Slipping into Kerrin's tent with a groan, he ruffled the donkey's ears as he passed.

"So what did happen?" Ashe asked quietly. He looked guardedly about, making sure the other outlaws present did not hear. Touching them both on a shoulder, Elion ushered them away from the clearing. Once they were back in the forest, Kerrin and Ashe bent their ears close.

"It's bad, I am afraid," Elion began, pulling on his left earlobe nervously. "Carwell has tightened his grip on the city and is already gathering the army together."

Kerrin gasped, looking at Ashe in disbelief. "That is madness."

Elion nodded sadly. "And that's not even the worst of it."

By the time Jarion Kail and Elissen returned from their foraging, the camp was full of outlaws, all of them waiting about, quietly sharing their thoughts on why Devlin would have called such a gathering. As they stacked their armfuls of wood to the side of Kerrin's tent, they caught sight of Elion Leigh, as he talked quietly with Ashe, Kerrin and Balan.

Jarion's pulse stirred thankfully, then, as Elissen hurried away from him without a word, faltered, leaving the bitter taste of his envy in his throat. When Elissen threw her arms about his captain and gave him a relieved kiss to one cheek, he felt his stomach knot.

With Elion away risking his life, Jarion had enjoyed the solitude of the forest and the time he had spent with Elissen. As each day passed and their friendship deepened, Jarion was certain that the woman he had fallen in love with, despite the turmoil she had suffered and the heavy sorrow that she still bore, may well have begun to feel the same way about him.

His constant attention, his kindness and flattery were all gratefully received with shy smiles and thanks and Jarion could sense that perhaps their friendship was just the beginning of something more.

As he watched Elissen and saw the colourful joy fill her pale face as she pulled back in embarrassment from Elion Leigh, a cold well of despair settled in Jarion's stomach as he realised it was more likely that his love for the girl from Eastbury would remain his own to guard, never to be returned in kind.

Forcing a smile, Jarion went to greet his captain and, whilst his joy at Elion's return was heartfelt, he could not fully bury the resentment that was starting to take root in his mind.

Eventually, Devlin Hawke deemed to appear, a cheer rising as he raised his hands in greeting and then lowered them gently, calling for silence. When he was satisfied, Devlin cleared a few outlaws from their stools by the fire and cleared his throat.

"Brothers!" Devlin called out, his clear voice rolling out across the camp. He paused, spying Elissen, where she stood next to Balan. "And sister, my apology," he grinned, offering her a graceful bow.

Many heads turned to the girl from Eastbury and she hid her flushing cheeks behind a veil of her chestnut locks.

"As you know, I have been to Carwell, with our good friend here, Captain Leigh," Devlin continued, drawing everyone's attention back. "I am afraid to say I didn't get the chance to dine with Henry Carwell, who was far too busy dreaming up ways to execute me–," a perfectly timed pause to allow laughter to ripple through his audience, "I did however, get to share a fine claret with a man many of us held respect for before he retired from office. Elion Leigh's father had dark news for us, confirmed the next day by an ally from within the city. Carwell prepares for war. The armies are being gathered and the Reven people, fingered as the enemy in all of this, are being executed in Raven Square and hung from crow cages along the Great East Road outside the city."

A wave of unease rolled through the camp and Elion met Elissen and Jarion's horrified looks with a regretful nod of confirmation.

"So what does this mean for us?" an outlaw called out from amongst the throng. Many heads bobbed in agreement.

Devlin eyed the speaker. "It doesn't mean anything right now, Ben," the outlaw leader began, looking about his men, "but in the coming weeks, mark my words, it bloody well will. Carwell's lust for power and ambitions are tearing this country apart. His allies have already sown the seeds of this in Karick and the high duke, a man many of us once respected in a previous life, is no longer in control. His strongest ally is dead and his enemies gather about him. In time, if he's not already, Karian Stromn will be dead and when that happens, which it will, there will be nothing anyone can do to stop the Valian armies marching north."

Devlin drew breath, allowing his words to sink in. He looked up at the sky, darkening overhead and closed his eyes, listening to the whispers of muttered debate that began to rise.

When he spoke again, Devlin's voice was full of conviction, though heavy with his anger. "Henry Carwell is a bastard, we all know that. The Lady knows we have pissed him off for many years now. But this is a new madness – the killings, tortures and brutalities. This is not something we can simply ignore, my friends, and I for one will not ignore it! Tomorrow, Elion and I will ride to Havensdale, where a rebellion is stirring. We shall deliver the terrible news we have discovered to them and formulate a plan that will see us strike back, before we find out that we cannot."

Elion looked about the camp, his heart racing madly. He hadn't realised just how many men Devlin Hawke had, but many of the outlaws looked uneasy now. Some of them even rose up and walked from the camp. Elion felt his hopes begin to fall.

Devlin watched several of his men leave, his eyes glittering as he swept his gaze about those who still remained.

"Anyone else lost their balls?" he asked calmly.

When nobody else moved, he nodded his head. "Good! Then, this, my brothers, is what we shall do. From tomorrow, we will hit any travellers on *our* road. We shall strike out from our sanctuary to the east and west, attacking any of Carwell's forces where we find them. The more we can do to disrupt and distract them from their preparations, the better it will be."

"But we haven't said yes, yet boss," Trell pointed out, his own answer flashing in his eyes, evident in his smile.

Shaking his head ruefully, Devin Hawke stepped up onto a stool.

"Forgive me, my friends," he said. "I will stand against Carwell. I will fight him wherever his stench resides and I will do all I can to aid those who would do likewise. Will you join me, brothers? Shall we make sure that we go down in history together?"

The huge roar that filled the forest and startled the scrawny donkey suggested that they would.

Savinn Kassaar cursed as he fumbled for the wine decanter with a shaking hand and knocked it from his desk. For a time, he sat in the darkness, listening to the sound of the fine red emptying across his carpeted floor.

Groaning, he buried his head in his hands, wincing from the stabbing pain that rose and fell with each ragged breath he took.

He was drunk! Beyond the stupefying effects that a single bottle would have inflicted upon him, well beyond any measure of coherence. Since the news, he had lost count of the bottles, of the days and of those who remained in his employ, coming and going like recollections, with their concern etched on their blurred faces.

They had tried to cover it up, but Savinn still had his contacts in the city. It had taken a lot of coin, but the silence and his fears were finally confirmed. Dia was dead! Killed, no doubt, in her brave and yet, ultimately, foolhardy attempt to kill the chancellor.

Relan Valus was alive, still tightening his grip on those who would stand against him and Renald Gardan, unleashed upon the city now without compunction, had stamped his Carwellian boot upon their supposed enemies.

Only three days ago, reports had reached Savinn's ears that public hangings had started, happening in each of the squares by the main gates leading in to Karick. Reven prisoners, dragged before the chanting mobs, had been strung up in their dozens, hung without trial, sent to their doom by the condemnation of the masses.

"Oh, Dia," Savinn whispered, stifling a sob.

Savinn moaned, clenching his frustration tightly in his clammy fists. He knew he should eat, even through the fog of his inebriation, but his stomach heaved at the thought, his appetite only craving an escape from his sorrow and the dilemma that faced him now.

The whispers were that Henry Carwell was on his way to Karick. Several guards drinking at the Jade Eagle had been heard talking about it and the information had been swiftly passed on by the proprietor there, Fenton Avery.

If it was true, then all would be lost, Savinn knew. And with Dia, with her no longer in the high duke's keep... all was already lost.

It was getting more difficult to get news, the past two days, and Riyan, when he last came to find his master, signalled that Gardan's men had started hunting the sewers, for any sign of Reven traitors. Only a week ago, Savinn's men had found a Reven man and his Valian family, hiding and starving in the eastern sewers, and they had given them sanctuary, before smuggling them out of the city to safety.

Sighing, the merchant-thief sank back in his high-backed chair, listening to his heart. It filled the lonely darkness with its foreboding beat, drowning out the thoughts in his tormented head.

The only hope there was, was that Lucien Varl and Khadazin could rescue Karian Stromn's family. It was the only move they had on the board, a countering strike that would sow uncertainty into the mind of the Brotherhood. With the son still alive, there was hope – just a faint sliver, but one nonetheless.

For them, maybe...

Savinn smiled and shook his head, immediately regretting it as pain lanced across his forehead. Clearing the dryness and need for another bottle of wine from his throat, he fumbled for the hand bell on his desk, finding it eventually amongst the empty bottles. Gritting his teeth against the pain that would follow, Savinn rang the bell heartily.

Eventually, when he had wrung the pain from his head, Savinn began to hear the nervous approach of feet, started to detect the faint lifting of the shadows in the darkness. As tendrils of light slipped under his door, Savinn shielded his eyes, waiting for the knock that followed.

"Come," he commanded, his voice hollow. As the door cracked open, he picked out the silhouette of the girl before him and with a faint smile that did little to chase the fear from her eyes, Ellie hurried into the room, the candle she carried revealing the chaos inside.

"Don't be frightened, girl," Savinn soothed her, forcing a painful smile to his face.

Wide-eyed, Ellie nodded her head obediently. "You sent for me, master?"

"I did," Savinn replied, waving a shaking hand. "Sit down a moment; I need to talk to you."

Barely masking her surprise, the young waif sat down at the desk, finding space for the candle holder and the flame she carried.

Sifting through the upheaval, Savinn found a sealed letter, one of its corners stained red by spilt wine. He frowned at it, before passing it across the table into the girl's reaching hand.

"Things are bad, very bad, Ellie," Savinn began,

swallowing his grief as he reached into a drawer and pulled out a pouch. "I want you to take this note and purse of money and go to the Jade Eagle tavern. The barkeep Fenton Avery is a friend, as you know. He has instructions to find you safe passage on a merchant caravan to the South Vales, Silver Falls first and then on to Blackmoor. This note will see you to safety, to a friend of mine there, who owes me many favours. I have asked him to find you work, to take care of you... as I am afraid I no longer can."

Ellie looked at the note, though Savinn knew she could not yet read letters, having only just mastered writing her first name. Her brow furrowed in confusion and she wrinkled her nose as Savinn passed the heavy purse across the desk to her.

When she looked up, Savinn could see the hurt in her eyes, the sadness brimming there.

"But this is my home, here, with you and everyone else, master," she stammered, her lips trembling. "I do not want to leave, I want to stay and help."

Reaching across, Savinn brushed the tears away that started spilling down her cheeks. He sighed.

"You must not stay, Ellie. I do not want you to be part of what is to follow."

Ellie sniffed, wiping her nose on the tattered sleeve of her faded dress.

"But I am scared," she mumbled.

"So am I," Savinn replied, his grief choking his words. "You have been a good girl, Ellie and there is enough money in that pouch to ensure that you have a good life. Always remember who you are, what you have had to endure and the lessons you have learnt. Be everything that you can be in this life, Ellie, don't become everything that you are not."

The young girl frowned, though Savinn could see that she would remember his words, even if at this moment, she did not understand them.

"Send Riyan to me, if you would," Savinn said softly.

Bobbing her head, Ellie rose up. She held her master's gaze for a moment, before hurrying away. It wasn't until she had gone that Savinn realised she had left the candle in the room. He smiled.

Riyan came into the room, as he usually did, in silence. Savinn ignored the look on his face and rose on unsteady legs.

Master? Riyan signed.

"Two things," Savinn said, pulling forth a leather scroll case. He looked up again, so Riyan could read his lips. "Firstly, I want you to see Ellie safely to the Jade Eagle, today. After that, I want you to ride north with this scroll case, to Havensdale. Re-join Cullen and the stonemason. There are two scrolls inside, one for Cullen, one for Lady Byron. As soon as Cullen has read his message, he will know what to do. If he delays, you must order him north to Highwater, at once. Do you understand me?"

Riyan took the scroll case. He studied it for a time then looked up, nodding once.

"Good," Savinn said. Drawing in a calming breath, he tossed the mute a large bag of coins. "For your loyalty, my friend, and my thanks."

Riyan frowned, then picked up the bag. His eyes widened as he felt the wealth in its weight.

I do not understand?

Savinn smiled sadly. "You will, in time."

Reaching out a hand, Riyan took Savinn's hand and shook it. With a calm smile, he nodded his head in farewell and spun on his heels, heading for the door.

Savinn stood, resting his palms on the desk, watching as the mute closed the door. After a time, he collapsed back into his chair and let out a long, deep sigh.

Wincing, Savinn drummed the fingers of his left hand across the desk. The other letter he had penned was already on its way to Ilithia, to his wife, and even now the words he had scratched down filled his heart with abject sorrow.

Closing his eyes, Savinn Kassaar steadied his nerves, cleared his mind of everything that might stray him from his chosen path.

"One last thing," he whispered. Rising up again, he sent a look about the room, his bleary eyes falling upon the painting of the wolf.

He smiled, shaking his head. Turning away, he stumbled from his study and went in search of another bottle of wine. He could afford himself some time, just a few more moments alone, before he played his final hand, made his final move.

CHAPTER THIRTY EIGHT

Thou Shall not Fall

Aren Bray wiped the swirling rain from his face with a gloved hand, a hand that shook from the anticipation roaring in his ears. All about him, *his* men formed slowly into line and stared ahead through the driving rain towards the wagon and the riders gathering defensively about it.

Licking his lips, he sent a look along the line, seeing that the faces of his comrades were set in sodden masks ranging from anticipation to uncertainty.

Aren swallowed down his own uncertainty, hawking up his derision for those that still fought to cling on to the old ways. Gardan and Chancellor Valus had been explicit in their instructions to him and the men he had carefully chosen under his command.

Find them. Bring us their heads.

Aren scowled. There would be no place for weakness, honour and peace in this new realm they were forging. Only the strong would survive. Setting his jaw in determination, he guided his stallion forward, turning him to face his men.

"It appears Commander Gardan's fears were well founded," he began, stabbing a meaningful look over his left shoulder. "There are still those who would work against all that we are trying to do to protect the Four Vales from harm. There is weakness still, cowardice and disloyalty festering here and together, today, we must cut it out. We all know our orders, you are all willing to see it done, or you would not be here now. Strike fast, strike hard with me brothers and let none of them leave this land alive."

Slowly, Aren drew his sabre, the heavy rainfall drumming on his armour. Wheeling his mount about, he raised the dull blade into the air and slashed it purposefully towards their prey.

"For the Brotherhood!" he screamed.

"Horses to the rear," Taryn Malak ordered calmly. Any riders still in their saddles leapt from their mounts and harried them to the rear of the wagon.

The woodsman looked back at Lady Stromn, who, even now, was still looking at him with wide, bright eyes full of conflict. Before she could say anything, he slid the short blade from the sheath hanging from his right hip. Reversing the blade, he passed the hilt into her hand.

She stared down at the blade, then looked up at him.

"You still remember what I taught you, lady?" he asked her, forcing a thin smile across his face.

She glowered at him. "Of course I do."

"Then defend your son and kill anyone who does not have their back to you," the woodsman said, turning away before she could reply. He paused momentarily and then, when there was no answer forthcoming, he hurried away.

Despite the danger, Fawn Ardent and the riders from Havensdale were working well with Taryn Malak's men. Acting as one, horses were quickly tethered to the rear of the wagon and each other.

Nodding towards Fawn, the woodsman hurried away to Lucien Varl's side, where he leant against the front wheel of the wagon.

"You are too weak to fight," Evan observed, clapping a supportive hand on his sagging shoulder. "Stay in the wagon with Lady Stromn. Protect them, my friend."

Lucien bristled, grimacing. "You forget, *my* friend, I do not take orders from you any more."

Ignoring the barb in his tone, the woodsman grabbed him under one arm and forced him to the rear of the wagon.

"No, that is true," he said quietly, having to tighten his grip as the captain struggled. "But you should listen to my advice."

The canvas curtain at the rear of the wagon parted, as the high duke's son peered out.

"Help him up," the woodsman ordered, forcing the captain up the wooden steps. Tobias' mother appeared at his side and together, they began to pull Lucien to safety. The woodsman turned away, hesitated, then looked back.

"And don't let him leave," he added, ignoring Lucien's curses and the look Lady Stromn dealt him at being given orders. Curling her lips, she allowed the curtain to fall without a word.

With the driver's seat cleared by Taryn Malak, Tania leapt up beside Khadazin and Rellin, watching as the stonemason fumbled nervously for the crank at the side of his crossbow and began winding the string back. As she slipped a feathered shaft from the quiver at her side, she began to hear the rumbling approach of danger. Reluctantly, she drew her eyes to the south east, her fear rising up through her body as images of the horrors that were about to fall upon them and those that she would be forced to exact herself, clawed at her mind.

She was not hiding in the trees this time, she was in

the open, as naked as the blades that the riders thundering towards them had in their hands.

Fitting the arrow to the string of her bow, Tania found a breath, drew it in for comfort then slowly, calmly, allowed it to escape.

Those without bows quickly formed a defensive ring about the wagon and horses, brandishing weapons and raising shields. Taryn Malak strode to stand beside Fawn Ardent and the woodsman, watching as the riders bearing down on them split into two groups, one of them circling the wagon, towards the north.

Taryn Malak looked to the defenders, dragging their eyes away from their attackers momentarily.

"They will have to fight us from the ground, as long as we do not break rank," he growled defiantly, the rain dripping down his broad features. "No matter what happens, they do not get through our lines, they will not claim their prize."

Though many of them had lost their voices, he saw them nod in understanding. Turning to Fawn and the woodsman, he offered them a faint smile.

"Lovely day for it," he said, shaking his bald head.

The woodsman nodded, wishing he hadn't given Cassana his bow. "Shall we?" he asked, gesturing to their enemy.

Fawn followed his sweeping arm, her heart in her mouth as the eastern group of attackers slowed their charge some hundred paces from her and began leaping from their saddles.

Shivering, Fawn felt the woodsman's hand gently touch her arm and looked down at it dumbly, feeling his strength flow through her. Looking up, she saw his smile and, with a steadying breath, she joined him in the line.

The enemy's screams and collective battle-cry, echoed across the bleak landscape, filling the gloom and silence with hatred. Brandishing their weapons, they raised them to the dark sky and then, with a thunderous roar, they charged.

Time slowed as the wave of violence rolled towards them through the swirling, sheeting rain. With his heart drowning out the attackers screams, Khadazin raised his crossbow, sighted and sent a bolt into the dark line charging towards them. Without wanting to know if he had found a mark, the Redani began winding the crank back again, the rain running freely down his face.

Twin shafts leapt into the enemy ranks from the snapping strings of the archers standing on either side of the stonemason and as one of the attackers went down, lost to the mud and rising screams, the enemy crashed into the defenders lines with a dull, ringing crunch.

Blocking a ferocious cut before her face, Fawn Ardent threw her opponent back, the stinging blow of steel throbbing up her arm. As the man came at her again, she could see the bloodlust twisting his features, burning away any clarity of thinking once held in his blue eyes.

Gripping her Valian Longsword in both hands, Fawn turned the man's blade away again as it slashed towards her belly. Sweeping his weapon aside, she slammed an elbow into the man's throat as he stumbled forward.

Choking, the man recoiled and as he brought up his sword to protect himself, Fawn slipped her blade past his defences and ran it through his ribs. Groaning, the man dropped to his knees, all anger slipping from his eyes as he looked up in confusion at Fawn as she drew away from him, taking her bloodied steel with her. As the young attacker fell forward into the mud, the din of battle rang loud in her ears again and before she could gauge how the defenders were faring, Fawn was forced to fight for her life again.

Kallum Campbell fell back as his opponent's axe split the air where his neck had just been and followed that attack up with a scything blow that nearly wrenched the sword from the man from Havensdale's grasp. Recovering from his fear and allowing his instincts and training to take over, Kallum stepped inside the reach of his attacker, burying his blade deep into an exposed armpit. Grunting, the large man, his long hair plastered to his face, drew back his head and thundered a defiant butt into Kallum's right cheek.

Kallum reeled back, his vision swirling as the chaotic dance of death continued to weave before him. As he fell to his knees Kallum saw Liyam Tallis deal his attacker a murderous blow that cut deep through his side and exited in a trail of thick crimson.

"Stand firm," Liyam shrieked, as another man came at him, opening up his defences to leave a cut in his right shoulder.

Blinking away his pain, Kallum rose up from his knees, growling angrily. Wiping the rain from his eyes with his free hand, he stepped into the breach, not even aware of the man dying underneath his feet.

Tania cursed, reaching quickly for another shaft as her previous effort was lost to the earth. At her side, Khadazin was trying to find an easy shot in the writhing chaos before him and his lack of experience with the crossbow was showing.

Looking about, Tania could see that the defenders were fighting bravely, the bellowing broil of battle punctuated far too occasionally by a scream or grunt of agony. One of Taryn Malak's men staggered back, clutching at his throat and Tania sent her shaft into the attacker that broke through their open ranks. As both men dropped to the sodden ground, quickly churning now under foot, she glanced back over the wagon, to see that behind them, the attackers were starting to gain advantage.

"Rellin," she hissed. The young woodsman followed her haunted eyes and nodding, they both sent arrows arching over the defenders towards the attackers stalking about, waiting for their chance to join the attack.

"We cannot keep this up for long," Khadazin growled, as he cranked the string back for a fifth time, his crossbow empty with failure again.

"We have to," Tania said, too calmly for one so young. In one fluid motion she sent another shaft over the back of the wagon. "If we lose now, we die."

Baring his gritted teeth, Khadazin threw his crossbow away and pulled his masonry hammer from the sash about his waist. Images of a time, many years ago now, flashed across his mind and leaping down from the wagon, he rushed to aid the defenders, Tania's curses chasing after him.

Bran and Bren Fal fought like a mirror, the two brothers fending off each other's attackers with timely blocks, or saving ripostes that, so far, had kept them both alive. Beside them, Janth and Liehella also stood firm, their Carwellian comrades fighting madly, their cries and defiant screams repelling their attackers each time they came for them.

Stabbing a look along their ragged line, Bran could see that all of them had suffered, however. Liehella, though she seemed not to notice, had a deep cut in her right cheek, the blood running freely down her pale face and neck. Janth's left arm was hanging limply by his side, though the sabre he gripped in his right, still flicked out effortlessly, as he fought off a thin-faced, balding warrior, dressed in heavy ring mail, who wielded a Valian Broadsword with an ease that suggested at his skill.

Sensing the danger also, Bren went to Janth's aid and his brother was thankful that the injured Tristan Farn had not ridden with them, despite his protests after wrenching his shoulder whilst helping to dig the defensive ditches around Havensdale.

As another attacker rushed at him, Bran's momentary relief was swept away by the madness again.

For a while longer, the stoic defenders held firm, though they had paid heavily for their bravery. On the west flank, several of the enemy suddenly broke through and rushed towards the wagon. Realising the danger, Tania and Rellin dropped two men with telling shafts and watched on forlornly, helplessly, as Khadazin rushed to meet them.

"Are you trying to get me killed, Redani?" Cullen snarled, appearing at the stonemason's side as a man came at him. The short man stepped in front of his charge.

A shout suddenly went up from the enemy's ranks.

"The Redani is here! Claim your reward!"

Though his chest was tight with fear, Khadazin's masonry hammer felt light and comforting in his hand. Horrified, he watched as Cullen stepped by his opponent's hesitant lunge and grabbed the offered wrist. Pulling the attacker in close, Cullen buried his dagger into the side of the man's neck and dragged it brutally around his throat. Wrenching his blade free, he threw the dying man aside, ignoring the blood spraying across his face.

Turning from the body, Cullen tripped a man who was racing for the Redani, allowing Khadazin to drive his hammer deep into the man's skull. Recoiling from the wet, crunching sound, the Redani stepped away, watching as Cullen leapt upon another man, punching him in the face and stabbing the warrior rapidly in the stomach.

Horrified at the brutality, Khadazin stepped back towards the wagon, memories of his revenge upon the torturer Borin resurfacing to haunt him and underline his own harboured guilt.

Taryn Malak's voice cut across the clashes of steel and dull drum of blade upon shield.

"Close ranks," he roared and the defenders instinctively tightened their protective circle.

Cullen stepped back alongside the Redani, his face spattered with mud, his beard dripping with blood.

"Stay close, Redani," he grinned, wiping his bloodied dagger on the stonemason's sleeve. "Father's balls, but we might yet survive this."

Falling back beyond the horses to form a tight defensive ring about the wagon, Liyam Tallis fought for a breath, his heaving chest on fire, his hands and face covered in the blood of whom he was still not sure. Looking about, he could see that Kallum had been separated from him now and he offered a comforting smile to the blonde female who stood wearily at his side.

"Are you alright, lady?" he asked her, flicking a wary eye to the enemy, regrouping beyond the tethered horses.

Liehella bobbed her head, fighting to stay upright. Looking down, Liyam could see that she had a deep cut in her left side and her shaking hand, clamped tightly over the ragged wound, did little to stem the flow of blood.

"Stay by me," Liyam said, reaching out to place a comforting hand on her shoulder. She dealt him a weary, almost vacant look, but somehow found a smile. She was about to say something when the attackers roared their battle cry and charged amongst the horses, cutting through the mounts, who screamed and kicked madly as they fell beneath their blades.

"Bastards!" Bren Fal screamed, away to Liyam's right. Raising her blade feebly, Liehella watched helplessly as the enemy cut down her own mount and came for them once more.

Arrun Hawksblade reined in his horse, dragging the hood from his sodden head. His eyes widened as he surveyed the battle taking place before him and he sent a startled look across his saddle towards Jessica, who rode beside him.

"We are too late," Arrun panicked.

Shaking her head, her face bared to the soothing rain, the Reven girl dealt him a withering look.

"Well sitting here is not going to save him, is it?" she said, not trying to hide her disgust.

Arrun glowered at her. By the Lady, she was the most annoying, though, at the same time, quite stunningly beautiful creature he had ever met. She had accosted him as he was about to ride out of Havensdale and had insisted she came along. Trusting his word that Rellin was in mortal danger, and that he knew where the Ashcroft Estate was (as his family had dined their two summers ago), Jessica had deserted her post and rode westwards with him.

Nodding his head, Arrun gripped his reins and kicked his heels urgently into his mount's broad flanks.

Aren Bray let out a euphoric roar as he heard the shouts go up that the Redani was here. *The Redani*?

He couldn't believe his luck. Surely the Father of Storms had blessed him. From where he watched the battle, he could see that the defenders were vastly outnumbered and that their strength was waning. Gardan would give him anything he wanted if he killed the high duke's family *and* brought back the Redani's head.

Scanning the lines, Aren's eyes fell upon the hooded swordsman who fought like a Reven devil. He watched on as the man's blade impaled one of his men, then spun the man about to hurl him away into another attacker. It was then, as the warrior saluted his fallen adversary, that Aren realised who he was... the mysterious swordsman from the bridge in Havensdale!

As Aren's mind began to reel at the implications, his eyes fell upon the woman, fighting alongside the bald-headed warrior who was rallying the defenders.

"By the storms," Aren chuckled, as he realised that Fawn Ardent was also here. Havensdale was indeed stirring with rebellion. Grinning, he strode through the storm towards her, his sword cutting through the curtain of rain in twirling, confident arcs.

With Taryn Malak defending their line away to her right, Fawn watched in horror as the man who had been fighting bravely to her left was cut down. Listening reluctantly to his fading screams of agony, she slashed her blade across the side of his killer's head, splitting the helm and skull beneath. Fawn recoiled instinctively as a thrown spear glanced off her shoulder and punched through the space where she had been standing. Wiping the bloody rain from her face, she fought against the heavy weariness in her arms and, for the first time, realised that their enemy's superior numbers were starting to take their toll. Bodies filled the voids in their defences now and during a brief lull in the fighting, Fawn watched with a sense of confused detachment as one of the attackers from Karick crawled away through the mud, his blood trailing behind him, his entrails dragged along in the wake of his desperate, futile attempt at escape.

Disgusted at what Valian was inflicting upon Valian, Fawn looked down at her shaking hands, her sword and gloves thick with blood. A scream rose up, filling the dark skies and as the ring of battle was joined again Fawn heard the telling dullness of steel striking flesh away to her left, framed by pleading cries of agony.

Fawn turned to watch the woodsman, transfixed, as he fought his way through two men who came at him, dealing out death and signing their warrants with a fatal cut here and a mortal blow there. Saluting his fallen opponents, the woodsman stepped back into the thinning line and sent a hurried look about him, his eyes widening as he found Fawn amidst the chaos.

"Watch out," he cried. Fawn snapped from her trance and turned to face the large warrior who stalked confidently towards her.

"The day gets better," Aren Bray grinned as he strode towards his prey.

"I think not," Taryn Malak said calmly as he appeared, stepping gallantly in front of Fawn Ardent.

Ignoring her protests, Taryn strode forward, hefting his shield high, his blade resting on top of it. As the two warriors came together, Fawn watched as Taryn caught a sweeping cut on his shield, then missed with his counter as the large attacker spun by him to plant a kick to the back of his left knee.

Before she could leap forward to distract Gardan's man, he plunged his curved blade deep between Taryn Malak's shoulder blades, twisting the steel triumphantly.

Screaming, Fawn hurled herself at Aren and sent a rising cut towards his head, which he easily ducked under. As they parted, Aren stole the momentum from her with a furious punch to her stomach that left Fawn down on her knees in the mud.

Spitting his disgust at her he turned away to put a muddied boot into the depths of Taryn Malak's back. Ripping his blade from the dying man, Aren turned to Fawn, raising his bloodied sword above his head.

"Gardan will give me Havensdale, when I bring him your head as well."

A feathered shaft appeared in his chest as Fawn looked up defiantly. Confusion spread across the man's face and as he roared, Fawn rose, slashing her blade up between his parted legs.

With her breath lost, Fawn turned away from the

screaming man, as he fell to his knees and stared at the warm pool of blood, spreading rapidly in the mud beneath him.

Looking to the wagon, Fawn spied the beautiful young archer as she nodded her head in her direction and reached for another shaft. Finding her lost breath, Fawn raised a trembling hand in thanks, her relief freezing in her throat as a warrior jumped up onto the wagon beside her, brandishing a long blade.

"No!" Fawn screamed. Tania recoiled as the man's sword cut through her right arm and sent her tumbling into Rellin, who was knocked from the wagon.

Turning from the man he had just killed, the woodsman heard Fawn's scream. Following her eyes, he saw the warrior wound the young huntress. Cursing anyone who was listening, he took two paces through the mud, reversed his blade and hurled it though the air, watching as it tumbled through the rain, pommel over point.

The enemy warrior lashed out at the girl as she fell backwards. Wrenching his steel from where it was buried deep in the driver's seat, he stepped forward to finish the archer, catching the woodsman's sword deep in his chest.

As the man stared down, Rellin rose up from the ground, turned and sent a muddied shaft through the man's right eye.

Tania rolled onto her front, looking towards the woodsman as he hurried to reclaim his sword. Nodding her thanks, she turned to Rellin as he stared open-mouthed at the man he had killed, his face covered in thick mud.

"Good shot," Tania gasped, her teeth clamped tight with pain. She pushed herself up onto her good hand and then both knees, with a shaking arm.

Rellin closed his mouth whilst he searched for his words. Reaching down with a shaking hand, he picked up

Tania's fallen bow and handed it to her.

"I was aiming for his chest," he blurted.

Ignoring Lucien Varl's warning, Lady Strom parted the canvas curtain at the rear of the wagon, staring out through the rain at the carnage beyond. Covering her mouth to stifle her disgust, she watched as the remnants of the brave defenders finished off the last of the attackers who still came at them from the north.

Grunting, Lucien dragged himself to her side and looked out, shaking his head sadly as one of the Carwellian riders stepped over the writhing horses that had been hacked down, ending their misery with swift, merciful cuts to their throats.

Behind the wagon to the south and east, the fighting still continued, though the raging din was settling down now to a weary, reluctant trill.

"Are we winning, mother?" Tobias Stromn asked, his young, educated accent somehow out of place amongst the brutality of the late, bloody afternoon.

Lady Stromn put her sword down beside her and nodded.

"I think we are safe, my love," she said, her eyes bright and full of tears as she took his trembling hands in her own, "for now, at least."

Two men raced through the dead and dying, screaming as they charged towards the wagon. Before Rellin could react, the woodsman stole the blade from the scabbard at his side and rushed to intercept them. Slipping one of the two remaining arrows from his quiver, the young archer stepped over a dying man and tried to get a good line of sight on one of the woodsman's opponents. As he drew back on his bowstring, he heard someone rushing up behind him and spinning he sent the nocked shaft at the man who came for him.

The arrow went wide of its mark and as the man swung his broad axe at him, Rellin panicked, throwing himself back. Reaching down for the knife concealed in his boot, Rellin sprang up to meet his attacker, watching in astonishment as his opponent staggered forward, a sliver of steel punching from his chest. Gasping for breath, the man dropped his axe and stumbled to his knees as another blade cleaved into his back.

"There you are," Arrun Hawksblade scolded him, his voice full of his own revulsion as the man he had just killed pitched forward into the mud between them.

Jessica stepped up alongside the young swordsman and, despite the carnage about them, dealt Rellin a rare smile.

"And you don't believe in prophecies," she scoffed, her smile slipping from her features deep into her disdain.

Two attackers stepped back from the last remnants of the defenders and threw their blades down. One of them, an aging warrior with a face scarred as testament, held up his bloodied hands.

"I know when we are beat," he said, his gravelly voice breaking across his shame. "We offer ourselves into your care."

Lowering his blade, the woodsman stepped towards him and was about to say something when a cry rose up from the north. All heads turned as two riders from Karick thundered away through the failing light towards the south, thick clods of earth throwing up into the rain to guard their escape.

"Tania?" the woodsman roared. Sweeping his cloak back over his shoulder he waved Fawn and Bren to apprehend the prisoners. If the riders escaped, got back to Karick with news of their failure...

The young huntress ran forward and it was then that the woodsman saw the extent of her injury. Cursing, Evan grabbed the bow and her final arrow from her. Fitting the shaft to the string, he drew back on the bow and sent the arrow on its way, watching as it arched through the gloom and plucked one of the fleeing riders from her saddle.

Looking about, the woodsman found Rellin. The young man ran obediently to his side, looking down at the last shaft in his quiver. He looked up with wild, pleading eyes.

"I–I can't," he began, flicking his fear to the south.

Resisting the urge to take the arrow from him and make the impossible shot himself, the woodsman clamped a hand on Rellin's shoulder

"You can do this, lad," the woodsman said softly, as he stepped away.

You have to! He waved Fawn towards the enemy's horses, just in case he could not.

Nocking the arrow, Rellin turned, staring through the rain at the retreating rider. One arrow, one shot, one chance.

Letting out a slow, steadying breath, the young archer drew back on the bow string. Nestling the feathered shaft under his chin he raised the heavy bow and sent the shaft on its way.

CHAPTER THIRTY NINE

The Man who Would be King

Scarlet Moore leant against the lantern post, staring out across the lands to the south of Havensdale. With the crops finally harvested, the land looked lonely and barren, scarred only by the empty road and river that chased each other away towards the south.

Havensdale had changed beyond recognition and the recruit sighed, allowing the stiffening breeze to distract her, as it playfully tugged and tousled her loose hair. Sighing, Scarlet ignored the cramp setting deep into her lame leg and sent a look along the wall away to her right, her lovely features creasing with sadness as she found Sara Campbell.

The grieving girl had volunteered for any watch that was available, had even turned up for those that were not. Since the departure of her brother Kallum, Sara had watched the empty horizon to the west each day, until the light had failed and she could see no more. Searching for signs of her brother and for those who had volunteered to go, the young Campbell had to, on one occasion, be dragged screaming and sobbing from the west gate by

Sergeant Manse.

Swallowing down her sorrow, Scarlet looked away. She had tried to offer comfort to Sara, but with her brother, Rellin and as it transpired, now Arrun and Jessica also in danger, the grieving girl's worry was too great for her to be able to find any fleeting moments of joy and happiness.

Banishing her own dark thoughts and fears, Scarlet consoled herself with the sight of the breathtaking sky to the south-west. The clouds scattered across the low sun were edged by gold and blushing with a myriad of red and purple hues. It was an autumnal sky, for certain, one that heralded the last throes of summer, though there were, in truth, still a dozen more rallying days left.

"A summer to forget," Scarlet sighed, though she knew Havensdale never would. Lost to her thoughts, she watched as the dark shapes of several crows chased the last embers of the day westwards.

The sound of approaching riders dragged her attention to the east, tugging at her heartstrings as she leant over the palisade for a better look. Staring through the fading light, she counted six horsemen approaching along the shadowy line of the Moon Glade Forest towards her, the first falling leaves swirling about them in the breeze. Looking to the other sentries on duty, she roughly drew them from their own thoughts.

"Six riders coming in!" she hissed, watching as one of them, Aden, was it, hurried off to raise the watch officer.

As the riders steadily approached, Scarlet felt her fears begin to rise. The defences were in place now, but the ghosts of the attack on the town still haunted all who had been at home that terrible, bloody morning.

When she saw the handsome, haggard face of Elion Leigh look up at her and smile, however, Scarlet let out a long, deep breath and hurried to open the gates.

Chancellor Relan Valus walked slowly through the double doors that led into the Old Royal Chambers, his breath lost in his dry, constricting throat. With his pulse itching he walked forward on legs he could not feel, his sandals scraping over the marble flagstones, his robes offering little respite to the anticipation and fear fighting for dominance in his thin body.

Relan started as the sentries brusquely closed the doors behind him, the sound bounding gleefully about his majestic surroundings. Uncaring of its familiar beauty, he followed the fading echoes towards the council table, licking the nerves from his lips as he saw the seated figures rise up to greet him.

The last light of the day spilled through the Great East window, falling upon those waiting for him. Large tallow candles in tall, iron pillared holders chased the deepening gloom away, their still flames rigid and somehow comforting. The chancellor felt his legs work, even if the rest of his body was failing him.

As he stumbled up the steps to approach the council table, the man sat in the high duke's chair rose up, spreading his arms wide in greeting. The Kestrel stood behind the chair, to the left, her arms folded across her breast, her cold eyes watching him intently.

"Brother, you are most welcome," the tall man said. Around the table, Relan could see the familiar faces of Lady Rothley, Renald Gardan and, to his surprise, Baron Crowood. They all acknowledged him with warm smiles and the chancellor found their welcome unnerving.

"I have long dreamt of this moment, my lord," Relan said, offering the tall man a calm smile. Inside, it felt as if his heart was about to fail and to underline his discomfort, his stomach forced his nerves towards his bowels.

"As have we all, my friend," Henry Carwell smiled, his handsome features filling with glee.

Relan studied the man, his master, with fresh eyes. He had not seen Henry Carwell for nearly three summers, since his last visit to the capital to attend the annual games. They had met in secret, before he had departed, carefully formulating the Brotherhood's plans for the long game ahead.

The years had been kinder to the lord of the East Vales.

Clad in elegantly stitched riding leathers, Henry Carwell clasped his large hands together, the gold stitching in his leather vambraces glowing in the failing light. An imposing presence, Henry Carwell always dominated a room, his strong features framed by his square, bearded jaw line and his piercing, captivating blue eyes always held your attention, whether he was looking at you or not. His short dark hair was free of grey, impossibly so for one nearing his sixtieth winter and his wide, hawked nose often channelled his scrutiny towards you, long before his crisp, resonant voice gripped you in its thrall.

This was the man who was meant to lead the Valian people, Relan thought, feeling his excitement rise. This was the man who would lead them to glories, well beyond the dreams of those who grew fat on the prosperous, yet insipid ambitions of Karian Stromn.

"Forgive the lateness of my arrival, lord," Relan said, falling onto one knee. He bowed his head respectfully, calming his wild heart with shallow, slow breaths. "I was at my estate, tending to my affairs, the messenger–,"

"Get up man," Carwell growled, cutting through his apology. He watched the chancellor rise up stiffly, studying the thin man wasting away before him.

"I have only arrived recently and thought it prudent to gather you all together for our first council meeting," Henry Carwell continued, sweeping his eyes about those gathered at the table. "We have much to discuss and even more to plan."

Lady Rothley inclined her head, smiling. "Indeed we do, Henry. It has been a trying time, but ultimately, a successful one. I think that whilst we have the momentum we should strike fast and hard, sweeping aside those who might dare to stand against us."

"And that is what we shall continue to do, Lady Rothley, have no fear of that!" Scowling, Henry Carwell lowered his hands, forcing them to sit back down. He remained standing, turning his head slightly, as he flicked his attention towards the Kestrel and directed her to take a seat beside Renald Gardan, the seat once filled by Lord Farrington.

Not hiding her delight, the Kestrel slipped slowly around the table, stabbing her glee towards the chancellor, who watched her with eyes narrowed with envy. She collapsed into the high-backed chair with a grateful, thankful sigh.

"Finally," she purred. The Kestrel licked her lips as she dined slowly on her rising pleasure.

Relan Valus, failing to hide his dismay, looked towards his master, his eyes wide with confusion, brimming with distress.

Henry Carwell smiled, his eyes glittering. As he sat down, he waved a hand across the Four Vales, to Alion Byron's vacant seat.

"Come join us, my brother," the lord of the Brotherhood ordered.

Before he realised it, Relan Valus was sat across from his master, his thin hands spreading lovingly out over the beautifully carved wood, tracing the length of the Great Divide with a shaking finger.

When the chancellor finally looked up from his reverie and smiled, those gathered at the table began to applaud heartily.

Fawn Ardent stifled a yawn, staring blankly into the flames of the writhing fire. It was late now, deep into the night, but the clearing skies overhead breathed a crisp sigh, filling the darkness with hopeful stars.

They had travelled hard following the battle, as far and as long as their waning strength would allow them. Leaving the dead to the storm and hungry crows gathering above them, the survivors pressed on, taking the empty mounts of their enemy with them.

Shuddering at the thought of those they had lost, the captain drew her knees up under her chin and hugged herself tightly. Listening to the angry spit of the fire, the hushed, sporadic chatter and distant, rumbling snores of Cullen, Fawn closed her eyes and shook her head sadly.

The shot Rellin had made had been impossible, but somehow, much to their relief and the young archer's revulsion, the shaft had found its mark. Slowing both rider and confused mount, those who watched on through the rain held their breaths, thinking that the escaping rider might carry on. But finally, as the silence lengthened agonisingly, the man slipped slowly from his saddle and lay still.

Biting her lip, Fawn banished the thoughts of the woodsman, walking away from her through the storm, his sword hanging at his side as he went to make sure they were both dead.

A sudden movement startled Fawn and she clutched at her shock as the woodsman approached her, his face hidden beneath his hood as he raised a hand in apology.

Nodding her acceptance, Fawn beckoned for him to join her and for a long while they sat in silence. Eventually, stirred by cramp, Fawn turned her eyes towards her companion, searching his face, wreathed in shadows and dancing flame.

"We have paid a heavy price," she said softly, idly flicking the settled ash from her boots.

The woodsman nodded his head. "But one we had to pay," he replied quietly, turning his head towards the wagon and the campfire beside it.

Lady Stromn sat before the flames, talking quietly to Lucien Varl. Her son, Tobias, was sleeping, his head cradled on her lap.

Fawn followed his lingering gaze and swallowed nervously. Despite her threats, Lady Stromn had not followed them through yet and had the woodsman arrested. Stoically avoiding him, she had given up their wagon so that the dying woman, Liehella, could spend her last few hours in this life in what little comfort they could afford her.

Shaking his head, the woodsman looked back, holding Fawn's attention with a calm, yet unreadable gaze.

"Must I fear you, woodsman?" Fawn asked before she could stop herself.

She saw the corners of his eyes crease with anger, but he calmed himself quickly and picked a long blade of grass, turning it thoughtfully through thumb and forefinger.

He finally shook his head. "You have nothing to fear from me, Fawn Ardent, nobody here does."

Fawn frowned, looking carefully about as she spoke, "But what of Lady Stromn's threats?"

The woodsman heaved a long deep breath and held it close before sending it away with a resigned sigh. He picked the blade of grass apart slowly, losing his thoughts to the flames again.

"I was in love once," he began, his voice wistful and strained. "It was the love that only those who have found it could ever truly understand, a bond that went beyond the physical, beyond any rational, palpable understanding.

I was a man of some worth back then, a gentleman of note, as some would call me. It was because of this, of my family name, that I met Karleth, the love of my life, the daughter of Lord Ashcroft. It was because of this that my life would ultimately be destroyed."

As the woodman's voice faltered, Fawn edged closer to him. "Please, you do not have to–"

The woodsman looked up, his tears burning in his eyes. "I want to, I have to!"

Fawn nodded, watching as he fought against his inner turmoil and gathered his waning composure.

"Twelve summers ago, I was captain of the high duke's guard, commander of his city's militia. I had my life before me, I was happy and my family's name was prospering. It would be, however, the dark, twisted taint of envy that would shatter all I was and all that I would come to have. In the end, it was my brother who would destroy me."

Fawn gasped, covering her shock with a swift hand. "Your brother?" she asked, her eyes widening.

The woodsman almost smiled. "Our family was once close with the Ashcrofts', close enough that my brother mistook Karleth's kindness and friendship as more than all it was. When Karleth and I finally admitted our love for one another, my brother's rage, his jealousy and anger at my apparent *betrayal*, poisoned his mind. Seething at Karleth's rejection, of my success and possible union to a rich, powerful family, my brother did all he could to besmirch my good name."

"You are certain of this?" Fawn flushed at her question as it slipped from her lips.

The woodsman nodded. "I am! He confronted me one day in the high duke's gardens, the first time he had spoken to me in months. We fought then and he came at me with a knife. I struck back, telling him to '*sheathe his anger*' as I disarmed him. I–I do not know why I am telling you this, Fawn, but please, I need to – let me finish." He headed off the questions flashing in her haunted, lovely eyes and waited for Fawn to nod, before continuing.

"I told my brother that I loved him, that he was everything to me. I pleaded with him to stop his madness, admitting that we had never meant to hurt him, of how Karleth and I had loved each other for many years, but had never found the courage to share our feelings. He spat at me then, clawing at my face. As he hurried away, I can still remember his words to this day. They haunt me still because I did not heed them… I should have done something, but I still believed he would see reason. 'I despise you,' he shrieked at me. 'And know this, *brother*, I will have what I desire, you will not stop me.'"

Fawn reached out, taking the woodsman's trembling hands in her own. She could not hold back her emotions any longer and she spoke through her tears as her mind began to slowly prick from a distant memory.

"I am so sorry," Fawn whispered, as her realisation began to claw at her.

The woodsman looked down at her hands, drawing the strength he needed from her. He looked up, saw the sorrow haunting her eyes and nodded his head.

"When Karleth… was found murdered on the thirty-second day of spring, just two days before we were to wed, I was arrested, my bloodied sword found beside her body. Without alibi, or proof of what I guessed to be, that my brother had finally made his move against me, I was dragged before the Chief Justicar–," he paused, snorting at the irony, "Lord Ashcroft, and sentenced to death. The scandal of the murder tore the city apart, the political divide it caused on both sides of the table irreparable. With help I escaped and much coin changed hands to make it look as if I had been killed in the attempt."

Fawn followed the woodsman's eyes, as he sent a guarded look towards Cullen. The man no longer slumbered and was sat with his back to a tree, watching them with glittering eyes, as he drank deeply from a wineskin.

"That man has a hold on you," Fawn observed, drawing the woodsman's face back to her. Seeing her tears, he reached up with a hand and gently brushed them from her cheeks.

"No longer," the woodsman whispered. His breath was suddenly heavy. "My name is Evan, Fawn Ardent. My family name is known to many, as is my brother. His name is-,"

"Relan Valus?" Fawn whispered reluctantly, silencing the admission on his lips. His eyes blazed as he nodded his head subtly.

Despite her shock, Fawn said, "What will you do?"

For a time Evan was silent, his eyes closed as he took Fawn's hands and held them tightly.

Finally, he pulled away. Reaching out, he threw some sticks onto the respectful fire.

"I will protect the high duke's family, though they might not want me to and we will find a way to rescue Karian Stromn. We will stop this Brotherhood, before it is too late."

Is that all? Fawn thought, quickly swallowing her rising guilt. "And what of your brother?" she dared to ask.

With fresh shadows and flame alive in his features, the former captain of Highwater held her gaze.

"Despite never having my body as proof and with nothing to suggest otherwise, the chancellor will have come to believe the lies that I am dead." The woodsman paused, gathering his composure. "I will find the man I once knew to be my brother, I will find him and drag him to the justice he deserves – not for myself, but for Karleth. I owe her that much, at the very least."

Unable to control his emotions, the woodsman looked down into his shame, his shoulders heaving with freshly raked grief.

"You are a brave man, Evan Valus," Fawn whispered, gripping his hands.

Looking up through his sorrow, the woodsman raised her blistered, bruised hands gently to his lips, kissing the fingertips tenderly.

"I am a coward, lady," he smiled sadly, "but I still thank you for it."

CHAPTER FORTY

The Weakest Hand

Devlin Hawke sat back in the chair with a satisfied groan. Reaching for the tankard on the table before him, he flicked a look at the barkeep, who was still eying him suspiciously. Raising his drink, the outlaw drained the ale in one pull, smacking his lips theatrically. The proprietor looked away and Devlin chuckled, shaking his head.

Elion Leigh's return to Havensdale with the leader offering the services of a band of brave men and women who were willing to aid them, had caused quite a stir. Guarding Devlin's identity to all but the mayor of the town, Elion had managed to convince Dekan Ardent that Havensdale had enough problems without word getting out that the most wanted man in the Four Vales resided there, also.

The news they had brought with them of the terrible atrocities taking place in Carwell, of the army being unlawfully marshalled there, soon diverted the mayor's thoughts.

"How are we to contend with the might of Karick and Carwell?" Dekan Ardent had asked them forlornly.

Devlin had been about to say something pithy, but Elion had silenced him with a sharp look.

Dekan Ardent's news quickly changed things, also. His report that the fugitive Redani was now allied to them, that Chancellor Valus had captured and tortured the high duke's captain, Lucien Varl to find out the location of the high duke's family, had even silenced Devlin Hawke for a time. When they were told of the rescue attempt, of those who had gone to prevent further murder, Elion Leigh paled visibly, his concern for his comrades flashing through his wide eyes.

Seeing his friend's distress, Devlin had imparted further troubling news. During the first light of the morning, on the day they were to leave Greywood Forest, Devlin's scouts had witnessed a large force of Carwellian soldiers, near to three hundred swords, moving south towards the distant shadows of the Sunset Hills.

"So Carwell has indeed started," Dekan Ardent had whispered, unable to control the fear in his voice.

Elion had nodded. "He has, my friend. He may already be in the capital. We cannot be certain..."

Devlin grunted, drumming his fingers across the worn wood of the table at which he sat. There was too much uncertainty to make any decisive plans yet. From the outside, to Devlin, it seemed that the rebellion stirring here had many of the pieces they needed to win this game, but not the strength, or determination to achieve it. They had the Redani, who was competing for his crown as the most wanted man in the Four Vales and who, apparently, could testify against the high duke's chancellor, bear witness of his duplicity and treachery. They also had another witness, who had seen Renald Gardan murder, had heard him divulge that it was Valian insurgency, not Reven, behind the attack on Eastbury and then later, the unwarranted assault on Havensdale. They even had Lucien Varl, who had been tortured by the chancellor and the mysterious woman with the scar on her face. Was this also the woman, marked as the assassin of Alion Byron? If it was, then the lord of Highwater's blood was also staining Relan Valus' hands.

Devlin was convinced that they had enough firm evidence now and that, had the high duke been in control in Karick, they could take it and their witnesses before the council to try to stop the coming march on the Reven lands. But their enemies, this Brotherhood and their allies had moved far swifter than they had anticipated and it would be almost impossible to find a peaceful way of averting civil war.

Distracting his settling melancholy, Devlin Hawke caught the barkeep's attention, waving his empty tankard at him. Nodding his accord, the man hurried to pour him another *Campbell's Own* – a local ale that Devlin quite enjoyed, though it did not have the rough honesty of his beloved *Notorious*. As Joseph Moore rushed over to him, Devlin noticed Elion slip through the doors to the inn. His face was ashen, his eyes reddened by his sorrow.

"You had better make that two," Devlin sighed, shaking his head sadly.

Khadazin headed away from the temple, his footfalls heavy, his heart aching. The young rider Liehella had made it back to Havensdale, had survived their journey only to die as the priest tended to her wounds. Leaving Elion and his comrades to their grief, the Redani spent some time with Tania, who was recovering in a tiny antechamber, her arm cleansed and freshly bandaged. When the young woman slipped away into a deep sleep, Khadazin left her side, in need of some air. He was troubled deeply by the silence of the temple and unnerved by the beautiful workmanship of the masons that had built it.

The former mason was heading over to the well in the

centre of the tent-filled market square, when the young rider from Carwell, Liyam Tallis, came hurrying over to him.

"Redani," he panted, catching his breath. "There is a messenger at the gate for you."

Khadazin frowned, shielding his hand against the bright sun, high in his eyes. His heart began to stir as the warm morning air suddenly cooled. "For me?"

"We think so," Liyam said, looking back towards the ramparts of the South Gate. "He doesn't appear to be able to speak... a funny messenger to send if you ask me – but he pulled his left sleeve down to, ahem, to indicate a..."

Khadazin gripped the flustered man by the shoulder and flashed him a relived grin. "It is okay! I think I know him. Let him in, but keep him at the gate. I need to find my friend. We will meet you back there."

Khadazin watched as Liyam hurried away. Listening to his heart, he gathered his composure for a moment then went to find Cullen.

Cullen was in a foul mood by the time Khadazin found him and managed to drag him away from the ale he was nursing on the porch outside the Arms of the Lady. As they approached the south gate, Khadazin glimpsed Riyan and raised a hand in his direction.

The mute observed their approach, flicking a friendly smile towards the Redani, studiously avoiding the cantankerous look on Cullen's face.

Brushing the dust from his leathers, Riyan came forward under the watchful eyes of the guards, clasping Khadazin's outstretched hand gratefully.

"It is good to see you, my friend," the Redani said, smiling.

Riyan nodded his head vigorously, then, releasing Khadazin's hand, turned his attention to Cullen.

They shared brief hand signals and Khadazin,

watching for any tell of what was being said, saw the frown on Cullen's face as Riyan produced a scroll case. Snatching the case away, Cullen looked about at the guards who were wandering away, checking that nobody else was looking on too closely.

"What is it?" Khadazin asked.

"It's from the boss," Cullen said quietly, as he untied the leather laces and opened up the case. There were two scrolls inside, both sealed by black wax and stamped with the effigy of a wolf's head.

Cullen eyed the name elegantly written upon one of them and grunted.

"This one's for me," Cullen began and Riyan nodded. "The other one has no name..."

Riyan met Khadazin's quizzical gaze and offered him a sad, knowing smile.

Cullen handed the nameless scroll and case back to Riyan, then hurriedly broke the other seal, rolling it out to read the message penned for him. As he read, Khadazin saw Cullen stiffen, then look up to find Riyan, who nodded his head slowly in affirmation.

When Cullen spoke, his voice was choked and Khadazin was certain he detected a tear in the man's good eye.

"The capital is in chaos, Redani," Cullen whispered, faltering, "and Dia... is dead."

"*Dead*?" Khadazin gasped. "How?"

Cullen ignored him, returning his attention to the message.

"The boss has instructed me to deliver the other scroll north, to Lady Byron. He mentions also that he has heard reports that Lord Farrington of the South Vales never returned home and is, along with his men, suspected dead. He suggests that, should Lucien Varl have succeeded, I also take Lady Stromn and her son with me to Highwater, as it is the only place now where she will be safe. Taxes have been raised in Karick, to fund the gathering army that will help solve the *Reven Problem.* He writes that hangings in the squares of the capital are commonplace... that many Reven traitors, men, women and children alike, have been sent to Durrant's Field, to work the mines there..." Cullen could not read on. He shook his head bitterly. "There is a message for you, Redani. He wishes you well and hopes that you find the peace you deserve. He finishes off by saying–,"

Cullen handed Khadazin the scroll, who read the last lines with a sense of rising dread and fear for his friend. The words did not register at first, so he read them again, whispering them aloud to settle his fears.

"I have few cards left to play, my friend. My hand is weak, but I will try one last trick."

It was signed *S.K*

Khadazin looked up at his companions. They stood there looking at each other, their concerns mirrored on their faces.

The town was very quiet as a nervous chill came upon them. Overhead the sun settled behind a cloud.

Relan Valus, the former chancellor of Karick, newly appointed member of the Brotherhood's Council, strode towards the council table in the Old Royal Chambers, his legs full of confidence this time, not apprehension and fear. Since Lord Carwell's arrival, word had quickly spread through the streets, whispers forming into cries of joy that there was fresh strength and determination in the capital, it seemed, to finally fight back against the Reven.

It was so easy to whip the mob up into a salivating frenzy of anticipation. They screamed their delight and cheered until their throats were raw as Reven prisoners were hung before them. Walking through the streets in the north of the city earlier that day with his bodyguards in close attendance, Relan was delighted he could taste the expectancy of the coming war in the air.

Lord Carwell was alone for once, sifting through despatches and keenly studying a parchment he held away from himself at arm's length. His advancing years reminded him that although his hunger for absolute power and control was still as sharp as the blade he carried, he was, much to his annoyance, not a young man any more.

As Relan approached, Lord Carwell sighed, laying the parchment aside.

"There are some things that even we cannot control," he said bitterly, motioning his guest to the seat beside him.

Relan accepted and sat in the offered chair. He had a pair of spectacles to assist him with his own failing eyesight, as many years of pouring over letters and accounts in poor candlelight had certainly taken their toll.

"I fear for the day when I will not be able to read," Relan said, his mind drifting away momentarily. When he returned, Henry Carwell was watching him curiously.

"You will be far too rich to worry about that," he chuckled after a time, his smile creasing his features, but the coldness in his eyes lacking the same warmth.

Relan smiled, covering the relish of that prospect as he politely cleared his throat. "You wanted to see me, lord?"

Carwell nodded his head. "I wanted to discuss recent events with you, without the others present," he paused long enough to allow the fear to reach the chancellor's eyes. "It troubles me that there are still pockets of defiance in the Four Vales, some threads that continue to elude our grasp."

"My lord, I-I can assure you that–," Relan blurted.

"Do not interrupt me again," Henry Carwell cut in, lowering his voice to a menacing hiss. He held the man in his glare, refusing to let him recoil. "The Kestrel, to her credit, has spoken in your defence and, as you well know, because of this, I have been patient enough to listen. She would be first in the line to cut your throat and her testimony has shown me what I always knew to be true, that, without you and your quick thinking, our plans would be far from realisation."

Relan found his breath, blinking in confusion, then hasty relief, as Lord Carwell's demeanour changed from one of foreboding and anger, to calm serenity. He reached out and clapped a heavy hand on Relan's shoulder.

"I am... relieved to hear you say that, my lord," Relan gasped.

Pulling his hand away, Henry Carwell sat back in his chair. Resting one elbow on the ornately carved arm, he stroked his thoughts through his beard.

"It was a masterful touch, my friend, to mark the Redani as a fellow conspirator to the Reven threat. He will not dare risk a testimony now and it is only a matter of time before we have him," Lord Carwell paused, raising his thoughts to the vaulted ceiling high above him. "After all, the people barely trust each other. They will never believe the word of an immigrant stonemason."

Relan nodded his accord. "If I may, my lord, might I suggest that you make a speech soon – something that will show the mob that there is now strength in the capital's leadership? That despite the increase in taxes, we only have their vested interests and welfare foremost in our hearts."

Lord Carwell smiled thinly. "A sound idea, Relan. It is no secret that I am here now and we must stamp our intent on all who would waver. I want our armies ready to march as soon as possible, before the first snows. By the dawn of winter, I want to be in Highwater."

Relan felt a stab of anxiety. He licked his lips nervously. "Lady Byron still defies us – we intercepted a letter from her a few weeks ago, bound to an unknown recipient in the city. It said only of her desire for information on how she could stop our march to war, how she would be grateful for any assistance from her ally, *again.* The courier died before he would tell us anything of interest, so we are still none the wiser."

Henry waved his hand dismissively. "She is a girl pricked by grief, nothing more. Her defiance and intent will count for nothing, once your letter has flushed her out into the open. What we should be more concerned about is what Gardan has set in motion, how he has stirred up rebellion in Havensdale."

"Havensdale and her allies will be swept aside, lord, once the army marches north. It cannot stand against us, despite her alliance with Highwater." Relan eagerly seized on the fact that the focus was now directed elsewhere.

"And what of Elion Leigh?" Henry Carwell asked quietly and Relan delighted in the underlying tone of regret that he detected there.

It was Relan's turn to wave a dismissive hand. "From what Renald has told me, he is a man who covets his honour. We have taken away that honour and destroyed his reputation. I suspect, although we must remain wary, that we should not fear him, my lord, no matter what evidence he and his allies may or may not have gathered against us."

Henry Carwell smiled, evidently satisfied. "So then, we must only wait for Gardan's men to return. Once Karian's family are dead and the news made public, we can send him to join them. The people will mourn their high duke and then, when their sorrow turns to anger, we shall have our war and, finally, the Reven will have an end to their pitiful existence."

Threading his hands together, Lord Carwell sat forward, resting his ambitions on the council table before him. Relan studied him for a moment, as he slipped away to visions of the riches that awaited them across the Great

Divide. Henry Carwell was a dangerous man, always one action away from madness and he could see it now, in his hard eyes, as he lost himself for a time.

With the North Vales standing alone now, Relan could not see how they could withstand the might of the rest of the Four Vales. Farrington was dead and the South Vales had sent swift word of their sudden desire to support. The West Vales, under the control of Lady Rothley, were ready to march, and Baron Crowood, now that his 'murdered' family had miraculously returned safely home, was eagerly back at her side. All the pieces were on the board, only Highwater and the Byron girl stood in their way.

The Valian navy, though small in comparison to the military might of the Four Vales, was already being deployed along the western coastline – ready to ship smaller numbers of forces north to attack the Reven lands from the sea. Had they another year, the Brotherhood could build a fleet capable of landing the entire army on the Reven shores, but Lord Carwell was an impatient man and did not want to delay. He did not want to give their enemies more time to dig in and raise their evidence against them.

'*Strike fast before the weight of uncertainty can stay your hand,*' Karian Stromn's father had said to his men all those years ago. The Valian armies had indeed done that, scattering Reven Skarl's clans before them. But, with the Reven lands open to them, the Valian might had turned homewards towards peace, ignoring the chance to claim what was there to be had.

There will be no second chances for the Reven race this time, Relan thought gleefully.

The large doors at the south end of the great hall opened wide as a guard came hurrying towards them. Both men looked up from their thoughts and Relan could see the annoyance staining Henry Carwell's features.

"My Lord Carwell," the man panted, his face pale, his ragged breath choking his words.

"What is it?" Henry growled, rising up.

The sentry flicked his eyes between the two men as he reached for his breath. "There is a man to see you, my lord."

"This had better be worth my time," Carwell growled to himself.

"He said you would want to see him, lord," the guard added hastily.

"Who is it?" Relan asked. Could it be Gardan's men? Had they finally returned to them with news and proof of their success?

When the guard answered, however, Relan's eyes widened and Henry Carwell's anger was lost to his evident surprise.

"It is Savinn Kassaar, my lord."

CHAPTER FORTY ONE

Never Say Goodbye

In the gathering light of a misty morning, Evan Valus made his way towards the small group of people gathered near to the carriage and horses, tethered outside the Arms of the Lady Inn.

Having spent a quiet night alone in the Moonglade Forest, much to his surprise, the woodsman found himself yearning for company. As he neared, he could hear the hiss of anger from Fawn's lips, could see her vented frustration billowing in the cool air before her. Her father stood before her, enduring his daughter's rebuke, whilst those gathered near turned away to hide their discomfort.

As the woodsman reached Elion Leigh and Khadazin's side, Dekan Ardent ushered his daughter up the steps and into the inn to continue their *conversation* in private.

The Redani nodded a solemn greeting and Elion Leigh stamped the cold from his booted feet.

"It seems the captain is still angry at our decision," Khadazin said regrettably. The woodsman nodded his head, his haggard features grey.

"It is for the best," the woodsman sighed, running a nervous hand through his beard. "Havensdale cannot stand against the might of Karick and Carwell – we must guard our cards well, if we are to play our final hand."

Elion eyed the woodsman, keenly aware that the news he and Devlin Hawke had brought with them had done little to settle his nerves. Following the blatant attempt to kill Lady Stromn and her son, it was clear that any hope for a political resolution to the problem they faced was no longer on the table.

Elion scowled. It had never been on the table, if the truth were to be told...

Before the Redani could say anything further, the woodsman gathered his cloak tight about his frame and wordlessly headed for the inn. Khadazin sent a look towards Elion.

"There is more to that man than I can tell," he said guardedly.

"Indeed there is," Elion replied softly, ignoring the itch of his own curiosity.

Dekan Ardent turned as the woodsman entered the inn and Fawn bit off whatever else she was about to say. Turning away from her father, she stalked across the empty taproom to stand before the cold hearth.

Shrugging, the mayor passed the woodsman, shaking his head sadly.

"Talk to her Evan," he said quietly. "Make her see the sense."

The woodsman gripped his friend's shoulder and nodded. When Fawn's father was gone, he turned from the closed door and crossed to join Fawn at the hearth.

Clad in travelling leathers and a long jade cloak, her lean frame was shaking with fury and she passed her annoyance from foot to foot.

"My lady?" Evan asked, as he studied her pale features. The cut on her cheek had healed well since the attack on Havensdale and he lost himself in her face for a time, seeing the ghostly flames of the empty hearth alive in her anger.

Fawn threw him an irritated look, then turned her head away. Her dark, loose tresses writhed.

"I cannot believe he is sending me away," she snapped, pacing away, unable to meet the woodsman's gaze. "I should be here, with my people. I must protect them. It is my duty to do so, the very least I can do after what has happened to them."

The woodsman remained silent for a time, letting Fawn find a calm breath. When she stopped pacing for a moment, he moved towards her.

"Normally, after what has happened to this town, I would agree with you, Fawn," he began hesitantly. "But you should not let your guilt cloud your judgement. Havensdale cannot stand. It will not stand once Carwell marches north. You must safeguard the high duke's family and, even more importantly than that, you must go to Cassana. She will need people she can trust around her for what is to come. She will need *you*, Fawn. You have a strong bond, one that will see you both through this madness together. If you decide to go, as I believe you must, tell Lady Byron for me that '*she was right*'."

Ignoring the look she gave him, the woodsman reached out a hand to gently touch Fawn's shoulder. She stiffened, but did not pull away.

Evan watched her for a time, listened as her ragged breath came and went as she fought with her emotions. When Fawn eventually turned, there were tears brimming in her eyes.

"But what if I don't want to leave?" she asked. "What if I want to stay here with them... with you?"

She blinked, her tears spilling down one cheek. With

his breath lost in his throat, the woodsman reached out and brushed them away.

"For a time our paths must lead us in different directions, Fawn," Evan whispered and he could hear the regret lacing his words. "But when all this over, if I am able to, I will come to you, if you would like?"

Fawn held his softening gaze, her bright eyes flicking about his features.

"I should like that very much, Evan Valus," she replied, leaning in close to kiss him on one cheek.

Khadazin could feel Tania tense as Cullen came towards them. Behind him, the final preparations were being made as the woodsman helped Lucien Varl towards the carriage that would bear the captain of Karick and his charges north, towards the sanctuary of Highwater.

Cullen offered them a smile as he stopped before them, though it did little to improve the warmth of his countenance.

"Well, I guess this is it then, Redani," Cullen said, fighting for a breath as much as his words.

He reached out with his right hand and took Khadazin in a firm handshake.

"Luck to you, stonemason," he said, nodding his head once.

Khadazin grinned. "Safe journey my friend, and thank you."

Stepping away from his discomfort, the squat man fixed his eye on Tania, who shuddered under the weight of his lecherous scrutiny. He flicked a final look over her slender figure for good measure.

"I've enjoyed travelling with you, girl," he said gruffly, jabbing a greasy thumb at the stonemason. "Look after him and the mute for me... I hope your arm heals quickly."

Tania nodded her head curtly, watching as Cullen

turned and hurried away.

"If I never see that man again, I shall be thankful for it," Tania hissed, shuddering.

Khadazin watched Cullen, as he headed towards the woodsman and stood waiting patiently for him to finish his conversation with Lucien Varl.

It was clear that something had passed between Cullen and Tania and, despite the fact the man had saved his life, the more Khadazin thought about it, the more his stomach turned.

Unsure of what to say, Khadazin put his arm about Tania's shoulders and pulled her close.

Lady Stromn watched impassively as the woodsman helped Lucien Varl into his seat inside the carriage across from her, pretended not to listen as they shared quiet words. The recent news of the death of the brave woman who had rescued him from the Old Royal Dungeons in Karick had broken Lucien's will and drained the last of his strength. As the woodsman turned and stepped from the wagon, she cleared her throat politely to gain his attention.

"My lady?" Evan enquired coolly.

She reached out a gloved hand to him, which he took gently, kissing her fingertips as her son and Lucien Varl watched on.

"Find my husband for me, woodsman," she said. Leaning in close she whispered, "If you will forgive me, I swear to judge a man by his actions in the future, not to mark him with the whisper of what one has heard to be the truth."

Releasing her hand, the woodsman nodded his head once and stepped away, closing the rocking door gently behind him. With his heart gripping his chest, he turned.

"I will take care of them, *woodsman*, as you know I will," Cullen said. Stepping close, he gripped Evan's hand before he could pull away. "Be sure to see that you take care of things for me in the capital."

The woodsman pulled his hand away. "And if I do? Are we even?"

Cullen grinned, narrowing his good eye. "I should say so, *captain*."

Shaking his head bitterly, Evan stalked away. Old memories came back to haunt him and as the face of a raven-haired woman flashed foremost in his mind, he went to stand beside Dekan Ardent.

All heads turned as the western gates to the town were hauled open. Patting her mare's sleek neck, Fawn whispered soothing words and sprung up onto her saddle. Gripping the reins in her left hand, she turned her mount about, sending a slow look around Havensdale and towards those that had gathered to see them leave. Eventually, her eyes fell upon her father and the woodsman.

Pressing her gloved fingertips to her lips, she gathered a kiss and sent it towards them. Turning her head and mount away, she rode through the open gates, the carriage, driven by Cullen, rattling across the cobbles after her. As the escort of six riders trotted after them, Dekan Ardent turned to the woodsman.

"Something tells me that that kiss was not meant for me," he said, a rare smile dancing across his sombre features.

Evan sighed heavily, but did not answer as he watched Jessica and Sara close and bar the western gates.

By mid-morning Fawn quickly began to realise that their journey northwards to Highwater would take a lot longer than she had hoped, thanks to Lady Stromn's insistence that they stop every hour so that she could partake in a well-needed *constitutional.* Whilst Fawn didn't doubt that the rutted roads offered the old carriage's inhabitants an uncomfortable journey, she could not hide her own impatience to be under the protection of Highwater and see Cassana again.

By the time they had stopped for a fifth delay that morning Fawn was all but ready to throttle her. Under a calming, gentle sky, they waited by the roadside whilst Lady Stromn and her son stretched their legs and enjoyed some fresh air.

Unperturbed by the delays, Cullen wandered off behind a tree to relieve his own discomfort, whilst Sergeant Calen and his men watched the wooded roadside guardedly. Meeting the man from Highwater's eyes, they silently shared their frustrations.

After a time, Lady Stromn returned to the carriage, hitching up her long skirts as she stepped up into the carriage after her son. Fawn choked on her relief as Lady Stromn looked back out.

"I feel much the better now, captain, thank you," she said with a polite smile. "Perhaps we might stop for lunch soon?"

"Of course, Lady Stromn," Fawn responded dutifully, her pale face failing to hide the words she had wanted to say.

With an almost knowing smile, Lady Stromn closed the door. Moments later, she thumped the roof of the carriage to let everyone know that she was ready to depart.

Cullen threw a roguish look at Fawn as he flicked his reins viciously, dragging her discomfort away from her for a few moments. Drawing a calming breath, Fawn watched as Sergeant Calen and his men fell in on either side of the retreating carriage. Listening to the chatter of the crows in the treetops for a time, she fought against the strong urges to return home and finally, reluctantly, followed her duty northwards.

Before they could find a suitable place to stop for some refreshment, Sergeant Calen drew Fawn's attention to the hazy horizon, the twisting road filled with a caravan of wagons heading southwards. Shielding her eyes against the high sun, Fawn watched intently as they drew near. As a bead of sweat ran down her left cheek and trickled down her neck, Fawn sighed with relief as she recognised the brightly painted wagons and began to hear the musical jingle of belled harnesses.

Wayfarers!

Thoughts of a time before any of this danger was truly realised rose unbidden in Fawn's mind and she swallowed down her grief, as she thought of the conversation she had shared with Cassana, Kallum Campbell... and Colbin Wicksford, as they drew near to Karick and the supposed sanctuary that was meant to be the capital.

A cold flush cooled her skin for a time and she shook her head sadly as the wayfarers approached them.

Sergeant Calen, his broad features hidden under the shade of his hood, drew them off to the roadside and guided his mount back to Fawn's side.

"It's just wayfarers," he reported, his tone neutral.

Fawn nodded. "Perhaps we shall share some news. I am keen to find out what is happening in Highwater."

"As am I," Sergeant Calen replied. Fawn dealt him a look. The quiet sergeant had been Alion Byron's man and had not been pleased when his daughter had sent him away to protect Havensdale.

Reaching across, she gently touched him on his left arm. "We shall have you home in a couple of days, sergeant," she promised him quietly.

He grinned then, the years falling from his face. "Not before winter at this pace," he replied, dealing a look towards the carriage.

"Greetings on this fine day," the tall man in bright clothes called out, sweeping off his wide hat to underline a deep bow. "How fares the south?" he enquired, as he straightened and offered them the customary wayfaring greeting.

Fawn guided her mount forward, as the wagons came to a slow halt behind their leader.

"I fear the kind weather masks the storm clouds you will find," Fawn replied, raising her own hand in greeting.

The man nodded, sweeping his keen eyes over the carriage and then the men that guarded it. He ran a hand through his forked beard.

"We have heard much tell of this, lately," he said. Jumping off his wagon, he strode forward. Fawn slipped from her saddle and wandered forward to meet him.

"We have met many a refugee on the North Road," the wayfarer continued. "All bring dark tales with them, of the chaos that is rising... and of the persecution in the capital."

Fawn nodded her head, sighing forlornly. "I fear that I cannot dispel these rumours, sir, only add to them. The road south is full of peril. The capital stirs with talk of war, war against a foe that is not really there."

The wayfarer looked about guardedly, before returning his attention to the world-weary woman before him.

"Seek you the safety of Highwater?" he asked softly. Fawn read something there, deep behind his lively green eyes.

"We do," Fawn admitted. "We hail from Havensdale – seeking sanctuary before the Valian armies come north."

The man frowned at that. "So it is true!" he mused, paling somewhat. He nervously tugged at the golden earring, catching the sunlight from his left earlobe.

"Where are your people headed?" Fawn added into the silence. "I would advise avoiding Havensdale and Karick. It may be those of Reven heritage that are being persecuted currently, but I fear for the days ahead and what the future may hold for all peaceful, free-thinking people."

Clearly troubled, the wayfarer fiddled with the hat he still carried. Sweeping it back onto his head, he reached out and took Fawn's hand. He kissed it gently, smiling.

"Thank you for the information, my lady," he said floridly, so that those behind might hear. In a lower tone, he added. "The north has its own shadows and you would be wise to have a care. If Alion Byron was not safe in his own keep, then nobody will be."

Fawn nodded slowly, her throat dry and coarse. "My thanks to you and your family, sir – may your road be safe and the stars above it bright for you."

Humbled by her knowledge of his people, the wayfarer released her hand and bowed slightly.

"Safe journey, lady," the wayfarer replied, stepping away. "May the sun always be before you and your troubles far behind."

Tilting her head, Fawn turned away and they both silently headed back to their people to continue their journey.

At the rear of the wayfaring caravan, sometime later, Arillion woke with a start as a rock kindly threw him from his dreams. Growling, he closed his eyes, willing himself to fall back into the arms of his dream and the embrace of the three women he had been sharing it with. When they failed to return, he sighed, sitting up stiffly in bed.

Above him, the lantern swirled rapidly and he felt his stomach knot as the swaying momentum of the wagon unsettled him. Falling from his bed, he limped over to the rear of the wagon and threw open the door, allowing the bright day and fresh air to settle him.

Sitting on the rear steps, he looked out at the Valian countryside, losing himself to the distant hills to the west. As he dragged his thoughts north and to everything he had left behind there, Arillion spied the dust, rising up on the horizon.

Standing, he held on to the roof and swung out on the step to look south at the wayfaring caravan.

"Did I miss something?" he called out. "Hey?" he shouted, when no answer was forthcoming.

Finally, Lia peered around the wagon, from where she drove them onwards.

"What is it?" she said crisply. She was still, evidently, angry with him.

"I said 'did I miss something'?" Arillion asked again, guarding his annoyance.

Lia nodded. "It was a group from Havensdale, heading north, escorting a carriage. You were too busy snoring to hear anything."

Arillion smiled his bitter thanks and swung back from view, watching for a time before the dusty horizon was lost, the road twisting behind a small copse of trees.

"I wonder who that was?" he mused, pondering if they would be any safer in Highwater, once the inevitable civil war began.

Shrugging, Arillion ducked back into the wagon. As Lia started to hum a merry travelling tune, he began to go through his exercises again. If he was going to creep into the capital and end this war before it could begin, he was going to need his strength, his wits and, above all else, a bloody great deal of luck.

CHAPTER FORTY TWO

Conflict

The knock at the study door roused Cassana from her thoughts. Massaging the weariness from her eyes, she stretched the tension from her cramped back and shoulders. Sitting up straight, Cassana placed the dispatches she was reading to one side. Plagued by doubts since receiving the mysterious letter, Cassana had barely slept of late. All her waking hours and many of her sleeping ones were spent trying to deliberate on what, if anything needed to be done about Lysette. Years of friendship stayed her hand, though it would have been folly to simply dismiss the letter, however. Caution and bitter experience had shown her that.

But, and this was the problem, when it came down to the harsh reality and lack of any evidence other than the word of a stranger, Cassana could not help but doubt that Lysette could ever truly be the spy. Even now, whenever they were together, when Cassana probed her friend for advice on matters that might reveal any dark intent towards her, there was never any hint of anything other than Lysette's caring, undying support. There was never a telling sign that Lysette could have had any involvement in her father's murder.

Cassana had even suggested that she seek to make peace with the south, if only to find a way to avert the imminent threat of war. Lysette's response had been swift and full of candour 'You would be wise to find another route to peace, Cassy. I fear you would not survive a second journey to the capital and I do not know what I would do without you.'

Surely that was not the response a treacherous spy would give her? Or was it?

Cassana blinked free of her dilemma, pushing herself away from the desk as the door heaved impatiently.

It was getting late, the candles lighting her dark thoughts now lower than the waning sun outside her window. Rising up stiffly, Cassana tried not to wake Shadow from his deep slumber underneath her desk and called out for her visitor to enter, relieved when she saw Edren step into the room. He had been keeping himself busy of late and she had not seen him nearly enough.

"Have you been up here all day?" he asked her, though she could clearly see he already knew the answer.

She had not eaten for many hours and suddenly realised that she must have looked a sight.

"Too many hours, I fear," Cassana admitted, as she self-consciously began adjusting her tangled hair.

Edren shook his head worriedly and as he stepped forward into the light, she noticed the cut on his left cheek.

"What have *you* been doing?" she demanded, reaching up on her toes to examine if the stitches were holding the blistering cut together.

Wincing, Edren leant forward and kissed her disarmingly on one cheek.

"Erith and I were sparring the other day," he said

ruefully. "The tip of his blade snapped... I was actually quite lucky – it could have been my eye."

Edren saw the concern in Cassana's eyes and hid his shame over her right shoulder as she drew him into an embrace. Images of his encounter with the arrogant hooded man flashed before him and he suppressed a shudder as he felt the warmth from Cassana's body ease his fears.

Even now Edren was not entirely sure why he had given the wayfarers the truth, or at least part of it. It would have been far easier to give them a false name, to lead them on a merry chase through the shadows and then have the Brotherhood kill them. It would have been the sensible move – but, and this was the problem, if he was honest with himself, he wanted to stop Lysette claiming what had been promised to him, before it was too late.

Despite the fact he could not resist her, Edren knew that Lysette would eventually betray him. She would never spare Cassana's life and he doubted that his parents would be safe, once the city was taken. If he had the courage to search his feelings deep enough, he would discover that he expected Lysette to have him killed as well.

After all he had and would come to sacrifice, Edren was not about to throw it all away. He knew that Lysette, should she be arrested, would never give up the Brotherhood, no matter what they did to her. He also knew that she would not give him up either, as to do so would jeopardise all that the Brotherhood had achieved in Highwater, thus far.

Edren believed that if he could stay in control, if Lysette's hunger and thirst for power was kept out of this, then he could still find a way to keep Cassana alive.

Edren sighed. Well, that was until he received the messenger from the chancellor that morning and the scrolls he had borne swiftly north with him.

Sensing their embrace was lingering beyond the

bounds of friendship, Edren pulled away from her and cleared his eyes of any guilt.

"A message has arrived from Karick for you, Cassy," he said, pulling the scroll from his belt. He held it out to Cassana and felt a great burden settle on his shoulders as she took it from his shaking hand.

There would be no turning back now, Edren thought sadly, though even now, he still had to believe that he would somehow be able to save her.

Her curiosity at the blank wax seal flashed in her eyes as Cassana offered her thanks and headed back to the candlelight to read it.

"Was there no other word from the messenger?" Cassana asked without looking up, as she broke the seal with a thumb and unrolled it.

"None," Edren said, watching Cassana's eyes, as she began to read. "I had to persuade him to give me the letter, as he was insistent he deliver it personally."

More lies, Edren thought, as Cassana murmured and pretended to acknowledge she was listening. Edren's heart was in his mouth as she read the message further.

Please don't let it be Kassaar, Edren pleaded silently. If the chancellor's wild gamble proved to be right, if Savinn Kassaar had actually been the one to rescue Cassana and thwart the Brotherhood's plans in the first instance, then Cassana would surely fall for the trap and it would be difficult to stop them finally killing her.

When he saw the surprise on her face turn to one of hope, Edren knew that he faced a difficult decision in the next few days.

"I will leave you," Edren said, eager to be away from her now.

She stayed him as he reached for the door. "Please, Edren, don't. Stay a while, I need your help."

"Should I send for my father?" Edren asked as calmly as he could.

Cassana rose up and hurried over to him, all her weariness gone, all her despondency and doubts beginning to lift.

She could barely contain her excitement as she passed the scroll into his hands and forced him to read the words he already knew to be penned there.

Edren maintained his look of surprise as he read the scroll obediently. When he looked up, he could see the hope burning in her eyes and, even though he wished it were not so, he could not bring himself to extinguish it.

"Is this right?" he stammered, shaking his head. "Are you telling me that this letter is to be believed and that it... it was Savinn Kassaar that rescued you from Madam Grey?"

Cassana's excited breath rattled in her throat and a rare, beaming smile lit up her face.

"Yes," she whispered. "He had me rescued from the high duke's keep, he saved my life and now he has information that might yet save us all."

She threw her arms about his neck and held him tightly. As Edren Bay clutched his childhood friend close, he began to cry gently. He loved Cassana – had always loved her and now, to the depths of his disgust, he was probably going to lead her to her doom...

Dekan Ardent had barely sat down in his chair when an urgent knock rattled the door to the militia headquarters. Sighing forlornly, the mayor of Havensdale bade his visitor entrance. When Sara Campbell's drawn face peered in, he offered her a warm, comforting smile.

"There's a group of travellers at the West Gate, sir," she said quickly, "they asked for you personally."

The mayor frowned, pausing for a moment. "Thank you, Sara. Let them know I shall be there shortly."

The recruit nodded her head and fell back from view.

Dekan wrinkled his nose thoughtfully and gathered himself. It had been many years since he had been involved in running the militia and he had forgotten how demanding it was. Since Fawn's departure, he had not found a moment's peace. There was always some matter that needed attending to, some advice being sought, or dilemma to solve.

Running a hand down his face from brow to chin, he drew in a steadying breath. It would have been easier to hand over the captaincy of the town to Sergeant Manse, but not the right decision. When Dekan announced that he would take over his daughter's duties in her absence, he could see the relief flood his sergeant's face. Larne was a good, dependable man, but he was not a leader, and, much to his credit, he had never pretended otherwise.

Rising up from his seat, which groaned in protest, Dekan Ardent strode from the small room and went to greet his visitors.

The sun was gathering up the early morning mist as the mayor reached the top of the steps to the ramparts. Warming his hands on his breath, he strode forward to stand between Sara Campbell and her brother, Kallum. Gripping the palisade with both hands, the mayor stared down at the group of five travellers that stood in a huddle before the closed gate, speaking in hushed whispers.

"Fair morning, travellers," Dekan greeted, his voice echoing in the silence of the early morn. "I am Dekan Ardent. I am told you wished to see me?"

He scanned the hooded heads that looked up at him, but did not recognise any of their faces. One of the men came forward, lowering his hood and Dekan studied the thin face that looked up at him closely.

"Indeed we did, Mayor Ardent," the man said pleasantly, his forked beard splitting into a smile. Even at this early hour, his eyes were bright and, despite his advancing years, he held the look of a man to be wary of. The man offered the mayor a slight bow, before continuing.

"We have heard tell of the misfortunes that have befallen your peaceful town and, whilst I understand that you would be wary of strangers calling at your gates, I would urge you, Mayor Ardent, to at least hear what we have to say."

"I am listening," Dekan replied, licking his lips nervously. He sent a look about the surrounding lands, fearful of any possible danger.

Sensing the discomfort, the tall man held up his hands. "We mean you or your people no harm, quite the contrary in fact. I am Kaspen Shale, leader of a large wayfaring family. We have recently travelled south from Highwater and have information that may well be of use to you and your cause."

Dekan's skin pricked and beside him he could feel Kallum Campbell fidget nervously.

"These are trying times, Mister Shale, and, whilst you are indeed well informed of our misfortunes, you must forgive me if I am sceptical as to your intentions," Dekan said evenly. He looked about, scanning the north. "I would start by asking where the rest of your family currently are?"

Kaspen clasped his gloved hands together, his breath clouding before him. "Of course, as well you should be. It has been several winters since my family last visited this region and I doubt you would remember us. As to their current whereabouts, they are camped a few leagues north, near to the hamlet of Lowdale. Despite my best intentions, they do not, ah, how shall I put it? They do not agree with an involvement in matters that should not concern us."

His curiosity piqued, the mayor folded his arms across his mailed chest. "I must agree with them. It is not usually the way of your people to involve themselves in the affairs of the wider Vales."

Kaspen Shale inclined his head in agreement. "But then these are not normal affairs, Mayor Ardent."

The man at Kaspen's left limped forward, his grey eyes glittering with impatience.

When he spoke, his icy words were laced with irritation. "Do you want our help or not, man?"

Kaspen threw a dark look at his comrade, then offered up an apologetic smile. "You must forgive my friend. It has been a long road for him and his patience and manners are sadly lacking."

Dekan Ardent reined in his own irritation. Sighing, he looked to Kallum Campbell. "Open the gates and rouse some more men," he said quietly. Turning to his visitors he smiled. "I will hear what you have to say, Kaspen Shale. You and your family are most welcome to Havensdale... but your weapons are not."

The newcomers' arrival in town garnered much interest in Havensdale, even at such an early hour. As they reluctantly handed in their weapons at the gates and the mayor led them to the militia headquarters, Ashe Garrin headed away from the well with his full bucket of water and went in search of Elion Leigh. The remnants of the patrol from Carwell had been allotted some tents, behind the chapel. Here they had gathered together to quietly mourn and share in the loss of their friend, Liehella.

Elion was already awake and sat before the small campfire. A pot of water bubbled away over it and the burly sergeant licked his lips at the thought of a nice cup of tea.

"A group of wayfarers just arrived in town," Ashe said, grunting in pain as he leant over and carefully put the bucket down.

Elion eyed his friend. His back was still hurting him

after several days camped in Greywood Forest and their current home did little to improve his discomfort.

"Wayfarers?" Elion pursued.

"Aye, five of them," Ashe replied, as he searched for a wooden cup. He found Elion's gaze, saw the curiosity there. "That Kallum lad said the wayfarers had been in Highwater, asked for the mayor personally. They had some help to offer, apparently."

When Elion went to rise, Ashe grabbed his wrist. "Sit your arse down, captain," he said with a grin. "If it's important, then they'll send for us, if not.... well, that means you get to cook me breakfast again."

Elion shook his head, struggling to find a smile. There was no sign of Devlin Hawke rising from his bed yet, but he glanced over at Elissen, as she crawled from her tent and began stretching the stiffness from her thin limbs. He suddenly felt the warmth from the fire for the first time and sitting back down again with a resigned sigh, Elion ignored the knowing look that Ashe dealt him.

Scarlet Moore was usually adept at eavesdropping on her patrons' conversations. She prided herself at her skill of appearing to attend to the mundane, whilst listening intently and gathering up the local gossip of the day.

The group of travellers who had arrived in town recently now huddled close around a table over their ales, somehow managing to keep their conversation below a whisper that would not carry to where Scarlet idly rearranged the bottles behind the bar. In fact one of them, the handsome man with the piercing grey eyes, the one who seemed to hold court over his friends, made it perfectly clear that he knew she was listening to them and, on several occasions, had caught her looking over to their corner by the western window and winked mischievously at her.

Flushing deeper than her name suggested as he caught

her watching again, Scarlet flicked a bold look at the group. The winker, despite the scar on his left cheek and the limp that had borne him to their table, was a man to be wary of. He carried himself with a poise and fluidity to his movements that left him always on guard, never relaxing for a moment. The other man that garnered her attention was not the tall, polite man with the forked beard, who had chatted amiably to her as he ordered food and ale. Nor was it the jovial, often smiling blonde-haired man, who dressed in garish leathers and shared a joke with the young traveller, who looked like he was more nervous than Scarlet felt in their company. No! It was none of these men. It was the giant man with the ruined face, who looked unhappier than the bear he wore about his shoulders. Scarlet could not take her eyes from him, could not believe that a man with such a gruff, cantankerous demeanour could talk so loudly and yet still manage to guard his words enough for only those he directed them to.

Admitting defeat, Scarlet picked up her cloth and lovingly attended to the oak bar. Her mother would have the strangers' food ready soon and she could already smell the roasting beef, could taste the sizzling meat in her mouth. Licking her lips, Scarlet braced herself for the scrutiny and the looks that would soon come her way again.

As intent on the bar as she was, Scarlet did not see Elion Leigh and his mysterious friend, as they quietly entered the inn.

"We shall just have to see what happens at the meeting tonight," Arillion said, trying to hide his exasperation. He drained the last of his ale and slammed the tankard back on the table. "It is no good debating what we do not know and I, for one, shall not waste my breath."

Kaspen threw up his hands and looked at Agris. "But

we should prepare what we will say at the meeting. If what the mayor has told us is true, then our task will be all the more difficult."

Agris shrugged his huge shoulders. "But if Carwell is in Karick, Kaspen..." he curled a huge fist about his tankard of ale. "This is the chance we have agreed to take. We can end this war, as Arillion has suggested, before it can begin."

"Just like that?" Kaspen hissed, clicking his fingers before his friend's nose. The wayfaring leader growled in frustration, looking around the table, searching for another voice of reason.

Agris had already made up his mind. The giant would travel to Karick on his own if needed and, if he had the chance, would walk up to the keep and ask to see the chancellor and lord of East Vales – so there was no reason to be found there. Tomlin loved Agris and would follow the large man wherever he went, despite the danger they would face. Evan Mor's son, Aven, had been the only other wayfarer who wanted to come to Havensdale with them. Following the heated meeting with the wayfaring family outside Lowdale, there was the distinct prospect of a vote looming, should any of them ever survive to return home. The young wayfarer was keen to prove his worth at the fire, should there be one left to welcome them back. Though Aven would probably side with him and seek patience, Kaspen doubted it was from anything other than loyalty to the memory of his father.

And as for Arillion...

Kaspen met the assassin's gaze and saw the stony look of determination there. He would not change his mind and would head south in the morning, with or without them.

Arillion looked as if he was about to say something further as the door to the inn opened and the late summer sun spilled eagerly into the taproom, chasing away the dimness of the lanterns and candlelight. Kaspen saw the swordsman's eyes widen and for the first time, he observed confusion and shock on Arillion's rugged features. As Kaspen and the others at the table looked to the door, Arillion rose up slowly.

Curling both his hands into fists, he forced his knuckles into the table.

"By the storms, you are the luckiest bastard" Devlin Hawke said, as he strode into the inn and stalked across the taproom towards the wayfarers.

Elion watched on as the man with a scar on his face crossed the wooden floor towards the outlaw. They stopped before one other and the former captain of Carwell could taste the tension in the air.

"We heard you were dead," Devlin admitted, holding out a wavering hand. His mind was racing and he couldn't control his heart as he studied the ghost scowling away before him.

Arillion folded his arms across his chest, ignoring the offered hand.

"Well here I am," he said, his words edged by anger. It looked like he was about to say something more, then gripped Devlin's hand, pulling him into a warm embrace.

Elion watched the reunion, sensing that out of everyone in the inn only Devlin and his friend had any idea as to what was going on.

Devlin clapped Arillion on his back warmly and then pulled away. He studied the face before him, noting the pain lurking there, seeing the fresh scar on his cheek.

"I survived, though not without paying a price," Arillion said quietly. He released the outlaw, glancing once at Elion, before looking away dismissively.

"I'm on my way south. I have coin to collect and old scores to settle," the assassin continued, shaking his head incredulously. "But what I can't fathom is what you are doing *here*? Why aren't you in Greywood, chasing rabbits and shagging deer?"

Devlin stiffened, though managed a smile. "A long tale for a large tankard, I fear," he replied. "In short, you have a young man to thank for that."

The outlaw fished through his pockets and pressed a note into Arillion's hands. The assassin's grey eyes looked down, then flashed up with a question.

"Destiny has brought us together again, it seems my old friend," Devlin offered, watching nervously as Arillion read the note.

For a time the assassin stared at the faded parchment, reading the words that had been penned there all those years ago. When he looked up, his face was veiled in anger.

"Now do you believe me?" Arillion asked, not trying to hide his contempt.

Before Devlin could reply, Arillion stepped in close and punched the outlaw in the face.

CHAPTER FORTY THREE

The Last Supper

The Arms of the Lady Inn was busy, the tension in the crowded taproom thick and palpable. Candles glowed proudly from lanterns and flickered from sconces on the walls and the shadows were heavy with expectation. In the centre of the inn, the tables had been dragged together by Joseph Moore and his daughters, to form a large, rough circle and the old beams in the eaves were freshly laden with rushes, to ward away the Father of Storms and protect those gathered below.

With cups of wine and tankards of ale in hand, those summoned by Dekan Ardent found stools and chairs at his behest, all looking to one another with concern and guarded apprehension as the scraping of wood filled the silence of the inn.

Pleased that something was finally happening, Arillion sat in his chair, beside Kaspen Shale and Agris Varen. With hooded eyes, he watched as Elion Leigh and Devlin Hawke sat across from them and Arillion buried his thoughts and found a smile, as he saw the cuts on the outlaw's lips and the swelling of angry bruises under his eyes.

Sensing the attention, Devlin Hawke scowled across at Arillion, though there was no malice there. He had accepted Arillion's earlier anger without retaliation, admitting at the time that he would, if rather ruefully, '*allow him that one.*'

Tearing his eyes away from his past, Devlin leant in close, studying the nervous, clean-shaven if cut, face of Elion Leigh. The captain looked younger again, since losing his pathetic beard and was perched on the edge of his stool, drumming his fingers over his cup of wine nervously.

"Take a breath, or a deep sip," Devlin advised quietly. Elion failed with the first, but raised the shaking cup to his mouth and whetted his fear.

Beside Elion, Elissen drew her shawl tighter about her features and hid herself away in her tresses. They had spoken at length before coming about what the meeting could mean for her, what she may be asked to do. She had replied that she was ready to do whatever she needed to have her revenge on Gardan, even if it meant she died in the process. She had met Elion's stricken gaze with only a shallow, weary smile.

Swallowing his own fears, Devlin looked towards the stonemason, seated at the far end of the ring of tables. He was sat next to the young huntress and the mute, his eyes fixed firmly on the wood before him. His dark brow furrowed, glistening in a cold sheen.

As if hearing nearby thoughts, Devlin looked back at Arillion, following the assassin's eyes back, as he too studied the Redani fugitive. Shaking his head, Devlin stifled a laugh. He knew Arillion, knew him far too well and could tell that he was sizing up the gold coin on offer in Havensdale. Right now, he was probably deciding if he had chosen the wrong side – contemplating if he should turn in the Redani and his old friend, the notorious outlaw

Devlin Hawke to the Brotherhood and claim the small fortune of crowns on offer.

If he thought about it for a while, Devlin was quite tempted to allow him.

Dekan Ardent, satisfied that everyone he had invited had now arrived, rose up from his own seat and clapped his hands together. Many people had tarried long into the early evening, their reluctance and hesitancy to confront what needed to be done understandable.

"Thank you all for coming," Dekan said, calming the last of the subdued chatter. With all eyes drawn to him, he rubbed his hands together. "Time is against us, as we are all aware, and I shall not dwell on the finer detail of what we all know. We are here, plain and simple, to decide what needs to be done, though our consciences may not like it. What must we do to stop Carwell and this *Brotherhood* from plunging the Four Vales into civil, and then, wider war?"

The mayor watched those gathered, seeing the looks they shared, hearing the whispers of discontent. At his right, Dekan heard the woodsman stir and could sympathise with his discomfort, knowing of the decision he had pledged he would take to him, earlier that evening.

"Before we continue, I would welcome new friends to our town," Dekan continued. He swept his left arm towards the wayfarers who had gathered at the table. "Kaspen Shale and his companions have news for us and before we decide on what we must do, I would ask that you listen to them. Kaspen?"

Kaspen drew in a calming breath and scraped his chair across the wooden floorboards as he rose up. Beside him, Arillion fixed his attention on the table, picking at a knot in the wood.

"Thank you, Mayor Ardent," Kaspen began, sweeping his gaze about the room. "Firstly, may I offer my sympathies to all of you gathered here, for all that you have been through and suffered to be here at this moment."

At his side, Kaspen heard Arillion sigh impatiently and decided it best he press on.

"As a wayfarer, I have many contacts, many methods of hearing what is said in private, listening intently to the winds for changes in the air. I have heard much tell of Havensdale's misfortunes, have heard rumours at first and then, firm evidence of what is happening in Karick and Carwell. I know of the attacks on Eastbury, of the duplicity that has brought the Four Vales to the cusp of war. I know of many things, but, most of all, I know that I cannot stand aside whilst others fight for the freedom my family so cherish."

Dekan Ardent saw several at the table nod their heads at the wayfarer's words, though some shared looks of confusion.

"Would you please recount to the meeting what you told me earlier," Dekan asked, the following silence filled only by the sounds of the meal they would soon share, being prepared in the kitchen.

Kaspen nodded, wringing his hands together. "As a token of our intent, I bring you news from Highwater. Following the murder of Alion Byron, we set about delving into the shadows, to find out who was responsible."

"And did you?" the woodsman asked, drawing attention to himself.

Kaspen nodded, aware that Arillion was suddenly paying keen attention to his surroundings.

"We did, sir," Kaspen said quickly, as he heard the assassin draw in a breath to speak. "Through a reliable source and with much coin, we discovered that the spy in the Byron household, the person who, even now, offers threat to Lady Byron, is none other than Lysette, the daughter of Lord Astien."

The following silence was soon swallowed up by mutters and guarded whispers, as many heads turned to their neighbours in surprise.

The woodsman failed to hide his own shock and rose up quickly. Dekan offered the table to his friend and sat down.

"And you can vouch for this information?" the woodsman asked. "Forgive me, but many have tried to find out the spy's identity, all have failed."

Kaspen smiled sweetly. "It is often easy to look my friend, though usually difficult to know where to search."

The woodsman tilted his head. "Your point is well taken, sir. Might we know what you did with this information?"

"We sent anonymous word to Lady Byron, to warn her of the danger she still faces." Kaspen said. "We could do no more for Lady Byron and thought our services would be better suited elsewhere."

Arillion rose up, leaning on the table as he swept his steely intent about those gathered. "Unlike my friend here, I am not a man to shuffle my words. I will get straight and plain to the heart of the matter, the reason why we are here."

"And that is?" the woodsman asked, his eyes flickering.

As Kaspen groaned and sat back down, Arillion smiled, searching the haggard face that glared down the table at him.

"We are here to tell you that in the morning, we will head to Karick to finish this war, before it can truly begin. You can be a part of it or sit here and pray to whomever that we succeed. Either way, we shall try."

"And why in the storms would you do that, wayfarer?" the woodsman asked quietly. They faced each other over the table as the temperature in the room began to cool.

Arillion grinned. "I am no wayfarer," he said, throwing a look at Kaspen and Agris. "And my reasons are my own. Suffice to say that I have unfinished business in the capital, business that, luckily for you, coincides with all that you stand for. In the morning, I will head to Karick, I will enter the city and I will kill Henry Carwell and anyone else I find there that is tearing this country apart."

Even the activity in the kitchen went quiet as the assassin's words settled on those gathered at the tables.

Seeing the impact of his declaration, Arillion pressed home his advantage. "There is no easy soloution to what you face, no simple resolution. Havensdale will fall, if you allow it to. You must strike now, before the armies can gather, before Carwell can sweep his madness north, crushing everything and anyone that would stand against him."

Elion Leigh found his feet. He looked askance at Arillion, before sweeping an imploring look about. "This man speaks of murder? Are we to give our blessing to such an act? Where is the law that governs this land? How can we stand against all that we abhor, when we stoop to the depths that have led us to this very point? We have gathered here tonight to find a way to bring the evidence we now hold to court, not to skulk in the shadows and draw crimson lines in the throats of our enemies."

Arillion liked the sound of Elion's last observation and nodded his head. "I am just telling you what I am going to do, son. You don't have to agree with it."

Dekan rose again, raising his hands. "This is not getting us anywhere. Before you decide on this course, sir, I would ask that you listen to what others have to say."

Arillion offered a slight bow and flicking a look at Elion and the woodsman, he sat back down, spreading his hands out on the table. At his side, Kaspen kicked his foot under the table in annoyance, whilst Agris offered him a broad, twisted grin.

The mayor turned to the woodsman, nodded, then sat back down again.

Licking his lips, the woodsman drew in a faltering breath. His heart hammered wildly and the heat in the room made his head swoon. Sipping at his ale, he wiped his mouth on the back of his sleeve.

"We have many enemies," Evan began, "those we can see, those we know and many we can only perceive. Recently, because of the bravery and sacrifice of others, we have been able to strike back at Carwell, at those who now hold tightly on to the reins of power in Karick. What is clear to us is that we have all the evidence we need to bring down this so-called Brotherhood. We have the testimony of Khadazin Sahr, the Redani who overheard Chancellor Relan Valus, as he plotted to have Alion Byron's daughter Cassana kidnapped. Thankfully, the Lady deemed that neither Khadazin nor Cassana Byron would fall foul to his machinations. This enabled, for at least a time, their plans to be thwarted."

As the woodsman gathered his thoughts, Arillion looked at Kaspen, his eyes full of mischief. Leaning in close he whispered, "And here we all are."

"In Eastbury, supposed Reven insurgents raided a town, the spectre of fifty years ago, it seemed, raising its head once again, to strike at the Four Vales. Again, the Lady intervened, Captain Leigh's patrol saving the town and setting into motion a chain of events that would lead him and his allies to this very table." The woodsman offered a gentle hand to where Elissen sat. "This brave young lady witnessed Renald Gardan murder the man who led the raiders – heard from his own lips, his damning testimony that marks him as an enemy of the law."

Elissen shied away from the attention and the surfacing memories, though her eyes shimmered with angry determination.

"Fawn Ardent, the kind captain who unwittingly escorted Lady Byron into the clutches of her enemy, was then marked by Carwell as a Reven sympathiser and her town attacked. Gardan visited murder on the people of Havensdale and then fled to Karick to poison the ear of the high duke, whose health and wits, even then, were failing."

Devlin Hawke rose up, clearing his throat. At his elbow, Elion Leigh looked up, startled that the outlaw had decided to speak.

"Might I intervene?" Devlin asked, though it sounded like he was going to speak anyhow.

The woodsman nodded, sitting back down.

"Captain Leigh has always been an honourable man," the outlaw began. "I have come to trust his judgement and I admire what he has achieved. I count him my friend, though I fear that we see matters from different sides of the same coin. When we journeyed to Carwell, we discovered that the city was already preparing for war, with or without the council's permission. As is the same in Karick now, all of Reven heritage have been arrested, many hung without trial, or never seen again. With my own eyes I witnessed the corpses lining the Great East Road outside Carwell."

Mutters rippled across the taproom as Devlin drew in a deep breath. "I have many men who will fight for peace and I have the desire to see those who would visit such horrors on our Vales, fall. I do not come here lightly, as I am not a man to abide by the law Elion Leigh so cherishes – though circumstances at this juncture would not find me anywhere else. My name, for all of you who do not know me, is Devlin Hawke and the men and women of Greywood Forest will stand beside you, no matter what you decide here this day."

Arillion's eyes sparkled with mirth as he saw the shock

and then more than a few crowns of greed flash momentarily in the eyes of those present.

Dekan Ardent rose once more, calming the startled uproar.

"Thank you, Devlin. Your aid has already proven invaluable and your assistance is greatly appreciated. I think now would be a good time to decide if our new friends should be privy to what we have achieved recently, as having spoken to them at length already today, I know that they do not know it yet."

Khadazin raised his hand. "I would allow them to stay. We are, all of us, drawn together for this very purpose. We have all suffered to this point in time and I believe, by their actions already, they have a right to sit at this table."

Arillion nodded his thanks in the Redani's direction and smiled.

If anyone objected, as clearly some did, they kept their tongues silent. Satisfied, Dekan Ardent looked to the woodsman, silently asking for him to continue.

Evan rose again. "We have an ally in the city, an ally marked as a traitor, though his actions have proven far nobler than any other found in the capital of late. Savinn Kassaar orchestrated the rescue of Lucien Varl, from the Old Royal Dungeons in the high duke's keep. By the Lady's grace, Lucien survived his journey north with Khadazin, to report that it was Chancellor Valus who had him taken, tortured by a woman who matched the description of Alion Byron's murderer.

With much barbarity, she forced him to reveal the whereabouts of the high duke's family so that that they might be found and killed. This, we have managed to prevent and as we speak, Lady Stromn and her son are safely on their way to Highwater with Fawn Ardent. The Brotherhood sought to kill them and blame Reven attackers again, this we know as we discovered items on the men sent to murder them – Reven items that would be left at the scene of attack, to stir up the people into bloodlust once more."

Arillion whistled, cutting off the woodsman's next words. "With their deaths they could then kill the high duke, make it look as if he died from the shock of their murders.... clever!"

Evan nodded his head. "Indeed! Should the high duke still be alive, we now have a brief moment of opportunity to rescue him. If we can save him, the people will have their rightful leader, a man who will be able to light the flames of justice once again, the only man who would be willing to listen to our testimonies. What is the best way we can achieve that?"

Before anyone could answer, Arillion rose up. "I think it is time to stop dancing in circles and before I offer a suggestion, allow me to lay my cards on the table, if you would?" He did not wait for permission. "My name is Arillion and I work for Savinn Kassaar. It was me who rescued Lady Byron and guided her, well almost, safely home. Unlike some of you, I didn't do it because it was the right thing to do, I did it because I was getting bloody well paid. It is the reason why I can think so clearly. Kassaar and the Byron girl still owe me a great deal of coin and I will collect that after this is all over. If you want to rescue the high duke, if he is still even alive, then I can help you. But, as the woodsman has said, your time is running out. When the Brotherhood realises that the high duke's family are in Highwater, which they will, as Cassana has not arrested the spy yet, Carwell *will* kill the high duke. If that happens, all the evidence in the Vales will not stop the march to war and Havensdale and Highwater will burn."

At the far end of the tables, Khadazin fought for breath, his eyes drawn to the enigmatic speaker.

"You are thought dead, swordsman," Khadazin

pointed out.

Arillion smiled. "It wouldn't be the first time." He offered the stonemason a bow. "It is good that you are here, Redani. I will be happy to help you claim your vengeance."

The woodsman frowned, his heart racing. "It seems that all of our fates are entwined with Lady Byron's."

"Our destinies," Arillion corrected, bristling. "If you want me to, I can show you a way into the capital. A way that will give us the advantage of surprise, allow us to strike at our enemies, before they can react."

"And just how much coin will this cost us?" Ashe Garrin growled, his anger painted vividly on his face.

"This one is for free," Arillion smiled calmly, though inside he was fighting for control. The revelation that Alion Byron's killer was also probably in the capital had completely unsettled his confidence.

"You speak of murder and coin in the same breath," Ashe pursued. "Are we to simply trust you at your word and follow you blindly into your shadows?"

Arillion shrugged. "It makes no difference to me, big man. You can, or you won't."

The woodsman felt his throat constrict as he coughed and drew attention his way again. "Karick is a dangerous place now and will be full of soldiers. We cannot simply walk into the keep."

Elion Leigh was on his feet again. "I cannot believe we are seriously contemplating this!"

Arillion sighed, raising his hands for peace. "Years ago, I was hired by someone to locate a man who had disappeared. I did not succeed in this hunt, though for my troubles, I was given plans as token payment, plans that showed the original layout of the high duke's keep. I don't have these plans anymore, but I have them up here," Arillion tapped his temple several times. "It was how I got in the keep to rescue Lady Byron, and it is how I intend to get into the keep again."

At that, Arillion could see the flash of possibility burn in the woodsman's eyes.

"A small group of people could get into the city, via the sewers and enter the keep to rescue the high duke without raising the alarm," Evan mused, running a hand through his tangled hair. "But this does not solve the problem of Lord Carwell and Renald Gardan. Their men have a choking grip on the region. Even with the high duke safely away, there is no guarantee we will be able to stop them forcibly taking over control of the Four Vales and marching to war?"

Devlin rose up to stand beside Elion Leigh. He rested a calming hand on the man's shaking shoulder.

"Elion Leigh and I have an idea, if we may?" the outlaw offered.

Dekan Ardent waved his accord.

Elion's throat was heavy as he drew the attention on Devlin his way. "The terrible news of Reven prisoners being used as slaves in the mines of Durrant's Field gave us an idea. We believe that a small force could easily capture the mines and free the prisoners being held there. If we could do this, allow one of the guards to return safely to Karick to report what had happened there, then Lord Carwell would be forced to react. There are other mines, of course, but with the Reven free and safely on their way to Highwater, with the mining of iron and the production of weapons and armour halted..."

"Carwell would be forced to send a sizeable force to reclaim it," Dekan Ardent finished off, rising from his seat.

"Especially if it is known that it was Elion and Devlin who captured the mines," the woodsman said, chewing his lower lip thoughtfully. "Gardan would come for you, surely?"

Elion smiled wanly, aware of Elissen's eyes upon him.

"I would place much coin on it! He will not be able to resist finally having me in his noose."

Kaspen, silent now for quite some time, spoke up quickly. "But surely that would mean you would be trapped?"

Elion nodded his head slowly. At his side, Elissen reached out and took his hand, squeezing it gently.

"It may not come to that," Elion said, though his voice was strained with the realisation of what would probably happen. "With the outlaws of Greywood and, I daresay, a great many Reven to bolster our numbers, I believe that we can hold out long enough for word of the high duke's return to reach the attackers."

The woodsman's mind was racing now. *Could it work?* Could they slip into the capital? Could he and Khadazin have their vengeance and thwart the march to war. Looking at the other hands offered to them, it might well be the only play they had left...

"We have former riders of Carwell," the woodsman observed. "We also have many uniforms from the Carwellian soldiers who died attacking Havensdale. There is a chance this could work, a slim chance, but one that we must decide if we are willing to take."

He sent a look about the room, where most people present were now on their feet.

"Who will offer themselves to this plan? Who will lay their lives on the line for the betterment of all?" The woodsman raised his own hand up high.

"My part in this tale began in the capital and it should end there. I will go with the wayfarers to Karick," Khadazin announced, raising his one remaining hand.

Arillion nodded his head, feeling his blood stir with excitement. As he looked on, all present raised their hands into the air, sharing a look of determination with their neighbour and offering their declaration of support. The room fell silent then, not a breath could be heard and only the sputtering flames from a dying candle sounded.

"It is decided, then," Dekan Ardent said finally, not truly believing what they were about to try, what people were about to sacrifice. "A small group of brave souls will travel to Karick to rescue the high duke, whilst the remainder head to Durrant's Field to draw out those poisoning the capital. There can be no peace it seems, without further sacrifice and we must act now, before our chance has passed."

"May the Lady guide and protect us all," Elion Leigh whispered, squeezing Elissen's hand.

CHAPTER FORTY FOUR

The Bitter Pill

Fawn Ardent's return to Highwater was tainted by the memory of her last visit to the capital of the North Vales and of the time she had spent with Alion Byron. As she rode under the towering gates of the city, the carriage and entourage clattering over the cobbles behind her, she swallowed down her sadness, burying rising thoughts of how Cassana must be feeling, of how she would have coped, had her own father been brutally murdered.

Despite the unrepentant heat of the high day, a cold fear swept through Fawn, knotting her stomach and drawing her deep into a shudder. How would she cope, when the time finally came, with the loss of her own father?

Allowing the reproachful sting of guilt to engulf her, Fawn guided her charges through the bustling, though sombre streets of Highwater. Familiar with the route to Byron Keep, Fawn allowed her mount to guide her, oblivious to the people who stopped to stare at the carriage, ignorant of the curious pointing fingers as many tried to guess the identity of the possible dignitaries hidden away inside.

Fortunately, and without delay, which had been the normality of the frustrating journey from Havensdale, they reached the keep without incident. As the guards at the high gates strode forward with raised hands and pikes, Sergeant Calen rode ahead. Short, hurried words were exchanged as Fawn sat in her saddle, listening to the distant roar of the city, its veins throbbing with life. After a moment's delay, the gates were ordered open and the sergeant waved them forward into the grounds of the keep.

Fawn rode alongside the sergeant, his relief at being home and the prospect of a reunion with his wife evident on his sun-kissed face.

"A messenger has been sent on for us," Calen announced, reining in his smile for a moment. "Lady Byron and William Bay will be told of our arrival."

Fawn's heart cantered with apprehension at the thought of seeing Cassana again. How was she faring? How much had she changed in the dark days they had been apart?

William Bay hurried down the steps to greet their guests as the carriage was guided to a halt before him. With the sun in his eyes, he sent a smile towards Fawn Ardent and a quizzical look in Sergeant Calen's direction at his unexpected return.

"Fair day, Sir William," the sergeant greeted as he and Captain Ardent approached.

William inclined his head, opening his hands wide in greeting to them both. "Well met," he said, though his eyes betrayed his concern. "I am gladdened to see you again, Captain Ardent, though, I must admit, perturbed somewhat at your arrival."

Calen turned his head briefly towards Fawn, before looking back. "I think it best we not tarry in plain view,

Sir William."

A crisp voice cut through the silence, as Lady Stromn stepped down from the carriage to escape her confines and ordered her son to do the same.

Fawn looked back at William Bay and saw the look of surprised horror that at first smoothed and then cut deeply into his ageing, weary features.

"W-we had better go and see Lady Byron," William stammered, licking the concern from his lips as he bowed low to kiss the hand that Lady Stromn came forward and offered to him.

With his guests keeping good pace behind him and his wife summoned to tend to Lucien Varl, William Bay hurried through the Long Hall of Byron Keep, heading for the grand staircase that swept gracefully upwards to the upper levels of the household.

Close at his heels, Fawn found little time to admire the beauty of her surroundings, of their constrained opulence. A magnificent oil painting to her left caught her eye however, and she regarded the beautiful woman that watched her ascent, marvelling at the skill of the painter and chilled by the resemblance the dark-haired woman had to Cassana.

They quickly reached a carpeted hallway, Cullen and Sergeant Calen close behind. Lady Stromn huffed and sighed as she tried to keep pace and her son hurried after them, distracted momentarily by a painting of the Valian armies, fighting bravely on the plains against the Reven hordes.

"Erith?" William Bay called out, bringing the group to a walk, as a man dressed in chain mail came towards them. "What are you doing here?"

Erith Taye came to a halt before them, throwing a look over the faces of those familiar and not, afore him. He frowned.

"I am just heading to check on the roster for this evening, William. Is there something wrong?"

"You were entrusted to care for Lady Byron, where is she?" William asked, his voice rising anxiously with each word he spoke.

Erith ran a hand through his beard, frowning. "Forgive me sir, I was told you had been informed. I was relieved of my duties by your son, this morning."

"My son?" William asked, looking back as Lady Stromn announced her displeasure at the delay and of having to stand like a common guard in a corridor. "I was not aware of such things."

Fawn watched as the cold light of worry lit up Erith Taye's features. "He told me that he and Lady Byron were to spend the day together, that I was relieved of my duties for a time. I believe they are still in Lord Byron's... her study."

As William Bay ordered Erith to accompany them, the growing party headed back the way the sergeant had just came.

"Lady Byron?" William called out, knocking urgently on the study door.

There was no answer forthcoming and after only a moment's hesitation, he tried the ringed handle. It was locked.

William looked over his shoulder, frowning. The study was never locked during the day. His chest began to tighten.

Ordering those closest by to step back, he and Erith Taye began kicking at the door, the old oak eventually and truculently giving way with a spitting snap of disdain. Hurrying into the study, William and Erith sent fearful looks about the empty room, filled only by the testimonies of history and scattered in ribbons of golden daylight.

Fawn stepped in behind the two men, Cullen curious

at her side. They saw William plant his hands on his hips, turn his head about, frowning.

"I am always made aware of Lady Byron's movements," he said aloud, though more to himself. "Where are they?"

Erith grunted, pointing to the unfurled scroll on the large, antique desk. Everything else there, the papers, the tomes, the pen and ink pot, were neatly ordered, but the parchment was not.

Sweeping it up, William hurriedly devoured the words and then, with his fear caught in his throat, he turned to those gathered behind him. His face was ashen, his eyes wide with fear.

"I believe they have gone to meet with Savinn Kassaar in the Great Divide," William spluttered, the hand clutching the scroll, falling forgotten to his side.

"That's not possible," Cullen growled firmly, as Fawn gasped. "She hasn't received his message yet."

Rather theatrically for a creature of his reputation, the squat man pulled Savinn's scroll case from his tunic and brandished it high for all to see.

Shielding his eyes against the high sun, Edren Bay drew gently on the reins, clasped far too tightly in his gloved hands. Cassana had drawn her father's mount Storm to a stop and was staring at a large rock at the side of the broad sweeping path that rose up before them through the mountains towards Highwater Keep.

"Is everything alright?" Edren asked, his throat dry and tight. When Cassana failed to answer, he guided his mount alongside her, the sounds of its hooves echoing in the uncomfortable silence.

"Cassana?"

Edren reached out to gently touch her shoulder, hidden away under a vest of dark leather and peppered with iron studs. She flinched then and as she turned to him, he could see the tears brimming in her brilliantly blue eyes.

"I was thinking back to another time, when Squir... when Karlina and I were coming down from the mountains," Cassana hesitated and sniffed back her emotions, as she saw the ghostly reminder of a thin, brightly-haired girl fast asleep on the rock. "We were so exhausted, Edren, scared from our feet by what we had been through. I honestly thought she had survived the worst of it, that I could keep her safe..."

Edren looked away, swallowing his guilt, drowning in his own wild, raging thoughts. His heart rolled and lurched in his chest like angry thunder and he could not hear the rest of what Cassana said.

Before he realised it, Cassana had gathered her composure, straightened in her saddle and was guiding Storm up the path away from him.

Edren shook his head free of his indecision and, casting a final look at the barren rock, he followed his childhood friend to meet her doom.

Cassana was unable to hide from her unease as she led Storm by his reins up the narrow trail that would take her back to Highwater Lake. So many memories lurked up here, hiding away in the sharp edges of the mountains, whispering to her of all that had happened, teasing her with ghostly images of what had become of him, as he stumbled away from her, back down the twisting, treacherous trail.

Feeling her control slip away from her, Cassana drew in a commanding, determined breath. The sun was at their backs now and she sent a look back over her shoulder towards Edren, her hair snapping wildly in the stiff breeze.

The sight of the jagged peaks and hazy land, falling

away before her stole from her lips in a gasp. Following her gaze, Edren took in the magnificent view, his eyes picking out the dark shape of an eagle, as it glided lazily over a distant chasm. In the serene silence that even calmed the turmoil in his heart, Edren could hear the beautiful Raptor's cries, as it called out for its mate.

"This is why we stand and fight," Cassana whispered, drawing Edren's attention to her. "This is why we cannot allow Carwell and his ambitions to destroy the peace and harmony of our lands."

Edren licked his lips, his determination drying up as he began to realise what was about to happen. "There is no guarantee that Savinn Kassaar will have what you seek, Cassy. We may be hoping for something he cannot deliver. It could still, even though you have said it not possible, be a ruse to lure you out. Perhaps you should allow me to go in your stead?"

Cassana bristled, waving a gloved hand dismissively at him. "My protector," she smiled. "Even now you still act as my brother, watching out for me. I do so love you Edren, but you worry too much. It is not possible for anyone else to know about what Savinn Kassaar did for me. He forbade me speak of it and I have not told a soul, other than you. For him to have contacted me, and at this time, tells me he has important information for our cause. He would not risk contacting me if he did not."

Her chest heaved with the excitement and hope burning away in her eyes and Edren hung his head in shame, the final, brittle link breaking. Slipping from his saddle, Edren fell to his knees and began to sob, his body trembling as he gave in to his heart's demands and turned his back on his ambitions.

Cassana stared in shock at her friend's behaviour, her certainty lost to her confusion.

Slipping deftly from her saddle, she hurried to Edren's side. Falling to her knees, she reached out to him, feeling his body tremble and twist beneath her hands.

"By the Lady, Edren, what is the matter?" Cassana asked, stroking his back. She went to pull him close, but his head snapped up and he pushed her away.

"Get away from me, Cassana," he cried. His eyes were red, his disgust running from his nose and flying from his lips. "I am poison to you, I have wronged you greatly."

Cassana recoiled, rising up and stepping away from his vehemence.

"What are you talking about?" she asked, watching confused as Edren stared up at her. "I do not understand what you are saying. What is the matter, my love?"

"Love?" Edren laughed, spitting his distaste onto the ground. "I love nobody but myself Cassana. You will come to find that I have proven to be a poor choice of friend to you and I hope that you will, one day, be able to forgive me."

"You are scaring me now, Edren," Cassana stammered. "Why are you saying this? Why now? I love you like a brother, there is nothing you could have done that I would never forgive you for."

Before Edren spoke again she could sense his desperation, see the needful truth in his eyes and Cassana began to wonder if perhaps she might be wrong.

"In my desire to be a better man, to rise above my father before me, I have shamed you, Cassana. I have betrayed all that is good in the Four Vales and all that it means to be Valian."

Cassana could hear the deep turmoil in his words, sense the madness lurking there. Throwing off the shackles of her shock, she went to him again, reaching out to console him.

Snarling, Edren rose up, pushing her away. With eyes wild with fury, he clawed at his face, tearing at the accusatory voice hissing in his ears.

"I have betrayed the north, Cassana," Edren said, his

voice soft and suddenly calm. "I have betrayed you and your father, my parents and Highwater. I am the spy in your household. It was *I* who intercepted dispatches from the capital, who worked in the shadows with Carwell and Chancellor Valus. It is I, your dearest friend, the man you think your brother who let the assassin into the city, changed the watch and distracted them with fires, so that your father and, but not for the misfortune of your friend, you, Cassana, could die in your beds."

Cassana recoiled, her eyes darting wildly about as Edren's words buried deeper than the longest blade ever could. With her breath catching full in her throat, Cassana stumbled back from her horror and revulsion.

"No! Oh, no, this cannot be? Why are you saying this, Edren?" Cassana demanded, her hands clasped before her as she prayed he was, even now, not himself and delusional.

"I received two letters from Karick, Cassy," Edren said, tears wetting his cheeks. "One I allowed to be delivered to you, the other was for myself. Savinn Kassaar did not write that letter. For all I know, he may even be dead. It was a desperate last act to prise you from the city, so that the Valian armies could march into the Reven lands before winter, without having to lay siege to Highwater."

Cassana blinked, looking about worriedly. "You cannot mean this? Where are you taking me, Edren? Are you going to kill me? Is that how the Brotherhood plans to win this civil war, before it has truly begun?"

Edren nodded his head grimly. "Chancellor Valus is a resourceful man, Cassy. He recruited me many years ago, when I saw all around me had better prospects. My respect and honour was slowly poisoned by him and turned to bitter envy."

Cassana shook her head despairingly, her voice rising angrily with each word she spoke. "But my father thought you like a son. He never treated you with anything less than love. How could you do this to us? How could you do that to him?"

Edren offered up his empty hands to her and shook his head sadly. "I wanted power, Cassana, and until this moment, I believed that I could still have it. But at what cost? What price would I be truly willing to pay? It all counts for nothing at the end, if you do not have your honour. It is not about wealth, not about power, but about the people, the prosperity and the law that protects us. I threw all that away on the day I betrayed you and your father, sullied the friendship of our two families."

Edren fell to his knees again, looking up pleadingly at Cassana as her hand drifted nearer to the blade sheathed at her hip. Her face was pale, hardening into anger before him now.

"There are men waiting by the tarn to kill you Cassana. I am a coward, a coward who loves you and could not do the deed myself. You must get away from here, my love, go back to my father and stand firm against the Brotherhood."

"But we will not be able to win if the armies are allowed to march on us," Cassana whispered, shamed at the sound of her own despair. "I can never forgive you, Edren, for what you have allowed to happen to my father, to Karlina, to me. You have put us all in danger, betrayed our love and trust... but I love you still and you can make amends, if you tell us all you know."

Edren shook his head bitterly. "I am, and have always been but a pawn – I see that now, Cassy. I could do little to help you, save one thing."

Cassana frowned, before the cold realisation of what he was about to do stained her face.

"No!" she hissed, rushing to his side she clutched at his mail sleeve. "Not this! Come back with me, make amends and peace with yourself. You can still be the man you were."

Edren pulled Cassana into his arms, felt her stiffen and shudder as he kissed the top of her head. Stroking her tangled hair, he tilted her face back, seeing her hatred drowning in the love filling her eyes.

"Go now, my lady," Edren whispered. "Tell my father the truth, tell him what you will. I will seek my honour in the mountains and before you leave, you must know this, Cassana. I did not work alone, you have been betrayed, closer, even still."

Cassana pulled back in his arms. "Tell me," she breathed.

"It is Lysette! She has a greater hunger, a deeper depth of desire for power than I. I have fought to protect you, to find a way to somehow keep you alive in all of this. But she, Lysette, she would happily hang you from the gates of the city, my father and mother along with you."

Sensing her shock and turmoil, Edren grasped her left hand and kissed it. Stepping away he retrieved his mount and passed the reins into her hands.

"Do not let her have her throne, Cassana," Edren said. Casting one lingering look out to the south, towards where he knew Highwater rested, he drew in a deep, calming breath, pulled his long red cloak tight about his frame and headed up the trail.

Stunned, Cassana let him go, watching the trail long after he had gone. When Storm came over to her and nudged her back to her senses, Cassana wiped her eyes, cleared her lungs and led the horses back down the mountains to have her reckoning.

Twelve men, heavily armed, stood around in scattered groups by the glistening, calm lake, whispering amongst themselves and unaware that Edren Bay was coming up the trail towards them. As the Captain of Highwater stepped out onto the rocky plateau, the leader of the group, dressed in long black robes, dropped the hood from his head and strode towards the spy, the sun filling his sight.

"Where's the Byron bitch?" he asked, fighting against the purple blotches in his eyes.

Edren looked back over his shoulder, just to be sure. Seeing the trail empty behind him, he smiled, let out a long, cleansing breath and turned back.

It was beautiful up here, a place he should have visited more. Somewhere Cassana and he might have found a love, deeper than the bond they already shared. Sighing wistfully, Edren raked a hand through his long, tangled dark hair.

"She's not coming," he said quietly, his emerald eyes flashing with sudden menace.

His blade flashed up from beneath his cloak and Edren sent it deep across the man's throat.

CHAPTER FORTY FIVE

Rebellion

Ashe Garrin warmed his cold hands together, wrapping the reins tightly about them. Despite the waning hour, the day was still bright, the sun unaware of the discomfort of the twenty two riders who made their way silently southwards across the lowlands, towards the distant hills.

"Won't be long now then," Ashe observed, dealing his captain a swift look. Elion rode in silence, ignoring him, as he had since leaving Greywood Forest, earlier that morning, his face drawn tight with worry.

Shaking his head, Ashe looked away helplessly. Since the meeting in Havensdale, Elion had fallen into a dark, brooding silence, barely able to answer beyond a nod, or distant murmur. Blowing his discomfort from his lips nervously, Ashe tried to focus on the events that were beginning to move more quickly than he could keep abreast of.

That decisive night in the Arms of the Lady, before his supper was even served, Devlin Hawke left the meeting, stating his intent to ride ahead to Greywood Forest and prepare his men for what was to come.

Leaving quiet instructions for those who were to follow, the outlaw had left those who remained at the inn to their hunger and thirst. Elion had risen to go after the outlaw leader, but Ashe had stayed him with a firm hand and a warning look.

The following morning, a grim day and omen to be certain, had seen Elion and the remnants of his patrol ride south with those other brave souls who had volunteered to rescue the Reven prisoners. The assassin and his party had left well before them and the road was empty for the Carwellian riders. Escorting two wagons, heavily laden with supplies and a dozen empty mounts they would need to carry out their plans, the comrades made swift their time, reluctant to see the task done, and yet, as Ashe had observed wryly, unable to avoid its call.

Chewing his top lip, Ashe discovered crumbs from his earlier meal, still caught in his moustache. Grinning, he looked back at Kerrin Thorn and sent him a smile. By the storms it was good to have the old tracker back. There had been more than one occasion recently, when Ashe had wondered if he would ever see his friend again. He was relieved, once they had rejoined Devlin and his men that Kerrin was well enough and had agreed to go with them, despite his reluctance to leave the donkey (who the outlaws now saw as a friend rather than their supper) and the boy Balan behind.

Beyond the heads of the Fal brothers and the rest of the Carwellian patrol, of which he now counted Elissen part of, Ashe could see Devlin Hawke, riding silently alongside Trell. The outlaws were clad in the livery of Carwell and looked just as ridiculous as they did uncomfortable. Behind them rode Kallum Campbell and his friend, Liyam Tallis, flanking the two brave recruits who had volunteered to come and act as leverage for their plan – Rellin Steelblade and Jessica Silvermoon.

Ashe could still hear Arrun Hawksblade's pleading

cries from the ramparts as they rode away, begging his friends to come home safely to him. The young swordsman had chosen to stay in Havensdale, his love for his friends second only to that of his father who still grappled fiercely with the Father of Storms, but would not, it was said, survive long enough to see his son return home, should he leave.

So much sacrifice, Ashe thought sadly.

A mournful breeze howled about them as they rode on, the lowland meadows silent, watchful of them as they turned their mounts towards the southwest, chasing after the setting sun that cast its final farewells out over the Crescent Hills.

"I've never been to Durrant's Field," Ashe admitted, soothing his mount as it lost its footing momentarily. "Have you?" he turned in his saddle, fixing his friend with a narrow look.

Feeling the weight of the stare and the depth of frustration in the question, Elion found his friend's face and couldn't help but smile.

"Not as yet," Elion said, shaking his head free of a chuckle. "I can't say that I am relishing my first visit."

Ashe nodded. "Aye, I hear you, Elion. I dread to think what we will find there, but we will find it, nonetheless."

Elion fell silent, brooding as always at the sacrifice they were making, not just to their lives, but to their honour as well. Ashe had spent long enough with his captain, his friend, to read him like an open book and he quickly turned the page before he settled into silence again.

"We have no choice, Elion, you see that don't you?"

The captain grimaced, looking away, avoiding the sergeant's eyes. When he eventually turned back, his eyes were haunted, though he nodded.

"I see it, Ashe," Elion admitted, though he didn't

sound like he did. "I just cannot believe that there is no other way, no lawful means to claim our victory."

Reluctant to embroil himself in yet another futile argument, Ashe decided upon a subtler approach. "I cannot either! I had always hoped, despite what was happening around us, that the high duke would see reason; that Gardan and his masters would bring their ambitions down upon their own heads."

They both fell silent for a time before Elion stirred. "But the high duke did not," he said, sighing. He ran a hand up over his face, massaging the tension from his temples.

Ashe nodded. "No, he was blinded by what was happening – succoured, as many were, into believing all that he was told, whilst all around him his supporters were being ostracised and murdered. It is a tragedy that we did not know all we know now, sooner – we could have avoided this. But it is clear to me Elion, that Carwell is beyond the courts now, he will not stop unless he is *stopped*."

Elion saw the regret on his friend's haggard face and nodded. "I will be honest with you I abhor that man, that assassin and what he is going to do. The thought that we will use his kind to achieve all that the law has not. What is it that separates us then, if we give our blessing to such murder? We are no better than our enemies."

Ashe growled, though remained silent long enough to rein in his anger. When he spoke, his voice was gruff.

"Listen to me Elion, I won't say this again. I have spent my whole life protecting these Vales, longer than you have and there is nobody more disgusted than I at what is happening. I am an honourable Valian man, also, though I don't polish it as frequently as you do," catching his breath and cooling the anger on his cheeks for a moment, Ashe looked away, before gripping his captain under his gaze once more.

"It is not an honourable thing, to take a life, least of all in cold blood. But what is honour if you cannot defend the people? The law has forsaken us, turned a blind eye to the horrors being inflicted upon the innocent so it can justify a war, but it does not mean that we cannot still try to do its bidding. We will do good, even if it is only this one thing – even if, after all our efforts, the hardliners still have their war and the Reven lands are conquered. What matters is that we kept our honour, that we did our duty and that we gave our lives for what we believe in."

Ashe gripped the wild heart beating furiously under his armour. "Your honour will still be there for you to find, Elion, once what needs to be done has been achieved. History will look kindly upon us if we try, though she won't be as forgiving if we do not."

"By the Lady," Elion gasped, puffing out his cheeks in surprise. "I don't know how to respond to that."

Ashe fixed his friend with a mischievous look. "Then don't," he chuckled softly. "Just think on what I have said. We can still uphold the law, you and I. There is still hope."

Elion smiled faintly, his thoughts drifting back to the hills before them. Falling silent, the two friends rode on, drawing their comrades ever closer to their destiny.

Despite the weight of tension hanging over him and his comrades, Khadazin's second return to Karick was somewhat easier. Travelling off road and journeying through lowlands and hills to avoid patrols, the small group from Havensdale made swift time, encountering only a few shepherds and cattle along the way.

On the second day, as the afternoon lengthened and the sky began to fill with heavy clouds, the group of eight riders began to reach the outlying farmsteads to the east of the Great Road.

At the head of the riders, Arillion led them silently past several smallholdings, his hood pulled up close about his face, his scarf covering his nose and mouth to ward away the stench.

The air was thick with their disgust as they reached a fourth farm and in silence, they rode past three burnt-out buildings, crossing the empty fields, left stubbled from the harvest and unattended by the tenants, who were hanging from the large oak tree by a paddock.

"This is why we act as we must," Arillion said quietly, looking over his shoulder towards Kaspen Shale. The wayfarer said nothing, his face pale and his revulsion wide in his eyes.

The woodsman rode beside Riyan, feeling his anger broil within him. Heavy with his own guilt and his bitterness full in his mouth, he looked at the mute, who sensed his attention and dragged his disgust away from the five corpses hanging from the tree.

"Was this here when you rode north?" he asked softly.

Even if he could have spoken, no words were needed and Riyan simply shook his head.

The woodsman looked away, staring ahead through the settling gloom towards the distant shadow of the city. For so long he had managed to forget about the tragedy and betrayal that had happened there. He had locked it all away, burying who he was deep into the recesses of his mind, encasing his heart in a cold shield that he hoped would never be pierced. And then he had woken to find The Seer sat across his fire from him...

Nodding towards Riyan the woodsman rode alongside the assassin, trying to bury the resentment he felt towards him, of the irritation scratched raw every time he tried to speak with him. The man had a way of getting under your skin and could find a mark with a cold barb in even the simplest of statements.

"If I had any doubts as to what we face and why we face it," Evan began, his breath ragged in his throat, "that family reminds me why Carwell must be stopped."

Arillion followed the woodsman's lingering gaze back to the dead family and nodded.

"They look like a Valian family," Arillion growled, "killed only because they worked for a Reven landlord, or perhaps were friends with one."

"I cannot believe it has come to this," the woodsman muttered, dragging himself away from the grisly sight. "Valian killing innocent Valian."

Arillion chuckled and found a deep mark under the woodsman's skin.

"There's nothing new there, believe me, I should know."

The sun was still breaking through the clouds as Arillion led his charges into the sewers of Karick. Relieved to be away from any scrutiny and the chance of being spotted by a patrol, he led them by meagre torchlight through his domain.

By the storms it was good to be back, Arillion mused, the only one in the group revelling at the stench and enjoying the cold water that dripped from the darkness above to somehow find a course down through clothing to bare skin.

In truth, he could have led them blindly through the darkness, each turn or break in the path as familiar to him as the curves of Cassana's hips.

Grinning, he took them through a deep pool of Karick's deposits, where the path sunk lower than the river of filth and he threw a glittering look over his shoulder as the woodsman followed him, then turned gallantly to offer a gloved hand to help the huntress Tania across.

Without waiting, Arillion carried on, trying to ignore

the feeling that if he had handed the woodsman the torch, he too, would have been able to lead the way.

By the time the assassin reached the seemingly blank, featureless wall, his leg was throbbing and his left shoulder was stiff. At least this time he hadn't had to carry Cassana all the way...

Several kicks to the hidden door brought hasty footsteps down the steep staircase beyond and as those behind him gathered their breaths, the wall slid away to reveal an old, toothless face glowing in the fresh lantern light before them.

"Talin," Arillion greeted, pulling his scarf down his face.

The thin-faced old man regarded the ghost before him for a moment, then looked at those gathered in the scattering shadows behind.

"We heard you were dead," Talin grunted.

"So did I," Arillion replied, smiling. "Take us to your boss."

"He's not here," the old man responded, shrugging. "He's been gone for some days now, though nobody knows where."

Arillion dealt his comrades a worried look, before Talin drew him back.

"He said that when Riyan and the Redani returned, to let them in and give them sanctuary."

Without offering them further explanation, the old man turned away and, for a man of his years, began to bound effortlessly up the steep, narrow stairs before him.

Flicking a hand, Arillion motioned for his comrades to follow them and Riyan, hanging about worriedly at the rear of the group, quickly pulled the secret wall back into place behind him.

At the top of the stairs, Talin offered them a seat at the old table, then hurried away to find refreshments. Arillion grabbed one of the four chairs and settled down on the creaking wood with an elaborate sigh.

Riyan motioned for Tania to follow him and as they slipped away through the door beyond the table, the woodsman, Khadazin and Kaspen Shale took up the vacant seats.

A weary, thoughtful silence settled on the room, as those standing found a cold wall to support their weary bodies. Drawn to the flickering candle waning away on the table before them, each man slipped away with his own counsel, lost to the events witnessed that day, pulled beyond to what would follow.

"So what is the plan, Arillion?" the woodsman asked finally, tracing a knot in the wood of the table with a forefinger. He looked up to see the grey eyes flick to him. "What should be our next move?"

Shifting the cramp from his left buttock to the right one, Arillion sat forward.

"Until word reaches the capital and Gardan falls for the bait, we will watch the city, find out what is happening in the streets and observe the movements of those we seek." He flicked a look towards Khadazin and offered the giant Redani a lop-sided smile. "Well, most of us that is."

Khadazin returned the smile. "I understand that I cannot walk about the city freely anymore and I shall remain here until we are ready to act, waiting for my friend's return."

"Where could Savinn Kassaar have gone?" Kaspen asked, stroking the fork of his beard thoughtfully.

Arillion's worry flashed in his eyes. "I do not know," he began. "But he would not have fled the city. He is not that kind of man."

"He said in his letter he had *'one last hand to play'*," Khadazin offered. "Perhaps he is trying to find support for our cause?"

The woodsman nodded. "Let us hope so, as our numbers are few and we face a great many dangers."

Arillion turned his head, his eyes flashing with something.

"I wanted to ask you, *woodsman*," he began and delighted when he saw his prey squirm. "Why are you here? Why *did* you get involved? Why do I get the feeling you have been here before?"

"What do you mean?" the woodsman asked quietly in return, tensing.

Arillion looked about the table for support, waving a hand airily. "Well, for one, you were not surprised by the hidden wall and you do not seem taken aback by this hidden complex, deep under the city. Why is that, I wonder?"

The woodsman's face was pale, haggard and world-weary as he looked down at his trembling hands. He sighed and looked up again.

"I have an old debt to settle, assassin, as have you," Evan began hesitantly, his heart hammering away. "I can see why you have stayed alive so long, you perceive a great deal."

Arillion dismissed the praise with a shrug of his hands and his continuing silence forced the woodsman to carrying on speaking. The others in the room watched on, drawn to the conversation, but wishing they were somewhere else.

"And you are right to say that I have... been here before," the woodsman continued, stumbling over his explanation. "Even though it is not your business, I shall tell you all why. We are comrades in this now and you deserve to know the truth."

Kaspen dealt an accusatory look at Arillion and the assassin replied with a knowing wink.

The woodsman cleared his throat. "Many years ago my life was in great danger. I was, still am loyal to the high duke and because of this, Savinn Kassaar had his men rescue me from certain death. The man Cullen was one of them and he brought me here, hiding me away until it was safe to get me from the city. I met Savinn once, on the day I left..."

Arillion clapped his hands together triumphantly, not trying to hide his delight.

"I knew it, I knew I recognised you," he said, his face calming down into a smile. He looked about the table, settling his eyes on Khadazin. "You have a strong ally, Redani. May I present Evan Valus, brother of that bastard chancellor you want to get your hands... err, have your reckoning with."

Khadazin's dark skin paled somewhat. He blinked and looked at the woodsman, but could not find any words.

The woodsman sighed heavily, a weight lifting from him. He nodded towards the assassin, who inclined his head in return,

"My brother, as he has so many others, betrayed me and coerced others to send me to the gallows," Evan said. "Savinn Kassaar saved me. He saved me as he did Lady Byron, as he did you, Redani. It is criminal that his loyalty to the high duke should be poisoned by those who would see every Reven hung from a tree. Without his aid, our cause would already be lost and we should reward all that he has done for the Valian people by finding him and finishing this, before it is too late."

Arillion rose up, drawing attention to him. He glanced at all present, seeing the determination flashing there.

"And tomorrow, that is exactly what we will do," the assassin turned to leave, but Evan's call stayed him.

"A moment, Arillion," the chancellor's brother asked. "I feel it time you shared your knowledge with us, knowledge of this scarred woman, the woman you say you know, the woman you believe to know killed Alion Byron and tortured Lucien Varl. We may all die soon and such knowledge should not be lost."

Arillion stiffened as a coldness, more chilling than anything he had felt for some time, swept through his body. There was a note of goading in the woodsman's voice and he felt his hackles rise.

"Yes," Kaspen Shale added, amusement flashing in his eyes. "Tell us, Arillion. It could be very useful to us."

Arillion turned about, his eyes glittering with disdain and his anger directed at the wayfarer. Kaspen had pestered him before about her identity, so much so that he had been ready to cut his throat and hide him in a ditch.

"Very well," Arillion growled, folding his arms across his chest. He held the woodsman's eyes. "But you won't like it."

Crossing back to the table the assassin sat down. "I know of this woman, that much is obvious, and I *do* believe she is the one who murdered Alion Byron," he admitted, his eyes hooded.

"How can you be so certain?" the woodsman asked, leaning forward.

Arillion smiled bitterly. "Because I gave her the scar."

Kaspen looked about the table, seeing the looks on Khadazin and Evan Valus' faces. He flicked his nerves towards Agris Varen. The giant wayfarer leant against the door frame, his thick arms wrapped across his broad chest. Agris met his friend's warning look and tensed.

"You gave her the scar?" Evan asked, perplexed. "Then who is she? Why do you seek her? Why are you willing to walk towards certain death to do so?"

Arillion forced a smile. "For the very same reason you do, captain."

"What do you mean by that?" Evan asked reluctantly.

Closing his eyes, Arillion gathered his breath. Sighing, he rested one hand on the table, whilst his other strayed below and to the knife hidden in his boot.

"Years ago, I was hired to kill an important woman, one whose worth was more than my weight in gold," the first spark of fear in the woodsman's eyes began to flare. "Back then I worked with a woman, we shared marks and we shared everything, if you take my meaning. We did not know why the woman had to die, that is not important to our kind and I did not stop to think about it beforehand, though with hindsight, I wish that I had."

Evan Valus' distaste dripped heavy from his tongue. "And just when I was starting to like you."

Arillion threw a cold look across the table. "Do not judge me, captain. There is more honesty in what I do than any claim you can level against me. Where were you when the high duke needed you most? Why have you not acted sooner against your brother? Had you found the courage and not hidden away in a forest, we would not be in this mess. Do not seek to besmirch my actions when your inaction is just as great a sin."

Evan recoiled, his anger draining from his face. He glanced about, seeing the looks others dealt him and clenched his fists.

"Just tell me what you know," Evan sighed wearily, his shoulders sagging. "Why you are so certain she is the one."

Arillion chewed his top lip, drumming his right hand across the table before him. *It would be easier to spare him the agony... wouldn't it?* Arillion chuckled inwardly. *True! But not nearly as much fun*!

"As you wish," he said. "I was hired by your brother, all those years ago, to kill your woman, Lady Ashcroft."

The woodsman rose up angrily, his chair tumbling across the wooden floor boards as he drew his sword. Arillion was just a swift, his eyes glittering from across the table as the rest of the room reacted.

"Stay your blade," Arillion hissed, revealing his own weapon and putting it down on the table between them.

"I did not kill her, but my woman did. I was betrayed as we stalked through the sewers to enter the keep. She had a lover, it turns out, and they planned to take all the gold. They attacked me and I barely escaped with my life. Badly wounded, I fled, surviving only by throwing myself into the sewerage, flowing out to safety with the rest of the shit. It took me many months to recover, but I did and I knew, one day, that I would have my revenge on her, give her back the blade she had buried in my back."

The woodsman stepped back, clutching at his throat with his left hand and trying to free his breath. Kaspen Shale stepped close and prised the sword from his forgotten hand.

"It is to her, and to your brother that you should direct you vengeance, Evan," Arillion said, his face full of regret. "Her involvement in this started many years ago when she started taking the Brotherhood's coin. I admit it, I *would* have killed your woman, but destiny had other ideas and I did not. My lover betrayed me, as your brother did you. Together, we shall make them pay for what they have set in motion and after, if we are both alive and you still think I must pay also, then we shall settle matters, you and I."

Evan Valus stared at the assassin, looked at those gathered close to him. Shaking his head, the weight of the past bore down on him again and he broke down before them.

CHAPTER FORTY SIX

Reap What You Sow

The sky was still holding on to the last embers of the day as Cassana led her mounts down the trail towards the group of people rushing towards her. With her mind scattered by recent events and her senses drowned by Edren's revelations, she did not register the words that William Bay cried out to her, nor did she truly believe that Fawn Ardent was there, following behind Sergeant Calen's men and Erith Taye.

"My lady," William said, his relief evident on his drawn, ageing features. He pulled Cassana into his arms and held on tightly to her. "We have been so worried about you."

Over his shoulder, Cassana saw Fawn, peering over the heads of the men before her, her eyes bright with joy and her eagerness to see her friend again stayed only by her sense of duty. Dealing Fawn a beaming smile, Cassana pulled back to hold William at arm's length.

"How did you find me?" she asked, looking about the men gathering close, seeing their own relief flashing on their faces.

"It has been a busy day, my lady," William said. "When Sergeant Calen returned from Havensdale with Captain Ardent, we sought you out. It was then that we discovered your absence, of the fact things... were not as they should be."

"We were forced to break into your father's study, my lady," Erith Taye elaborated. "It was then that we discovered the letter."

Cassana shuddered, drawing her attention back to the question on William's lips.

"Where is my son?" William dared to ask.

Cassana took William's hands in her own to find that he shook just as much as she. There was a light growing in his eyes, once filled with uncertainty and now laced with abject fear.

"Oh my dear friend," Cassana whispered, shaking her head sadly. She hid behind her tresses for a time, gathering her composure. "Edren was taking me to the chancellor's men. He is the spy, William. He told me so, before he sent me away."

William blinked, oblivious to the gasps of horror rising from the throats of those gathered near.

"I do not understand, my lady?" William said dumbly, stepping back. "My son is the spy? There must be some mistake? We know that it is someone else."

Cassana gripped his hands tightly, stepping close to him again.

"I am so sorry, William. Edren confessed to me, before he saved me from certain death," Cassana leant in close, whispering in his right ear. "But he confirmed that which we know. He and Lysette were working together. She is the real threat to us all. She will see us all dead before too long. Edren was torn apart by his betrayal – he could not live with our blood staining his hands."

William flinched, as if he had been dealt a stinging blow. Fighting with his emotions he pulled away, staring for a time across the Great Divide. After a brief moment, he straightened his shoulders and spun on his booted heels.

"Sergeant Calen, you and your men will follow me to find my son," William barked crisply. "Erith, I want you to safely escort Lady Byron and Captain Ardent back to Highwater. Wait for us there."

Both men saluted as William nodded, turning back to Cassana.

"Wait for me, Cassana," her father's old friend said, finding a hollow smile. "There is much we must discuss, a great deal of news we need to dissect. Captain Ardent will explain more along the way."

Cassana looked back up the trail, fighting against the urge to demand she went with them. Sensing her dilemma, Fawn came pushing through the men and dragged Cassana into a deep embrace.

"By the storms, I have missed you," Fawn said and their smiles and joy at their reunion overcame their worries for a moment.

Cassana held her friend tightly to her, taking strength from Fawn's wild heart. Pulling back to study her features, she lost herself in her smile.

"I cannot believe you are here!" Cassana laughed and sobbed at the same time.

Fawn, tears running down her cheeks, caught the look William dealt her. Sniffing, she slipped an arm through Cassana's, as Erith Taye took hold of the two horses' reins.

"We have so much to talk about," Fawn said. Squeezing her friend's hand, she steered Cassana down towards the wide trail that fell through the mountains towards Highwater.

Erith Taye saluted his comrades and followed after the two women, the horses' hooves clattering over the uneven ground behind him.

"Come, Sergeant," William whispered sadly to Calen. Turning to look up the narrow trail to the east, William drew his Valian steel and went to find his son.

Devlin Hawke guided his mount alongside Elion Leigh and Ashe Garrin, as they reached the boundaries of the mining community know as Durrant's Field.

"Keep riding," the outlaw hissed, as the column slowed in horror and disgust.

The sun had not settled yet and the sky was blushing with purple, throwing its sadness on the smouldering pyre a mile to the east of the high wooden walls of Durrant's Field.

Kerrin Thorn had been the first to pick up the charred smell of death on the wind and as they came closer to the distant tendrils of smoke, the riders' throats and nostrils became choked by their disgust.

Unable to tear their eyes away, despite their revulsion, the patrol rode silently by the spitting pyre of charred and smouldering bodies, thrown together without ceremony or care, most likely without word to guide them into the next.

"Who are they?" Elissen whispered, shocked beyond her emotions.

Jarion Kail, as always not far from her side, reached out to touch her shoulder.

"Reven prisoners," he said angrily. "Most likely the ones who have died whilst working the mines..." he trailed off not wanting to add that it could be the ones who were not fit enough to work there.

Elion Leigh heard their exchange, as the riders grouped together. With his voice barely containing his anger, he threw a look at all gathered close.

"If there is any doubt in any of you of what we do, this barbarism serves as a stark reminder."

Turning his mount away from the pyre, Elion raised a hand and signalled they continue.

Devlin Hawke caught Trell's look of disgust and scowled.

"Just get me inside those walls," he hissed, clenching his fists tightly about his fury.

The news that Fawn divulged to Cassana, as they reaffirmed their deep affection for one another, only hastened their safe return to Highwater. As they began travelling through the busy streets, Cassana could only listen wide-eyed, as Fawn told her all that had happened, of the risks that had been taken and of the sacrifices that had been made.

The news of Khadazin's safe return and of Lady Stromn and her son's rescue helped dull the raw wound of Edren's confession and of Lysette's betrayal for a time.

"I can only thank you and the Lady for your timely arrival," Cassana mused, as they made for the distant towers of Highwater Keep. "I fear for what might have happened had you not."

Fawn smiled, her eyes still searching the lengthening shadows for sign of further betrayal.

"I feel we should all place our thanks on Savinn Kassaar's table," Fawn said quietly. "Cullen's letter he bore north for you should underline that even further."

Cassana nodded, thinking of the squat, ugly man who had so unnerved her when she last met him. Dragging herself away from a forming image of Arillion, she promised herself that she would never judge people by their appearance again, only by their actions.

"Mister Cullen has aided me twice now," Cassana murmured. "I feel I owe both him and his master a great deal more than I can ever truly repay."

Erith Taye, following behind them both, spoke up.

"You should know, my lady, that Lucien Varl is being tended to, and his wounds, whilst terrible, should not claim his life. He has strength, that one."

Cassana sent a smile over her shoulder. "Indeed! I am most keen to meet and thank him, also. Tell me, Erith. Is Bryn Astien still in Highwater?"

"Yes, my lady," Erith replied. "He has taken personal responsibility for the protection of Lady Stromn and her son."

"Good," Cassana said, nodding thoughtfully. Her mind wandered for a long while and she did not see the worried looks Erith and Fawn shared.

"As soon as we arrive home," Cassana continued eventually, "I will meet with Mister Cullen and read his letter. When Sir William returns, we shall have much to discuss."

"As you wish, my lady," Erith replied dutifully.

Cassana began to look away then hesitated, her eyes narrowing.

"Tell me, Erith... Edren had a deep cut on his cheek. He told me that he received it during a spar with you. Was he telling me the truth, or was that also a lie?"

Erith sighed, shaking his head, his answer clear in his eyes.

More lies...

Cassana chewed her lip, squeezing Fawn's hand for support and reassurance. Edren's betrayal had wounded her deeply, but his last act, his final attempt of redemption had given her the chance to endure, to survive and strike back at her enemies.

Letting out a calming breath, Cassana sent a rallying smile to her companions, her path clear before her.

She would speak with Cullen to find out what Savinn Kassaar had to say and then, then she would go and see her dearest friend, Lysette.

"Follow my lead," Elion Leigh hissed from the corner of his mouth, as he led his 'Carwellian' patrol towards the gates of Durrant's Field.

The sun was low behind the Crescent Hills now, a fading blush that clung to the dark horizon. But, even amidst their rumbling approach, the patrol could still hear the distant echo of the work continuing beyond and see the smoke curling away from the hungry smelting furnaces.

The guards on the ramparts stirred finally, featureless black shapes that reacted with slow curiosity, rather than a hurried, defensive call to arms.

Over the rebellion in his chest and the whispers of caution hissing in his ears, Elion Leigh drew his patrol to a crisp halt. Standing in his stirrups, he raised a hand in greeting.

"A fair eve," Elion called out, his voice loud in the settling hush.

The guard nodded his agreement, though Elion could not make out the man's features

"Better than the storms we've had of late," the guard agreed, leaning against his spear. "You are a long way from Carwell, captain – what brings you to this cesspit?"

Elion smiled. Pulling off his riding gloves he ran a hand through his tangled hair. He threw a weary look at his comrades, blinking.

"Orders, I am afraid," Elion answered, looking back. "We have been called to Karick, to aid in the preparations. Thinking to hasten the journey, we cut across country–," Elion turned in his saddle, motioning to Rellin and Jessica, who cast their eyes downwards compliantly to their hands, bound and lashed to the pommels of their saddles, "and found these two running like hares towards Greywood. Are they yours?"

The guard leant over the wall for a better look. After a

moment's study, he shrugged.

"Probably," he spat. "We've had a few rats escape recently, due to overcrowding. Those we weren't able to shoot down, we let run."

Hiding his anger, Elion forced a bright smile. "Well you are welcome to these two. Put them back to good use or hang them for all I care."

The guard turned to his companion and they spoke quietly for a moment. In the silence that followed, which lasted what felt like days but in truth, probably only a few heartbeats, Elion dealt Ashe and Devlin a swift look.

Grim-faced, Ashe nodded his head slightly, whilst the outlaw leader flicked him a look full of bloody murder.

"We could always do with a few more hands," the guard called down, finally. "You are welcome to water your horses and share a fire for the night, if you wish?"

Offering hearty thanks, Elion waited impatiently as the order was given to open up the gates. Every second that passed stirred with the prospect of something going wrong and it wasn't until the gates were hauled open, that he found a calming breath.

His throat dry, Elion waved his patrol on and with their hearts in their mouths they accepted their invitation and rode without a fight into the enemy camp.

The sight that greeted the patrol from Greywood sickened them to the last and Elion tore his eyes away from the desperate scene that greeted him. Wary that they had not yet succeeded, he knew that the abject conditions hundreds of Reven slaves were being forced to work in could only be rectified once the guards were overpowered.

The air was thick with the smell of filth and squalor, acrid with the glowing forges away to his right. Filthy Reven scurried under the lash of a couple of guards, up and down the narrow slopes that rose to various dark tunnels in the hillside – a weary stream of the enslaved, who shouldered their sorrows and heavy burdens with vacant, lost stares. Elion could also see hundreds of wooden crates, many already full of weapons, ready for wagons and the war that would surely follow if they failed.

Casting a look about the guards nearby, he counted only ten, noting several more towards the mines. Unaware of the newcomers, they stood idly chatting near the pens where many Reven would be forced to spend the night.

Slipping from his saddle, Elion landed heavily in the deep mud and marched a smile over to the guards who came towards them.

"My thanks," Elion said, offering a hand to the sharp-faced man who reached him first.

"Always glad of the company," the man who had spoken smiled, highlighting the scar above his left eyebrow. He was early into the summer of his life, a lean fellow with sandy curling hair, dressed in leathers that bore the crest of the high duke.

As they shook hands, Elion was aware of his comrades dismounting. Holding the guard's sapphire eyes, he glanced about casually as Trell and Jarion made a good show of abusing Rellin and Jessica from their saddles.

"Likewise! We'd be obliged only for some water and a moment's rest then we shall be on our way," Elion stated, cocking a curious eye towards the many mining tunnels gouged into the earth. "How is it going? You seem to have enough of the scum to do the work – though perhaps not the men to guard them?"

The guard threw a look to the mines and sighed. "I don't think we will ever have enough of them for the amount of weapons Karick wants – but then I am only a soldier and we do what we must with the men that we have been given."

Elion bobbed his head, watching as Trell and Jarion forced their prisoners onto their knees.

"They are all yours," Elion observed, forcing enough

gratitude into his words.

Waving some of his men forward, the guard turned to Elion.

"I'll show you to the water, captain," he made to leave, then paused. "I have some dispatches, if you would deliver them to the city for me?"

Before Elion could reply, he was aware of movement beside him and Devlin Hawke appeared, sword in hand. He levelled his blade at the man as Ashe and the others leapt upon the unsuspecting guards.

"I think we will let you take it yourselves," Devlin hissed, twisting the tip of his steel under the terrified man's chin.

"W-what are you doing?" the man stammered, his eyes wide with fear and disbelief.

Elion looked about, seeing that the few guards left on the ramparts were being ordered down at bow-point. To his right, Jessica rose up from the mud and spat in the face of one of the guards before her.

"We are taking over Durrant's Field," Elion said, smiling. "Order your men to surrender their weapons, or we will give you to your prisoners."

The guard looked about, his eyes flicking wildly for any help he could find. When he realised that he and his men were outnumbered, had been taken by surprise, his shoulders slumped.

"Alright," the man whined, gulping. His voice faded under the strain of his defeat. "I'll get the others to throw down their arms. What do you want from us?"

Elion took the spear from the man's limp hand and waited for Devlin to lower his blade from his throat.

"I want you to take a message for us to Commander Renald Gardan in Karick," Elion smiled. "Tell him that Durrant's Field is now ours and that he can come and claim it back if he has the spine and courage to do so."

"Oh," Devlin said absently, as he was turning away.

He clicked his thoughts through his fingers. "And tell him that Elion Leigh and Devlin Hawke will be waiting for him."

Before the guard could respond, the outlaw leader drove his fist deep into the man's stomach.

"There was no need for that," Elion growled, reaching down to help the retching guard up.

"Yes there was," Devlin snapped, throwing a look back into the plains and the distant pyre of burning dead.

The dark lines deepened under Elion's tired eyes as he nodded and searched for Kerrin Thorn. The old tracker was watching him expectantly and nodding his accord, he pulled the hunting horn from his saddle bag and blew three, long deep blasts.

William Bay forced his legs up the narrow trail that would take him and his men to Highwater Lake. Each step he took grew heavier, every breath he found fought for life in his chest.

The sky overhead was low, full of circling crows and dark clouds that brooded over the departing day. As he stepped up onto the rocky plateau, a cold wind picked up his senses, dragging his eyes from the jagged horizon and still waters of the distant lake towards the bloody battleground before him.

"Have a care," William warned, his old training flooding through his cramping muscles. As Sergeant Calen and his men spread out warily behind him, they made towards the bodies, listening for sounds of life.

The dead were everywhere, offering their wordless testament of the brutal fight that had taken place. Stepping around a severed arm, still clutching a Valian Longsword, William picked a wary path across the bloodied rocks, sweeping the corpses for a sign of his son.

Overhead, the crows watched on for their supper as

the Valian men knelt beside each body, searching for Edren Bay. One man turned over a corpse, startling the rat that was feasting upon the dead man's split belly. Crying out, the soldier stumbled away, doubling over to retch away his disgust.

Gripping his sword tightly, William Bay turned away from a headless corpse, spying, for the first time, the thick trail of blood that splashed over the rocky ground towards the shores of the lake.

A dark shadow lay by the water's edge and with his breath lost to the wind and his heart forgotten, William followed the trail of blood towards his son.

"Oh my boy," William sobbed, as he turned over the body, cut deeply by many blades, pierced by several arrows. Pulling the still body into his arms, William roared his anger to the heavens, scattering the crows overhead.

Edren flinched, thick, dark blood bursting across his lips as he coughed up a breath.

"Edren?" William cried in relief. Holding his son close, he stroked his blooded, matted hair.

At his cry, several men made to go to William's aid and then, respectfully, stayed where they were, their heads bowed low in sorrow.

"I am sorry, father," Edren rasped, spitting blood. "I was trying to protect Cassana, shield her from the danger – but she was too much like Alion. Forgive me!"

William could not hide his shock and his tears flowed freely. "What have you done, my son?"

Growling, fighting with his agony, Edren clutched at his father's mail, dragging him down to hear his fading words.

"Is Cassana safe?"

William nodded. "She is, fear not, my son."

Edren sank into his father's arms, a crimson smile broad across his pallid features.

"That is good," he murmured, closing his eyes. "At

least there is some good left in this world."

William took Edren's hand, the one that had fingers left and placed his own sword into his son's grasp. At the touch of the blade in his hand, Edren's eyes flickered open and he gripped the hilt with the last of his strength, clutching it to his chest.

"Tell me why you betrayed us, my son?" William said, his hand reaching for the dagger in his right boot.

"I wanted to be someone, father," Edren whispered weakly, his body stiffening.

"But you are someone, Edren," William replied softly, tears streaking down the lines in his face. "You are my son!"

Pulling his only child close, William Bay slipped his blade deep into his son's heart.

CHAPTER FORTY SEVEN

Friends will be Friends

The last time Cassana had seen Cullen was in the dark quiet of a wood outside Karick. Not able to recall the name of the copse and unwilling to recount her emotions and fears on that cold night, she hurried forward to greet the short, fat man whose appearance, it seemed, had not improved.

Cullen turned away from the painting he was inspecting, his nose wrinkling as he offered Cassana a faint smile, lost amidst his thick, red beard.

Dragging her eyes away from the lewd tattoos on his bared hairy arms, Cassana stepped close and hugged the man, ignoring the dust of the road, the staleness of his breath and the stench from his clothes that she suspected he had worn the last time they were together.

But, despite all of that, Cassana could not help at being overjoyed to see him. Cullen was, she came to realise quickly, one of the last physical pieces of tangible proof that Arillion had been real, that their journey and flight northwards from Karick *had* happened and was not just a cruel figment of her imagination. This man before her had known the assassin. He too understood who Arillion was and what he had been like.

Thinking of Arillion suddenly raked up images of Karlina, of her grandfather Galen and then, much to her torment, of her father and Edren. Reining in her fraying composure, she pulled away from recent events and Cullen's timid embrace.

Fawn watched as the repulsive creature shuffled his discomfort and surprise between his feet, offering Cassana his shy greetings, caught somewhere between a half-bow and curtsey. As Kassaar's man handed over the scroll case he had been guarding, he stepped respectfully away, his good eye darting furtively about the great hall as he stated his genuine joy at finding her safe and tugged nervously at his fraying trousers.

"I cannot begin to thank you for your timely arrival, Mister Cullen," Cassana said, as she broke the dark wax seal and unrolled the scroll case.

"Very timely, I am told, Lady Byron," Cullen responded dutifully. His eye darted to Fawn over a smile that was not altogether reassuring.

Fawn looked away, watching as Cassana slowly read the message from Savinn Kassaar. As her wide eyes reached the end of the letter, they filled with tears.

"Is everything alright?" Fawn asked, as Cassana struggled with her composure.

Cassana shook her head, the letter and her hand falling limply to her side. "There is much to be comforted by in Savinn's letter, of the evidence that we now have. But the cost we have and will all continue to pay has been underlined deeply by news that... that the woman who helped me when I was being drugged by Madam Grey, Dia, is dead."

Fawn put an arm about Cassana's shoulders and pulled her close. Kissing the top of her head, she looked across at Erith Taye and Cullen.

"She was a brave lass," Cullen said, bowing his head to hide the glimmer in his good eye.

Two servants entered the hall and came slowly, respectfully towards them as Cassana gathered her composure.

"Can you tell me where Bryn Astien and his daughter are?" she asked of them as she gently pulled free of Fawn's embrace.

"Lord Astien attends to your guests, my lady," the elder woman said, as she curtseyed. "I have only recently returned from taking refreshments to Lady Lysette in the Reading Room. She has retired there for the afternoon to read some poetry."

"Thank you, Mary, that will be all for the moment," Cassana said, dismissing them both with a warm smile. When they were gone, she turned to her protectors.

"Erith? Would you go to Lord Astien and kindly ask him to join me in the Reading Room at his earliest convenience?"

Erith straightened to attention and slapped his right fist above his heart dutifully. He began to hurry away, slowed thoughtfully and then turned back.

"Beg your pardon, Lady Byron, but I should stay with you, Sir William was most explicit that..."

Cassana cut him off with a flippant wave of a hand. "It will be fine, Erith. I have Captain Ardent and Mister Cullen with me. We shall wait for your return outside the Reading Room before proceeding."

If he harboured any doubts, Erith hid them well and spinning on purposeful heels, he hurried away to the east.

Fawn watched him slip hurriedly through a door, then turned back to regard Cassana.

"Perhaps we should wait," Fawn advised.

Cassana shook her head, loose strands of her thick hair swirling about her face. "I have waited too long," she said softly. Turning, she headed for the sweeping staircase, leaving Cullen and Fawn to hurry after her.

It did not take long, such was Cassana's haste, and she soon led them to an elegant landing, furnished by a soft, deep red carpet and white walls decorated by paintings. In one curtained alcove, an alabaster statue of a naked woman playing a harp drew Fawn's attention as they passed. Cullen lingered as the women swept away from him and then, remembering where he was, shuffled after them.

Cassana slowed before a large oak door, its frame ornately carved and fashioned into the image of two trees, their branches spreading above the doorway to cradle a bronze plaque which read 'Reading Room.'

Fawn eyed the twin sofa adjacent to the door. "We should rest a moment, wait for her father to come," she offered quietly, watching as Cassana stood before the door, her hand straying to the short blade, hanging from her right hip.

Cassana half-turned, but could not meet her gaze. "Wait here for me. I need to speak with Lysette, alone."

"Is that wise?" Fawn protested quietly, fearful that they would be overheard. "You have been through so much today and may not be able to think clearly."

Cassana came and took Fawn's shaking hands in her own. She gripped her friend tightly, holding her eyes with a look of sad regret.

"I need to see the truth in her eyes before her father comes and her defences go up. Bryn Astien dotes on his daughter and would never believe that she is the spy. It would be too easy now for her to blame it all on Edren and I shall not allow that to happen."

Fawn searched Cassana's face, could see a determination fixed there that had never been there before. Her friend had been through so much, suffered danger and great personal tragedy and it had changed her, shaped her into the strong woman she was becoming. Fawn realised that the Cassana she knew, the one she cared about was no longer there. She was like a freshly forged blade, cold, strong and ready for battle and it was unlikely anything she said would divert her from her course.

"We will be outside," Fawn sighed, releasing Cassana's hands.

Cullen shuffled forward. "Call us if you need us," he added gruffly, fingering the pommel of the dagger, sheathed at his hip.

Offering her thanks, Cassana turned. She placed a tentative hand on the ringed handle, drew in a deep breath and then pushed her way inside the Reading Room.

When Cassana locked the door behind her, Fawn realised she may have made a grave mistake.

Cassana's heart was racing as she turned to lock the door, her eyes falling briefly towards the woman who languished serenely on a low sofa, her attentions drawn from the small leather book she held up before her face and the momentary shock that flashed there.

Fighting for breath, Cassana cooled her rising anger against the wood of the door and tried to calm herself down by thinking what Arillion would do.

Head before heart...

Steeling her nerves, Cassana unclenched her fists and pulled her forehead away from the cold comfort of the door, turning to look at Lysette, as she regarded her curiously, a warm smile spreading across her features where there was no longer any beauty to be found, only the calculated mask of betrayal.

The room was bathed in candlelight, the velvet drapes flanking the tall double window to the south, still kept apart to allow the final warmth of the day to seek out any words attempting to hide on the page.

"Where have you been, my love?" Lysette enquired, setting aside her poetry book. "I have not seen you all day. Where is Edren?"

As her words found their mark and Lysette swung her feet down to the marble floor, Cassana suddenly knew what Arillion would do.

"Come, my dear," Cassana said, a ghostly smile dancing across her lips. "You know perfectly well where I have been, though I daresay you expected Edren to step through that door, not I."

Lysette snorted, rising gracefully from the sofa, her silk gown glowing in the light. As always she looked pristine, her features pale and regal, her long sunshine hair neatly pinned, her jewellery carefully chosen.

"I can assure you that I have no idea what you are talking about. You have clearly had a bad day, my dove. Come, have some honeyed wine and sit beside me." Her childhood friend forced a jovial jingle into her words, though as she patted the sofa with a shaking hand, they sounded more like steel dragged upon stone.

"Will Edren be joining us?" Lysette continued nervously, as she moved away to a sideboard and picked up a decanter of wine.

"No," Cassana said, seeing Lysette's bared shoulders tighten, "he will not – but I can take you to him, if you like?"

Lysette turned, her eyebrows narrowing, an empty glass in her left hand, the half-filled decanter in her right.

"Well, where is he?" Lysette demanded impatiently.

"He is dead," Cassana growled, brushing her right hand over the pommel of her sword.

Lysette's face paled even further and both glass and decanter fell to the floor with a clatter. The glass shattered, the decanter surviving, its contents spreading out like blood across the floor.

"Not quite how things were planned?" Cassana smiled

dangerously, her words chasing Lysette's downcast eyes through the silence.

"I do not know what you are talking about, Cassana," Lysette said, finally meeting Cassana's withering stare. Her mask was back in place, though the shock still lingered in her eyes.

Cassana stepped closer and Lysette's attention flickered to the blade Cassana wore.

"Spare me the lies, Lysette," Cassana hissed. "Edren confessed to me what you have been plotting all these years, what you and he have done to this household – of your complicit betrayal."

Lysette tossed her head back and laughed, a deep throaty cackle full of bitter hatred.

"And just how do you think you are going to prove it, now that my lover is gone?"

Cassana recoiled, seeing the disgust and loathing burning the amber from Lysette's eyes. Her mind began to spin, her breath caught in her throat.

"But we have been friends since we were young!" Cassana nearly choked on her words.

"A necessary evil, I am afraid, one that I knew I would have to suffer, even at such a young age," Lysette smiled, flicking imaginary dirt from the fingers of her left hand. "You have no idea how difficult it has been all these years, watching your father gain the power he reluctantly wielded, whilst my father stood in his shadow and I, drowning in your selfishness and self-pity."

Cassana bristled. "You were always the ambitious one," she snapped, rallying. "But this betrayal, your deceit, the suffering you have caused. How could you do this to us, Lysette? How could you do this to the Valian people?"

"Believe me, Cassana," Lysette chuckled, regarding her former friend with a pitying smile. "A few years spent with you and I would have been willing to betray myself."

Cassana laughed, turning aside the barb with a shrug.

"Spare me your petty words, they mean nothing to me now. All that matters is that I and everyone else will know what you are, will hear of your betrayal before the end."

Lysette sighed, as if bored with the conversation. She tilted her head to one side and fixed her friend with a look of confidence.

"With that fool Edren dead, there is no proof, no evidence for that which you claim, Cassana. My father will not believe you, he will never be able to accept what I have done."

"We shall find out, when he arrives," Cassana smiled, watching Lysette's confidence wane. "You shall discover what side he supports, will see that his honour is stronger than any love he may have for you."

"Still the little girl," Lysette snarled, advancing towards Cassana. "You, like your father before you are blind, you cannot see what is happening in the Vales, what is about to occur. My father will, when the high duke is dead and he finds that he has no political allies left to hide behind. He will know then which side to choose, he will quickly come to realise where the real power in this land now lies."

"That will never happen, Lysette," Cassana spat, standing tall against her friend's advance. "Your allies, this *Brotherhood* will never cross these mountains whilst I draw breath. We have all the evidence we need to reveal the real traitors to the Valian people. You will hang, like they, for your crimes."

"Cling to your fanciful dreams, Lady Byron," Lysette smiled, her eyes flashing menacingly. "Your father was blinded by his honour and loyalty to the high duke, growing fat on the peace of this land. He, like the high duke, will fade to memory once the Valian might rises up to smash the Reven and claim their lands."

Lysette turned away, striding over to the cabinet to pour a glass of wine from a fresh bottle. "It is not too late for you to choose the *right* side, Cassana. To become a part of history, not fall afoul of it."

"And what would you know of sides?" Cassana hissed. "You know nothing of what is occurring here, Lysette. You bask only where the sun shines brightest. You know and care nothing for friendship or loyalty! You are nothing but a common traitor and I will see you hang for what you have done to this house, for what you allowed to happen to my father."

"I am not a traitor," Lysette screamed suddenly. Turning, she hurled the glass she was filling across the room, forcing Cassana to duck.

"You are a traitor and a liar!" Cassana goaded and before she could react, Lysette was upon her, slapping her across the face with a stinging blow that echoed about the cold chamber.

Cassana recoiled as Lysette pressed her advantage, her painted nails clawing for her face. Stepping back swiftly, Cassana halted Lysette's stumble forward with a punch to the face, both women oblivious to the shouts of worry rising from the corridor outside.

Lysette recoiled, her face wide with shock as she blinked back her tears and stared dumbly at the blood spilling from her split lip to searching fingers.

As Cassana gathered her breath, she became aware of the booted feet echoing in the corridor outside, heard, for the first time above her pounding head, the hammering on the door and pleading shouts.

"You are about to find out that it is you, my dear Lysette, who have chosen the wrong side." Cassana thought Arillion would have been proud of that one and turning, she made to move for the locked door.

Lysette's maniacal laughter stopped her after three steps.

"Oh how I cheered when I heard your father's throat had been cut, how I wept when I heard you had somehow survived, again. It was your father who chose the wrong side, Cassana, and led you to believe there was any strength left in Karick."

Tensing, Cassana turned, her eyes flashing like steel, her hatred fixed upon her twisted features as Lysette threw her a bloody smile and continued speaking.

"But there is power in the capital now, no longer controlled by weak Valians seeking to *barter* with our enemies. The shame of it! You know what the Reven have done to us before and will do one day again, mark my words. And yet... still you seek to protect them, to allow them to flourish as we wane. And you call me the traitor?"

Screaming, Cassana broke from her tether, launching herself at her friend. The door began to shudder as Bryn Astien roared out his demands to know what in the storms was *going on.*

Cassana dealt Lysette another deft blow to her face and watched as she recoiled, blood spilling from her nose to hand.

"It's a shame your father did not show the same spirit," Lysette laughed hysterically as Cassana leapt upon her, reaching for her throat.

They came together, their screams drowning out the panicked cries outside the room and, amidst the tangle of claws and teeth, Cassana's fist found Lysette's chin.

Falling back, Lysette slammed against the sideboard as Cassana came for her again. Fumbling blindly, Lysette picked up a heavy candlestick holder, smashing it into the side of Cassana's head, sending her reeling.

Snarling through her bloodied teeth, Lysette leapt upon Cassana from behind as the door crumbled and Bryn Astien and Erith Taye spilled into the room.

"Lysette? What are you doing?" Bryn Astien cried, his eyes wide with horror as his daughter wrapped an arm about Cassana's throat and pulled a long hair pin from her tumbling tresses.

Lysette smiled, her face twisting. "Something I should have done weeks ago, father."

Before anyone could react she plunged the needle into Cassana's neck repeatedly.

CHAPTER FORTY EIGHT

The Price We Pay

The crowd was silent, standing together in the large square before the scaffolding, waiting eagerly for the next display of justice that had encouraged them from their homes. The afternoon was cold, though many fought for breath amongst the press, lightheaded from the rising body heat. Those with room enough to move fanned themselves rapidly as the anticipation in the cobbled square began to build.

From his respectful position, one pace behind Lord Carwell, Chancellor Valus watched the pathetic mob before him with thin arms folded together, seeing the delight on their faces as they pushed hungrily against the shield wall and the guards who stood vigilantly in front of the waiting nooses.

Relan shook his head faintly, running a tongue over his dry lips. It had been an interesting, troubling few days, though with his lord's assurances, he was starting to relax a little, beginning to believe that it would all be over soon.

When Gardan's men did not return from their mission, a furious debate erupted between the two men across the council table, before the watchful eyes of the lord of the East Vales.

"Yet more incompetence," Relan had pointed out waving an accusatory finger. He was fighting against his rising anxiety and drowning in the worrying prospect that if the high duke's family were allowed to live, all they had strived to achieve may yet prove to be for nothing.

Gardan's face had twisted furiously in response, his eyes burning paths across the table as his derision dripped from his quivering lips. "Careful, chancellor," he had retorted angrily. "You are not so free from blame in all of this as you would like to think. Time and again you have allowed our enemies to slip through your fingers and it is only by your bewildering luck that you are allowed a seat at this table."

Over their ensuing argument, Lord Carwell had summoned the Kestrel, finally silencing them with a withering gaze.

Later that day, the Kestrel had set out north, alone. She was yet to return.

For two days, Henry Carwell toyed with helping the high duke over the threshold he lingered on, keen to end the uncertainty, but was, in the end, wise enough to remain patient. Until Karian Stromn's wife and child were dead, when he could be certain the people could no longer be swayed by their enemies, the high duke would be kept alive, a beacon of anger for the mob who loved him, were willing to do anything to avenge him.

Relan wisely kept to his own counsel, not wishing to jeopardise his position and allow Gardan any extra length on his reins.

When the news of the uprising had arrived the previous day, Relan, despite his worry, was glad to see the back of Gardan. Ignoring the chancellor's warnings about the reasons behind the rebels capture of Durrant's Field, reasons that he suspected were far less simple than the desperation that Henry Carwell and his commander believed, Relan was happy to watch the volatile commander ride from the city, his hastily amassed army marching purposefully after him towards the north east.

Not one to wait idly, Henry Carwell grasped the chance offered to them by their enemies and made it known that the Reven threat to the Valian people (this side of the mountains at least) was about to be dealt a telling blow. Allowing the dust of Gardan's departure to settle, Lord Carwell had waited until this very morning to have it known that the leader of the Reven uprising in the Four Vales had been captured, that, before the very people he had terrorised and on this day, the penultimate day of summer, he would answer for his crimes and meet his fate before them all. That had skilfully ensured the attention of the crowds that now gathered in the square and spilled into the adjoining alleyways and streets.

Rubbing the tension from his eyes, the weary chancellor looked behind, nodding his head to Lady Rothley and Baron Crowood. They, too, had been summoned by Henry Carwell after he had declared that he wanted *all* of his pieces on show for this decisive move in the game.

Relan shook his head, thinking back to the previous week and their unexpected visitor. He was still not sure why the man had done it, why he had given himself up to them so readily...

The first ripples stirred in the crowd and Relan turned his nagging doubts away from events he could not control. Before him, Henry Carwell blinked from his thoughts and all eyes turned to the east, towards an archway, guarded by shadows. As the tall tenement buildings that surrounded Merchants Square seemingly leaned in close for a better look, the tension and the anger began to rise.

Arillion elbowed someone in the side of the head as they attempted to push through the throng towards the scaffolding. As the large man, dressed in a tanners apron rounded upon him and flexed his broad shoulders in the tight confines, Arillion pressed a swift knife under his chin.

"Just try that again," the assassin hissed, his eyes narrowing angrily.

Swallowing down his fear, the rough-looking man blinked an apology and stepped away from Arillion's fury, suddenly deciding he had somewhere else to be.

Arillion watched him leave for a moment then turned his attention back to the north, as the crowd surged forward and the screams of misplaced hatred began to rise.

"We are supposed to be keeping a low profile," Kaspen chided the assassin. Behind them, Agris Varen let out a throaty chuckle.

For three days, whilst Khadazin and his allies remained in the sewers, Arillion, Kaspen and his men had watched the city, lining the pockets of those willing enough to part with information. News from the streets was proving difficult to obtain, however, as it seemed that '*Carwell's Wrath*', as the Reven cleansing was now being called, had silenced people's tongues for fear of losing them.

Frustrated by the lack of information about what was happening in the high duke's keep, and as to the whereabouts of Savinn Kassaar, it had meant, whilst Arillion visited his favourite brothel, that Kaspen and his men had to spend many hours watching the keep, noting the chancellor's frequent comings and goings and following him to his estate in the west of the city.

When news reached their ears that morning of what was going to happen that day, Arillion's fraying temper had snapped.

Above the roar of the crowd, Kaspen saw the first stones fly, watched the slow arch of horse dung and rotten vegetables being thrown at the unfortunate guards who were escorting the hooded prisoner towards the wooden scaffold.

Arillion fixed Kaspen with an anxious look and then turned his attentions back, his eyes drawn with murderous intent towards Henry Carwell and his allies. Sighing, Kaspen clamped a firm hand on the assassin's shoulder and, with the mobs' hatred ringing in is ears, watched and waited for what was about to unfold.

Savinn Kassaar stumbled as he was shoved roughly from behind. Something heavy slammed into his head and although he could not see what it was, he heard the crowd cheer as he dropped blindly to his knees.

Before Savinn could gain his senses, he was dragged to his feet again and sent forward on his way with a sharp punch to his back and venomous words in his remaining ear that was, thankfully, drowned out by the jeers and blood-thirsty screams from the crowd.

Enduring more abuse, pelted by more missiles, Savinn stumbled on his way, his manacled hands, their fingers all broken, clutched protectively before him. Through his hood, the merchant-thief could see little, only the faint grey of the bitter day beyond, and as he tripped again, he felt his bare feet touch a wooden platform.

Showing some compassion, one of his guards grasped him gently by one elbow, saying nothing, but guiding him with some kindness up unseen steps and onto the scaffolding.

"Wait here," the guard shouted over the roar of the crowd and before Savinn could respond through his sodden gag, he heard the hasty retreat of booted feet.

Savinn drew in a faltering breath through his nostrils. He was, for the first time in days, it felt, finally alone.

The crowd began to quieten and soon the market square was silent, but for a calming breeze and the distant call of gulls that had been drawn from the coast of late with the promise of rich city pickings. They had become a blight upon the city, as many citizens had been attacked earlier that spring by gulls protecting their urban nests. Lucien Varl had, it was reported, been trying to petition the high duke to allow falconers to hunt with their birds, though before any decision could be made, other dark events had taken precedence.

Savinn snorted. *Such a thing to think about now...*

Shaking his hood, Savinn let out a long breath, his senses picking up the familiar scents of roasting, spiced meats as he drew some air in through his ruined nose.

Savinn smiled fondly. Old Kaden still ran his stall, under the eaves of *The Cutlass* tavern, on the western edge of the market, near to *Spinnaker Row.* He had, to Savinn's knowledge, run his meat and fish stand there for over thirty years, never missing a day, always the first to arrive and the last to leave, as the sun set.

Inevitably he thought of his wife, of the first day he had seen her. Savinn flinched, slipping away from the crowd's renewed fury to better days.

Growing up in the city had not been easy for Savinn, his heritage marking him out as a bastard, a half-breed, viewed no better than the mongrel that had whelped him and far worse than the father that had spawned him. Angered by the abuse of his youth, Savinn's sharp mind fashioned his rage into a keen edge. Working the streets as a labourer, clearing away the horse dung and rubbish, he toiled (and stole) for two summers, earning enough coin to rent some space on a merchant's ship for whom he had ran errands for. This small, dark, rat-infested corner in the hold of the ship allowed Savinn to start procuring a small amount of Redani spices. In time, he had enough stock to set up a spice stall in Merchant's Square, the very place his life had changed, the very place his life would end.

A deep pain ran through Savinn's body, worse than any agony the woman known as the Kestrel had inflicted upon him, these last days, as the Brotherhood sought the information that the *Wolf of Karick* (as the chancellor now called him) had, but would never give to them.

Even now, all these summers later, Savinn could still recall that busy day in the market, just before the mid-afternoon lull in trade, when he caught a faint scent of rose petals that hung in the air just long enough to be detected over the smell and stench of the fishmonger's stall, that seemed to have embedded itself into the very cobbles beneath his feet.

But the scent was there, nonetheless, and then was gone, stolen away by the heavy crowds. Savinn had scanned the multitude of faces around him curiously and was about to turn his attentions back to his customer at hand when suddenly the crowd seemed to part before him, allowing his gaze to fall all the way over to the far side of the market.

For a brief moment he caught a glimpse of her, of his Elisha, and then she was gone, obscured as the crowd of vendors and customers joined together again in a noisy dance of barter and trade.

But it had been enough. That one solitary glance, even at such a distance, had captured his heart and led him on a search to find out who the mysterious beauty was.

Savinn smiled, his joy safeguarded beneath his hood. A daughter of a rich grain merchant, Elisha Maye was a regular customer to Old Kaden's stall and it had not been difficult to cajole him into making an introduction. The handsome, charming young man had made the most of his opportunity, despite the storm such a union would eventually cause. But Savinn's life would change, he would marry the woman he loved and would come to covet the depth of the purse he had acquired from such a union.

From behind him, Savinn could hear someone approach and he detected a ragged breath at the right of his sagging shoulders. The merchant-thief tensed as the hood was ripped from his head and he shielded his blinded eyes with his ruined hands. Savinn recoiled as the fury of the crowd overwhelmed him and he was shoved roughly forward onto his knees.

The merchant-thief was dressed in long dark robes to hide the cuts, the burns and the bites she had inflicted upon him during his torture and although Savinn could sense people close behind him, none came forward to help him stand.

Struggling to rise up through his pain, Savinn growled defiantly and slowly stood. Straightening his ruined frame proudly, he stared fixedly over the heads of the assembled crowd.

It was a grey afternoon, the clouds close and watchful as his ragged breath gathered nervously before him. Several missiles were thrown from the crowd and he stood where he was, listening as the throng's hatred passed him by.

Savinn became aware now of movement behind him and the crowd's vitality quietened to an expectant murmur. Stiffening at the booted approach, Savinn focussed on those gathered below and began to pick out individual faces in the throng – their expressions twisted by such a fury that he felt his faint hopes for the future of the Four Vales fade. Some members of the merchant's guild were there, also, their faces stained by the shame of their treachery.

He had just spotted Old Kaden, his head bowed behind his stall before *The Cutlass*, when the guard at his shoulder shoved him forward once more. Savinn kept his footing this time, but the momentum carried him across the wooden floor of the gallows and ever closer to the empty noose that awaited him, stirring gently in a mournful breeze.

Savinn stared at the long gallows and swallowed down his disgust. With the demand for Valian *justice* high, the gallows could hang four unfortunates at a time and a putrefying corpse, hung days prior, still spun gently from a noose.

Savinn snorted. *Someone to share my last dance with...*

The guard pushed him closer across the wooden floorboards, closer to the stool that would lift him to his doom. Savinn was several paces from the noose when a commanding voice echoed about the square, silencing the screams and jeers.

"People of Karick," Lord Carwell roared, coming to stand on the edge of the platform, away to Savinn's left. "This is a day for you, the people. This is a day to rejoice. Our summer ends tomorrow and it has been a terrible one, a season full of threat, a time of murder and of great upheaval that has threatened the very peace of this land."

Carwell swept a broad arm to where Savinn watched him and as their gaze met, the lord of the East Vales, the man who would take the people gathered below to war, smiled gleefully.

"But we Valian are strong. We will not be intimidated by treachery, we will not be broken by the wickedness of our enemy and today, today my dear friends, we shall begin to strike back at them."

The crowd surged forward, screaming angrily, forced back roughly by shield and haft of spear. If they broke the line, Savinn knew that he would be torn to pieces long before he could hang.

As Henry Carwell preached to the crowd and outlined the clear case for justice this day, Savinn looked for Old Kaden. The old man, despite his clear sorrow, could not look anymore and he was busy selling sizzling meats to those with room and enough iron in their belly to keep it down.

Savinn suppressed a fond smile. He had made a lot of money from the city, from her people's pockets and it would be someone else's chance to turn a profit for a change. The members of the sycophantic Merchant's Guild were keen for a seat at the new table of power, hanging on to the scraps and desperate to win Carwell's favour. They, too, would profit from what was to follow, though, much like Savinn himself, their conscience would one day come at a great price.

Savinn looked up at the clouds, offering up a prayer that his sacrifice would not be in vain, that there was still some justice, some honour to be found in the capital.

As Lord Carwell finished his speech, Savinn closed his eyes, listening to his heart, strong and rapid in his ear. He had placed all his hopes in this one final chance to speak to the people, to sow the seeds of peace that he hoped his allies would give a chance to grow. If not, then his final hand would indeed count for nothing and the Brotherhood would finally have their time in the sun.

Savinn thought then of Dia, of her bravery and of her sacrifice... her strong face appeared in his mind and he smiled. He had loved that girl like a daughter and he could not have any regrets now for the grief-stricken, wine-induced choices that he had made.

Lord Carwell moved closer to the prisoner, his arms raised high to the crowd. At his side, the shadow that was his chancellor lingered, whispering words of counsel that could not be heard.

"The law dictates that the prisoner may speak, that his final breaths in this life do not follow him on the path that led him to his doom," Henry Carwell cried, "but this man has stirred the Reven against us, has unleashed the past to strike fear into our hearts once again. Do we allow his wicked tongue the chance to ask our forgiveness?"

Savinn chewed furiously on his gag, as the crowd roared their answers. As Lord Carwell lowered his arms slowly, gesturing for quiet, a silence settled on the square as all gathered looked to one another to see if anyone had courage to speak.

"Let him speak," someone called out suddenly and Savinn's head snapped towards the voice. The crowd looked for the speaker, who was lost in a sea of turning faces.

Off to the east, another voice echoed the sentiment and then another which sounded like Old Kaden, until finally, those who still held on to their honour found the courage to call out. As the calls died down, Savinn found the thin face of the first speaker, a tall man with a wide-brimmed hat. The man was not known to him but it was then, as Savinn nodded his gratitude and looked away, that he saw the cold grey eyes glittering from within a dark hood beside him.

His breath lost in his throat, Savinn could not stop his smile and it spread across his face before he could catch it.

Arillion. Savinn could not mistake those eyes, though the man's face was hidden beneath a scarf. *He was still alive! There was still hope...*

Resisting the urge to laugh out loud, Savinn nodded once in the assassin's direction. Arillion's turmoil flashed brightly across the crowd in response.

"Unlike our enemies we still abide by the law that governs this land and as the people have spoken, we shall allow this traitor to speak," Henry Carwell decreed, ignoring his chancellor's hissed protests.

A guard was ordered forward to remove the prisoner's gag and Savinn thanked the man hoarsely, as the pale, somewhat familiar man retreated, his eyes downcast.

Gathering in his courage, Savinn whetted his lips, drew in his lungs and moved forward. Stepping up onto the stool, he reached out with his useless, trembling hands and somehow managed to slip the noose about his neck.

Relan Valus looked at his lord in horror as the crowd murmured its appreciation.

Savinn, despite his abject fear, ignored the rope's caress around his throat and sent a solemn look about the crowd.

"I am dragged here before you today as a traitor to this city and her people," Savinn began, surprised at the clarity and calm in his voice. "I have, I am told, given breath to this Reven uprising, given direction to the chaos and murder we have seen. It has been a terrible time for us all and many of you will, like me, have been horrified by the blood that has stained our streets. I come before you today to die, marked for death by supposed crimes, but I leave you as a man with a clear conscience."

The merchant-thief waited for his voice to finish drowning in the silence. He heard Lord Carwell draw breath and he continued, before his chance was lost.

"I am not, as you are all led to believe, a traitor and the leader of this uprising. There *is* no Reven uprising, only the duplicity of a minority of people who would have you believe it so. They have waited for many years to destabilise the peace of the Four Vales and lay claim to the lands across the Great Divide and if *you* allow them to take this bloody path forward, allow them to march upon the Reven Lands, you will unite the clans there like no chieftain has been able to do for fifty years. You will unleash a war of attrition upon the Four Vales like no other before it."

A gull screeched its agreement, wheeling high above the square. Savinn allowed his words to fade and looked up at the bird, watching it as it slipped away over the rooftops towards the south. Sighing, he looked down at his shaking hands, broken like his hopes and ambitions.

"We should not have allowed him to speak," Relan Valus whispered in his lord's left ear.

Henry Carwell remained still. "Give it a moment," he

breathed calmly.

The first boos began to rise up from Carwell's supporters among the crowd and then, like the sheep they were, the rest of the throng began to bleat along with them. Stepping to the very edge of the platform, the lord of the East Vales seized his opportunity.

"And thus the condemned man speaks, his final words still laced with the poison of his lies and treachery," Henry Carwell bellowed, waving a sweeping arm across the crowd and pointing his disgust to Savinn Kassaar.

"There will be no negotiations with our enemies; there will be no *peace* with the Reven. All will fall before us, all will pay for the crimes they have inflicted upon our lands and the innocent blood they have spilled."

Raising his hand high, Lord Carwell looked to the guard stood behind Savinn Kassaar. The merchant-thief met his triumphant gaze, shaking his head sadly.

Arillion tensed, his anger unchecked, as he shrugged Kaspen's hand from his shoulder and reached for his twin blades.

Kaspen and Agris both grabbed the swordsman by his wrists.

"There is no point us dying here today," Kaspen hissed in the assassin's ear. Arillion tore himself from their grip and turned, not wishing to see what was to follow.

"We end this, tonight!" he snarled, stalking away to the south.

"Justice be done," Henry Carwell roared, sweeping his hand down.

Savinn winced. Closing his eyes, he imagined the sweet smell of rose petals.

With a regretful sigh, the guard kicked the stool from beneath the prisoner, dropping Savinn Kassaar into the arms of his oblivion.

CHAPTER FORTY NINE

Fate's Destiny

Ashe Garrin eyed the sullen sky as he stepped up onto the ramparts above the gates and joined his captain at the wall. Dealing him a faint smile, Elion turned his attention to the south, his thoughts clouding before his face with each slow breath, as he hid deeper within his cloak.

"It's a cold one, to be sure," Ashe said, as he rubbed his large hands together and tried to blow some life back into them.

Elion nodded, but remained silent and, realising his friend was not for conversation, Ashe joined him in his vigil, watching the grey, misting horizon, searching the bleak land for a sign that Gardan had accepted their challenge.

It was early afternoon, the third day since they had allowed the men guarding the mines to ride safely from Durrant's Field to bear their message with them. Following their departure, Colm had answered Kerrin Thorn's hunting horn, bringing with him the rest of Devlin Hawke's men and women, two wagons of food, supplies and warm blankets and clothing for the Reven prisoners.

Not really believing their luck, but offering thanks to the Lady for sending them their saviours, the weak, emaciated prisoners had crowded about their rescuers, eagerly accepting their care and kindness through their joy and tears.

Amidst the chaos and squalor it took a day to organise things, but by the end of the next afternoon, Elion and his comrades had gathered some thirty extra swords from the ranks of the prisoners, those with strength and anger left in them enough to be willing to fight and have a chance of vengeance. The rest, some hundred or more men, women and children alike, who were too weak, too broken to stay, were guided away from Durrant's Field by six of Devlin's men and Rellin and Jessica, who would see them safely to Havensdale. Once there, they were to be entrusted into the care of Sergeant Calen's men, who would guide the refugees north to Highwater to seek the sanctuary they deserved.

Elion chewed his thoughts. With the thirty extra swords, a mixture of Reven and Valian, staying to fight, the defenders numbered just over a hundred.

Looking along the long palisade, Elion knew that it would not be nearly enough...

"Anything?" Devlin Hawke enquired, as he startled both men with his sudden appearance.

Ashe shook his grizzled head. "Not even a Kestrel," he growled, trying to hide his rising impatience. The waiting was killing him, the long, silent hours dragging away like days, tugging at his fraying nerves, toying with his composure and doubts.

Better to get on with it now, see it done, one way or another, he thought.

Elion rubbed his chin with a gloved hand as he pondered what would happen if Gardan did not come. Knowing Gardan, that was something that would not happen and when he came, they would have to stay alive as long as they could. They could not afford to buckle under the first assault, lest the Valian forces return early and stop their comrades from ending the war before it had truly begun.

Ashe bade his farewells, stating he wanted to make sure the wagons they had dragged behind the gates had enough crates of weapons on them to stop the wall being breached. Elion grinned, knowing that his sergeant had already checked them four times that day, but allowed his friend to depart and deal with the agony of waiting in his own way.

At least we won't run out of weapons, Elion thought, suppressing a wry smile.

Devlin, his hood drawn up about his head, watched the burly sergeant leave and then turned back to stare out across the plains.

"What will you do if we succeed?" Elion asked finally, when it seemed like they had only the cutting wind for conversation.

Devlin turned his head slightly. "Trell and I have spoken about this," the outlaw smiled. "If Arillion succeeds, no, don't look at me like that, if they do succeed, then my reason for exile is over. There is no reason for me to strike out at the authorities anymore."

Elion chuckled, ignoring the flash of irritation in Devlin's eyes. "Forgive me, my friend, I just cannot see you leading a quiet life."

The outlaw accepted Elion's hand of apology with a shrug. "Carwell wronged me many, many years ago when I was young and impetuous and I have struck back at him and all that he stands for ever since. Turns out that I was right to, too! But if the time comes that we can leave the forest, share our lives with the people again, then I should like to grasp that chance. Trell and I might start up an inn, '*The Wanted Man*,' perhaps? We could brew and sell our fine cider there. Earn some honest coin for a change."

Elion turned, leaning on the palisade. "You've thought a lot about this, haven't you?"

"I have," Devlin nodded. "I am not reluctant to admit that I have yearned for it, Elion. Dared to dream there might be a time when I would not have to hide behind my mask. You have given me this chance Elion Leigh, and I thank you for it, no matter what happens to us in the coming days."

"Well, if we survive this, I would be honoured to join you there for a drink, my friend," Elion said, his throat tightening.

Over their smiles, the outlaw and the former captain shook hands.

Arillion did not bother to look up as Kaspen Shale opened the door and stepped into Savinn Kassaar's study. The assassin was still in a foul mood over the coin he had lost, his irritation stamped across his handsome features as the scar on his cheek twisted with raw anger.

"It won't be long now," Kaspen observed, keen for the waiting to be over. It was only an hour since they had returned from the execution and the wayfarers had not dared tell Arillion what Henry Carwell had ordered to be done to Savinn's body, once he had stopped kicking and jerking before the strangely silent crowd.

Arillion continued to stand over the magnificent desk, studying a large sheet of parchment and the wayfarer drew his frustration away from the assassin to admire the painting of a wolf, howling from the wall and shadows behind him.

Eventually Arillion looked away from the crude charcoal drawn map, offering up a smile that failed miserably.

"Dia's last gift to us," the assassin said bitterly,

indicating that Kaspen was allowed to have a look.

The wayfarer dutifully obliged, staring down at the detailed map, though failing to be able to read the small, untidy handwriting scrawled upon it in the poor light.

Arillion snorted and stabbed the parchment with a forefinger. "We will be entering here, the '*Moon Suite*,' and from the last we know, the high duke is being kept here, in his study, under armed guard."

Kaspen frowned. Across two wings to the east, one floor higher. It would be a miracle if they reached there without raising the alarm...

"Once we are sure he is safe, Brother Valus will go with Khadazin to seek their revenge, whilst we..." Arillion paused, to tap a finger slowly on the Old Royal Chambers, "...we will head to finish things off once and for all."

Folding his arms across his chest, Kaspen glared at the assassin.

"You make it sound all so easy," he said.

Ignoring the wayfarer's sarcasm, Arillion straightened his aching back. Picking up one of his dark, studded arm guards, the assassin pulled it into place on his left arm. Pain clawed at his stiff shoulder and he winced.

Kaspen watched quietly as Arillion fished about in one of his pouches, pulling forth a small ball of what looked like rolled leaves. The assassin grinned at him as he popped the leaf on his tongue and rolled it about his mouth.

"Just a little something to see me through the pain," he said, his eyes flickering in the candlelight.

Trying to hide the worry in his voice, Kaspen drew in a breath, steadying his nerves. "As this may be the last chance I get, I wanted to ask you something, swordsman."

Arillion sat on the corner of the desk, continued chewing and waved a hand for him to proceed.

Inclining his head, Kaspen smiled.

"It is clear to me that you are full of surprises,

swordsman," Kaspen observed, licking his lips. "And, whilst your involvement in this tale is now well known, it occurs to me that you have been involved in this tale a lot longer than many could have expected."

Arillion's eyes narrowed and he fixed them on the wayfarer.

"That's as may be," the assassin agreed. "But I fail to see what it has to do with you."

Kaspen ignored the warning and spread his arms and smile wide. "Humour me a moment, my friend. You owe me that, at the very least and, if I am to survive this tale, I would know a little more if I am to write your ballad and sing the song of your adventures."

Arillion sat back a little, the faintest smile lighting up his pale features. "Guess I had better keep you alive a while longer then," he grinned, folding his arms across his proud, leather-clad chest. "So, oh mighty saga-spinner, what do you want to know? How many throats my blades have caressed? How many thighs I have caressed, perhaps?"

It was Kaspen's turn to grin, his eyes laced with mischief as he spoke.

"Tell me about the woman," he said.

The assassin stiffened and Kaspen could see a pain, much deeper than his wounds, steal through his body.

Arillion winced in remembrance. Shaking his head he looked down at his boots, lost to the past.

"It took many years to get over her betrayal – it is a wound that has never fully healed, one that I thought never to re-open"

"Who is she?" Kaspen dared to ask, then seeing the look that crossed Arillion's face, he held up his hands. "It is not my business, my friend. Forgive me for asking!"

The room fell silent for a long while, then, with a weary sigh, Arillion looked up. "It won't matter soon as she will be dead, so what difference can it make. I spent many years in my youth stealing horses in the East Vales, it is there that I met her, Alyssa – it is how I met Devlin Hawke. She is the Hawke's sister you see, the reason why he and I were at daggers for the last few years. When she failed to kill me, she went to her brother, told him that *I* had tried to kill her.... bitch! The scar I gave her was compelling evidence though. It was a canny move, too, as Devlin was my only real friend and, well, as you can imagine, he did not take too kindly to the news I had tried to murder his sister..."

Kaspen fidgeted as Arillion pounded his clenched fists on the desk, gathered up his composure and met his friend's eyes once again.

"It took many moons to get him to even speak to me and that was only years after he and his sister became estranged over her involvement with the Brotherhood. After rescuing Lady Byron, Devlin and I planned to ransom her to her father, share the gold he would surely spare for her safe return."

Kaspen whistled, tugging nervously on his earring. "You really have not led a dull life, have you? I can only begin to grasp how you must be feeling right now, Arillion, though there is one thing I cannot fathom... why you threw the punch, not Devlin Hawke?"

Arillion laughed. "I was not for farming, for the quiet life and I am certain I shall not be for a normal death, either. It's funny how things work out. The man who led the attack in the mountains on Lady Byron, the man I carried to his death, was Alyssa's lover, Tobin. You have to laugh at that irony! During the fight there was a young man in the hunting party, whom I spared. He found a letter in Tobin's belongings, a love note from Alyssa all those years ago, saying how once I was dead they could finish the mark and claim the reward for themselves. She always was persuasive. This young man and the letter somehow end up in Greywood and, well, let's just say that

Devlin now sees things from the other side of her coin and I owed him for not believing me all those years ago."

Letting out a breath, Arillion smiled, feeling the weight of an old, heavy burden lift from his shoulders. His eyes glowed with relief as he folded his arms across his chest once more and fixed his friend with a look.

"My turn," Arillion stated. "You have given up the quiet life, the freedom that you have and, quite possibly, your head at the table of your family for this perilous venture – have *you* any regrets now, Kaspen Shale?"

"The Lady works in mysterious ways," Kaspen observed, delighting at the irritation igniting on Arillion's face.

"My luck does," Arillion responded, grinning. He rose up and clapped a firm hand on Kaspen's shoulder, hesitating before drawing him into an embrace. "Stay close to me wayfarer and we might just live through this."

Or die a terrible death, Kaspen thought, turning his grimace into a wry smile.

Elissen was the first person to spot the subtle shift in the shadows to the south, a darkening of the horizon that turned the steel grey afternoon towards night. For a time, she simply watched the army approach, lost to her fear, though kept on the ramparts by her rising anger.

Shuddering, the refugee from Eastbury hugged herself, pulling her fraying composure close about her thin frame. Since leaving Havensdale, after declaring her intent to stand alongside Elion and his friends, her sleep had been filled with old doubts and haunted by whispers and vivid memories from the past. Any hopes she had began to cherish that she might be able to find peace with what had happened, that she may one day be able to forgive, soon scattered when they reached Durrant's Field.

Elissen blinked rapidly, hoping she was seeing things,

but the army was still there, filling the gloom with their approach. Others on the ramparts were stirring to the threat now and the alarm had been raised.

Lost to her grief and sorrow, Elissen stood where she was, as the world hurried on about her.

It took well over an hour, but the column of soldiers finally reached Durrant's Field and were led to the east by several riders, their faces hidden beneath their helms. Elissen had remained where she was, watching nervously as the army from Karick filled the plains before the mines, forming diligent ranks in the mist and gloom before her.

She was unaware that the ramparts had been cleared and that, far away along the wall to her left, only Elion Leigh, Devlin Hawke and Ashe Garrin now stood up there with her. Below her, the defenders waited out of sight, ordered by Elion Leigh to stay there, so that the enemy could not know their true numbers.

Sighing, Elissen brushed tangled strands of her lank hair from her eyes and allowed a breeze to caress her face. Scanning the enemy ranks, she could see that they were not setting up camp, were not resting before attacking.

Several officers stalked along the lines, barking unintelligible orders to the waiting soldiers and the ladders many of them carried in their foremost ranks.

She was about to turn her fears away, tear her eyes away from the massing ranks, when she saw him, stood amongst his men, his helm tucked under one arm. Her failing breath choked her, filling her throat with hatred and disgust and, as the plains before her began to spin, she stepped back into the arms of her fury.

"Are you alright?" Elion said, steadying her as she stepped back to the edge of the walkway. She turned her wide, haunted eyes towards him and he stiffened in shock.

"You should join the others," Elion offered, trying to not show his horror at her appearance. There had been some colour in her cheeks recently, a softening of her turmoil and grief, but no longer. Her pale face was gaunt and hollow and only her eyes showed any colour, as they burned brightly with a dangerous, maddened fire.

"I-I am alright," Elissen managed, looking back towards where Gardan stood, laughing with a tall man. "I just did not think they would come."

Elion followed her gaze and swallowed hard, ignoring his own fears for a time. He simply nodded, slipping an arm about her sharp shoulders.

Elissen drew some strength from his touch, trying to banish the whispers echoing in her head. As she attempted to wrench her gaze away from the man she had sworn to kill, Elissen saw her sister for the first time in many weeks, walking slowly through the enemies ranks, her loose, chestnut hair blowing in a breeze as she searched for something.

Shuddering, Elissen stepped away from Elion's embrace. "You should make ready," she said without looking at him, her voice suddenly calm. "They will come for us soon, Elion."

Elion disguised his hurt and worry, touching her once on the left shoulder. She did not turn her eyes away from where Renald Gardan stood, though she reacted slightly to his touch.

"Please, Elissen," Elion pleaded. "Join the others below for now." She nodded subtly, but did not move.

Sighing, Elion hurried away along the ramparts to rejoin Devlin and Ashe.

Dressed in a long, pale dress, Meredith twisted her way through the ranks, finally coming to stand beside Gardan. She reached out a bloodied hand, touching the commander on one shoulder, who, oblivious to her presence, continued to laugh at some joke.

"Kill him!" Meredith hissed suddenly in her ear and sobbing, Elissen turned from her vengeful demons, hurrying down wooden steps to join Jarion and the others.

"Can you believe that bastard?" Devlin Hawke swore. His face flushed with anger as Gardan and two others mounted their steeds and began to ride slowly towards the walls of the encampment. "He doesn't even ride under a banner of truce."

Ashe sighed, flicking a nervous look past the outlaw towards his captain. "That's because they have no intention of letting us surrender," the sergeant growled, seeing Elion flinch.

Devlin spat over the ramparts, then pulled his scarf up over his mouth. Gripping his bow in his left hand, he slipped an arrow from the full quiver at his side.

"I could end this now?" the outlaw suggested, looking for the answer he knew Elion would give him.

Elion sighed, shaking his head. Despite the enticing offer, he knew it would not help their cause.

"A tempting offer, my friend, but we must hold on to our honour, for the moment at least," Elion whispered.

Gardan raised a gloved hand, bringing his small party to a halt, some forty paces or more from the closed gates. As he took off his silver helm, his thin, pale features spread into a smile as he looked along the empty wall.

Leaning forward, he patted the broad neck of his black stallion.

"There you are, Elion Leigh," he said, his clear voice echoing away through the silence of the fading afternoon.

"Here I am," Elion replied, resting his hands on the sharp stakes of the defences.

Straightening in his saddle, Commander Gardan idly tugged off his gloves, slapping them into his upturned helm. "By the Storms, boy, you have the luck," Gardan said, not trying to hide his disappointment. "I have to admit I am actually impressed that you have somehow stayed alive, that you have even managed to find some fools to believe your fanciful tales," Gardan paused, turning his attention to where Devlin stood. "I must also thank you for this, you have given me the opportunity to rise even higher than I ever thought possible – *the man who caught the Hawke and smashed the rebellion.* Capital move, Leigh. I am indebted."

"Say your piece, Renald and be gone," Elion said crisply, putting a calming hand on Ashe's shoulder. "We will not give up Durrant's Field. We will not allow your treachery to the Valian people to go unanswered."

Gardan scowled, before he chewed a fingernail thoughtfully. When he spoke, a ghostly smile lit up his face. "You see, that was always the trouble with you, Leigh," the commander sighed, waving a finger up at them. "You never knew your place in the grand scheme of things, always polishing your honour like silverware, always thinking that life was that simple." Gardan looked about, feigning disinterest. "After today, no one will remember your name. I will strike it from the history books and bathe in the delight of your death."

"You really must have pissed him off," Devlin chuckled quietly.

Elion glared down at his tormentor. "At last the wolf bears his teeth. I shall be waiting for you, Renald. Come and find me."

Gardan made a show of pulling on his gloves and helm, baring his teeth in a smile.

"Until then, make sure you stay alive," he said. Nodding, Gardan turned his mount about. Elion watched them ride away to the east, before finally letting out a ragged breath.

"You should say something," Devlin said quietly. They had watched the army from Karick for a time, seeing that they were readying ladders and preparing to attack.

Elion turned to look down at the defenders, gathered

below. A sea of faces looked up at him, eyes full of fear, bodies stiffened by anticipation.

"Just don't tell them we face at least five hundred men," Ashe added out of the corner of his beard. "Best not win Gardan's fight for him."

Elion glared at his friend, before turning back to the makeshift courtyard below. Swallowing hard, he raised his arms for silence.

"Our destiny has arrived," Elion began, trying to keep his hands from shaking. "The wolves prowl at our door and soon, very soon, we shall have the chance to avenge the injustices inflicted upon the Four Vales. I will say nothing more to you, my friends, only that we will fight and we must stand. Although we may die today, we will act as a beacon of hope to others, fanning the flames of justice that have been trampled under the boot of treachery. It will be bloody and it will be brutal, but we *must* stand."

Elion drew his sword, raising it high above his head. "I will stand and I will not fall. Who will stand with me?"

Swords flashed in the fading light, rising silently to join Elion's. The few muted cheers that rose up from the remnants of Elion's patrol were drowned out as the Valian army attacked.

CHAPTER FIFTY

Death Becomes Us

Eran Dray barely reacted as the front ranks of Renald Gardan's army roared their battle-cries and raced away through the gloom towards the walls of the mining encampment known as Durrant's Field. As the first screams pierced the din, Eran blinked, as if waking from a dream and he watched sadly as the dark shapes on the walls of the encampment directed further death towards the charging attackers.

It would be a cold night, Eran thought, as he watched his breath trail away into the greying sky. At his side, he suddenly became aware of Wen. The old man had not left him to mourn since he brought the news of Dia's fate, his guilt and need for forgiveness as keen as his desire to make amends.

Eran flicked him a grim look, sensing his comrade's nerves. If the first two attacks failed, Gardan would send them to bolster the assault and as most present had never faced battle before, it was a daunting prospect.

Eran sighed, offering a faint smile to the old man. Despite his initial anger, Eran could feel no ill-will towards his friend. Wen had not intentionally sent Dia to her death; he had only set her on her path in innocent, passing conversation.

Eran's stomach knotted as he tried to fill the void in his heart with thoughts of their love, of their time together, but each time he did, the darkness was filled with the cold realisation that Dia had probably not loved him, had only seduced him to find out information about the chancellor and his scheming.

She had tried to kill Relan Valus, it was said by those present, then had jumped to her death to avoid capture and worse. Wen had told him of that night, of the sadness on her face as she realised she had no other choice.

Eran winced, his face tight with pain. It was whispered that Dia was spying for the Reven, was working for Savinn Kassaar and was a traitor, attempting to kill the chancellor for her master.

The heavy shroud of darkness drowning his soul lifted momentarily as Eran thought that he would have liked to help her in her attempt.

Since her death, Eran had not been approached, but his superiors, Esten Oswald and Renald Gardan had made it perfectly clear that they did not trust him. He was followed constantly by hooded men, watching him from the shadows to see if he, too, was a traitor to the Valian people.

Two days ago they had tested his *loyalty* to its limits. He had been one of the guards, forced to brave the mob at Savinn Kassaar's execution. He had been the one they sent to kick the stool from beneath the proud man's feet and stand close, as the merchant kicked and fought to hold on to his final breaths.

More screams filled the plains, the roars of battle joined as several ladders were thrown up against the wooden walls of the settlement, then repelled by the defenders.

Eran swallowed his grief and disgust, as images of what they had done to the merchant's body filled his mind and he was thankful that they had not forced him to defile the corpse, also.

"Make ready!" Esten Oswald's voice roared out, as the initial attack faltered.

Eran smiled weakly at Wen. "Not long now, then," he observed. The thin man simply nodded, gripping his sword far too tightly.

Eran hefted his shield and drew his own blade. Dia's beautiful face filled his mind and chased away his fears and doubts.

Despite everything, he sensed she had loved him, knew it deep down in his heart, beneath the shards of doubt that pierced him.

He had thought to come here and take out his grief on those that did not deserve it. The men and women who had captured the mines had rescued the Reven slaves, not persecuted and killed them like the madmen who now controlled the capital. There may still be hope for the Four Vales...

No! Eran thought. *I will not be a party to this madness.*

If he was to die, he would prefer to die on the point of an honest sword, rather than get sucked into the genocide that would follow.

Elion Leigh hurled the ladder away from the wall before too many attackers could weigh it down with their ascent. As he did, he leant out over the stakes, glancing briefly down at the sea of angry faces glaring up at him. He pulled back hastily, sucking in a shallow breath.

At his side, amidst the chaos, Ashe grinned, his face flushing from the exertion of keeping the wolves from their walls. Forcing a smile, Elion stared out across the dark plains, his heart faltering as he watched the waiting lines of men, still ready to join in the assault.

Along the wall, the outlaws continued reining their death upon the attackers, black barbs of disdain that caught in throats and chests with unerring accuracy. The ground was now thick with writhing bodies and shafts, their screams of agony and groans of pain drowning under the din of battle.

Far along the wall, Elion could see a ladder had found its footing, several enemy soldiers hurrying up it as the defenders sought to repel it. Before he could react or cry out a warning, Devlin Hawke realised the danger.

"Bring them down," the outlaw roared and several of his men hurried along the busy ramparts, bows bent with deadly intent.

Elion sent Devlin a nod and then turned as the ladder was thrown up against the defences again.

From nearby, Trell leant over the wall and sent a shaft into the throat of the first man who began to climb. As the startled man was swallowed up by his comrades, Elion and Ashe grabbed the top of the ladder and began pulling it up over the wall.

Ashe snorted with laughter. "That's one way of stopping them," he grunted, his bearded face splitting in a broad grin, as they dragged the ladder away from desperate, grasping hands.

Elion grinned, his face youthful again for a time. He was about to say something pithy when Ashe jerked, a dark bolt appearing in his right cheek, just below his eye. Grunting, Ashe let go of the ladder, staggering back into the arms of his shock. As Elion cried out and reached for him, his friend stepped back and fell from the ramparts to the ground below.

Time slowed for Elion as he lost his grip on the ladder and stood there dumbly shrouded in ice. Below, some of the waiting defenders rushed across to aid Ashe, where he lay crumpled and still.

Time caught up with events as Elion let out a

screaming breath. As he turned back, another bolt whispered a warning and Elion ducked low.

"Skirmishers," Trell called along the wall to him, his large bearded face grey with worry.

He sent a shaft in their direction and dumbly Elion followed it, seeing the line of some twenty crossbowmen, ducked down low behind the raised shields of their comrades, as they reloaded their slow weapons.

Trell sent an order along the wall, as Devlin Hawke reacted to the danger, also. As the crossbowmen rose up from behind the shields, a hissing cloud of shafts leapt forth, peppering their line. Several of the attackers fell back, clutching at feathers before they could loose their bolts, but many replied in kind.

As a ladder was thrown up against the defences again, Elion heard the screams on the wall as some of the deadly bolts found a mark. A spear struck the wall suddenly and nearby, one of the Reven defenders fell back, fingers curled about a thick haft buried deep in his stomach.

It was palpable. He could taste it in the air.

As a shocked Elion Leigh fought to hurl the heavy ladder away, his skin pricked. The tide was already turning in the attackers favour.

By the time Arillion had led his comrades through the sewers and up the steep steps towards the shadowy door, his injured leg was burning painfully. Popping another leaf ball under his tongue, he turned, sweeping his torch about to watch the faces, gathering grimly in the shadows below him.

"We are here," he whispered, putting a finger to lips, hidden beneath his scarf. Banishing images of another, more enjoyable moment on the steep, narrow staircase, he turned back to the secret door and pressed a hooded ear to the cobwebbed wood.

Evan Valus reached the small landing first, his hooded head bent low as he gathered his breath and fought against his nerves. He too was caught up in the past, his thoughts dragged back to distant memories of the flight from the high duke's keep and the brave men who had spirited him to safety through the sewers.

As the rest of their party waited nervously on the steps behind him, the woodsman saw Arillion's eyes sweep back to him.

"Are you ready?" he asked, his gaze burning in the torchlight. There was no mockery to be found there, only the flint grey intent of one who relished the chaos that was to follow.

The woodsman nodded, but could not find breath enough for words. Satisfied, Arillion turned and slowly, quietly hauled open the secret door.

In the fading light of the grim day, the defenders somehow held the walls, their limbs weary, their blood flowing freely. Three times the attackers had gained the walls, each time driven back by arrow, shield and sword. As the evening stretched on and the defenders' strength waned, Elion ordered those weariest from the walls to rest, replacing them with the last of their fresh men and women from below.

Elissen now stood beside him, her tangled hair tied back behind her neck. She stared out into the thickening dark, counting the hundreds of torches burning there. If she had not known what they faced, she would have thought the scene beautiful, a shadowy horizon of flickering fireflies.

Ashe was being tended to by Jarion Kail. She had reported that his wound was life-threatening, though the burly sergeant tenaciously refused to '*miss out on all the fun*.' His body and pride were also badly bruised by his fall.

Troubled and yet somewhat relieved, Elion had been forced to turn his thoughts to even heavier burdens, ordering the dead to be carried from the walls and laid to rest in one of the empty store houses, on the eastern side of the encampment.

At the last count, they had lost twenty-six brave souls... the enemy at least three times that number and he dismissed grim thoughts of when someone would be forced to count him amongst the fallen.

Sighing, Elion stared at the enemy lines and shook his head. Gardan had, for some reason, recalled the attack an hour ago, but had not sent a white flag and men to reclaim his own dead. They lay in the gathering gloom, forgotten and used by a man who cared little for their honour and dignity.

"Will they come again tonight?" Elissen asked softly, her breath trailing away to the north.

Elion met her eyes briefly, lost there for a moment, before turning away again.

"We can be sure of it," he said sadly. "They have the numbers to attack us through the night. As our strength wanes, they will send fresh men to our walls and, eventually, they will overpower us. We must hold on to our courage as long as we can, delay that moment as long as possible."

Elissen studied Elion's face, feeling her hopes drain. The once handsome man, the man who, every time he looked at her, stole her breath away, had changed since Eastbury. Gone was the winsome, boyish smile, his youthful features now haggard, drawn tight under the weight of pressure and the burden he so readily carried.

As she spoke, Elissen wondered how she must seem to him and she stumbled over her words.

"I-I," she began, her thin face furrowing with frustration. Elion turned his attention back again, his eyes lingering this time.

"Are you alright, lady?" he asked quietly. The wall was quiet, conversations nearby muted and guarded.

Sniffing, Elissen nodded. She reached out a shaking hand and gripped Elion's hands together.

"If I die, no please, let me finish! If I die, will you take me back home Elion Leigh and bury me beside my father and sister?"

Elion swallowed hard, licking his lips nervously. Bringing her thin hand to his lips, he gently kissed her fingertips.

"You have my word, Elissen Fenn," he promised, though he doubted he would be able to.

Horns sounded and roars shattered the silence of the evening. Like a coming storm, Renald Gardan's army thundered across the plains to attack them again.

The guard blinked, swallowing his fears down over the tip of the blade pressed under his chin. One moment he had been drifting off to sleep, the next, he was rigid against a wall, several hooded figures gathering close about him.

"Where is the high duke being kept?" a voice hissed in his left ear. The blade twisted meaningfully, drawing both blood and a garbled answer.

"Quit your jabbering," Arillion hissed impatiently, replacing his blade with a broad hand about the man's throat. "Just tell me if he is still being confined to his study? We are not here to harm him. You have my word on that."

The man rallied defiantly. "It's hard to believe that when you have your hand around my throat."

Arillion chuckled beneath his scarf. "And my blade between your ribs," he whispered, his eyes narrowing as he prodded the man with his sword.

The man blinked as Arillion tightened his grip. About them, the hooded figures glanced around their brightly lit surroundings nervously.

"Time's up," Arillion snarled. With wide eyes, the man nodded his head rapidly. He struggled under the assassin's grip to free his voice.

"He's still in his study, under guard," the man admitted, reaching for breath. "He waits on death's door. Please, don't hurt him. He is not a threat to you."

"I know he is not," Arillion scoffed, driving the pommel of his sword into the guard's temple.

Kaspen Shale threw the unconscious man over his shoulder and hurried away down the wide hallway to hide him in an empty room, next to a staircase that swept down to the lower reaches of the West Wing.

The woodsman stepped close, gripping Arillion's shoulder. "We must not tarry," he said softly, flicking a look towards Khadazin. "Our luck is going to run out soon."

Arillion nodded his head. "Follow me," he whispered. Turning on painful heels, the assassin led them away down the hallway.

The woodsman peered about the corner and ducked back again, meeting Arillion's eyes fearfully.

"How do we get there?" he asked quietly.

Four guards stood in the wide, carpeted hallway, dutiful, yet evidently weary of the charge they had been given whilst many others in the keep celebrated the momentous day for the Valian people. As the group of rescuers had made their way to where they hoped the high duke was still being kept, they had heard much distant merriment.

Two further guards had been overpowered without the alarm being raised and any blood being spilt, much to everyone's (except Arillion's) relief. Both confirmed that, as the assassin had rightly predicted, the keep was celebrating Savinn's demise and the inevitable crushing of the rebellion. *What better time to strike?*

Slipping past parties and muffled moans from bedchambers, the group had somehow made their way to the hallway that would take them to the high duke's study.

Khadazin watched as Arillion deliberated. Each second they wasted offered further chance of being detected. He flicked a wide, fearful look at Tania. The young huntress met his fear from beneath her hood with a calm shrug and slipped an arrow onto her bowstring.

Arillion finally muttered something, slipping his blades back into their sheaths. Rolling the tension from his neck, he swore.

"We may not be able to avoid a fight," he hissed. Before anyone could react, the assassin stepped out into the hallway.

Swords leapt from scabbards and a spear rose up in challenge as the hooded figure walked down the corridor towards the high duke's study. A challenge went unanswered and the figure came closer.

"You have no business here," Callin Vane called out. As if this night could not get any worse. Stuck on duty, when all about the city celebrated...

Any frustration was tempered by the hooded figure's approach. He was probably lost, drunk, or both.

"Are you lost?" he called out, sending a look to his comrades as he chose the former.

The hooded man stopped several paces from them, oblivious to the weapons pointing his way. A pair of open hands spread wide, revealing the leather braces guarding the strong arms hidden beneath the cloak.

"I'm exactly where I need to be," a calm, lucid voice replied. From the shadows of the hood, a pair of eyes glittered. "Don't react, don't attack, just listen to me for a moment."

Callin frowned as the guards shared confused looks.

As he went to speak, several hooded figures filled the corridor before them.

The hooded man before them folded his arms across his chest and drew their attention back.

"We know the high duke is inside," Arillion began, staying calm as a spear turned back towards him. "We also know that he has been poisoned by the chancellor. We are here to protect him as after this night, his life will be in even greater danger."

The guards stiffened and their resolve hardened.

"What nonsense is this?" Callin growled, his patience fraying.

Arillion sighed as his comrades reached them. "Look, we don't have time to debate. Just know that I could have walked down here and killed you all, but I didn't. I must be getting soft, or old, or both. All you need to know is that Carwell and his lapdog Gardan have betrayed the Valian people. Chancellor Valus has schemed and plotted, undermining everything the high duke has strived to protect and has been poisoning him for many days. There is no Reven uprising, only the duplicity of those who would have it so. They have had Alion Byron murdered, they recently tried to kill Lady Stromn and her son. They kidnapped and tortured Lucien Varl to give up her location."

The guards looked amongst themselves, their faces ranging from outright distrust to confusion and shock.

"And what makes you think we will believe any of this is true?" one guard growled, his mistrust fuelling his anger.

Arillion sighed, reining in his impatience. "We are here to stop the Four Vales plunging into civil and then, wider war. We are here to stop Carwell claiming his *throne.* If you are loyal to Karick and the high duke, help us get him to safety... if you are loyal to Carwell, then you must prepare to die."

Stood behind the assassin, Kaspen Shale hid his grin, not daring to meet Agris Varen's eyes.

Callin lowered his sword slightly. "We have no love for what is happening to Karick since Gardan arrived, that much is true. We are all loyal to the high duke... were loyal to Lucien Varl."

The woodsman stepped forward. He raised calming hands and slowly lowered his hood.

"Lucien Varl is alive. He is safe in Highwater, as is the high duke's family. We *must* protect Karian Stromn. We must ensure that he survives this night. Will you help us?"

Callin looked to his friends, who threw looks at him for guidance. Ever since Lucien Varl had disappeared, the city had descended into madness and the streets had run with blood. *Could they be telling the truth*? Or were they working for Carwell, seeking to have the high duke killed?

"Who are you people?" Callin asked, sheathing his sword with a shaking hand.

The woodsman stole Arillion's words away. "You knew me Callin, many years ago, before my brother betrayed me and framed me for a murder I could never commit."

"*Captain*?" Callin baulked, his eyes almost popping from his head as he studied the haggard, familiar face before him. A breath of shock escaped one of the older men stood behind also. As one, the remaining guards lowered their weapons, allowing everyone to breathe.

The study was cloaked in heavy shadows, one futile candle casting a ghostly pallor across the room. The woodsman swept a gaze about the shadows, his weapons left with the guards as sign of his intentions. The lock had been broken to force entry and the stench that escaped the study had overpowered all outside. The guards explained that only the chancellor's physician and cook were allowed entry into the room, giving further weight to the former captain's words.

Cold fury swept through his body as Evan spied the weak form, slumped on a sofa to his right. He had very nearly not seen the high duke, as emaciated and thin as he was. With the hems of his cloak covering his nose, the woodsman hurried to his former lord's side.

"What have they done to you, Karian?" Evan whispered, choking on his disgust.

The high duke's lashes fluttered at mention of his name and his eyes, once bright with strength, flickered weakly.

"Lucien? Is that you?" the frail man croaked. "Where have you been? Why did you leave me?"

"I am here now, my lord," Evan lied, brushing the matted hair from the high duke's eyes.

"Thank the Lady," Karian whispered, his head lolling. "I fear I have not been well."

Evan fought back his tears and held the high duke gently in his arms.

"You are safe now," he said, his anger flashing through his eyes.

Arillion reached out and shook Khadazin's hand. They held each other's gaze for a moment.

"Happy hunting, Redani," Arillion said, nodding his head.

Khadazin swallowed his words nervously and could only tilt his sweating head in response.

Releasing his hand, the assassin swept his gaze over those gathered down the hallway, away from the high duke's study. The guards were inside, along with the young wayfarer, Aven, preparing to move their charge to the *Moon Suite*, safely away from those who would soon seek him harm.

"Luck to you," the woodsman said. Reaching out he gripped Arillion's offered hand by the wrist.

Arillion grinned from behind his scarf. "And to you, Evan. See you on the other side of this."

Releasing his wrist, the assassin turned and sent a nod towards Tania and Riyan. His eyes lingered on the mute and Riyan nodded his accord, as Arillion flicked a meaningful head towards Khadazin.

Without another word, the silent party set off back the way they had come, heading in search of the chancellor's offices and a long overdue reunion. Arillion watched them leave, feeling his heart begin to race. A chill swept through him, but he dismissed it with a warming growl. He turned to regard the three wayfarers behind him.

"Shall we?" he chuckled, sweeping a broad arm in the opposite direction.

Only Agris Varen returned anything that resembled enthusiasm. Kaspen and Tomlin's faces were pale with worry.

Sighing, Arillion threw back his dark cloak and drew his blades, stepping into the eastern corridor. He drew up suddenly as he spied a tall, elegant woman dressed in a long gown of ivory coming towards him. Two guards hesitated at his unexpected, threatening appearance.

"Lady Rothley," Arillion called out in greeting. He bowed mockingly as the venerable lady of the West Vales eyes widened in horror.

"Such a pleasure," Arillion snarled, advancing towards her.

One of the guards drew his blade and stepped in front of Lady Rothley as the other turned and ran back down the corridor.

"Assassins! Assassins!" his scream sounded.

Moments later, a panicked bell began to cry out.

CHAPTER FIFTY ONE

A Good Day to Die

Elion sent a deft cut across the shadowy face of an attacker, as the man leapt over the palisade. Screaming, his foe dropped to his knees, vainly trying to keep his nose and left eye in place. With the din of battle ringing in his ears, Elion buried his sabre in the warrior's throat and then ducked low as another man leapt from the ladder onto the ramparts, his axe cutting murderously through the cold air.

Tristan hammered his shield into the large man as Elion recovered and together they cut the attacker down, dragging their blades free as another corpse cluttered up the walkway.

Finding his breath, Elion offered his thanks. Clutching momentarily at the wounds he could no longer feel, he spat blood from his mouth. As roars rose up about them, Tristan turned and fought his way along the ramparts to the north. Slipping past Trell he went to aid Janth, who was furiously fending off two attackers who had managed to capture several feet of rampart and were defending it madly to allow their comrades to join them.

Below, Elion could hear the rhythmic thud of axe on wood as Gardan's forces continued to hack at the gates, protected from the outlaws' arrows by shield bearers.

If the gates are breached...

More attackers gained the ramparts in several places as their numbers began to overpower the waning defenders. Amongst the throng, Elion spied Elissen. She was fighting near Devlin Hawke now, carried away from him on the rolling tide of battle. Her face was running with blood, a tapestry of dark and light that framed eyes bright with fury.

"More coming up," Trell reported, his bow snapping in disdain. He found Elion's eyes, as they both drew in rallying breaths.

Puffing out his bloodied cheeks Elion nodded wearily. They had long since dispensed with trying to repel the ladders, conserving their strength for the attackers that climbed them.

Raising his blade, Elion saluted the fight to come and sent a pleading look up at the dark sky, scattered now with broken cloud and stars.

"Just a little longer, Lady," he pleaded.

The only response he heard was the telling bite of axe upon wood.

Arillion danced by the guard's hopeless lunge, spinning past to cut both blades across the man's back. As the startled man dropped to his knees and Agris Varen drove his staff into his skull, Arillion licked his lips in delight, feeling his blood sing through his veins.

How wonderful it was to dance with death again, he thought as he turned through his pain to stand before Lady Rothley, who shied away from his bloodied blades.

"I beg you sir, please!" the proud woman said calmly above the distant clamour of the bell. "I know who you are and can guess as to why you are here. Spare me, I beseech you, and I will tell you all I know about the chancellor's corruption."

Arillion stepped close, driving both blades deep into her breast. "You just did," he whispered in her ear as he lowered her slowly to the ground.

Kaspen Shale dragged the assassin and his blades away.

"That was not a noble thing," the wayfarer hissed, glaring at him.

"I am not a noble man," Arillion responded. Yanking his good shoulder away from Kaspen's grip, he turned from him and cleaned the blood from his blades on Lady Rothley's silk gown.

It had been many years since he was last there, but without recent renovation, Evan Valus knew his way about the keep, knew where the chancellor's... his brother's offices were. Any caution was abandoned as the bells began to echo all about them and with his blade in hand, the woodsman led Khadazin, Riyan and the young huntress Tania down through the keep.

Drawn to the sounds of distant fighting, several guards rushed by the bottom of the spiral staircase and Evan paused only long enough to allow their shadows to slip from view.

Stepping out into the hallway, the woodsman sent a look after the guards, who turned a corner, oblivious to the threat they had just left behind. Tania stepped out first behind him, a feathered shaft to her cheek. Letting out a breath, she relaxed her bowstring and did her best to ignore the tight complaint from the stitches in her wounded arm.

"Follow me," the woodsman ordered, his concern flaring in his narrowed eyes. He led them across the hallway and down a short flight of steps into a narrow corridor. A lantern flickered from the wall beside a large wooden door, as Khadazin leant close.

"Is this it?" the Redani enquired, as he slipped his crossbow over his shoulder and pulled his hammer from his belt. His voice was dry as he imagined what would happen inside if it was. He had never seen the offices from this side, only from the courtyard, outside the keep.

Evan's hooded head bobbed once and he strode forward to throw open the door.

They hurried inside, weapons readied, searching the two empty side rooms, before spilling into the room heaving with parchments and flickering with candlelight and dancing shadows.

Riyan dragged a young scribe out from underneath a large desk, hauling him up to throw him towards Khadazin.

"Where is the chancellor?" Khadazin growled, his heart hammering in his chest. The young man nearly fainted in his grip.

"T-the chancellor?" the scribe stammered, his jade eyes wide with fear. "He has retired to his estate for the night. He was suffering from a terrible headache and he left the celebrations early."

"*Celebrations*?" The woodsman spat his distaste, glaring in frustration about the chamber.

Khadazin stared at the man he held in his grip, unsure of what to do. He released the thin man, who fell to his knees with a whimper and began to retch before him.

Sighing, Riyan stepped close, hammering the hilt of his dagger into the scribe's head. The man collapsed without a sound and the mute offered Khadazin an apologetic shrug.

As one, they looked to the woodsman. Evan met their stares calmly, as he chewed his top lip. Shaking his head, he let out a long sigh and ran his frustrations through his beard.

"Back to the sewers," he muttered grimly, turning angrily away.

The sounds of approach stirred the elegant hallway beyond, as Arillion found his breath against the blood-smeared wall. Kaspen watched the assassin as he reversed the grip on his left blade and calmed himself down from the trail of bodies they had left behind.

At the wayfarer's side, Agris Varen loomed large, his staff gripped tightly, the iron-shod ends covered in blood and wisps of hair. Tomlin skulked behind the bear, his eyes and bow trained on the servants' corridor behind them.

Looking at the rapier he carried in his gloved hand, Kaspen swallowed his disgust. The alarm bells had fallen silent now, as they carved their way down through the keep towards the Old Royal Chambers and those they had come to silence.

Sighing heavily, Kaspen looked to Arillion once more and fleetingly wished he had not headed up the slopes of the Great Divide to relieve himself that morning. *Life was so much simpler back then*! But then the Lady had deemed he pay attention to what was happening in the Four Vales, become a part of history, for better or for worse.

Arillion drew the wayfarer back to the present, stepping into the hall as shadows lengthened across the corridor before them. He plunged his left blade deep into a startled soldier's chest, leaving him impaled on the sword as he stepped by the man to send his right blade through the throat of his comrade.

Spilling into the fight after the assassin, the wayfarers found themselves in a broad hallway, carpeted and beautifully decorated. Lined with fine artworks from a different age, several statues watched the fight from shadowy alcoves.

Arillion blocked a blade that would have ripped his

throat out and disdainfully whipped his steel deep into the belly of his attacker, slicing it free to draw a scarlet line in the side of the guard's head.

Kaspen rushed forward into the fray, his rapier flicking deftly out to open up a man's cheek, turn aside another's lunging spear before finding its mark in the first attacker's neck. As the man stumbled back, a futile hand clamped over the gouting wound, Agris Varen roared, the bear about his shoulders seemingly alive once more as he barrelled into the spearman, swatting aside the spear to pummel the man to the ground.

"P-please, no!" the guard pleaded, raising a weak hand. Agris smashed the man's pleas back into his throat as his staff pummelled him brutally.

A shaft hissed over Kaspen's shoulder, dragging his horror away as Tomlin's skill felled a soldier running towards Arillion, who had danced his way through two more men, his single blade just as keen for blood without its twin.

Irritated, Arillion turned, his hooded eyes flashing as he regained his senses. Nodding his thanks, he found a breath as a telling silence settled on the hall. His left leg and shoulder ached as he walked back through the dead and dying, his pulse racing and his surroundings weaving before him.

Reaching Tomlin, he nodded again, before turning to the soldier he had impaled. The man was on his knees, his chin resting on the steel that had claimed his life. Transferring the sword he held in his right to the weaker hand, Arillion pulled the sword free, watching as the dead man toppled over.

"You are wounded," Kaspen Shale observed, coming to his side. Behind him, Agris watched for further danger.

Arillion scowled, following Kaspen's eyes to the cut in his side. Irritated, he looked back up.

"There will be time for pain when this over," he

hissed. "Come my friends, we still have the worst before us. We are near to the Old Royal Chambers and can take the servants' corridors to avoid the main entrance."

Kaspen liked the sound of that.

Arillion was already heading away again, whispering words of encouragement to Agris as he hurried by him.

"Are you ready, Great Bear?" Arillion asked as he swept away down the hallway.

The grizzled wayfarer nodded, his ruined face flickering in torch-lit determination as he followed the assassin. "I'd rather die fighting for something, than live a life that counts for nothing," he answered.

Ignoring his own wound, Kaspen grimaced at Tomlin. The younger wayfarer smiled faintly as he reached for another arrow.

"Well, you wanted a song," he pointed out solemnly.

Devlin Hawke gripped the palisade with trembling hands, watching as the attacking Valian forces regrouped before them momentarily. Reaching out for his sword, forgotten against the stout wooden defences, he picked it up again, staring at the notched steel, swimming in blood. It was a good blade, one he had rarely had cause to use until his bow had snapped whilst desperately fending off an attacker.

It was a good bow...

The clearing night sky and fulsome moon told him that it was past its zenith now, well beyond his need for sleep. His body felt like it was not his own anymore, the cuts and bruises belonging to somebody else. Two times more Gardan's forces had gained the ramparts, two more times the valiant defenders forced them back, giving their blood and lives to reclaim what was lost.

Devlin blew out his sorrow, thinking of the friends he had lost that night and those that he was still to say farewell to. During the last attack, Trell had fallen, the giant outlaw racing alone to repel the attackers who had slew several defenders to gain the northern wall. Sensing the danger, Devlin had looked along the chaos, seeing his friend's moonlit charge. Trell had cut down four attackers, sending them back to their comrades before he was overwhelmed. As Elion and several other defenders raced to his aid, Trell, pierced by axe, spear and sword had wrapped his huge arms about two of the men who were stabbing him and carried them from the ramparts to their deaths below.

Too tired to grieve, Devlin licked his dry lips, shaking his head. About him the defenders made the most of the lull in battle, tending silently to their wounds and thoughts. Elion Leigh was still standing, Devlin was happy to see. The young Carwellian captain was talking quietly to two of his patrol, flicking occasional looks towards the torches of the enemy, as they reformed into determined ranks.

One blessing to count in their favour was that when Durrant had built the mining community, he must have used the stoutest oak from the East Vales as the gates had still held, blunting both the axes and determination of their wielders.

Their numbers were waning badly now and Devlin knew that soon they would be forced to seek the protection of the upper tunnels in the mines. Once the walls were lost, the gates would be lost and then...

"I am sorry about Trell," Kerrin Thorn said, coming to lean on the palisade and stare out into the night.

Devlin nodded his silent thanks, unable to find any words. For a time they stared out into the torch-lit plains together, before the old tracker turned to him again.

"I think this last attack will be the one," he said quietly, his weathered face shamed at his words.

Devlin nodded. "Aye, friend, I fear it will be. It is a

shame we did not have another fifty souls to defend these walls with... I believe we could have held out."

Kerrin nodded, wishing he had stayed in Greywood with the boy, trapping and hunting to the end of his days, living the quiet life with the donkey for company.

"One thing's for certain," Kerrin said, "at least we won't run out of weapons..."

Devlin Hawke chuckled. Their enemy attacked.

The first tell that something was not right was when William came late to his study, carrying a Valian sword in his hand. Looking up from his papers over his spectacles, Chancellor Valus could see the fear in his retainer's eyes, flashing urgently in the shadows.

"William, what is the matter?" Relan asked. Taking his spectacles off, he placed thin hands on the desk to propel himself from his seat. His headache, his excuse for leaving the revelry of the night had been forced, aiding in his desire to be away from all the premature celebrations.

Savinn Kassaar's death had been a telling blow, one that would hopefully see the end to any rebellion in the city, but the Kestrel had returned a few hours before with further unsettling news that did little to aid his appetite for celebration. Her report that the high duke's family had survived was apparently of no concern to Henry Carwell, as he would soon announce that Karian Stromn was dead, enabling him to usurp the 'throne'. There would be plenty of time to seek them out and lace their suppers with poison once the Brotherhood had cemented their control.

Highwater also remained strong, with or without the Byron girl's determination, and news from the mines of Durrant's Field hinted further at an organised, determined uprising. If his plan to draw out Lady Byron had failed and she still lived, Relan feared it would be a long winter for their ambitions.

There were too many pieces on the board unaccounted for, too many unseen moves yet to be played out...

"Lord Chancellor, the estate, it is being attacked," William said, crossing the study to grab his employer by one sleeve. "Your wife waits for you – we must get you to safety, through the rear gardens."

Relan's mind spun. *Under attack? How could this be?* His thoughts stirred with warning. Did Henry Carwell no longer have any need for him, now that he had secured his seat at the head of the council? Who else would dare to make their move so soon?

William had his master from the study before he realised it and Relan was herded roughly through the mansion towards the rear gardens and orchards. Two guards waited nervously with the chancellor's wife, who was dressed in a diaphanous nightgown, her indecency hidden only by the dark cloak she reluctantly wore.

"Husband! What is happening?" she demanded, her raven-black hair as wild as her fearful expression. She planted her pale hands on slim hips, indicating she was in one of her tempestuous moods.

"I do not know, my love," Relan admitted, holding up his hands. Hurrying to his wife, he reached for her and pulled her close. "We must err towards caution and find sanctuary. All will be well, I promise you."

He looked towards William and nodded. "See her to safety, William, see–,"

His words were cut off as the sounds of fighting drew near to the front of the mansion. A cry split the silence and Relan flicked a fearful look to his wife.

"Let us flee together, my love," he stammered, his fear getting the better of him.

Taking his young wife's slim hand in his own, Relan Valus followed William out into the grounds of his estate as screams pierced the night.

Kaspen Shale had always wanted to see the splendours of the Old Royal Chamber, had dreamt at the marvels of its architecture and purported beauty of the great hall. As he and his fellow wayfarers followed Arillion down the narrow servants' staircase and out into the magnificent chamber, Kaspen wished he was as far away from there as possible.

The expansive, domed marvel was wreathed in shadows, the edges of the night lit by candles that did little to warm the cold. As they slipped from the cover of a huge pillar across the marble floor to the next, they were all aware of the ominous silence of the chamber.

Agris Varen lumbered along behind Tomlin, casting a worried look behind him towards the huge double doors that remained closed. His skin itched with worry as he stared through the shadows at the flanking pillars that lined the chamber, unable to pick out the threats that he sensed were lurking there.

Arillion slipped silently across the marble floor, uncaring of the beauty of the place, unseeing of the artefacts worth more than any coin he could have possibly ever earned. Shafts of moonlight spilled through the windows of the huge dome over their heads and, as he began to spy the council table on the dais ahead, he felt his lust for blood and his emotions take control.

"We are walking into a trap, swordsman," Kaspen whispered at his ear.

Arillion nodded his hooded agreement. There was no harp or fiddle being played, no cacophony of celebration to drown out the sound of their approach.

"Be ready," Arillion murmured, barely beyond a breath. With swords glistening in the moonlight, he led them on towards the grand table where the Valian council had decided the Reven's doom.

Tania watched, mesmerised as the woodsman parried a sentry's wild attack with crossed-blades, swept his attacker to one side effortlessly and cut him down with his shorter sword. At her side, Khadazin gripped his hammer, his breath ragged from the efforts of their swift race through the sewers and the climb over the high walls of the chancellor's estate.

Several guards had fallen to their unexpected attack, though they were rallying now, and, to her disgust, Tania had felt no shame as her shafts had killed two of them.

Riyan fought silently beside the woodsman, following him as they cut down the final guard outside the mansion house and headed up marble steps to the door. The mute had fought well, the long knives he bore effortlessly flashing in the moonlight.

Khadazin hurried to aid the woodsman and Riyan, as they beat upon the barred double doors. After a moment, their combined strength and need won out and the wood gave way with a sharp crack of complaint. Faint light spilled across the porch.

"No time to think, just act," the woodsman hissed. "Take Tania and enter from the rear of the house to cut off any escape."

Khadazin's heart was racing. Everything he had fought for, all the agony he had endured had led him to this moment and now that it was here, he was not so certain it was what he wanted.

'*Sometimes*,' his father had once said to him in a rare, lucid moment, '*the need for a drink is often a greater reward than the drink itself*.'

Four guards faced them through the shattered wood beyond, swords drawn, shields held high.

As Tania led the Redani away, Riyan and the woodsman surged forward into the fray.

"Why don't you come and join me for a drink?" a deep,

rich voice asked, echoing about the chamber.

Arillion started, looking towards the dais. He could see two people there, one sat on the far side of the majestic round table, the other stood behind, hooded and watchful.

Arillion's heart began to race and he fought for breath. Flicking a look behind, he met Kaspen's wide eyes. The wayfarer held up an empty hand and shrugged forlornly.

Sighing, Arillion stepped from behind the pillar and led his comrades towards the council table.

At their approach the candles around the dais began to stir and fill the shadows. As Arillion put a tentative foot on the first marble step, he could see that it was Henry Carwell sat across the far side of the table in the high duke's chair, one hand stretched forth on the ancient wood, toying idly with the stem of a wine goblet.

One step higher and the assassin could see the slender, hooded figure, cloaked in shadows at Lord Carwell's shoulder. Their eyes met briefly and Arillion could not feel the feet that took him onto the dais.

As Kaspen joined him there, his sword hanging in hand by his side, the double doors behind them groaned open and all heads turned to see a dozen soldiers hurry through, led by a squat, dark-haired man dressed in obscene finery, his fat bejewelled hands clutching a goblet in one hand, a rapier in the other.

"I have this," Agris Varen growled, turning to face them. Tomlin bent his bow in their direction, also.

"Gentlemen, gentlemen," Henry Carwell purred. "It doesn't have to end like this. We are, after all, not the savages. Join me for a drink and let us settle this like men."

Arillion fixed the would-be lord of all the Vales with a withering glare. "That's exactly what we intend to do."

Henry Carwell sighed, turning his head slightly to the

figure standing at his right shoulder. Arillion met the familiar eyes that watched him intently from the hood with such hatred, that the shadow, *she*, took an involuntary step backwards.

Henry Carwell raised a finger in the air and as he spoke, a dozen more guards appeared from the darkness behind him, spreading out behind their lord with weapons drawn and faces determined.

"It is a shame, assassin. Had destiny deemed us allies, not enemies, I believe we could have become good friends," Henry Carwell said sincerely, "alas, fate has decided otherwise for us..."

Arillion swallowed, as the tension in the chamber became unbearable.

The lord of the East Vales raised his goblet to his lips to whet the anticipation in his throat.

"Will somebody kill these imbeciles for me?" he asked, smiling devilishly.

CHAPTER FIFTY TWO

We All Fall Down

The night was bitterly cold as Chancellor Relan Valus hurried through his orchards towards the northern wall that would take him to safety. As he pulled his wife through the darkness with only the moon to guide them, he wished that he had not been so grandiose in his ambitions and had chosen a smaller estate.

As they fled, one of the guards cried out a warning and stealing fearful looks over their shoulders, he and his wife could see two figures chasing them through the misty night.

With a hiss of warning, a shaft sped through the dark, catching the guard who had called out in the left shoulder. With a cry of pain, the man turned, clutching at the arrow.

"Flee, my lord," the guard shouted, as he turned back, brandishing his sword bravely.

As William ushered his charges away, the second guard turned dutifully to stand beside his comrade to protect their escape.

With his chest tight with fear and his skin crawling, Relan Valus fled into the night.

The Old Royal Chambers erupted with angry roars as Henry Carwell's men rushed forward to carry out his command.

Arillion watched the men spill about the ancient table to either side of him, a raging river parted by a solitary rock. As Tomlin's bow sang and the first attacker fell, the assassin met Henry Carwell's triumphant smile and noticed *her* eyes flash fearfully.

Arillion flicked a calm glance at the approaching soldiers, caught sight of Tomlin and Kaspen rushing to meet them. Looking back at Henry Carwell, the assassin winked.

Screams echoed about the chamber as Arillion leapt up onto the council table, ignoring the fiery protest in his left shin. Springing towards Henry Carwell, the tide of battle raging all about him, Arillion could see the fear creep into the lord of the East Vales eyes as he realised what was happening.

Two more steps and Arillion dropped onto his good knee, sliding forward across the Four Vales, scattering goblets and silver plates full of delicacies. Henry Carwell went to rise from his seat, his confidence lost, fear etched on his face.

Arillion slid forward, burying both his blades into Carwell's chest, pinning him to the high duke's chair.

"The King is dead," Arillion spat, watching the disbelief drain from Henry Carwell's eyes. The lord of the East Vales pawed at his killer's face, coughing up words choked by thick blood.

Arillion turned his attentions on the woman stepping back into the arms of her shock.

"Long live the King," Arillion hissed vehemently, as he ripped his right sword free.

A long knife appeared in her right hand, slipping from underneath her dark cloak. Instead of attacking, however, she took tentative steps away from him.

"Hello, Alyssa," Arillion snarled, pulling down his face scarf to reveal his bitter hatred.

Turning from her duty, the Kestrel flew for the shadows.

The night was cold, though Elion Leigh was not, as he slipped on the grim realities of battle underneath his feet. Janth saved his life, lunging over his left shoulder to run the attacker through who towered above his captain, broad axe raised high.

Elion could barely nod any thanks, his limbs and body burning from fatigue as he found his feet amidst the dead, their limbs and entrails.

Throwing a despairing look along the wall, he could tell that the moment had come, that everything they had fought so valiantly for was lost.

"Janth, get Tristan to safety," Elion said, turning to his friend. Together, they hauled Tristan to his feet. The wounded rider from Carwell slumped against his friends, clutching at the deep wound in his belly.

Janth almost carried Tristan to some nearby steps. "Get Jarion to move the injured to the upper tunnels," Elion shouted after them. "He won't have long. We'll hold the wall for as long as we can."

For the briefest of moments, Elion was alone, with only the dead for company. His nostrils and throat were full of death and sighing, he glanced up at the stars overhead, brighter now than his own prospects.

The sounds of fighting filtered through the haze and blinking, Elion watched dumbly as two soldiers gained the ramparts before him. As they charged towards him, two of the remaining freed slaves rushed by, their swords flashing in the moonlight. Elion blinked, watching as the wall was saved, though at a heavy cost. At the end, only one defender remained, his bared chest running freely from his wounds.

Elion went to the man's aid. "Thank you, my friend," he said, clapping the Valian man on one shoulder. "What is your name?"

"Athen," the man rasped, his face contorted.

"Get to the upper tunnels, Athen," Elion ordered, casting a sad look at the still form of the man's friend. "I will join you there soon."

As the man stumbled for the stairs, Devlin Hawke roared out, dragging Elion's attention back.

The outlaw was fighting alongside Elissen, Bran, Colm and several other outlaws. Over the chaos of battle, Devlin met his gaze.

"We have to fall back," he cried out, deftly blocking a rising cut from his opponent. Devlin rolled past his adversary, cutting him down from behind as he forced his way along the cluttered rampart towards his friend.

Elion ran to him, hearing the screams of more attackers behind him now.

Two men pulled themselves over the ramparts between them and Elion charged forward, burying his sabre in a burly attacker's ribs. Screaming, the large man growled defiantly, smashing his forehead into Elion's right cheek. As Elion fell back, his surroundings spinning, his blade snapped as he tried to drag his sword free.

"Takes more than that to kill me," Fuller spat, coming after his opponent.

The sweet song of a blade caressed Elion's cheek as he ducked low, barely avoiding the large man's attack. Pressing home his advantage the bald-headed man chuckled, forcing Elion back towards more attackers.

Realising the danger, Elion blinked free of his daze. Stepping inside Fuller's reach, he rose up on his toes to ram his broken blade into the man's stout neck. Throwing the dying man behind him, Elion stumbled towards

Devlin Hawke. The outlaw dragged his sword from his opponent's belly and tossed his friend a fallen blade.

"We have to go, now!" Devlin said grimly, his face spattered in blood.

Elion nodded, his senses drowned by the roar of battle. The order went out, filtering along the wall and as the defenders hurried for the steps, Gardan's men finally claimed his prize for him.

Khadazin rushed forward, his throat raw and his jaw set tight with anger as he caught sight of Chancellor Valus for the first time since that fateful afternoon in the grounds of the high duke's keep. The thin, pale looking man, the orchestrator of so much misery in the Four Vales hurried away from them, his eyes wide over one shoulder like twin moons.

Tania drew back on her bow, a shaft tight to her nose as she let fly, guarding the stonemason's charge. The second guard fell back as the arrow found a lethal mark in his chest and as Khadazin reached the other guard she felt for another shaft, hurrying past them both.

Barrelling into the guard, Khadazin knocked the man off-balance as he felt the sting of a blade bite into his left shoulder. Ignoring the pain the Redani fell on top of the man, whose face twisted in panic as they grappled on the ground.

Snarling, Khadazin pinned the man down by his throat with his ruined wrist. The Redani stared down into the man's pleading eyes and before he realised it he smashed his hammer into the side of his head.

Standing up, Khadazin fell back from the dead man and looked for Tania. She was hurrying through the trees away from him. Calling out in alarm, the Redani raced after her.

William cried out a warning, as an arrow struck an apple tree beside him. He threw a look over his shoulder as they weaved through the maze of trunks, hurrying for the wall that stretched across their misty vision now.

Another shaft missed its mark and William shouted madly for them to pick up pace. As they ran on, the chancellor's wife stumbled and fell over a bent ankle to the sodden grass. For a moment only, the chancellor hesitated, before turning away to carry on with his escape.

"Husband?" Lady Valus screamed. She tried to pick herself up as the chancellor disappeared through the shadows.

William hurried back to the stricken woman as the archer reached them. He stared in disbelief, laughing.

"You're just a girl!" he snorted. Raising his sword, he stepped before his charge.

Tania scowled, her face hidden by the night, her eyes bright from the moon.

"No," she said calmly, sending a shaft deep into the man's face. "I am a woman now."

Arillion threw himself from the ancient table into the soldiers, as they stared in disbelief at Henry Carwell. Cut badly, Kaspen also pressed home his momentary advantage. Driving his sword into one man's heart, he leapt back, barely avoiding the blades that turned his way and watched as Arillion cut the hand from one man, before blocking an attack with such ferocity, that it sent the attacker's blade back up into his own face.

"Go after her," Kaspen panted, parrying an attack. He fell back to the steps, as he was overrun.

Cutting another guard down disdainfully, Arillion hesitated, throwing a look about the Old Royal Chamber. They were holding out, despite the overwhelming odds. He looked past the macabre form of Henry Carwell, towards the rear of the great chamber and the archway the

Kestrel had fled through.

Saluting his friends, Arillion kissed his bloodied sword, turned and limped towards his destiny.

Tomlin's skill with the bow kept his pursuers at bay as he ran between the pillars. As he hurried through the shadows, reaching for his final arrow, he heard Agris Varen's roars.

Turning, the wayfarer could see his giant friend, standing against a tide of attackers. Agris charged into their midst, his staff light in his hands as he spun one attacker's head on his shoulders and swept the legs from underneath another. Thirsty blades drank from the huge wayfarer, flashing as they stabbed from all angles. Roaring defiantly, Agris pulled one man close, smashing his forehead into his opponent's nose. Tossing the man aside, he drove his staff into another attacker's belly, sending him reeling. More blades fell upon the wayfarer, as the fat man standing nearby took another sip from his goblet, enjoying the spectacle.

Tomlin turned his bow on the man, drawing back on the string. As he nestled the shaft against his cheek, he felt a blade cut through his back. The arrow went wide as another blade cut through his shoulder. Screaming defiantly, Tomlin dragged his sword free as he was wrestled to the marble floor.

Baron Crowood drained the last of his wine and threw the goblet into the shadows. It clattered away as the huge wayfarer dropped to his knees, the four remaining soldiers circling him warily. Glaring up at them, the giant spat blood from his mouth, dealing them a bloody grin.

"Come a little closer," he growled, his staff falling from his hands. His head lolled and a guard stepped close, driving his spear into the bearskin covering his back.

Barking an order, Crowood strode forward, taking the

bloodied spear from the man's grasp. He moved around to stand in front of the dying man, his boots echoing ominously.

"Renyard Crowood, bear-slayer," the drunk baron nodded in satisfaction. He raised the spear high, aiming it for the wayfarer's bowed head.

Agris Varen lashed out. Pulling Crowood's feet from underneath him, he crawled on top of the fat baron as swords and spears fell upon him.

"Not today you're not."

Roaring his last, Agris Varen bit the throat from the whimpering man beneath him, spitting out a bloody smile as the steel and shadows claimed him.

An owl swept silently away through the night as Chancellor Valus stumbled towards the wall, his robes hitched up about his knees as he ran. Behind him all was silent, his wife's pleading screams absent now as the night gathered close about him.

Fighting for breath he hurried to the wall, staring up at his freedom. As he fretted on how to climb over without William's aid, an arrow struck the wall above his head, dragging his last breath from his throat in a strangled gasp.

Shuddering, he turned, watching as a young woman stepped out from the tree line and trained another shaft on him.

Dropping to his knees, Relan Valus held up thin arms, shaking his hands pleadingly.

"Please, do not kill me," he faltered, his voice gripped by fear. "Whatever you are being paid, I can give you more. You don't have to do this!"

The woman watched him silently, her deep brown eyes narrowed between wild strands of her long tresses.

She barely reacted as a huge shadow reached her side, though she relaxed her bow string slightly.

Relan Valus stared in abject horror as the huge figure stepped into the moonlight and he saw the broad, broken face that glared at him.

"*Redani*?" the chancellor gasped. Falling back, he scrambled on his haunches tight against the wall. "P-please, don't do this. I can give you the life you deserve, the money, the status..."

Khadazin bellowed and rushed forward, all of his anger shaking though his body as he raised his hammer high above his head.

"No!" Relan Valus begged, reaching out with trembling hands.

Khadazin blinked rapidly, his veil of rising madness parting as he looked down at the pathetic creature beneath him.

"Khadazin," Tania's soft voice called out.

The Redani lowered his hammer.

"I do not seek riches," Khadazin spat, his wide eyes still white with anger. "I have only ever sought peace and happiness in this land. It was you, *you* who are guided by power and greed, who stole that chance from me. I should bury my anger, my thirst for revenge deep in your heart, but I come to realise now, here, at this very moment, that I do not want to. There are others who lay darker claim to your life than I. I want only what you and your allies have stolen from the people. I only want the truth from your lips."

Throwing away his hammer, Khadazin seized the chancellor by his robes and threw him back across the ground towards Tania.

Sobbing in relief, Relan Valus looked up at the young woman. She glared down at him, then stepped away as a hooded figure appeared from the darkness of the orchard.

"There can be no true happiness found in lies and deceit," Evan agreed striding forward. He lowered his hood slowly, barely able to control his fury.

"Hello brother," he greeted, dropping his voice to a menacing hiss.

Relan stared up in disbelief, then began to snivel and whine, as a breath caught in his throat.

"Evan? How can this be?" the chancellor screamed, his hands clawing at the grass as shock and terror writhed through his body.

The woodsman, who was once a captain, was barely able to look at the man, the brother who had ruined his life. Time slowed, the shadows of night softening at the edges as dawn began to stir in the east.

"Lady, forgive me," Evan sighed.

He strode forward, his sword raised in his shaking hand. Stepping in close, he slammed the hilt into the side of his brother's head, watching dispassionately as the chancellor crumpled amongst his robes.

"Not here," Evan hissed, turning away. Tears slid down the lines of his bloodied face. "Not in this place where nobody will know."

Khadazin smiled grimly.

Fear chased the Kestrel up the spiral staircase, any certainty she may have held lost to the blades of her former lover. Reaching a bare room, marked only by an adjoining stairwell and lit by a solitary torch, she hesitated, drawing in a deep, calming breath.

Below her, the sounds of battle raged on and the Kestrel chewed her bottom lip, hoping for the telling silence that would suggest her former lover's little rebellion had failed.

Her former lover?

The Kestrel smiled bitterly, shamed at her own cowardice. If he survived, if the Brotherhood's quest for power was now over, he would never stop looking for her. She would never be able to sleep soundly again.

Did she want to spend the rest of her days looking

over her shoulder and become a victim, like all of those she had killed since the night of her betrayal?

Testing the weight of her trusty long knife, she drew the crescent-shaped dagger with her bandaged hand. Steeling herself, the Kestrel strode back to the spiral staircase and became one with the shadows.

A whisper, nothing more, but it saved his life, as Arillion fell back, a knife raking sparks along stone. His sword hissed in return, finding only shadows as the darkness before him shifted and he heard the light step of retreat.

"Nearly," Arillion called out, his voice echoing. "Perhaps I should turn my back for you?"

Arillion grinned as he heard the sharp intake of angry breath on the staircase above him. Griping his blade, he hesitated, popping his last opium ball into his mouth. His body dripped with wounds and his injured leg was crying out from all of his efforts.

Just one more score to settle...

When he reached the top of the staircase, she was waiting for him, stood in the centre of a circular room, her hood about her shoulders.

Torchlight framed her cold features, the flames highlighting the scar on her beautiful face.

"Still remember me, then!" Arillion observed, stepping into the room, his sword hanging casually by his side.

The Kestrel nodded, smiling bitterly. "I have never forgotten you, my love."

Arillion spat his distaste on the stone between them. "And neither have I, you, Alyssa."

"I am known as the Kestrel now," she pointed out.

"What is it with your family and birds?" Arillion asked, his eyes betraying his fury. He flicked a look at the crescent blade she carried in her right hand.

The Kestrel followed his anger to the blade and

frowned. She looked back at Arillion, saw the revenge in his beautiful eyes, recalling a time when they were bright with something else for her.

"Of all the abhorrent things I have done in my life," she began sadly, "I regret killing the girl."

Arillion fought to remain calm. "As do I," he said coldly.

Silence filled the emptiness between them.

"What happened to Tobin?" Alyssa asked finally.

"We went for a little chat," Arillion responded, his eyes blazing.

"If you ever see him," the Kestrel said, "apologise to Lucien Varl for me. He is a brave man."

Arillion inclined his head, drifting now with the opium coursing through his veins.

She came at him, knife and dagger opening up wounds in his left arm and right leg as he twisted by her.

"Not bad," Arillion grunted, nodding.

Panting, the Kestrel, once Alyssa Hawke, turned to face him, grimacing as she became aware of the deep wound beneath her left breast.

She smiled thinly. "Even with one blade, you were always better than me."

The Kestrel leapt at him, her knife opening his left shoulder as he turned away the dagger and buried his free elbow in the side of her head. As she stumbled to the floor, Arillion was behind her, plucking his dagger away from her dazed hand.

A vision of a flame-haired girl filled Arillion's mind as he drove his sword into her back and pulled her into his arms.

"Do it," the Kestrel sighed wearily.

Arillion kissed her cheek and drew Squirrel's dagger across her throat.

CHAPTER FIFTY THREE

The Bitter End

"They are retreating," Bren Fal observed grimly, as he dragged his blade from the chest of the wiry man who had leapt over the palisade at him. As the dying man muttered a desperate prayer to the Father of Storms and fell into his eternal embrace, the younger Fal looked along the ramparts for his brother, seeing him hurrying down the steps before Elion Leigh.

Smiling, Bren puffed the relief from his cheeks.

More attackers filled his vision and as another man came cautiously along the ramparts towards them, several others appeared over the tops of ladders to block the stairs they would need to flee to safety.

Kallum Campbell, his sword arm weak from fatigue, wiped away the blood running down his face. At his side, Liyam Tallis, his left arm useless now, caught a heart-beat's worth of breath and cast a forlorn look at the men, as he leant wearily on his notched Valian Longsword.

"That's that, then," Liyam sighed, hefting his sword in his shaking hand. The three men shared abject looks, raised their swords to salute each other and then turned on their enemy with ferocious, defiant screams.

In his haste Elion Leigh leapt down the last few steps onto the roughly churned ground. The biting sound of heavy axes on wood continued to tear at his nerves as a spear buried in the mud beside him.

Throwing a worried look behind, Elion could see the ramparts filling with attackers now, their dark shapes framed by the first signs of the dawn stirring in the east behind them.

Cursing, the former captain of Carwell turned, chasing after Devlin and Bran. He was relieved to see that most of the defenders were already hurrying up the torch-lit slopes of the mines, towards the tunnels that would be their refuge and then, inexorably, their tombs.

As Elion hurried away from the wave of helplessness that threatened to drown him, Bran hesitated, as Devlin raced by them and swept up a bow, resting against a barrel full of rain water.

Elion slowed, his ears also detecting the screams of battle. Reluctantly, he turned his head back to find that three defenders still fought their way along the ramparts, desperate for the southernmost steps that would offer them a way free of certain death.

Elion gripped Bran's arm as they both watched on, oblivious to the enemy that rushed down nearby steps towards the weapon-laden carts blocking the gates.

"Oh no," Bran moaned, as he realised who was trapped on the wall...

Kallum Campbell felt the sharp stab of pain in his side as he forced an attacker against the palisade. Glaring at the soldier he wrestled with, he managed to drag his blade across the man's ribs and throw him to the ground.

Yelling defiantly, Liyam blocked a vicious blade before his face, his steel singing and his good arm throbbing as he shouldered a man from the ramparts, ignoring his screams as he fell away from him. Ducking under a hungry axe, he drove his steel home into a man's groin, stumbling forward onto another blade as he slipped by the mortally wounded attacker.

Grunting, Liyam fell to his knees, barely aware of Bren Fal. The Carwellian rider jumped over him, his sword flashing across an attacker's face, as he drove several men back with his screams.

Fire spread through Liyam's chest as he clamped a hand over the blood flowing from the deep wound. Snarling, he forced himself up onto legs he could no longer feel and was aware of Kallum at his side.

"Come on," Kallum grimaced, his dark hair matted with blood. "Let's get you to safety."

Bren watched as the men before him, forced to fight one at a time, stepped back warily. Stepping through the dead, Bren brandished his bloody blade defiantly. The first man before him, realising that he could not step back any further, turned his reluctance into attack and leapt forward, his short stabbing blade thrusting out from behind his shield.

Bren turned the attack aside, rolling past his opponent's raised shield to throw himself onto the attackers gathered behind. As Kallum cut down the stranded shield-bearer, Bren drove his sword into the shoulder of another man, wrenched it free and barely avoided a spear, thrusting from the line of attackers before him.

As Kallum came to his aid again, he threw a look beyond the wary warriors before him and saw the stairs, but a few blades beyond.

Crying out madly, Bren charged forward.

Elion growled, gripping Bran firmly as he made to go back to the ramparts to aid his brother's escape.

"It's too dangerous," Elion stated, his face pained as he realised what he was asking Bran to do.

Devlin Hawke was at their side again. Drawing effortlessly back on his bow, he sent two shafts in rapid succession towards the wall, clearing the way to the steps.

"We have to go," Devlin hissed, eyeing the growing number of attackers who were trying to haul the weapon carts away from the main gate.

Bren ordered Kallum and Liyam down the stairs, covering their escape as he fought off another attacker.

Steel rang out across the settling silence as Bren fought a rear-guard down the stairs, cutting the ankles from beneath a tall warrior, who fell from the stairs with a blood-curdling scream.

Without another word, Devlin Hawke hurried for the torch-lit slopes of the mine. Rushing forward, Elion and Bran spread out on either side of Kallum and Liyam, guarding their stumbling retreat, as Bren reached the ground.

Dozens more attackers filled the ramparts, their spears and a crossbow reaching out for the retreating defenders.

Elion felt the sting of a bolt, as it creased his right calf. Ignoring the fierce pain, he hurried away, hearing, but not seeing Bren Fal go down, a spear deep in his back.

"NO!" Bran screamed. Elion twisted at the cry, meeting Bran's searching eyes, as he turned away from him.

"Good luck, Elion Leigh," he smiled sadly.

Before Elion could react, Bran raced for the stairs and the brother that crawled through the mud towards him. Caught up in his shock and shackled by his responsibility, Elion watched on as attackers fell upon Bren, their dull blades hacking and stabbing down mercilessly.

Bran leapt amongst them, his sabre opening up a deep wound in one man's forehead, before snaking out to cut the elbow from another's arm. His brother was dead, he could tell, his body pierced and cut in many places and Bran did not even feel the sword that cut through his back.

Driving his sword into the face of a bearded man, Bran threw himself through his attackers, another blade opening up a wound in his throat.

Dropping to his knees, Bran coughed up thick blood, reaching through the blades and boots that stamped and cut down on him.

"I'm here little brother," he whispered, as he grasped Bren's lifeless hand.

Elion's sword was forgotten in his hand as he turned through his tears and away from the brothers. His heart was in his mouth as he stumbled for his hollow sanctuary.

Bran, Bren, Liehella and Eban... all of them gone to join Clarissa, who, much to his bitter acceptance, most likely waited for them in the next life.

Behind him, the attackers cheered, their bloodied weapons raised in triumph as they claimed the walls for themselves and found some momentary respite from the bloody work ahead of them.

Not feeling his wounds, not accepting their pain, Elion stumbled on, the cheers cutting through him deeper than any blade had.

They had been so close, had fought so bravely and yet still, even now, it would not be enough. Gardan would soon have his victory and his cold, callous boot would stamp out their little rebellion. The Brotherhood, should the others have failed, would tighten their grip on the Four Vales and choke away the last remnants of honour left in the land.

Snarling, Elion took three steps forward and fell to his knees. His sword was heavy in his hand now, as he directed his anger up at the stars.

He had always believed that everything that had happened to him had been for a reason, a higher, greater purpose the Lady was keeping from him lest he lose faith, become a victim of his own code and honour.

How many more people would have to die, before her intent was made known to him?

"What more do you want from me?" Elion screamed, tears washing the blood from his cheeks.

Shaking his head, Elion drove his blade into the earth and forced himself to stand. Ignoring the shallow wound he felt again in his calf, he turned and walked back towards the ranks of the enemy amassing on the palisade before him.

His heart was racing as the carts were finally pulled aside and toppled over, spilling their crates away from the gates. As he strode towards the palisade, the gates were slowly, ominously hauled open to reveal the soldiers waiting outside.

Elion Leigh cocked his head to one side, listening to his drumming heart and the eeriness of the coming dawn. Drawing in a calming breath, he raised his sword in salute, kissed the bloodied blade and then, very slowly, he drew a purposeful line in the mud before him.

As Arillion stumbled down the spiral staircase, back towards the Old Royal Chamber, he could hear only the telling silence that the battle below was over. Slumping against the cold stone, he almost fell down the final, twisting steps, leaving a trail of his own blood there to mark his passing.

Sheathing his sword, Arillion left behind his vengeance and the anger that had very nearly undone him. Stepping out into the chamber, his eyes narrowed, sweeping the carnage before him.

There was nobody left standing, no guards waiting to

cut the last of his luck from him. Frowning, Arillion listened to the silence, unsure of why there were no reinforcements, uncaring of what he would do should they arrive.

Falling across the marble, he made his way to the council table, dragging his eyes from the corpses and limbs that littered the chamber beyond.

Reaching Lord Carwell's side, the assassin pulled the small fortune from his lifeless fingers, filling his pouches with a long overdue reward.

Lifting up the dead lord's head, Arillion leant close, staring into the unseeing eyes.

"All the designs of men count for nothing in the end," Arillion quoted, though he could not recall where from. Pulling his blade free, the assassin turned away as Lord Carwell slumped forward onto the table.

History, it seemed, always had its say in these ancient halls...

Searching the chamber, Arillion quickly found Kaspen Shale. Surrounded by his enemies, the rangy wayfarer was slumped with his back against a pillar, head bowed, broad hat fallen by his side.

Kneeling on the bloodied marble, Arillion gently lifted the wayfarer's head by his chin, tilting his face towards the candlelight.

Coughing, Kaspen opened one eye, the other crusted shut by the blood running from a head wound that had lifted his scalp.

"There you are," the wayfarer observed above a faint smile.

Gripping his friend by one shoulder Arillion could only nod, his throat too thick with emotion.

Kaspen flicked an unseeing look about the great chamber, his breath shallow and elusive.

"Tomlin and Agris... they are dead," the wayfarer sighed. "Soon, I shall join them beside the fire..."

Arillion noticed for the first time that Kaspen's side was open, his entrails ripped from him.

"Rest, my friend," the assassin whispered, choking on his sadness.

Kaspen dragged words free. "Did we succeed?"

"Aye," Arillion nodded, "we did."

Kaspen murmured. "Thank the Lady. Tell our family... tell them we did a good thing here."

"I will sing a song for *you*, my friend," Arillion promised, though Kaspen would never hear him.

Looking about through his tears, the assassin found Kaspen's fallen rapier and curled the wayfarer's lifeless fingers about the hilt. Leaning close, Arillion kissed his friend on the forehead, rose up on unsteady feet and left the wayfarer to rest with the eleven men he had killed.

A feral wind accompanied Eran Dray into the mining encampment known as Durrant's Field, his weariness forgotten, his heart hammering as he stared about the mines and the squalor the Reven would have been forced to work and die in. Eager comrades rushed by him, their cheers failing in their throats as they slowed and looked in confusion at the solitary warrior who stood in their path.

Eran shot Wen a wide look and his pale friend looked back in astonishment.

"What's he doing?" Wen whispered, watching as the blonde-haired warrior, bathed in blood, drew a line in the ground.

"He's making a last stand," a grizzled warrior with one ear and barely any teeth in his head grinned proudly at them both.

Eran shook his head in wonderment and was tempted to go and join him. Both he and Wen, once ordered to attack by Esten Oswald, had made for the gates. When it came down to it, neither of them were keen to throw their lives away amongst the carnage on the walls and had spent the night shielding the axe-wielders from the archers' shafts – remaining there to protect them long after the defenders had given up trying to stop them and Esten Oswald's body had been recovered from the fighting.

For a few heartbeats further, Eran and Wen stood with the warrior who had spoken to them, all captivated by the brave man who strode slowly along his defiant line in the dirt.

Eran heard the distant approach of rumbling hooves behind him and barely managed to hide his distaste as he saw Commander Gardan riding through the dawn towards Durrant's Field. He and his personal guard had finally deemed, now that the walls were theirs, to join the men in battle.

Eran looked away, disgusted. Gardan had repeatedly thrown men at the attack, uncaring of the men and women who died for him. He personally checked the wounded who stumbled back to their lines during the night, sending them back again if he thought their injuries not serious enough.

How many more lives would he demand, before winter was done?

As his commander reined in his mount outside the mines and slipped from his saddle, the solitary warrior's defiance was broken, as an impetuous attacker threw a spear at him. Eran held his breath, watching its arching flight, but the bloodied warrior stepped calmly to one side, stamping on the fallen haft in defiance.

Silence settled on the encampment momentarily before his heroic stance and the respect he had garnered was lost to a roar that rose up in the throats of some, quickly spreading along the watching line.

Screams filled the dawn as nearly thirty of Eran's comrades surged forward.

Aven Mor looked up as he heard the quiet, urgent discussion in the chamber beyond. Flicking a look at Callin Vane, they stared towards the closed door, draped in thick shadows. Swallowing, the young wayfarer whetted his lips, gripping his short sword before him in trembling hands. At his side, Callin moved to the bed the high duke rested in, turning to protect his charge with his life, if circumstance dictated it.

The door cracked open, torchlight spilling into the bedchamber to chase away the shadows and fall upon the high duke, who lifted his head from his pillows.

A shadow filled the light, slumping against the doorframe.

"The city is yours to claim again," Arillion hissed, feeling his pain now as he directed his words at the high duke. "You must send out word that you are alive and are, once more, well enough to rule. The attack on Durrant's Field must also be stopped and that murderous bastard Gardan is to be arrested."

The high duke coughed heavily, overwhelmed by what he was hearing. He dabbed at his mouth with a handkerchief, staring at the bloody apparition before him.

"Who are you?" he demanded quietly.

Arillion ignored him. "There is little time left to you, lord. You must act now, before your enemies can regroup and strike back at you."

The assassin could see his words had found their mark and grunting in pain, he turned to leave. He hesitated, turning again to rest in the doorway, the same doorway he had watched Cassana sleep from, all those days before.

Arillion inclined his head at the young wayfarer, motioning for him to come with him. As the pale young man dutifully came to his side, Arillion turned his attentions on the high duke once more, the blood from his wounds dripping on the elegant carpet.

"I will come and find you for my reward when you are feeling better, my lord," he stated, his eyes glittering.

Turning, Arillion stumbled away from Karian Stromn's confused thanks and headed for the safety of the sewers. Unbeknownst to him then, Arillion would never set foot inside the high duke's keep again.

Elion Leigh stood calmly, listening as a roar swept through the enemy's ranks and they surged forward. As he prepared for his last, brief stand, he felt suddenly at peace, reconciled with his decision and ready to face the Lady and accept her judgement. That was until he heard someone come to stand beside him...

"Ashe, what are you doing here?" he gasped, as his friend stumbled to his side.

The burly sergeant growled, his pale face covered by a sheen of sweat and blood, his cheek plugged by a dark, matted rag.

"I'd rather die by your side, than up there," he grunted, as several arrows hissed by them into the charging ranks.

As they were swept up in battle, Elion heard the rallying roar from behind him, as those still able to stand, came charging down the slope to fight one last time with him.

Devlin Hawke and Colm rained shaft after shaft onto the enemy as Elion and his comrades were swallowed up in the storm. As they loosed their last into the melee, the outlaw leader caught sight of Elissen. The young woman fought alongside Jarion Kail and Kallum Campbell, her hair wild and loose now, as she ducked under a spear, buried her sword deep into her opponent's stomach and wrenched the steel free.

Flicking a look amongst the madness, Devlin picked out Elion as the Carwellian danced through the throng, his blade cutting though the enemy with assured, deadly intent.

"What do we do, boss?" Colm asked. He cast a look back up the slope and to the sharp hills above the mines. It was a tempting climb, but almost an impossible one.

Devlin threw his bow aside, drawing his Valian steel. He eyed each of his friends in turn. "My destiny waits down there for me," he shouted above the din of battle. "I won't hold it against you if you choose no to, but I would be honoured to have you by my side one last time."

The outlaw turned. Gripping his blade before him, he ran down the slope. After a moment of hesitation, the last of his men from Greywood Forest raced down to fight by his side.

Kerrin Thorn buried his blade into the back of a warrior, barely wrenching it free in time to turn aside a spear that would have ripped his throat open. As he fell back, Janth cut down the spearman, hacking his way into the men that ran at him.

Ignoring the pain from his injured shoulder, Kerrin joined Janth and back-to-back, they fought off three more warriors, spinning to and fro to ward off danger.

"There are too many of them." Janth cried out, grunting, as an attacker found a breach in his desperate defences, carving out a deep mark in his right arm.

Spinning to his aid, Kerrin hacked the fingers from Janth's opponent's sword hand, driving the man back into the masses. Two more took his place and sharing, a forlorn look, the riders from Carwell fell back towards the slope again.

Overcome with anger, Elissen ignored the wound in her left cheek. Parrying the tall warrior's next attack, she drove her knee into his groin, falling back, as Jarion Kail came to her aid and plunged his sword deep into the man's back.

Nodding her thanks, Elissen swept her tangled locks from her eyes and sent a look about the fighting for him. As the battle danced and swayed rhythmically before her, she could see Elion Leigh, deep amidst the chaos, his friend Ashe by his side. Kallum Campbell leapt before her as a man in heavy mail peeled away from the defender he had just killed and rushed towards them screaming. Oblivious to everything about her, her emerald eyes blazed as she saw the tall, white-haired figure pushing his way impatiently through the enemy ranks towards Elion.

Her breath failed in her throat and her skin began to ripple, as she found herself again outside the hut in Eastbury.

Shrieking madly, she raced into the throng as she tried to cut her way through towards the man she had sworn to kill.

Ashe hammered his sabre into a woman's neck and dragged his steel free. Wiping her blood from his eyes, the burly sergeant blocked a man's lunging attack from his left, hurling him back with a growl before turning to send his blade into the spine of a warrior fighting Elion.

Elion turned, ducking wide of an arching axe to cut his sword through a man's thigh. Screaming, Elion's opponent went down and as he regained his balance, Elion noticed that the wary attackers before him began to retreat.

Confused, Elion found his breath, trying vainly to calm his wild heart. All about them, the fighting was still fierce and, much to his horror, Elion noticed the warrior Athen and Tristan nearby, their bodies still, pierced by many blades.

"There you are, Leigh," a crisp voice called out above the fighting.

Clenching his bloodied hand tightly about the hilt of his sword, Elion looked up, his eyes blazing as Renald Gardan strode through the ranks of his parting men, his elegant sword gripped lightly in his gloved, right hand.

The first light of the bloody day caught on his mail as he came forward and the tall man's hawked face split into an eager smile.

"I have to say," Gardan admitted, looking about to acknowledge his own admission. "I am still impressed, mightily so."

"You have nothing to be impressed for, Renald," Elion responded, dropping his own sword to his side. "Only ashamed for what you have done."

Gardan smiled, shaking his head. He clicked his tongue reproachfully.

"You see, again, that is your problem, Leigh," the commander sighed, "always worried about the men, never thinking about the wider world and the issues that *truly* matter."

"Forgive me if I don't have the time to listen to your excuses or swallow the vitriol of your misguided hatred, your lust for power," Elion glowered, spitting on the ground between them.

"That's more like it," Gardan laughed. He swept his free hand through his short, ivory hair. "Shall we?"

Gardan raised his blade and nodding, Elion brought his own blade up to accept the offered point. As their steel touched, Ashe backed away, eyeing the ranks of nearby attackers, who watched on eagerly.

"Take his head off," Ashe growled, ignoring the look his former commander dealt him.

Renald Gardan's reputation as swordsman was not embellished and Elion fell back, barely fending off the flashing blade that cut and tested his defences. Flicking a desperate response back towards Gardan's face, Elion was amazed at the older man's speed, disheartened by the ease in which he turned aside his attack.

"You'll have to do better than that," Gardan smiled, striding to and fro before him.

Remembering his training, his need for patience, Elion raised his blade, beckoning Gardan to him.

"Why don't you come and show me?" Elion asked and before he realised it, Gardan was upon him, the tip of his sword deep in his left shoulder.

"Too easy," Gardan gloated, as Elion dropped to his knees before him. He flicked a look at the men behind him, throwing his head towards the startled sergeant.

"Kill that man for me," he hissed and with a roar, Ashe was set upon by several warriors.

Elion raised his head, gritting his teeth as Gardan twisted his blade, forcing it deeper into his shoulder.

Gardan smiled sardonically. "After all you have achieved, I really thought you would make a better show of it!"

Pulling his steel free, Gardan kicked Elion's sword from his hand and raised his blade high.

"Traitor's end," the commander cried.

He staggered back as a dark shape appeared from the fighting and sent a sword through the side of his face. Screaming, Gardan backed away, clutching at the deep wound in his cheek. Spitting his fury and bloodied teeth from his mouth, he stared at the woman who stood between him and his execution.

"Remember me?" Elissen asked. She glared through her tangled veil of hair, delighting at the horror that crept into Gardan's eyes.

Before he could respond Elissen attacked, her father and sister's memory guiding her blade as she opened up a wound in Gardan's left arm. Recovering from his shock, the commander blocked her wild, eager attacks, turning them upon her to open up a deep wound above her hip.

Grunting, Elissen fell back towards Elion and Gardan

pressed home his advantage. He opened up a cut on her opposite cheek and watched in satisfaction as the girl fell to one knee, sobbing.

"You should have chosen the rope, girl," Gardan spat, raising his sword.

Elissen leapt up, slashing her blade across Gardan's chest. Grunting, the commander stumbled back and dropped to his knees, staring up at the woman who glared down at him.

"Help me," Gardan screamed, desperately. He looked about, frowning when nobody came forward to help him.

Elissen followed his searching gaze, delighting in the fear that crept into his eyes. Behind her, she could hear Elion calling out weakly to her, but her head was pounding and she could not make out his words. She did not see Gardan's hand moving slowly to his boot.

"For my family and for Eastbury," Elissen cried out, brandishing her sword high.

Gardan drove a dagger deep into her stomach and rose slowly, wrenching the concealed steel up with him.

"I'll take that, girl," Gardan whispered in Elissen's ear as he plucked the blade from her hand. She stared down at the life flowing from her, glanced back at her killer in confusion.

Stepping past the collapsing woman, Gardan watched on dispassionately as Elion tried to rise. Staggering back to the young captain, he smiled down through his pain at him.

"The day gets better," he admitted, resting the point of Elissen's sword, her sister's sword, against Elion's throat.

Jerking violently, the commander stared down at the point of a blade that burst from his wounded chest. Blinking, Gardan shared his disbelief with Elion, who looked up in shock, watching as blood ran from the commander's ruined mouth.

Coughing, Gardan fell to his knees as the blade was ripped from his body. He stared at Elion for a moment, before the light faded from his eyes and he toppled to one side.

Blinking, Elion stared up into the rising dawn at the warrior who had just saved his life.

"This man had no honour," Eran Dray shrieked to his gathered comrades, pointing his bloodied sword at Gardan's body. "Where is *your* honour?" he demanded of those gathered near.

Eran went to stand beside Elion Leigh. Turning to face the Karickian ranks, he helped the wounded man to stand.

"This madness must stop!" Eran bellowed, his eyes ablaze. "We cannot keep butchering our own, throwing our lives away so that those who crave power can take what is not rightfully theirs."

A few men raised their weapons angrily, muttering the word '*traitor*' as they came closer. About them now the fighting was easing off as others were drawn to what was happening and former enemies stood beside one another in confusion. Devlin Hawke forced his way free of the crowd, staring wide-eyed at the scene that greeted him. His sword fell forgotten by his side.

Eran pointed his sword at Elissen's body, banishing thoughts of how Dia must have looked at the end.

"These brave people did not come here to steal riches. They came here to die so that strangers, and perhaps peace, could live. I will not become a pawn in this power struggle. I am a simple man, an honourable man, loyal to Lucien Varl," he paused, directing his hatred down at the man he had just killed. "I will not kill my own for *them*."

Eran threw down his sword in disgust by Gardan's body then looked up defiantly. For what felt like an eternity nobody moved and then Wen appeared from the silent ranks. He walked forward and threw his sword and shield down on Gardan's body.

Eran smiled at his friend, as he came to stand by him. Devlin Hawke, his body bathed in bloody cuts, stumbled forward to join them, casting a sad look at Ashe's body as he passed.

Elion gritted his teeth as he stooped down to pick up his fallen sword. Looking at Elissen's still body, he felt tears well in his eyes, could not look at Jarion Kail, as the man rushed forward and gathered Elissen in his arms, his strangled sobs shaming all who watched him.

Elion threw his sword down beside Gardan and looked at Eran Dray.

"I don't know who you are, friend, but I thank you for it," he stammered, giving in to his grief.

Eran wrapped an arm about the injured rider and watched as the ranks of the surviving defenders and attackers became one, piling their disdain on top of Renald Gardan's body.

CHAPTER FIFTY FOUR

Echoes of a Storm

Arillion eyed the solitary crow, studying the bird, as it watched the crowd with eyes far more intelligent than many gathered below in the square would give it credit for. The bird looked on, its keen black eyes fixed on the promise of food, cocking its head to one side as it watched a large man wave a leg of chicken about in the air, as he made some unheard point to the woman stood next to him under the shadowy protection of the statue of Valan Stromn.

Uncomfortable in the rising heat and the itching from his tight wounds, Arillion folded his arms across his chest and looked at the Redani, stood in contemplative silence beside him. The giant stonemason looked at peace. His broad, broken features softened by recent events and his freedom from those who would have seen him hang from a gallows, similar to the one the large crowd now gathered before, that afternoon in the cobbled square.

For three days the city had continued to hold its breath, letting out a huge sigh of relief when the violence that had consumed the streets finally abated and the high duke's allies and supporters reclaimed the city from those still loyal to Henry Carwell and the Brotherhood.

With his strength slowly returning, the poison and his need for it finally free from his veins, High Duke Karian Stromn had made a firm declaration of his return to power by announcing to the people and the wider realms what had occurred in the city, what had happened to him over the last days of the summer.

The public were angered by what they heard and the militia struggled to contain further violence for many days, peace and order only restored when Evan Valus returned to public life. News of his bravery, of the wrongs done to him and the dignity in which he carried himself, settled the populace's rage and the woodsman, somewhat regrettably, hung up his woodland cloak, knowing that his days in isolation were now over.

Arillion smiled. Though his thoughts were dark for the friends he had lost, he could not help contain his joy that their plan, *his* plan had worked. The Brotherhood had been crushed, its surviving supporters either in chains or in hiding. There was still a great deal of work for the assassin to do, a lot of unfinished business to attend to, but, with Carwell dead, the high duke's supporters had rallied about him, no longer fearing for their lives as they had done since the moment '*chaos had ruled the city*.'

The Valian armies had returned to Karick earlier that morning, news of the bravery and sacrifice at Durrant's Field spreading through the streets of the capital, embellished with every recount, until, some would come to say that only twenty men had fought against Gardan's armies, their swords and shields strong and true, as they stood firm against the tyrant, repelling the attackers in the Lady's name.

Arillion scowled. There was nothing worse than a wagging tongue and a man's need to always seemingly want to tell the story better than the man who had passed it on to him.

Elion Leigh and Devlin Hawke, along with several of the remnants of those who had set out for Durrant's Field had not travelled to the city. Some had taken the glad news back to Havensdale, whilst Kerrin Thorn had returned to Greywood Forest to be with his friend the donkey and the boy Balan. Devlin and Elion Leigh had, it was said, journeyed back to Carwell to ensure that the city did not remain in the hands of those loyal to Henry Carwell. Talking quietly to a man called Wen, Arillion also heard that they would stop in Eastbury along the way.

The crowd stirred as the high duke and his supporters appeared, walking out to take their places on the scaffold, accepting the polite applause and cheers that began to fill the square. Arillion picked out the woods... Evan Valus amongst the throng, stood once again at the high duke's side, supporting his weak lord. Even from here, the assassin could see the strain on his clean-shaven features.

Arillion watched the crow, as it took to the clear blue sky and winged its way westwards across the rooftops. He turned his hooded head towards the Redani, watching his face fill with turbulent emotion.

"What will you do now, Redani?" Arillion asked him. He knew the answer already for they had shared a drink earlier that day in the Mason's Inn, the place where Khadazin's adventures had begun. They had spoken at length about what the future would hold for them both.

Khadazin turned his head, sweat running down one broad cheek.

"I am a free man now," he began, smiling subtly. "I think I will enjoy a peaceful life, one that does not involve danger and a price on my head."

Arillion grinned, clapping the Redani on his left shoulder. Like the men of Greywood, who had been pardoned for any crimes by the high duke, the stonemason no longer had a bounty on his head.

"I think, more than anyone, Khadazin, you of all people deserve such a life," the assassin said, hesitating. "Though I still think you should contemplate the high duke's offer."

Khadazin's eyes narrowed, hinting that he was not willing to talk about the matter again.

Chewing his top lip, the Redani sighed and looked away. "I wish Savinn were here," he sighed, shaking his head sadly.

So do I. Arillion thought, though for different reasons.

"It is a shame," the assassin agreed, "that he could not finally take his seat on the council. Though, I daresay, his presence will be felt at that table for many years to come."

As will mine...

Khadazin nodded his head several times, smiling. It was said by many that Savinn's sacrifice, his words that fateful day, had sown seeds of rebellion in the city – rallying together many of the high duke's supporters and a great deal of the populace. When Arillion and his allies had attacked the keep, plans were already underway to seize back power in the high duke's name.

Any further words between them were drowned out by the angry jeers that filled the square, echoing out loudly across the city as the chancellor was dragged towards the scaffolding in chains.

Arillion gripped the Redani's arm. "It's been a pleasure, Redani. I am, as Savinn would be, happy you are safe."

Khadazin was pushed forward as the crowd surged towards the platform. When he turned to thank the assassin, Arillion was gone.

Relan Valus, the former chancellor of Karick was thrown to the wood before the high duke. Drained beyond any perception, he stared up at the man he had served, the man he had betrayed, the man he had poisoned.

Word had reached him in his dark cell that his man in the kitchens of the keep had admitted his part in the plot, of how they had poisoned the high duke's tea, of everything he and the chancellor had done, giving credence to the suspicions of Madam Grey's suspected involvement in the Brotherhood's plans. The cook's evidence had damned them all, though he had been spared the noose for his testimony. It had not saved him though, as the man was found dead in his cell the day after, his throat cut from ear to ear.

Collapsed before his lord, the hatred of the crowd ringing in his hears, Relan Valus gathered himself together, drawing close the tatters of his composure. Raising his head proudly, he stared past Karian Stromn and fixed his defiance on his brother.

"People of Karick, my friends," the high duke called out, his weary voice gaining in confidence with each word he spoke. "We stand here today, not on the cusp of chaos, as we have done for so many long days now, but on the threshold of a new dawn for the Four Vales. So very nearly the peace of our land, the prosperity we have all shared these last years, was destroyed by the ambitions and the treachery of our own. Deceit, lies and, worst of all, betrayal, by those who were entrusted to protect us, those we believed had our best interests at heart."

The high duke paused, looking about the crowd who watched on in silence, captivated by his every word. Lowering his raised arms, he pointed a condemning finger at his former chancellor.

"But they did not have our best interests at heart, they cherished only their own greed and thirst for power. They duped us into thinking there was a plot by the Reven to conquer these lands, when, in actual fact, it was quite the reverse. They wanted the Reven lands for their own personal gain, they poisoned our minds, they poisoned your lord and they murdered the innocent so we would believe it so. Without the bravery of others, of whom much will be told in the coming weeks, they would have had their war. But, my friends, today we can stand here together, today we can breathe the fresh air of freedom from their designs. We are Valian, we are honourable men and women and we will not take from others what is not rightfully ours."

Karian lowered his shaking arm, staring down at the man who had betrayed him. Even now, he could not quite believe that the frail creature before him had been so cunning, so quick to throw away the friendship and status he had given to him.

"I am sorry it has come to this," the high duke whispered, shaking his head sadly.

Relan Valus' eyes blazed. "This will not be the end of it," the chancellor hissed, laughing madly as he was hauled up and dragged towards the noose.

The crowd began to cheer and Karian sent a look towards Evan, seeing the anguish on the former woodsman's face. Steeling himself, Evan walked to his brother's side, helping the guard to haul him up onto the stool and slip the noose about the sobbing man's thin neck.

"In accordance with our laws, we will allow the prisoner to speak, even though by his actions he has robbed himself of that honour," the high duke decreed.

The crowd fell silent.

Piercing laughter rolled across the square as the chancellor cackled, his eyes boring into the crowd.

"You fools!" he screeched. "How can you listen to this? How can you stand there as Valian and let these imbeciles tell you all will be well? Mark my words, it will not be. This is not the end. This is only the beginning. The Brotherhood will have their day, we will have our war and the Reven will fall, mark these words."

Relan's screams broke down into sobs as the high

duke waved away his brother and the guard.

Moving slowly to stand beside the prisoner, Karian Stromn looked out at the silent crowd.

"Justice be done," the high duke cried out, kicking the stool from beneath Relan Valus' feet.

The crowd cheered and a bell of celebration rang out across the city.

Fawn Ardent attempted to rub the weariness from her eyes and only succeeded in making things worse. Smothering her deep yawn with the back of one hand, she drew in a fulsome breath and reached across the silken sheets to hold Cassana's still hand.

The room was quiet, its peace broken only by thin ribbons of daylight that speared through the darkness to fall upon the bed Fawn had sat beside for many days now.

Outside the chambers, events moved on swiftly and the news reaching Highwater from the south was incredible. The Brotherhood's plans had been thwarted. The high duke was, once again, well and in command.

Even now Fawn could not fully believe the news, did not wish to believe it, should it prove to be more lies and deceit, a way to get Highwater to relax its guard, to take its eyes from the shadows and the enemy threatening from within the Four Vales. But, should the whispers be true, Havensdale, her people, her friends would be safe once more...

Fawn eyed the letter that had arrived for her the previous day, felt her heart race as she picked it back up and read it for the hundredth time.

It was from Evan. His flowing handwriting bore credence to the rumours, telling of the events that had transpired, of those who had sacrificed themselves bravely so that peace could settle on the land once again.

Lady Stromn had received swift word from her

husband that all was well in the capital and had set off immediately with her son and a sizeable retinue without even coming to check on how Cassana was faring.

Fawn put the letter down on her lap, gripping Cassana's hand tighter. For twelve days, since Lysette's attack, Cassana had fought against the Father of Storms. The physicians William Bay and Bryn Astien had brought to the room had tried everything their knowledge would allow them, all leaving with the same prognosis that only by her sheer will, did the lady of Highwater survive.

Twelve long, hard days since the attack and still Fawn could not forgive herself for allowing Cassana into the room alone.

Haunted images filled her mind as Fawn again found herself looking on, horrified as Cassana's friend repeatedly plunged her hair pin into her neck, each bloody strike slower and deeper than the previous.

What had happened next was to remain a secret, lest the Brotherhood hear news of what had transpired, and Fawn could still see Cullen react, as everyone else stood watching, transfixed by their shock and horror.

The squat man had rushed into the room, pushing aside Lord Astien and William Bay. As Lysette struck again, Cullen threw his knife, the spinning weapon plunging deep and true into her right eye as she screamed deliriously. As Lady Astien fell away, Cullen leapt to Cassana's aid, catching her in his tattooed arms, as Lysette twitched her last beside them.

Fighting back her tears, Fawn rested her head on the bed, kissing Cassana's hand. As she drifted off to sleep, so hard to find of late, she did not hear the door open, was not aware of the shadow at her side until it reached out and gently touched her shoulder.

Starting, Fawn recoiled. Aghast, she stared up into the shadows of the hood, seeing a masked face and the pair of bright, beautiful grey eyes that stared down at her.

"Do not be alarmed, captain," the calm, commanding voice whispered. The man held up empty hands to reveal strong forearms, clad in leather wrist guards. "I am here only to see Lady Byron. I mean her no harm. Had I done so, I would not have woken you."

Fawn quickly recovered her composure. "Who are you? How did you get in here?"

The cloaked figure folded its arms away beneath dark cloth and tried to hide its irritation. Fawn could smell the road on him and she felt her pulse stir with warning.

"I am known to Cullen," the man said softly. "He will vouch for me, as would Cassana were she able."

Fawn rose up onto weak legs. "What do you want, sir?" she asked, her eyes straying to her sword, hanging from a chair far too many steps away.

"Only a moment alone with Lady Bryon," the man requested, following her eyes. "Cullen?" he called out.

The door to Cassana's chambers opened and the flame-haired man ambled in, Shadow loping in beside him.

"It's okay, cap'n," Cullen nodded, his beard split by a hideous smile. "He means her no harm, on my life, I swear it."

Fawn looked between the two men. Sighing, she nodded, stooped to retrieve her fallen letter and followed Cullen out obediently into the hallway beyond.

Arillion waited until the door closed behind them and eyed the hound briefly before lowering his hood. He hated to admit it, but it was good to see Cullen again, a reminder of other, more simpler days.

Swallowing, Arillion moved to Cassana's side. His heart raced as he stared down at the pale, beautiful face he had never been able to forget. Her head lolled to one side, her dark hair loose across the pillows, her neck and shoulder wrapped in freshly dressed bandages.

For a time, the assassin looked down at her, struggling

with his thoughts and emotions. Sighing, he leant across and kissed her gently on the forehead.

Taking her thin hands in his own he curled her lifeless fingers about the crescent knife and rested them on her breast.

"Hello, princess," he whispered sadly.

Staring down at her still form, Arillion untangled the knot forming in his throat. Scowling, he stared up forlornly at the ceiling. Pulling his hood back over his head and the scarf up over his mouth he took one final look at Cassana then left the room without a word to Fawn and Cullen.

He was not present some hours later when Cassana's eyes fluttered open and she smiled weakly at the knife she held in her hands.

EPILOGUE

Khadazin Sahr stood in the cobbled square, the sun on his face, the city and the clamour of life vibrant around him. Overhead, the proud statue of Valan Stromn watched with him, casting a shadow across the throng of bickering merchants, the boisterous hawkers and the impatient citizens who hurried about their business on such a fiercely hot autumn day.

Listening to the bark of debate, Khadazin mopped his brow with the sleeve of his robe. Through the busy dance before him, he caught sight of two children, chasing each other through the crowds, their laughter ringing out.

Khadazin smiled, watching them play for a moment, before their cries and hoots carried them from view. It was a sound that had been sadly lacking in Karick for many, many days.

Eyeing Valan Stromn and silently thanking him for the brief respite from the sun, the stonemason made his way through the crowds, politely steering himself across the cobbles towards the safety of the Valian Mile.

Ignoring the stares and pretending not to hear the whispers, he reached the broad road, staring up the hill towards the high duke's keep.

For thirty days he and the Four Vales had known peace. There had been no uprising, no response from those still loyal to the Brotherhood. With their leadership slain and their hopes of war in tatters, Khadazin suspected it may be many years before they did.

Sighing, Khadazin stood under the eaves of a tall tenement building, enjoying the shade and his thoughts for a time. It had been a long thirty days for him, trying to reclaim his place in society, trying to rebuild his workshop that had been routed by thieves and defaced with the hatred of those who had very nearly destroyed the city.

Khadazin smiled bitterly, looking down at the leather cap, covering his ruined wrist. No matter what the future held for him, Karick and the Four Vales was his home. He would never be able, even if he had wanted, to find passage across the Western Reaches to his ancestral home. His people, the people he did not know, would never accept the man, a man who spoke another tongue, a man deemed a thief in their eyes as he only had one hand.

There was much to be thankful for, however, Khadazin mused, unable to contain his joy. Following the bloody night, Tania had remained at his side until the morning of Relan Valus' judgement. They had shared a tearful farewell, before she returned home, bearing with her a letter that she promised, once she was able to, she would deliver to James and Brother Markus.

Two days ago, a letter had returned, the neat script bearing news that James and Brother Markus were coming to the city to be with him. James' desire to be a stonemason was still strong and already the Redani was excited at passing on his knowledge to one so young and eager to learn. One he thought his own son.

Stifling a tear, Khadazin thought of Lady Byron, of the news that she was recovering from the attempt on her life. She could still not walk unassisted, it was said, but she was planning to journey to Karick in ten days time, to attend Karian Stromn's first council meeting and to help decide its new council members.

Evan Valus had journeyed to Highwater three days after his brother's execution, returning only days before with news of the woman who would be his bride and bearing word from the Lady Byron that she was eager to meet Khadazin, the stranger who had saved her life and the man she hoped would be her friend.

Khadazin wiped away his tears as he thought that he would like that very much, also.

Thoughts of the *New Council* soured his mood, stirring up the dilemma of the offer that Arillion had thought he should take.

The high duke had been very gracious with his offer, one that had taken Khadazin completely by surprise.

A Redani on the Valian Council... The very thought was preposterous, even to him. The people would never accept it, just as the members had not accepted Savinn Kassaar.

Or w*ould they*?

Shaking his head free of his turmoil, Khadazin thought of Arillion. Since that day, when the assassin had slipped away from him into the crowd, the Redani had not seen or heard from him. Arillion, and Riyan, had not been seen again.

News of fresh murder filled the streets, only fifteen days following the death of Henry Carwell. This time, however, it was not the supporters of the high duke who suffered. It was the prominent members of the Merchants Guild who died, those who had betrayed Savinn Kassaar so readily on the hollow promise of position and favour.

One by one they died, the last being Loren Kalis, the man who had been such a political thorn in the high duke's side. He was killed in broad daylight by a hooded figure, dressed all in black. With twin swords the assassin had cut the merchant down, witnesses claiming that the killer had placed a gold crown in the merchant's mouth, before calmly walking away through the stunned, parting crowds.

The swordsman, the assassin, was wanted by the high duke now, dead or alive to the sum of thirty thousand crowns.

Khadazin, though disgusted by the killings, could not feel sorry for the victims and he secretly hoped that in the coming days, the assassin would remain free from capture.

Elsewhere in the Four Vales, the news was less bloody. Elion Leigh and his allies had returned to Carwell, seeking to liberate the city from the shadow of their former leader, only to discover that his father had not been idle. In Henry Carwell's absence, Marten Leigh had returned to the political arena, rallying those loyal to the high duke, of which, it transpired, there were still many.

With the aid of Lucas Rhee and Reyn Cross, the city had gladly accepted the uprising, embracing the chance of freedom from tyranny with open arms and raised swords. Without any blood being spilled, Carwell had fallen back into the hands of its people.

The last news Khadazin had heard of Elion Leigh and Devlin Hawke was that they were riding to Highwater. The former captain was keen to take up a lady's offer and the former outlaw, happy it was said, to find a suitable place to pour a peaceful tankard or two.

Aware of the eyes upon him, Khadazin turned his thoughts to Lucien Varl. The brave captain of Karick had recovered suitably from his torture to travel home and had arrived in the capital two days prior. He was currently at home with his mother, convalescing before his return to public life.

Khadazin swallowed down his nerves, whetting his lips for the words he suspected he would struggle to find.

Turning away from the square, he was about to head up the hill when he hesitated. Looking back towards the high sun once again he was sure, just for the briefest of moments, as the crowd parted, that he caught sight of a thin, scrawny looking apparition, watching and grinning at him from the shadows of the gatehouse.

The crowds drew together before him again and pulling in a deep breath, Khadazin smiled, turned and headed up the Valian Mile to keep his promise.

The End

About the Author

Anthony has always loved reading stories and from an early age, since reading The Lord of the Rings, he has been inspired to write his own. He states that his favourite author is David Gemmell and his style of writing has been inspired by the sadly missed author.

Anthony lives in Wales with his wife Amy and Mertle, the cat. He is about to start work on his next novel, The Last Tiger.

You can keep up-to-date with his news here:-

Website: http://alavisher.wordpress.com

Twitter: @alavisher

Facebook: www.facebook.com/lavisherauthor

Made in the USA
Charleston, SC
03 December 2016